the Unsung.

Written and Illustrated
by Harley J. Sims

Kurtisiani
(1979 - 2007)

hic
habitabamus
et etiamnum
vivis.

S

Table of Contents

withstand
oblivion

S

The Languages of the Story

The Unsung is a fantasy of language as well as a fantasy of setting. Its use of words, as with its approach to reality, has been altered to effect new circumstances.

There are many languages (or *tungs*) in the novel: the Allmal (or Common Speech, in its various dialects); Linguish; Ignish; Hálish; Vakhish; Saffish; and others. Some of these languages tell the story. Others are simply mentioned, or are represented by one or two words. These are the languages of the story's own world. They are not—as with J.R.R. Tolkien's works, for example—analogues into which the story's indigenous languages have been translated and modernized. Unless otherwise stated, the words the characters speak in *the Unsung* are the words they are actually using.

Many, but not all, of these languages have correspondences within our own world, and are comprehensible to those who already speak them without much translation. The Allmal coincides with English, Linguish with Latin, Ignish with Welsh, Hálish with Icelandic. They are not quite the same, however, and their differences reflect the strange and secret ways in which they came to coexist in a reality not our own. Footnotes have been used, at times extensively, to guide readers through, and at the same time to preserve the disorienting familiarity of the world's own wordcraft. **There is also a sizeable glossary in Appendix A.**

Vocabularies, including idiom, afford the most obvious discrepancies between our forms of these languages and those of the novel's world. Many words common to us, for example *mountain* and *magic* and *reality*, are rarely heard in the Kingdom of Knaks, and are instead represented by other words (*berg*, *dreecraft*, and *itness*, respectively). Furthermore, expressions such as *scared off one's branch* and *woody as a squirrel tree*—which can be explained through a little contextualization—share space with sayings such as *something sameworked is samwrought* and *no min, never been*, which require more thorough translation.

In addition, there are discrepancies in evolution, culture, and influence, often contradicted by our own linguistic models. For example, Modern English and Old English do not coexist on Earth as spoken languages, but in Knaks they do—as Allmal and Braccish. Ráma and Smað are realms of wondrous anachronism, whose variety touches even the tongues of its characters.

That said, this is not the right place for a treatise on language and its special pertinence to fantasy literature, alternate worlds, and Smað in particular. I will eventually write such a thing—pieces of it can be found in writings I have already done—but here such an essay can only divert the reader from the insular experience of the story, as well as seek out insurance for its own experimentation.

Subjecting audiences to alternate experiences is the goal of any artist, and while it is arguable that the writer attempts to go deeper and further than any other artist in doing this, he is often thwarted by the very medium that makes it possible. Suffice it to say that language has always proved the last barrier between imaginative reality and the reader's own experience simply because that barrier must also serve as the bridge. All fiction reshuffles reality's deck of cards, but fantasy introduces new rules to its games.

It is deeply hoped that, in time, the reader will become acclimatized enough to the languages of Knaks and Ráma that deeper and deeper plunges into their gardens will become possible.

English, Braccish and the Allmal

As stated above, the English of *the Unsung* is known as the Allmal. Like English, it is a mixed tung whose blend can be separated into national, regional, historical, and other strains. Of the regional strains, it is the Braccish which has been most influential in the Kingdom of Knaks, though the other *Medths* (provinces) of the kingdom have also contributed to its wordhoard. Most of the Allmal can generally be considered Knaksish.

The novel's footnotes and glossary distinguish many of the language's branches from its basic roots. It is possible to go deeper than the divisions specified, just as one might break down Old English into Anglian, Kentish, Northumbrian and other dialects. Such work threatened to turn variety toward pedantry, however, and was avoided in these pages. As it stands, some readers will recognize a consistency to the division of Braccish Allmal from the Knaksish.

The central characters of *the Unsung* are better travelled and nimbler linguistically than most Knaksmen, but in various peoples and places of the kingdom certain tungs and their influence on the Allmal will appear more concentrated. For the most part, and for now, readers have been spared immersion in these more distilled and isolated pools of the Allmal.

There are two exceptions. One is in the Bulletins (variously called *lathings*, leaflets and *looknows*) following Chapter Three. Although the gist of them should be clear without too much help, they are written in more formal and regional strains of the Allmal and may require more thorough reference to the glossary to be translated fully. There are no footnotes in this section.

The second exception is in Chapter Five, which brings readers into the court of the Isentron and the presence of the King of Knaks himself. The King is a purist of the Braccish Allmal, as his comments make clear, though he is being more casual with his choice of words than he can be. The footnotes in this chapter are the most extensive in the novel.

Pronunciation

As with vocabulary and spelling, the pronunciation (or *swettling*) of names and other words—including very important ones—varies across the land. While *the Unsung* places less emphasis on how to say its words out loud than on how to define them, a few likely to prove confusing are:

æw – AH (less like UH than AW)
Arsask – AR-sask (also AR-sash)
Brac – BRAWK
Braccish – BRAWK-ish (also BRAWCH-ish)
Hála – HOW-la
Knaks – KeNAWKS (also NAWKS)
Ráma – RAWM-uh
Smað – SMAWDTH

Abbreviations in the Footnotes

AB – Braccish Allmal   **B** – Braccish
AC – Colonial Allmal   **L** – Linguish
AH – Harandrish Allmal   **H** – Harandrish
AI – Ignish Allmal   **I** – Ignish
AK – Knaksish Allmal   **K** – Knaksish

Western Norráma
(Northwestern Ráma)

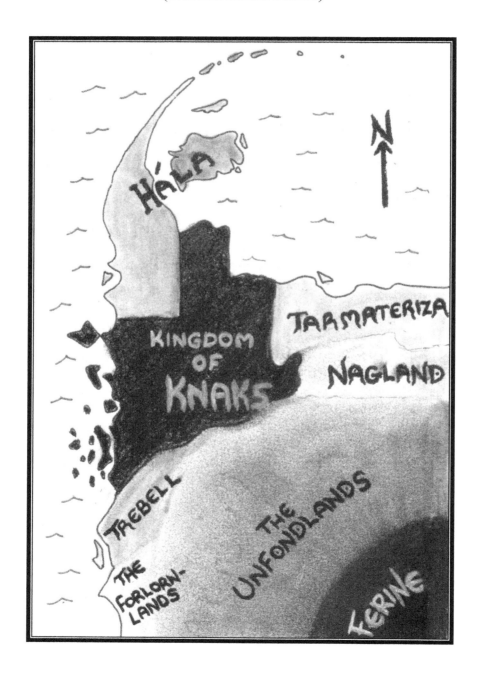

𝒮

The Medths of the Kingdom of Knaks
(Provinces)

Weightiest Happensteads of the Tale
(Most important sites)

Nid yn unig y dechrau ond hefyd y diwedd
A Prologue that is also an Epilogue

The girl left the woodshed, and the man knew she had no memory of him.

He watched her split the eaves' curtain of rainwater and disappear into the fog with her bucket.

He sighed out his very soul.

Then he sank back down between the stacks of firewood and listened to the downpour their voices no longer drowned out.

He had asked her not to turn away, and what she had not understood of his words he had put into gestures. But she could not stay any longer. Her family already missed her, and they would come looking.

It was on hearing this that he had given in and let her go. He knew he could not face them, not even the way he was.

He had watched her eyes as they left him, and she had not turned back as she had headed to the doorway. He had not called out to her as she went through it. He had not wished to startle her. Nor had he wished to start over again.

The droning of the frogs sent the memory of her creeping across his every thought. He was not sure how old she was. He reckoned somewhere between twelve and fifteen. What had happened in Shebril, it still tied knots in his timeline.

He was lucky her name had come back to him[1], odd as it was.

An Ignish name.

Tes. Short for *Tesog*.

"So it was the day she was born," Rhianys had told him.

He had come off at the time like he knew what she meant, but even now he had no idea. No one spoke the Ignish tung[2] outside of Ignam, and how it was spoken there differed not only among its shires—or *cantrevs* as they called them—but also its towns and valleys.

"Tes," he had said to the girl. "Tes, we have met before. Do you know when your sister went away? It was with me. Rhianys went with me."

The words sounded stale, he had held them in his mouth for so long. Part of him believed they wouldn't work.

She had looked him over peacefully, but with a confidence he had found unsettling. "Rhianys is gone," she had said.

"Yes, Tes. With me. Do you know me?"

She shook her head, but not in reply. The Allmal came slowly off her tongue, picked from scant but adequate stores. "She went from us with you. And now she is gone from you too."

He had to think about it for a moment, which clearly caused Tesog some impatience. She began to clarify in her own, wet language, but by then he had already understood.

---

[1] The Knaksish conceive of memory as a recovery of old thoughts, analogous to the return of Woden's second raven, Myne, or Mune, at the end of each day. Such returns they call *Mins*, and the process *minning*. A standard Knaksish idiom is "If Mine comes back…" which means "If I remember correctly…".

[2] *(AK):* language; *tung* (language) can be distinguished in writing from *tongue* (the organ of the mouth), though they are pronounced the same way.

Somehow, she had heard that her sister had been killed soon after leaving with them.

"She is…all-gone," Tes stammered.

"Yes." He held her eyes as hard as he could but made no attempt to approach her. Either she would trust him, or she would flee.

"But you," she said. "You are still here."

"Yes."

He wanted to say more but willed himself to stay close to what he had rehearsed. She did not appear to resent him. She looked intrigued, perhaps a little wily, which reminded him of the young woman—this girl's older sister—he had met at this croft around two years of his time ago, and five or so of hers. It wasn't until Tesog bit her whole lower lip, however, that the face of Rhianys appeared upon her own. He had forgotten that awkward habit of hers, and found the sight of it pained him.

"Five men were there when Rhianys went away," Tesog continued.

The man nodded. "They are gone too."

"Dead?" she asked.

Her use of the word took him unawares. That, and it was hard for him to recall on the spot whom exactly she meant, for there had been several thoftmen[3] before, after, and during her sister's own short stint with them.

"Three of them, yes. Maybe all. I don't know."

"What for are you here again?"

He smiled, but only to himself. He had very often had to mend her sister's speech as well.

"You mean, *why*," he said.

"Yes. *Why*. That is the word. Is it you want me now? That like Rhianys the *arwydd* is on me?"

The *arwydd*. The gift of wild dreecraft. Magic.

The man's heart leapt. And for the first time in months, it was not from anger or fear.

"Yes." Tesog was proud of it—very—unlike Rhianys, who had taken the gift in stride. With a whiff of sideshowmanship he might elsewhere have laughed at, the girl narrowed one eye and whispered, "I have the *arwydd*. See it."

---

[3] *(AB):* An ally; a comrade; a partner in toil. A *thoft* is a bench on a rowing vessel, upon which men sit and grip the oars. A fraternity of thoftmen is a *thoftship*.

She carried a bucket of oats at her side, and, one by one, her fingers uncurled from the handle. When at last her hand fully opened, the bucket did not fall. Tesog folded her arms across her chest, and it hung there, aloft, just over a foot above the ground.

The man took a step forward, his hands trembling. "Tes, you must listen to me. Rhianys spoke of a learninghouse for wizards—a school for those with the *arwydd*, as you call it. She said it was here in Ignam—*Yngmwn*—" he mended when she frowned at the elseland name for it. In hindsight, he didn't reckon slaughtering it with his Harandrish tongue made her any more grateful. He went on nonetheless. "It was in one of the eastern townships. The headburg, maybe. Its name hasn't come back to me. Do you know—"

Tesog's mind lost its steadiness, and the bucket thudded to the ground. Oats leapt up, and her eyes dropped. He shrieked, and bolted forward.

"*Look at me, Tesog!*"

Indeed she did. She also fled backward two steps of her own, and stood, gathered like a deer, against the rain of the hollow doorway. For the next few heartbeats, they eyed one another, him fearing she would flee or cry out, and her clearly believing he would not let her. What kept her from trying, he could only hope it was tenderness.

"Tesog," he said, and put down yet again the rasher ways of staying her. "Please. You must not look away."

"Why?" Her sternness came of misgiving rather than of fear. It was the tone of one who pitied a leper but was not entirely sure it wasn't catching.

Though he had told the tale a hundred ways, he now chose the words carefully. "If you do—if you look away for more than a blink of the eyes—I shall leave your mind. Everything I've told you will be gone. You will not remember me."

"A *melltith* is on you." Her look struggled between a fear of the thing and pride for having known its name.

Whatever separated her understanding of a *melltith* from his true condition, the man was convinced she had at least named its breed. "Yes," he said, settling back onto his seat. "The mother of all *melltiths*. It's a ban of a kind. A curse. Someone laid it on me so that I could not warn anyone about him."

Tesog answered first with a slow, sage nod, the likes of which she might have seen in a playhouse. Now she was clearly less bothered by the *melltith* than enthralled by her own part in all this.

"To take away a *melltith*," she said, "a ban, as you say—this is not my *arwydd*. Me and Rhianys, we move things, but not touch them. Like this…like this…"

She motioned towards the bucket as she tried to think of the word for it.

The man's sigh had gravel in it. "I know, Tesog. I know. I know you can't get rid of it. I didn't think you could. I came for the school. You must know the school. Rhianys spoke of it often. She wanted to go, but your mother and father had no means for it. It was why she went with us, to find gold, to get into the school."

His throat closed on him. Her shattered, bleeding body. It was all too awful.

"You must know it," he said. "I've come so far. I could not tell you in ten days what the road has put before me. Please, Tesog. The *school*. Your mother and father must have spoken of it."

Though her face held a wisdom beyond its years, Tesog remained a very proud young woman. That it was information he wanted and not her talents clearly put her off, and she did not appear to think about it very hard before letting her mind wander. She glanced about the shed as if to see how he'd been keeping the place, quickly and sparingly enough that he did not leave her field of sight.

"You come the morning, today?" she asked, spying his rucksack and the unwound sleeping roll in the corner

"Yes," he answered, patience simmering. "But I've been in the cantrev for more than a week now. I could not remember where you lived, and no one here speaks the Allmal."

She seemed to find that funny. "No one wants the Allmal. But you hear it in the burgs some. In Wythdeg. And in Kilko with the bookhall. Full *gwyr o bant*—"

She went into a brief travelogue, entirely in Ignish. He picked up a handful of words, none too close to another to make any sense of the whole. He said her name and kept repeating it until she reined her tongue back in.

"I can't understand you," he pleaded, maybe even whimpering a little. His fingers curled into the dirt.

"Rhianys owed you the lore," Tesog pipped. "You wanted her tung, yes?"

The words were weird, and the man chilled beneath them. Tesog seemed to have grown darker for a moment, as though what she said had needed to part her outer fleece in order to be heard.

"*Clywaist ti fi, Ddorn,*" the girl taunted. She leaned down towards him with legs unbent, a heron inspecting the peat. Her hair fell about her face, and her eyes were very different from her sister's. Her neckline sagged, and he saw the Ignish scar-nodes on her breastbone.

The man held her stare, unwholesome as she now seemed. She was more hayseed than dryad, however gifted. Whatever her game was, he had gazed into faces she could not imagine.

"What do I need to say to make you help me, Tesog? Everyone in my thoftship[4] is gone. I'm so far from home, I don't know the trees or the birds anymore. Your town is days from the highroad, and there aren't enough folk to get by on. I need to steal to live now, and I don't know if I can get away with that here for very long. If they catch me, and they lock me up, they'll forget about me. It's happened before, Tesog. More than once. The last time, I had to kill someone to get away. It was either that or starve to death."

The girl's eyes were not still but studied his face like a detailed drawing. The rest of her did nothing.

"Tesog, listen to me. I didn't come from Arsask. I followed the ayflood, the river, up from the south, from Bayerd. From *Bayerd*, Tesog. I don't know what you'd call it. Do you know where Bayerd is?"

She nodded twice, slowly. She was still a heron, and he was a talking fry.

"There are no roads out of there anymore. Not anymore. They are choked with death. I had to follow the ayflood."

"You said that before," she murmured.

"Then help me!" he snarled, startling her a little. "Stop gawking at me and do something, one way or the other!"

The girl drew herself back up with a flicker of boredom. "The school I know the name," she said. "But the name will not help you. The name will not find the school. It hides all around."

"Then, Tes, Rhianys's sister—" he reached for her long fingers, "please help me find it. I'll do anything. I'll give you anything."

"You will do the thing now," she demanded, upending the pail and seating herself with knees wide apart. The oats made a moat for the rustic throne; she even propped her chin on her fist. "You will show me in words why I owe it."

---

[4] *(AB)*: band; fellowship; especially in difficult matters.

The man rolled backward, coming roughly to rest against a stack of firewood. It had been freshly cut. Inhaling its green scent, he sighed furiously, and could not help but glance over to where he had hidden his weapon. He had left it there so as not to frighten her. Part of him now wished he were a more drastic sort of man.

"They will have to be my own words, Tesog," he grumbled, still looking at it. "A lot of them you can't understand."

"The words, or what the words tell about?"

The man chuckled and beheld her again with grudging affection. For a blink of the eyes, he saw Rhianys again—thinkress from the fens.

"I reckon both," he said. "If only in that you won't believe them."

But her face was like a kept child's, brightening as if before the gleam of open pages.

Beskak-lin [1]
The Innocents

"Do you see it?"

"No."

"There, before us."

"No. Your eyesight is blessed. I've told you so many times."

"A kestrel has not the eyes to spy it where you're looking. Look down, by the road."

"I can't see it. Let's keep moving."

"Is a lot of mist. Too much mist. Can't see. Can't smell. Shard use dree[2] to push it away."

Too nuch nist, was how it sounded. *Can't snell. Shard use dree to sush it ayay.* As a kattid[3], Níscel lacked the lips to make some of the sounds of Mannish speech and improvised using other parts of her mouth. She tended, for understanding's sake, to keep to those words she could speak well, but today much of that wont had fallen by the wayside. It gave away her unease long before she began to unravel.

"No," Toron said. "The mist is good. Come. Come along, Níscel. We've yet to reach the gates, and already you're dragging behind."

They kept to their forward drift, the stones twinning and retwinning their footfalls, and to the ears it was as though some mighty throng of men moved with them. To the six alone who were

---

[1] From the extinct *Aftheksish Reekgish* tung (transliterated from the *Rekghnakghlokh* script): ignorance; unknowingness.

[2] *(AB)*: magic. The practice of magic is *dreecraft*. A magician can be a *dree* as well, but is more commonly called a *dreeman*.

[3] Name by which the sapient feline race is known to most outside races and, in Níscel's case, the name its members use when introducing themselves to Men. The katkin of The Kris's Cusp in Zaota (whence Níscel hails) call themselves *Sesh''mak-howrool* (as best can be represented in this script) and speak among each other a pidgin formed of Hattic (the local human tung) and bestial feline sounds. The name of their race translates to *sand-foundlings* in the Allmal.

there, it was a heartening sound. Not even the grackles sang anymore, if indeed their mad barking might have been called a song.

The mist was thick atop the gutter of their path, its ghostly wool having fattened and frayed over the long while they'd walked. The whole highberg[4] now wore the hood it had knitted, smearing the sunlight to a glow. A stonescape of horns and spurs jutted through the murk like great, scuttled prows, the nearest necking across the road. It was among these outcrops that the narrow way had wound after leaving the woods, swinging to and fro like a river does in meadowlands, looping back toward itself but never athwart, dipping behind ledges and climbing steadily. From where the thoftship now was, it could be seen only for another furlong or so. After that it banked into the heart of the mountain and swethered[5] between two great shoulders of stone.

"You see how the road ups and dives," Shard said. His lowered voice scratched the mind, whispering like a devil of dry leaves. "It made anyone who neared the city come into sight and stay there, after which he was laid open within this bowl until he reached the gates. Were he a foe, he'd have made an easy mark for the shooters."

Níscel craned her neck, her nostrils blinking.

"Shoot they not everyone, theyn't?"

"No, I don't believe so," Shard answered. "Otherwise, they wouldn't have bothered themselves to make a road at all."

"Made?" Kurtisian said. His eyes swept the pathway, his face blunt with doubt. "You mean they cleared it."

"That is not what I said."

Kurtisian scoffed and looked to his brother Justinian, a younger man, but huger to the brink of trollishness. Near to seven feet tall he stood, and more drowning in muscle than bound in it. The closest word Knaksmen had for him was *priest*. But unlike the preachers and churchmen of this Eld of Life[6], he pushed no creed, peddled no writings, and had no temple, and was more like the goddy landlords of old, who still lived further north, and shaped sagas and fulfilled rites in a way that needed neither books nor timber. But unlike even they, who pledged troth to the Powers for the might it gave them over other men, Justinian was more ombudsman than ambassador, sworn to a god long a backbencher in the lawhouses of heaven, who

---

[4] *(AB):* mountain. To be distinguished from a *burg*, which is a city.
[5] *(AB)*: disappeared; faded away.
[6] *(AK)*: Age, or Era (of Life)

was as content simply to be known by Men as to be worshipped by them. Seisuma and the Brasmat were two of His names. He was a puckish deus, and a bit of a clod, and though His best Ages had passed, He was happy in his aphelion, and kept a petty lordship over earth and stone. In bygone days His followers might have torn whole lands asunder, but those powers had long ago dwindled to a knack for small shakes and rockslides. *Sumoi* they were called among the southern colonies, each one a *Sumo*, the name a witty falsening of an original *Shûme-ho*, from a tung no one in the order knew anymore[7]. Being a Sumo made Justinian something of a knowhow when it came to building with stone and earth, for though he was no mason himself, he knew the quirks of rocks and soils—their moods and their bents, verily as a ranger knows the wildlife—and might say whether this here was good for that there, and how far it might go to meet what was needed of it. The only other token of Justinian's godtroth[8], besides his steerlike beef, was the Allmetal—a burly medallion of mongrel steel whose surface roiled tirelessly, and suggested strange runes.

Catching his brother's glance, Justinian peered down at their path, and halted to bounce his bare heel from its top. Of groan and trembling, there came no answer.

"I don't think so, Shard," Justinian said. "It's what we call granite—I guess they'd call it cornstone up here, or something like it. Damn hard to quarry, and near rooted to the world. Adamant don't get much harder." He stomped it again. "I couldn't crack this if you dropped me off a cloud."

Kurtisian nodded, and his eyes were fixed to the back of Shard's head. "We knew a mason in Salpes who needed a gem-toothed blade to cut it. Took him days."

They talked of colonial masonry for some time, speaking of prices and fashions and the fickle tastes of the governors. Which stone was favoured in which neighbourhoods; which colours were reserved for the highborn. No one seemed to be listening, but neither did they keep walking. Toron looped back when he saw he was

---

[7] In the Linguish tung, which is spoken in the Southern landholds, *sumo* means, among other things, "I am eating"—Sumoi are notorious for their appetites, on which they rely to reach and maintain their abnormal size. Along with *Seisumite*, *Sumo* is the usual term for a clergyman of Seisuma. Within the holy order itself, there is also a loose hierarchy of Sumoi, with each rank denoted by a title.

[8] *(AK)* religion; commitment to a god or gods.

alone, and he brought Gorrh to a grudging halt. In all, Justinian concluded, the road indeed looked as though it had been delved out, but that simply could not be so. There was no stonecraft or tool of which he knew that might carve a trough out of granite so smoothly, and of such size, like the work of a colossal carpenter, who might gouge such a channel into softwood for the joining together of furniture.

Shard's eyes narrowed, but not at his naysayers. He was scrutinizing the two great stacks enclosing the path ahead.

"Yes, it is," he answered, transfixed by what he saw. "Granite, that is. And, yes, the road was most certainly made—by stonecrafts, young Chaldallion, long gone from this world. Behold."

The outlander raised both of his six-fingered hands, pointing to show two things. One by one, as his companions looked ahead and were seized by the sight that befell them, they stared, and became as still as the rocks themselves. The mists had thinned, and they could see that it was not between bluffs that the road led, but between two stone heads. Each had a face, each chiseled to a Mannish likeness, and so masterly was the craftsmanship that they appeared less as carvings than as titans petrified and beheaded. They were enormous. Were they dislodged from the spur on which they lay, and rolled down the slope into the valley, they would strangle it, damming the river and pushing travellers to the hillsides to get around them. It was not only their vast size that made them awesome, however, nor was their size the most awesome thing about them. For even as awe is a stew of fear, worship, and wonder, fear is a simpler thing than both others, and will rise to the top the more the awe is stirred.

The faces screamed. Made of stone, they screamed without sound, but the lack of whatever hellish noise they might have made did little to lighten their horror. The flinty skin of their mouths stretched near to tearing, their tongues breaching like great whales in flight of a rising abyss. Beneath the colliding folds of the brow lay sightless eyes, stuck skyward and bulging. All of it was cracked—blitzed with the bloodshots of horrible arousal. Their lips split. That they were lifeless seemed moot to their breed of panic, for no living thing, however gruesome its torture, might make such a face without the puppeteering hand of a demon.

"Fergh and Hern[9]," Toron swore.

It was more than the look of the things that stole the heat from his blood. They had appeared too suddenly. For their vastness, they should have been seen from the valley floor, two days ago even, when the mist was thinner, and this journey was in the making. Instead, they had taken shape in the bounds of a few steps.

Níscel loosed a series of pitiful mewls. Shard, without hiding it at all, used his strange finger-prayers to call courage into his body. Justinian threw up his hands and turned away, his face blank with shock.

"Well, that's that. It's there forever. Though I'd have thought getting my brain tattooed would have hurt a little more."

"This is it, isn't it?" Kurtisian said, looking from the faces of stone to those of his fellows. "What that old man told us about Aftheksis's sleepless watchmen? That's these two, yeah? This is Aftheksis?"

"Must be," Toron answered, and needlessly.

Using his swordstaff as a prop, he climbed off the saddle. Even through his footgear, the ground was colder than icelocked sand. Shard, having stood a few steps ahead of the thoftship, now backed slowly into the ring of them, and when Toron caught a glimpse of the outlander's eyes, he knew with dread that it was the first time he had ever seen them uneasy.

Shard, who had once cowed a mob without ever drawing his sword; who strode into hinterland nights as though they were days in a kingsburg market; who had lived the lives of three Men in a row. That man—the Highbred, as he called himself—was now, and openly, afraid.

Justinian stepped forward, finger raised toward the sentinels. "How in the Hells did they make those?"

Níscel whimpered. "No how. *Why*."

"They didn't make them to look like that," Shard said quietly. "It's what those faces saw, in the last moments of this dead city, that shaped them so."

Shard, turning his back to the dreadful immortals, used his fingers to trace their stares to a common point overhead. Whatever had come, it had come on the wind.

---

[9] A common oath of the Eld of Life, referring to the Lord of the Eld (*Bluharyn*, or the *Heron*), and the spirit of Life over which He presides (*Fergh*).

Níscel slipped beside Toron, her claws finding the links in his mail. "Toron, I want we must turn. We go back."

The man felt their pricks and looked down at her. What he saw softened him. She was wretched with fear. Her ears stood hard upon her scalp, leaning apart from one another as they swept the silence for any chance to flee. Her eyes bulged from her skull, her nostrils flitted, and her fur seemed to become glassier with every passing heartbeat. All in all, she looked far more the quarry of a hunt than the keenhearted huntress he had known at the foot of this highberg.

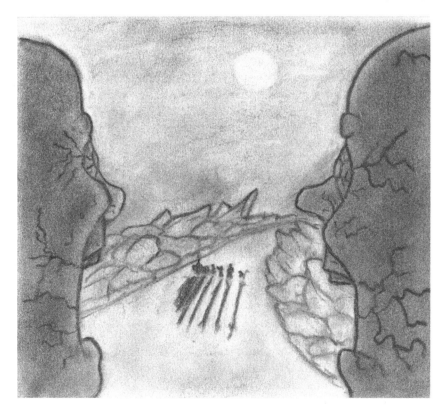

"We're not leaving," he said, his jaw knotting as Níscel rounded him and stared into his eyes. "We're going in. This is Aftheksis. It must be."

"I care not any," she cried. "I want to go to the town. This is too much for us."

"Then go," Kurtisian grumbled, tightening one of his wristwraps.

The kattid had not wanted to leave the Shebrish farming town in which they'd spent the night three days ago, and the Chaldallions had felt she should not be urged to. Leave her here, one had muttered. Give her a ball of string to pass the time, added the other. Shard had spoken not a word, though his hush had said more than enough. An unwilling thoftship was not thoftship at all, he had once said. It was thralldom. Toron had egged her onward nevertheless. They were all one, he pleaded with her. Her gifts were needed—her ears, her eyes; she could not let them down. Now, as he weighed her burden upon the lot of them all, as he watched her shudder and whimper and fight back the tears her Mannish mind bid her shed but her cattish body could not make, he found himself standing upon the threshold of renown, and could not bear turning back.

"Four months, Níscel. Four months to find what we have found here." Toron raised his hand toward the watchmen, but it balked halfway. "We're almost out of silver. We're two days from the town, and weeks from the border with Arsask. It would take us days to climb out of these bergs again."

Gorrh grumbled at that. Toron hadn't carried himself more than the last few feet.

"On top of everything else," the man said, "it will be night soon, and that's no king's garden down there. It's hinterland. Something will come at us again, and it might be no better than what's beyond those…those things up ahead."

He said it, but he didn't believe it. Nor did Níscel, whose scoff sounded like a noseful hiss.

"That like every night on the road. Shard and me see in the dark. And Gorrh too. We hear far off. Nothing come at us we not hear and ready for."

Toron felt his forbearance buckling. He took a breath. "And what are we going to do back at the town? Shall we sit there and hope some fiend comes loping out of the woods and attacks the pig yard behind the inn? So we might earn the hearts of thirty townsfolk and their eighty-year-old burgreeve?[10]"

Kurtisian snorted. "If I were one of those farmers, I'd be angry at us if we did save them. You'd think if your days were spent up to your waist in pigshit, you'd at least give Hell a go."

"I care not what we do!" Níscel said. "I want to go away from here!"

---

[10] *(AB):* Borough-reeve; mayor of a city or town.

"There's nothing down there for us!" Toron snarled.

Níscel's ears went flat to her head, and she cowered as if he'd struck her. He hated himself then, but not enough to take it back. She was as forthright in heart as anyone he had known, and he loved her for it, but such goodness was woven simply, like a child's, and it itched at him to wear it for long. Whether her cleanness of mind was a thing owed to her kind or to her own onely soul, Toron did not know. She was the only kattid he had met, and likely ever would meet here in the north of the Rámish world. What he did know was that she did not peddle any easy beliefs, which was a thing seldom done by simple Men.

He made his hand go higher and showed the watchmen with a stiff wave. "You see those? They're dreadful. They are one of the most frightening things I've ever put my eyes to. You, Kurtis? Justin?"

Both men nodded, and without waffling. Shard fully turned from them then, and did not need asking himself.

"Then let us go back!" Níscel pleaded, the trifoil toes of her boots turning by half-inches.

"Why, Níscel? That you're frightened? Gods! How do you hope we make anything of ourselves if we run from what frightens us?"

The kattid followed his hand, this time not to the watchmen but into the misty gap between them whither the road led. She took in a great, shuddering breath, and when it came back out again, it sawed from her throat in an angstpurr.

"Not only they. Not the faces. Not only. Elso. Something. Something elso." She turned her stare back upon him, and her eyes were possessed. "Can not you feel that? That? That that that that that—"

She caught herself, and Toron fought the grisly feeling that inched its way into him. Forewarnings breathed through his bones. For a handful of heartbeats, he thought he could disown it—that he might belittle that dreadful shawl that was gathering, fold by fold, about them. He had no qualms against kindhearted lies. He had said them before. But never before had he known such a feeling as he felt now, one that came at him both from within and without, and filled him with an awe whose share of wonder hardly kept his mind together. The fear in it—the fear was so much worse.

As a child, he had spent far less time among fellow Men than he had with the petty beasts and livestock of his father's homestead.

Long before the Rine had tethered his soul to Gorrh's, he'd had a feel for the quirks and ken of cats, and how their wits went beyond the weave of Man's own world, reaching into pockets and wrinkles of itness[11] forever hidden from Mannish minds. Now, having grown up, his being since bound by the will of the Heron to that of a tuskcat, he knew without dent of twain[12] that beasts were seers beyond his own seeing. So it was that he did not gainsay what Níscel felt, not only because he believed her, but because Gorrh—and through Gorrh he himself—felt it too. It was evil, and cunning, and full of hate. And it was older than the rocks they walked on.

"It's that very feeling we were hoping for," Toron made himself say. "Now let's move on." His hand gave a final swish at the screaming watchmen, then fell back to his side. "We can't become sung just by looking at something's handiwork."

Níscel's eyes kept sweeping his face, patting about for unlocked doors, and he turned away lest they seek to ransack the rooms of his mind. He set to tightening Gorrh's saddle, wary she still watched him.

"Toron," Shard called, and Toron, shaken, looked over as sharply as the summons was soft.

Weak but grandfatherly was the Highbred's smile. Fond but heavy with the doom of greater years, it was the smile of one knowing much, but who was not sure whether those with whom it spoke were knowledgeable of what they chose, or simply willful in choice.

"Toron," Shard began again. "Have you given it a thought—as to what in the Age of Life makes an unliving thing scream?"

The question struck Toron like a blow, and his chin fell to his chest.

Thoftship, and all that. Shard did not stray, least of all from his own wisdom.

In the half-hush of the winds, upon the burnished links of his byrnie, Toron beheld a hundred reflections of himself. He watched them warp, cloud over, and return beneath the slow, snowing wash of his breath. Behind his eyes, and for the last time on this road, his fear fought his hunger, and lost. Perhaps if he had felt this foreboding down below, before they'd left the valley floor, and not

---

[11] *(AK)*: reality.
[12] *(AK)* idiom: without a doubt.

so close to the end, he might have heeded it. But he hadn't, and something told him there was meaning in that. Every mail had its chinks, and everything slept, however great it was. This bank of fear was a warning, and nothing bothered to put out warnings for those it did not fear the trouble of. This thing they hunted, perhaps it was frightened too.

That they stood on the brink of something great was what mattered. That, and not Toron's own mettle, was their touchstone now.

> *The Red Collector came to reap their stock,*
> *To swallow hearts and blood and broth of thought,*
> *Entomb their Soul within Its hellish hide,*
> *and giggle screams to foam within Its veins.*

Four months ago they had heard those words. They had come as a share of a much longer lay—the *Sherk*—one chanted by an old scop[13] in a tumbledown inn just outside the walls of old Gatherdsburg. They'd heard many such yarns, some sung, others spoken. Knaks was a kingdom of tales; you could not take two steps without tripping over one. But the matter of this tale had bewitched them, gripping their very minds with both hands. Afterwards, they had all sat about the hearth until morning, shaken and shuddering, fearful of the sights that might have met them at the marchlands of slumber.

The lay told of a yoreland, in days out of Eld, whose people farmed stone itself. Aftheksis was its name. Its lords had made the choice to defy the ruling Gods, whom they believed to be corrupt, and to wall out the greater world. The Gods had answered not with sanctions but with an executioner—a fiend known in the poem as Havsikt, the Red Collector. It was a devourer of peoples—the Thede-Eater—one who swallowed not only the flesh and bones of a race, but also every trace of its pith and marrow. When It was done, it was as though Its food had never been.

The thoftship found they could not shake their minds of it, and they had agreed to look into it further. Indeed, Níscel had felt it more strongly than everyone, saying it was time they put Rhianys's death behind them, and hallow her memory with a newfound will. Given

---

[13] *(AB)*: poet.

the way by the innkeep, they had tracked the scop to his home, finding a shanty mouldering within a glade many furlongs from any road. It was the house of a hoarder, choking with old books, and they had smirked to stoop inside it, ushered in and offered tea by an old man more than willing to sing his song again.

Though the seeking and the way there proved long, the unraveling of the yarn had not. Only the Medth of Shebril, the old man pledged, held promise of such a place as the poem told. A 'rock of white mist'—a *Sherk-narsk-wirth* in the dead Aftheksish tung— was Aftheksis's crib and grave, and though many great fells and highbergs might be found within Knaks, only the easternmost chains wore mists worth such a byname. In the eight fortnights since, they had indeed eaten away at their will, feeding on its fresh hopes when starved by the endless road. But just as their stores had been threatened, they'd found the trail—word of a ruin on a nearby mountain, which no thief dared to burgle.

And here they were.

Toron's face rose hardened, and, shooting stern eyes among his thoftmen, he climbed back into Gorrh's saddle, and urged the cat onwards into the fear. Footsteps followed, and he was thankful for it.

The watchmen grew larger but no more daunting as the band drew closer. It was as though the first dread had been a wave, and once broken ashore needed time to gather itself together again in the trough. No chip or facets did the stonework show, not even when the band passed between them, and drew close enough to touch them, but did not. It was nonetheless there that a weight fell upon their living flesh, as though new moons thronged the skies, making their limbs and their marrow feel heavier. Past the heads they went, till the heads too were swallowed by the fog.

Before them loomed a mighty barrier. It was like the great Ringwall of the Leafapanz, whose gardened woods hid the Isentron of the King. Yet this was far greater. Here they stopped again, and beheld this godly curtain that dammed from cliff to cliff the wide defile down which they walked. Its top was lost to sight, becoming one with the murk, but at its foot was an opening—a tunnel so small upon the face of the whole that it seemed no greater than a mousehole. Its gate, had it ever owned one, was missing, and what lay within not even the sharpest of their eyes might see. The thoftship kept to their tracks, and as they drew nearer saw that the doorway was much greater than they'd reckoned. So, by that

balance, was the wall, whose height—what they could see of it—
Shard put at near to three furlongs. Choked with shadows, its doorway stretched the height of many Men; four-cornered it was, and flat
were its four sides. It was a block of hollow, with no arch or lintel to
be seen.

The thoftship halted again fifty yards from the threshold, for it
was there that a breeze could be felt, breathing through the wall's
single bore with a whine. Though Toron had felt uneasy in mind
before this, it was here where he first began to feel ill.

"What's that up there?" Kurtisian said, marking a less-weathered
patch above the entrance.

"I would say it is where the marker used to be," Shard offered.
"It might have been a tablet with the ruling family's houseshield, or
perhaps a board bearing the city's name. Either way, we could not
have known or read it."

"Well, why in the Hells would it be gone?" Justinian griped.
"It's—what—a couple of hundred feet across? I don't see any rubble
around. Who could have packed something like that away? And now
we can't tell for sure if this is the right place."

Kurtisian gave an overwrought laugh. "You're rizzing[14], right?"

"Come," Toron egged them. "The thing we're after isn't hiding
outside."

Shard gave a start, as though stung from inside his clothing, and
Toron did not see how oddly the outlander looked at him.

"*Alfresco*," Shard whispered. And then he repeated something to
himself—a portion of the *Sherk* the old poet had murmured beneath
his beard, and which the Highbred alone could have understood in
full:

enim inir versti vargar
aldri al fresco mithe
autem in tenebris
frá augunum solanna
firenweorc wite in withe.[15]

---

[14] *(AC)*: kidding; joking
[15] From the Braccish, Linguish, and Hálish:
> *For the worst criminals*
> *never hide outside,*
> *but in shadows*
> *do their evil deeds,*
> *away from the eyes of the suns.*

Justinian's face soured. "What did you say?"

Shard blinked it away, the memory of a half-remembered dream. He turned to the much younger man with blithe weariness. "*Alfresco*, Chaldallion. It's a late Linguish word. Spoken among the Shoeswap Islands[16]. It means 'in the fresh.' Outside. Under the sun."

Justinian nodded slowly, not taking his eyes away. "Benny.[17] Thought you meant that herb horses eat. Didn't think it would bother hiding *that*. Stuff tastes like feck."

Kurtisian's eyes went white as they rolled. "Gods, you're an moron sometimes, Justin."

"Yeah, and you knew what it was. You've never been to the Islands."

Kurtisian halted dead in his tracks. His look was of simmering wrath, as though his brother had hurled at him the worst of slurs, and in a tung that only sounded like the Allmal they all knew. He spoke without turning his head, shaping the words as one angrily chews a meal. "I knew that it wasn't *alfalfa*, you walking gut. Just purse those gansy lips of yours and swallow it next time."

Now it was Justinian who stopped thunderstruck. His hands clenched into hammers.

"You wanna utter that *itrem*?"[18]

And before anyone might step in, there came a flurry of sound, of feet scraping stone, and grunts of swift movement, whereupon the Chaldallions stood chest-to-chest, or more to it, chest to stomach. Such a duel might have seemed whimsical, were Kurtisian not the magician he was. The full weight of his body he put into his man, and he glowered up at him to wither the day. The share of flesh that doled them was lopsided two times; Kurtisian might have been a child seeking to uproot his father's house. Justinian kept his head and saw this, but he saw the blue throb in his brother's eyes too, and knew along with everyone watching that if Kurtisian chose to unleash his magic, the bigger man's bulk would count for nothing more than making it hard for his attacker to miss.

Justinian swallowed for all to see. "*Fra*, you need some calm—"

---

[16] *Le isole scusawappi*—the rocky archipelago, known for its soaring bluffs and manors, lying to the east of the Colonial mainland. Commonly referred to as *le isole*, and *The Isolas* or *The Islands* in the Colonial Allmal.

[17] *(AC)*: Okay.

[18] *(AC)*: 'You want to say that again?'

"Shut it, *pantex*. Just shut up." Using the hand that wasn't a fist in his brother's stomach, Kurtisian rapped Justinian on the ear. "You hear me? *Fra?*"

Níscel slipped between the warring siblings, then seemed to unfold and enlarge herself there, wedging them apart a little. "Ease, Kurtisian. Why say you these awful things?"

With the slightness of her frame and the switching of her tail, the kattid was like a thing of rope between the two men, but she seemed more at ease dealing with this than she had been on the path a while earlier. Her eyes, always wet, always shining, and thrice the breadth of any Man's, had the uncanny power to soothe and soften any onlooker. Like the faces of three sad, honest children they were, all staring up and imploring at once. It worked here, as it always had, but as Kurtisian backed down, he blinked long and slowly, like one fishing himself out of a deep sweven[19]. With every opening and closing of his eyes, the blue light dampened, until at last and again they were wholly his own. He stared at his brother in a stun before turning himself away. Justinian let his hand steal to his stomach, and slowly let out his breath.

"Let's get on with it," Kurtisian said quietly, as to himself. He strode past Shard and Toron, as though he would storm the stronghold alone. His cloaked frame, black tethered to black, was a ghost against the murk of the doorway.

They did not bother to share glances, but went after, stepping onto the tongue of mist that seemed to reach out the moment they had all made up their minds to follow. One by one they entered the open mouth of the wall, each looking up and around at its edges as though wary of fangs or collapse. And Toron, as he always did before gaining a building or other hampering place, leaned his swordstaff up against the outer wall, and left it there.

Inside what might have been called the stronghold's gatehouse was a plug of whiteness that stretched on for too long. Slowly they trod, and very gingerly, but with every footstep they made, they knew the wall atop and about them was that thick, and it beaded the mind to think of it. Not the Ringwall, nor the unbreakable Sigyards of the Hálishmen, nor even the yorechewn rubble of the forlornlands along the Sundarsund showed such uncanny

---

[19] *(AB):* a vision while asleep; often the neutral term between a *dream*—which is joyful—and a *nightmare*—which is distressing.

workmanship. Showing neither grain nor seam nor crack, it was as though the stone had been made molten, thinner than gruel, and poured into a form the height of a highberg, there to set as ice does. No wright or orthank[20] they knew of might have wrought what they saw. Yet it was only a shell for the greater wonder it guarded.

As with the road up, the insides of the tunnel played with the sounds of their passage, making every clink and rasp and footfall much louder. Even Shard and Níscel seemed walking rackets. And it was more than some prank of the stone that saw to it. Not a mouse, they felt, might have come upon this stead unheard, just as nothing seeable might have come before that wall unseen. Following each other's shapes in the gloom, they at last breached the white curtain of that terminus, looking to step out from beneath the strongwork onto a flat of fog—a swamp of ruins, with bones weltering in shoals of smog. But instead, and to no great wonder given the things they had already seen, they found themselves ushered into a realm so open and clear that its sight bit the eyes.

A burg of towers and of pillars, a city still and soundless, stood just beyond the greatest courtyard any of them had ever dreamed. That open place, as flat and as dark as an underground sea, fanned open from the gate, edged in by the faces of the cliffs and reached fifteen furlongs or more before ending at the foot of the burg's own battlement. The vastness of the yard, like that of the stone curtain under which they'd walked, threatened the worth of their own menning[21]. Every Man and being they had seen in all their lives, gathered up as one whole throng, might have stood upon that field, and easily. And yet that place was only an apron of sorts, a showcase for the work at its yonder end.

The burg itself was foremost an upward one, with spires by the scores—fingers of stone both thick and thin, like the very hands of those titans whose heads flanked the incoming road. Knuckled with inner chambers they all stood and bulged, some not altogether straight, some outreaching others, their skin wrinkled with the brims of outlooks and walkways. A cunning network of black threads ran among them, many knotting into hubs, and which, for being seen from such a faraway stretch, must at closer look be thick, and solid enough to hold up many Men. Some were catwalks, and others were

---

[20] *(AB):* skilfulness and ingenuity, especially in matters of engineering. *Orthanksmith* is the *Allmal* for both a master architect and an engineer.
[21] *(AK):* civilization.

roofed bridges. Houses of a kind were stitched up in the weave, like small birds in a great spider's web. And for every building that lent many sights of its kind, there were onely ones too—singular sorts of steeples and landings and overpasses that, standing out from the others, made for a balance between onemindedness and freedom.

A roof of sorts overshadowed the deadburg. Piecemeal it was, and upheld by six pillars of heaven. If, for the thoftship now looking upon them, the outer wall of that place had cast new touchstones for all that was both manmade and huge, these pillars broke it, and in its stead put themselves. In two rows of three they stood, staggered evenly across the burg's breadth, their ankles among the buildings, each reaching up no one might reckon how far, the fog gathered about their necks, the tilted panels atop them like the black caps of vast, underworldly mushrooms. The edges of the great sheets did not meet, but by tilting and overlapping each other at varying heights, they worked both to let in the daylight as well as to hood from any storm the great canyon in which the burg lay. Their undersides— those that might be seen from where the band stood—showed themselves veined with black vessels. Fixed to the lowermost edge of each panel was a trough, from which ran many sluices. These led into single pipes which ran down the height of each pillar into the burg below. Ledges lipped out beneath doorholes. Stairways open to the air, and railless, wound and zagged from one hole to another. In only a few places did the black bridgework of the burg's towers touch the six pillars. From this it was clear, as well as from the rawer look of them, that the larger structures were workmanly buildings, and not, like the towers, for living in.

A cold sweat scampered across Toron's body as his eyes, leaping from one share of the roof to another, came to land upon the one their path would lead below. He felt the ground shiver as Justinian moved closer to him, a feeling he knew well, but one he found he did not welcome here.

"Gaia's mams," Justinian muttered. "How old are those columns? How old did the poem say this place was? 'Cause, Heron, if that thing falls—"

He brought his hands together slowly, from top and bottom, then slammed them together with a bloodcurdling clap.

Níscel leapt the height of a man.

"Stitch them, Justin!" she shrieked. She took a step back towards the wall whence they'd come.

The man chortled, but it had no heart. "What? If it falls, it falls. It's not like talking about it's going to make it any more likely to happen."

Shard's cheeks caved in between his teeth, and he looked swiftly from the roof to his most youthful comrade. "In my goings, Chaldallion, that's often what happens."

The Highbred began to fish for something within his vest pocket. Scoffing, Justinian looked about the rest of them, but found himself besieged by frowns, some angrier than others. Most of the magic their thoftship knew, including many of his prayers, had their strength unleashed by words.

Justinian bristled. "Prime. Then I'll talk about it only because I'd rather be squashed by a couple thousand tons of friendly stone than swallowed by some race-devouring dra—"

The Sumo's mouth finished, but his voice did not. For in the half-heartbeat it took Shard to toss a pinch of rabbit fluff into his face, he found himself struck dumb. Bringing a hand to his throat, Justinian flushed as his lips wove soundlessly. Shard dusted the rest of the white fuzz from his fingertips.

Kurtisian watched his brother with mock fascination. "These are the most intelligent things I think I've ever heard him say."

"He can still hear you," Shard said as Justinian gave up trying to speak and eyed his brother with knotted jaws. The Sumo then looked over at the Highbred who had hushed him, his look somewhere between hurt and hate. Shard returned the stare without fear, but also without ill will.

"Easy, Chaldallion. It will wear off in a while. And by then you may have a better understanding of what we face here."

Justinian snorted, and when he found he was able to snort, began to show his anger with a riot of wet, loathsome noises. He wasn't at it for long before he began to laugh at himself a little, which they all shared in.

Toron smiled too, but it was not glad. Never before had Shard wielded dreecraft against one of their own thoftship without leave. He'd done it to heal them and to hasten them and to knead their hearts when the fears or sorrows were too much. Though all were helpful things, he had always asked. But since they'd heard the *Sherk* and begun to seek its roots, Shard had become unlike himself. He'd turned grim where once blithehearted and was often impatient with the youthful thoughts they put to him. He had held them together when Toron broke—after they'd buried Rhianys, and made the memory of her into kindling, a fire both to warm them and to drive their hopes out of hiding. But he had not spoken of Rhianys for months and seemed to have forgotten her. He slept less, and ate more, and wandered away from their camps. The others swore they'd heard him talking to himself, and in a tung none of them knew, or had heard him speak before.

Whatever the Highbred might do next, it surprised Toron not at all when the Sumo, even in mid-laugh, lunged at him. Shard easily evaded the giant, waltzing out onto the outyard with steps that looked to be avoiding unseen snares.

"Shard," Toron called to him, clearing his throat, "maybe you should let him speak again. He's learned better, I think."

"It will only be for an hour or so," the outlander replied. "With any luck."

And he pulled on his cowl and tied his scarf around the lower share of his face. Once that mask was in place, Shard did not speak. It was all Toron could do to cast Justinian an unhappy look and to nod for everyone to move on toward the burg.

He felt they had little to fear from the ruin itself. Its hush and the forbidding look of it made for little more than a rueful kind of wonder when beheld without thought of the *Sherk*. And seen with that thought, everything beneath the suns seemed to scream. He knew he had to push it from his mind, at least until—

It then beheld a cave, an open bone
Of Smað Herself where marrow ore was sucked
And worked by all the hands It had consumed
Into Aftheksis of this Sherk-narsk-wirth.
In Mother's veins th'Infanticidal wormed
Whilst cackling, cackling, dragging squealing souls
To stew and seethe and slumber 'thin Her womb.

The burg wore its lifelessness well. A place of steel and stone, no share of its body had ever lived, and even the footfalls which knocked ringing from its many faces showed its grudge to host life now. Their brains hammered by those sounds, the six souls made their way across the outyard towards the burg's innermost wall. Unlike the outer wall, its front showed seams, but met tightly together without grout or sign of tack.

So widely swept the commons that its floor seemed to dip on all its sides, like the face of the sea, whose flat bends round behind the head of the world. Its tiles were not all the same, neither in size nor in shape. Even their hugeness changed, with some stretching for tens of ells, in forms unlike anything, with others having four sides only, and small enough for a man to lie upon. Frost traced a few of their seams, as though leaking up from below, and though ice was cold, and no more alive than stone, life was its domain, and its sight was not unhappy. It was hard to tell whether they were made of metal or stone. They seemed a bit of both. It was one of the few times Toron bethought himself to ask Justinian about such a thing, and Justinian could not have answered.

Toron gave up trying to reckon with the work that had made all this, for to look upon something he could not understand was to know he had flawed means to grasp it. It was the same when he sought to ween[22] the forges of the gods, which he knew Men called forges only because Men had no word for what the gods themselves must wield in the making of things.

Crossing the yard took long enough for Toron to think of singing a tidesong[23] and then to sing the one he chose ten times over. He hummed it to himself as his head swung everywhere, seeing things lurking in the corners of his eyes, things skulking like shucks[24] among the many shadows and edges of the looming deadland. He bungled the pace of his singing, he was sure, but around four toes of a daytime[25] went by as Gorrh padded across the grounds, and though the many uprights of stone grew and sharpened before them, Toron still, through the legs and shoulders of that soulless crowd, could not spy the burg's furthest end.

In the freedom of that bleak place, he and Gorrh spent some time seeking to better the cat's legwork. Unlike the sharing of their minds, riding was something the two of them had given a lot of work. It showed not only in the onely make of their saddle, but also in the unwonely[26] way in which each carried himself. No fourlegged

---

[22] *(AB):* imagine. The *Knaksish* is 'insee,'— to see within the mind.
[23] *(AK):* A song of a certain length, sung in order to measure the precise passage of time. Many of the Knaksish folk still use them; in the burgs, however, they have largely been replaced by *Timekeepers*.
[24] *(AB):* unknown monsters; bogeymen.
[25] About forty minutes (one toe being ten minutes).
[26] *(AB):* abnormal; unnatural.

thing was less suited to be ridden than a cat, and Toron could not have stayed in the saddle for more than a few rough moments were Gorrh to step in his wonted fashion. Built to skulk, crouch, and leap, the beasts' legs seemed fixed to their trunks from the sides rather than below, the great humps of their shoulders pitching and heaving beneath a scruff of skin too loose to grip firmly. The barrels of their bodies were lithe and snakelike, made to bend and twist with the demands of the four limbs, and narrow to keep its innards from harm. The backbone itself was thick and mighty, a sight clear to all as it stood up along the creature's length, blades to dishearten all climbers. And then there was the head—the great, tossing flesh-churner which fronted the whole like a prow, less the stem than the core itself, and dragging the rest behind it. Since first climbing aboard Gorrh, Toron had come to weigh every redbloodeded thing he met as a steed, and deemed that almost anything, including bears, brocks[27], spiders, and ground-birds—anything save snakes, bats, and maybe fish—would make for better riding.

At long last the thoftship came within arrowshot of the inner wall. In height it was like the walls that safeguarded their lands' own burgs, but here seemed less a battlement than a kerbstone between outyard and inner. Rather than a single barrier sweeping from one cliffside to the other, it ran between fortlets and gatehouses. Of the fortlets there were twenty-four, each with a brooding watchtower whose heights opened onto the crest of the wall, which, it seemed, might be walked, but was not crenellated. Of the gatehouses there were five—five for five gates—built at even stretches, but not wholly alike in shape. The greatest was not the middlemost, but the one to the left of it, and it bested the others not so much in height as in width and the lounging sprawl of its stonework. Like a lying lump of a beast it seemed, all bulk and mounds, windows here and there, stirring to behold, but with no further meaning. Though the thoftship had drawn closer to another gatehouse, this was the one their eyes were drawn to. Shard, having ended the unsettling sideways slink by which he had made his own way across the outyard, stood akimbo and closest to it. Toron brought Gorrh beside him, wondering what his better eyes saw.

"Not the guestiest looking place," the younger man said.

---

[27] (AB): badgers.

Shard pulled down his scarf. "That or the contrary. Judging from how hard it was to get in unwelcome, I would say that whatever hospitality these people gave must have been hearty indeed."

Toron looked back across the outyard. "Odd that the inner wall is so far back from the outer one. The way we would build them in Knaks is to put them close together, or at least build a few more between here and there. Having a field like this before your own gates—it's a gift to your foes once they've broken in. Somewhere to muster."

Shard nodded. "Yes. If walls were your only fallback. But these," and he waved a six-fingered hand at the chain of strongworks before them, "are an afterthought. You'll see there are no gates."

Toron squinted. He could barely make out the emptiness within the shadows of the gatehouses, but the Highbred was right.

"What do you mean?"

"The floorstones," Shard said, tapping his split-toed boots, "aren't all anchored. They are some cunning sort of trap, though they no doubt need men to work it."

Like a landed fish, a chill twisted its way up out of Toron's skin. "What do you mean they're a trap?"

No one save Shard seemed easy with the news, but it was Justinian, likely having felt such a thing with every step, whose face suddenly looked as though he were standing atop the grave of a restless body. He moved swiftly to remove himself, and his wide steps toward the inner wall were like those of a thief slipping across a room full of sleeping dogs. Níscel and Kurtisian froze where they were.

"Trap? Trap is? Under us?" the kattid mewled. Her tail wrote panic behind her.

Kurtisian seemed more impatient than afraid. "Well, should we move or not?"

"As I said," Shard replied, his quicksilver eyes seeking something in the nearby wall, "I don't believe it's something that one simply springs by walking across it. It is more like a drawbridge than a snare. A mechanism, some might call it."

Toron braced his feet in the stirrups, readying Gorrh to leap. It brought him no balm to hear a word he did not understand.

Shard gave Níscel a bit of a look. "You say you did not feel it? Not at all?"

All owned and aghast, she did not feel his barb. "A trap? No. No! The floor? The floor is it?" She went high from foot to foot, a cat with something on its paw, and a new huntedness came into her eyes. "The floor, not all down! Feel it walking over! Something under? Under?"

She went over the same words, and again, and Toron called to her, told her it was no plight. Kurtisian laughed at that, asked if he meant this one moment. Of course they were in danger. If not here, then soon enough.

Toron climbed down from the saddle and made a show of putting his feet on the same tile as hers. He stomped on it twice, proving its trustworthiness, but the kattid's fright was unbroken.

"Níscel—" he pleaded.

"Name!" she shrieked, a rag of voice whose tattered edges caught on every corner and surface within earshot. "Not my name!"

One side of his mouth smiled. "Níscel, I know that's not your true name. You know I can't say your true name."

She smiled too, such as cat can, then said, "this place is evil."

Yet again the words went into him like a slithering thing, and he backed away lest she feel it slip back out of him. He closed his eyes to get a hold of himself but found that the darkness did nothing to banish something he might have felt without eyes.

"No," Shard pledged, appearing beside them. His eyes made a ring up and over all their heads. "It is not a place of evil, but a place that has been scoured of everything else. Goodness, holiness, the softest hues of its past. These things have been shorn away, and flayed, and scraped to the bones of what you see left, and that which is left has been salted by what hides here. It cannot be revoked."

"If it's irrevocable," Kurtisian said, "then why are we here?"

Toron answered. "The old man himself said that we could not free Aftheksis. That which has been eaten, it cannot be unswallowed. We could only make sure it would be His last. His last meal. The Thede-Eater."

Kurtisian nodded, as one brooks the story of a child one does not believe or much like. "And this thing, this Red Collector, took this whole city. Without scratching the stonework and without its people even springing their defenses."

"And many other cities," Shard said, and recalled the lines of the *Sherk*:

and not simply burgs but whole folkdoms fell,
to his hunger, whose food whets not slakes it.

"Word for word," Kurtisian said, nodding wry credit. "I heard it first in a dirtfarmer's tavern and again in a smelly hovel and thought nothing of it either time." He looked around, the resolve draining from his lips and leaving them dry. "Guess I should have kept my eyes shut. My eyes, at the least."

Shard looked to the nearest gatehouse. "The way is open," he said, and slipped forth with less sound than he made replacing his scarf.

The gatehouse, which indeed housed no gate they could find, opened onto what looked to be the deadburg's mightiest street. Walled in by low buildings of mottled gray, the road stretched far into the yonder, arrow-straight, until it seemed to come to a point at the foot of the cliffwall at the end of the defile. From its mouth, the urban canyon into which they stepped seemed a sleeping gauntlet, something which, though now dormant, had been built to chop away to the very gist of the unworthy. The doors and windows on the face of it were like so many eyes, and where there were eyes, there were arms, and hands to seize. The skyline was a piled throng, a cluster of mushroom-like rooftops, stone-shingled, and beyond them the columns, smooth as river rocks, standing among them like the trunks of so many World Trees.

Someone said, "Toron, look at the walls," and he did so, stepping closer to one of the two buildings that cheeked the mouth of the street, and beholding a sight both grand and awful. Works of choicest craftsmanship adorned the building's skin, like the scar-nodes of the Ignish, which Rhianys had shown to him hidden beneath her sleeves. They were not carven, but risen, things brought forth from the stone as though called from its depths, and inlaid with gems and iron, and other things mined from the innards of the world. And bringing back his eyes to the greater sweep of the burg, Toron beheld the grays of the yonder walls, and made out ornamentation there too. Every building he could see, save for the mighty pillars, stood decked by cunningest skill.

Right before him stood a likeness of war, and so like life it bulged that it threatened to leap onto the street alongside him. Among the many things it showed were a band of stocky little men, wielding hammer and pike, braving a pair of giants—what

Knaksmen called *thurses*—which snarled soundlessly. Between them aloft the two monsters held a great tree, uprooted and brandished as a club, its trunk bleeding resin of amber, and roots trailing clods of brown gemstones. Four moons and a thousand stars overhung their skirmish, while a somber, bearded man whose cowl glittered, oversaw it all from higher still. Some of the company's armour had been overplated with steel, and every eye glinted, whether blue or green or yellow-red. The thurses' loincloths were trimmed with silver slag, and the trunk of their tree was a length of petrified wood. Glitter of sundry shades dusted the heavenly bodies overhead, which made them glimmer with every shift of Toron's eye. And shift they did, for the workmanship overwhelmed him. No inch of the thing had been made without utmost care—from the tendril-threads trailing from the tree's roots to the creases and abrasions on the thurses' knees.

Stepping between Toron's eyes and the wall, Kurtisian ran light fingers across its face. "A more festive theme on the one behind you," he said. "I like this one better."

Toron looked around to find the rest of the thoftship fixed on the gayer sight he spoke of. It showed fierce, almost frantic, merry-making, with thickly bearded men and braided women jigging wildly atop the same long tables at which their cheering onlookers sat drinking. Chips of white gemstones overlaid the foaming heads of their ale, while several ewers of the stuff were in many stages of flipping through the air. Six minstrels, or *gleemen*, plucked and stroked string-things with real strings. Their music was a tangle of rubies and owlstones, which like a whirlwind ensnared every frolicker.

Kurtisian made a sound of disgust. "What was that?"

Toron looked back. "What was what?"

He saw his thoftman's fingers smeared with what looked to be soot. Kurtisian rubbed them together, and black dust hung in the air before him.

"The icon's beard." Kurtisian pointed at the lordly figure overseeing the battle. "It's turning to ash or something."

Toron reached up and ran his own hand along its stormy locks. He had foreseen them feeling sharp, like the long filings left on a blacksmith's bench. Instead, they were crusty and loose, like paint flaking from an old fencepost. A clump broke away, showing pocked stone beneath, and fell to the ground before a trail of powder.

"There's some on the tree, too," Kurtisian said. "And under the footsoldier's helmet. Third one from the right."

Indeed, ashy clods hung from both.

Kurtisian called to his brother, asked if he saw any where he was. Still unable to speak, and knowing Kurtisian knew it, the Sumo responded with the waggling, two-fingered gesture the two often made at each other, and whose meaning was much more clear than how it worked. Kurtisian made the answering sign, which was just as cryptic, and each returned to his perusal of the wall before him.

Toron watched them coolly but then had to blink, swearing he saw Shard next to Justinian one heartbeat, but not the very next. A darkness slinked in the stillness not too much further away—a shifting of shadows—and then suddenly there was something leaping across the rooftops. Had Toron not seen Shard do so before, in towns as well as in trees, he would have thought it a prowler. He had to calm himself no less, however, nearly leaping from the saddle and bringing Gorrh's hackles up in alarm.

They kept to their path, and made their way through the southern quarter of what had to be—what could only be—the burg of Sherknarsk-wirth. Every step made that sooth more sure, for Aftheksis had been a wonderhouse of ingenuity, and all that they saw, even dormant and in vestige, was beyond their menning to remake. They had to stop themselves from stopping, so many wonders they passed. Nothing—neither door nor eave, nor sash nor streetlight—had been given in boredom to an everyday make, and these were but the things they recognized from their own worlds. Most of what they saw they did not understand—things both great and small, some painstaking, others simple, some fitted with pipes and belts and wires and toothed wheels, some sitting in the street where likely they had moved in some way, and others fixed to houses and to the ground itself, seeming like chests save that their insides were full of working parts. As for images, every brick and tile had a face, and every wall told a tale, even the many-storeyed buildings, as well as those for business rather than living. Some impressed more than others, a few so thorough as to draw the buildings themselves—their framework, and gables, and windows—into their play. The best they beheld was a two-floored dwelling that showed the duel between a lone thegn and some sort of wyrm. The fighter seemed little more than a pair of boots and a cloak huddling beneath a great shield, whose panel twinned as the building's front door. The fiend he braved took up the rest of the building, its head tilted, its one eye a dormer and the other an oriel, its belch of flame a widow's staircase that made its way down the wall from its throat, which stood black-gated within the shadowed jaws of a landing. Its wings were peaks enclosing a rooftop outlook, its eaves hanging nearly to the ground on two sides.

This was the one the thoftship dawdled longest to admire, and the last for which they stopped altogether to do so. They passed words among one another like bland waybread, feeling it dimwitted to be speaking of artwork at such a time, but having never seen anything of its like. They spoke of its differences from the others. Whereas every other building seemed to raise the people above their foemen, this work was unmistakably more concerned with glorifying the monster.

Kurtisian crossed his arms. "I wonder what Muse asked for that one." He gave a halfhearted look around. "Whichever it was, it doesn't look like they listened to her again."

Toron shrugged. "The better the baddy, the bleader the boot."

Kurtisian shook his head like a small bug had gotten inside.

"Means the bigger your foe, the more you take home. Even if you lose."

Some inner part of Kurtisian tried to laugh, but the outer part showed only the ripple of a smile. "Only if someone hears about it."

The two kept walking, leaving Níscel to stare at it from one side of her head, toddling from one three-toed foot to the other like a child who had to pee. Justinian tried to say something, and, finding himself still unable, restoked his glower and threw it Shard's way.

Such onely buildings were not wonely[28] within the burg. With every passing row, with every face that resembled its neighbour, it became more clear that for those who had once lived and built here, togetherness was greater than selfdom—that one song sung by many voices made the mightier sound in life. Though the stagger of their windows and doors would differ from one building to another, some dealt toward this side, some toward the other, the difference among them was like the faces of the felefedborn[29], which only those closest to them might know or care to tell apart. In shape, most of the houses hunkered to the ground like half-kegs, as though dumped from an alemonger's wagon outside the doors of taverns not yet open. The taller dwellings, perhaps those of wealthier households, were two and three of these barrels stacked up, though the etchings and byworks upon them sometimes tried to hide the seams. Railed overlooks and windowboxes made ledges over the street. Walkways joined a handful of rooftops, while the uppermost floors of some lay partly open to the air, showing chairs and shelves and other empty things. All lay shadowed beneath the heavenly roofsheets, whose great undersides seemed as the keels of airships frozen in midfounder. The mind played tricks on whatever eye beheld them, and made them tremble where they hung, or inch, slowly and terribly, toward the ground.

The burg's lack of life bedeviled every thought, breathing out the blackness of what had purged it. But every now and again even whispering devils must take breaths, and when they did so, other lacks than life slumped forth to be heeded. There was, for one, no writing. No markings at all told one door from another. No signboards stood before or above them; no wayboards named the streets. No runes or staves of any kind gave tell to the carvings upon

---

[28] *(AB):* normal; habitual. At times, wonely can also mean 'natural.'

[29] *(AK):* children born as multiples, such as twins, triplets and quadruplets.

the walls. Their lack, in this clever place, was unright. No such
cunning as gave rise to such works might have done so without at
least rime of numbers. The streets ran straight, and where they joined
they did so smoothly, like two locks of hair braided together. Such a
thing was not at all like the tangle and riot of burgs elsewhere and
yet living, whose streets had grown out of need and frayed without
foresight, and came together into waymeets[30] that simply dumped
travellers into each other's paths. Though it was not beyond belief
that the people of Aftheksis simply grew up to know their burg
without needing outward means to guide them through it, and that
guests from away were too seldseen or unwelcome to be cared for, it
seemed as unlikely as boatless vikings that they had not found the
means to make letters.

A few toes went by before the street could be seen to end, where
it fed like a riverbed into the empty lake of another burgyard.
Squinting toward it, Toron fell in alongside Gorrh and slipped a hand
beneath the tuskcat's barding, spidering his fingers to dig past the
fur. He set fingertips against the axling thews of the beast's shoulder,
shaped his pace to his lumber, and closed his eyes. When he opened
them again—or rather, when his sight came back to him—he saw
what lay ahead with fourfold the sharpness. It was not quite Gorrh's
own sight, nor might it be said simply to better Toron's own. Rather,
it was through some weaving together of their flesh and their souls,
whereby all were pulled straight side-by-side, their sinews made taut
with warp weights, and the threads of their spirits wefted to and fro
among them. It was not without worry, this thing the loom made,
and could only be done with care and deep thought. They called it
the Rinesight, and it was one of four gifts that the Heron, somehow
and without word of why, had seen fit to give them.

Through it Toron saw new things, and none of them was
heartening. In the courtyard was a dry springwell[31], round and many-
stepped, its shape slouching before the face of something grim and
yonder. Behind it, peering down the length of the street they walked,
was a great dark façade—a face of sorts that seemed to have been
gutted onto the burgyard. The sight of it made Toron's blood jolt,
and he steadied and strained his sight to make it out fully.

It was only a hall, but one whose two dark windows and open

---

[30] *(AK):* intersections; crossroads.
[31] *(AK)*: fountain.

doorway between them gave it the look of a misshapen face. The dark runs of rubble lying before each of the three hollows had long ceased to flow. It soothed Toron only a little that the building was not indeed a skull that had been boiled to make its insides flow out, for he could think of no way why the heaps should lie before it as they did.

The sight was a gust of wind upon his smoldering uneasiness, for it was the first token of wreck, and not simply of forlornness, that the thoftship had found. He swallowed hard and caught a stir upon the field before him, and then there was Shard, standing next to the spills as though he had blinked there. Each spill at its deepest was the height of two men. Toron broke the Rine and shook the fog back into his own eyes, turning toward his thoftmen as he heard them shuffle up to him for word.

Níscel's voice came first, rasped not spoken. "Bastet, Toron! There is something at the end! It watches us!"

"It's only another building," he said. "But there's something dumping out from inside."

Kurtisian stepped up. "What's that? Something's ruined up there? An actual bit of wreckage?"

"Yes."

"Any sign of Master Mysterious?"

"He's already there. Looks like he's waiting for us."

"Hey, Thorn, you know that smart, black silk shirt you bought in Eksar?"

"What? Yes."

"Can I have it?"

Toron turned and found Kurtisian weirdly in earnest. "Can you *have* it?"

The southerner looked back at him as though he were the odd one. "What?"

"What do you mean, 'what'?"

"What were you talking about?"

"You asked if you might have my black shirt."

"Did I?"

"Yes, you did."

"Hm."

"No, you can't."

"All right."

Toron looked away and back at Kurtisian a few times, awaiting the twist of his mouth that gave away a prank. He saw no such thing and had to wonder if the same dread that made himself forget such things as clothing and trade and belongings was beginning to unhinge the others. Now that the whim of handsome shirts had been pushed into his head, all Toron could think about was his own burial, or balefire[32], and the likelihood that whatever he wore now was what he might be wearing at his first dinner in the Hereafter. He found he was able to banish the thought readily enough, but only because the dread of this place, begrudging of other cares, was too eager to chase everything else away.

Turning back to Níscel, he saw from the way she stood that she had less will to go further than he. Rather than a soul quick and fleet, she looked a plant happily grown there, and might not but for the death of her be uprooted.

"Come along, Níscel. There is no one there. I swear to it."

"Gods, Toron, I heard something."

Her eyes were halved eggs, the yolks poisoned black.

"Gorrh heard nothing," he said, and did not lie.

"You do not only hear with your ears, you know."

The words curdled him. He knew she'd talk back, but he hadn't foreseen any wisdom in it, and Níscel's wisdom, when it came, was as unsettling as a child's prophesy.

"Well," Toron answered, struggling to smooth himself, "if you're listening with your mind, then you're bound to frighten yourself."

But underneath his mail, his gooseflesh kept its sweat. Rather than hide his shudders, that burnished steel threatened with its shimmering to highlight them. Before he could speak, however, Kurtisian stormed in. His eyes were fey and furious, and he pickaxed the catwoman's sternum with his fingers.

"Listen up, you overgrown rat. If we need to keep changing your swaddling rags every ten steps, I'm going to stop warming up my hands to do it." He clenched both teeth and fist, gnashing as though to withstand a great pang of mind. When it was over, he seemed calmer, but no less caustic. "You know, you won't hurt anybody's feelings by turning around and going back down to that pisswater village, so those plebes can skin you. And you know it'll happen

---

[32] *(AK)*: funeral pyre.

without us there. That's you, gattagat. Always the needer, never the donor."

Toron had no meaning for *gattagat*, but what he had understood of Kurtisian's words was scornful enough. Though it went against his better reckoning, he bellied up to the man and glowered down at him. "Hold your tongue, southman," he snarled, and bit back the lestword[33] that would send it all south of Hell.

Níscel needed no backer. Had Kurtisian's words been hooks, they could not have drawn her eyelids back any further, and the look with which she answered her assailant threatened a storm of its own. She leaned around Toron and swan-beaked the southerner's chest with her own paw. Its thudding was ominous.

"Who are you think you fool, apeman? You think I smell not *your* fear? You hide it with your words, but you fear as much as I do. Fear stinks, apeman, and you stink so bad, you shit in that suit and it would not hide it."

Kurtisian raised his left hand, and Toron saw the face he wore. He threw himself into the dreeman as swiftly and as hard as he could.

Kurtisian's everyday ire was like a pan of water on the boil, running up from smooth toward a foam for all to see and avoid. But his hottest anger was like the dry ice of orthankship[34], which when given to air burned straight to a fume, overleaping thaw and showing nothing of a simmer beforehand. Once it boiled there was no unboiling it. Only heat itself might burn off that steam, and the rage consume itself upon the pyre it had ignited.

Toron had seen the telltale flash of blue and thrown his elbow into Kurtisian's mouth. He knew the southerner's dreecraft needed two such flashes to happen, the first of which was a silent kindling, and came as the dreeman went from thought to deed. That flash merely unlocked the gates to the weird powers waiting behind them. It was the second flash that mattered most, that which needed words, and which called those powers down the halls of Kurtisian's own flesh, to be discharged irrevocably upon whatever the dreeman put in their path. So it was that Toron had meant to keep Kurtisian from speaking, and was dismayed when their struggle somehow tore itself in half. Each man tumbled his own way, a clatter of cloth and steel.

---

[33] *(AK)*: a contingent warning; an 'or-else'

[34] *(AB)*: the practice and/or product of *orthank*; can refer to both alchemy and engineering, including chemistry and physical products of ingenuity.

Kurtisian went into the wall of a nearby building, and when he turned, Toron stood before him with both swords drawn.

Kurtisian's grin was diabolical. Both men knew the blades were of middling use against him, less against his the dreeman's own weapon—the *Carno*—an edged horror he could summon at a word, and which was named from the Linguish for the meat it carved so greedily. The sorcerer eyed his thoftman from where he propped himself. The decorated wall at his back showed a solemn feast, in their midst a singer frozen in midsong. Kurtisian's hand lay hard on her breast as he pulled himself up.

Justinian had caught up to them now, but stood well away, a grimful kind of helplessness flickering across his face. Not far from him rose Níscel, uncurling herself up from where she had leapt the moment Kurtisian's eyes had glittered. Gorrh, hackles boiling, watched them all from furthest back.

"Jumpy, jumpy," Kurtisian proclaimed, looking from one of them to the next and gathering swagger with every drop of their unease he drank in.

He then made a long show of dusting himself off, but only with his free hand. The other he kept where it lay, glancing from it to his onlookers with a leer so overwrought that Toron knew not what to make of it. He did not stow his swords, and halved his mind between keeping Gorrh at bay and trying to recall those feats of swordsmanship Kurtisian knew least. Not for one blink did he break sight with the dreeman's eyes, but rather bobbed to gather strength for the burst he would need to close the gap in time.

No one in Knaks, Kurtisian included, knew what kind of dreeman Kurtisian truly was. All knowledge of his craft came from one booklike thing, a grimoire he called *Marat*, which he kept strapped to his back like a nursling too dear to put down. He'd found it on a dead man, or so he said, and his armour too, and by sheer strength of yearning gained some knack to use both. Bound in red tegument that shed hues with the light, and written in some ink like the silver blood of errandghosts[35], *Marat* was not of this Where. Its writing was unbreakable, but its worth was without question. Merely to touch its pages thrilled the flesh, even if everyone but Kurtisian swore it left a bad taste in the head.

How Kurtisian had come to wield its lore at all was something no one, not even he, had told out, though it occurred to Rhianys, and from she to Toron, that *Marat* itself was the key. Whether from loneliness or ill will, it had wanted to be read, and like some *meinwen y coed*[36], exposed itself only to lure away, and seduce, and enslave. Whatever the truth, Kurtisian could make use of only a sliver of *Marat*'s pages—the first five of five hundred or more—and in so doing called himself *fuhrbido*, a word he could not write, though he believed himself to have read it. And however silly it all might have seemed, as with a man who claimed to know how to make himself invisible only when no one watched him, all snickering ended with the flash of Kurtisian's eyes, and the proof that what he claimed worked indeed.

The fuhrbido was a monstrous foe. Even unfledged, as Kurtisian's dint of it was, the shadow of the fullgrown thing lay

---

[35] *(AB):* The messengers of the gods; angels.
[36] *(I):* lit. 'maiden of the woods'; nymph; rusalka.

upon his every toddle and flutter, as though *Marat* watched him
grow, and not at all like a parent, but like something that awaits the
ripening of what it wed. Its dreecraft was heartless and slaughterful,
bent upon suffering and the mockery of health. Its spell-like
onslaughts, which Kurtisian called the *Ultrices*[37], made a game of
the flesh, kneading and tearing it like clay, dealing with the bones
beneath it only as tinder for the lighting of pain's worst extremes.
Whatever Where whence it came, *Marat* was a neighbour to Hell,
and from watching what Kurtisian did to his foes, Toron dreaded the
day he should ever face the southerner one-on-one. It was a dread
which had soothed itself through too much forbearance with the
man's moods, urging Toron to say nothing even when Kurtisian's
quips nipped at the very hamstrings of their thoftship. The
swordsman had no idea whether the fuhrbido shared his qualm, but
from a reckoning of those woes each man might inflict on the other,
Toron saw no sake for which Kurtisian might fear him.

Brushing the last bit of grime from his shoulder, the dreeman
looked up through his eyelashes. His eyes were hardly his own.
   "I've told you how much I love those swords, haven't I, Thorn?
Shempy names, though. Tuger and Mortha. Like a pair of
famsapping hamsters. I'd have no idea where to begin using them,
but it was the same way with the *Carno* when I found it."

---

[37] *(L)* avengress; she who punishes (sg. *Ultrix*). *(AB)*: Wreakress ('Ladies of
Pain').

He made the word a summon, and the weapon came to his hand from nowhere, with such haste that Toron, to the sinking of his heart, could not hope to have stayed him. The flash of light was a blitz—a blink so brisk its shadow burned sight—and then that grisly thing was there, reeking the dewsteam of where it had been left lying, and gloating as only something without a mouth, but plenty of teeth, might do. It was a sword of sorts, and gripped with both hands, but so eldritch in shape that no one might believe it governable who had not first seen it wielded. A sicklemoon of steel it was, four feet between the cusps, with inside edge honed for shearing, and grips flat along the spine. Blinding was its sheen, like quicksilver, only that it did not, like a looking glass, echo images around it. Instead it was opaque, and moltenlike, and throbbed with an inner fire. Like *Marat* its manual, the *Carno* had been drawn from some other earth's veins; it was lighter than leather, and gore beaded upon it, to be shaken off like weevils. Rust went nowhere near it. And no matter where it was dropped, and in however many shards, it came back to its lord whole, at beck and call, like a beast whose faith in its master broached the walls of death itself, and who would rise ever and again to make meat of anyone unwise enough to cross him.

Though Kurtisian's grip on the *Carno* seemed mild, Toron did not slacken, but kept his blades up between them like a two-log stockade. He had seen the dreeman hurl that thing before, and because the thrower was able to recall it again and again until he got it right, it mattered little that he landed it only half the time. As to whether the *Carno* might shear through his own blades altogether, Toron had no two thoughts about it. But he kept them up nonetheless, even as he would do with a pair of sticks, or a chair, or his own arms, if nothing else were at hand.

"They're good swords," he thwore[38]. "I like them too. But you can like the look of something without seeking to own it. I grew up at the knees of the Wottrámish Alps, and I never tired of seeing them. But they are not mine."

Kurtisian gave a sour little puff, which, however bitter, seemed to vent some of his bale. "Not much of a choice there, Thorn." He stood fully away from the wall, holding the *Carno* by one handle, downward like a gripsack.

---

[38] *(AB):* agreed. The verb is *to thware*, and conjugated like *swear* (*thware, thwore, thworn*)

Perhaps marking his brother's boredom, Justinian chose then to move himself closer, not quite breaking the line between the two men, but putting himself within a lunge of both. It was Kurtisian who held his eyes, however, and the Sumo tightened with every fidget of the dreeman's fingers, as might a stringdoll who had yet to be untethered. The sight of his unease seemed to restoke Kurtisian, and the fuhrbido stepped away from the wall, beginning to ring the men who risked him, passing the *Carno* from hand to hand and making it wheel edge-out. The weapon whined, though no other thing might have done so while moving so slowly. Like a hound at bay it whimpered, the passage of its blade making Kurtisian's face flicker, that of a fiend gloating behind tentflaps. The rasping of his gloves joined the scrape of his boots, and gave nightmarish music to the sight. With each pass of the bladed curtain, Kurtisian's grin seemed to widen, soon threatening to tear from his cheeks and escape into the world. Though Toron did not turn his body, his eyes followed the man unswervingly, watching as Níscel crept swiftly to his side when Kurtisian drew too close to her. Kurtisian, meanwhile, seemed not to acknowledge her until she stepped beside Toron and Justinian, and chortled loudly as the heads of the gathered trio obliged him like seas giving their tides to a common moon. Gorrh he hardly heeded, which was odd.

"But, Thorn," he began again, and the pleading of it was like being baited with one's own flesh. "What if you might one day have the Alps? Call them yours. Put the Powers before you who raised them up, who call them theirs, and carve the lease from their starry fingers. What is ownership but a *chop*—" he axed the *Carno* one-handed "—and the picking up for yourself whatever someone can't keep hold of anymore?"

"Much." Toron fought against the trembling in his limbs, and to look as though he had the calmness of mind truly to think about what the dreeman was saying. "After the laws of this land, anyroad. Take whatever you want, but they say you're an outlaw to do it."

By now, Kurtisian was right behind him, and everyone but Toron swiveled to follow. Suddenly, though, Shard was there too, face unscarved, standing next to the fuhrbido like a piece of statuary no one had noticed. Kurtisian leapt a little, but the subterranean part of him had to have recognized who it was, for he showed no stomach to attack the Highbred. Instead, he let the *Carno* fall to his side, like a child whose father has discovered his wicked game.

Shard, for his part, regarded the lesser dreeman with a coldness far flintier than any stone, saying everything to undo him, but none of it in words. Though half a head shorter than Kurtisian, and in body a poplar to the Man's oak, Shard's look alone sapped Kurtisian's stance, bringing his shoulders to slump, and emptying the wind from his chest. His silver eyes were lancets that pierced him, draining off whatever had bloated him, and leaving him deflated but with the look of the cleansed.

"You're in the shoals of it here, Chaldallion," Shard said at last, and the hardness of his look became tradesmanly. No longer was he seeking weakness, but rather probing for broken bones. "However will you fare in the trenches?"

Kurtisian licked the insides of his shut lips, answering the outlander neither with his eyes nor with words. Shard gave the shadow of a nod.

"Make no use of magic" he bid, then called over his shoulder as he turned away, "this mana is corrupted."

A shudder went through them all, no less than if he had told them they had passed into the gullet of the beast some time ago. Kurtisian let out a windy breath and tossed them all a nod. It was the closest thing to an apology he was capable of, and his thoftmen nodded back, unbegrudging. If Shard could forgive him his outburst of feyness, or at the very least vouch for it, so could they.

Mana had no homelier word in the Allmal, at least none that Toron had heard, but his talks with Knaksish wizards were few, and those dreemen would no sooner speak to him of magic than a shepherd might speak to his sheep of shearing.

Mana was everywhere, the life-breath of magic. Whensoever a dreeman worked a spell, he drew some in—inhaled it, as it were— and made its lightning the blood and tinder of his creation. As with the air, mana was sundry, and might come in many strains both clean and foul, and smack[39] of things put into it. But whereas the air trailed scarves of smells and wetness, and burned the lungs with heat or cold, mana was a soulish stuff, and wore a weave of ideas, and feelings, and the meanings it once had worked for. Were it a soundscape, its valleys might deafen—crowded with the clamouring of gods, its skies aflame with philosophy, and its middle ground buzzing with the disputations and moral madness of all those caught

---

[39] *(AK)*: taste (both a verb and a noun).

in between. But mana was not hearsome either, for its sway was over senses beyond the flesh, appertaining to that discarnate shadow of the self which coexists in other Wheres and Whens, which has senses of its own.

Once upon a time, in what was then the most fearful place his thoftship had ever suffered to overnight, Toron had had mana laid out for him. It was in the heart of a dead thorp somewhere between Ignam and Arsask—a village far from the highroad, emptied out long ago by some black illness. Half the homes had been burned. Shallow graves, looted by wolves, pocked the gardens. Bones lay mouldering on beds. There was no mistaking the tokens of what had happened.

The woods all about the townlet were swamp-bottomed, and the thoftship had been grateful for its island—that is, until they saw what had befallen it. It was Shard who had pledged that no ghouls were about, and that they might camp on the village green unharassed.

But wield no magic, he had warned the band's dreemen, lest the mana of that steading's tragedy unhinge every door of grief the mind had a frame for.

That night as they doled out the grouse stew and kept their eyes to the black windows that watched them, Toron had asked Rhianys what Shard had meant. Was mana so sundry, and dreecraft so unsafe, that casting one spell in the wrong spot might break a dreeman's mind?

A dreemaid herself, having been taught for a short time in a wizarding garden, Rhianys had known mana by another name, but it was clearly the same thing. Mana was unsteady, she had thworn, but it was not fickle. It had a root stock—a broth brewed and salted by the Lord of the Eld, which was his right, and which all who worked magic within his Age must drink to ply their trade. What it did to those who drank it, and how it shaped their work, were his fee, but most of the time its sway was narrow, and showed itself only in the spells it quickened. As for the mind of the dreeman himself, a fair deal of mana, and of a strong kind, was needed to budge his mood markedly—a mood which was more often shaped by the success or failure of whatever dreecraft he needed the mana to carry out. Some spells it strengthened, just as some broths bring the best out of some things stewed in it. Others it soured, or drowned.

Rhianys had stirred her stew the whole time, and Shard, sitting on her other side, had listened without blinking.

In the Eld of Life, she went on, spells of healing were like dumplings, sopping up the Heron's mana and swelling with its richness, always doing the best they might do, no matter how simple the dough, or how callow the cook. As for the magic of death and undeath, those were like toadstools and wormwood, which begrudge any brews but those of their own steeping, and in others smack of nothing unless heaped in by the handfuls. This was why warlocks and devilcleppers[40] were skulkers among dreemen, having to wreak their foul craft out of sight.

As Rhianys had raised the spoon to her lips, however, and shown that her talk was at an end, the Highbred had broken his hush, and what he had given them was a scolding without spite.

What she taught was true for the most part, he had said. Mana, like clay, had power over what it might make, and did not shape the maker. But, he went on, breaking off a wedge of waybread, the sculptor soils his hands with every lump he seizes, and not all of it comes off on the work. Shard thus began twisting the bread into a form, making a show of the crumbs as they fell. Most of it, he went on, washes off in time. Its mark was almost always faint, and rarely dwelt long enough to stain. But—and his face had darkened—rarely was not never. Sometimes, in the eldritch hollows of Ages past, or in places where reality has been riven and scarred by happenings too meaningful to keep single names, the mana indeed became perilous. Unbounded by recipe or cauldron, its essence took to the strengthening of itself. Breaking its tether with the worldly things to which all things magic are shadows, it thickened itself beyond saturation—it became a self-feeding food, a drink to devour its drinkers.

And he had placed his sculpture, a little man made of bread, into the edge of Rhianys's bowl, where it stood kneedeep in stew as he had continued. Unchecked and unbalanced, he had said, this essence might grow as much as it pleased, overrunning ethereal dikes and drowning even non-practitioners of magic—*magentiles*, as the Chaldallions and other southerners called them.

Not always was it evil, he had said. Havens of serenity were examples where the forces of goodness and peace had permeated the mana in a comparable manner. To come upon them was to lose oneself in wellbeing, perhaps never to leave. But the most

---

[40] *(AB)*: devil-summoners; diabolists; practitioners of goetia.

frightening were those impregnated by malefaction, places where the very potential for virtue and temperance had been razed, sites of unspeakable cruelty and suffering. Such mana, envenomed, might unhinge a magentile, and cripple a magician's mind. Depending on the mental strength of he who drank it, even the small amount needed for a simple spell might bring on a *devilgrip*—what Shard called demonic possession. Carrying out lengthy or high-tier sorcery under such conditions guaranteed it. And such conditions could not be rinsed.

Following his silver glance back down to the bowl, Rhianys and Toron found the bread man still standing, but now black and hideously twisted, in a way that only a cantrip[41] might have made it. Rhianys had put the bowl down. Shard, nodding sorry, had offered her his. But they'd all had so little hunger left anyway. The sadness of the thorp begrudged them it, shamed it from them, even as the distraught folk of that nameless place must have forgotten everything but their suffering. And mana was to that feeling what boiling water was to stock.

Little of that talk had come back to Toron ere now. The weight of its truth, the sharpness of its foresight, staggered him.

Goodness—the very worth and hope of it—had forsaken Aftheksis. Evil had moldered its grain and could not be washed out. Even if the deadburg were purged of its illness, it could never be healed by crafts such as theirs. Its heart could only be rid of the bloated worm that had hollowed it out, and in the emptiness left to find the peace at last to die.

Recalling that Shard himself had used dreecraft to silence Justinian, Toron put away his swords, picked up his feet and jogged past Kurtisian to the outlander's side. As Toron learned—simply from being able to catch up—the Highbred was in nowhere near the hurry he had been during his first trek down this road.

"What of you?" Toron asked him. "Are you well? That spell you made earlier—"

"Yon broken building was a lorehouse," Shard said, marking the structure with an unwavering stare. "The people of this place seem to have etched their learning on leaves of stone and copper. There are thousands of them, spilling out from broken walls."

Toron's heart fluttered. "Can you read them? Any of them?"

---

[41] the simplest of magical spells, whose effects are comparable to parlour tricks.

Shard answered nothing but with a twitch of his head, as though what he wished to say would not go near his mouth.

"Shard?"

"They tell me things, yes."

"I don't understand you," the Man said. "What do the leaves say?"

"Nothing."

"They *say* nothing or they tell you nothing?"

"They are empty," Shard answered, but only the last word had any sound. He spoke them again, and carefully gave voice to all three. "Whatever lore they once held has been erased. And not simply struck out or filled in, nor even unscarred from the metal by some healing geomancy, but *scoured* away, like to the great inscriptions on the walls of our oldest ruins, which are blasted by the weather, and even so, after many eons, might still be read. It is a faulty likening I give you nonetheless, for even had these leaves lain open to the weather since the breaking of Wottráma, and not stowed with care on dry shelves, they should not have appeared as they do now. What you will see, you will call it no wonely thing.

"Theirs is the emptiness of something stolen. Were it the absence of some trinket, a bauble pilfered from a barrow hoard, or an idol snatched from off the pedestal of a buried church, it might sicken the heart, but this, Toron, *this* sickens the immortal soul. This was *lore*," for he saw the ghastliness settling into his young friend's face and knew it for the wrong sort of fear. "Just for a moment, forget the how of its theft, and consider the why. It was names and histories, and crafts and creeds, and maps, and compendia, and gatherings of knowledge—oceans of learning so deep and so wide that no minds were trusted to hold them all. Now gone."

Shard wobbled where he stood and pulled his eyes to the dead wonders about them. "Look around you. What you see here will not be seen again. That it is still whole means nothing; its health is that of something falling from a great height, which has yet to strike the ground and break apart. Look around you and try to see the steps and deeds that made these things. Deduce the alchemy of gold; behold a living thing and tell me how to make one. And even that is easily done compared to the hearing of songs, and of tales, whose tungs have been torn out."

Toron heard him, but felt like a child whose father's fondness presumes too much of his understanding. He shook his head. "What does it mean?"

The Highbred beheld him, and the Chaldallions, and Níscel besides, all of whom by now had caught up. They gathered about as Toron asked this. All looked at Shard, and they saw the terror that gnawed him. He made no bid to hide it. At the mouth of this place, before the great, gaping heads of the watchmen, he had simply been afraid. No longer. His deadpan was merely a shield, and it cracked before their sight even as they tried not to see it.

It was not a terror he greeted. He fought it, clearly, but it was like the fight of one who seeks to withstand an overwhelming grief. He trembled with inner throes, and tears fled the boil of his mind. His eyelids met and withdrew, laying bare the full gape of his hunted silver stare. His gaze, fluttering about Toron's face like a wounded moth, could not stay fixed, this of a man who might once have turned a basilisk to stone, whose pupils now leapt like fleas trapped in glass thimbles. His jaw hung loose, not the knotted mandible of yesterday; the gray skin of his face no longer stone, but sealhide wet from chase. Amidst the whelm of this dread, the only rock left to cling to was that Shard welcomed none of it, instead continuing to allow things unspoken to harry his senses, to wrench his head about like that of a thrall whose neck is bound to a dozen wrangling chains.

He began again, in the whisper of a hostage whose captor is near. "For four months now, I have suspected something I have told none of you. Now I know, in what little way I might understand it, that my suspicion is true. The sage outside Gatherdsburg, who told you all of Havsikt, the Red Collector—it was no new tale he told. He did not meet my eyes any more than he did the rest of you, and I sensed nothing overly odd about him. Yet he said things that only I could have understood, and I had feeling that he was speaking more to me than to any of you. I believe, were we to leave this place and seek out his house again, that we would find no one there, and no house, or a ruin at best. I believe he wanted me here, for this reason and for other things I have felt since, and that I have a role to play which I cannot, with every step we have taken, refuse."

He took a breath, and when the words came back, he seemed with their new bearing to have found a steady shoal from which to speak. "In the land of my birth, among my womb-mother's people, there are more old stories than there are even here. Many my sire's people laughed away as yarns, but some must have come down to us from Ages long before ours, perhaps told by outsiders, or by the gods themselves, who are the only ones who might have overlived the great harrowings between aeons. But even to the *nyhrrdoiv*, who believe all their own tales to be true, many of their lessons have gone flat, and find no palate in an Age of new tastes." And with that likening, Shard looked to Toron and smiled, and showed he remembered their talk of mana. The smile then simply blew away, like a line drawn of dust.

He went on. "The oldest myths tell of a monster. So old he is that the year of his birth lies amongst the ashes of an Age forgotten many times over. The gods do not rule him. His taskmasters are Gods to gods, and They must make way when he comes. And when he comes, it is the end. He cannot be stopped.

"More than one tale names him Avarnok, but such a name would matter little to one from beyond the stars, half of which are younger than he. Bloodthirsty and unquenchable, and utterly without ruth, he is no mere roving butcher, but an executioner, punishing those guilty of a sin older than *sum*[42], of violating a covenant far beyond the laws of any one Age. Such a covenant, or rather the way of living it upholds, I have heard here called the æw[43], but the æw is a sweeping word, and tangles together many such bonds. Avarnok only cares for one, that which the *nyhhrdoiv* would never violate, and of whose holiness my blended blood is living proof—that the peoples of this world were not meant to cleave to their home fields, and to mass and sway together like rooted grass, but to go forth, to explore and to mingle, whether in war or in trade, and so prove their clay worthy of the soul with which it was animated."

Shard's eyes glimmered faintly with pride. Then he shrugged. "It's as foolish to believe all such tales to be true as it is to believe them all fiction. They're not all lodestars, as benevolent as their lessons may seem, nor is all their farlandish whimsy the lovecraft of distant shores. I see the game in them too. As peoples, we are all the gods' long horse race. What we can know of that scheme, we know darkly, and that includes the folkmingling I speak of. Some gods, such as the Heron, seem to hold to it, though in his own way. Other powers, of the pettier or more headstrong sort, seek to defy it,

---

[42] *(L): I am.* The very state and recognition of being.
[43] *(AK-* pronounced as in *ah,* not *awe*): natural law; a multifarious concept, which is revisited in further chapters.

believing their tenures beholden to nothing, all from scratch, and that no oaths or framework bind them. The tales of the *nyhhrdoiv* account for them too, saying they do so at their peril, for not even celestial flesh, one tale tells, is beyond the shear of Avarnok's jaws."

The name, spoken anew, seemed to bring dread rolling down every road. The thoftship bristled, glancing about. Shard rooted his voice and went on. "It is said that should a people wither toward selfdom—should they know the world and turn away knowing, closing border and mind, to make a world only of their own—that after a time, *he* will come to unmake it. Some tales say he comes from the sky, others from the sea, still others from the igneous blood of the world which remains untouched during the cycling of Ages. In his wake, however, he leaves not a trace of those he consumes. He is effiat; the ontoclast; the nothingmaker. He does not simply eat. He uncreates. Their breaths he unbreathes. Their words he unsays. Their bodies he unbegets. Whomsoever he takes he tears from the Weave, leaving not their absence nor their void, but their entropy, the very gaping need of them, ragged in the itness, which can never again be fulfilled. And thus do the brokers of souls repossess what they consigned, not through extortion or murder, but through the annulment of genesis."

Despite the horrors he breathed, Shard looked tenderly upon the faces of his companions, like a man who has scared his children only in the hope their fear might one day save them. None of them said a word, but returned his look pleadingly, begging him go on to the part of the story where all is made well again.

But Shard would not lie.

"It was Avarnok," he said, "who came to Aftheksis. He, or the one the tales are shadows of. Only such a creature could have done the things we have seen. Worse is to come. And somewhere beneath those mountains before us, he is waiting for us. Of that there is no question."

Kurtisian erupted at last. "But we can't defeat something like that."

Justinian made a face mocking how obvious that was.

Toron nodded. "If someone sent you here, Shard, he sent you here to die."

"Of course, you are right Chaldallion," Shard answered. "But, young Toron, things are not as they seem. The affairs into which you have stumbled stand beyond the reckoning of your senses. This place, you must know by now, could not have been found ere today. It was revealed to us only as we approached. At other times, it must lie in pockets of forlornness, which like the slow stomachs of a stag, fret it away from the outside in. Who showed it to us, I do not know, but for one to believe it were Avarnok himself, one must believe oneself so crucial to an all-powerful being that it be worth him this whole ruse to draw us here.

"If Avarnok had wanted us dead, he might have brought it about a thousand ways by now. His power is beyond our reckoning. With his thoughts alone, he might reach out and pull apart our minds. His dreecraft, might we call it that, is godlike. Were he to wish it, he might have blinked the whole of this mountainside, and us on it, into the nethermost hell Hell harbours. As for his bodily strength, I can imagine nothing that might bind or wound him. And that he has not risen beneath us like Leviathan, and cast off this burg like water, tells me the most of all, for such brute strength would be the first and last resort of one whose higher powers have been shackled. But he has done none of these things. So it is that something is amiss here, and I am not sure it is against us."

Kurtisian's nods gathered force. "That was something I thought about too—how it is that something as unstoppable as the Red Collector simply hides away when he might be done with all of Knaks in a handful of months. Something is keeping him here."

Toron frowned. "But I don't understand. If the Collector does the bidding of the gods, as the *Sherk* says, or of the gods' Gods, as your mother's people say, then whose bidding do we do to hunt him down?"

Shard yielded with a sigh. "There are too many discrepancies to trust the stories alone. The Avarnok of the *nyhhrdoiv* is an empyrean offsend[44], a dogstar on a leash, howsoever he loves the slaughter. The monster of the *Sherk* is something else—not so much an avenging angel as a beastly privateer. What he takes into his jaws he does not fetch for his masters, but swallows for himself, and grows hungrier. It is why the *Sherk* names him Havsikt, which I suspect to be no more than a contrivance on the poet's part, for I know the word, and it means the desire to own all that one sees.

"But whether Avarnok or Havsikt, it is likely both accounts are wrong, or, rather, each only a little right. I can answer nothing,

---

[44] *(AK)*: representative, messenger.

northman, because I know nothing. I am older than you, but in the ears of Heaven, only by the whisper of one grain of sand falling. I have my hunches about what might be afoot, but they have been cobbled together from the echoes of godlore, whose meanings, like to the figures of constellations, are given by those who cannot see them from their other, innumerable sides. All that I can say for certain is that I shall not turn back from this. Something compels me, and my own will seconds it. I do not ask you to come, and I do not warn you from it. I simply say what I do, and that I believe it is the right thing."

With care, he tied his scarf back about his mouth, which was smiling to make a memory of him, and nodded to each of his companions.

He turned, adjusted his scabbard for an overhand draw[45], and headed north toward the lorehouse commons. For a few moments, they watched him go.

Then he wasn't alone anymore.

---

[45] Shard's rigid scabbard, made from a stalk of kadu plant (a bamboo-like grass native to equatorial lands), is secured to his back with an elaborate suspender-and-swivel system. Attached to the intersection of his suspenders is a circular clip which extends through an opening in the back of his suit. Mating with this clip and secured there with an anchor pin is a similar device attached to Shard's scabbard. The system allows Shard to rotate his scabbard in any direction fifteen degrees at a time; a spring in the anchor pin prevents it from turning without deliberate effort. Should the scabbard be turned upside down, mated clips on its orifice and the sword's guard prevent the weapon from being released without a deliberate pull-and-twist. Shard usually sets the scabbard at 30 degrees to the left of down, allowing him to access his sword with a left hand, cross-body reach. The scabbard-pivot technology is unknown among Knaksish weaponsmiths and, Shard alleges, would largely be dismissed due to the stealthy intention of its design.

II
Disposition
A Bad Place

He no longer knew whether he walked or crawled.

The tunnels dripped and gibbered.

Ghosts weltered in puddles of drool.

He would give anything now to get out.

He clung to the thought that only beings had souls. What he felt around him, dragging at him, was the spillage and stir of them, an eddy and current of the bodiless. It was the better belief of two. He did not want to think it was the rooting mindsuckle of the place itself. He had felt the moods of places ere now, but he had held them to taste and not truth. Howsoever unwelcoming the graveyard, or how thrilling the inn decked for a holy day—it was all, he had believed, given by one's upbringing. Those who did not like the dark had not spent enough time in it, and the fear of something wicked around the next shadow was no more the fault of the shadow than the lushest forest answers for the beasts who live there. It had to be so. If the Age of Life was indeed an age for life, why might the gods suffer souls to walk unfleshed?

He thought he'd had the answer at one time. It was talk of mana that first had rattled him. Now something rattled him again, and shook a share of him loose. It was the inkling, no, the certainty, that whatever shaped one's feelings at any given time and stead, mana— at least as mana was said to be—was only half the story. The knowledge flattered his feyness. Whatever was happening here, and whatever it was doing to him, he knew near to no one had ever felt it. Fewer still had lived through it. So it was that the lore of it was shaped without the word of its best witnesses, even as the books of death must be written only by the living.

None of that mattered now. All that mattered was that places too had souls, and, like the people who walked among them, they too might be twisted, and damned.

Never had anything become clearer as the thoftship had made its way beneath the deadburg. The path had gone before them, but the walls did the walking. Their hearts beat in moments, but time cowered in place. Their bodies shrank from the cold, and their lungs sawed at the air to find kindling. Then came the swelter, as though the burrow were a great pipe, half-melted and misshapen, laid snaking through a balefire's embers.

Sweat and breathclouds, mist and phantoms.

The ghosts they breathed in with the reek, who tantrumed on their tongues.

They tasted madness.

The underway wound and twisted like the crampadder[1] of a crone. It crumpled and dived, swung to and fro, and never gave headway for more than ten steps. Its walls and floor were so rough, they seemed wormed out, not hewn. The only tokens of delving were the stopes—the nooks here and there where broken rock had been stowed, whose drifts slouched across their black thresholds as frightful, half-melted shapes. Some of these closets were empty, and withdrew for great stretches of their own, their frameworks ringing overhead like the bones of a windpipe before narrowing down to nothing.

He had not drawn his weapons, for there was hardly room to swing a fist in here. It happened too often, and he knew it, that his boyhood choice of the biggest swords he could find had put him in such a plight. A sax-knife, or even a longmeech—which to him had both seemed puny to a greatsword—had in hindsight been much wiser. There was nothing for it now. He had been no yarl's son, and in Harandril the King's Boarsmen[2] had had no body of men to throw in with, a mere day with whom might have taught him his misreckoning.

He fought now only a little better than he had learned to fight as a boy in a glade—with great, whistling strokes, and sideshow-

---

[1] *(AB)*: varicose vein.
[2] The Knaksish military, whose divisions are known as *wereds*.

manship, trusting as much in threat as in thrack[3] to clear the field of
his foemen. It had been good enough in his homeland, at least for the
short time he had roved there after becoming a young man. But the
outlaws and unhiresome[4] things of Harandril were not like those of
Knaks elsewhere. They were few, and they were watchful of their
skins. More often they fled than crossed swords, for wounds were
worse where healing was hard to come by, where wortcraft[5] was
dear, and dreecraft untrustworthy. This dearth of healing was how
the bearsarks—the hidewearing madmen of old stories whom
Hálishmen called *berserkir*—were indeed as woody as a squirrel
tree[6]—not for the strength of their strikes, but for fighting without
fear of suffering.

But outside Harandril a craftier and angrier world had awaited
him. Magic worked there, and he'd met dreemen such as Kurtisian,
the full bloom of whose devilry might one day redden whole fields.
Ways of fighting were arts, and hundreds of years in the making.
Men learned from childhood how to deal death best, whether at the
laps of fathers who made a living of it, or in swordstables—fighting
schools—they had to pull strings to get into. Of the two ways to
learn, the schools were less trustworthy. Toron had found early on
that being taught was not the same as learning. He had clashed with
these smug tincake swordsmen, so-called for having been made in
rows one batch after another, half-baked it seemed, and found that
hall-taught fighters, however crafty, could often not overcome his
raw wherewithal. They were the wolves to his brockwolf[7]. He had
been made of starker stuff.

So bedrudged were the swordstables that the hungriest fighters
did not bother with them. Some sailed to masters overseas and came
back with weird blades. Some had learned means to win empty-
handed. Still others fared overland in search of old heroes and
squatted at their doors in hopes of being thrown a scrap of teaching,
beneath whose dust they might find something worthwhile—perhaps
a himely[8] bit of knowhow that had never failed, or better yet, a
wreath of wiles clipped from a whole lost field of fighting lore. As

---

[3] *(AK)*: violence; force.
[4] *(AK)*: monstrous; savage; uncivilized (*Braccish* unhearsum).
[5] *(AB)*: herbalism (also called *wort* and *worting*).
[6] (AK idiom): crazy ('wood' itself is a synonym for 'mad')
[7] *(AK)*: wolverine (lit. 'badger-wolf')
[8] *(AK):* secret; private; kept to one's self. The *Braccish* equivalent is *dighel*.

such, these scroungers had struck the motherlode. They might very well have happened upon heaven itself, gaining Gladhome and the courtyards of Walhall, there to soak up the wisdom of the fighting loneharriers, who bego bloody arts without fear of death, and unflaw themselves day by day, ever honing and hardening, in readiness for The Rack of the Ranes—that teerful slaughterfest at the dusk of the End of Days.[9]

From such expeditions men might return unbeatable, as had Unwinn the Unyielding, and Fiddick Morwa of Lakeland, both of whom died lossless in warm beds, but who, Toron deemed, would have been hard put to it with Shard, whose nimbleness and speed were so dizzying that he once scratched a word stave by stave into the forehead of a foeman he did not wish to kill.

But that was all child's play in the face of what lurked here, whose thirst drank men and menning alike, learner and lore, one who had withstood the gods themselves, one for whom fighting with weapons was a butchery dance among meat dolls. His swords, these beaten metal things, meant nothing whether he had room to swing them or not. He nonetheless kept in mind the old dagger he had strapped to one leg, and between his hand and ankle looped a thew of wariness by which, unthinking as a kneejerk, he might reach for it at need. Every mail had its seams, he told himself, which the narrowest of needles best found.

A year had passed since they'd stood aboveground.
Or a handful of hours.
He didn't know, and it likely did not matter.
Whatever toll time had paid to open the roads into this place, it was not a straight barter. One to four; one to ten. Were he to come out of this alive, and Toron did not look to, he might find Gorrh too old to ride, or a heap of bones lying faithfully where he'd left him. The Rine held for now, but it was tangled in the maze of this place, their thoughttalk drowned out by its riddles. All he could do was to push on, and to cling to the last rags of sunlight his eyes had given

---

[9] The northern deities known as the *Æsir* to the Hálish are called the *Ozmen* by many of the peoples of Knaks. The body of beliefs, practices, and stories surrounding the Ozmen is known as the *Oztroth* (**H** *Ásatru*). These are their Knaksish names, followed by the Hálish names by which they are better known to the reader: Gladhome (*Glaðsheim*); Walhall (*Valhöll* [*Valhalla*]); loneharriers (*einherjar*); The Rack of the Ranes (*Ragnarök*).

him. Those sights of the upper world came back to him, less whispered by minning than croaked from faraway.

After making up their minds to follow Shard, the thoftship had walked on. Aftheksis had lolled out before them like a corpse freshly freed from deathlock[10], and the lorehouse commons was the last of the open places they had crossed. It was four-cornered in shape and fronted by shops whose lower walls bellied out like sacks. Streets spoked off among the buildings and ended in other burgyards faraway.

The springwell at its heart, the likes of which none other seemed to have, had been a masterwork. It stood thrice the height of a man and had been made to appear as though four great chunks of stone had been tossed into an unsteady pile. A closer look showed the whole thing to be molded of a single block of metal, its every face roughened through art, only to seem as stone. Why the smith had bothered when so much stone was at hand would forever be a riddle. It stood within its dry basin now, a token to thoughts unthinkable.

Behind the springwell stood the lorehouse. It was hard to say how grand it might have been when it was whole. Its black walls were broken, their rubble mingling with the gutted spill of scoured tablets. Though wreckage, it was too tidy. Toron had seen great landslides, and the shattered curtain walls of keeps as well, and neither had kept to its place so cleanly as the ruin he saw before him. Nothing nearby had been scarred by its smashing down, and the loneliest piece of rubble lay but inches from the heap. Unless the brute had swept up afterwards or had surrounded the hall with a dam of sorts before storming it, Toron understood no means by which the building might have been holed out so neatly. It was nonetheless the first token of foul play they had seen—the first toothmarks of a mouth which up till here had been content simply to lick.

Shard led them left. He gave his thoftmen little time to look around, not even when Kurtisian had leapt among the tablets and, digging, found some of them uneffaced. The Highbred's speed, never backlooking, made it clear he would leave them behind if they did not keep up. Toron climbed back into Gorrh's saddle, but bid the cat go no more quickly than he must. Shard had led them a winding chase, cutting across the open thoroughfares and sticking to the

---

[10] *(AK)*: Rigor mortis.

backways behind buildings. He'd leapt a gate at one point, its panels made from a slatelike pith that flew apart tinkling when Justinian spurned to vault or open it. Not even the uproar of its destruction was enough to bring Shard wheeling back to them.

In time they found themselves before one of the great pillars of the Aftheksish sky. It had loomed toward them for blocks, its foot always behind the next row of buildings, growing and broadening, till its breadth filled the eye. At last, the houses broke to reveal its toes, and the thoftship stood before it, its mightiness devastating, its orthankship enslaving. Its base went around three furlongs or more, its height so dizzying that its taper seemed to bend, the roof atop it balanced as if on the tip of a quill. As with the buildings mushroomed about its foot, its body was piecemeal, backbonelike. These vertebrae themselves showed seams, like eggs broken and limed back together. The whole length of that godly leg wore a threadbare stocking of black and silver pipes, the meanings of which they would never learn, while from its knee ran the strings of the walkways, leading to other pillars. Near to the ground, atop short ramps and stairways, was a number of doors, inlets so tiny against the whole that they seemed as gated pinholes.

They had left that sile behind them and walked abreast until they reached the outer edge of what they had named the Dwindling. It was Shard who first marked the dreadful wonder of it, raising his fingers, then bringing his hands together and down, twiddling, in the gesture of something falling away. They followed his beck and saw that the stonework of the outer buildings had begun to diminish—not like the wearing away to which stone was heir, but in the way bright hues are whitened by the suns. It was no wonely thing. It seemed at first a prank of the eye, how something standing before them, which they might walk up to and handle, was fading away in the manner of a drawing. The likenesses of men and women, so sharp and bold upon the walls of the buildings nearer to the gates, here stood bleary, as though molded of some loamy fog that was slowly letting go of its shape. Within a short time whence it began, this dwindling had spread to the walls themselves, and then to the roofs, and onto the flatbricks of the roadway, till everything lay within a haze of half-thereness, and only a ribbon of a causeway led through it. This they walked singlefile, shunning the Dwindling as both briar and plague, as something they might snag, and bring into their flesh, and unbone their legs in ten steps.

The thoftship had followed the road out the eastern bounds of the burg, which had no wall, where the buildings had ended like the trees fringing a clearcut. There they had stood before a wide, open flatland. The grassless meadow stretched on for miles, to the foot of the great bluff that walled it in. A lonely road cut across, meandering a little around the swells, sending off shoots here and there to small knots of buildings that looked to be thorps in the waste. Lines made of ditches and stoneworks wrote of farming, though the croplands could no longer be told from the pastures. Blowing grit and dust devils were all that grazed there now, dashing themselves against the dikes where their bodies noisily broke apart. The wind carried no smell, but it moaned where it caught, and it bit those who breathed it.

"Their earthyards," Toron said, his tongue hugging a word from his childhood. And because his youth had been fed with tales spoken and not read, his mind easily called back the words of the *Sherk*, though he had heard them but twice:

> *And crops and wells and mushroombeds bled dry*
> *Whilst kine and aurochs gnawed thr'own wasted bone*
> *As limbs Aftheksish ceased to pulse with warmth*
> *When Sherk-narsk-wirth did stain the rictus foul,*
> *The have-all hellmouth of Collector Red.*

They went on, and the bluff had risen slowly before them, like one of the great banewaves said to drown whole coastlands. Its white crest was toothed, and its trough, where it met the ground, was the black sill of death's door. Despite the cold, and the nagging of their fears, it hadn't taken them long to reach it. The Dwindling went unseen, having little to eat here, though they did not look for it in the thorps, in whose houses and sheds it most likely lurked.

Not far down the road they had come upon a vast boneyard that had once been Aftheksish livestock. The parched hollow that had served as their watering hole swept out across both wings of the pasture, its edges littered with ribcages, and with skulls tipped over from the weight of their mighty horns. The remains were dark and mottled, shimmering with old frost. Flaps of skin and hair clung to them like old pennons. All the bodies seemed whole, and to have died where they lay. The wind had half-buried most of them, with hundreds of empty eyeholes and sharp-edged nostrils gawping up through the dust. Two kinds of orfkin[11] were there, the greatest hayrick-sized. The overlaying of enough cloth might have made a tent-town of the ribs. These were the aurochs of the poem—mighty oxen which still lived wild and in scattered herds throughout the Knaksish lowlands. The other kind of carcass, whose bulk was that of a run-of-the-mill cow, lay strewn about the bonehouses of the aurochs like litters of calves.

The sight of dead bodies had not heartened them. Though they clearly had died in a more straightforward way than the people who had herded them, the livestock had not died easily. The broken ground and the overturned mangers showed they'd starved, having spent the last days of their lives gathered about the ponds, gulping and wasting away with full bellies.

If, as some say, the baying of the wind might be called quiet, the stretch of road had gone by quietly. Shard had stayed well ahead of the rest of them. Every now and again, a length of low wall had risen alongside the road, on which the Highbred would leap and speed, his soles flashing to show the quick swap of his feet, his body becoming a ball as he went end-over-end, alighting hands-first and tumbling from fingers to feet again, all atop a pathway the width of one's wrist. They had all seen him do these things before, but never so freely, and it was a sight to stir them a little from their gloom. None of them, not even Níscel, had the knack of it. Shard was a halfMan, but the other half was of eight kinds, and if his body had been a gamble among all nine players, his soul had won big in the begetting of it, and in the womb got a body that was the best of all worlds. A wonderwork of the flesh it was, a miracle of humours, the brawn of the mightiest stock driving the lightest's bones, which bent like green boughs, and did not break with the torsion of it, all put to work by a mind that learned even as it slept. A onely man he was, unprecedented and irreplaceable, whose blood was alchemy and not simply blended, nerbefore and neragain, both essence and antithesis of the Aftheksish folk themselves, who could not be remade.

Upon seeing him leap, Toron had leaned onto Gorrh, and through the Rinesight better taken in his dance. Toron knew what it was to show off, but as a homesteader's son, he had also been around enough animals to know when something was simply scared off its

---

[11] *(AB)*: bovine creatures.

branch.[12] He had seen meat rabbits race about their hutches when the smell of their butchered brethren crept into the breeze, and more than once had he fought to calm the goats when a bear, or a bergcat, had passed through the woods nearby. This was no show Shard staged, but a fidget to suit his cunning. For all the wonders of his mind and body—despite his might, his tungs, and his sweatless dreecraft—he fared no better beneath the thumb of Fear than did any of the Heron's children.

And then, past a rise, the caves had appeared. Though mines at one time, they were mines no longer, just as a garden retaken by the wilds from once it had been housebroken might no longer be called a garden. At one time, the foothills before it had held a town, a river running through it, and the town had been the threshold of that underground half of Aftheksis which the *Sherk* sang to be greater than the half above. No longer. Though heaps of ore lay there still, and the holes in the cliffside remained, the Dwindling had fed deeply on their craftsmanship, fretting tunnel and building alike, until their shapes seemed to slouch upon the table of Being, like clay that would not set. The gnaw of it was far hungrier than anything they had seen before, splitting into the marrow of what it ate, and it was with no small share of dread that they followed Shard onto its very tongue, and strode across the dwimmer they had the touch of ere then.

Toron had felt a shudder as he did so but could not pare it from the lepsy of his soul. Whether it was his own fear, or the latch of the Dwindling itself, either was a leaf amidst the gale of Havsikt's nighness, and it was all he might do to put one foot ahead of the other, and not crumple to his knees and plead for mercy. Erasure was in the air, and he breathed it, and he found himself forgetting things he had only just beheld. Simple knowledge fled his grasp, as only it had done in times of reeling drunkenness, then surged back, bringing to his awareness things he always should have known. His mind was soft bread upon the boil of this cauldron, afloat only for being lighter

---

[12] An idiom of the Age, or Eld, of Life; the Bluharenites postulate the existence of an enormous, eldritch tree upon whose tier-like branches is arranged the hierarchy of all living things. From the trunk of this *Alleverwood* extend branches for every order of creature, and upon each branch is housed the Progenitor and Archetype of each, from whom all living descendents draw their character. For a creature to be "scared off its branch" is thus for it to behave in a manner either atypical, or akin to some lesser type of creature.

than the bones and rubble it knackered. In time, if in time such a deed might be reckoned, even the valley itself would be melted away, its whole eld and folkdom turned to glue, and swallowed, and made to bind the inner pieces of a Thing whose essence was nothing but to unmake. And then, whatever its true name, that Thing would wriggle loose, and worm its way out from below, unfurl loathsome sail, and ride infernal updrafts to the next Aftheksis. Perhaps it would be Knaks itself, which with the wars of the Onelatching not long ago had brought the Bracsriche under one kingdom.

Shard had pointed. A hole in the cliffwall, gaping like a narwound[13], waited. Instead, Justinian had cast his eyes about the blighted town, whose chimneys and great heaps of ore showed signs of smelting, and of steelmaking. The Sumo sighed to show the return of his voice. The Brasmat was a god of metals after all, and the lodes and blends of Sherk-narsk-wirth offered exotic fruit.

Kurtisian had chuckled mirthlessly. "No reason to investigate, fra. Not enough there anymore."

Justinian had sighed again. "Procrastination is a reason."

Shard had since made it to the cavemouth, and stood there, waiting for them, for the first time since they'd gathered at the foot of the great column in the heart of city. At one time, that cave had lain within the deepest part of a vast bay, the throat of a wide, welcoming grotto which had been delved from the foot of the cliffside. Its entrance had been surrounded by statuary and ornamental dripstones, overhung by a mighty spur which itself had been a honeycomb of windows and breezeways. Now, that excavation had been dealt with as a cavity, and scabbed in by the Dwindling, made to caulk itself, choking the great underroad it gated, and shrinking what once was a wide and fearless underhill passage into a squeezeway that was less than a smial[14]. Its chthonic wind had shown itself as it played with Shard's clothing, but it made no sound. Nor had it forewarned them any token of its deeper bane, as they stepped before the gap and fell straightaway to their knees. Gorrh staggered like a shot horse, and Toron slipped from him. Kurtisian fell more cleanly, as though robbed of his feet by grief, but Justinian collapsed to his haunches like an overladen mule. Only Shard had managed to stay upright. Níscel reeled to a crouch.

---

[13] *(AH):* literally "corpse wound"; a fatal wound, with which a victim may suffer for many days before dying.

[14] *(AK):* a burrow, as of a small animal.

"Toron," she had strained, "there is a saying of my people." She uttered a bestial string of meows, growls, burbles and clicks. "In your Allmal, it is, 'no good merchant has the stores that will match his spirit to sell them.' It is not too late. We can turn still around."

Toron's head had hung low, the warning like an executioner's blade. He rolled his eyes toward Shard, turning his head because he could not lift it, wondering whether the Highbred had not warned them, or simply could not feel whatever this was. He had seen the masked man making a finger prayer, and had thought of the mana he had told them not to risk, but then self-mastery had returned to him, and he had risen slowly, warily, back to his feet. The rest of the thoftship had followed, but sundrily—Justinian loosing a great cloud of relief while Kurtisian, smoldering, looked about his own body like a centurion thinking to decimate the troops that had failed him.

Pushing past everyone, he had clamoured into the darkness. "If I wasn't going in before, I'm going in now. I smell your breath, privy-ningler, but I'm still going to be your *irrumator!*"

Bellowed into the chasm, his challenge had splintered among echoes, and in pieces bounced away. The retreat of it had continued for more than was wonely, shrinking and shrinking but refusing to disappear, but it was not until it began to regather its strength, and to crawl back out of the cave again, that the thoftship seemed to recognize what was happening.

By the time the noise reached the cavemouth, it had become something else, and shrieked forth from the gash as the song of a mutilated choir. At first, all the voices were Kurtisian's, and simply mislayered, dissonant, but then their sound began to warp, as heat does to things seen, and the voices changed. Within a handful of heartbeats, they became those of younger men, then broke, and shrilled into childhood, from there garbling, and becoming the babble of infants, their notes shortening, their breaths shallowing, until at last silence, but only for a moment. Then it all reversed itself, but faster now, running the vocal gamut of man's mortality— through infant, child, juvenile, and adulthood, becoming again the trumpeting, slightly nasal boast of a Kurtisian in his prime, its strength lingering before lilting, and taking on a quaver which widened, and blighted, and wizened, and finally throttled its former might within a soft, geriatric wheeze whose lungs slowly played out. And then it was over, its gasp lapsing into the wind, as though reminding them with mockery that silence itself was the sound of innumerable voices heard no more.

Kurtisian had chuckled, but it was cheerless, a pair of sounds pushed out of his mouth. "That was not my voice."

Their eyes would not meet as they recovered. The fear was gone, and in its place was some nameless feeling that the gods, perhaps out of mercy, had never shaped their minds fully to perceive. Whatever it was, it was cold and unhurried, like the trudge of an ox through a winter storm. It had no imagination, but it could be pointed the right way.

And now deep inside, where he had aimed that feeling before it had fled him, Toron staggered into a wall and heaved like a man washed ashore. Light spidered about him, and gave no hope, and he knew how it was that a fire within darkness might only show that darkness to be endless.

It was all right. He did not rue his coming.

There, before the cavemouth, was the last time he had asked himself what they were doing here. He had done so knowing it was all up to him. He had only to say one word—nay, but to wheel about—and everyone save Shard would have followed him. With haste, they might have reached the treeline before midnight, finding the food and gear they had hidden under a mound of scree. By the next eve, they might have reached the inn, got drunk next to the hearth, and forethought warmer places, with better roads, and weaker foes. And like all starving hopes, that feeling had ransacked his mind to feed itself, flensing his soul, and shaving tinder from the walls of his will to cook it. In its selfishness, it sought only to save itself, and gave no heed to shame. So it is when the uttermost spark of life feels itself guttering, and commandeers the man for the sake of the beast he betters, and drives him to forsake beliefs and friends alike, that he might redeem himself another day, and not die for the both of them, the ox and the ploughman together.

Toron had felt that low thing wheedle him, for the shrines of his troth he had locked fast within his heart, and it wanted the keys. He would not yield them up willingly, and it began to tell him he did not have to, but even as it began to find the wherefore of its witherspeech—to grope out the words most likely to win him— something uncanny had strengthened him. It girded him, joisted him, built a framework beneath his feet. It held up the best of him and caged the worst down. It put a hull between himself and apostasy. And even as it worked from below, it had worked from ahead, firing a beacon before him, egging him onward, throwing its beam onto the road between them and showing it to be rugged but straightforward. Unbidden and at first unwelcome, its light warmed him, then filled his heart like a burning drink, outdoing his thoughts of petty ease as much as a sunrise outshines a lick of flame. A reckless will was what it kilned, and Toron had felt his flesh tighten about its cure. It had no longer mattered what they were up against, nor did the likelihood of a fall hold any shame with which to threaten him. Nothing they had done had yet paid off in the world, and nothing they might otherwise do held a hundredth the payoff as this.

It was not simply the fiend they faced here, but the finding of it that had to be reckoned with. Most tales told merely of the fray, the pitting of such-and-such a swordsman against this devil and that cutthroat. Only the wandering, true-to-life slayer himself knew that finding one's foe often posed the greater hardship, and that some monsters, no matter their might, would never be caught in the open to be fought with. Many, even the big ones, were skulkers and slinkers, striking only at night, or from the thickets of hinterlands whither roads did not lead. Toron knew not how it might have been in other Elds, when Man was less, or how it was when Norráma had been won from the wilds, but monsters now were a black kind of gold, and had to be sought by those doughty few who would profit by them. Havsikt, even with the odds at a hundred-to-one, was worth the game, if only because the game had never been played before.

Gorrh had come with them as far as he could, until the narrowing of their pathway had threatened his safe return. Backtracking a little, they had left the tuskcat at the gullet of the cavemouth, to watch over the *Carno* until Kurtisian had need of it again. The dreeman's hands had been put to better service for the time, adopting an *Ultrix* which cast light without heat, and the only one he knew that did no harm.

A heavy hand fell onto Toron's shoulder, but it did not startle him. He knew it was Justinian. So stifling was the sense of unlife in here that his thoftship, even those of them who did not carry lights, hollowed out the murk around them like glades.

"You good, Thorn?"

"Benny," Toron replied, using the southerner's own lingo. "Pulling some breath in, is all. Can't seem to catch any for long."

Justinian gave him a reassuring rap on the back and left his hand there as the Knaksmen gulped his lungs full. When they kept moving, it was together, though the passage didn't go on much further. After another bend, it emptied into a great cavity, one so wide and deep that the light could not find its boundaries. Their words, when they spoke with them, fell into the murk, and none of them dared speak loud enough to seek an echo, and so prove the void was not infinite. Across this swallowing abyss, their path became a bridge, still of stone, but smoother. Metal laths winked up from where it was pitted. To and from this bridge ran other bridges, like the walkways webbing the great pillars aboveground, some wide and some like threads, all leading they knew not where. In any other place, such a road plighted ambush, but in no place like this had they walked before. Its otherworldliness threw them, and so it was that they entered the gap bewildered and not wary, treading no less boldly than before, knowing that if something had the knack to waylay them here, such a thing was their doom, and far beyond their powers to withstand.

As they walked, Níscel had halted. She said she spied great towers in the gloom rising all around them, with windows too many too count, all black and sagging. Only Shard and Gorrh might have spotted them too, but Gorrh was not there, and Shard said nothing. Kurtisian had reached out with his shining hands, and Toron had strained to see by them. He thought he glimpsed some of the black holes, but their pattern frightened his mind. The min that came back to him whispered of a man he had once found hanged in the woods, several days dead, whose flesh dripped from its skull like a mask of molten wax.

They kept on walking, and saw other things, but everything they saw asked more than it answered. Great shapes loomed into the halflight and fell back again into darkness, deadheads slowly sinking in a swamp of tar. Mountains reached down from overhead, seeming as dripstones, save that no sea in a thousand thousand years might have dripped to shape them so mightily. Landings appeared alongside their path, like lilypads floating in the murk, showing railings but no bridges by which to land on them. Pipeworks leapt in and out of the stone. Half-buried things stood out as growths. The thoftship marched up and over archways which looked more the

products of wind than water, rounded the lip of a basin which
projected from a wall like a trough, and twisted up an enormous
pillar using a long, coiling channel.

They lingered over none of it. Shard kept well ahead of them,
and where first they had followed him because they had not wanted
him to be alone, they now followed because they did not want him to
leave them behind. Whatever it once had been, that vast underground
place drifted slowly away, blinking into the light one last time,
shifting shape and swethering back into the void. Even as its stone
seemed to glisten, the light seemed to corrupt it, bringing out dead
hues, fallows and duns which bleached the mind even as it banished
the darkness. Twice had Toron looked down at his hands—at his
own skin and fingernails—and thought he saw them paling, as
though this place, starved of life and light, would drink every drop
from them of the realm it was denied, wringing them out into
troglodytes whom the sun would burn, and who might never return
to an iridescent world.

At long last, their light fell against something that proved to be a
wall, and the emptiness ended at a cliff face pocked with caves.
Their pathway kept going into the largest of these holes, but it was
not the one they took, for Shard diverted at the last moment onto one
of the lesser walkways and followed its stairs high overhead. Little
more than a bough the route put beneath their feet, supported only at
its ends, and as wide as a gangplank at its narrowest. Its edges were
unrailed, and Toron felt no shame in crawling, knowing that
Justinian was rooted only by his faith in the Brasmat, and that
Kurtisian, the light of his hands blinking in and out of sight, was
doing the same up ahead. Níscel and Shard walked the rib steadily,
and without hint of worry, the kattid turning around to check on the
Men over and over, her tail swapping sides to offweigh her body,
and her mood thankful to show off. It was after the fifth time she did
this that Kurtisian, from all fours, accused her of it, which she
snorted away, but did not deny. The fuhrbido promptly stood, took
two steps, and nearly fell off the path, and returned to his dog-stance
with a snarl.

The path led into the most inhospitable cave of them all, whose
roof and floor sent fingers of stone towards each other, over which
they tripped, and which caught at their clothing. They kicked
through these growths where they could, but their speed was halved,
and not even Níscel could keep from staggering. More than once,

they tripped and fell against the walls, and saw that these too were in flux, ribbed to the touch, like the lips of many mouths pursed, sewn shut to keep from telling their secrets. At length it was these walls and not the floor that hindered them most, narrowing and tapering. Over and again Toron felt they were closing about him, and he had to stop, his arms and legs braced, to prove to his fears that this was not so. Its lessening was no bother to Shard or Níscel, both of whom were short and slight, and moreover had bodies that flattened like those of mice, but Kurtisian had to bow, and Toron to stoop, and Justinian to wedge himself through. The priest made it all into an occasion for lewd jokes, which his brother did his best to turn against him. Toron found himself in the middle of their filthy trade, but for their choice of southern words and homecloaked meanings understood only half of it, which was more than enough.

They kept on, the cave begrudging them more and more, and at length would yield no banter, but only the staking of pain and curses. Justinian expressed concern he might soon become stuck. Now moving sideways as well as crouching, the Sumo was white with powder from having to break through in many places. Were his skin not unbreakable by normal means, it would have bled. He could no longer turn around, and were he not a faithful of the Brasmat, for whom a landslide might seem a rough sort of hug, the tightfear[15] of the cave would have driven him mad. Toron worried for him, but also for them all; if Justinian became stuck, none of them might get out. He could not see past Kurtisian, whose body filled the passage like a bulkhead, and he risked a shout to those ahead of him, asking whether this wretched smial ever ended, or at least began to widen again. Níscel's answer, from further ahead than where he thought she had been, was that it opened into a hall big enough for a group. She and Shard were there now, she said, but the last bit was not going to be easy.

With that, the three Men pushed on, and after twisting themselves around one more corner saw ahead of them—and not far—the twin, lambent disks of Níscel's eyes. Kurtisian held up his hand, its flame illuminating the edges of the fissure that framed her like a half-open door. The squeeze was tight, but not hopeless. Its teeth were more forbidding than its mouth, and its teeth, as they had learned, could be dislodged. They went for it, no longer walking as

---

[15] *(AK)*: claustrophobia.

men, but rather twisting and lurching like legless things. To make
room, Toron unbuckled his swordbelts, and passed them ahead to
Kurtisian, who had to thread them up through a gap under his arm
before Níscel might receive them. So near to freedom himself, the
fuhrbido fell to wrenching and thrusting where he ought to have
inched with care. He became stuck, and his swearwords lilted toward
panic. Níscel urged him onward, with both encouragement and
behest, her voice nearly shrill enough to drill through the stone that
held him. So doleful was his plight that his words joined hands with
hers, and he let her rule him, and was slowly and gratefully
delivered.

Toron waited for his turn. Kurtisian was a little bulkier about the
chest and shoulders, and if the fuhrbido could make it, so could he.
He did not know, however, from the crush and the scrape of it, how
Justinian might follow them, and he could not turn around to see
how bad the clog of him was. The Sumo's breath was shallow, his
lungs crumpled into whatever shape his twisting body had made of
them. He had ceased to speak, even to jest, and that was a worse
token than anything.

At last Kurtisian pulled free of the passage, leapt back to his feet,
and with his hands lighted the way for the two men still inside. He
and Níscel called Toron forward, telling him where to put which
hand and which foot, but he had not crawled for long before the
fuhrbido simply grabbed him by both wrists, planted his boot against
the outer wall, and hauled him out onto the floor like the world's
worst midwife.

The flames about the dreeman's knuckles guttered for a moment,
bouncing the world in and out of darkness, but they did not burn
Toron, for they gave no heat or smoke, and ate no air, as was their
master's choice in a place such as this. And so thankful was Toron to
be free that he forgave Kurtisian his torn brow, which bled quickly
into his eyes. He rose, wiping the wound with a sweaty hand, and
looked about for his swords. He saw the tips of their scabbards
glinting from where they lay, but before he might reach them, he
found himself comforted by the sound of Shard's voice, which part
of him had not expected to hear again. Though recognizable, the
voice was strange, and not only because the Highbred spoke through
his scarf, which he had never done.

"There are mandrels about," he said, brandishing a stout-helved
pick with which he pointed into the darkness. "Retrieve one, and

have at it, or young Chaldallion will not be joining us."

Toron climbed back to his feet and caught his drift, witnessing in
Justinian's plight a sight no less awful than a titan being swallowed
by the underworld. Kurtisian's light, flashing as in a nightmare's
soundless storm, showed him to be trapped between the stone
pincers a full three feet from liberty. The remaining distance was
congested with outgrowths, and at its narrowest point inadmitting
even of the Seisumite's thigh. Of the whole man, only one foot and a
hand were close to making it out, and both of these flopped, their
digits fiddling, to show how violent the wedge. Justinian's face was
slack to feign calm—still the mien he might show at a card game—
but the blear of his eyes had always been his tell, and they bloated
now, their shine redoubled by the light. They seemed to belly out
like his muscles, as though his spirit pressed against them from
within, and would abandon that sturdy house now a prison. That no
one could get back through the tunnel seemed less a dilemma than
that Justinian might never escape it, and Toron groped through the
darkness whither Shard had pointed to find the tool that might
somehow help him. The hall was not wide, and his fingers readily
found a handle. But when he turned to wield the pick, Kurtisian was
there to receive it from him, muttering thanks before pushing Níscel
aside and attacking the stone with hatred.

At the outset, it looked desperate, but Kurtisian's third blow tore
out a slab so massive that he had to leap from its path to save his
legs. They saw then that the rock was not at all durable, and found
hope. Still, the absence of leeway made good swings difficult, and
the widening of the tunnel had to be from the outside in. Progress
was not swift, but it was steady, and because Justinian did not fear a
wounding, and gripped the Allmetal to be sure, Kurtisian swung with
impunity, worrying only that he might break the pick against his
brother's limbs, and not vice versa. He let no one else do the work,
and there was only room for one axer, so with nothing to do but
every so often to clear away the debris, Toron and Níscel passed the
waterskin, and again attempted to wash the old fear from their
breaths. Shard lighted a torch for them, whose flame fed on the
windy disturbance of the toil. Its light throbbed like a pulse, and
Toron found it dizzying, and closed his eyes. But what he found in
that darkness was worse—the hoarse breathing of the fire, the
hoarser breathing of the axer, and the chipping, cutting cadence of
the pick. Things were said, and that broken talk shambled, but there

was something else too, something beneath it all, which moved like the ground itself, and gave his mind nowhere to stand. He began to feel ill.

When Níscel asked him where he was going, he said he wanted to find another pick. The one might break, he said, the thing was so old. He then slipped out of sight of them all and felt his way around a bend. There, he could not see at all, but still he felt his ken reeling, spinning in a drunken way. After a few steps into the black, he dropped to his knees, sent the weight to his head, and threw up the worst he had ever done in his life.

Whatever it was, it needed to be out with. He fought the first heave, which tore its way out, and after that he gave himself up to it, no longer caring whether anyone heard. In the darkness, the croaking echoes of his retching was like the laughter of hidden goblins, and it felt as though every ounce of what he carried inside him was being rifled through, and weighed, and jettisoned if unneeded, as if by an arbiter who had no heart for softer things. Whether the better part of him was doing the purging or being purged, he did not know, but when it was over, and he pushed himself back to his feet, he felt wondrously lighter, not so much as unburdened as unbeholden, like a man whose arms are freed from things he once cleaved to.

He nearly forgot the pickaxe before going back. His fellows seemed not to have heard him in his throes, or if they had, they feigned it well.

Kurtisian had made much headway in the time he was gone, and Justinian now lent his own hand to the excavation, battering the stone where he could. He talked more now, and was encouraged, and inch by inch, the tunnel's scarring was stripped away, until he lay within a foot of release, and began to growl and thrash. Able at first only to dangle an arm and leg out of the gap, he gnashed his teeth and tried to wrench himself through, becoming less a titan than a housebreaking ogre who sought to devour the refugees within. Despite his violence, it was in vain, and Kurtisian chastised him with a kick, reminding him he had already tried that himself, herding his brother back into the recesses of the passage to allow him room to finish widening the exit.

Chink, chink, chunk. The pieces rattled. Shard held the torch aloft as Toron ducked beneath the pick and removed them.

Níscel looked down the hall and screamed.

"Bastet, Bastet, Toron, Toron, something is there! Something is there!"

Shard was before them with his sword drawn, the blur and the grind of it coming half a blink later. What he had held in his hands—the torch and the second pick—struck the ground behind him, and there the flames guttered, and were chewed down by the dark. The first axe clattered as Kurtisian threw his aside. He dumped more magic onto his hands, and they flared up brighter than before, but what they illuminated was an empty passage, Shard's shadow undulating into its open throat. Toron was aghast to find himself still swordless. His whats[16] had failed him, and not for the first time. He had not shrunk from the threat, but nor had he leapt to arm himself. He had simply stood there, frozen, his fists half-made, as though whatever it was could not be withstood or even fled, but only met, and embraced, with a hope for a weapondeath, teerful and tearless. And worse was the knowledge, ripped from its finery by his fear, that such a death, in such times, proved merely the dwaledom[17] of bold mice.

"What is it?" Justinian bellowed. "*Pedica me*, get me out!"

Shard slackened a little. "I sense nothing there. What did you see?"

Again, Justinian clamored for his release, tearing apart several gods in the demand. Níscel inched forward, head bobbing, her tail as thick as a chimney brush.

"I—I know not," she murbled, her eyes moonish with light. "It was…I know not."

Kurtisian scoffed so severely, it had pinched his vocal cords. "What do you mean *you know not*?! What in barathrum did you see?!"

"I thinked—I thought I see—I saw something move," she stammered. "But I smell nothing, I hear nothing. Sorry me. Sorry, Shard."

"Don't be," the outlander assured her. But his sword he resheathed, and he retrieved the torch from the floor. He cast a wary eye down the tunnel, put his back to the wall, and nodded at Kurtisian to continue their work. Toron had already retrieved the axe, however, and had at the wall with all the thrack of his self-loathing. Four bites he made and Kurtisian stepped in as well,

---

[16] *(AB)*: instincts

[17] *(AB)*: willful foolishness; something made up to avoid pain; a delusion.

working from the other side. The dreeman was what the Harandrish in their Allmal called 'cockhanded' and the southern colonists called *skeevy*, each of which was as unflattering as it sounded, but which meant simply, when stripped of their connotations, that in one-handed work he used his left, and not his right. And so from both sides they went at the wall, and made a contest of it, their faces reddening, their grunts building, with Níscel manning the torch, and Shard standing watch in the penumbra.

One pick thudded, Kurtisian pried, and half the wall seemed to break away. Dust went up, and from within its cloud, Justinian Chaldallion stepped free. His skin was chafed but unbroken, and begrimed where the sweat had made mud.

"Seisuma—" the priest prayed angrily, smothering the Allmetal within a fist "—the rocks are Your flesh and bones, but I'll piss on every boulder I find if they imprison me again."

Shard spoke without looking at him. "Do not antagonize your Patron, Chaldallion. If in these doldrums of faith your god sails beside you, His favour is mighty indeed. The rocks of Sherk-narsk-wirth are no longer His bones than the head on a hunter's wall belongs to the creature it was cut from.

"Even now, many things should not be. This fire, the air we breathe, the mana which now is clean, but too clean, like refreshing water utterly without taste. It is as though our needs had been seen to, and we stand within the larder. Or, rather, it is a pocket that goes where we do, sewn to this scrap of the Weave with stitches unfixed, and drifting wheresoever we wander."

Justinian opened his hand to look upon the Allmetal. Its surface was not glossy, and it did not echo light. So it was that its inner gleam could not be mistaken, and it smoldered even now, its lambency rippling like slow lava.

Kurtisian stared at it. "How do we know it's not a trap? That we're not being led in by the Collector himself?"

Shard shook his head. "The Collector cannot replicate these things. No more than you can learn to make a meal simply by eating it. And there is more—a way forward, for one, which goes as though kept open, as clearly as if cloths had been stuffed into doorjambs. Look to any other route, from the city gates onward, and you will see it choked off—hedged in by the Dwindling, grown over, or with bridges severed. Do you not see that the way to the Collector's own room would be the first It would close? And now, it is the only one open."

Níscel, but half-listening, gave another start. She scrambled back from the void, staring at something her eyes had never left. The thoftship leapt to arm itself again, flashes and grinding, and this time, Toron did not fail. Tuger and Mortha cheered as he loosed them from their stockades one-by-one, their double-edged blades— each the height of an eight-year old child—made to stretch and to play on the walls. They were twins, but unlike—what the Harandrish called two-edged twiborn—and his wont was to pull them out both at once. He had yet to buckle them back on, however, and there was too little room here besides, so little indeed that he worried to wield even one of them and made ready to drop Mortha if needed.

Níscel scootched back among them, keeping her torch if not her wits, and she held the brand forth like a banishing wand. They all waited, and waited again, their shadows writhing across the disfigured stone, and the slick eyes of the living glistened in the gloom. From inside the shaft whence the thoftship had arisen came the brief and sudden clatter of a delinquent bit of stone. The sound wrenched their heads to one side and left the fingers of their weapon-arms twiddling. Their breathing sawed frantically at its own cloud.

Still nothing came.

"Pardons, pardons," the kattid warbled. Her fur, ruffled upon hackles, burst from shirtsleeves and collar, making her seem far too big for her clothing.

Kurtisian snarled and stomped his foot, half of at it at her. His tension, overstressing him, needed somewhere to go, and the messenger was all that there was. The *Carno* shimmered as he shivered, still atatter with vapours from whatever midwhere warrens it had crawled through.

Níscel took a breath, and said "I thinked—," but the words were caught up in a chain of soft chirruping, which emerged from within her as irresistibly as a hiccough. Twice she sought to catch herself, and twice again the pangs interrupted her words, these times more loudly, and they made the stone walls to knell. The thoftship glanced at her sideways and would have stared were their wariness not trained elsewhere.

The torchfire bent backwards. They all heard something now.

"Voices!" Kurtisian hissed.

"And a draft," Shard added. "Vented from the direction of the bait."

"Bait?" The leather about the grips of the *Carno* creaked. "What do you mean, bait? Bait for what?"

Níscel's nostrils winked, and the nose-sense, as it sometimes did, took hold of her. Her head bobbed. "Smells of skin-water. Very strong. *Yech!*"

Shard lifted his hand for silence, and everyone listened. The torch crackled, and their breathing, however hard they meant to hold it, rasped at the walls like a spitless tongue.

Toron strained his ears, and with such ruthless suddenness that he wricked his brain on both sides. All he heard for it was the closest thing to a hush a living soul might hear—the heartbeat in his skull, and the crowding of the blood about his eardrums. Whatever the voices had been, and whatever they were saying, they had gone dark again. Only the draft remained, and its thereness, for its reek, could not be mistaken. He felt it first as a push against the dampness of his face, and he gingerly took a sniff. Indeed, it smelled of sweat—a rank and frightwrung strain which, for its strength, he told readily from the thoftship's own.

"Smells like a knocking stable[18] around midnight," Justinian offered.

"Or you an hour later," Kurtisian bettered.

The younger brother sniggered. "Tie me a hangknot."

"But what are its bellows?" Shard asked himself aloud. He unstiffened and stood within the draft with the kind of easiness one might wear on a beach. Resheathing his sword, he then pulled back the upper share of his cowl, and his metallic tresses caught and scattered the torchlight. The brilliance danced across the walls, and went into the darkness, turning dungeon to ballroom, and himself to a beacon in the drear.

Dappled by light, the rest of the thoftship slackened a little too. That the Highbred had ever made his living by skulking and eavesdropping and going otherwise unseen now seemed as gainly as fielding a seal at gymkhana.

Toron cleared his throat. "What—what do you think we ought to do, Shard?"

Shard looked back at him. His scarf made waves as he spoke. "What else can we do, northman, but trace the breath to its lungs?"

---

[18] *(AK)*: brothel; whorehouse.

Then, with his katana stowed, the halfMan sauntered into the brackish smell and was slowly swallowed by the blackness. The shimmering of his hair shrank down, like a bright thing sinking far into deep waters, and at last went out.

Níscel mewled softly, juggling her eyes between the lightless path and the tight-jawed faces of the Men around her.

"You'll stay with us from here, Níscel," Toron said.

She nodded, and they crowded into the bladder of her torchlight. Toron goaded himself to the front, having never put away his own swords. Their blades reached into the blackness like the prods of a beastkeeper, who keeps at bay things too mighty for chains alone. Kurtisian, unhappily but unasked, buckled his two baldrics back onto him. Before doing so, the fuhrbido leaned the *Carno* against one wall, where its slick sheen bled between darkness and radiance, and its liquidy surface looked as though it would snag, swallow and assimilate any flesh that might touch it. Those who saw it felt it looked more sinister than usual—blushing, perhaps, in chthonic air it loved—and even Justinian stood back from it, and waited until Kurtisian picked it up again, and went on ahead, before moving himself.

They traced this new hall for what felt like some time, murmuring at how—despite the decay in the shaft that joined it—it appeared to have been delved out yesterday. Its walls rose flush, at right angles to the floor, and merged nine feet overhead as a slightly uneven vault. None of its surfaces might have been considered smooth, but after having spelunked for miles through the dreeish karst of the underburg, they found these gouged faces almost friendly.

Their observations were clipped, however, when something new rode the draft. Again, it was a sound, and again one so faint that it was more like an inkling than the thing itself—something lurking just within the threshold of the knowing mind and lairing among the suspicions. These hearcrafty gremlins gave no heed to the thoftship's onely and sundry talents. Níscel seized them no better than Justinian, and at times they all would stop and cock their heads, turning their ears into the draft but hearing nothing more than the supping of the torchfire. Four times they halted and listened without fulfillment, their blood cold in their hearts and their hearts drubbing to splinter their ribs. Their sight thrested and bleared, and at last it became too much. They halted as one and vowed not to go on until the bogey unhooded itself.

Loath to do it but dead-ended, Toron called out to Shard, first softly and then boldly, remembering what had happened to Kurtisian the last time one of them had thrown his words into a gap. He did not wait long before an answer came, but it was neither Shard's speech nor his own. Instead, it was the jabber that had baited them, skirmishing no longer but now driven fully to earshot, rushing and pelting about them as when a door is thrown open by a storm. They all cowered in its path, as though the sounds were ice and stones, but even amidst such a squall, they heard words in the din, though in a tung none of them knew. As the roaring purl of it went on, and brought nothing in the way of foemen, the thoftship rose from the single knot into which they had tied themselves. None of them spoke amidst the uproar, but questioning looks went among them, all of which were met with shrugged shoulders and shaken heads. Only an *Allmaller*[19], or one of the many tung-changing magic spells, had a chance.

Nonetheless, the braid of voices held them, and seemed to plead for disentanglement, for much can be said in the very sounds of speech, whose breath, unlike language, is at home in every Man's throat. Were a child brought up wordless, his tongue undressed by that silver mantle we mistake as inborn as a caul, there would still in his utterings be the seeds of all Man's meanings, which tamer men have in their settled places grown into gardens. So it was that the thoftship stared into the dark gullet of that weird chorus, and gave their ears to their hearts, and by that reroading heard much.

There were tens of voices, not hundreds, both aboil and in throes, their waves made by something deep beneath them, which showed itself only in their deepest, sametimely troughs. Rather than simply crest and pitch into blarings and hushes, they blistered the whole while, foaming up with whimpering wherever the spaces between them widened. Their turbulence crashed at the soul, black billows of salt at cliffs of chalk, and even Kurtisian crumpled toward tearbreak. Still the thoftship withstood it, and hearkened deeper, and upon the chop of its face new flotsam emerged. These were the voices, told clearly, of both men and women, and beneath them of children as well, whose chirms are weaker but sharper than those of the

---

[19] a magical item that carries spoken language into the *Allmal*; a universal translator.

fullgrown, like the teeth and claws of whelps, whose end is to prod those who care for them. Though sundry in years, the voices were all one in woe—the building, baneful kind of dread felt by those stripped of hope and thrown to poach in a vat of their own mindsight.

Then the voices split open, and their insides ran out. The cries became lunatic, unlunged with suffering so mordant that they bit gobbets from the minds of those who heard them. They rang in all pitches, some running out of breath as others recharged, but it wasn't long before every one of them united in a single, ululating howl which was its own dirge. The hearing of it was enough to forswear hearing itself, inghasting things to melt one's meanings, and to give to that unsong one's own, shredding cry. Crushing his fists to his ears, Toron forgot he held swords, and nearly took the heads off his bystanders. Níscel, though, had shrunk to a heap at his knees, and the Chaldallions staggered back together, both gasping and exclaiming in disgust of their own horror.

Suddenly, each of them heard his own name—uttered once, but with power—and everything, both air and mind, became silent again. Blinking away the blear, they looked back down the tunnel, and heard the voice clearly.

"It is Shard!" Níscel cried. "He calls to us!"

Toron caught his balance, then his breath. With care this time, he lowered his hands and swords, and called forth to the outlander, whose voice he heard again.

Words returned from the gap ahead of him. "Come. I have discovered something. Something you and the Seisumite should examine."

His heart still thundering, Toron took no chance. "What's your name again?"

A moment bellied, one whose child was laughter.

"Thyrsabyn-Sairtys," came the reply, giving the full name of which Shard was a shard. "Toron, Avarnok has no need to ventriloquize."

The name struck him like cold water, unaddling him at once. He looked behind him and saw that everyone was shaken but whole. The Chaldallions, impatient and full of fight, urged him forward. Toron put aside one sword to help Níscel back up.

"I am wellsome," she said, dragging the words out by their scruffs. Still, the sound of Shard's voice had bolstered her, and she went on ahead, the torch up to one side so as not to blunt her own, sharper eyesight. Her cloak, from its midpoint down, glittered with the dust of where it had heaped.

Having footed so tenderly before, their thoftship now all but jogged, rounding a bend in the hall and loping down a slope whose floor gave them long, shallow stairs. But that downward flight went on for too long—too long, it seemed, for Shard's words to have climbed it so breathfully. Their pace slowed beneath the weight of their qualms, this as the torchfire blazed a trail, its light writhing like the limbs of a berg-splintered dawn. The path screwed downward, straightened, and screwed downward the other way. The four faces of the passage shed all marks of unlikeness, and seemed now all one, as though the thoftship walked through the same place over and over, through a rehappening web, seamless and endless.

But at long length there arose the tang of wet stone, and the air dankened. The torchlight spread wide wings, and the tunnel emptied into a hollow—a jagged gutting of the stone whose ancientness sniffed at their marrow. The room was the crossroads of three other shafts, which stood against the far wall as empty sockets. At its core was a dark pool, eyelike, as of a fiend peering up through a hole in the world's hull. Its rim folded fattily where it had not been cut by runnels, dripping down into puddles which shone as oily as their motherhead. Dripstones fanged every surface, whose skin heaped like drosen[20]. A droplet of water fell into the pond, sending ripples slithering across its black skin. The stead reeked of foreboding. Níscel stopped hard at its threshold, but Toron stepped past her, walking as on a lake's first freeze. The cavern was too small for swordplay; Mortha's blade chipped the ceiling as he put her away. Tuger he kept out, but apart from wielding the great sword as a spear, Toron saw no way to swing him without risking his thoftmates' lives.

His thoftmen quarreled behind him.

"Go on, Níscel," Kurtisian urged. "It's only another room."

Níscel said nothing. The torchlight stayed where it lay.

They heard shuffling, and slapping against stone. It was Shard, making noise so as not to startle. It was a kindness he seldom did them, but he did not forgo it here. He all but stomped from the darkness of the leftmost shaft, his hair showing first, catching the

---

[20] *(AK)*: sediment; deposits.

fire again and will'o'wisping out of nowhere.

The Highbred beckoned. "In here."

Toron made his way across the cavern, his feet seeking ridges on its floor. The air was warmer in here, but it did not hearten. Its heat seemed to emanate from the pool, which Toron felt in his blood he ought not to go near.

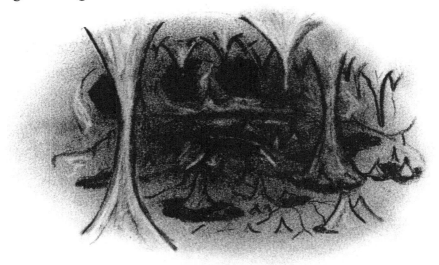

Behind him, Justinian groused at Niscel, telling her if she wasn't going any further, then at least to step aside and let him in. He demanded the torch, and she refused. The room's light fluttered as they fought over it. Kurtisian told his brother to relax, and rekindled one hand, cupping his fingers to direct its beam, and making ghostly twilight where the two radiances overlapped. The Chaldallions left Niscel there, and not until she seemed likely to be abandoned with her firebrand did she pick up her feet. The threshold she crossed, and the cavern walls slinked as she moved.

Toron ducked into the shaft behind Shard, bracing himself against the wall with his free hand. The coldness of the stone bit through his handshoe[21], stinging his fingers, and it was then that he saw the cloud of his breath had become thicker.

"Shard, the screaming."

"I heard it," replied the darting darkness ahead. "In truth, I provoked it."

---

[21] *(AB)*: glove.

"You what? How?"

"By tracing the draft to the site you are about to behold."

The shaft went on for only ten yards, and wound to a dead, black end. Nothing seemed odd about it, and he waited, and when Kurtisian came close enough, they saw by the light of his hand that a single stope made a burrow in the wall. A mass of rubble lay strewn about its mouth, and a crawlway had been cleared to within. The hole, even before they looked inside, was hellish. Its sight blackened Toron with its unlight, and he shrank from it unwittingly. Shard crouched beside it and waved their eyes within.

"Behold," he commanded. "Behold the refuge of the last Afthecksans."

They had all gathered close, but still they could not see—indeed, they did not want to—and Shard seized the torch from Níscel and thrust its flames into the cavity as if to cauterize it. What lay within was profane. Justinian looked away.

It was a shrine, makeshift and crude, hollowed out in haste by the picks worn to nubs still lying there. At its heart was an *ofgod*—what in the south they called an idol—though only the foot of it remained. The rest of it lay in rubble, ransacked by some godawful force. That same strength had rent the walls asunder and broken the rings of runes that had been carved there. Toron eyed the gashes fearfully. Harandril was a land of bears, and he had seen such wounds on tree trunks.

But these.

He could reach into these up to his armpits. Such a bear to make these would outstretch the walls of a keep.

But the way in was so small. Were they what he thought they were, he saw no way such a fiend might have reached in here and made them. He pulled his eyes from the gouges, and they fell upon an unbroken patch of the wall's surface. Its writing, like the walls and floor themselves, was crude, messy, chiseled out in haste. He looked closer. There weren't many staves. Only five or so, over and over again, covering everything, warding the evil away, ringing the one, round wall in an endless loop of forwishing.

A prayer.

"They fled here," Shard told them. His voice was cold and drained. "Hunted from behind, they were cornered. They knew they were the last. They stopped up the entrance, and made pleas to an old god, one they'd abandoned long before." He chuckled sadly, an unlikely sound. "They hardly remembered His name."

Withstanding the dread only because he couldn't fully name it, Toron leaned a little closer to the floor and saw it to be scratched all over, faintly and in rows, as by many four-toothed combs. The Aftheksish, whatever their make of mankind, had had strong fingernails.

They'd been dragged from this church they'd made. One by one.

Toron pulled back, his flesh crawling. He looked to Shard, and the Highbred's eyes were no longer his own.

They iridesced, their irises ruffling and glistering like feathers.

"It didn't work," He said, and His voice was full of pity.

Toron fell onto his backside.

"Who are you?" the northman cried.

Kurtisian screamed.

But he was looking behind them, back toward the room they'd known was watching them all along.

III
Εὐθάνατω
Two Good Byes

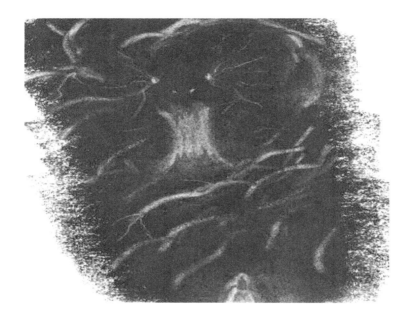

When the cavern disappeared, it left nothing behind. There was only the darkness, and of a kind they had not yet seen. This was turbulent, amniotic, both empty and full, and like a storm it had its own radiance, though it could not rightly be called light. The tunnel opened into it like a hollow needle.

The One who was no longer Shard went the first to its threshold. They let him pass, then crowded about the portal, both cringing and gawping, like children watching their father's first duel. A narrow bridge grew out beneath his feet, with neither a rail nor a parapet at its edge. He went out to its end, and so walked the plank to his doom.

Something moved within the murk. Its stirring muddied the cosmos.

The One who was no longer Shard spoke, but what he said, they did not know. The tungs he chose were legion, and many of them only the Endless know now. He had selected them with care, to show his Enemy that the memories of what It had stolen still lay with someone. And what he said in those tungs he arrayed in all the lost bounty of their uniqueness, flourishing grammar and idiom, a paradise of rhetoric. Nouns sprouted verbs burst skyward whorling wordforms. Tenses blew as winds; moods monsooned. Syntax enmeshed it in vines and white water. Their phonologies bruited, and Eden rang. Archaeopteryces sang with the lizardbirds. Seacows lowed from lagoons. Extinct allusions walked again.

And though it could not last, its linguistic symphony brought joy to the face of old Creation, as to a man in his bed, spent and worldweary, into whose hands is pressed something life has taken from him.

It was a key to a memory, by which a sealed door reopened. Sunshine poured from within. The pale universe blushed with old happiness.

But then the room of memory bled out, and it was dark again. The light puddled, shimmering as it extinguished. The old Judge sank to His knees in it, and all the hope He had left went into the hatred of what had despoiled Him.

He set the Laws aside for a moment. He looked the other way.

He has done it before.

And though few things tend to happen at such times, big things can be achieved by those who know He has done it. As with worldly laws, suspension of the rules does not benefit those who do not know they have been suspended. Anarchy is not inertia; most things continue along the trajectory of their expectations. Things fly as they were thrown. But for those in the loop, who stand with feet ready and eyes on the clock, it is a time of infinite potential, when impossible things become not just possible, but easy, especially if the target itself is unaware of the opening.

It is at times such as these that the Deathless can be killed.

The One who was no longer Shard finished his performance. The Judge's reward, the chance He afforded, would in the end echo louder than any cosmic fanfare.

What he said is ineffable. These mouths of ours cannot convey it, not with its poetry and hatred both, not with all the shearing force of its mordancy, and the sardonic bitterness of its slander. Like an onion it gave pain to peel, its many layers thickening and darkening with depth, till the unfleshed heart of it dripped, and its pungent drifts made a tearjerking broth of the air.

But this is what he said more or less:

"Across a hundred thousand worlds we have hunted you. From the meadows of one world to the cities of another. From moons tethered to empires of stars to huts among the bulrushes of riverbeds we have tracked your carnage. Forever you evaded us. You slipped in and out of doors we could not follow, reaping and vanishing, and took refuge in Wheres beyond the knowledge of light. To find you we had to learn to look in places we did not know, and then dare to tread them. We badgered and ferreted you. We nearly had you once. You remember the time. But we balked at the threshold you crossed. As you see, we have stooped to cross it.

"We have baited and gaffed you. We hauled you up out of the cosmogonic sewage, and landed you here, in a domain of my making. Look about you, filth, if your shrunken eyes can bear the gleam of something so clean. Into its precious flask I have decanted all that is best in me. The dregs I withheld, and I chew them now to brace my hatred of you. There is soundness here. The roads are straight from life to death, no perversity, no bending, no *vilomas*[1] sanctioned. I am Lord here. And you are a freak. Bow before me, freak! And then grovel before the rest of us, all of whom authored such realms, and whom you bereaved, made *horim shakulim*[2], took our children to be your veal.

"The quest for you has consumed us. But you kept us going, you filth. Most of us you would not deign to remember. We are faces in a crowd. We hail from all Quanta, and the thing that brought us together is you. Your ilk seeks to corrupt what we have made, but you—you want to unmake it. That makes you the worst; your greed is the vacuum that pulls everyone in upon you. You make allies of us. Fire and water would link arms to hunt you. We did not need to agree on anything other than to want something for ourselves. We shall throw our weight behind anything that opposes annihilation, for to save something from oblivion is to keep open the possibility of its redemption. One might free whoever has been enslaved. One might redeem the fallen. One might heal the sick. But one cannot work with what has been unmade.

---

[1] *Vakhish*: unnatural things; perversions.

[2] *Safish*: bereft parents; parents 'widowed' by the loss of children (sg. *horeh shakul*).

"We hate you for more than for what you have undone. We hate you for what you have made us do to ourselves. To be able to follow you, we have accepted mutilation. Our minds we have injured, that we might act without understanding. We have gouged out our eyes that we might not see where we had to walk. I have had to prune things, and to uproot within me what cannot be regrown.

"Ere this, the sunless places you inhabit were but a well for us, into which we stared for reflection, and trembled, and screamed, 'you shall not have us', and turned away to do our work. Its nothingness is the gap Creation works to fill, and eternally oppose. But you made us leap, and plunge into the dark. We held our breaths to sound the abyss, and when we came back, we were not ourselves. For the role of Creator is to create, and to do that thing in the lee of life's hard winds, in the havens of silence and deep thought. Soft fingers one needs, and an open heart, toughness only in softness— the will to keep care through hardship. I challenge any destroyer to undo what he does. Uneat what he swallow; unkill what he murder; unburn what he put to the torch. Do not flatter yourself, filth— creation and destruction are not counterparts. One is something; the other is but a parasite. You are less than nothing, for nothingness is the canvas upon which I work. At best, you are its thrall. You are oblivion's catamite.

"We know what you are doing, and it is not to your benefit alone. Your foul kind are furthered by it, as a windfall of your glut, just as the master gets clean plates when a dog is let in to lick them. We know what you are doing. You seek to load the dice. And you seek to do it long before the dice are cast. You would win the game not simply by cheating, not simply by assassinating its players, but by erasing their forebears. You seek to foreslay them—a weary scheme of dastards wherever dastards wield prophesy.

"But you do not see how deeply this goes. How could you, with eyes ever crossed upon your meal? You drink dry the rivers that the baby's bathwater might never be drawn. You take too much. How might you understand what it is to pluck out whole patterns, to unravel bloodlines from the fabric of the Weave? In what way might you even feign to comprehend what fills their absence? For when a plug is pulled from this world, it is drawn away by its cord, which is a vital tether. It links its dependent to the Unity, and so it is umbilical, but it is also a pendulous chain, one of a finite number by which Being is withheld from the ravening jaws of the true

Devourer. You pull them out, and you uncork Creation, and you drink what bleeds out. The vessel falls further with the draining of it. What you swallow, vile sot, is no preserve, but preservation itself. On this bender of yours, there is nothing that is not the soma of seedcorn.

"The burden of you weighs Us all down, down into the maw of Finality. Let the stars constellate Our deposition:

"We have no choice. Here We do what We must do."

When he finished, there was silence.

Then came a response from the brume. Its sound was seismic, whalesong *basso profundo*, of underworld pipes moaning out through their welds. Its organ was ancient, and long abandoned, pressed back into service as bolthole of speech, as when one whose arms and legs have been chopped away, and his tongue ripped out, beats head against floor, spelling out the dots and lines of an obsolete code. Whether it was the Beast speaking, laughing, or simply readjusting the coiled miles of Its body, they could not tell. Only an immortal might recognize it as language, the rules of whose grammar antedated the laws of starbirth. For everyone else, it spelled madness.

But He protected them, the One who was no longer Shard. He shook His head and would not hear it. He raised His arm, like a showmanly gladiator demanding his due, and out of nowhere came music, of a kind to armour the heart. The invincible black voice warred with it and failed, for the music did not seek to overpower it, but entwined and entangled it, put its bass body beneath its own, wrapped staves about its length, in whose lattice blew blossoms of tenor, alto, and treble, whose cadences flexed at need, and so rode the lowing hulk through its every bucking pitch. So it was that the music yoked that unbreakable force, neither by civilizing it nor by teaching it taste, but by enthralling its savagery to great beauty, just as the same drums throbbing at a cannibals' feast might be made to adorn the symphonies of maestros, and the lard of vermin made to brace maquillage.

He who once was Shard gloated, boasting into the gloom one last time. "See, filth. See how there is no weapon you might wield that I cannot hammer into ornaments. So with rot and ordure and ash, which are the rightful sigla of your ilk, I have Here made the tinder of the phoenix fire, which gives rise to new life. I have seen to all of this. I have evolved by your predation. I have adapted to the chase. And I have pressed my hatred of you into the love of what I make— as when a miller grinds the rats right along with the grain, and finds miraculous leavening, whose bread, disinfected by the baking, feeds more mouths than ever before. I—"

The gangplank of stone exploded, swept asunder by the awful passage of something immeasurable. So massive it was it did not seem movement but stasis in the midst of movement, as though the thing itself merely glowered, and world itself stepped aside.

The thoftship cried out, in voices they had never made before. Shard was gone—not dashed or flung or plucked away, but simply engulfed by the violence of that cataclysm. No token of him followed, and no tidings beyond the first bursting of stones. The fragments of the bridge never sounded from below. The place seemed netherless, a pocket unreckoned, where things might fall out the bottom of itness and time. The endlessness now eddied with maelstroms, but they could not see what owned it—whether what had flicked Shard away now writhed in glee, or whether, like oared water, the ether kept its spin from the push.

But the music did not stop. Instead, it stacked up, and new instruments joined in, adding to that boisterous symphony many new strains. Some of their sounds were familiar, but also outlandish, with deep blasts and fierce, fretful strumming, as of horns and lutes the shapes of which were never to be seen, theirs like the voices of divas, perhaps many-headed and necked, and with corpulent lungs, whose deformity in sight is a sacrifice to heavenly powers of sound. And as such, the mystery of them made their tones even more beautiful, and the music found awesome power. It entered the heart and stirred even the most curdled blood, causing it to race and to cascade, to leap sparkling into the coldest valleys of the self, as a river freed from icelock, which will in time circumvent all obstacles, and carry away the things it cannot thaw.

It was a symphony for life. The kind that sings fiats to the void.

The little band felt themselves lighten as the music melted their oppression. Their spirits sprang back toward willfulness, as from the hibernation fear had chased it, and basking stretched their legs in this new atmosphere, whose cultivation was proof against savagery. Before them stretched the same galactic roil, if anything more turbulent now, but its menace had been foiled by the music, fenced

its villainy with theatre. Upon them the band felt the eyes of many
spectators, though they could not see them, and beneath that
supervision they felt the duty of a role. It empowered them and
brought them back to the parts they had begun to choose for
themselves when they had first closed their fingers about weapons
and clad their soft skin in cold armour. And it told them that all
rightful choices must forget themselves, and become performances,
abandoning the choice like an open eggshell, and trading fear of
regret for fear of failure.

They hardly noticed as the tunnel disappeared around them,
lifting like a fog, and found themselves exposed atop a threadlike
jetty, much like the one from which Shard had been swept moments
before, save that it no longer had any shore to anchor it. A sole
filament of Creation in the chaos it lay, the swallowing storm on all
sides. The greatest commotion in that cloud remained before them,
however, its swim the silhouette of the leviathan, and so they kept
their chests trained upon it, locked like so many ballistae, from
which they were prepared to sling their own hearts, if the script so
demanded it.

A sinister rain began to fall.

Most of it went from nowhere to nowhere, from topless sky to
bottomless ground. Some of its drops struck the jetty, however, and
rang out tinnily, like the strikes of a tinker's hammer. The air shrilled
with their noise. At first the murk's dark light betrayed little, and the
rain seemed merely to splash and to scintillate like any other. But as
the downpour grew and the sound of it thickened, it became clear
that it was not rain. Some of it struck those standing there, clinking
off Toron's mail like pebbles, and where it struck skin, it stung.
Everyone but Justinian took bewildered refuge beneath his own
cloak and saw from the shelter of those awnings a shower of coins.
Most of them leapt back into the void, but so many there were that
small heaps began to accumulate, rolling and arrested by
irregularities in the floor. Brilliance peppered, then paved, the dark
stone beneath their feet.

Squinting through the shimmer, Toron kept his eyes on the
cloud. Its treading currents lasted, but they did not hasten, and
though he could not explain it, he did not fear an attack. If anything
toyed with his expectations, it was the music, whose movements
kept building, and circled the scene like sharks, their scales

glissanding towards some grand finale, a catastrophic fugue whose overtones frisked with apocalypse.

Swifter and richer the seconds unfolded, and Toron watched the coins pile up around him. They tinkled in different tunes as they met with his swords and each other, drawling as they struck his cloak. He reached down and picked up a piece, braving the torrent with his handshoe, and held it into the gloaming to inspect it. It was not a Knaksish gildenbit, nor a Hálish gullkona, nor even a farthing from the forlornlands, a few of which he had seen. It was egg-round, with a knurled edge, showing on both its faces the laurel-framed profile of a hawk-nosed man whose chin and scalp wore tightly curled locks. Toron marked an inscription as well, but before he could make out any more, the coin was struck from his fingers by another, which was big enough to hurt. He withdrew his hand and continued to weather the strange storm, glancing over at the Chaldallions, who gave him looks as baffled as he was. After a short while, the fall subsided, and the giggling of the pieces gave way to a few scattered clatterings. Toron wasted no time and rose from one knee, molting a fleece of mintage which cascaded loudly into the drifts surrounding him. With a jangle, he disinterred his swords, and stood to behold more wealth than any story had ever given his mindsight.

Heaps of coins had snowed them in. They swamped the whole platform, undulating from ankledepth shallows to mounds higher than the waist. The coins were of many shapes—some round, others faceted, others just shy of square. Some were worn faceless, while others seemed to have been minted but an hour ago. Some were as broad as Tarmaterizish moths, whose wings went wider than a man's two hands. Such coins must have been thin, or their gold diluted by tin, or else they would had brained everyone they had rained on. Others, however, seemed lesser than the eggs of hummingbirds, and filled the gaps among their betters as pebbles do wherever mountains have molted. A few were blank, but most showed images, and from what they knew of this place, the thoftship felt they looked upon the shadows of ghosts—the reliefs of monarchs, strange beasts, and majestic cityscapes—ringed by letters no soul in the Wheres could read any more, riddlers from the past, whose voices have been reduced to the mere vibrations of their echoes.

The thoftmen dusted themselves off, picking the coins from their collars and belts. A few fell from their hair, while those that had slipped into their clothing were given the same writhing shakedown as ants. Their faces were all stunned and wary, even that of Justinian, who stood with legs braced wide, a harbour colossus in the shimmering high tide. Níscel had the look of a fox in a chicken coop, one mad with starving but with wits enough to suspect that the hens had been dusted with arsenic. More than anything else before it, this tortured her, and she stood with wide eyes, frozen, a selfmade statue. Her nostrils winked, and again.

"It smells strange," she said. "The coin it smells strange. It is not right."

"Give me anything right about this place," Kurtisian crammed through his teeth, "and I'll show you a dead dragon."

There came light laughter, not as a gladdened storm might make, but a man. It came from below, rising like an unsinkable thing dragged down and let go again. It was Shard, or Whoever wore him. He rose even with the bridge and hung there, floating but for the lack of a bob or yaw, as though simply drawn, with the solid ground yet to be put beneath him.

"It is plunder," he said, addressing both them and the one that had not yet shown itself. "He has hoarded it into these vaults of his own making, shut up within these pustules between Wheres. Its reek is the rot of its uprootedness, the sweat and wither of anything that has been thrown into a box out of time." The One who was no longer Shard turned his head fully to the brume and laughed, now hysterically. "You thought you could pluck a thing from its own reality and believe it stays what it was? Like a child who jars a mouse under his bed and knows not why it smothers and rots. And of all things *coin!*" The word was uttered like a base bit of gibberish, and the One's eyes glistened with disbelieving mockery. "*Coin.* Of all you might have preserved, of all you have undone, you save coin. Not lore nor tech, nor bottled cities. Not a harem of the embalmed. You save coin." The speaker's voice staggered, as beneath its finery its composure was gnawed by the lifehating madness of it all. "Old habits die hard, eh old wyrm?"

The coins clinked again, though none new had fallen. The One who was no longer Shard swung his head back toward the band, and beheld Níscel, broken at last. She was on her knees amidst the money, ladling as much as she could into her foodsack. The food, dumped out, lay next to her.

"Do not take one!" the One who was no longer Shard commanded.

"Good," Níscel retorted. "I will take a thousand!"

The music began to muddy, and with its muddying the black thicket reroiled.

Something was wrong.

"Do not make me stop you," the One warned.

Justinian growled. "Don't make me stop you from stopping her."

Toron too saw the kattid's misdeed, but rather than something he might halt, it seemed something he might only watch, as a memory, or as a stageplay he had no right to interrupt. His swords, his arms, his whole body seemed a whimsy of matter here, an assembly of things that like so many breaks in the clouds had come together as a mere window onto beyond, and not a means to act there. The unheavenly skies boiled on all sides, upwelling colours which blistered, ruptured, and bled, and with every burst the music shrank back, as before the thrashing of a beast whose savagery its melodies no longer had the power to calm.

Showing yet again that he was not himself, Shard would not be ignored. His voice uncloaked itself of its lordliness, and he spoke to the thoftship with desperate mercy. "Níscel, everyone, I implore you. The Collector fears for its life. It has offered this plunder in exchange for our withdrawal."

He was on the verge of laughter, he clearly found it so preposterous, but the coins kept ringing, Níscel kept scooping, and every clink was a hammerstroke that flattened out his smile.

Níscel leered. "Good. Good. We accept."

"Sand child, you do not know what you are saying."

Toron blinked and stretched his eyes, as if to banish a drunken vision. He no longer felt as before, emboldened when the music had steeled him, nor had he yet come back to himself, the hint of whom hid deep within his mind, like a child among the storage. He felt instead both adrift and arrested, something caught between witherly winds, whose stasis is no stability, but a prison of their conflict, the crushing calm between two storms. Buffets from each broke loose and shuddered into him; his seams began to ache. And he observed with the distraught patience of one frozen that the two sides were not even-tempered, but that one was monstrous, and sought only to shatter him, while the other did all it could to hold him together. Toron's whole self shrilled, whining like a harpstring strummed to snapping, and he knew by that awful strain that the friendliness on one side of this contest was for naught, and that its backing would do

nothing more than to give the monster a solid surface against which
to grind him.

With every passing moment, what was sound around them
drained out, as from an unstoppered tub, its trappings dashed to
wreckage by the widening of the breach. In that gap lay the madness
of unfixed meanings, that aetherstock, inchoate, which is itself the
wombwater of all worth and knowledge. But beyond the churn of its
inflow waited something much worse than that, eye-lanterns
blinking behind the spray, for whom that unseeded stuff was simply
a medium, and pressed its belly to the only road that did not burn it.
It waited, waited for its world to flood out the other, like to the
dreadfish that circles the foundering ship, whose engineers had
sworn was unsinkable.

The One who was no longer Shard could not hide his dismay.
His otherly eyes glistened, and his head twitched with the blows of a
hundred thousand cares. Whichever bearded star he had tugged, its
roots were stronger, and went deeper, than he had thought. Its
upheaval, were it any slower, might bring down the roof of Heaven.
He, they, had to act, lest their window be closed. Whether this tick
broke, however much of its body left behind, however Pyhrric the
victory.

They had to pull.

So through the warring confluence of it all came a sweet blast of
encouragement, like the voice of an old teacher, long gone and
beloved. Simple and firm, it rose up to support them, a floor
reclaimed, even as the hand of a god plucks up the drowning ship,
and sees the dark waters run shapeless from its deck. The music
struck up again, and this time the loudest, bursting from what
strangled it, as a hero wrenches free from a smothering curse. It was
a kamikaze tune. The winds that went through its pipes were the last
lungfuls of their minstrels, even as the fingers that sawed and fretted
its strings were themselves sawed and fretted. Its percussion
thickened the air, grumbling like the grandfather of thunder, pulsing
as the heartbeats of billions made synchronous, as though the
hemispheres themselves were the faces of its drum, and its thrashing
meant to butter Creation. Furious was its tempo, and unstoppable
while it held, a juggernaut bleeding out, whose heart its puppeteers
gave their own blood to sustain. But it could not hold up for long, the
influx of that spirit too utter, causing its vessel to bloat with
desperate hope, its hide to fissure, till one return blow might burst it,

and all its holy charge strew asunder.

The gooseflesh simmered upon Toron's neck as something in the empyrean squalor tossed itself about, this time something definite, a meteoric blackness within the lesser gloom. And before he might warn his thoftmen, a new shining—a dreadful blush—entered their skies, an inflammation in thin skin, which flames brightest before it breaks. He quailed, forefeeling the brunt of it, and knew he would not overlive it, but before its anger burst, his backer threw its balm upon it, and the malignancy flattened.

What happened after that they did not know.

They had to recollect it in pieces, scraping them out from beneath the thresholds of their waking minds, and, most frighteningly, from memories that blitzed through the windows of the calmest thoughts. What they assembled of that event could not be called a dream, for its basis was not wholly in vision, nor could they call it a revelation, for they had partaken of it. It was instead some species of sublimation, election to a hallowed tenure perhaps no more than a few minutes long, whose incumbency had taught them traumatic truth and power, the enormity of which would not fit into their minds all at once.

The darkness had unloomed, and become visible. Its threads separated, and again, and became ever more delicate, parting as if before countless hands running out through the tresses of night. The gaps between them widened, and they became living lines, curling and slithering, undulating in the winds of the music, until in concert they settled, and were cinched down, becoming the things from which hidden shapes were limned. The colours were there already, blooming even before the lines had fenced them, new colours, which seemed to drip in clean from elsewhere, making dinge of the hues they displaced. Before their eyes of flesh an illustration was extorted, a sight that fought to stay unseen, but was pulled into the light by its tail, whose thrashing appendage was made to spell out its name.

Slowly, and with rancour, the thing came together before them. Its dimensions became ungodly, and kept building. The canvas of the Weave writhed to show it, and buckled beneath its weight, a mule nigh to crippled by the criminal it bears to the gallows. Its growth craned then strained the necks of its beholders, and still it kept waxing, gathering size and detail so ruthlessly that its revelation made a lag in existence, as though reality struggled to find the stuff for it—like to a colourman who seeks to fulfill the demands of a mad artist, one whose easel is a mountainside, who strips the world bare of ochre, and burns what is left for his charcoal, to meet his buyer's impossible vision. Still it grew, and grew, and the walls of the world were moved back to contain it, and again, and finally they hinged, splitting open as though shucked, and the tumour within its husk was fished out, spiny and glistening like a bezoar. Its enormity was not black, nor red, but something like the bloodless blush of crabshell. The hue unfurled like a cold dawn, owning every horizon, its innards bulging outwards, a frenzy behind its curtain, limbs distending from its membrane, a husk re-inflating with bones. At first, it seemed a great, writhing anemone, an eight-armed devil from the abyss whose brain is in its body, and whose mold is nothing like Man's, but within moments its thrashing chaos had recovered its old schematic, and its extremities pursued their own bearings. Legs wound downwards, four twisters descending from a single storm; wingstalks rose, handwelded and batlike; neck and tail snaked out from the core, first stubby like maggots from a fruit, then like the ends of a single serpent, whose bloat halfway was the melting remnant of some swallowed prey. Atop one of those ends, two distant stars kindled, and their light was ghastlier than darkness, like screams made visible. Where their light met, a rift opened up, whose pit was omnivorous, and whose edges were the sawblades to bring down Yggdrasil. The thing's hide boiled, and its swelling became scutation, its every limb leavening and hardening, baking, then kilning, beyond iron to adamant, patterns racing and cascading about, ants running wild from the torch in their midst.

And then there was a blink of sorts, the sudden and unanimous establishment of what came next, as the thoftship found themselves clinging to the floor of some vast arena, whose walls enwrapped them, and whose crests reached higher than stars. It had the look of the newborn ancient, that flinty curtain, as though age were something it had been given along with shape. The light was everywhere now, and it was good, not that hellish illumination that was worse than blindness.

Before them stood a monster, titanic but plainly revealed, its regrowth almost complete, its boundaries anticipated and prebuilt. Whether Avarnok could be called a dragon was beyond mortal knowledge—it was as likely that dragons could be called the pettykin of Avarnok—but he had the look of a dragon through and through, sail-winged and scaly, snakecatlike, with the aspect of a living rock, and not a hint of that softness and fellowship for which the milkfeeding share of creation was known. Even where its body ranged and thinned, its appendages seemed more like roots than boughs, which for their limberness are in many ways tougher than the trunk itself. Impenetrable in every way he seemed, and no spear, whether wielded by archangels or forged in the fires of heaven, could be imagined to do anything against his armour but to shatter. That there should be meat and blood beneath that mail was hope's cruellest whimsy, and were it there, it was likely as insensate as vulnerable, the withered umbilicus of an infancy long ditched.

All about and above them the great Thede-Eater stiffened. Its neck snaked to a clef, and the scutes atop its body floated outwards on a rising tide. What it did there, they learned, was to draw breath, and what Avarnok made of that breath was nothing less than alchemy. The hammer of its noise brought clots to the eyes, that which had no name but Roar, and from the edges of its strike leapt that bright, ashing agent whose worldly echo is fire.

Not yet did they suffer a fraction of its brunt, against whose stress they stayed shielded. It was the scream of one cornerthwarted, whose all-too-mortal feeling and all-too-mortal lungs encouraged the mortals before him like nothing had done before.

Till now they had felt as intruders, led far up from the grottoes of their own dark world and into one their eyes had not been engineered to witness. But now they knew, with the sound of Avarnok made fearful flesh, that their own world was kin to this one—its redaction perhaps—the painstaking edition of some body of works too vast for a single binding. And Aftheksis was testament to other editions, of which perhaps there were many, some yet open on cosmic lecterns and others forever shelved, all of them kept in a single gallery of Creation whose walls lit a beacon in the void. Behind its threshold were the Editors, emaciated by their task. And harrying that bookhall were the hordes, the swarm of them boiling over every hillside, whose only business is to overturn everything the scrupulous have sought to set upright.

Of this lawless mass there could be no true lords. Avarnok seemed but a festering curd of it, a cell swollen to self-awareness where its malignancy knotted and metastasized.

The titan muttered and raked, but its movements were tremulous. Either unseen tethers bound it where it stood, or it grudged its

poachers greater effort. The One who was no longer Shard stepped
out before them all, and faced the thoftship with hard, smiling eyes.
At his back was the nightmare of gods, whose bane outstripped the
feelings of Men, but in the Shard-One's eyes there was only
righteousness, as though it were all indeed a dream, and what
mattered was not appearances, but the will to see through them.

He raised up his hand, the six fingers a fist. The thumb rose, and
he swung to display that sign, not only to the thoftship, but to all
those watchers whose eyes could not be seen. His pace, unhurried,
was the antithesis of chaos, whose deeds are without custom. *See
here, all ye summoned* it seemed to say, formal and premeditated,
with the grace of a ceremony. At last he showed his hand to
Avarnok, turning back to face that living fireberg, and the beast, for
all its enormity, seemed as rapt by the sight as the rest of them. And
when Shard's thumb turned downwards, it made the monster twitch
to behold it—that gesture so simple no sentient thing can mistake its
meaning. Past the furnished halls of all learning it reaches, to make a
shadow off the hearthfires of thought itself. The gesture caused the
Shard-One to tower, an icon of judgment in the medium of flesh,
gripping not scales but standing *verso pollice*, demanding no quarter
nor mistake of pity. And with his judgment the judge became the
giant—he whom the accused once dwarfed now eclipsed the
convict—even like a shadow, the size of whose maker is no
limitation, whose distance from the fire lets it grow.

And then the Shard-One had returned to their midst, and the
music settled to a simmering melody. Both expectant and insistent,
its every repetition was like the tapping of a foot, with an occasional
boiling of fanfare, crescendo and haunting, whose insistence was a
jewelled goad. Avarnok had awaited them, his eyes flickering with
their inner light, feet braced wide, with the look of a quarry whose
trappers have returned. The thoftship had stood beneath the hulk,
knowing what it was they were bidden to do, and thrilling with the
warrant, as children whose parents have given them hammers and
blades and every other tool hitherto forbidden, given leave to wield
them against something grand and intact, and not to skimp, but be
gung-ho. For in that demolition was no vandalism, but only justice,
the execution of a sentence by one's righteous betters, whose
fulfillment is a privilege, and no dirty work.

How they struck Avarnok, and wounded him, was something
none of them could fully recall, and each recalled his pieces of it

differently. Their need to talk about what happened nonetheless dwindled over time, till the pain dulled, and talk itself became the grief, and was done only at day's end, sometimes weeks between them, when the ache of old wounds is at its strongest.

Justinian spoke of it jovially, more as an observer than a participant, miming the mêlée blow-for-blow until its conclusion, where the sorrow seemed to surprise him every time. For him, it had been a glorious uproar, like to the battle-theatre of the easternmost kingdoms of Ráma, whose productions are orchestrated bloodbaths, where every blow falls as it should, every duel is a dance, and every wound a sacrifice to Muses strange and sanguivorous. When he struck, his foe recoiled as though directed. When his foe retaliated, the Seisumite knew how it was coming, and stepped aside, sometimes lingering for more dramatic effect beforehand, and watching it miss him by an eyelash. The passage of those blows made winds the like to unroof houses, and cratered where they struck the ground, but still Justinian dodged them, or else gripped the Allmetal and felt no harm, wriggling himself laughing out of the dirt he'd been nailed to. As for his own blows, they clobbered the beast, mauling where they struck, against which no armour was proof, but rather a messenger, passing blows past its walls like to some devastating news, jarring and jelling their contents, till the innards lay pulped, though their shields were unbroken.

For Kurtisian, the remembrance of it became an obsession, embittering him, with every retelling more jealous than the last, till the truth of it was lost to the fish tale. What was clear was its spree, an indulgence of power lent him but limitless, whose taste was sweeter for the promise that one day, keeping care over his life, he might come to such power on his own. Glimpsing that inheritance—plunging his hands into its wealth—had changed him, and in a way that could be told apart from the changes the expedition to Sherk-narsk-wirth had wrought on them all. He recalled summoning the *Carno*, whose apparition shook him with its ferocity and eagerness, panting beneath his hand. Kurtisian swore the weapon had even looked different—larger, crueler—whose new raiment was proof of his promotion. He had held it before him with both hands, and its crescent was a bodiless leer. And oh how that mouth had bitten its meat, hissing even with full jaws, and great sprays of black blood. Against its edge, the fortified alps of Avarnok were merely the bloat of something overcooked, whose hide burst with a prod, and whose heavy skin as it fell dragged the wounds wide open. As for the sorcery Kurtisian was let wield, and the *Ultrices* which shot him like a slingstone to all heights and reaches of the towering devil, he could no more recall the knack of it than one might invent something by knowing what it does. He could only assume the secrets lay deep within *Marat*, staring up at him from those pages to which he remained blind.

Of the thoftship, it was Toron who was most guarded about his memories of the strike, who presented every newfound scrap as before the eyes a hardhearted appraiser, shyly risking that flotsam to be called rubbish, though every listener was in the same boat. For him, it had been an exercise in perfect camaraderie, with mates and mentors all one and eager, the work of whom was near to a game, and the pleasure in it so pure that past, now and yet-to-come became a trinity while it endured. Tuger and Mortha had smoked as he drew them, and he had felt the strength of a hand on each shoulder, and low voices in his ears, whose reassurances were Allfatherly, telling him they would work, that Avarnok was small here—not he, not they—and that the honest sweat of humble origins was a rinser, and would unstain the Weave like no lye ever mixed. And for the size of him he knew not how, but he had struck, and mightily, finding the beast's tenderest spots before him, as if they had been led to him on a rope. All around him his thoftmen had blitzed, shooting to and fro like lightning, and there were others there as well whom he did not know, beings of light and darkness both, but alike in majesty, and the air was full of their laughter.

To Níscel it was least clear, for she was given the fewest epiphanies with which to rebuild. If she helped to strike, she did not remember it.

What she remembered most was when, by whatever means or lapse of bondage, Avarnok found the strength to resurge. She had seen it coming, marking it in the monster's movements, which she had been able to describe with mesmeric detail. Its shuffling steps had found roots and willfulness; its wings had unfurled as a membranous sky. There that vault had stretched itself out, fluttering darkly, and fulgurant with bloodshots, a banner of vermilion and sable which had heralded the coming assault. Its body had swollen, chest plates rippling, and the gates had opened to let the storm in, its maw becoming greater and greater, gaping, unhinging, phantasmagoric, until it seemed that that void might engulf all life and matter—

a Jezi Baba, chin sinking to the Pit, jaws widening to scrape the walls of existence.

They all remembered what had happened next. Across the world drew a curtain of flame.

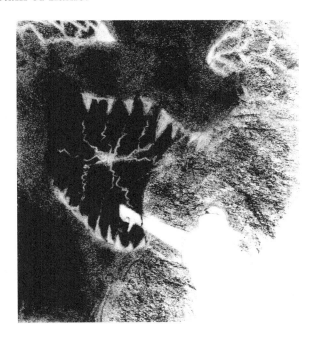

Blue and yellow and blinding, its flutter was the breath of a storm, and its sweep caught them all. Their guardians again had shielded them, putting empyrean backs to that meat-eating light, and sheltering them in shade and lee. And though they survived it, they all remembered its terrible heat. It hit them like a fist of the sun. Their bodies bore its tokens for days afterwards, with withered hair and scalded faces, their mail and weapons forever burnt blue.

But Shard had not been as fortunate as they. Before that hideous brunt he had had no escort beyond He who wore him, and that guardian could not shield him with his own flesh. The channel of death had engulfed him, and though he had endeavoured to wrap himself in some shell of magic, its wall was not fully proof against such an onslaught, and it failed—not wholly, as might have been merciful, blasting him straight to vapour, but in its mortar, through whose gaps the heat sent its tongues, which licked away his outermost layers like frosting.

The deed had taken its time. The lungs of Avarnok are not emptied quickly. A wail had gone up from the blinding torrent where Shard had been drowned, audible even above the typhonic chew and swallow of the fire in air, at first unyielding, but then distraught, and finally agonized, as the bristles of its defiance were melted down to their roots.

The fires had receded, not because the jaws ever pinched the torrent off, but because their reservoir ran dry. The hoarse howl of their pour had ended, and their blinding hell-shadow dimmed, leaving the walls of the arena to undulate behind the fumes, and the towers of Avarnok to shudder before the music that its fires had warped. In air chewed to its marrow, every noise had rung hollow— the pop and sizzle of burnt stone; the shuffling of feet on charred earth; the abysmal rumble and paw of the cosmic animal who had sought to break its pen and butchers. The Shard-One's keening became laughter, though he lay as a heap black and steaming. Its sound was neither gleeful nor fey, but a crippled halfbreed of both, like to the cackle of the berserker as he tugs a spear from his own guts and admires it. The thoftship had heard its sawing titter before they knew what it was, as they stepped from beneath the hems of Those who had saved them, and made sure that the tingling of their own flesh was not its melt.

And then they were at Shard's side, and it was Shard, and not the One, who had addressed them. His scarf had fallen off, its wrap burnt away on one side. He had risen to his feet, and that movement they heard in his skin. There was no smell, only the piteous sight. His magnificent body was a ruin, unsalvageable. They knew not how he lived. His face, however, had remained untouched, save for the unimaginable pain and cares of one in his place. Haggard was his look, with the rueful weariness of one whose long journey is at end, but who fears the loss of whatever purpose it had given him.

Whither the One who had worn him had gone, they had not known. Expectation was still in the air, in the answering minstrelsy, and Avarnok had not slipped his bonds again. Perhaps he had never done so, but like a five-legged thing had simply hidden one limb from the stocks, one whose freakishness had let it go unforeseen, and had lashed out with it when the chance arose. He raged now from beneath redoubled chains, his hide leaking where riven, his great serpentine neck knotted and bowed, and held as though by some invisible device akin to a scavenger's daughter. His head was forced low, jaws grinding, his neck stretched for the bonesaw, but despite all he had done, and whatever was at stake, the guardians had hung back for a moment, some even a little sheepishly, and gave their agents a moment to foremourn.

I began to miss you even as this began, Shard had said, or something like it. Each of them recalled different words, and Toron believed it was because he had somehow spoken to them both together and sundrily—as he would have done if all the time he had needed had been lent to him. He spoke to them of innhearths and road banter, and bid them not forget the things about their lives that were most easily forgotten—not to let the shouts and the blows, which move and shape us so violently, to drown the whispers and caresses that make us whole.

And when the guardians had thronged, and in the hands of one there was presented a sword no mortal smith had forged, Shard had held his thoftmen's eyes through its radiance, and told them he was sorry he had brought them here. And as the figures shut him off from them, pushing them back, the thoftship reminded him they had chosen it, shouting it through closing shoulders, past starry hoods and nimbi, over the heads of the cabalists and gamblers whom they'd served as knights, or as pawns.

Back, back, they'd been herded, displaced by that burgeoning knot of conspirators and players, not a one of whose faces was turned to them. They craned, and they pushed back with what strength they had, and they cried out, but no more could they resist its swell than that of a mountain pushing up from beneath them. Back, back they'd been pushed, at times stumbling with the haste of its growth, till the heart of it seemed worlds away, and stars began to kindle between. They had watched the throng roil. A light had streaked up from its heart. It had drifted forward, building rather than moving, till it pooled about the living rubble of Avarnok, where it grew to encase him like a fog.

There were words, and cries of triumph and hatred. They echoed through the starry void as light does.

And when they awoke on a cold hill's side, it was in a glade open to the Shebrish valley they knew of yore, where a lake lay black beneath the flameless sundown. Gorrh was there too, with less memory than they of what had befallen them.

They stayed there for a time, saying nothing, staring stunned and heartsick into the gloaming, and hearing no birds sing.

But elsewhere...

Viloma
The Rainbow shall herald the storm.

the Unsung.

The Red One has been murdered.

the Unsung.

Nonsense. The invincible cannot be murdered.

And yet it is done.

Nonsense.

IT IS TRUE. I HAVE HEARD TELL OF IT.

Call for him.

He does not answer.

the Unsung.

the Unsung.

So be it.

They shall pay.

They shall pay.

THEY SHALL PAY.

They shall pay.

They shall pay.

the Unsung.

They shall suffer.

And so we went on.

We made our way back to the world of Men, and found that what time had gone by in Sherk-narsk-wirth was not like a dream, whose passage is greater inside than out, but rather like the sleepdeath of a dwall[1], which is the other way around, and from which there is often no awakening. Years had gone by.

But that was all so long ago.

Where to go to next…
Oh, yes.
What was left of our thoftship was making its way through one of the many passes of the Eksarish whorlberg—the one the Knaksish call Teakenmaley—on our way to the elderburg of Eksar Arsask.

---

[1] *(AB)*: coma.

From the Old Headmedth of Brac, a lathing dealt among its towns and burgs:

READ THIS, ALL YE HIGHT MIGHTY KNAKSMEN

SILVERN YOUR POCKETS
REDDEN YOUR SWORDS
SPREAD THE WORD
DO YOUR KING A THEGNING

THE MARCHLAND MEDTH OF BAYERD IS BECOME A BITELAMB OF LATE, CHEWED BY LESSER FIENDS AND NICKERS FROM THE UNFONDLANDS AND THE SOUTH. THEY KILL LIVESTOCK AND HINDER THE HARVESTS. THEY REAVE, AND THEY RANSACK. THEY SET UPON WAYFARERS AND DRAW THIN THE KING'S BOARSMEN, WHO MAKE HASTE TO ANSWER EVERY PLEA.

THOSE WITH FIGHT TO SELL, MAKE YOUR WAY TO THE BORDERMEDTHS OF IGNAM AND LANDON AND PYNDAMIR, AND THENCE SEEK OUT THE BOARSMEN'S HEREWICKS, WHERE YOU SHALL FIND WORK, BOARD, AND A GOOD LYING FEE.

BY THE BOOKMEN OF THE KING AWRITTEN
AND SENT FORTH BY KNAKS-HAWK
FROM THE ISENTRON ITSELF

From the Eastern Medth of Ignam, a looknow tacked to the piers of the Nawponts:

READ AND LEARN, UNBRACCISH FOLK OF KNAKS
AND SPREAD THE WORD IN YOUR OWN TUNGS

TELL OF SOME UNSEEMLY CLAP HAS REACHED
THE EALDORMAN, AND SO THE VERY EARS OF YOUR
KING. THIS CLAP IS OF YOUR BROTHERMEDTH,
BAYERD, AND OF THE HARRIES OF THE UNFOND-
LANDERS FOR WHICH CLETHMEN HAVE BEEN HIRED.

THESE HARRIES AGAINST BAYERD ARE AS
WONELY AS THE TIMMERS, FALLING AS LEAVES IN
AUTUMN, AND NO BLIGHT OR YETH. YOU ARE THE
FOLK OF MARCHLAND MEDTHS YOURSELVES, AND
KNOW WELL THE PERILS AND NEEDFUL BOLDNESS
OF WHERE YOU LIVE.

KEEP HEART AND HOLD TONGUE.
THE BOARSMEN SHALL OVERCOME.

BY THE BOOKNAPS OF OSTASGARD AWRITTEN
AND SENT FORTH BY KNAKS-HAWK FROM THE
AVONLAYS OF SHEBRILLE

From the RingsMedth of Arsask, a leaflet posted at the Edgeburg of Booril:

FOR THE UNDERTHEDE, WHO ARE MY FOLK

AND

BOLD OUTLANDERS, WHO ARE MY GUESTS

I KNAKS SAY FORTH

LET IT BE KNOWN THAT THE MARCHLAND MEDTH OF BAYERD IS BECOME A NEITHERLAND, AND THAT ITS EARTH, AIR, AND WATER ARE TO BE SHUNNED AS UNKIND THINGS. ALL WHO GO THERE, AND ALL WHO STAY, THEY DO SO AT PLIGHT TO THEIR LIVES. THE BOARSMEN HAVE DONE WHAT THEY CAN TO BRING THE BAYRDISH HAVEN-SEEKERS INTO NEIGHBOURING MEDTHS, WHERE GREAT HAVENWICKS ARE IN THE MAKING. BUT MANY MORE WOULD RATHER DIE THAN FLEE THEIR HOMESTEADS, AND I FEAR THE SELLSWORDS IN THE SENDING SHALL FIND IN BAYERD A BURDEN BEYOND THEIR STRENGTH TO OVERCOME.

I SAY FORTH AGAIN, THAT THE BOARSMEN ARE NOT OVERCOME. THEY ARE SIMPLY OVERDRAWN, AS WOULD BE ANY MIGHTY THING WHOSE TASKS OUTSCORE ITS LIMBS AND TEETH. TOO MANY UNRIGHTFUL THINGS SAP ITS STRENGTH TO DO ITS RIGHTFUL THINGS FULLY—IT CANNOT DO THE THEDISH WORK OF THE BOARSMEN, AND AT THE SAME TIME SHIELD THE ROADWAYS, AND BE THE BURGWARDS OF EVERY TOWN.

---bottom portion torn away---

$\mathcal{S}$

From the saddlebags of Toron the Belkol, got while passing through Booril from the east:

THEREFORE I CALL UPON THOSE WHO HIGHT HELETHS AND TEERSEEKERS, UPON THE ONELY WOLFHOUNDS AND SHEEPDOGS WHOM I KNOW ROVE MY LAND, WHO ARE STEERED LESS BY WEALTH THAN BY DARING, FOR WHOM THE LOVE AND TEARS OF A LIFE SAVED ARE THE GODS' OWN GOLD.

YOU I CALL TO THE ELDERBURG OF THIS MEDTH, WHICH IS

Eksar Arsask

THERE TO MAKE YOURSELVES KNOWN TO THE BURGREEVE, WHO IS BIDDEN TO HOUSE AND TO FEED YOU, TILL COMES THE DAY OF RECKONING, WHEN YOU WILL BE SENT TO STARE DOWN THE UNFOND-LANDERS AS YOUR OWN MEN, BUT WITH THE THOFTSHIP OF THE BOARSMEN, AND THE BACKING OF THE RINGS.

KNAKS AWRITTEN
AND SENT FORTH BY KNAKS-HAWK
FROM THE ISENTRON ITSELF

IV
Contraction
Pulling together

The sky was the hue of waleberries, which grew on the lee slopes of Harandrish dells in early fall. Pale blue-black-red, it stretched to every skyrim, scratched at the edges by the highbergs, whose teeth were a ring of jawbones. The two falltime suns were its eyes, drifting closer then wider apart as the day lengthened, becoming predator-faced then cyclopean as their bodies merged to their hottest before straying again. Starmath and Ansend were their names. Unwhiskered by clouds they shone down upon a woodland still giggling with the dizziness of summer.

The thoftship came up from the southeast. Their road was an old one, and unkept. Split by creekbeds and knotted with tussocks, the ground pitched and wove beneath a heavy bower of branches and woodbine. The bordering thickets rose and fell upon waves of earth, stretching for short lengths as moss-bottomed groves where shafts of sunshine broke through into glades. Beyond the land withdrew into wolds of birch, spruce and firwood, which in thousands climbed the hills their road cleaved through. Hairy roots and old stone slouched from the walls of these clefts, dribbling water which made puddles at their edges. Bulrushes grew, their long heads bobbing with dragonflies.

Strange prints and scuffings in these wet places showed that others had used the road, and lately, but not many, and not so lately that the thoftship looked to come across anyone. The birdsong and sighing of leaves made things seem colder and lonelier than they ought. The thoftmen saw other paths, some greater than their own, which came in and split off again. Those byways ranged into the thicket, swethering amidst the undergrowth and coming into sight again faraway, as pale cuts in the hillsides, and breaks among the trees. Though they seemed to weave a great maze at times, all paths drifted one way, making for the same gaps in the whorlberg's ring, whose coils there was no getting around. The trees were tall and thick, and the path set deep among them, but there was no time at which those great stone fells might not be seen or felt, those dusky walls of the skybowl which melted down into the wood's own shadows.

This was Teakenmaley[1], and it was to the embrace of the highberg's stony arms that the bowl owed its steadfast warmth. Wrapping and winding, their many folds stood as ramparts against the cruel Norrámish winter, their heights—put forth like bait to draw the beast and save the body—keeping the worst of its bites away. No string of highbergs alone might have done this, nor two, nor even a stakewall ringed by ten, for the whorlbergs of northern Ráma were wonderworks, and Teakenmaley was their king. Their many walls in truth were but one—a single, skyscraping length of ridge, which went around and around like an untied scroll, putting before the landsweep of weather rampart upon rampart and shield upon shield, standing against the wolves of Unsummer not as mere men, but as *hekatonchires*—the hundred-handed ones of southern godlore—with endless arms to spare.

Among the northernmost of the whorlbergs, Teakenmaley lay in the mideast of the Arsask—the Kingsmedth—its cool greenery speared through by stonecroppings and split by the screeslides of its ever-winding battlement. Though the peaks of the inner coils were middling in height, many of the more outlying fins rose so high aloft that they stretched the neck to look beyond. There were folks who said that some of them outdid the Wottrámish Alps themselves, though none that said so had ever climbed either. Snug among the Teakenmalish dells were many homes, from the wintering grounds of elseland birds to the year-round dens of Men. The whorlbergs had been won long ago, the worst fiends purged more or less. Fattening within that dearth of maneaters were no fewer than thirty towns, and many more hamlets. Both great and small these were, among them the sleepy, cleveland thorp of Hopehold, and the old, thursebuilt stronghold of the Tusker's Airy. The latter, at one time a nest of devils, was haunted only by the King's Boarsmen now. Shaped by the winds to seem a crooked stone steeple, it was daunting to behold and likely worse to live in.

---

[1] (*Old Braccish* Ticianmægle [which itself is of unknown provenance]). Also known by many other names in the Allmal alone, including Surtskrone, Thusandell, and the Brakwyrm's Coils. It is also known simply as the Whorl and the Coils, although these names are also applied to other Knaksish mountain-crowns by their respective residents.

A thin yet sturdy network of roads and pathways linked most of the Whorl's settlements, their threads winding among the bushy wolds of leaftrees and evergreens, across the toes of giant ashes, puckwoods, and willows. They led through the berg-gaps upon mighty bridges, and trickled past the lonely laps of shrines, monkstows[2], and the many standing stones of faiths both living and dead. Among these footholds of menning were wetlands—fens, marshes and tarns, themselves connected by a web of waterways which made for roads of their own. Hidden within the Whorl were lands which only these waters reached, and which only those taught could find. Old river kingdoms held out there, petty but no less proud than before the Onelatching, some of which traded with the Knaksmen, and others which kept to their own, sheltered halfworlds. For the most part, it was they who kept up the wharves, booths, and storehouses on the banks of the waterways, many of which were curtained by the willow boughs, and drowned from sight amidst leaping foam and wet rock.

Folks who spied the buildings often took them for a resurgent share of those ruins winking beneath the screes and mosses of the Whorl, for Teakenmaley was one of those landsteads where Time's reign was not even. Just as its mountains stymied the incursions of winter, so too did they muddle the passing of Ages, branching and splintering its tide, and slowing and muddying what sought to flood in. Olden times held out in backwaters and in pools, some disappearing overnight and others flickering in and out of being, often cruelly, as those who found joy in them learnt. To the Braccish it was a Tidewonder, but most Knaksmen called it the Timebriar—a place that catches the cloth of time's passage, tearing off scraps which flutter and fray, but never wholly vanish. One petty kingdom in Teakenmaley knew it as *nonjuloft*, which is "karst of memories." A hidden realm of eyots and crannoghs whose folk the Knaksish called Rivrishmen, its lore maintained that this spotting of time reached into the mind as well, and that the harder tempers of the Knaksmen were simply wont to deny it.

For the northerners who now owned the Whorl, the wonder was a mere glammer—a scop's delight, and a mapmaker's annoyance—whose manifestations kept to the mists and did not usually happen within burgs. Whatever the sooth of it, the wonders of the Timebriar

---

[2] *(AB):* monasteries; monks' hermitages.

were not alone in Ráma, nor even in Knaks, where the folding of stone and the oversowing of histories had made a palimpsest of the land itself. What was clear was that at least one northman in the beginning must have found the Timebriar pleasing, for *Eksar* was an old word meaning "no pain". A trading post in early times, it had become the folkfullest steading in Arsask, most of all during the coldest months when it became a winter haven for the highborn, and headburg of the Medth. Walled though never threatened, Eksar hunkered in the depths of a trough-like valley, amidst orchards and croplands, and flanked by dour, scree-bellied cliffs. It was toward this lonely but lively seat the thoftship now headed.

The hillocks huddling about the path seemed welcoming, however dumb and shaggy they stood. The branches windling overhead were pale-skinned and aromatic, their wide dark leaves waving like the perfumed fronds of far southern lands. The footfalls of the thoftship's passage frisked through the copses, and leapt loudly from pools hidden among their roots. Every now and again, those sounds were joined by the drumlike wingbeats of grouse, and scolded by the otherworldly gossip of four-winged songbirds. Through warrens among trees and over shallow seas of grass the wayfarers kept their trail, and by and by found themselves on a wider pathway which they hoped would soon lead to an open road.

Theirs was an unlikely route to an elderburg. Had they come at Eksar from any other side, they might have availed themselves of the wide and guarded highways by which the menning of these wilds was best shown. Sturdy bridges and stonework; crushed gravel in the potholes to spare the ankles; mountainside run-off troughed underground rather than left to hollow out the pathways; roomy inns and churches for the weary; signboards and milestones to give the bewildered their bearings back. This was the frover[3] that followed such a wealthy Medth as Arsask, by which chapmen[4] came from all around, and sold the wintering highborn their trinkets. As such, most of the ways in were tollroads, and many had muttered what good it had done to chase all the monsters out of Teakenmaley when Men charged heftier fees than any bridge-trolls had ever done.

No, the going was not for the thrifty, least of all by the

---

[3] *(AB)*: consolation; benefit.
[4] *(AB)*: merchants.

Swansbawn[5], but this was not why the thoftship had picked such a wild and lonely inroad. They had been many days from that highroad's inlet when they had chosen to come to Eksar, and met among the foothills skirting Teakenmaley a fellow wayfarer, who for his looks kept to lesser-known paths. He was an outsider, most clearly, and did not hide it well. He said he knew a road to Eksar which he had taken before, and on which he would lead them, if they wished. The kingdom's greatest burgs, those near the shores and marches above all else, were better wonted to outsiders than those inland, and he feared harassment by the rangers and Burgwards of the Whorl. Aside from that, he had sworn to them that his way would take half the time of what it would take to reach the inlet of the Swansbawn. His only fee was their wardship, for although the Whorl was not a threatening place, its least trodden hinterlands were too hazardous for a single wayfarer, especially one the height of a ten-year-old Manchild.

Deeming their own worth and gear too paltry for it to be a trap, the thoftship had made the deal, and following their steersman had come in from the south, advancing steadily through wilds which at times were trackless, and amazing with trails. True to his word, he led them through gaps in the Whorlberg they had not known were there. Their path hardly climbed into the mountains at all, but kept to the footlands, however dim and snarled they became. At nights they had slept in uncanny glades, inside old rings of stone. Some had lain through the underbrush, many furlongs off the path, and had prickled the skin to enter. Their whereabouts the pathfinder knew by heart, and it was only when they had found one of these sought-after havens disturbed—a circle long broken and the undergrowth having crept into the breach—that he seemed at all ruffled, and urged them on to find the next one before nightfall. That evening and the next, the thoftship learned why, and were told to ignore the sounds around them in the darkness as they readied their meals. Cold eyes gleamed from the black thickets, rushing toward them and drawing back angrily, unable to enter yet insulted beyond retreat.

Whether they were warmblooded reavers or undead bound to the night, their pathfinder spurned any talk of them for blither things. No greater wrong, he declared, do we do the gift of speech than to discuss those who would silence it. He paid heed to the shucks only

---

[5] The highroad and inlet into Teakenmaley from the East.

once thereafter, when the thoftship raised their weapons against a singly loud and willful encroacher, and warned them not to hope for the same safekeeping within these groves without one such as himself to vouch for them. He had then gone back to his gleemanry, with a zither-like thing which lay on his lap. He'd plucked at its strings as one might tweak a cat's belly, singing away in a child's voice as the bushes all around thrashed and gibbered till daybreak.

One such as himself. Not until later did they truly learn what that meant.

Now was the day he had promised they would reach Eksar before nightfall, and the thought of lighted streets, clean beds, and food eaten from crockery instead of dirty hands gave bright new hues to the last leg of their journey. It had been grim going since the loss of Shard, who had known wayfaring magics and could do such plain but priceless things as ward off insects, repel rain, cook food, and perk one's wits in the morning. Best of all had been his knack for banishing the aches of sleeping on hard ground. Their thews and bonelocks[6] throbbed all day now, the soreness never wholly being walked off before it was time to lie down again. Though their sleeping rolls were better than nothing, so was a slough to a man thirsty enough to drink it. Without the Highbred, their travels had soaked, sapped, starved, frozen, and bitten them in ways it had never done, leaving the Chaldallions—who had joined the thoftship shortly before Shard, and had never journeyed far inland without him—threatening to go back to the Colonies.

For now, however, they were deep within the Whorl, the summergreens around them having yet to shed even their uppermost fronds. The waters of the nearby stream did not smoke at sunup, and the breeze was crisp without sharpness. Black oakwerns[7] chattered as they harvested, and the evergreens were skirted by moats of their own cone-scales. Masked towhees and chickadees shrilled their names from the brambles while deer nosed through the greenlife of the floor.

All at once the animals stiffened, feeling the nighness of a great hunter in their midst, some mighty eater of flesh whose name lay folded among the memories of their forebears. Whatever it was, it

---

[6] *(AB)*: joints.
[7] *(AB)*: squirrels.

plodded along a path made for two-footers, impressing the earth with four thursish paws. Its musk took the breeze in a devilgrip, storming among the trees to spook the nostrils of the mossgrazers. Within a blink the deer were off, bounding through the woods like long-legged hares, their white tails swallowed by the undergrowth.

The tuskcat heard them flee. He hearkened to the twigs breaking, to leaves tearing from the bracken, to the split hooves drumming the moss. He was hungry, but he let them go as he had all the others. His barding, worn as it was during long travel, was too much of a burden to hunt in. Had he given chase, even at speed great enough to make up for it, the jangling of it would only have spurred the game faster. He had done it before and would do it again if needed, but now was not such a time. Besides, this was a valley for lynxes and bergcats, and other hunters at most a tenth his bulk. The trees grew too closely together for a landwhale such as himself. The deadfall was too tangled, and the creeks too plentiful. The moss lay too loose to leap from. His was the craft of waylaying prey rather than tracking it down or tiring it through a long chase, but there had never been one without a little of the other two.

And so he kept walking, his shriveled belly begrudging his restraint. He had lapped up some frogs from the path in the last little while, about ten or so, shoveling them onto his tongue with the swift sideways swipe of his head that had taken years to master. The slimy things had been cold, and they weren't sitting well. The first two he had swallowed whole and alive, and they were still squirming by the time they slid into his belly. Their twitching made him retch, so he crushed the heads of the next few between his shearteeth before downing them. The taste had been worse than the twitching, but he had eaten worse things. He hadn't had any worthwhile prey in almost five days, and he craved meat, any meat, at least two stone of it. Even a little azflesh[8] would be better than nothing. The thought of finding a fat haunch in the dirt, sticking out from where some other hunter had buried it. It made his tusks run.

"Gorrh's drooling all over the grass," Justinian griped, stepping to the margins of the path to avoid it. "Are you sure those frogs he was eating weren't poisonous?"

Toron passed his swordstaff to his other shoulder and worked the free limb awake again. He hated the weapon sometimes, which he

---

[8] *(AK)*: carrion.

seldom found the chance to wield. He had to think about what *poisonous* meant. *Attery*.

"He wouldn't have kept them down if they had been," he answered without much thought. "His body can tell."

Half-turning as he walked, Justinian held an imaginary frog in his hands, pointing at it. "They had yellow stripes on the back. I know of painted frogs back in Salpes that don't look much different, and nothing goes near them."

"He's good," Toron grunted. "They just don't taste like honey, is all." Grimacing, he switched to carrying the weapon by its middle.

"He looks ravenous," Urien said. His voice piped among the Men.

The tuskcat looked around its hulking shoulder and stared at them all, his green eyes like cracked gemstones. His long, barbed tongue scraped hearsomely against his front teeth, and made its way about his chops from one side to another. Two more threads of drool unwound from his scythelike tusks, and blew about like torn spidersilk. He beheld the little creature which would be so easy to grab, but probably not so easy to swallow. In truth, it was Gorrh who had guessed their pathfinder was a leaf off some lower branch of the fayfolk, likely a changeling raised at least in part among Men, and whose sight reached those unseen realms of the hidden folk without quite descrying its doors. Toron had put it past him, Urien had offered a cryptic smirk, and Toron had gathered from that unmistakable chagrin that the little wight[9] was not used to being pegged.

Justinian nodded gravely at the little man abreast of him. "I think he wants to eat *you*, Urine."

Neither stopping nor slowing, Urien deviously surveyed his marching partner. "No, I don't believe so. You are the one with all the sleen on your bones."

"All the *what*?"

"Sleen. Kine give beef, sheep mutton, swine pork, and the flesh of Men," he grinned, flashing his sharp little teeth, "is sleen."

Justinian laughed, casting his mirth toward the thickets from side to side. "Sleen, yeah? So, do they have different names for the cuts, like the sirloin and the brisket?"

"They do."

"What do they call the penis?" Justinian glanced swiftly back at his brother to make sure he was being overheard.

"You mean the pintel?"

"Yeah, the blood-sword. The collared cyclops. What do they call it?"

"The manbits are known all as tenderfleshies. They might be seethed or stewed, but they swiftly wither in open heat. They are odd dainties. As with the sweetmeats of livestock, most cooks do not bother with them."

Justinian's nod was slow and facetious. "Ever eaten one, Urine?"

"Indeed."

"Yeah? How does it taste?"

"By itself, not like much. Its bulk differs among the thedes, but most of it is only skin. It has this odd chewiness that is unlike anything else one might eat. I reckon it borrows most of its flavour from whatever it is cooked with. I have eaten bits from soups and found nothing between the flesh and the broth itself. Some cooks use

---

[9] *(AB)*: living being; any person or creature. Distinct from the undead monster (*barrow wights*, etc.).

them only as skin for mearies and wursts, as with the innards. The best way to ready them, I believe, is to seethe them in sleenbroth until they swell, and soften. Be thildy, for it takes a while. Take them from the wrekin, and overstuff them with a stir of cooked sleen, knobleeks, fenroot, choicest crides[10]. Pick strong ones. I go for shredded graxroot, black pepper, even a pinch of mandrake eye, if you happen to be someone it does not kill. Let them sit for a toe, and the skin will shrink around the stuffing. A little like haggis. They're lovely, and if you eat them carefully, you won't even need a dish."

"Prime," Justinian grunted. He looked a little put out, and from his own game yet. "You get all that, Kurt? Poor Kurtis. He's been eating them raw all these years."

Though his sight was trained elsewhere, Kurtisian flashed his brother the thumb-finger. As for Urien, his mouth went back to its wonted pursedness with a flicker, his pale jaw the only share of his face unshadowed by his hood. He seemed again to lose himself in the peacefulness of their setting, and as a great breath filled his chest—opening the breast of the cloak enough to reveal a brass-buttoned scarlet blouse—his sandals rose a few inches from the ground. He kept forward at walking pace, his sandals gyrating in air, and it wasn't until he released the breath again that he touched back down.

"Wish I could do that," Kurtisian mumbled, though his eyes seemed still on the thickets. "Just to hold my breath and let the wind blow me to the city." Switching his own pack from one shoulder to the other, he appeared to wait a moment before saying something that had clearly been on his mind for a while. "Odd that we haven't seen any traffic up there all this time. No griff patrols from the city, or anything incoming either. And what about the ranger wardens? If we're only a day from Eksar, you think we'd have seen a few by now."

"Maybe," Urien said, who was walking aloft again. Spending his breath in speech, he touched back down. "But these paths are not well travelled. The Swansbawn is hard beyond that ridge. I'm sure you'll find your guardsmen there."

Kurtisian scoffed, aiming but failing to catch Toron's eye. "And no doubt that they'll be guarding the path as he we leave it,

---

[10] *(AK)*: spices.

wondering why we chose a brigands' route instead of the main road."

"Maybe," their guide said after a moment, but that was all he said.

The thoftship went on without word for much of the afternoon. Their going slowed only the handful of times Gorrh stopped for a drink, stabbing the waters with his tusks where the stream widened into small pools, and tonguing its surface with all the splashing of a millwheel.

Urien and Justinian kept their distance from the grumpy meateater, but remained side-by-side, and from behind seemed less like a father and his child than a trollish bodyguard and his tamer. In hemp breeches and a belt of rope, Justinian dressed as modestly as his flesh-flaunting faith would allow, the neck chain of the Allmetal bob-winking atop the thrawny waves of his upper back, and his bare feet flashing their dirty soles as he lumbered on. A few yards behind him slogged Toron, who walked as though his footgear was made of lead. Every now and again, he would stumble over a stone or an old root, things which no one else had found any hardship in stepping over. He had caught himself each time, though not without making a crutch of the swordstaff—tripping, pitching its end, and stumbling past it, wrenching it back out again with a burst of wet earth, and swearing. Justinian looked back whenever it happened, Gorrh along with him, but the only time anyone said a word was when, after a singly thrackful stumble, the swordstaff flew out of Toron's hand, forcing Kurtisian to duck as the weapon spun sidelong over his head. The thoftship stopped, and Toron had waited, his weariness grudging, as Kurtisian fished it out of the tall weeds with no friendlier a look than he might have retrieved it from a dung heap.

Kurtisian shook it off as best he could and offered to carry it the rest of the way.

"Thank you, no," Toron muttered, taking back the lance and heading past him.

Kurtisian stayed behind for a few moments, letting the distance between them build as he nitpicked tiny burrs from his clothing. His arms went up. "I'll just give you some room, then, if that's all right."

Toron sighed, bringing his head up only with great striving, and putting his face into the sunlight. The furrows beneath his eyes were full-on blue, his eyes like lumps of coal laid atop white dishes that had been broken and put back together with red lime. His hair lay limp and oily, rough even for the road, forelocks stuck to his brow for want of a wash. To his jaw clung a half-mane of tawny bristles, seeming less a beard than moss he had picked up from sleeping on the forest floor. His shoulders slumped beneath his cloak, and wrinkled leggings told of many nights spent clothed, and tossing.

Only his shieldwear showed any token of liveliness—a breastplate and pair of greaves which glinted beneath his gloom like something half-swallowed by a bog. They were mismatched, all of them, likely hailing from three sundry Medths, but their differences were simple enough that only a lingering eye might have marked them. Though dented here and there, they showed a grim, almost garish, polish, which showed they were new to the man who wore them. They'd come to him that way. For his mood, their shine could no more be mistaken for Toron's own work than a bedridden man could be trusted to have rethatched his own sickhouse.

He had bought the gear only weeks ago, from a blacksmith in the Whorl's foothill hamlet of Barrin. The smith was a blithesome man, with a youthful heart, who had made a hobby of combing through old battlefields nearby, and of beating old weapons and shieldwear back to life. He was neither a teerseeker nor a wyeman[11], nor had he ever fought anyone to the death. Barrin was a breadbasket, after all, and his business was in plowshares, coulters, and the metal fittings of handcarts, among other things. Though it was not unwonely for restless laymen to indulge dreams of fighting in some way or other, most did so in a manner that was whimsical and barren—doing swordplay on their scarecrows, or reading books of petty magic by the light of tallow candles. A little sad, it was no different from the way in which a ploughhorse, unwatched in its stall at the end of the day, tosses its mane and rears like the free thoroughbreds it has seen in neighbouring meadows.

This man, however, had wed his craft to his whims in a way that was both praiseworthy and gainful, finding there to be little fineness—but patience and heart only—in the pounding out of dents and the sanding away of rust. Among his wares were his one go at a byrnie, which he'd mended with hundreds of heavy nails he'd hammered into rings. Having taken him months if not years to do, it must have weighed four stone, and was far too heavy to gamble

---

[11] *(AK)*: a teerseeker is an adventurer. A wyeman is any soldier, whether burgward or Boarsman, for whom fighting is a trade.

one's life on, but his eyes shone so brightly when he spoke of it that Toron felt something prick his heart. His own mailshirt was freshly wrecked, but he knew the craftsman could not mend it well enough, nor could he swap it for the homespun deathtrap put before him. So it was that he had chosen the dusty threesome of shieldwear stacked atop a nearby crate of rivets, one piece each for the body and lower legs, to fill in for his tattered hauberk. Thus he left the shop twenty pounds heavier and a gildenbit lighter, which would have been the other way around had he seen a proper shieldsmith.

He was not sorry for it, at least not yet. It was shortly before that time when the band had become enlightened to the plight of Knaks, and his soul became, for the first time in two months, a shade above black. Through the gloom an opening shone. The Isentron was looking to put down some kind of reavery in Bayerd, and all the kingdom's would-be teerseekers were bidden to the headburgs, to be given tidings and the backing of the Rings, whether a weapontake or whatever that was. Much about the call was cloudy, but one thing could be seen. A marchland Medth was in peril, and the Boarsmen themselves were on their heels. It was the stuff of sagas, the grounds on which landmarks were built. No shadow of grief could blind Toron to it. It was what they had been waiting for, and his thoftship would be there.

That he walked as one in chains had nothing to do Bayerd. That he walked at all, and had fared so far to get here, was proof enough of his hopes in that undertaking. Instead, his mood had everything to do with his thoftship itself, whose bench had been shortened twice in as many months.

Behind Toron, well behind him now, was Kurtisian, gamefaced and smooth-chinned, his hair a proud and unbound riot about his head. Cloaked and armoured in his dour hues, dusty black upon unilluminable blackness, he seemed more a specter of Toron's grief than a thoftman.

Behind him walked no one.

This was all they now were.

The day dragged on, and the mountains swapped garments as the suns slid their own ways, the slightly golder burn of Starmath withdrawing from the western bergsides, and casting its mantle upon the eastern snowcaps. The breeze picked up mightily as the valley stepped down into another, and the path became a shushing hallway of leaves and grass, ashudder with the wingbeats of birds, which went among the boughs for shelter from it. The greenlife to the right of the thoftship began to thin, giving glimpses of lowlands which, though said to be near Eksar, showed no marks of farming. Nonetheless, and after days in the shade, all the creeks seemed eager to get down there, and shot bubbling across the footpath in beds of naked stone, to leap off of edges they heard, but could not see. Since the deer that morning, most of the wildlife seemed to have kept well out of sight, with only a few smaller things tarrying on the trail and creekbanks long enough to be spied. Most plentiful were the wingbugs—the great bees, flies, and dragonflies strong enough to withstand the lusty winds—and it was only because they seemed everywhere that the forlornness of the backroad did not seem too odd.

Casting his tired eyes about him, Toron was not heedless of it, but he had yet to feed his hopes the natter of any misgivings. Though the heart of Teakenmaley had been rowdy with life the last time he had been to Eksar, it had been on other roads and earlier in the summer. As late afternoon neared, however, and their path drew close enough to the cliffside to begin its drop toward Eksar's own valley, there still was no token of menning. Not a single plume of smoke; no flights of griffmen overhead or afar; no roosters crowing; no cattle lowing; no bark of axes splitting firewood. He wondered aloud, in a voice he barely breathed into, whether Urien might have led them down the wrong road.

Hardly had the halfshaped words made it past his beard when the Rine rang out in his mind, and Gorrh stopped dead on the path. The feeling of it was like a shout which drags one out of dreams, and it jolted Toron to a halt. He snapped his fingers and hissed at those before him, telling them to draw themselves back. Justinian and Urien stopped, as much at Toron's beck as for the roadblock Gorrh became. Something, some *things*, were ahead, hidden behind the bend of the path, and although Gorrh did not know the smell, he knew it was not good, and that Teakenmaley was not the right place for it.

Its threat was unlike those gaunts that had come out during the night to harass them from the edges of Urien's groves—creatures for which darkness was its own world, whose presence was no less natural than that of fish in a place nightly flooded by tidewaters. These things up ahead were outsiders, whatever they were beyond that. The thoftship had been lucky with the wind, Gorrh said through the Rine, which had bent as the path wound east, and now came at their faces rather than at their backs. Gorrh was a hunter and a tracker, a soul shaped from the nose back, and for him to be waylaid was a blow against his very being. His worth still limped from the loss of Níscel, though the winds that day had been awry—a thing that Toron, even through his own grief, kept reminding him. What was harder for Toron to bear was the awareness that Gorrh was coming to see himself as a defender, something utterly at odds with his selfish kind, and something he only could have learned from his bond with a Man. That sense of safekeeping which saw others as the most vital parts of one's own body—such a thing was unsuited for the animal's understanding, like a living thing brought over oceans to new shores, and in that unused land taken root, perhaps to overrun what lay before it, and in time either shape a new land, settle into balance, or bring it all to ruin.

For now though, Gorrh's one thought was to prove himself anew, and putting his body across the breadth of the path, he made a wall behind which the men gathered, and tossed their packs into a heap.

"I can't believe it's a monster," Kurtisian said, flexing his fingers and staring down the path at what he couldn't see. "Within, what, ten miles of the city? Five? This place is supposed to be a watched like a fortress."

"It's said to be," muttered Toron. "But we haven't seen a ranger since we stepped into the Whorl. If we could go this far without meeting one, why couldn't something else?"

Kurtisian remained incredulous. "Last time we came, there must have been a dozen outposts within two days of the city."

Toron looked to Urien, and the pathfinder did not meet his eyes right away. "Are you going to tell where we are, swapling?"

Urien chuckled, but there was no swikedom[12] in his look. "Eksar is past the next rise, I swear it. The road is—it's not one you've ever been on before."

"That does nothing to tell us what these things are up ahead," Toron said. "Do you know?"

Urien shook his head easily, and Toron felt his blood rising. All along, their pathfinder had kept an air of confidence, ignoring or dismissing the thoftship's cares as the captain of a ship might treat a

---

[12] *(AB):* deception; fraudulence; treachery.

passenger's complaints of wind and high waves. Now, it turned out, there may have been something wrong all along, and leaks in the hull too big for a bailout.

"Well, how many?" Justinian asked, craning his neck as he looked down the bend. "Can Gorrh at least tell us that?"

Kurtisian snorted. "What difference does it make if you don't know what they are? Five goblins or one dragon—which would you prefer?"

"There are four," Toron said, his voice not his own. Up ahead, Gorrh nodded as he sampled the air, his eyes slitted and his tail writhing like a newly beheaded snake. "Four thurses, ringing their kill."

Both Chaldallions tensed. Kurtisian swore filthily in Linguish.

"Thurses?" Justinian echoed, dangerously loud. "As in giants? Giant giants, or are we talking more like trolls?"

"Two-leggers," Toron added, then in his own voice, "and smaller than what you call giants. If they were ettins or thurses or reeses, you should be able to see them from here. Might be hobgoblins, might be…might be trolls. Might be ten other things, maybe something we've never met before. Gorrh doesn't reckon they've heard us yet. We can linger here a while and see if they keep on going." He sighed windily. "But if they do, it will likely be towards us, since they're not likely to get any closer to the burg. Whatever we do, we're going to have to make our way closer if we're going to find out what they are, and how best to deal with them."

Kurtisian stretched his neck with a pop, his tongue trapped beneath his teeth and lower lip. He seemed ready to explode. "Let me lob a few *redballs* down there…"

His eyes flickered as he named the *Ultrix*, and Urien started at the sight.

Toron found that odd—a wight of dree somehow spooked by it—but had no time to reflect on their guide's newly cracked façade. "That might do nothing but give us away," he said. "And coming at them unawares might prove our best hope."

He looked to Justinian, who only a month ago had called upon the Brasmat to bring down half a cliffside onto the heads of their foemen. The thoftship had been utterly outmatched at the time, and the feat had saved the lives they had left. As it was, Toron had never before witnessed his youngest thoftman perform such a mighty deed, and had his misgivings about whether he could repeat it.

For the most part, Justinian trusted in fear to send his foemen running. His knack to set the ground trembling, and to send out small, unruly waves of earth were not wholly dreeish, but more like the gifts to answer prayers, and made him a terrifying stranger even to those familiar with sorcery. He would often yell at his foemen, and let them hear the outlandish warp to his voice, or he would chant the Linguish itself, and make them think he was calling devils out of nowhere. For all his enemies knew, and for the bewitching cadence of that language, his cries might open a crevasse beneath them, or shape vengeful golems from the clay like the rabbis of Saffish lore.

In tales of the southern landholds whence the Chaldallions had come, magicians known as geomancers could ensoul the surrounding rocks, causing them to detach from nearby hillsides like dryads from their trees—stepping forth as invulnerable brutes who advanced upon the enemies of their master with eyes of coal, and mouths dangling roots and spiderwebs. Even for those who knew nothing of these tales, however, Justinian the man was an awestriking specimen, wearing no armour and carrying no weapon, but walking as though an army were at his back. Dreeish or not, he was fit to break bones like branchwood, and twist heads clean around. The mere sight of him was enough to cure hiccups, and to inoculate against ill will.

These things were all true with Men as their game, but giants were not Men. They were vulnerable to much less, and slow to recognize what those fewer things were. Justinian sucked his cheeks as he played absently with the Allmetal, then at last met Toron's eyes.

"Don't know how much help I can be, Thorn. No bare stone on the northern face, except up above the treeline. Anything I might be able to knock loose wouldn't make it through the trees to the path. If we catch them close enough to the edge, I might be able to dislodge a piece of it and send them over."

Urien chose to speak up. "I am not so sure whether the rangers will love you for burying a stretch of the road down below. They're sure to look into it."

Kurtisian made a noise through his nose. "Could be overkill, too. If these things are shrimps, best we erase them quietly. I say we crash them."

Toron nodded, not in thwareness[13], but in having foreseen the fuhrbido's plan. But for the *redballs* he had already offered, the dreeman was stuck with hand-to-hand attacks only, and would have to get close to find glory. The day should soon come, Kurtisian had once told Toron, when he would unlock the deeper secrets of *Marat*, past the first few pages he could currently use, and he would, like an archer, find means to rain blows upon his enemies from a distance safe and sound. Until then, if and whenever that might be, he was bound to close quarters with his foemen, and for that he usually summoned the *Carno* rather than unleash the *Ultrices* that made a weapon of his own body.

The unease and the afternoon heat became a single, pressing burden as Toron went through all the choices before them, calling back to mind every time they had faced an ambush, and every time they had set one. There had been many, for although the highroads of Knaks were mostly free of fiends, the same could not be said of highwaymen and other outlaws, who hid among the kingdom's own folk, and like weeds sprang up without anything to overshadow them.

At times the thoftship had stripped Gorrh of his barding and set him to circle around. At others, they had sent one man ahead to draw the foeman back to them. They had called out to barter. They had winged it. They had made a show of strength to send their robbers fleeing. They had brought about plots cooked for hours, and redes hatched raw, but none now seemed better than any other, as each happening had been unlike the next. Even in the handful of times they had been caught unawares, and had fought like brockwolves to save their skins, they had always carried the day. Most reavers, at the end of it all, would only hazard so much to win a fight they had chosen, and withdrew when threatened with wounds enough, or death.

After a spell of silence the Chaldallions had born more than patiently, Justinian cleared his throat. "What do you say, Thorn? Day's getting on, city's just over those hills. Rather not spend another night in a fairy's ring."

Again Toron sighed. He was tired too, and in more ways than Justinian meant.

---

[13] *(AK)*: agreement.

"To Hell with this," he said. "Gorrh and I shall sneak up the path until we can see what they are." He used his swordstaff to push himself up from his knee. "The trees are too thick to go around them on the north side, and we can't leap off the cliff to get around them on the south. If there's a chance we can take them, we shall."

Justinian nodded, and Kurtisian clapped the northman on the shoulder as Toron went past. He worked swiftly to unbuckle the sundry packs and gear hanging from Gorrh's saddle. Among them were his small crossbow which, next to his rope, was the thing he had carried longest without ever having needed. Even if he had the quarrels for it, it would be no good here; nothing stronger than a shoat, and narrower than a barn door, had anything to fear from such a weapon while he wielded it. Throwing everything to the side of the path, he pulled himself into the saddle and crammed his footgear into the stirrups. His swordstaff he kept—its blade was dull, and would not glint—and kept his swords sheathed on his back as Gorrh began to skulk down the path half-gathered, more like the stalk of hunting hound than the belly-bottomed slink of a cat. As they neared the bend in the path, Toron closed his eyes, and clenched them together until he heard the blood in his ears. Thus he drowned out the meddling of his own feelings as he gave his mind wholly to those of Gorrh.

The Rine saw to it that no wall in the world might bar their words from each other's thoughts, but when they were this close, each brooked the other's senses as well. Toron could peer through Gorrh's sharper eyes, and listen through his ears, and know all the business of a place which seemed empty to his own sight and hearing. Gorrh, on the other hand, could judge what he saw with all the cunning of Man, understanding laws and orthank and other things no wonely beast could ever learn. Neither was fully at the home in the mind of the other; the tungs of musks and spoors were still a babel to Toron, while the pecking orders and manners among men were knots Gorrh lacked the thumbs to untangle. Were the beast of houndkind rather than of cats, Toron reckoned he would face the shared world with more kindness, but, as it stood, the hunter looked on life as a lonely, grudgeful business, and saw little worth in folkdom, or the customs that came with it.

As they drew closer, Gorrh kept his eyes on the bulge of thicket through which the scent drifted, but he could spy nothing through the tangle, and would have to creep to the very edge of the bend itself.

Lower and lower he dropped as the curve came up, and Toron laid himself along the cat's length, lifting his footgear and stirrups from the ground, and wincing at the soft, jangling drag of the barding on the grass. It was not loud, but to Gorrh's ears it was deafening. So it was that when the cat at last halted, the sound of speech startled them both. It was much too deep to be Mannish, that talking, and seemed less to ride the air than to roll through the earth. Roomy lungs such voices needed, and stembands[14] thick as mooring lines, intoning a rumble which shook one's thoughts. Still they crept further, till they heard beneath that talk the burble of inflowing waters, and of winds rushing up from the valley. It was shortly before the very top of the bend, through a haze of ferns and other leafweeds at its edge, that they at last spied the first stirrings of what blocked the last leg to Eksar.

Urien and the Chaldallions rose expectantly from their crouches as Toron and Gorrh returned. Toron's face was troubled and already lost in more plotting.

"Well?" said the brothers at once.

"They look like some kind of manshfretters," Toron said. "Not giants. Underthurses. Ogres, I reckon you'd call them.[15] Four of them, all gathered around some bloody heap of slaughter they just clubbed someone into."

"*Pedica me,*" Justinian swore. His eyes were starry, and mystified with contempt. "How the Hells did they get in here?"

Kurtisian dressed his sneer in a laugh. "Let's go up and ask them. Who *cares* how they got here? What matters is how they're leaving. Say it with me."

"Death's door," Justinian recited along, bled by rote of any enthusiasm.

"That's right," Kurtisian said, mock-motherly. "And we're the famsapping ushers."

His face hidden, Urien seemed walled up in cares of his own. Shaking his hooded head, he looked down the path they had all taken and traced it, slowly, all the way back to the forbidding bend before them. "No trail, no tidings. They aren't likely to have come this way, I'll stake a pot to it."

---

[14] *(AK)*: vocal cords

[15] The Trebellish term, by which the monsters are most widely known in midwestern Ráma. *Ogre* (*orcus* in the *Linguish*) is nevertheless a generic name for any humanoid creature halfway in size between Men and True Giants.

Even if he had said something they understood, the Chaldallions would have ignored him. Their goodwill towards him was gone, and Toron barely trusted him not to backstab them.

Justinian was already limbering up. "How big are they?"

The Harandrishman shook his head. "Hard to tell without someone standing next to them. Looking at the trees, I would say around ten feet. Thick, though. Thick as you. Maybe a little more."

"Slow, then," Kurtisian concluded. In his eyes, he was already among them.

Urien piped in. "Unless they have something—dreeish gear, or a spell that hastens them."

It was a warning meant to help rather than hinder their rede, but Kurtisian's scoff misted the air. "I wouldn't ever tell you how to cook a dick, changeling. So don't tell me how to fight an ogre. They're *monsters*. They're as likely to have eaten such a thing as they are to have figured out what it does." The magician imitated their guide's childlike voice. *"What if it has a ring that can turn us to stone? What if it can breathe fire?* Trust me, we start thinking like that, we sit here all day."

Urien's hood showed the slow shake of his head, and Toron, racked as he was between weariness and worry, saw in him someone to hear out. Not all the fayfolk were hundelds old and worldwise; Urien might only have been a little older than he looked. Nonetheless, his kind stood closer to the eldritch domains of fiends than to those of men, as his talk of cookery had made plain. For all his boasting, Kurtisian had never fought ogres hand-to-hand, not ogres like these, which spoke to one another at length, and moreover had sneaked to within a stone's throw of a headburg. Toron knew there was much that Urien was not telling them about himself, and about where he had led them. Himeliness[16] was not the same as untruthfulness. They would lose no face in giving him half an ear.

"What were you saying, swapling?" he muttered, fiddling with his saddle and shamming for Kurtisian's sake to seem less than heedful.

Urien looked over at him, his white chin wobbling in the shadow. "Even in this world, the ogres of the Farthest East built cities and wrote down their tungs," Urien pressed. "I have heard that

---

[16] *(AK)*: secrecy.

their ships trade at times with kingdoms around the eastern rim of this very landbody."

"Fascinating," said Kurtisian as he limbered up his neck.

Urien's white face dawned as he pushed between Chaldallions. His voice had become shaky. "Have any of you fought a manshfretter before?"

"We've fought shabshucks," Toron said. "They're what some Knaksmen call trolls. About the same height. Skinnier."

"But not an ogre," Urien said. "Not four of them."

The thoftship looked at each other, then grudgingly shook their heads.

Urien nodded, knowingly, but not without ruth. "Any of you seen one before today?"

Justinian's brow went up as he called something back to him. "Yeah. Yeah, from a distance. A couple of times. I think they were ogres. One was working as a longshoreman at the docks the day we left Salpes. Remember, Kurt?"

Kurtisian shrugged, nodded. Urien let the silence steep a little, then tossed in a few more words.

"They're mighty strong, aren't they? Even stone-for-stone."

Justinian gave the tightlipped nod of an appraiser. "He was running freight up the gangplanks. Bushels, hampers, jars, everything. Yeah, some of those sacks had to be fifty stone. Maybe more. They didn't need the trochlea[17] at all. The captain was asking how he was supposed to unload everything once he got where he was going."

The Sumo laughed, then frowned when he realized what Urien had done.

"Well, you're no kitten either, fra," said Kurtisian. "And none of them has an Allmetal around his neck."

Justinian cleared his throat. "What—" he began, then lowered his voice. "What about weapons?"

"Clubs. Ugly-looking. Tree trunks full of spikes."

"Of course they are," Kurtisian grumbled. He began to hop on the spot, and threw a few punches.

"All of them?" said Justinian.

"I believe so."

"Armour?"

---

[17] *(L)*: arm-and-pulley device used for loading heavy weights; essentially a crane.

Toron shook his head a little, his voice as bloodshot as his eyes. "Shieldwear. Yes. It's—looks homemade. A little like lamlar. Plates, stitched to leather and hide somehow. Rivets, maybe. Patchy. Should be able to find openings. Stab, don't slash, if you can."

Justinian's face kept souring. "Can't do either," he said.

Turning toward Toron, he let slip through his eyes a glimpse of his own exhaustion, and Toron, in all the days and weeks of his own weariness, had never reckoned the baldrish[18] man prone to it. But there hadn't been many such thoughts at all—of the way they lived, and of the points at which wills and the bonds of brotherhood broke. There had only been the voice of his inner taskmaster, driving him on at whatever the toll, telling him he could count his friends at some table up ahead. Now that such a board lay only a short way away, he saw that what he had taken for strength of will had been as much a deadening of the heart, not so much a willfulness as a drift and stowing-of-oars. He had been coasting for a month now, heedless of his thoftmen save when they did things to sap his headway.

"Almost there, Thorn," Justinian said, and although Toron knew that the plea in his voice was not to him but to the gods, Toron felt his shoulders slump, and knew it for the awful weight of the oars he gripped anew.

His mind did a walkabout through his flesh, as does a ship's headman through the ship before the clash. It was a dreadful awareness, which he'd felt often ere this, and which being waylaid indeed spared him—to know that this might be the last time he would see his body whole, and uncrippled. He heard Kurtisian propose some sort of distraction for the enemies ahead, Justinian rule it out, and Kurtisian suggest another. He heard their pathfinder protest its gamble, and Kurtisian's angry retort. He heard the weird birds keep calling out, as if gloating in their freedom from the brewing thrack. What he did not hear any longer was his own whingeing, nor any of Gorrh, who hated qualms and tarrying, as he brought the tuskcat about in a wide eastward wheel, and began to pelt down the path with his swordstaff raised.

He held the swordstaff fully lowered lest it tangle in the outreaching greenlife, and its broadleaf-shaped blade bounced only slightly as Gorrh fought his wont to lope. The tuskcat while ridden kept his body firm, and his head stiff like a ram as he closed the

---

[18] *(AK):* jovial; good-natured; easy to like.

stretch between themselves and their would-be killers. His legs rolled like wheels, his rhythm relentless, his tail switching from side to side as if to keep it all in time. The end of it all, far from funny or even weird, was something dreadful in its deviance, as with the sight of a wolf who, its prey having fled to the lower branches of a tree, puts out longer claws and climbs after it.

They gained the bend in the path within heartbeats. Toron took the collarbar in an undergrip with his free hand and held on for dear life. The manshfretters came into sight, and he into theirs. The path had widened into a clearing where they gathered, and they took up its room like four standing stones, the uprights of a henge whose capstones—the clubs on their shoulders—lay off-kilter. Great bellies of brawn sagged from their limbs, which Toron might have taken for fat, had he never seen Justinian tauten his own. As it was, the bloat of all that meat stiffened when the devils saw him, and rose readying into its thews. It sickened Toron with sight of it, of these fiends for whom bloodlust was such a maddening, hardening thrill.

But as he rushed forward, and showed them no fear, they seemed to shrink a little from the size his loathing had given them, their eyes widening and arms slackening as they saw he would soon be upon them. They were nevertheless much taller than the tallest of Men, and together they stepped out from their ring, and made a gate across the pathway for the man who meant to crash it. A lesser body lay among them, its red soak seen even from thirty yards. One of the ogres shoveled the broken thing into the brush with its foot. The long stretch that it flew, its dead limbs flopping like a doll's, was the first show of their awful might.

Even at full gallop, Gorrh's paws were a mere patter above hush, and the sound of the creatures' speech was dreadfully clear. Each stave was the grumble a bull toad might make were it the size of a mastiff, a rumour of thunder through the whistling of the wind. One of the ogres, the leftmost, was a little swifter than the others. It recovered fully from its startle and pounded its club against the ground. Dirt flew up, and birds fled the shiver of nearby branches. A black gash lay where the weapon had struck, and a gouge deep enough to bury a dog in. Two blinks of the eye later, the greatest of the brutes broke line, and began to work itself into an onward rush— a barging, ungainly lope which might have been funny had the creature carried half a fourth of its bulk. As it was, the sight shocked Toron's fingers even tighter about the shaft of the swordstaff, his grip edging against the stays, pulling the graper hard against his side. He sent his mind to his feet, found them still in the stirrups, and willed his thighs iron to stay saddled.

By now, the Chaldallions understood Toron was fully winging it, however unlike him it was, and unlunged roars to hearten him. In the stormfront of it all—as the ogres grew before him, inhaling life and detail like things touched by the quickening wand of a wizard—the northman thought maybe it would not have been so bad if Kurtisian had lobbed a couple of *redballs* down there, at least to bewilder only one of the four, whose gang had shaped itself into a wedge to smash-smear him in two.

But then Gorrh cleared the last stretch in what seemed a single bound, and drove them straight into the storm. The shaft of the swordstaff shuddered, its blade diving between the flesh and iron flotsam on the face of an oncoming wave, the wood buzzing in after, smoothly then suddenly pushing back, wrenching both shoulders, Toron letting go of it, monsters mountaining, toad-thunder in his ears, burying his face in fur, something black sweeping over him, tearing his cloak, and the great mass beneath him bending as it dodged among bergshadows. He clung to the cat with every bone and sinew he'd been given, and at first it was all clean, but then bad sounds began to break in, from both above and below him, and Gorrh dug in his heels before Toron knew he was clear of the fray. It was bad news to stop, for it meant a penning in. A soft dodge, then a feint the other way, thews tightening till they hummed, then the sudden, reckless, and twisting sort of leap the cat might only have made if it was death for him not to have made it. The world went straight up, and Toron was clinging to a wall. He felt a blow shake his seat, and did not know whether his steed took or dealt it. The world went right again, bounced one way, wrenched the other, then went up and to the side, and for all the white strength in his hands and his thighs, he felt his body coming loose from the saddle. In his mind he saw the riot that Gorrh fought to live through, but with the tuskcat's mind too busy to read, it was all a dizzying squall of sound, hue, and smell, their lines running together. The sky wheeled past, dawn and dusk within the blink of an eye, and Toron looked up to see the ground somehow falling atop him. Another thud, another blow, evil shapes on both sides, Gorrh's tail brushing past like a broom, as if all the cat could do was to give the spot his brother landed a quick sorry sweep before dumping him there. With no other choice but to be thrown off or crushed, Toron let go of the collarbar and dropped to the ground in a heap.

He found himself on hands and knees in broken dirt, half-bracing for the blow that would shatter his back, or the arms that would seize him and crush his ribs like a reed. He leapt sidelong when neither came, aware only that Gorrh was on his hind legs nearby, and that the snarling coming from the animal's throat was straight from under Hell's own bed. Whether they came from wounds or from wrath, their discord unwove the weirs of thought, and it was only because the din was from one of his own that he could keep from clamping hands over ears. Instead he churned himself toward what he thought was the shallow ditch at the edge of the path. Still burdened by his swords, he rolled like an unpruned log. His cloak twisted and gathered between his scabbards, and the weapons' handguards dug at his skull. The buckles of his shieldwear strained with the twisting, and a leafy wall sprang up. At once, Toron was through the weeds and off the open path, getting back his bearings only to find himself sliding down a bank, toward a pool of dark and slightly rippling waters. He had thrust himself so hard, there was no time to stop, and he pitched into the stuff a few inches off headlong.

The cold shocked him, even through all his dread and cares, and let him think for the first time since he fell from the saddle. It went through his mind to stay underwater, maybe to pull himself across the bottom to emerge elsewhere, but fear of the club found him, and he thrust his feet downward to find them. He rose from the waters, found them waist-deep, not knowing whether the babbling nearby was from an incoming stream, or if something was wading towards him. There was still snarling, but it was muffled now, and because he was no longer atop Gorrh, his own hearing felt weak in his ears. He reached for his swords, but his sight was bleary. He wiped his eyes with a hand and went back for them. Alas, the cloak was tangled deeply among them, for when he was on the road, he wore the garment over top of his swordbelts, and not the other way around. In his haste, he had not thought to swap them, and so he stood there with both elbows up, snarling and cursing as if to undo a stubborn neckchain, his eyes sweeping the mess he had fled.

The Chaldallions had not yet arrived, nor could he hear them coming. In hindsight he saw it had been folly to begin the fight alone, and to have rushed so far ahead of his thoftmen. Nevertheless, only two of the ogres he could see still stood, and one was longer for this world than the other. Run through by his swordstaff, the doomed fiend was trying to draw the shaft out of himself, learning for all its might that dry wood does not drag easily through wet innards and leather shieldwear, less so when the blade at its end lacked fullers, and was fixed by the sucking strength of a pierced stomach, lung, or bowel. A cowlike sound came out of the monster as it struggled, and Toron was struck by its hopelessness, having thought an ogre would only rip the weapon out, guts and all, and feel no hurt through its wrath.

As it was, the stricken thing gave no heed to the tawny slayer only a few lengths of its body behind it. Gorrh was back on all fours, head lowered, and though Toron could not see much through the tall grass, it was clear his brother had an ogre pinned down. Thick legs kicked up, and brown arms made a yoke about his neck from below, but none of it broke the tuskcat's throttling grip. For a short time Gorrh was still, chewing in for a deeper hold, the thing in his mouth muffling his growling. Then he leapt up again, ruthlessly dragging his quarry to another spot as the ogre impaled on the swordstaff at last crumpled to the grass behind him. That left one ogre standing which Toron could see, and he was further afield than the rest. With one eye on Gorrh the fiend waited, distraught, at the foot of the path, peering up its length with feet rooted and club twitching. It had to be the Chaldallions the creature had spotted, but whether they were rushing to join the fray or trying to bait the monster toward them, the sight was hidden behind clouds of greenlife. Of the fourth manshfretter, there was no sight or sound.

At last, Toron got loose a single sword, Tuger, and scrambled up the bank for a better look. As he broke through the wall of grass, he became dreadfully aware of the fourth, who had been knocked down but not harmed, and which rose at the same time he did from beyond the other bank. They spotted each other at once, and though its weapon was gone, the brute rushed him like a bull. It slipped on the bank and fell, but then it was up again, and angrier, and Toron knew there would be no way to dodge it. The hulking thing broke through the wildflowers like a warg from the thicket, dripping and muddy, and roaring to bloodshot the suns. The sight of it made Toron's soul squirm, and he grit his teeth to keep it all inside him.

Two bounding lopes the thing took, and as fearful as it already was, it seemed to grow, and gather awfulness as it took on speed. It was slightly misshapen, Toron saw, with one leg longer, and head fixed aslant, like a steer squashed alive into the shape of a Man, driven mad by the hellish suffering of it. The will to flee, and recklessly, nearly overwhelmed him, and he gave it a few inches east, putting between his teeth the tales he had heard of Thunor and other thurseslayers, and of the fighting schools and styles that were proof, however roundabout, of Man's might to overcome these devils hand-to-hand. He bit down on these yarns, made them balms against the pain, and then there was nothing he could see but the monster itself, its dirty skin full of blackheads, its head eclipsing both suns.

There was a burst of red-hued stuff which he thought was blood but gave off light. The ogre lifted its arms about its eyes, giving Toron the time to leap to his left. He somehow kept his feet, and the ogre crashed itself snarling through the spot he had left, going like a runaway wagon over the bank he had only climbed out of, and into the pool with the wettest of uproars. Half aware of what had happened, Toron stepped closer to the middle of the path, his heart pounding at the glass of his eyesight as he watched two more *redballs* break against the ogre at the bottom of the path.

The Chaldallions came charging down, Kurtisian in a sprint, and Justinian in the thigh-gyrating speed-waddle the girth of his legs restricted him to. It looked like a too-late dash toward an outhouse, but Toron was grateful to see it. The *Ultrices* Kurtisian had used were not strong, and pushed rather than burned what they struck, but the ogre, like most redblooded things, was wary of the sight of dreecraft, and gave a few yards of ground. As Toron had foreseen, Justinian was indeed small before the creature, his head reaching to somewhere around its collarbone, and the girth of his limbs was much less. But just as a kept and cultivated thing has its own, rarer magnificence—a subtler elegance and pride, be it a horse or a bloom—so it was that Justinian stood like a sculpture before the ogre's unkept chunk of stone, and topped it, though he lacked its raw mass. Kurtisian was a black shade at his brother's side, like a thing one glimpses in a lonely place from the corner of one's eye, and turns but finds it gone. His face was a blue lamp, bleached by the fires beneath his brow. His teeth he bared in a smile, his arm he outstretched from the closed curtains of his cloak, as though offering a trinket in exchange for the soul. He said something, and Toron knew what, as the *Carno* came together in that hand, an upturned crescent, a quarter moon of steel which he raised aloft and to the side like a giant cleaver. Behind them but with no less haste came Urien, his hood thrown back to show the chalk-white hair on a head white as bone.

Together, the three reached the bottom of the path and advanced into the wider roadway, the monster before them drawing back a little more as it weighed which one to attack, or which one would attack it first. The Chaldallions exchanged a few words and nods, then broke wider apart, Justinian flanking the creature on the left, with Kurtisian to take it head-on. Hardly any time had gone by since Toron's own foe had overshot him and blundered down the yonder bank, and now the churning of the water there became geyserish. He saw the ogre tossing to regain its crooked footing, its great arms clubbing the pool and sending up sheets which drenched the overhanging branches. Toron readied himself for whatever was coming, and hoped the sight of the newly arrived fighters would be enough to sap the ogre's fight once it climbed back out.

He made the most of the time he had. Throwing Tuger down, he tore the pin from his cloak, wrenching the sopping garment from about his neck and winding himself free of it. It made a wet sound as it heaped, the iron brooch ringing into the dirt somewhere. Pushing the hair from his eyes as his hands went past, he pulled Mortha's blade into the daylight as well. As he stooped to recover Tuger as well, he saw that the ogre he had speared lay all but dead, its hands still clutching at the shaft, but hardly stirring otherwise. A few yards from that, Gorrh was nearly done with his own game, but not so nearly that the cat let go. The tuskcat's mind was aflame with the thrill of it, and disturbing him then, even with the Rine, was like jostling the shoulder of a man in the midst of his deepest and most jealous pleasure.

It was with no small share of gratefulness that Toron saw Justinian coming his way, and that he might not have to stand alone against his own foe. The *Carno* alone seemed enough to keep the other ogre occupied, for it showed no wish to take both Chaldallions at once, and seemed to invite the chance to shed the larger of the two. Urien stood somewhere between the brothers, though further back, his cloak almost touching the leaves edging the path. Though Toron could not spy the look on his face, their pathfinder's willingness to get closer was clearly, and wisely, halfhearted. Even had he brandished a sword the full height of his body, and raised it aloft with arm outstretched, its tip would not have reached past the ogre's chest. As it was, the knife he held seemed the talon of a sparrow, visible in his white hand only when it glinted, and perhaps better suited to ending his own life were the monster to break past Kurtisian and seize him.

There was, as Justinian moved to join Toron, a narrow window of peace, where the big southerner gave a heartening nod and turned his body away from what became his brother's fight. Starmath put his shadow before him, and as Toron squeezed off a smile and scrounged about in his mouth for a lefthanded word of thanks, something awful happened which he saw before anyone else.

However it worked, its shadow came first. It appeared as a gauzy radiance about Justinian's own, then deepened to engulf it. The air itself danced, waving as if with heat, and behind Justinian appeared yet another monster, a colossal thing with skin like dusk. Toron's eyes gaped, for Justinian had yet to notice the darkness about him, and stood there half-aware as the news took the slowest route.

Like the ogres, it was manlike in cast, but whereas the others carried their brawn like dolls stuffed in a hurry, this one was fabulously muscled, the great bulges of its shoulders, arms, and chest straining against its skin. Horns were on its head, coiled and ram-like, and a ridge of thorny knobs topped the jut of its brow. Tusks stuck up from its lower lip like a crippled palisade, so crowding the face with bony horrors that the face itself was almost overwhelmed. Some of its garb was visible, but Justinian obscured the rest from its breastbone down, and for their common deal of muscle, the monster stood, more than the others, as an obscenity of what it threatened. It was the minotaur to his Mars. There was a tangle of brilliance about the beefy cords of its neck—golden chains embrangled with more grisly trophy-ornaments—all of which flashed as the fiend reached up, and gripped aloft the demon-king of all bludgeoning weapons.

The thing was an ogre like the others, but some kind of headman whose greater bulk and lordlier bearing were tokens of its standing. Much like wolves and other scrabbling pack-beasts whose fellowship was a pecking order—the backs of whose leaders whiten, and the tails of whose thralls droop to drag in the mud—so too did mannish thedes bear marks to show the rungs on which they stood. The Kings of Knaks themselves were said to tower among Men, but as they were athelings and kin to the Ozmen themselves, this seemed more a matter of blood than one of standing. Were the king slain or overthrown by a layman—and such a thing had never befallen his line—it would have to be seen whether the usurper would grow a yard taller the following night's sleep. With wildlife such a handover indeed happened, as it did with many fiendish thedes; whoever overthrew his overling found uplift, giving his body new means to grow, and greater strength, and other marks of lordship. It was why herds of deer were often seen led by elk twice their size, and why the killing of that sire one year—by hunters or by chance—left another in its place the year after. Priests of the Heron called this uplift a suchness of this Eld, where lifestrength could be sown and harvested like wealth. Through hearty living and overcoming deadly perils, one might build up a great hoard of it, by which he would live longer and more richly than his weakhearted neighbour. Called *Fergh* or *ferrow*[19] by the godlore of the Heronstroth, and Quicklife by Knaksmen, it was the kind of life that is itself alive, and not the kind only to tell a beating heart from a still one. *Fergh* and *life* were but one of many odd twosomes in the godlore of the Heronsmen— among them *fire* and *elled*, *water* and *ay*, and *air* and *loft*—which gave two such sides to the same thing. One was soulish, the other inanimate.

The thought that the devil before Toron was likely an earl among ogres and not a king dumped ice through his blood. For its might, he could not bear to insee how awesome their highest lords might become. Time itself seemed unwilling too, and forsook the place as Toron stared. What happened next, he came to understand, was a quirk of the Timebriar, whose workings he had never before witnessed so deeply. Something he did, or felt, seemed to have brought it about, even as the smell of fright brings things both predatory and pitying to our sides.

A wrinkle in time came together, and what he saw then he saw with his memory alone. It showed him a gangling fiend—what some Knaksmen called a troll, the first his own eyes had ever suffered. Harandrishmen did not call them by that name, however, and kept the word of *troll* for a hulking, clever folk not too unlike themselves. These devils Toron knew only as shabshucks, a name which like *fiend* and *devil* was shared by many unhiresome things too filthy to earn names of their own. He had heard tell and tales of them—of skulking, green corpse-gobblers who, like most devils, had fled the coming of Men and now haunted the sunless bowers and deepest

---

[19] *(AB)*: life as energy; the animating force (a form of *Fergh*).

back country of their realms. Though the stories had been overwrought as most stories are, he had never misgiven them. Now that he beheld one, however, he saw that the limner of his mind had failed, and that the thing was so much worse than what the words had made it seem.

He had heard it before he had seen it—a humming like a nearby hive—and as the monster slithered out from between boulders, a black haze all about it, Toron saw that the din was of the flies who followed it like smog. Even fed by the hinterland's teeming game, a thing of its size seemed too big. Its toad-green body spread itself across the sky like a spider seen from below, its lank limbs as thick as its trunk, its head narrow and too large, its face sharp like a swamphag's, with nose and chin jutting, and hooking like fins. The whole of its hide glistened and shivered wetly, crawling with the larva of the trollflies who weltered in its broken boils and fed upon the endless meal of its ever-healing, ever-cankering flesh. Horrible as it was all over, its face sucked up one's sight most, lying too low on its body, its neck like an arm reaching out and not up, its hair limp and oily, its redblack eyes bulging and bellying as if to burst. There was nothing in them but bloodlust—the kind that comes not from hunger or wont or hatred, but from the Pits beneath all understanding—and it was a wonder to Toron that those hideous windows served sight at all. Its mouth was a hinging gash, like a trap dug to catch game, and stuck full of spears, then forsaken to fill and to fester. Yellowish stuff came out of it, and the air seemed to crawl with the whisper of sickness. Even the flies shunned that reek, parting and regathering like living clouds. A sound rose within the drone, a disturbance of phlegm that became a gurgling, gathering snarl, and Toron saw that what he had mistaken for an overlong arm was in truth an arm gripping a cudgel the height of a man.

He stepped back, helpless, and it was not Justinian beneath that taproot of Hell, but Níscel. The young katkin rode Sofe her white horse, cradling the yellow kitten she had found on the road a few days ago. Her strange chirruping was a homeland song. She was the first among them to have become happy again.

The swordsman stepped back once more, heard himself cry out. The troll's weapon came down, and everything broke beneath it.

He never knew whether she had heard him or not.

He only knew that she couldn't have felt a thing.

Then frayed atop now, like a garment fast-aged, and Justinian marked the anguish in Toron's face. The Sumo saw the shadow fall across him, and soak up his own. His hand stole to his chest, his lips formed a breathless prayer, and he gripped the Allmetal like the hand of his god itself.

The ogre chieftain swung its club like a hammer, down-slamming half-sideways between neck and shoulder. The sound of it, dull, shook dragonflies from flowers a quarter-mile away. It was enough to mince flesh and mash bone into gravel—to shatter a Man like the mere likeness of a Man, and leave a pile of whatever had built him. As it was, it spiked Justinian to his knees in the dirt, but it did not break him. Instead, it bounced back wildly from the Sumo, as if he were granite, jarring itself from the grip of its wielder and whirling off to one side. Grunting thanks to the Brasmat, Justinian uprooted and wheeled, releasing himself into his ambusher, joining their bodies with the blunt slap of brawn and the extortion of breath. Caught offguard, the ogre staggered offbalance, and Justinian got his arms about its knees, dropping his hips and driving with all the strength of his thighs. As quickly as it had appeared, and with a snarl of frustration, the monster toppled over backwards, clawing and flailing at the little big man as it felt its legs being braided into a wrestling hold.

The fourth ogre's sudden appearance had startled everyone, and Kurtisian, his eyes for a moment drawn away from his own foe, seemed to have underestimated the creature's swiftness. In a blink, the monster had lunged across the gap between them, and the fuhrbido only had time to raise the *Carno* like a shield. The savage force took both his feet off the ground, but he flew cleanly, his cloak trailing like a flag, running in air as he hit the ground again, rolling, and releasing his weapon lest the tumble carve him apart. It chimed as it stuck upright among the weeds, perilously close, and Kurtisian cursed obscenely as he gathered himself up again.

By then, however, the ogre had made it to Urien. The monster seized the little pathfinder by the cloak and wound it round its free fist. The little white face stared up, bright eyes luminous in the living shadow atop him. Having reeled in its tiny quarry, the ogre lifted him high, Urien's legs kicking, his knife loosing from his hand as, behind his neck, he tried to prise apart the great fingers that held him. Though fierce, his struggling was silent, and seeing the weapon fall, the ogre brought him closer to its face, leering and croaking with something that might have been language.

"*Sibakhe khua!*" was about what it said, like the throat stretching and readying itself for swallowing. But whether the monster had intended to eat its prize like an apple, or simply to smash it to the ground like a gourd, Urien said something back, and its sneer went slack.

"*Khibak na,*" was what the changeling hissed, his voice muddy with phlegm, and Kurtisian and the ogre both watched in horror as the little creature's face went demoniacal. Its white skin stretched, and bloodied pink, the cherubic guise melting away to become the ghastly vizard which was no less his true countenance. The eyes became snakish, pupils knives of shadow. Its hair became a smoking black fire. But it was the *mouth*, the mouth that was most appalling, stretching the full virulent breadth of the skull, ear-to-ear like an assassin's cut, hinging in half to turn the stomach, and congested with white thorns. Row upon row of hooks lay within, receding like legions, the teeth of a shark, inexhaustible and horrid. A ribbon-like tongue writhed out, licking every one of those barbs, slathering them with whatever toxins oozed from the black glands visible in the mouth's inner reaches. No more soft and childlike the neck—that fiendish head stood atop a pillar roped and fluted with muscle, veins standing out like creeping plants—and where the little creature's forearms came out his sleeves, they too rippled with strength. Talons the length of paring blades had leapt from the manicured nails, and carved into the ogre's own fingers. All this, and the clothing at the changeling's back was thrashing from within, as though a hardshelled insect, its mandibles and forelegs labouring, sought to burst forth from the membranous egg which contained it.

The gremlinnish thing that was Urien growled once, paused, and spat, and peppered the horrified ogre with something sticky. The sputum at once began to hiss and fume upon the brute's skin, causing it to whimper and jig, to drop its club and clutch madly at the stricken areas of its body. For whatever reason, however, it did not release what it held, which Kurtisian saw was not wise. For as the ogre carelessly bent its wheeling arms, and Urien drifted close enough, the littler monster saw its chance. It lashed out with its claws, anchoring itself to both the cheeks of the bigger monster. Their faces met, and Urien began to feed.

The ogre screamed even before it could have felt the pain of it— a pitched, baying sound—which soon became chopped into short, shrieking pieces as its nose fell apart between the devil's teeth. Blood went everywhere, in specklets and as mist, and as Urien continued, his head sawing from side-to-side as a gory blur, it seemed as though he would burrow straight through his poor foeman's skull. Finally, however, the ogre succeeded in tearing the barnacle off. He hurled it away, most of its cheeks coming off along with it. The cloak came loose from Urien's neck, remaining bunched about the ogre's bloody hand as the little creature landed on all fours a short stretch away. The bigger monster's face was no longer there, but its eyes seemed intact. Its hesitation, as it froze, was not out of blindness.

Bearded by blood and fleshcurds, Urien looked between the ogre and Kurtisian. The fuhrbido, for his stance, seemed unsure which of the two promised him more pain. Urien's mouth had closed a little, but for the horror it did nothing. The back of his shirt kept tossing, and his tongue still lashed about like the tail of a half-swallowed serpent.

Kurtisian shuddered from head to toe as he weighed the metamorphosis.

"You are one creepy little bastard," he muttered.

Of all the things about Urien that had changed, the flower-coloured eyes remained most constant, but if there was any wit to the changeling's face, it was buried under beast. For all Kurtisian could see, his guide's new shape was something thoughtless and hungry and would not revert until heaped about with corpses. The corner of his eyes held the *Carno*—he had only but to call it—and whether the thing that was Urien saw his fear or feared for itself, it stood up straight and backed away from the fight. Its talons swiped at the front of its shirt, and the garment fell away, revealing the ivory musculature beneath, but also freeing the batwings at his back. They opened and stretched like fingers, their black membranes bleaching as they tautened, and began to flap. Falling back to all fours, Urien let them lift him from the ground with an onerous, lurching rhythm, snickering and slavering to clear his airways of butchery as he rose past the treetops. His misshapen shadow grew upon the grass until it draped the whole theatre in gloom. The winds brought the weird fire atop his head to a rage, showing with its smoke the westward blow, but no matter how high he rose his eyes still stood out, switching to and fro, rapidly and back again, like those of an imp in quest of more mischief. He swung suddenly westward, his mad muttering still audible, and retreated whence the party had come, drifting into the radiance of Starmath and taking his shadow with him. Four heads watched him go—or made sure he was gone—before returning to the red work still at hand.

Toron locked eyes with his own foeman. The manshfretter had climbed back to the pathway, and was no less awestruck than anyone by what it had seen. An ox-witted brawler, and unaware of what its face showed of its thoughts, the devil had a look of utmost wonder. Whatever manner of shapeshifter Urien was, the ogre seemed to think Toron might be one too. Toron meanwhile did his best to hide his own shock at what had happened. His swordsmanship came back to him, and he baited the giant with his weaker blade, making rings with its tip and running them through. Tuger he kept back, waiting for the kill. The ogre watched the lure but gave it nothing, and as hatred returned to its mug—its childish wonder swallowed by the devil—Toron knew he had only heartbeats before it would rush him again. Though the fiend wasn't the sharpest axe in the block, it doubtless knew that if the Man before it were a shapeshifter, he would have shifted shapes by now. The spikes of its club dripped, and the sound was like the tapping of fingers.

Toron baited once more, half-baited, then lunged, and brought down Tuger with every stone and thew his body owned. It struck but rang off, and the fleshy sky shifted. What smote him in answer felt less like a blow than like the world stopped and he hit it. Hurt's older brother set fire to his bonehouse, and such was the stun of it that he barely knew himself flying, or tumbling, or breathing in water. Somehow, he had been thrown back into the ditch, headfirst yet again, and he screamed and gagged to find himself there. He hands were swordless, his head gathering pain. At last he stood, retching and wheezing, and waded back to the edge of the pool. In a cloud of madness and hatred he stormed the bank, and readied to hurl himself devilmaycare into the devil that was becoming his slayer.

More than half his mind believed himself dead, his doom already laid and half-meted. It was all he could do to drag the ogre down with him, be it by the gobbet or the whole loathsome lot. In the mud of the bank his fingers hit something hard, and he knew it for the stockier hilt of Mortha. He took it in his right hand and scrambled up the last stretch, wild and giddy, like a seaman leaping gnawed from hungry waters.

He saw his foe. Its twisted hill of back was to him, a least a little. Up the path, something was coming—some new devilry was afoot. The manshfretter turned to meet the Man once again, but it seemed to have become bewildered in the meantime, or not to have thought its foeman could rise again so soon. The downward swing of its club was so careless it might well have hired heralds to foresay it. Toron needed only to tarry a step, to let it shovel itself into the ground before him, and to leap through the breach the bungled onslaught had left. The ogre's body embowered him, rooted on three sides where it had leaned into its swing. Toron had but to steer Mortha upward and drive, palming her pommel with his free hand and punching it into the meat of the monster's neck. The flesh yielded, and took a full foot of steel. The unslit howl of the manshfretter said he had missed the windpipe, but it mattered not at all. Unbelieving of its end, the devil sought to unstab itself, and its struggle made Mortha's edge saw. A dammed lake of blood burst forth. Toron towed backward with all his wounded might, reddening his hands to the elbows as the weapon came free. He backed away trembling from the tree he had chopped.

But the sky whirled then, and he fell to one knee. It was only as he stared steadily at the grass that he found that the blear in his eyes which he'd taken for water had not lessened. When the smudging grew wider he knew something was wrong, and that he'd not come away unscathed. Gorrh felt it too, but Toron no longer knew where the cat was. The man got back to his feet and sought to better his bearings, or at least to find Tuger before his head gave out. With his own foe down all the ogres were dead, busied, or deathstricken, and he thought the thoftship in good shape, all things reckoned.

But his foeman had indeed been distracted by something, and it didn't take long for that distraction to show itself and to demand the toll Toron owed it. A mad drumming of paws sounded from the east. There from the thicket just past the brook burst a pack of shaggy black fiends. They were smaller than the ogres, but there were more of them, and the halfmannish way in which they loped was heartboiling to behold—a fellowship of wolfish things so lank and shaggy that Toron at first thought them weirdly limber bears. They

moved like much wiser things than both, however, and Toron would
have pegged them for werewolves even if he hadn't spotted their
overlong legs and blunter muzzles.

As with the manshfretters, Toron knew their kind without having
fought them before. They were in many ways the flipside of the
ogres, cloaking themselves as Men to hide their man-eating lusts—at
one whim to help, the next to prey upon, those who called them
neighbours and friends. As with underthurses, many kinds of were-
thing were known to prowl Ráma, with all kinds of looks and moods.
Not all of them were harmful. Some could warp shapes at will and
keep hold of their wits, while others were thralls to the shift,
sufferers of that dreeish sickness called the wargening[20], which
twisted their minds as grimly as their bodies. The tales of these
worse wretches were better known those of their selfwilled betters,
where in the shapeshift all their feelings become one hateful hunger,
their most steadfast friendships deadheaded, and those the shifter
most loved become his most craved food. No lockup could hold
them, no chains bind or distance weary. Everyone closest to the
manbeast who does not kill him while he can is in turn made a meal
of, one change after another. Not all the tales went this way—some
told of those who had bent the wargening to their will, or those who
wielded it as the share of some mighty brotherhood. But whether
slave or lord of the warp, no werewolf Toron had ever heard of was
open with it, and instead hid it—an Unsaid, maybe, a blasphemy—to
the Age of Life and all that was wonely.

It was this inborn kind of wolfman that Toron knew he saw
before him, but they were not friendly. Gorrh was first in their path,
having only at last settled down with the kill between his teeth, and
begrudging the new fight upon him. He let go of the limp body, and
gathered down for the newcomers, every thew tautening like a
bowstring. The wolves were much larger than the sheepeating kind,
and larger even than the timberwolves that live where shepherds
field no flocks. But even had they been wargs, they'd have been
heifers to the tuskcat's ox, whose shape was more dreadful than the
bulk itself—not heaped in clumps about the haunches and chest by a
rancher given a go at gods' clay, but smoothed and braided with
bloodthirsty thildiness, every inch and limb at mangling's behest.

---

[20] *(AK):* lycanthropy—the disease by which one contracts wolfmanry.

The upshot was that Gorrh both outsized and outnimbled the pack, which saw him and slowed down markedly.

The cat fought the urge to break his oneman shieldwall and spear into them, and stood fast, deaf to their mockery as the dogthings scampered forth in a halfring about him. Bloodlust warped his face wickedly, drawing back the skin till it seemed nothing but teeth. Even as the madness tore at the harness within him, he had enough foresight to send out a bidding, to ask that he be freed from the saddle on which the wolfmen would likely find handholds to swarm.

Toron groaned, the strength of its urgency new pain, and he used Mortha as a crutch to push himself up to both feet. The ogre he had necked was down at last, having staggered and spun with both hands at its throat before tripping over the body of a tribesman. The two lay near each other, both still alive but not so still that Toron would go close enough to do their suffering a sword's kindness. His sight fought blindness as he staggered toward Gorrh, thankful at least he could not see fully what he was heading into.

Some ways behind him Kurtisian and his own foe had done nothing to close quarters with each other, one too bloodied and the other too stunned by the unfoldings to make a move. With the seven newcomers, however, both seemed obliged; each heaved a reluctant sigh, and they began to square off. The ogre dragged a forearm across its eyes, clearing away some of the blood, and picked up its club with a dutiful growl. Its would-be victim was disarmed, and Kurtisian could not, for his own show of shock and fear, try to pretend that Urien's transformation was something he had expected, much less a power he shared. Despite its injuries, the ogre would not be fleeing, and Kurtisian's look, while grudging, showed a hint respect. The sight of the bloodbent monster nonetheless brought his showman back, a devilish grin to his lips, and he wrenched his head from side to side, limbering up his neck, though he had already done so earlier. He held his eyes open wide, better to boast the blue burn which kindled and grew with each word, and finally, like rings of camphor candletouched, flared.

"I call for you, *Carno*," he declared, and the otherwordly weapon came. It melt-flashed away where it stuck up from the ground and coalesced in his hand top to bottom. The meateating metal steamed, the wetness it had picked up from the grass flash-boiled by its transit.

The ogre kept to its track and fronted the little Man, no roaring or lunging. Pain had taught it some patience. Both foemen feinted, baiting the maiden strike, trying to trap the other with his own carelessness, or perhaps hoping some distraction would arise. They drew within a yard of one another, their shadows swapping dominance as they went in a circle, overlapping and again like the game children play by heaping up hands.

No warning; Kurtisian bit. The *Carno* sang and struck so abruptly that the weapon seemed to blink from one side of his body to the other. A flap of the ogre's crude armour flopped open, and the monster started; Kurtisian, still leering, darted a glance at its midsection. Across its squash of a stomach was a thin red line, which didn't seem like much until the ogre sucked in a breath. That deed brought the line to leer open, and a red comb of runnels to escape its wet mouth.

Now the ogre was baited, and its breathing gathered pace. A windy brew of panic and rage began to boil behind its chest. Even without a nose, it smelled its death, and in the hopeless glaze of its look was the same proportion of mortal anguish as was the humanoid's share of Mankind. Its club went up for a squash-blow, all strategy gone, duel over.

"*I-eat-you-inside*," it voiced, and the broken words clattered down the gory hillside of its chin.

The black branches of Kurtisian's limbs began to shake at the ready. "I ain't that kind of dance partner, *pathice*. Buy me dinner first."

The club hit its peak, and seemed like the suns to have reached a point too high to fall. The ogre's body gathered and craned. An explosion began to build in its throat. It was all so ridiculously slow that Kurtisian could not hide his impatience. The *Carno* hissed twice, and the upraised club wobbled—a wet heavy sound, as of a great load of fish being dumped onto a dock. The fuhrbido had finished his task, and the ogre stood eviscerated. It stood there dumbly for a moment, poised like some infernal statue—a war-demon with wormy tongues lolling out of its gut—then crumpled half over backwards. Its roots severed, the club could no longer choose how it fell, and came down to bounce from its wielder's own head.

Already looking to the next battle, Kurtisian wasted no time in doing his foeman mercy, seizing the *Carno* with two hands to one slot, and axing it into the neck. The head did not roll, but the strike did its work. The fourth of the manshfretters lay dead on the grass.

He at once had to leap to safety as the grappling mass of Justinian and his own opponent came reeling from the west, an enormous tumbleweed of flesh—four-armed and four-legged—which caught its heels and went down into a spidering fury. The vast share of it was dark—a great storm meaning to swallow the small, bronze-coloured sun at its heart. The mighty ogre seemed to have enshrouded Justinian, and it was only when the monstrous limbs shifted, opening and groping for better purchase, that flashes of the Man met the eye. Kurtisian stalked the rim of their contest, hurling words into its heart. Tonics and bolsters he gave to his brother, reminders of worse battles won, and for the ogre savage mongrels of Allmal and *Linguish* whose teeth were likely blunted on one so thick.

So crippling were the odds that Justinian's strategy was one and only—to keep simply from being dominated, and so by not losing perchance come to victory. Even against an opponent one's own size, wrestling was an arduous trial. Its exertion enjoyed no reprieve, no opportunity to clash briefly and withdraw, to catch one's breath and await another opening. Once joined, the combatants fought with tension rather than with impact, one opposing the torque of the other, and endeavouring with sudden bursts and rearrangement to strike upon the slack underbellying every resisting part. Like the squirrel who, treed, seeks to keep the trunk between itself and its observer, one read and reversed his opponent's movements, taut and defiant not simply until caught but informed he'd been caught. So much a part of the game was contraposition and stubbornness that only an amateur or weakling was ever conquered by strength alone.

Justinian believed this as much as any true wrestler, and though a born ruffian and a veteran of the chalk ring since long before taking up the cloth of the Brasmat, he was as outsized in this contest as a ten-year-old child to a well-fed working man. His opponent, for its immensity, was able to drape itself over him, clutching at the backs of his legs even as Justinian faced into its stomach. The creature's body was everywhere, its girths uncircumnavigable, its strength dispiriting beyond the reassurances of strategy. Wherever it seized him, the crush of its grip reached the bone. Its force, when its lifting and pulling found leverage, was something that might tear Justinian apart if he relaxed for a moment the skeletal knit of his thews. On top of all this, the distraction of the thing's unMannish noises and odours was irrepressible. This bothered Justinian most, whose worst opponents had been known, among other tactics involving flatulence and unctions of pig manure, to resort to tonguing obscenities into his ear on vomit-baited breaths. This opponent, however, was no Man, and everything from the abysmal pitch of its snarling to the emasculating potency of its musk told him this was no storm to try to swim through. *Back off, gain a vessel and crew, tack about its edge if you have to*, it warned, but do not on your life measure this thing with your bare arms alone.

Such a deficit would, in any other wrestler, have justified recourse to the biting, scratching, and groping for soft stuff which made a fight of a contest, and enemies of contestants. Justinian, however, had kept it a competition, trusting in the holds and limb-locks which, put to an opponent this size, was like the tying of tree trunks into bows. Several maneuvers he had not been able to secure, and several others did no damage. Even with the monster's knees knotted firmly in a *nodus textoris*[21]—a hold which in normal circumstances might dislocate both joints—he could not, for all his strength, exert enough pressure even to distract the monster's own assault. He had been forced to forsake the hold, a dangerous decision from which the ogre had regained its feet, but since taking advantage of the body of his brother's victim to knock the creature down again, Justinian had somehow managed to close the *lamh-alef*—a combination ankle-hold and leglock which he forgot he had learned until he was in the perfect place to apply it.

His *palestra*[22] in Sallupus had considered it an exotic hold, and the *exercitor* taught it on a whim one Saturnday afternoon. It was a field submission maneuver, born in the desperation of disarmed combat far to the south, and because it could only properly be used against opponents much larger than its applicant, it was almost useless in a sport where contestants are pitted according to weight. It was, nonetheless, a punishing move, and a gambit. The *not-of-knots* it was bynamed, both for its penchant to undo an opponent, and to warn of the momentary vulnerability of whoever employed it. In occupying the wrestler's whole body to immobilize only the legs of his opponent, the opponent's arms were free to attack him. Once the

---

[21] *(L)*: "weaver's knot"

[22] *(L):* a wrestling school, similar to a *ludus* for gladiators, but for citizens rather than professionals or slaves. Called a *wraxl* in the Braccish tongue.

hold was secured, however—the one leg locked by the knee and the other twisted by the ankle, the wrestler strung sideways between the thighs of his opponent, and somewhat in the shape of the *Almuhit* character for which the move was named[23]—the torsion became torturous, and a Man might wring from a giant cries of agony and for mercy. Justinian had not been a submission wrestler—such a thing was held more akin to the slave sports than to the Games, and offered no respectable circuit—but even as a young athlete and the son of a noted vintner, he had entertained the teerseeker's life in which he now found himself, and had learned what he could to rack a foe's body. Now that Justinian had locked in the *lamh-alef*, and the ogre's thrashing served only to amplify the torsion of its knee and ankle, the Sumo knew enough not to pop the joints, but rather to do everything to keep them from popping—to push the bones and sinews to their uttermost strain, and back off before they came apart.

Kurtisian saw his brother's success and went wild, leaping once on the spot and craning toward the match like a trainer confined to his corner. It took Justinian's whole strength to do it, but he made the ogre bellow, its body flattening and its great arms drumming the ground in pain. Justinian backed off, as much to relieve his own exertion as to let the joint resettle. The ogre recovered the same instant. It sat up and reached forward, fumbling for purchase, groping for limbs to seize and pry open. When its fingers failed to find them before Justinian began to twist again, it turned to its nails, which were long and hooked, blunt-sharp like the claws of a dog. Bare against the Allmetal, Justinian's hide was protected by the Brasmat, but that blessed curing was not proof against everything— the ogre's hands, doubtless able to gut a tree trunk of its grainwood, was too much for its tegument. The claws pressed and trembled, and blood welled about their ends. Together, with the sound of coulters breaking through shale, they dragged deep ditches.

The blood ran into the deep valleys among the Sumo's brawn, but the wounds seemed only to embellish him. Justinian, less enraged by the pain than by his opponent's abandonment of the contest, began to wrench and flex the creature's joint to and fro, as one might do to rip a living bough from its trunk. "*Fraudatrix!*" he spat between bursts. "Famsapping cheater! *Edem merdam antequam*

---

[23] The alphabet in which a number of southern languages, including Biten al-Yasan, are written. One of these languages is itself called *Almuhit*.

perdam!"[24] At last, with the absence of sound that was all the grislier, the ogre's left leg achieved an unnatural angle.

The monster made a noise which, for its pitch, it was clearly unaccustomed to making. Justinian knew it for the worst horror the mighty can know—to be stranded between death and mending, crippled rather than scarred, and trapped forever beyond the dignity of a proud stand, much less a good death. Kurtisian's cackling whoop crowned the cry—a noise only slightly less wonted to its maker—and the fuhrbido applauded uproariously, having threaded one arm through the grip slot of the *Carno* in order to do so without disarming. Unshouldering the massive limb which now flopped like a beached porpoise, Justinian elbowed aside the ogre's fingers and shot both hands beneath its loincloth, seizing upon the broken rules of their match with disgusted zeal and bringing to an end his opponent's unmanning.

New discord escaped the ogre's throat, trillings of panic atop a sonority of rage. Even from such a place it was able to send out blows, however, and Justinian turned away his face as best he could to avoid the worst of it. Blood painted his arms and shoulders, in smudges and in runnels, but it was not until one swipe opened twin trenches across his brow that he seemed at all fazed. Now the red flood surged into his eyes, overwhelming the thick dikes of his eyebrows, and he tossed his head in an attempt to drain it. The distraction left him unguarded, and the ogre's next blow hit him like a ram. One of his hands came loose, and his head wobbled on his neck, causing him to reel where he knelt between the ogre's open thighs, dazed and bloodied and looking like a midwife hired to Hell. The Allmetal had disappeared, having leapt behind his back with the force of the blow. Its chain was like a garrote about Justinian's throat. Blood rimmed upon it, and droplets broke through like it had already bitten.

The Sumo was beaten. Had the next blow landed, it would have eggshelled his face. It was before then, however, that his audience forsook the stands to intervene. Not until Justinian had recovered his wits and begun drubbing away at the monster did he notice the brute's movements to be aimless. Still blinking away the red cloud in

---

[24] The fraternal motto of Justinian's wrestling squad, uttered together in a private circle which is closed to the *exercitores. (L):* "I'll eat shit before I lose."

his eyes, he went for a headlock and found his opponent without a head. His fierce lunge, finding no purchase, sent him sprawling.

The ogre's noggin lay a few feet away, face-down, and made to eat grass. Straddling the ghastly pumpkin was Kurtisian, the *Carno* dripping red beads.

"Sorry, fra." The fuhrbido looked genuinely contrite as he offered his brother a hand up. He mimicked the accent of Knaksmen. "You were in a plightly heap of peril there."

"No hard feelings," Justinian replied.

Shielding his bloodstained eyes from the sunlight, he reached up and took the hand, intending to pull himself up but proceeding to pull Kurtisian down on top of him. The smaller man made a tetchy noise and picked himself up again. He smoothed himself and prodded his brother, urgently but not unsympathetically, with a boot.

"Got to get up, fra," he said. "Gorrh has his mouth full of those lupins, and Toron took a bad one to the head. Don't know if he's still in it."

That made Justinian chuckle to himself, but not with any mirth. He loosed a titanically reluctant groan and rolled over onto one knee, exposing to view the many ugly splotches on that side of his body. His flesh bled beneath the unbroken skin wherever the ogre had clutched at him. His head lolled forward, staring at the ground. He looked like someone waiting for the chop.

"Just—just need a minute."

Seeing the blood still dribbling from his brow, Kurtisian planted the *Carno* in the grass and untied one of the leather bands from about his arms. He quickly ran it about his brother's head and knotted it in the back.

Justinian guffawed again as he finished. "Now instead of looking like I've had the shit beaten out of me, I look like a *mujahid*[25] who's had the shit beaten out of me."

"Come on, Justin." Kurtisian did what he could to put his arms about the man's enormous trunk. "Come on, fra. Not finished yet. A couple more flies to swat. The hard part's over. A couple more. Just a couple more."

With noise and effort on both sides, the Chaldallions lifted the Sumo back to his full height, and Justinian replaced the Allmetal between the mounds of his pectorals. He staggered a little but

---

[25] *(Biten al-Yasa*n): one who fights in holy war.

remained standing, and gave the corpse of his opponent a vicious kick in the thigh. The limb barely wobbled. So enormous was the brute that it was difficult to believe it had been able to sneak up on anyone.

"Aww, *gods*," Justinian whimpered, tracing the clawmarks on his chest with a finger. "I could pedicate Bastet and end up in better shape than this." He glanced back at the dead chieftain. "What was that you were saying before about monsters and enchanted items?"

But his brother had already charged away.

Down the trail past two more bodies, Toron knelt where he had fallen only moments before. The pain in his head hummed toward bursting. His sight had become a flickering smear of things—a black river flooding and foaming over bright rocks, shredding and swallowing the banks that kept it in. He could hear the sounds of the big cat holding back the newcomers, and he could, if he tried, grope his way toward the fray with his mind alone. He did not, however, know what good he might do there, for he did not as yet feel enough needfulness in Gorrh's plight to hurl himself blind into a grindstorm of teeth. Mortha he still had, but Tuger was behind him somewhere, and the weight of the wetness in his clothes and boots felt much heavier than it should have. He began to think about home, and knew it for the plea of a dying man to that share of himself that still had strength left to him.

Kurtisian gained his side first, dropping a hand across the man's wrist lest he lash out with his sword. "We're here, Thorn. Me and Justin. You hold it together just a little longer. In no time, no time at all, we'll be in the city biting coals[26]. No time at all. You hold it together."

Toron chuckled at the Harandrish saying, and nodded wearily. He pushed himself to his feet, and the fuhrbido stood before him as a black smudge swimming in the green.

"The ogres are all done with," Kurtisian said, laying the *Carno* blade-up across his shoulder. "It's just these hairy bastards now. Looks like they waited until we did all the heavy lifting before getting here." A shadow flitted across him, and he looked up. "Huh. There goes Urien again—back towards the city. Looks like he went

---

[26] A *Harandrish* expression — to be a coalbiter is to be a layabout, or one who sits by the hearth all day instead of working.

and got his pack off the trail. Better not have taken anything of ours."

Justinian arrived then as well, his own shadow flickering as he scooped up a rock and hurled it up at the retreating fairy-thing that had once been their guide. "Little prick. Led us and fed us, both to the dogs."

Kurtisian snortled. "That's a good one, Justin. We'll get you a stool and a feathered hat when we get to the city, and you can recite that shit on a street corner."

"Better'n what you sell on a street corner, *culibone*."

The fight roared up, and drowned their banter. Its discord had become infernal, as though it would shatter earth and sky. Gorrh seemed disoriented, and after watching two of their pack fall the remaining wolfmen were attacking him with abandon. Two of them had boarded the saddle, gripping its edges with prehensile paws as they sought chances for their teeth. One got ahold of Gorrh's ear. Another on the ground bit down on his tail and was jerked flailing from its feet. Three more of the things remained arrayed before the cat's eastern flank, pacing and striking and withdrawing again like a school of toothed fish seeking to bleed its prey out. Swatting the air so lustily that it fluted through his claws, Gorrh did enough to keep them from piling on or getting past him. It was clear, however, that he had become somewhat deranged, and those who knew him, and could see Toron slumping on his own feet, did not need it laid out for them what was happening.

Kurtisian swallowed wetly. "What does he want us to do?"

"He wants the saddle cut off." Toron fought to shape the words. "It's the thing I was trying to do before the blasted clover pulled me down."

Justinian took half a step forward. "Wherever those lupins are from, they don't seem too eager to get past him. Those two smaller ones in the back look like they don't want to be here at all." He looked to his brother. "Which *Ultrices* do you have left?"

"Except for the *redballs*, all of them. Don't know if any of them will do us any good here, though. Have to attract one of those lupins and put him right in front of me, and they all look pretty content with the mess they're in now.

Justinian took another step. "How long would it take you to crack open *Marat* and just get the *redballs* back?"

Kurtisian shooed the idea with a hand, grimacing like he had explained it all a thousand times. "Can't. Have to open the channels first, no matter what I want back. Whether—" and he had to pitch his voice above the noise—"whether you want a dozen eggs or just one, it still takes a long walk to the henhouse."

"The *Carno*, then."

The fuhrbido was nettled. "Do you see something in front of us that I don't? Because what I see is a millwheel of teeth and fur, a quarter of which we don't want to hurt. *Carno* or not, how are you or I or anyone else supposed to walk into that and do anything productive?"

Justinian seemed to deflate. "Can I throw rocks at them?"

"Not without hitting the cat," Kurtisian muttered, his head bobbing as he followed the wolfmen's movements. A sudden insight pulled at the edges of his mouth. "Seems to me, they're staying close to Gorrh because they know we won't risk hurting him by getting involved. Or risk ourselves."

"Still," said Justinian, "that's a damn nasty shield they're hiding behind. Why don't they simply take the chance to flee? Hairn, I'd let them go."

"I don't know. Maybe you should ask them."

And then one of the creatures was before them. It was the one who had seized Gorrh's tail in its jaws, and was thrown nearly at the feet of the three men in the same way an overthrilled angler might pole-snap a fish straight from river to shore.

The manner in which it alighted, however, showed no hint of unease. Its long limbs caught the ground and rolled like the spokes of a rimless wheel, the turning of its body unwinding the strength with which it had been hurled. The slavering thing recovered before it had even stopped, but Kurtisian had seen it coming. For a wide wasting sweep of the *Carno* there was no space, but the fuhrbido had foreseen that too. The wolfman half-collided with Justinian as the Sumo tried to leap to one side, but Kurtisian's eyes were already kindled, and his free hand shot out like a jab.

What he spoke was mired up in the mad snarlings of his target, but there came a clap like someone had opened a jar of thunder. The air itself shocked, and sent out a small wobble. Kurtisian, Toron, and Justinian had their hair blown back. The wolfman, still wheeling, looked to have struck a wall. Its body went flat while still upright, arms at its sides and neck craned. It stood there for a moment, then fell backwards like something chopped and wooden.

Waggling their heads and massaging swears from their faces, the three Men looked only slightly less stricken by the blow than the one who had taken its brunt. Toron went to one knee again, and Kurtisian sought to flex his eyes back into focus.

Justinian stamped his feet in a brief tantrum, like someone trying to shake rats from his pantlegs. "-ing *Hairn,* Kurtis! A famsapping *Thunderfist* and we're all standing right here—"

His eyes back in service, Kurtisian began to flex his jaw. "It worked, didn't it?"

The lupin lay there and writhed slowly, as if having a bad dream. Its blunt muzzle and low-set ears made it look more like a wingless bat—or one of the stone waterspitters of Tarmateriza[27]—than like something of houndkind. But its eyes were furious in its head, staring out of its stun like those of a prisoner within it. The noise rolling from its throat was bestial but not beastly, the unsettling sound an older infant might make when toying with the range of its voice. In the span of a single breath, the fiend regained strength; whatever had been done to it, the creature would soon recover.

With the sorry scrap of stealth he could muster, Justinian shook off his fit and crept away from Toron's side, coming up behind the thing and aiming to crush its skull beneath his heel. The fanged brigand disliked the idea, and snapped wildly at the Man's upraised foot. Justinian flinched, as much from the sudden mad racket as from its teeth. The following moment, the thing had somehow coiled itself about the Sumo's ankle, blustering and tearing as it sought to climb his leg.

Justinian bounded back a step, dragging the hateful monster along with him. "Leggo, you bastard! Kurtis! Getim off!"

One arm out for balance, unable to kick at the thing, Justinian shuffled back toward his thoftmen. His look was more repulsed than alarmed—that of a man who had stepped in something putrid and now sought an edged surface to scrape it to. Kurtisian complied, his face wincing with every gust of the creature's screaming.

The hairy body parted before the *Carno* like soft cheese. It gaped gore and fell from his brother's leg, and Kurtisian took off its head

---

[27] A coastal mountain kingdom to the northeast of the Kingdom of Knaks, known for its dour, towering stonework and statues which, devilish, are intended to frighten off the creatures they resemble. Known also as *gargoyles.*

with a butcher's indifference. The parts of the carcass each twitched a bit, and Justinian kicked the head toward the bushes on the south side of the path.

"Lycanthropes," he remarked, watching the corpse slowly lose its hair and shrink. The head, wherever it came to rest, would be found as the head of a man.

"All of them are," Kurtisian said, pointing with his chin towards Gorrh's arena. Both of the other fallen creatures had been replaced by the bodies of swarthy men, as pale and nude as they were broken.

"Naked as a baboon's ass," Justinian tsked. "How humiliating."

Kurtisian flicked beads of blood off the *Carno*. "A baboon's entirely naked, you idiot."

"If they're werewolves," Toron croaked from where he knelt, "make sure you cut off their heads."

"Will do, Thorn."

Toron crutched himself up again, swearing as he staggered the few steps between them. Though Justinian had warned him, he caught his foot on the wolfman's body and nearly went over. Kurtisian caught him, but the southerner's face was unhelpful.

"Maybe you should sit, Thorn. There you go. A nice, warm bench for you."

Toron felt the soft cushion of the corpse beneath him. The odours of the thing, both inner and outer, were strong, but they did not bother him. He was a homesteader's son, and no maiden to a slaughterhouse. "Can't bloody see," he murmured offwardly. "Can't bloody...where is my other sword?"

Justinian made to look back for it, but Kurtisian stopped him with a touch and firm shake of his head. Before them, Gorrh continued his blind war against the lupins, and although he had done well against so many, his foe seemed now to understand that the big cat had lost one or more of his senses. The knowledge gave them new strength and haste, and they began to open holes in his defenses, two of them drawing him with barks and half-bites while the others leapt to tear at the thews of his hind legs. The ring of them worked like one living thing, swapping tasks from side to side as their mark turned, each knowing his part without the other's speech or gesture. They would lunge, seize, and release before the cat could find his bearings, and as tufts of his hair began to litter the grass, and blood dappled his hide, it was as though Gorrh was trapped within their belly already, being eaten by an enemy who was everywhere at once.

Every few moments, one of the wolfmen would return to his back, tearing at his ears, and Gorrh would roll to dislodge him. Each time he did so, the saddle dug more deeply into the ground, making it harder for him to return upright before the creatures hurled themselves at his undersides. His roars, though still mighty, no longer lorded over the fray, but rose keening from its turmoil like the cries of one defiant but overrun.

One of the wolfmen, a black one, latched onto his hamstring and swung there like a pitdog from the throat of a bull. Toron flinched and reached for his own lower leg, rubbing it briskly like one might the sting of a bee. Gorrh at last knocked the leech loose, but the harm was done, and he limped as he wheeled, and that leg took his weight.

"Better toss him a rope," Kurtisian said, though very uneagerly. "He could probably finish them off himself, but those lupins are going to make a mess of him first."

"Get the saddle off of him," Toron urged. Each word was like an earthworm pulled from hard ground, squirming and half-torn. "He can do what's left."

His patience boiling over, Kurtisian pivoted and spat. "And how in the Hells am I supposed to—"

Justinian had time for a single bray of alarm, and the armoured, wolf-infested hillside of Gorrh was before them. The tuskcat had reached them with a single, guess-measured bound, and calmly presented his flank. Kurtisian took a swipe at the wolfman still atop the saddle, but the creature leapt to safety on the cat's opposite side. Wasting no time, and leaving to his brother the work of warding off the lupins, Kurtisian dropped the *Carno* and attacked with his hands the leather bramble of tethers and buckles lying beneath the rim of the saddle. A dozen riveted sections and straps confronted him, many caked with the dirt and grass of Gorrh's repeated rollovers. Some of the smaller bindings, it was clear, were for securing baggage to the saddle, and hung unused, but others were mired up, and may have belonged either to the saddle or to the armour winking beneath it.

"A mess in here—" Kurtisian reported, his voice a wave coming to shore.

Justinian ducked in. "Lemme see—"

A new squall of beastnoise broke out, and the hill tossed as Gorrh swatted at things on the other side. Toron had to scream to be heard. "There are only two bindings—the breast and the girth. Forget the others!"

Kurtisian echoed the instructions to himself, over and over, as he bobbed and probed to fulfill them.

"Right there! Right there!" Justinian said, then leapt back to his feet as a hairy arm swiped at him through the gap. "Find the buckle!"

"Shit, it's on the other side. It's on the other side!"

"Thorn, he's gotta turn around! He's gotta—"

And Toron's voice, scrambling above it all, cried, "Cut it, by Hern!"

Kurtisian grunted his approval and took up the *Carno*. One tip of his blade, pressed and dragged, was all it took, and the whole weave came apart. Straps fell like chopped locks of hair, and buckles bounced from the earth. A handful of chainlinks fell too, and Gorrh's roar reared up in delectation as his body rippled out from beneath every manmade trapping upon him.

"*Shee-it*," Kurtisian said between his teeth. "Took off a little too much, Thorn."

The saddle, tackle, and armour sloughed off like the shell of something shucked, and Gorrh's unbound entirety went wild with freedom. Like a tawny mass of smoke he seemed, flying and reshaping himself in the winds with no right side up, limbs leaping out from the core so quickly and suddenly that, had one not seen him at rest, one could not be sure of their number. He became inescapable, everywhere at once, and when one of the harried wolfmen again leapt to his back, presuming perhaps to seek refuge behind the hunter's own eyes, Gorrh went over like nothing born on land, crushing the creature ruthlessly between jaws of earth and brawn. In a blink, though, the legged serpent that was a tuskcat had regained his feet. The wolfman too sprang up again, like a tough trampled weed, returning to full height for only an instant before its limbs knew themselves broken. The wolfman began to crumple, but was uprooted entirely before it could fall, Gorrh's paw striking him so hard that blood stood in the air where it happened. The Chaldallions themselves gasped with the violence of it, and the broken monster ragdolled into the thicket.

"*Now* they consider escaping," Kurtisian said, watching the three last wolfmen back toward the woods.

Justinian chortled blackly. "But he's not going to let them."

And sure enough, Gorrh leapt through and ahead of them, blocking their flight and penning them between himself and the three Men he traveled with. The wolfmen's movements, so brisk before, now slipped hesitantly from one to the next, and looks of fearful frustration—looks unmistakably Mannish—tamed the bestial leers on their faces.

"Gods, thofties," Justinian said, "we could just let them go. City's around the corner. Beds, a little booze, all that. Gods, we could just let them go…"

"They weren't planning to let us go," Kurtisian replied, though he sounded a little sorry to say it.

Justinian sighed lustily, letting the air fart and flap through his lips. "Prime. You take the one on that side. Toron, tell Gorrh to go for the—"

The wolfmen made a mad break for it then, the three of them trying three different directions. Justinian went for the one on his left, then changed his mind with a shriek when he saw Gorrh opt and charge for the same one. The big cat's sight, however crippled it was, seemed no hindrance at all. Unharassed by the pack, he bore down the rangy creature without sport, and it became among his teeth and claws nothing more than another piece of meat.

Of the two other wolfmen, one headed right, into the woods leading down to the valley. It was the only one to escape. The other, perhaps hoping his packmates would split the two men still standing, pelted straight up the middle. Kurtisian let the first one go and confronted the last, knowing he would never catch a beast among the trees, and that the third would escape in the meantime, likely after mauling Toron on his way past. His chosen opponent gathered speed as it made for its freedom, and although the nimbleness of the villain threatened to send it past him with the slightest change of course, Kurtisian did not waver. He braced himself, and with his left hand hurled the *Carno* like a dinner plate. It flashed as it gyrated, wobbling without grace, and even if it had struck, it would likely have done so with its unsharpened side. Kurtisian had not, however, thrown to hit. When the wolfman dodged the blade, and did so easily, it had run out of room to maneuver, and the fuhrbido was there to meet it.

He and his foe both screamed at once, and their bodies met in a tangle. Limbs tied, and they went to the ground writhing and pulling at the knots, the wolfman clawing and snapping as Kurtisian sought slack for a strike, or for a soft place to bury a knee or elbow. The contest had hardly begun when the creature showed its advantage, its raw strength much greater than the Man's, and the reach of its arms and legs too long to restrain. Equally clear was its will to escape rather than to fight, with its body arching and lurching away from its captor rather than straining to close with him. So it was that Kurtisian, whether to set the wild thing free or merely to check his disadvantage, untied his own arms and let the lupin scramble off. But as it leapt back towards a run, the wolfman found its paths all closed, with Gorrh, Justinian, and even Toron arrayed in a half-ring before it, the latter wobbling and staring slightly in the wrong direction. Its lips peeled back, the thorny red gums shedding their rind. The thing seethed where it stood. Behind him rose Kurtisian, and the ring readjusted, the gaps between its parts each a trap to spring shut. Dead in its centre, the wolfman slowly turned, its eyes drawing burning lines among its four adversaries—from Gorrh to Justinian, to Toron, to Kurtisian, to Gorrh and over again—a game of roulette, but whose spin was unsound. So maniacal in motion, the creature seemed unreal while at rest, a ewe's vision of Hell, or a taxidermist's prank, but surely not something that walked with a beating heart.

"Nowhere to go, *canicula*," Kurtisian announced. "Just a choice of which block to put your head on."

The thing let out a growl, but one that sounded more like the clearing of its throat than a threat. Though shrouded by its beastly mask, thoughts could be seen to ripple across its face.

"Will it talk?" Justinian asked, addressing the wolfman itself as much as anyone else.

The creature's body went rigid, as if jerked by a leash. Its breathing slowed, its mouth closed, and it looked at the Sumo fixedly. Its eyes were black moons in a white sky, colours as backward as its nature. Several moments passed, till Kurtisian broke the silence, as well as the monster's gaze.

"It can understand us, it seems."

Justinian studied it. "Might not speak the Allmal though."

The creature half-turned to the fuhrbido, dropping nothing of its newly Mannish composure. It looked at him too, but still did not respond. Kurtisian returned the stare icily, his fingers flexing in their gloves. A few moments later and the corner of his mouth showed the collapse of his patience.

"Justin, what do you ask a castrated lycanthrope?"

"I dunno."

"O where, wolf, are your balls?"

"Good stuff, *fra.*"

"Wait, I have another one. In Linguish. *Cur verbum 'lupa' et pornam et lupum feminum adsignificat?*"[28]

Justinian shook his head.

"*Quia it ad lupabus ut sit cum canibus.*"

Justinian shook his head.

"*Canibus. Cunno bis. Audisne?*"

"Yeah, yeah, I hear it now that you've beaten it flat for me." Justinian glanced over at Toron. "Sorry, Thorn. Can't carry that one into the Allmal without killing it all over again."

Toron's groan sounded too weary to be unthildy[29]. Gorrh's roar, so furious that it blew the skeins of gore sideways on his tusks, did not.

Kurtisian sighed with mock irritation, an artist among the unwashed. "Never mind. It's over this one's head anyway." He reached up and undid his cloak, and when it withdrew he stood with fists cocked high. "Not going to talk, bitch? Then I'll make you sing."

The werewolf's eyes flicked to the *Carno*, lying whither it had spun. Kurtisian, half-following the glance, did not turn his whole head.

"Don't worry. It stays where it lays. I don't *need it*—" And his last words were jettisoned as the wolfman sprang.

The fuhrbido's tongue needed room, and he made it. It was only a small show, the *Ultrix* he invoked, for among the small number of incantations which Kurtisian could read of *Marat*—among the twenty-two dwimmers, strikes and maneuvers which took up the first eleven pages of that ponderous tome—it was perhaps the least marvelous, though doubtless one of the most useful. Kurtisian called it the *ictus anteprimus*—the blow that comes before the first—but the thoftship knew it better as the *Lightning Punch*, for it struck so quickly that one saw it a full blink of the eyes before one heard it. If one blinked as it struck, one did not see it at all.

Though unleashed by magic, the *Ultrix* struck with no magical

---

[28] "Why does the word *lupa* mean both prostitute and female wolf?"

[29] *(AK)*: impatient.

force. The strength of the blow was in the terrific speed with which it flew. Because of this, the *ictus anteprimus* was always a hazardous choice, with the striker in no way reinforced for the impact. The enormous load, unmitigated by the powers that discharged it, was born fully by the fuhrbido's own knuckles, bones, and sinews.

It was a detail, Shard had once explained, of which the dreeless magentile was commonly unaware—that a spell, like a recipe, had no foresight in itself. Whatever it made often left out some ingredient crucial to the caster's taste, and the dreeman had to brace himself for its shortcomings. A spell to up the strength of one's body might only affect the muscles and tendons, leaving the skin of the hands to split, or bones to splinter, if that strength were pushed too far. An enchantment to harden the skin against the penetration of blades might, like chainmail, fail to protect against bludgeoning and crushing blows. A charm that allowed one to breathe underwater might not allow him to sink to deep depths and rise again without contracting the same bubbling sickness of the blood that plagued oyster-divers.[30] Dreecraft was a perilous trade, and spells were the ficklest of tools.

The finding and—if possible—patching of flaws such as these made up the shakedown time of any new spell. It was also the most intricate task of the spellmakers themselves, whoever they were who coaxed new definitions from old chaos. Nonetheless, some spells began and stayed imperfect—perhaps the offspring of creators more intent on creating than on cultivating, or shaped for a deadline, or for a single, pressing use. Sometimes the flaws of a spell seemed innate, or essential, rather than owed to some negligence on the part of its maker. Such shortcomings were concessions of a sort, a weakening of its character in some area in order to strengthen others.

The lodes of magic were legion, as were the methods by which its powers were drawn and shaped—from the wild mages who plunged their hands into raw quintessence and sculpted anew with every casting, to the wizard-scholars who worked only in classes and categories, and from their endless, endless books. However chaotic it seemed, there was indeed a balance to it all, a heart to its many veins, which weighed effect against competence, and kept the tolls tidy. Some masterly magics could at times be wielded by apprentices, but with equally powerful drawbacks, for only as the

---

[30] the bends.

spellcaster became more proficient—only as his experience brought him greater authority among the legislatures of magic—did the workings of his spells become more dependable.

Whether *Lightning Punch*—or *Spark of Life,* or *Redball*, or *Djinni Kick*, or *Thunderpunch*—would become more powerful as Kurtisian himself improved depended on the nature of fuhrbido magic, and not even Shard had known enough of it to say. Perhaps, he had offered, the *Ultrices* were like single routes, and could not be redrawn—or, better, they were more like destinations, and could eventually and with further orientation be reached more quickly. In either case, they would remain ever the same, and find improvement only in their uses, like tools in the hands of different men.

But there was also the possibility that the dreecraft answered to the dreeman—that the magic was shaped by his skills, and not simply wielded by them. Each *Ultrix* would thus be like a pupil who would flourish beneath the fuhrbido's own growth, maturing as well as multiplying, and with every stage becoming something better, an maybe unforeseen. This, Shard had explained, was the most powerful kind of wizardry, whose magic had the power ultimately to write new laws, and not simply to play at their limits. Each spell offered a gamut rather than a single song, even as a deck of cards holds within it the chance of all possible hands, or a dictionary every story to be told. Such magic held the utmost potential, and its master the power for its uttermost expression.

Kurtisian, whose skills had not improved in several years, had seemed both encouraged and disheartened by Shard's claims, buoyed up but more than a little put off by the outlander's superior knowledge of his own craft. Toron though had been utterly enthralled, and spent many nights afterwards staring long and gloomily into the hammer-beaten metal of his swords. Such fromkinnish[31] things they seemed in the face of magic—little more than sharpened stones; the weapons of a firehuddler. If Rhianys had still lived, he would have begged her to teach him something of the *arwydd*, as she called her own gift—a single step of the dance, one line of the song—anything that might breathe upon the cold coals of his magentile's mind and make some share of it sparkle.

He would never know whether she could have done so, just as he never knew whether Kurtisian had challenged the werewolf to a

---

[31] *(AB):* primitive.

fistfight because he thought he could defeat it, or because he knew his thoftmen would not let him lose. Either way, and whether the *Lightning Punch* would one day improve to reinforce the bones of the fist that bore it, Kurtisian broke his good hand on the wolfman's skull, and it was no mild fracture.

The godflaying curse he sent up was in Linguish rather than Allmal, and although Toron had neither seen what had happened nor understood the word, its gist was unmistakable. It was at about that same moment that he found he could no longer stay standing, and went sideways and down as the gods—perhaps offended by the oath—tipped the world on its end. Most of what happened afterwards he heard from where he lay.

Kurtisian was disciplined enough not go to pieces when his wrist did, and mounted a hearty defense as the wolfman recovered and struck back. But with his grip and fist both a ruin, the southman could neither wield the *Carno* nor deal another blow. Bewildered by the storm of pain, his mind could not find its bearings, but groped from shock to fear toward the thickets of his whats, well away from any premeditated strategies. There was noise—a wet roil of cries both beastly and Mannish—and then the voice and shifting shadows of Justinian moving in. Swearwords wove together and tangled, enmeshing and muffling something furious beneath them. A trough of hush fell between the peaks, a wave rose again, and something shouted above it all. And then it was Kurtisian, his wrath stemming above the tumult, blooming and bursting and blotting out the sun of all sound, the disheveled music of a citizen giving it back to his madman. Then came the gruesomest hammering—the damp gather and smash—of the madman's assault on what met him.

Only as Toron's ears began to join his eyes in emptiness did the geyser of that fury abate. The cacophony shrank between the pieces of the world, and it all settled back into the picture he knew. A hush began to seal the cracks, followed by a last sudden uproar. The pieces leapt out of place then were calm again.

But this was a calmness that stung, like the spreading venom of a wasp crushed but not escaped. There was trouble in Justinian's comfort, and Kurtisian's answer, and Gorrh's own, aghast alarm.

The fuhrbido had not died, but on a whim had done something stupider.

He'd fed the wolfman his arm, baiting the lycanthropic bite. It took the invitation eagerly.

Toron went to the dark.

Heartbeats rapped at the windows.

Something jostled the dark.

"-rn."

"Thorn."

"*Hm.*"

"Thorn."

"Yes."

"Thorn. Sorry. I know you're not in a good way, but you're going to have to carry her. You and Gorrh. Kurt's broke his hand. We'll need a medic in Eksar. For all of us. But especially for her."

Before Toron could speak again, a spidery bundle of limbs was slipped into his arms. Cold hair brushed past his wet face and stuck to it, and he was engulfed by the smell of outland blooms, a florilegium for which he had no single names. The crook of his arm cradled a heavy head.

Beneath him twitched the mountain of his steed-brother, rising and falling with breaths still cooling from the fight. The cat's heartbeat throbbed like underground drums. Toron was back in the saddle, which was itself back on Gorrh. Packs crowded into his legroom, dangling where the Chaldallions had hastily secured them.

"A moment—" Kurtisian's voice broke in from the other side of him. It sounded pinched and far away. "I'm adjusting the collarbar. It's in the way."

He grunted with pain.

"Let me do it, fra."

"No, it's all right. Just have to put the *Carno* down. Don't want to. Keep thinking there's something else watching us out there."

"Here, Thorn." Toron felt the Sumo's smooth, heavy hands steering his own. "Keep pushing right here."

His trembling fingers were pushed to some coarse dressing, which was tacky and wet. He felt around with his thumbs and met the notch of a collarbone. When he tried to lift the dressing a little, a warm trickle met his touch.

"No!" Justinian snapped. "Here, push harder or she'll bleed out. There, keep it right there. Her neck is shredded, but she really did a dance on that wolf somehow."

"Wolf?" Toron echoed. He felt himself slumping, and put the weight of it into the staunch.

"Yeah, that one that got away. She must have been hiding by the path the whole time, and took him out when he ran past. Didn't hear anything, though. Maybe she was with the poor bastard those ogres clubbed into salsa back there."

Kurtisian finished adjusting Gorrh's collarbar and the woman settled evenly across Toron's haunches. Her head lolled.

"I didn't see a dagger, Justin. I should go look for it."

"No. Forget it, fra."

"I should see. How did she do that to him? I should see. She could be one of them."

"Why in the Hells would they tear the throat out of one of their own? No, let's go. Toron is dropping off again. You staying with us, Thorn?"

"*Sneh.*"

"That a yes or a no?"

"A *sic et non*," the Knaksman answered, and found it too funny.

"*Age*, Kurtisian," Justinian bellowed. "We have to move now. I don't like it here."

They bickered to a standstill, then decided to keep moving.

"Careful," said Kurtisian. "We've had to tie the saddle on with rope. Tell Gorrh to take it slow."

Toron nodded as they went, keeping rigid the litter of his arms, and witnessed the next hour as a broken stageplay, whose black curtains open and shut at random.

From *The Heron's Song*

Amidst the wrack of the former Age did Bluharyn find you, from hopeless yearning fallen and broken-legged, in irons wrought by denial of your own nature bound and by your refusal to breathe the common air strangled...

And Bluharyn said to you, "Your misery is the yield of an unsound tillage, for I ask of you knowing the answer: would you sow a crop in denial of the season, the soil, or your ability to coax its seeds to time of harvest?" And though your mind had broke beneath the onus of your misreckoning, you knew the answer was nay...

And Bluharyn took you by the hand and brought you to the wildest places of the world, and showed you the wuthering heaths and sunlit glades and the strands of the great ocean, its wrinkled sands dressed in the salty dulse, and all of these places were enlivened by the humble industry of wildlife...

And Bluharyn took you and showed you the glory that was the Alleverwood and how its branches, though busy with life and livelihood, went unsullied by those who lived there...

And as you watched them you were filled with a secret shame...

And Bluharyn said, "Behold! Behold them in their sundry tempers and bearings. Behold the vigilance of the owl and the ingenuity of the beaver. Behold the ant's tenacity and the cat's cruelty. Behold..."

"Behold them all and perceive the truth with your eyes alone, for you are not their better but their totality. Like them you eat and sleep, you mate, you bear progeny, and like them you shall always and inescapably die. Behold..."

"Know that your misery was and always will be the yield of ignorance and delusion — of denying the senses which you in the beginning were endowed with…"

"I say to you, then, would you come to happier times — deafen your minds and blind your hearts to all Those Who would instruct you otherwise, Those Who would set you back upon a staircase of Pages, up a rope of Words from which you will only fall again."

"…for even the best of Them are as the parents who wish more for their children than they are fit to obtain…"

Squandered and shameful you were found, and Bluharyn took you by the hand, and led you out from the pit of your fall. Beneath a verdant pall He laid away the wreckage of your cities that they might still be the footing of Life. And upon mended legs Bluharyn set you and told you you were loved, and still free…"

…and though your freedom is the very token of His absence, He set among you mortal proxies who shall until Exanima uphold the creed you cannot read but only see…and to remind you of the perils of closing your eyes again…

From the *Starkheartbook* of Brac the Sleepless

The Age of Life was for all living things, and for that the
Age of Men—the World—was in peril. Man was not a
neighbour to the beasts, but their conqueror. He would not
share. Those four-legged things who took the earth as it was,
and could not shape it, whose only flags were their shit, and
who mated with their own kin—these were not the peers of
Man in this life. They were his food, slaves, and sport. Earning
his affection or proving their use, they became his companions,
and deserved largesse, but were not owed it. For unlike Man, a
beast set free is only ever something shivering in the cold,
something that paws the rocks for its supper, bears its children
in ditches, and dies alone in worse places, to rot or be eaten
beneath the suns.

V
Ofermodig
Highminded

"*Ck'nacks*," the King of Knaks read aloud, and spelt it through a wry smile, "*is not an ancestral form. It seems to have been coined by a Landish poet in the first century of this kingdom—an Abois of the Fosswolds—for whom the Braccish tung was a strange and inconsistent mouthful.*"

The King looked up from the page. "Indeed poetic, Bookman."

"I thank you, King."

Knaks then glanced over at Kween Oyvarr, whose eyes, even in the shadows beneath her forelocks, gave the white flicker of a roll.

"I did not say it pleased me," the King replied. But he laughed heartily, and went on. "*The first occurrence of* Ck'nacks—*that is, with the high comma—is in the poem* Blavor, *'The Blue Boar,' which tells of the rise of the House of Knaks and its wars to unite the Braccish Empire under a single crown—that undertaking which the Braccish tung names the Onelatching.* Blavor *is of middling quality—*." Knaks smiled again, his mind lifting from the page. "Middling quality."

"King?"

Knaks leaned his whole body toward his head scholar. His eyes, whatever his mood, cut what they touched, and the Bookman's two helpers shrank beneath them. "I have heard the *Blavor*, Bookman, and I like it very much."

"It is a stirring lay, King."

Mighty bulk shifted beneath the kingly mantle. "Then why *middling*? And why such a reckoning at all in what is meant to be a book of namelore?"

Blacwell's eyes may have flickered towards one of his helpers. "A fair frayn[1], King."

But Knaks was not done. He seemed despite his baldrishness to be bothered by the matter, and everything in the chamber—from the handful of fires to the shoulders of the atstandands[2]—slumped as beneath a damp and stifling pall.

"I do not," the King went on, "bid my chartwriters and landmeters[3] judge the sights of where they go, but only to mark, tally, and set their findings down for the needs of others."

He stretched a great hand toward Ivrik, his Wyehead[4] of the East, who waited by the hearth. The elderthegn was doing his best to warm himself without seeming to be doing so. Having flown some thousands of furlongs, the Boarsman showed his face raw and chapped by the lofty winds and cold, and with indents still to be seen from the insulated headgear which, though worn to warm, did little at such heights and stretches.

"Do you reckon," Knaks asked, "that Ivrik, who is near to blind from reading such charts, has any care whether Bayerd smells splendid in the fall, or whether its summerly skies are the bluest in the kingdom? Do you, Ivrik?"

"No, King." Even beneath his beard, the thegn looked to have been flogged, and the King's badgering wearied him no further.

"If I should say so, King—" came another voice.

Knaks turned his eyes back toward the Bookman, who looked aghast. The scholar had not opened his mouth; the words had come half from behind him.

Knaks craned his neck in a show, and one of the Bookman's two helpers, a younger man whose white-and-brown robes hung creased and overpressed, took one step sideways out of the shadows of his better. The other helper, a balding man whose eyeglasses goggled what were normally smiling eyes, looked as though he were going to be sick right there.

---

[1] *(AB):* question.

[2] *(AB):* attendants; retinue.

[3] *(AB):* mapmakers and surveyors

[4] *(AB):* military rank, comparable to a general.

"Yes…?" Knaks drew him, the hearthfire popping the hush.

The youngest scholar cleared his throat. "If I might say so, King, the quality of *Blavor* is notorious. The name of the poet, as we now know it, is believed to be a pun. The word *abois* refers to the baying of a hound in the Trebellish tung."

The Bookman called Blacwell trembled slightly, like to a piece of ground being burrowed out deep from below. His words he pushed through the keyhole of a locked smile.

"Our King knows that very well, Arwill."

He spoke to his helper in the same way he might have sneakmurdered him—his words thin and hidden, but sharp and full of thrust. The handful of underlings gathered in the chamber seemed no less eager to stab the outspoken stripling themselves, most of all Kween Oyvarr, who looked even more put out by having to do the deed herself. Away at the hearth, Ivrik and his three marshals were more sullen in their scorn, glaring up and to the side from heads forced down and away, hounds of war long inured to the yipping of untouchable lapdogs in courtly places such as these, where blood could not be spilt freely.

Of them all, it was the face of Knaks that held the least ill will. Fixed high atop those shoulders, mighty for the yoke of the Dright[5], he looked down from above the others, all of whom he overtowered save Oyvarr, whose blood like his own was athelborn. Though his face could not with its iron beard and cloudless eyes be called friendly, it gave forth a light which fostered rather than cowed—a face to hearten his followers, not discourage them.

"Yes, Booknap. You are on the right path. But you stepped onto it halfway, and see where it goes without knowing the lay of the land. Our southernmost Medth is known to most as *Landon*, which means nothing more than 'long hill' in the Braccish tung. The Trebellish are wont to calling the whole Medth *Cascade de Sylve*, which is 'Fosswold,' and the name we give only to the firthland in its southernmost tip. You may find yourself bewildered already, but stay with me.

"The word *landon* is shared by the Braccish and Trebellish tungs, and many men in southernmost Landon speak both. Trebellish was indeed the first tung of that Abois of the Fosswolds who wrote

---

[5] *(AB):* the people of the nation; the royal *thede*. The five original bloodlines of the House of Brac are known as the *Yoredrights*. They are emblematized by the five *Rings*, for which the Kings of Knaks is known, and a byname.

the *Blavor*. And there, Booknap, *landon* has another meaning, which I shall teach you. It serves as a pun, but with two edges. Speakers on either side of the border, whether Knaksmen or *Trebellaises*, wield this word against each other. Landon is a marchland after all, and ever a place of jostling."

Knaks glanced over at Ivrik as he said this, and the eyes of both men were hard. And though this hardness was not against one another, but in thoftship, a dusk came over both, and the King, falling speechless, looked deep into the hearthfire, as though to bid its brastling flames to lure the lesson out of him.

He stood there behind his reading stand, his fingers, banded by the Rings, still spread over the book of namelore. The eyes of the Timekeeper throbbed upon the wall, making no sound, but marking the growth of the hush from loud to deafening.

Oyvarr's lips became a line and then a pinch. She softened as if to speak to her husband, then steeled again as her eyes stole among the many others in the room.

"It may be—" she said, but Knaks began to speak even then.

"A *landon*, Booknap, is to them a ring, at times fitted to a picket, to which the leashes of hunting dogs are bound. It holds them all at bay while the hunter takes careful aim, and from which they can all be loosed at once. For the Trebellish, then, the name *Landon* serves to mock those who bide the King's will, who await my bidding and so, as it were, live in leashes. It calls them dogs. For the Knaksmen, though, *landon* calls the Trebellish prey. It reminds them that I need only give the word, and let them slip, and that clever little land of love and winemaking will find itself between their teeth."

Knaks stepped away from the reading stand, and the scholars stiffened for the coming dismissal. The King, looking again to the Kween, made his eyes smile for the gift of the book. Oyvarr straightened, nodding. In that tenderness, her lips loosened into the pout which made her so winsome, and which she let no one but her husband see.

Merry Yearsday[6], *my King.* Her black eyebrow bent its wings. *Now send these men away.*

Knaks nodded, but again the trouble behind his eyes donned its black helm. Turning back to his bookmen, he moved to the top of

---

[6] *(AK)*: Happy Anniversary.

dais, and crossed his arms atop a chest so broad, no shirt or breastplate might wrap it that had not been wrought to do so.

"So it was, Booknap, that Abois of the Fosswolds was said to howl and bay. And not because his work was of *middling quality*. If Mine comes back, the *Blavor* calls the Isentron "the cyngdoms firy heorte kindled, in grunds coldest blod slain.""[7] He smiled. "That is not doggerel."

A man who had given his life to words, Blacwell was able to trap the gleeful groan with one side of his face only. "The Booknap thanks you, King, and for your tholemodeness."[8]

His conciliatory use of the old Braccish word escaped no one. He bowed, his eyes inching past the King on its belly. "And know, Kween, that the volume will be done within the year. We have already begun work on the northern staffrows.[9] Again, my deepest sorrow that it was not ready for today."

Though it had a woman's pitch, Oyvarr's voice, like the King's, seemed to the enthrall the air that carried it. "The Bookmen have had other duties of late, Blacwell."

"As we have, Kween. We leave you. Merry Yearsday."

After a moment's kafuffle—Arwill seemed unsure whether he should take it upon himself to retrieve the book or not—definitely not—the three slipped from the chamber, and the great door closed with an iron noise. Upon Knaks's brow, the clouds continued to gather, and though they all knew its weather, they knew not—save perhaps Blacwell, with his wordlore—the depths of its grip. For Abois of the Fosswolds had had another name among the northern Landishmen whose company the scop preferred, and where resided the Knaksish underking whose favour the *Blavor* gained.

It was a calque of sorts. *The Baying Bard.* In his twilight years, King Singrim had simply called him Bayard.

Bayerd.

It was utter chance, but it was there. All paths, though of different lengths, led back to the same place. There was no escaping it. Knaks vented some of the storm in a long windy, breath, loosening his flesh and easing slightly beneath the great mantle. Mores took the place of manners among wyemen, and before his

---

[7] (*Middle Braccish*): 'the fiery heart of the kingdom, kindled within the coldest, forged blood of the earth.'.

[8] *(AB)*: patience; forbearance; suffering through something.

[9] *(AB)*: alphabets. Also called *abecedes*.

thegns he could be more at ease. The thegns themselves, on the other
hand, seemed to have stiffened with the withdrawal of the Bookmen,
though there could be no mistaking that the marshals of the
Wyehead were much more at home before their King than the
assistants of the Bookhead had been.

"You deem these matters foolish, Ivrik." Knaks gave a nod
toward the bookstand.

The whole room seemed to look toward the Wyehead at once. It
may have been the firelight, and it may have been weariness, but
Ivrik's eyes seemed to have glazed over in the meantime since his
arrival.

He nonetheless shook his head with slow, solid feeling. "No. Not
foolish, King."

"Maybe you see it as untimely given the matters at hand. This I
do understand, Wyehead, and I shall hear your tidings soon. Know
until then that in my court I do not forgo the welcome of some good
talk first, and that on my Yearsday, upon which this news will fall, I
do not forgo the gift of my Kween."

"No, King. It is not untimely."

"What, then? Something gnaws at your care for it. What name
might you give it?"

"*Odd*, King"

"*Odd*," Knaks answered, nodding as though the word, despite its
opposition, found favour with him. He took the single step down
from the raised half of the room and joined his stewards and
atstandands on the main floor. "Outside the pale, as it were."

The Wyehead pondered this for a moment. "Yes, King."

Knaks, as he approached, did not quite leer. His proud face had
never learned to do so.

What touched his look, however—what stirred his features as
they went through the twilight of flame and flame glancing off
mail—was something predatory, like the look of a highwayman,
however well-bred, whose lure has been taken. Still, Knaks came to
a halt well before the bounds of closed speech with his elderthegn,
and his carriage was nothing like a man bent on feuding.

"You are spent, Ivrik. Your men too. They do their duty well, but
I see they barely keep their feet."

"It has been a long journey, King. And forgive me, the tidings I
bring must be heard. If you would—"

"When did you last eat?"

A shadow—mild anger—stained the raiment of the Boarsman's self-rule. "I am well, King." But then something touched his cares with a soft hand, and his eyes turned inward. "But these men," he said, shooing the tender thoughts out his mouth, "they have been with me from Vormsbal. They have had nothing for a day, at least."

Oyvarr stood at the edge of the dais, her snowy gown drenched in the blue glow of the Timekeeper. "I shall have food laid out in the hall. They shall eat while we speak."

It was not an offer, and the Wyehead bowed. His nod the Kween passed to the theow[10] at the door, who mirrored the gesture, opened the way a crack, and disappeared without a sound. The Wyehead, half-turning to the three men at his back, dismissed them with nods that, while grudging, were not spiteful. Murmuring thanks, to him and to the Kween, and casting down their eyes before the tower of their King, they trod from the room with as much might and presence as the bookish servants before them had lacked.

The door banged shut, and Knaks frowned down upon his remaining Boarsman. Like to the glower of a thunderhead over wilted land, however, it held a gloom which promised more sustenance than whipping. King by right of gods, Knaks was not a man to make mice of his own thegns.

"We are Men," quoth Knaks, and the weight of the words was like a great timber the Wyehead had once shouldered in the building of a hall. "And by the gods, we shall skoal one another[11] and have our talk as Men, however long the rude tidings must wait panting at the door."

Oyvarr appeared at his side, a bronze-yellow-haired elm, aging but still beautiful—*wlitifast*, they would say in the Braccish. In her hands was a drinking horn, a gilded tusk whose whiteness seemed grown from her own white fingers, floating before the tied-shut sleeves about her arms.[12] Ivrik's tired blood shocked to starch when he marked the vessel. It was no hollowed-out oxhorn for the guzzling of mead, but an Evertux, the tusk of an Ever—those great and dreadful boars which only the Kings of Knaks might hunt. Thick

---

[10] *(AB)*: free servant; distinct from a thrall.

[11] drink to one another (*Harandrish* expression, the *skoal* being a bowl from which one eats without a spoon).

[12] Oyvarr wears the gape-sleeved gowns traditionally worn by highborn women, but has bound them to her forearms with ribbon, in the fashion of the Kúloy highborn, who are known to do much of their own manual work.

as a woman's wrist, and the length of the arm from that wrist to the
elbow, it might have seemed a lean sort of goblet for a king or
fighting man. It might, that is, until one beheld the red cave from
which the thing had sprouted. Ivrik's eyes went a little to the right,
peering into the shadows beyond the King and Kween, and spying
the enormous head, eyes glinting, which stared stuffed upon the
faraway wall. A handful of such siggertokens[13] decked the halls and
chambers of the Isentron, the largest the head of Upstormer, the
Rioter, who had destroyed a town, and whose eyes stared down upon
the throne of the line that had slain him.

To drink from an Evertux was a great giftright, and the brew the
Kween poured was to ale as an Ever was to an everyday boar. Ivrik
took the vessel thoughtfully, mumbling something that may have
been *my Kween*, but was sapped of its strength by her eyes the green
of lichen. He raised, drank, and found it to be some brawny kin of
burned wine. A hotspring gushed inside him, and washed singing
through his veins. He felt its kneading edge unlock the cramps of his
body, clearing his throat to hide the easeful, thankful sigh.

Knaks left him to wallow for a while, such as a harried Wyehead
might wallow, then leapt while the man's wit was most supple. "You
call this learning odd, Ivrik. To the point I shall make, that is helpful.

---

[13] *(AB)*: trophies.

In the Braccish tung, which my mother's kin still speak, *odd* may be carried into the word *uncuð*, which, as it happens, means *unknown*. *Uncuðe mann* is a stranger, to be distrusted because he is not known to you. The Braccish highborn say it of unmarked fighters in the games—the black knights with no banners, who are bent most often on wrake[14], and wish to hide their Houses. *Uncuð*. We wield it in lawly matters, against wrongdoers whose right names are unknown, and to mean murderers, and other lawbreakers who take pains to keep their misdeeds hidden."

Knaks stepped before the oak carving of two of his longfathers. Both were of his mother's kin. There stood Morgenmece, a peerless wyeman, and the only man to bear that name before Knaks had given it to his own son. In hides and steel that sire stood, an axe in each hand, head turned down and away in what the Braccish called siggersorrow, or anguished victory. Beneath his foot lay the cloven body of Blæc-hafoc, his own sisterson, who had betrayed him to the thurses, and whose swikedom had forced Morgenmece's hand. *Aglæcan þær grislic aglæca guðode* its lettering read—"There, horribly, one godling slew another"—a line from the *Orgeldream*, which many scops had worked to shape, and which told of the heavy bloodshed and scant joys of the earliest Nethrishmen.

The King stood still before the mighty woodwork, his shadow thrown lapping at its cliffs. Its own shadow was a black, flickering claw on the wall beyond. As he beheld the likeness, and stood small against its dreadful show, he did not turn his head. His words carried backward nonetheless, as though brought forth from the vast lungs and throat of the wooden kinslayer he pondered.

"The *Allmal*," he said, and the name of the common tung was like two blats on a horn, "has rolled the old words in new herbs, and with them we say a man to be *uncouth* when he is rude and unlearned. He is one to whom the rules of good conduct are unknown, or seem trifling enough to be broken. And so he is, as the Trebellish have given us, *impolite*, which is to say that he is undeserving of burgs and township. Their walls and their rules and the wardens who oversee them; their streets and shops and goods; their depth of craft and lore and thought—all of which the Hálish call *menning*, which is the world shaped by Men—these things give freedoms and chances undreamed by the cavedweller, who chases

---

[14] *(AB)*: revenge.

the beast with a spear by day, and who frets away the dark nights on what food or warmth or health the morning may not bring. And better than any of their wealth, Ivrik, is the *might*," and Knaks boomed with that, "the *might* of these greatest steadings to lift up any man who beholds them, to breathe into him like a god and to kindle new fires in his mind.

"Yet the Man who is *impolite* is said to be unworthy of these glories—maybe the greatest glories the deathful world can give to those who are born to it. But to be uncouth, Ivrik, is also to be *uncivil*, which the Southern landholds have passed our way, which is to be unfit for household altogether. Unfit for fellowship, for the love of kith and kin; unworthy of wedding, and of elderhood to children; to be kicked away from the warmth of the hearth because he has an ill will towards tending to it. He seems, it is said, not to wish to be a man among Men, but to be a cunning sort of beast who has learnt to onhere[15] man's looks and manners. Such a wight does so only to gain food he did not hunt or grow himself, or a dry threshold he did not help to build, or to escape the whipping he knows his unkindness earns. The things we most take for granted as freeborn Men, even should we dwell far from elderburgs, are not for he who is said to be *uncivil*.

"But the grimmest of them, Ivrik, is a word of our own. It is *unhovely*, and though it is not often heard beyond the shires of Brac, its fire is shared among the many kindred tungs of this kingdom, and each of them carried with a different brand."

"On the Islands, it is *óhøviskur*," Oyvarr said, and her rise from hush was startling to Ivrik. She smiled at him softly, a slight leavening of her white face in the warm lapping light of the hearth. He was unsure whether she felt for his sake, or the look was wholly with the King.

On the skirts of her speech came a chain of others, one word each, like to the calling of a roll. "*Uhøflig*," was the first.

"*Unhoflich*," another.

Still, "*unhofleiko*,"

and others which sounded too similar to tell apart, like the same song sung not so much by different tongues but by the voices of different people. Not everyone in the room spoke. Only the elselanders, it seemed, fitted their words to the chain, and one only

---

[15] *(AB)*: mimic.

for each Medth, as though the song had all been gone over—learned and played through—many times ere the Wyehead had arrived at the Isentron.

"Unhovely," Knaks boomed, and the word was like three beats of a hammer, fitting a great iron weight to the end of the chain. "It says a man is unfit for court, and thus *discourteous*. Yet those are only the leaves of its truth, Ivrik. Traced to its branches, it says a man is to be turned away from all homsteads, be them yards or hovels—kept from other Men wholly, and not simply from the houses where they know themselves Men. But if you press your ear to the trunk, Ivrik, and listen to its roots, the word whispers a man to be unfit even for shelter—that his mood and his bearing are so like those of a wild thing, that he ought to live as one. A heathen, some would put it, a dweller on the heaths, with nothing between the weather and himself—no roof of sticks to hinder the rain and wind, not even a byre, which sheep and kine are too dizzy to seek for themselves, but will use nonetheless when herded to it.

"A beast we let indoors is said to have been housebroken, Ivrik. It is the only word touching on politeness for beasts, and, like the taming of steed, it is a word full of fight, of pressing and yielding. It speaks of crushing something within them, that we might call those crushed things our companions. We might crush our foemen, Ivrik, just as a master must break the will of his thrall. But neither of them do we afterwards call our companions. The best hope a beast has in the world is to be broken by Man. But the man who is unhovely...he is a man who is simply broken, not by men, but *to* them—as if his whole birthright were turned upside down, and given over to darkness whose rightful share was light."

Then Knaks turned, and he faced his Wyehead with the eyes of a different man. They were hard and full of belief, fresh from the sight of something true. Though his hands had come unlocked, they reached out like one imploring, and his stare was bitter, and brooked no defense. "Such is the wisdom of words, Ivrik, though they might fret the mind like so much grit, and at times grind away at the very bedwork of thought their heaviest stones helped to form. They are the soul of us. They tell us what it is to be Men. All we do that is brutish, Wyehead, is to forget ourselves as brutes—to lay those things aside, like the winning and clearing of tangled lands for the building of homes where we might sing and read, and welcome children, and wassail friends. It is where we gain neighbours, where we gather together and put to our workbench what have in common. It is where we grow together, where we toughen and we reach, and the world becomes to Men what the wold is to the tree—not a throng of single things, nor even their whole worth, but a world. And such a world where things come together to become new things entirely, as in the laboratories of my alchemists, and add to the glory of knowledge and being."

The words loosed, Knaks stood there for a moment, his great hands still raised, like a warlock emptying his spell into the inanimate thing he sought to quicken. Ivrik watched drink in hand, his look not altogether bored, but as one who awaits the lesson of a fable he likes but has already heard.

Knaks let his arms drop slowly to his sides, and the heavy ghost of his speech lifted from the room. He stood to his fullest. Leather groaned in the hush.

"We who fill our lives with lore, who break our minds and bodies on the gathering and winnowing of it—that is not odd, Ivrik. It is the opposite, the witherword, of odd. I say it is as much the burden of a Man as it is his right. Now, my friend—what would you say to this?"

Ivrik emptied the Evertux. "I should say, King," he began, and his eyes shone with drink, "that it is a very good thing for a king to think so, and that the folk should be glad indeed that their lord holds these things dear."

The eyes of Knaks gave a hint of narrowing. Beneath his beard was the face of a father whose child, though naughty, has said something very clever. "But you do not hold them dear yourself."

Ivrik looked about the chamber, marking the many atstandands who seemed to melt into and out of the shadows when bidden. "You know I am Harandrish, King."

The halting nod of Knaks showed the wariness of the baited. "Indeed—of the Smilkameers."

"Yes, King, like all the highborn of Harandril. But my folkland is further north. In the Kyaribo region. Timil Insee."

The words, though lightly dropped, fell upon the King like a firm hand, like that of a guardsman who bustling through the pomp of a court event catches the king in midmirth, to remind him that grave things are about. "Go on, man," he bid. "Do not let shadows and inklings speak for you."

Ivrik nodded, and the words came forth readied from the gates of his teeth. Like the standing armies he headed they bristled mailclad and grim. "King, Kween," he looked to each, "the home of my family's House is indeed to be found in the Smilkameers. Byornsgrav, it is called, on the edges of Kawsvad, within sight of the Three Ayfloods. Throw a stick into any one of those rivers and within days it will have drifted past the seats of all the northeasternmost Houses of the kingdom. Only Ostasgard holds a court worth speaking of, though many more strive to do so. None is greater than what a wealthy chapman might furnish, would he appear an atheling, but they are all proud, and they have kept their higher tastes.

"Some of these Houses are of Harandril, but not many. Most of them came south after the Eastern Wars, when they left their folklands for a wastumly[16] share of the Avonlays."

He marked the Kween's questioning look. "The Avonlays, Kween, are the booklands[17] given to them by the Rings, won from the pettykings of Shebril who fled away to the north and east. As the landcharts go, the Smilkameers straddle both Harandril and Shebril, but the Avonlays are wholly in Shebril. And so, though few will say it aloud, no one sees the highborn of the Smilkameers who came from Harandril as Harandrish any longer. Not those three or four strinds[18] born there, and certainly not the folk of Harandril—whoever and wherever they might be.

"Even before they came to the Smilkameers, most of the Harandrish Houses thronged shoulder-to-shoulder among the southernmost foothills of Harandril, hardly more than a week's ride from where they lie now. There, their hands were known to hover about the only breadbasket Harandril might be said to have had, waiting for something to appear within it, so as to snatch it up and tear it apart between them. An old saw of my thridfather's[19] likened them to the white bears who lazed about holes in the ice of the Great Lakes. Rather than hunt for themselves or fight one another for ownership of the place, they sat in small herds, utterly unwonted,

---

[16] *(AB)*: fruitful; fertile.
[17] *(AK)*: land granted by writ rather than inherited, conquered, or bought; a kind of benefice.
[18] *(AB)*: generations.
[19] *(AB)*: great grandfather.

and together awaited the mereswine[20] who must sooner or later rise for breath. One could tell a swine's age by the clawmarks on its back. They became deeper every year until it was caught or died of its wounds."

His bitterness scolded him, and he drank again. He looked into the fire, as though willing his confidence and his discomfort— mismatched like ox and drafthorse—to pull the words out of him. "These Houses came from the foothills of the south. But my family's lands lay in the Kyaribo, far among the alps to the north. Only one House lay further north than Timil Insee, and it was lost before all the others."

Foreseeing a story, Knaks showed him to the table with a single sweep of his hand. It was a longboard whose face was a single wedge of ironwood, and so mighty it was that thurses alone might have carried it into place. Running its length down the middle was the heartlode of greensilver, of which things might indeed be forged, and which was both like and unlike an iron of the earth. It glinted in the candlelight like still water, as did the woodgrain which ran out on either side of it, line after line like the strings of a harp, to the black bark at its edges which no manmade axe might wound. At the King's beck, all those in the room gathered without sound about the mighty board. Some sat in the chairs and others stood behind them, making it altogether clear which of them lorded and which of them thegned.

Both ends of the table were left open, and Ivrik took his place at one of them. As he waited for the King to take the other he sought the best way of holding the Evertux, which for its shape he could not set down. At last Knaks took his chair, his back broader than its own, with Oyvarr at his side and a thuften[21] at hers. An Evertux was in each hand of the Kween, and a ewer in the arms of the handmaid. The vessels were filled, and the Kween passed one to Knaks. The other she kept for herself. Both athelings drank, and blinked, and were still. The floor fell back to their guest.

"Byornsvey was our foremost hall," Ivrik said, "the old seat of one of the oldest lands of the Bracsriche. Our lore tells us it was the last one built by the Olallish themselves—that hardiest stock of Harandrishmen who first thwarted the Wottrámish Alps."

---

[20] *(AB)*: dolphins, of which they are many varieties among the great lakes, or *insees*, of the Kingdom of Knaks.
[21] *(AB):* maidservant; handmaid.

Something like the murmur of restless thoughts went around the table, for of course nothing could cross the Alps, whose summits lay always within starlight, and whose snows were older than the bedrock of the sea. Elsewhere, those hearing Ivrik might simply have jeered, but at the court of Knaks they knew enough to wonder, and not simply to disbelieve. For the first Bracsmen to stagger into Harandril had indeed found within its northernmost homesteads a tung not too unlike their own, whose folk told stories and spoke of gods most like to those of the Hálish. That happy kinship had led to a bloodless bonding with the Bracsriche, and the Kings of Knaks had never forgotten it. It helped that Harandril had had no kings of its own—its yarls having forsworn any use of the name—and that the Braccish High King had made the Harandrish folklands into ealdormanries headed by the inborn Houses rather than turn them over to his own kin. Nonetheless, and whatever the truth of it, the folk of Harandril had somehow come to be living on the southern side of the Alps, speaking words like those on the northern side of it, and without, it seemed, having come overland from west or east.

The gathering settled, and whatever the breed of their doubt, Ivrik seemed wonted to it, and went on. "As you know, Kween, King, many lands in the north and to the edges of the kingdom are not as they are here. Here the borders of the shires fit together like the spars of a hull, with no room in between. Elsewhere, though, they are more like islands in wide stretches of haunted sea, most of which no one wades into. Chartwriters spell lands in ink, not in blood, for the maps do not show these things, instead dealing out whole swaths of land to some seat or other whose true sway is but an islet in their midst. In some Medths, as in eastern Shebril, these islands themselves rise only in the warmer seasons, and swether wholly with the winter tides. The folk might remain, but the landlords seek warmer seats—as in the Smilkameers, or Eksar Arsask—and leave their lands to the wolves until springtime."

"The Houses of Harandril did not flee the snows in winter. The cold—it was as much a part of their lands as the trees and the fells, and ice enough could be found all year to keep meats and milks from spoiling. But the hold on the land was always with loose fingers. The shape of the menning shifted, like the wings of a palace, which are closed off at times with furniture covered to the dust, and brought back to life at need and cost." He chuckled, an awkward, unpracticed sound. "Though here, I see, the King's talk of courtesy has taught it to my tongue, for I have always likened this seasonal waxing and waning of the Harandrish lands to an ailing body, whose limbs are tied off to save the core, and which, burnt and blackened by the cold may not return to life once the blood is given back to them. As time passed fewer and fewer of its shires—which we called *filks*—were given back life with the spring. In the time of my thridfather's thridfather, seven halls—seven seats—were kept alive year-round. *Seven*." He spoke the number with awe, as one might the hidden name of a god. "Through snows higher than two men, and breaths from the highbergs so cold that watchmen could empty their drinking cups from the wallwalks and hear ice ring on the stones below. Seven. By the time my father's father came south to Byornsgrav in the Smilkameers, we had but two, and they were two too many."

"But such winters, Ivrik," Knaks said, and for seemliness had made his towering voice to sit as he did, "they are known across the lands of this kingdom, whether year-to-year, as in the north of this very Medth, or as sudden freaks whose wrath, however great, is heaped higher as the memories of them age." He waved toward the chamber's single, small window and laughed without mirth. "No fewer than thrice in my own lifetime has the Fimblewinter of the Ozlore[22] been at the walls of this very building. Or so the priests said."

Ivrik smiled with his teeth, a gloating smile. "No doubt, they were housed so deeply in their booklore that they forgot the look of the world it all came from. Were any of them here, I might tell them that I have put my hand between the jaws of an Arsaskish winter, and it is but a whelp to the Fenriswolf of Harandril. The pup may have the sharper teeth, King, but they are small, and do not grip for long what they seize. In Harandril, it does not let go. It only dies in the springtime, and goes limp, with you pulling free of it. Truly, nothing can be more savage and let Men live—the Fimblewinter, should it come, is three Harandrish winters, not a winter greater. But, yes, King. If I have learned two things as a Boarsman, it is that Knaksish winters are grim wherever one might be—that, and the Ignish can't cobble boots to save their lives."

---

[22] The northern gods, called the *Æsir* by the Hálish, by whom they are worshipped as other aspects.

The Wyehead snickered once and let the jester die, allowing its ghost to burn away somewhere above the middle of the table. He looked to the window, which as it happened gazed to the northeast, peering out through the small stretch of stonework joining the chamber's northern and eastern walls. Its sight was black, and in its glass was the cold throbbing of the room's many flames. Ivrik spoke while facing it, the Evertux turning slowly between his hands.

"But it was on learning and courtly things that we began to speak of this, and that is where I am headed. Many have heard tell of Harandril, and some of what they have heard is true. It is a land of highbergs and evergreens, with one moon and one sun. Dreecraft does not work well, and prayer is like a voice shouting through a storm—sometimes it gets through, sometimes not. No one knows why. The gods, and the ghosts, do not talk to us there as they do elsewhere. The land does not welcome us, but nor, despite the hardships, does it hate us. It is as though it was made long before us—maybe for others, or maybe for no one—and whoever made it forgot about it, or died, a thousand Elds before Man. But we found it, and made our homes there."

And then Oyvarr was beside him, and the ewer which her thuften had needed both arms to cradle was gripped by one of her hands. She began to refill his horn, and Ivrik thanked her.

"Why is it," she asked as the burned wine poured, "that a House cleaves to a place so forbidding? The yorelore[23] of the Bracsriche tells of Men warring southwards, in search of lands that did not threaten to freeze their children's blood if they wandered out-of-doors, and where crops might be grown for more than two months of the year. Why did your House cleave to Timil Insee, and why does it do you pain to speak of its loss?"

Ivrik started a little, as though the words held a sting, but when he met the Kween's eyes, he found them easing, and warm with a kindred fire. What she had put to him was not a jab but a spur, a prod toward the place he dithered over. She was of the Kúloys, after all, and knew what it was to love a motherland only its children might.

"This, as you see, goes to my point, Kween. Timil Insee was a land where the work was the only thing that kept Men alive. The gathering of stores, the mending of the walls and roads ere the coming of winter—the time not spent in the doing of things was best

---

[23] *(AK)*: history; old knowledge.

spent on the planning of them. As the seven halls of my eldfathers closed—as luck and life severed branches of my House, and hard choices were made to save those left—the court became the heart of the world in a way not so much as a saying, but a truth—a place to keep the blood of Man warm and moving. The worth of what things we did was reckoned by their gainfulness—how they made better use of men and gold, both of which are dear worth to a throne, but worthless without the other. There could be no waste. In Harandril, we had no great trumes[24], but we picked and provided for the hardiest of men to range the old wilderness, crossing paths with the mighty saint-hounds who carried casks of firewine beneath their chins. A body of outposts kept the fires of Man burning in every dark corner of the land, like so many candles in a vast black grotto. We called this network the *Magernatt*, after those nights when the sky holds only a handful of stars. Their light cannot warm you, nor even show you the road, but they are there, and like cinders give hope of day to come.

"The upkeep of these and other bodies were the whole sake of the court, and what we called our craft was anything—any work, scheme or learning—that made our lives steadier. Our skalds sang songs of warning and survival, whose verses were not just pretty garlands of words, but keys to overcoming death should one find oneself without fire or shelter, bitten by an addersnake, or in the throes of childbearing with the midwife far away. I know many of them, Kween, King, and they have helped me as a Boarsman more than any of the pinchlearning or roughnecking I did when I enrolled.

"And we staked our gold not to baubles, but to the making of things that might see our halls and outposts better speak with one another across the wide wastes, strengthen the roads, or bring more food from the soil. We needed warmer clothes, and houses which kept their heat, hearths which ate less wood, and better blades to hasten the gathering of it. Ways of carving through the thickest ice, or better, to melt the ice away, so to keep our wagons always moving among the halls and hamlets, and the feet of travellers from flying out from under them. The best of our minds found the best routes between places, and ways to keep the thundersnows from burying them. Nonetheless we had plows, and more wonderful tools, and

---

[24] *(AK)*: armies.

workmanly ways which were honed and proven over time, of keeping the white death at bay.

"And we bred the hardiest of beasts to be found in all of Norráma: a giant horse, the Ullris, whom the snows cannot stop, and a pony, the Langblod, whom the snows cannot kill. They are still kept in the northernmost places of the kingdom—they are in Shebril, on the borders with Tarmateriza and Nagland, but I have not seen them here. The mighty Adlergriffs are said to be of Harandril as well, where we called them *Stormskyer* in our old tales. They were even mightier than they are now, but there was none left in Timil Insee even when my thridfather was young. Other lands, Hála among them, have laid claim to them, but do not heed that chatter. Those feathered thurses are Harandrish, through and through.

"Beasts were not all we sought to harness everything. In everything from the heat of springs through the might of the winds to the weight of the ice we sought to make boon of hardship, and better root the foot of Man to the slopes of those godless fells. Happy indeed were those who came forth with something new that worked better than something old, for they might live by that trade. And so it was that every child of Timil Insee grew up a finder at heart, seeking new and hidden strengths within common things, and bending old crafts to new ways. Thus did a land thin of Men become thick with mills and lighthouses, waterworks which thawed as they led water, and cliff-strengthening walls that kept the woodroads from slouching off the highest slopes." He waved toward the hearth. "Here we build fires in the midst of us, as we might in any camp or roadside. But in Timil Insee it is said our homes somehow sat upon their hearths, nestled within the flames like salamanders, with leedrushes[25] for smoke, or steam, running among the rooms, open at many places, but breathing only heat, and not fumes. And there were villages, it is said, and outposts, which put these works beneath their very grounds, and so warmed everyone who came through the gates."

The eyes of Knaks were as pools into which the thoughtful peer. "There lives something of this craft in western Arsask, but only where the cold is middling," he said. "In Hála, it has been fullfremed[26] to keep every town in springtime even through Overwinter. But their earth is unlike ours. It is more like the peats of

---

[25] *(AK)*: conduit pipes. Also called *rushes*.
[26] *(AB)* perfected; fully made.

the eastern boglands, and can be delved and refilled, and will scatter the heat of whatever hot thing runs beneath them. When Edgebane my forefather wed Ísabitra of Hála, she brought with her workfrodings—men wise in the building of wondrous things—who sought to remake those great hearths within Knaksish earth. For she found the throneburg was too cold for her, and would not go outofdoors between fall and late spring. She, an atheling of the icelands, and she could not stand the ice. Nonetheless, they could not do it. Only a handful of steadings in this kingdom, they found, might take the works and do their task, and these were either barrens or farmlands which had no wise use for them. But Harandril, you say, shows the bones otherwise? I should be very pleased to see them."

Ivrik's answer was a rother[27] of a stare, corralled the long length of the table by the many silver grains of the ironwood. It took its time to find its way back to words. "I have never seen them, King. My knowledge of Timil Insee is from tale and lore, and from the few things I saw and heard tell of when I went among the remnants with my brothers and their sons many years ago. But it seems so. And it is woeful to me that such works might be of worth not only to you, but to the kingdom. The cunning of Harandril, you see, was not held with esteem—*arung*, as the Braccish has it—by any courts beyond our own. We are, to the greater share of them, more churlish than earlish, as the saying goes. This is not only because the Harandrish Houses are unathelborn. We are, as you can see," and his hands winged to present himself, a man of wonely height and breadth, "alike to the men we led, for we are of them, and wed freely. Our Halls did not need the wider doorframes and loftier rafters that those of your Highnesses do. No, it is not that. Even today, among the endless gatherings of the courts of the Smilkameers, it is there to be seen—that the courtly works of Harandril are reckoned low, and, for their bearing on worldly things in need of stiff scrubbing.

"They say that what we had sung before ourselves and our guests were not songs, but shanties and rote-rimes—knowledge put to pretty airs only to keep wandering minds from dropping it. Our stories, full of warning and quick wisdom in the jaws of peril, were called tales for the wide-eyed and unweaned. Though hard-won and winnowed by our longfathers, they were said not to be on the same footing as those airy sagas and legends which simply call one's

---

[27] *(AB):* an ox; a bovine animal.

longfathers mighty. As for the bodies of knowledge we had shaped, and the many works they had begotten, the many rouns[28] we had both stolen and won from our heartless motherland—these were called the tokens of smithies and of worksteads, and not the mathoms[29] of the court. And the wealth we gave as gifts—the waterproof footgear, the coats no cold could cleave, the little anlikenesses of our best buildworks, and writings of our knowhow—these were held between the fingers as coarse, dizzy things, like a mouse a cat leaves at the threshold. What we fed and watered with all our souls, King, were not blessed as arts. They were called knacks, or yepship, and at best orthank—"

"Which is a praiseword, Ivrik. Orthankship is not easily done."

"But it is, forgive me, King, a breed of handiwork. The orthanksmiths—the workfrodings, as indeed we say it in the Northway speech—they build castles and bridges and mills, and other wonders out of iron, stone, and wood, but their hands are as black as those of the cutters and wrights they drive. And the driver beds down with the oxen, so it is said, and not with those who pay him to drive. Moreover, *orthankship* is the same word of cleverness we give to ants and to beavers, and to other beasts that make more than trails and dunghills. It is the highest of the trades, but a trade it stays, and for touching worldly things it is deemed low by the eyes of the highborn. No, King. None of our tungs, neither Braccish nor Allmal nor even the snatches of the Northway speech we recall in Harandril, can do anything but scorn them. It was in the way of it alone—and now only in our memory of it—that their worth was upheld.

"And so, King, by the reckoning of my House, I call your namelore odd. Not foolish. Not worthless." He shook his head in an implacable way. "For even in Timil Insee, with all its rigors and burdens, we knew what it was to write books, to sing songs of love, and to frike[30], and to sound with moots of clever men the deepest pools of talk and thought. And it was to the hardships in our lives that we owed the bliss of these things, not despite them, for our work was like the common metal which grips and foils the pretty gemstone, and makes it something Man can carry with him always, and yet keep both hands free to grapple with the world. It was not

---

[28] *(AB):* mysteries; secrets.
[29] *(AB)*: precious object; treasure.
[30] *(AB)*: to dance.

only that the sweet smacks sweeter after salt, as we say, and that these joys were like a warm inn after many cold days on the road. This is a thing any beast might understand, and I do not mean to say that my House, in bitter thrall to itself, withheld from its children the mindfires which are the right of the highborn. No, King. They sat before the knees of their teachers, as do the children here, and learned the Braccish staffcrafts along with our own. Some took their wanderyears, such as they might in that deal of the world, but never so far astray that they might come to scorn their own homes. Others went straight to the grindstone, as it were, sharpening themselves for the trials that would ever be upon them as they headed their hall and filk, their body of men, or the House itself.

"It was a matter of pride, my thridfather said, that no one in my folklands was goaded into place, for the tasks were too great, and the shieldwall too needful, to risk the slack of anyone unwilling to do it. Rising before daybreak is hard for many, my King, but mornings in Harandril have dark hours of cold the rest of the world does not know. Day after day seeking cinders in the ash, and at breakfast the cares for whatever weather had come in with the dawn. A ranger, due with tidings of the outdales and freethorps, might not have come. The woodroads may have slouched, or the icerains entombed us. Roving outlaws might have struck, or uhters[31], or wolves—things that lurked, and poached, and murdered, and took time to *spore up*, as we called tracking them down. There was no biting of coals, for at every gate and doorstep waited a wheel for the shoulder, and the sort of work we could not call toil, only because toil is work without aim. Knocked ever backward, we swinked nonetheless, and hoped for a time that the heydays of headway might return to life—that halls might be reopened, or, as in the mightiest of our tales, new ones built, and filks newly born."

"And in such a life as this, King, with no emptiness in time, what we gave to dear things became holy. We had a bookman or two, and more in the endyears, when we chose to uproot, and took down all that we could of the lore of our land. And to us, these things were beyond dear worth. We could no more share them with outsiders than we could make light of them—the sort of cheapening lightness that comes from taking something up day after day, one of its kind after another, till it lies empty, or one is wearied of it, and tosses it

---

[31] *(AH)*: monsters.

aside. And it was the work, King, the work which gave these things their dear worth. You say we must work to lay those things aside in order to know ourselves, but I say that whatever we are, it is the tension between what we must do, and what we wish things to be. The sides are fixed, and the wishful things are coiled about pegs, as with a harp, to be tautened by whatever strength is in us to be both Men and good. Love, King, is the music we make upon those strings, and though they might be plucked while slack, and give ill sound, or weak, they cannot be made to sing if broken, or unfixed at either end."

Ivrik's mouth opened again, as if he would say more, but the echo of his words off the walls seemed to bring a peace to his face, and he was silent. His listeners were quieter still, but the hush was not leaden. Wreathed by the golden noise of the hearth, his talk hung aloft, and its substance was like the warmth of an olden truth found alive.

"Well said, Wyehead," Knaks said at last, and rather than break the silence, his speech seemed simply to overrule it. His voice retook the room at once, reminding it of his reach, but in such a way that he did not banish that spirit he had bid Ivrik shape. Instead, and despite the witherwardness of his own, earlier point, he seemed deeply taken. There was a gouge in his throat, which, like a sudden plunge in a riverbed, makes the stuff flowing atop it slow down and darken. "More you might say, and plainer, I ween, were you in less hovely company than ours. You shoot a rich volley, and all the sharper I say for returning those darts of mine which called you to arms. Some here may not have caught them, and to them I make it known that *emptiness*—which is the thing you say life lacked in Timil Insee—grew from the Braccish word *æmettig*, which in that tung is *rest*, or more forthly, the freedom from toil to which we most owe those courtly arts. And so the namelorist is stung by his own namelore." Knaks chuckled once. "And the wise say that learning is a weapon that will not bite its own master."

The King stood then, if indeed a stronghold could be said to stand, and despite his baldrish remark his eyes stayed troubled. He quaffed his drink of a sudden, elbow up like a rampart, the Evertux a lonely white spire atop the iron hedge of his beard. He smiled at the Kween as she took back the empty vessel. Whatever cares were in him, she took half them too, and her light bleakened beneath the braided ore atop her head.

"But I know you, Ivrik," the King spoke from their twinned gloom, his eyes staring into the shadows of the eastern wall. "As well, maybe, as you think to know me. We have not met more than twice ere this day, and were it not for the troubles in Bayerd, we might never have spoken further. But you are of a kind, my friend— a onely and selcouth[32] kind—which I look for in all those I name my Wyeheads. You are a ward—a hero in the olden way—a man who spies the darkness beyond every belt of sunset, and will not give himself ease." And with that Knaks looked upon Ivrik, and his stare was like the hammer that brings down a beloved mad steed. "In the seeds of what has grown between us here, I named you. 'Beyond the pale,' is how we tithed it when you called my namelore odd. The 'pale' is a stakewall, you see—that sharptoothed haw which keeps the fiend outside—and for you the worst thing in the world is someone who plays beyond it, mindless of what might lie in wait. But less worse only by a little are those who take their play inside, for theirs is time squandered rather than reckless—wood given to the flames of the hearth, that might have strengthened the wall.

"You are a sheepdog, Ivrik. You are one who hounds the wolves. And Harandril, be her grim face forever upon the halse of our ship, is the bitch who whelps you best. In what other share of the land might I find Men who, for duty, brook no joy? Men who see life not as things to be lived, but as games they need lose only once, and which therefore they must daily win, lest the sky fall upon every one of us? Yes, I know Harandril. Though far off from the other Medths and now nigh broken away, it is one of the ten spires of the Crown, and it is my business to know. All the while that Timil Insee was dwindling, my House was having its own dealings with that land. It was not forsaken, Ivrik, but like an unbreakable beast let go. It had always been unruly, as you say, but something else had come upon it, something like the full moon, washing ghosts and light between the boards of its byre. Or like the foaming madness, slipped into the blood by a bite overlooked. Whatever the root of it, it had begun to thrash within its stall, wounding wood and latch, trampling those who sought to calm it. It bit every hand it once had nosed. And when it began to kill, Ivrik—when its madness raised such of Hell that it threatened to spill over into the stalls of its neighbours—that was

---

[32] *(AB)*: rare; seldom met.

when its harness was removed, and we whipped that weird thing back into the gray that had grown it.

"That is the last of what I know, my friend, for that must be the time when your thridfather brought your House southward, and the thrawny highborn of Harandril became the bitter orchardlords of the Avonlays. But it was with thegns such as you, Ivrik, that the Rings came to know the true worth of that lost Medth—that its riches lay not in the barrens of its marches, but in the blood of those Men whose Houses had once called it theirs. There are fewer of you left than you know, but your thews have not loosened with the times. Even unbound among the courts of the Smilkameers, you woo without thrill or wantonness, and do not die to marry. You see childbearing as yiselry[33] to Wyrd, and have fewer children than you need. What of your days that are not given over to brooding on things lost are spent seeking the toothiest beasts, in whose mouths you gamble your heads. Those of you who seek theowdom—to serve with blead rather than to rule with blethefulness[34]—I do not fail to mark you. Do not wonder at why you made Wyehead so early, Ivrik. You are born thegns, and all of you have proven flawless in that role.

"I should bid you answer forthwith, but you have the look of a man who knows not whether he is loved or hokered[35]. So I shall not put that goad to your hide. But I shall nudge your cares with this. A night—" and he halted. Whatever he had stood to say, his pride had put a knot in its path, and Knaks threw down his eyes as he slowly untied it. Kween Oyvarr gave the hint of a start, as though, in the sight of all, she would come to him and embrace him, but she ruled herself and stood still. Nevertheless, to see the King so troubled by his feelings—to see him overcome by anything other than a fellow godling or a great wyrm—was as unsettling to the soul as a shaking beneath one's feet. At last, Knaks found his voice again, and though full of might, its edges were scratched, like one who has charged his way through thorns.

"A nightmare has had me since I became a young man—a dark, dreamless sweven that found me when first I could see the World from...this other place." His hands swept twistingly about the room before him, Ring-collared fingers writhing as he sought to hold something vile and shapeless. "It was no single thing that showed it

---

[33] *(AB)*: hostagery – "yiselry to Wyrd" is "hostagery to Fate."
[34] *(AB expression)*: to serve boldly rather than to rule timidly.
[35] *(AK)*: mocked; duped.

to me, but an understanding that loomed slowly and sharpened out of the fogs of childhood. The World, Ivrik, is a thing made by Men. The other thing was not. I do not know what it is. It is like the black, swallowing walls about a ship on nights without stars—the itness lurking behind all things we have shaped and named. When first I glimpsed it, my mind struggled to find its edges, and the worst was the sleeplessness that comes from struggling thoughts. It was not until I slumbered again that the nightmare showed me a likeness. And believe me, Ivrik, I came to yearn again for those nights when I could not sleep at all.

"It shows me a Hell that no gods we know made—a black Where, and endless, which I mistake at first for the shutness of mine eyes. But then a prick of light, and as it grows from mote to speck, I know myself borne towards it. You have heard, Ivrik, of the Earthfarers. I do not mean the Wherewalkers—those striders-among-worlds whose wizardry can part the weave of our own suchness, and find eldritch earths. I speak rather of those who have been said, by dreecraft or by wonderful vessels, to step from this dirt and to make their way among the heavens above us. One of the many tales I have heard is that the stars cannot be reached. They stand ever before you, drawing you on till the end of time, never to be caught or neared. Some say they are the fool's fires of the gods, drifting fro to match the speed of whosoever hunts them, but others, Ivrik, say they are indeed rooted, and lie so far away, and burn in a field so ormete[36], it merely seems that way. Ween such a field, but with a single star. This is what I see. The darkness is not empty, but something beyond anything your eyes were shaped to behold. It does not hide; your eyes hide it from you. Full of nothing, it leers. And once it has racked and broken your mind on its nameless endlessness, it shows you the fleck of light for what it is.

"It is a hill, a lonesome isle in the bleak. In any other sea, such a sight might give heart, but the look of this strand—even before one draws close enough to know it—it is what my eldmother's tales might name a *færgryre*, a thing of uttermost dread. What seemed a star is its peak, which is alight in such a way that its glow does not pierce the darkness above, nor that to its sides, but falls like a weak spray of water upon what lies beneath. For a time, it seems like to a hill shaped by many rains, wrinkled and furrowed, with no face that

---

[36] *(AB)*: vast; boundless.

is smooth. But only for a time. As one nears, one sees it to be a heap of Men. Those at the peak are alive. The beacon they hold aloft looks like to a mighty torch, and it shows the mass of flesh that is its lighthouse. The fewest of those wretches are those who bear up the great brand, who keep it straight and feed gobbets of stuff to its fire. Others bear those Men up as well, and still others those, the heap ever widening till sight of it dwindles below the reach of the light. From afar, the many bodies piled beneath the flame seem still— ridged and knobbed like wax, which after a thousand thousand candles has entombed its sconce within its melt. But as I am borne closer, I see that the wax is yet molten, and seeps. Closer still I see it is not wax at all, but skin, glistening and golden in the sputter. I see the shape and swell of naked bodies, of both men and women. Their arms clutch at one another, their feet claw and thrust at others beneath them. Some kick to oust, but most seek to hold on, or to hold others. Their heap is unsteady. It has no core, save the bones of the dead unseen. It shifts and it trembles, in places juts and swells. From the undersides of its ledges legs dangle and writhe. In the steepest places Men fall, one-by-one, and in whole shelves which slump and tear slowly away. Their bodies tumble and pitch into the nothingness, the arms of those who once had moored them trailing raw from the heap like to the open edders of limb torn off.

"Closer I draw, and now the shadows deal into faces and sharper things. I see both young and old, and all their looks are of woe. Caged in their eyes sob sinless souls, welcoming Death but not his touch—not Pain nor Unknowing, nor the many faceless others who throng beneath His robe. And the thought of this seems worse than any sight yet shown to me, for to seek freedom from sorrow is fit for a Man, as is some fear of what one craves. But when freedom lies with death, it does a foul thing to his heart. The boldness to seek what one craves becomes one with the fear of death. Thews twisted, a man seeks to embrace what ought to spur him; the heroes are then those who gut themselves on their own swords, and the heirs of the world are those too weak to fall.

"But, again, the heap. Elder and youth, they seem not to live asunder, but meng in their grind and pain, with longbeards and smooth-skinned alike toiling to keep the brand flaming. To what end I am not yet shown. On the banks scrabble children, their hands clutched by mothers with babes at their breasts. I see them given birth on those banks of flesh, brought in pain from motherly dark to this motherless black. Some slip from their mothers and fall beyond the light. Others reach. Fingers sometimes find them in time.

"And as I come closest, there is nowhere to land. I round their pile like a helpless healend, my pity and the mankindness that we share egging me with both lungs to wreck and to join them in their sorrow. That I cannot save them, I must join them—is that not the rightful way of the head, Ivrik? But as I near to do so, and as the swey of them at last begins to claw at the very drums and strings of what keeps me whole, the safer share of me at last bares itself, and gives me what strength it has. It is that seabed and bonehouse of our wit and health that is a true gift of gods, which grounds us and holds us together when all else is scraped away, and we believe that our tempers can brook no further blows.

"And in the hush of its leeward shore, Ivrik, it tells me a thing you might have foreseen—that even now I am wrecked upon that isle. I was born upon it, and I shall die upon it, as are you Ivrik, and as for us all, for it is a tokening of Man himself, and of the lonely and neverending war he calls the life of his kind. He is the food that fights the swallowing throat, the soft-bodied liver between the teeth. From darkness to darkness he grows, the torch his only hope and learning, which he builds of the bones of his forebears, and whose fire he feeds with his own fat. To live closest to it is to break one's back in the upholding of it, and to suffer the more for knowing its frailty. Better this, it seems, than to scrabble at its edges—to have one's back to the beacon, whether from hate or from selfishness or from swime[37] of birth—and to see only that part of its glow that brinks the gloom.

"But the worst that happens there is not the wasting of the idle, nor the angst of the unready, but a choicer evil. Not all those benighted lie barren. Some men, Ivrik, would rather seek fellowship with darkness than work to uphold the blessed fire they must share, and worse than any oathbreaking is swikedom such as theirs. To unlock the gates to the reavers would be a cleaner kind of backstabbing than to smuggle dark teachings into our shrines of hope and learning—to infect with devils' whispers the very lore that keeps us sound.

"Such men wreak works to wreck us all, fitting skeins of manfiendly darkness to the looms of manfriendly light, and weaving

---

[37] *(AB)*: vertigo; disorientation.

for us all robes of death whose cladding is worse than any hairshirt or iron maiden. What they do is akin to children who put their backs in the grass, willing whimsical things of the drifting heavens, and shaping worlds in the welkin to gladden their inner gods. But that is a sinless likening, Ivrik, for such children do no harm, and do not blunder in what they build. Those who draw our eyes to the darkness, on the other hand, and who use our own light to do so—they are more a threat than the darkness itself, and whose unhoveliness is like a wolfwere—a beast in the fell of a man, who wears it only to gain the indoors."

And with these words, the eyes of Knaks went somewhere among those seated along the table's northern edge, and held a look as close to loathing as the righteous might withhold. Ivrik followed the withering line of the stare, but could not see where it landed. The hoflings and hirdmen[38] about where it fell did not shuffle nor seem troubled by any reckoning, but seemed to know among themselves whom it was meant for. Ivrik would have peered deeper, but Knaks carried on, and the heed of them all was yanked back to him, like afterboats in the tow of great ship.

"Now, I am not so wet from the womb, Ivrik, as to take this sight for the One Truth. We have all been given such sights, those that move if not shake us, whether in the gray hours of morning after sleepless nights, or as our heads boil off the stews of too much drink and undercooked flesh. An eve or two later and the nightmares become dreams again, and we drift again through rest, grateful and hindsightless, like a bark on its way through the fickle seas. The gods at a whim might show us such things to better bend our knees, but They are too many and too selfish to show us truths outside Their own welfare. There is a single truth that binds Them all, however blind They be to it, and however unwilling They be to unenthrall us by teaching it.

"Such a truth as this is carried by this nightmare, Ivrik. And it is only for your talk of Harandril that I give it tongue before my court—of the wedge it drives between works and wratts[39], and of the binding it weaves to make one of craft and wisdom. You believe we two are at odds, but only in the drift of it all. For where we see with

---

[38] *(AB)*: courtiers and retainers.
[39] between works of practical value and works of art. *wratts (AB):* ornaments; treasures.

the same eyes is how merrow[40] a thing is menning—that in the black blast and howl of Being we are the soot that skirts a single, glinting ember. Upon that wretched isle I have drawn, you would keep your back ever to the brand, Ivrik, not to scorn it, but to put yourself between it and its undoers—its snuffers and scathers—to die upon its banks whether or not you yourself, or even your children's children, ever feel its warmth. And I, I speak of things that huddle near the flame—of things that brook fully its richness, and stretch themselves out in that undarkened place it has won. For what better way is there to hallow that site than to unhollow it with things of our own making, the more playful the better? To bear and raise Mannish worths, those whose twinkling the black itness would smother should wards such as you fail, to take back for itself the naughtness we seed. Though we have unsame outlooks, Ivrik, they belie our one footing. For the day I myself feel the fires of Man flicker—that crack in time when I feel the winds through broken walls, I shall tear up my floor to find stones for the breach, and melt down every thing I own to mend them."

And Knaks, though he had spoken staidly till now, all at once threw that stillness from himself, the hearthfires leaming as though bellowed upon by an inner self he had shamed. His fingers gathered into a fist, knuckled by the Rings, and were as the Five Yoredrights of the Bracsriche they betokened, becoming one onely wered, one folk and one army, whose thews and whose wrath could not be unsnarled. Both fists he settled upon the table, and made the ironwood fibres hum.

"I fear such a time will soon be upon us, for whatever unwonely thing fastened horns in Harandril has now turned its head toward Bayerd. I say it is unwonely, Ivrik, and I say they are the same in that both lands were long manned ere they bit our hands—and not only manned, but taught manners—and made to welcome us, its rightful lords, with both meekness and bounty. Unsoftly at whiles were those welcomes, Ivrik, and in Harandril most of all, but life in Bayerd is no oysterfest either, however blithe the summers. And this I know, for lands enough there lie in this world that do not suffer to be settled by Men at all, and drive his flags and every founding from their bodies ere they might take."

---

[40] *(AB):* soft; delicate.

And the eyes of Knaks, though their line did not break, showed the same leftward itch as before, and Ivrik again glanced among those seated there. This time, he saw someone shuffle—a man in a kirtle whose heavy beard hid his youth.

"So it is," Knaks went on with tongue newly bristling, "that I draw no hard lines between the land and the beasts who seem always to thrive within it. One is but a white shift atop the other, drinking its darkest colours, and settling into whatever shape the thing beneath it slinks to. We know those fourlegged wights that eat their own kind, that leave their young undenned to freeze, and that starve their own fathers when they can no longer help with the hunt. Not from single, dire needs do they do such hellish things—not in such plights that become gray tales, wherein some bloot[41] is needed, or where the ranger, his thoftship snowed in and starving, gives himself for the whole. They do this out of wont, unthinking as the thrall that does all it is told, and so forsakes what it is to be himself, and a Man.

"For Men we are!" he stormed. "And that means we shall break everything that seeks to unman us—break it or bend it, till it bows to our will, to our whim even. For what will not bend would seek to unman us, to make us more like itself than what we have learnt of ourselves! What should we be if we stooped for every branch in our path, and ate the weeds in the fields—how high to rise were we to hunt with our hands, or to flee flash and thunder?

"We should be *deer*, Ivrik, a word which in Braccish means all wild beasts, but in the Allmal means only those split-hoofed horsekin that flinch and start at every whisper—who as they run forget their only strength, and put between their horns and their foemen the softest and most beckoning part of them. So wretched they are that I myself will not hunt them. I have banished to the nethermost cellars of the Isentron all the hides, heads, and stuffed kills of those antlered mice which my forefathers gathered, however great in body. In their stead are the monsters—the rippers and spoilers and unmakers, and those who would eat the flesh of Men were their lusts given leash—and their lifeless husks I nail up and show with love, as stent to our menning, and as a warning to those deathless overseers whom some suffer to call gods that my world—the Age of Man—will not be so easily overturned.

---

[41] *(AB)*: sacrifice.

"For what is Man but a teacher and tamer—a soul sent in skin to turn all the pain of the middenerd[42] toward the pleasure-grounds whence his Maker sent him—to make one of heaven and earth, and so bring about the only end for which the dying can strive? From the day these eyes of flesh first reckoned, we have taught this world manners. Every chamber that bids us bend we have hollowed it out with our hammers. Every patch of fallow earth we have taught to yield our food. Every wedge of iron we have hauled sweating from the lodes of hell, and beaten into shape, whether into swords or as ploughshares, by which we carry out new work, till we have unlocked every chest the world holds, and so solved the riddles the gods have set before us."

Knaks drew breath to go on, the break in his talk like the waitful stillness between ythes[43], which crash ashore one after one. But from the trough of that wrath there arose from the table a new voice, and its strength was like that of a shoot which, though small and slender, housed fibres no raw strength could overwhelm.

"My King," it announced, "I believe I must speak."

To this voice Knaks gave the floor, throwing to it with civil scorn as he drank deeply from the Evertux. The break in his storming was nonetheless so abrupt that it gave the new speaker the hue of a dreeman, who with a shout from below might calm the angriest winds, and bring peace to the land bending below them. For a moment, the silence was a startled one, as though no one could believe it had been brought about. It was the hush in a room of great minstrelsy quelled, when a guest unwelcome but unbanishable strides onto its floor.

"What is happening in Bayerd—" the speaker declared, and twice cleared his throat as it caught, "what is happening in Bayerd—and what came to pass in Harandril, for that matter, Wyehead—was not the will of Bluharyn."

He spoke with the heart of a believer rather than the tongue of an orator. Such a voice might have come from any churl, who knowing an impossible thing bearing down on his village, cries it through the market as a warning, with no heed for his own reputation.

More silence followed, wherein the hallthegns about the table stood dumb in mouth and deafening in face. Not even the theows at

---

[42] *(AK)*: middle-realm; middle-earth; the land of mortal Men.
[43] *(AB)*: waves.

their backs could keep eyes unskewed, and looked about those seated for whosoever would take up the speaker's stone now that it had become red-hot. But through whatever mirth and aghastment they all showed, it was clear that this play was an old one, and that they knew its lines, however shuffled the pages were this day. Knaks wore a look of fatherly bitter boredom, while Oyvarr showed how faintly a face might show a feeling—her nostrils only a shade more open, but giving her a look of rancorous forbearance, as though putting up with a needful smell, whose stink keeps at bay something only slightly worse than itelf.

It was within this bellying moment that Ivrik weighed the speaker over—*yondthought* him, as the Braccish might say—and came up with little. His hair was mousebrown, spiked hedgehoggishly on top, where its points stood bleached as by dint of lime, which the eastern elselanders were wont to use. This alone marked him apart, for as to looks, his seemed a skin sewn for any soul to wear, railmade for modesty, and for blending in without hiding. He was neither handsome nor ugly. His head was a head's shape, with ears and a nose. His eyes seemed sharp, but not stabbing, and his brow made a slight ledge above them. His beard was simply the beard of a man—not of a thegn nor of a lawdeemer—and middling thick—neither the downy bib of youth's, nor the chinmane of an awnsman[44]. His raiment—were it indeed the raiment of the court rather than any frock or housecoat—was tawny and slightly coarse, and whether made from the wool of sheep or the wool of some tree or wort, Ivrik could not be sure either. His bearing, as with his look, lay somewhere between humble and haughty—not passing from one to the other like to some cunningly wrought carving that does so with the light, but truly afloat between most and least, and standing so thoroughly outside outstandingness that it seemed staged—like a man hidden behind the trunk of a tree only slightly broader than his body.

There were many answers for his looks and bearing. The man was a priest, and gods were wont to mark their followers, and especially their chosen, in unmistakable ways. To make one so plainly plain, however, so unremarkable as to warrant remark, went against Their swaggering tastes as Ivrik knew them. And only a god

---

[44] A Braccish term for those men who, by some blessing or gift of blood, are able to grow thick, mighty beards, and like to dwarfs and heroes of legend, might tuck them into their belts or weave them into braids as thick as their wrists.

above Others should be so odd—an artist whose fame is fixed, and who keeps his new work subtle and weird, so as to allow those who recognize it to congratulate their own tastes rather than the skills of the artist, and so makes his celebrity a bloodsucker of their own pride. It was this reckoning above all—not the man's words—that told Ivrik he looked upon a priest of Bluharyn, the God of Life in All Its Shapes, Who saw souls in everything, and, was, more importantly, the Lord of the Eld in which they now lived. Contrary to many lesser priesthoods—and contrary to priesthoods of the Lord of the Eld in Elds past—the Heron's holy men were neither so widespread nor so invested in the province of Men that one might ever meet hosts of them. Theirs was a bookless faith, their flock the whole of frumth and ferrow[45], and so it was that any ditch or bog might be their church, and any gathering of grubs their fellowship. Nevertheless, Ivrik found it odd how little thought he had given to the Heron's priesthood till now, and how naked that want made his wits.

Like his every father before him, and like the greatest part of the Knaksfolk, Ivrik bent his knee to no one god or other, but looked upon Them as so many trees in a mighty forest, about Whose feet he as a Man must walk. He was not godless. The *Ossalore* gladdened him still—the old sagas of the northern Drottens told by his folk, and which had thrilled every Harandrish lad—especially the tales of Ossa-Tor, who was like Þórr of the Halishmen and the Thunor of the Knaksmen, but which in the stolid mouths of Harandrishmen had become more hero than god—*helt* rather than *gud*—and shared in the pain and toil of mankind more fully than anywhere else.

It was to the Ozmen themselves that the athelborn of Hála and the old Bracsriche were in some deal kin, so it was not for lack of faith, nor for any spurning of choice that Ivrik kept his godtroth unpledged, but rather out of need as a thegn and a Wyehead. He was an overseer of many different men, whom he drove to shed blood far from their homes, and to do so in an Eld of many gods and other Strengths, where the ways and worths of bloody deeds meant a hundred things on a thousand fields. And so it behooved him to keep his own heart unhallowed—not in readiness for unholy things, but so as not to hinder holiness—to build no idol of his own to be unshelved or swallowed by the winds and fogs of war. Such worldly

---

[45] *(AB* expression): all of living creation.

freedom—selfwill, as it was known—was, along with quicklife, another suchness of the Eld. And though it was said to differ from Elds past, Ivirk had seen in his own lifetime many times where men seemed under threat—whether of jealous gods or other men—to pledge their faith to One.

Derkings[46] to many single gods could be found among the Boarsmen—to Tiw and to Thunor, and to other lesser known Lords among elseland wereds. It was no surprise that the Heron was not a god loved by fighters, whose livelihood was the ending of lives, and whose minds could suffer no misgivings if the hand were to wield a sword well. At the Heronsmen's love of life and the living the Boarsmen had slung slurs befitting the black gulf that middled their two camps, calling them sheepsarthers and treefuckers, and countless other things both worse and wittier. Filthy hearsay of their worship, and of their rites, made up some of heartiest glee about the campfires, little of which Ivrik had ever believed, but which he had never bothered to learn the truth of. All he knew for sooth was that the Heronsmen were forbidden from being weredspriests to Boarsmen, both by their god and by the King himself, though Ivrik was not sure whose ban came first, and whose was the withsake. It had at one time angered him that a priesthood given to life spurned his own trade, where the fight was always for peace, and where men who loved life enough to seek out its edges, and to gamble it for a richer lease, might lay chopped and dying, and craving unfed the great gospel of the Ferghsmith[47] before they passed away.

But Ivrik had soon yielded his grudge toward the Heronites, knowing that anyone who worshipped life as having worth unto itself, regardless of the liver's shape and choices, must of need stand at odds with Mankind. To such a view as theirs there could be no Mannish souls, but only souls in Man's skin. As such, all the living business of the world was menning, or none of it at all.

To this manner of worship, the plainness of the Heron's priesthood meant much that was workmanly and harmless. To Ivrik, however, it nosed somehow of spydom, and of the sort that meant harm. And though the Wyehead had never before met the man before him, so it was that he disliked him at once, and like the King and Kween glowered at him, but without fully knowing why.

---

[46] *(AK)*: sects; cults.
[47] *(AB):* The Lifesmith; Bluharyn.

As for the priest stabbed on all sides by their stares, he blinked the way a cat might do, and turned smoothly toward Ivrik. "Boarshead, the Eld of Life had its stirrings well before the Nethrishmen came south. Harandril was settled—and throve in its own way—even in Its midst."

Ivrik set his teeth, and the cheek-knots raised hackles in his beard. To have one's thinking goaded by a king was one thing, but this was rather another. "Both a king and his elderthegns know," Ivrik muttered onto the table, "that a country takes time to carve out. Headway is a fickle road, nowhere more than in Harandril, where it seems snowed-in two-thirds of the year." And with that he lifted his eyes, and thrust his look upon the priest with all the might of his post. Were his stare the thrust of a spear, he would have hoisted the man upon it, and let him dangle aloft, as the words slowly worked him through. "It may be, Heronite, that the headway was ours for that long, and hardwon it was. Then the Heron's Age came into its own, and the tide turned against us. But, then, I am no more a man of the cloth than you are a man of the sword. Who can say what oceans—whether blood or soma—laps each of our shores."

The priest was unshaken. He took Ivrik's thrust, but like one who feels no pain. "No, Boarshead. The Heron knows, I cannot speak to all things. But I can say this—Bluharyn is no emperor, no high king, as you might say. The Vitalic Age is no divine empire, but rather like a singing breath that serves to brace the weary, and to remind them what it is to be on borrowed time. He does not, unlike other gods in the past and given the chance, lord over every little thing. Though God of Life, He does not commandeer every living endowment—He does not overrule every quickening and heartbeat, every shoot and stirring, to His own ends. The proof of this is simple—that He did not overturn what was here when He came in. It is all as it was, but with new hues alone."

His drinking horn drained, Knaks laughed within the afterbreath. "Methinks, priest, the Wyehead does not believe you."

"He has a good head to do so," Oyvarr added, taking back her husband's Evertux and handing it to her thuften.

"King, Kween," the priest began again, and if anything irked Ivrik further, it was the strength of this man to keep his head beneath the storms looming all about him. "The Heron knows that Man is a child of this world, and a cunning child. And the Heron does not wish to set you at each other's throats, however wayward you be. It is not His will to see Man made an ape."

"So you have said ere now," Knaks answered. "And again I call it sotship and stuntspeech, at best made to keep the fleshmeat off my dishes, or my axes from the trees I put beneath them for my boards." He scuddered his fingers upon the mighty ironwood that once would have towered above him. "Again I say you this, and now I do it before my court: Man is not simply a child of this world, but its heir. What Age he lives, he inhabits, and it becomes an Age of Man. His earth is his yard, and there is nothing he cannot, or will not, lord over. For he is born with a craftiness and a cunning that are onely among redlife, and when whipped and unleashed, and given a worthy pack, he shall overleap any haw, take wing, and gain the very threshold of his makers. You see there can be no peace between gifts such as ours and a god who loves all heartbeats as one, for Man would must cut off his fingers and walk on his knees, and gut half his brains through his nose to live alongside beasts and not lord over them. We may be good herdsmen and hawkers, riders and kindhearted hunters, but we shall not take the gates off our byres and bring our livestock into our houses as brothers, nor shall we think for our children to share the meadows with wolves.

"You say it is to be an Age of Life, but I hear it is to be an Age of Beasts, where Man must make way and not grow, where he must stoop for the yoke, and go about on all fours. I see you shake your head, priest, and I ask you, if the Heron makes all the frumth and ferrow of Smað one kind, then what are the bounds of His reckoning? What lines has He drawn, that we as Men might cross them and cease to be what He makes us? Whatever they might be, they are the walls He has built for us, and they are the first stones our hammers will find. For the end of Man is to know himself, and not be told, and to gain the farthest thing he can ween in thought, and not simply reach with a grasp of flesh and bone.

"And it gets away from no one, priest, that you speak of Man in *you's* and not *we's*. You utter a tung of Men, you clad your nakedness in Man's garb, but only as an ombudsman to the fauna. It is why this court will not hear your Man's name. You have not earned one. And till the day you find means to write one in piss, as your beloved beasts do, and to do so before my housethegns unman you fully for such unhousebroken filth, you will have no name but *priest,* which is a word I shall want back and washed when you are done wearing it."

It was a king's abuse, and the priest took it as he must, reddening a little as laughter went around the table. For some, and for many of the gigglers no doubt, it had been enough to chase one from court, much less still his tongue there, but Ivrik watched the priest bear it, and saw in him a kind of man he knew well among Boarsmen, and indeed sought out whenever picking men for the hardest of tasks. It was the look of the unbreakable, grazed but unscathed—*thellich thildy thegn,* some song somewhere had it—for which the heat of arveth[48] and shame were as the fires of a blacksmith's hearth, melting from the heart all the dross and slag that yielded, and leaving behind a will of purest iron.

As Ivrik foresaw, the priest waited for the sniggering to die, then acknowledged the King's blow thoughtfully, touching his own breast and nodding with a smile as full—and, Ivrik believed, as misleading—as that of a pitdog.

"I give it you, King, that the Heron's government is unlike that of this kingdom, and of the Bracsriche before it, and of any upon Ráma save lands far too south to matter. And for that, its uniqueness may go unseen, for just as Men must judge others by means of their own wits, so must the mightiest kingdom judge other dominions by the might of their armies, and the reach of their marches, and the wealth of their coffers, and other such things of which I have little knowledge. But the Heron's Age is not a kingdom, nor is it a single era. At best I can liken it to a fellowship, wherein Powers of all kinds stake an interest, but Who work together to a shared advantage. And though this fellowship is always sundry, it is never stable, and its shape is not fixed. The heavenly hall where it musters is a place of storms, where bodies of Power gather and swell, and clash with one another, to crumble or merge like quicksilver, reshaping again, leaving those once inside out, and the other way around. And with every such shift, it may seem to us that a different Age has come in, or that different Ages live in different places, where old factions have learned to cling to corners, and conspire within the wings to overtake the whole once again. It is an Age of freedom that way. Untamed. We have it ourselves. And just as Man is free to make war on some share of Life's dominion, so too might some share of that

---

[48] *(AB):* difficulty; hardship; adversity.

dominion make benighted war on Man, not so much in need or in hatred, but in misjudging the Heron as a kind of gardener, whose shears are for the tallest blooms.

"And to those of His children who truly are under siege, and who know not whom is to blame, I repeat that the Heron overturned nothing, and that the land lies prowled by legions of things who stand beyond His dominion. The eldritch, the undead, the fayfolk, and the frumth of magic—the wyrms, and the griffs, for that matter—as well as the cunning creatures who speak the tungs of Men. These are neither Man nor Beast, as a twaining dole must make them, but something both and other, which gained their souls in other Ages, or in corners thereof, at other knees than the Heron's, and live, and thrive, despite what one might presume of His Age and tastes. Some of these beings—the soarcats of Tymnig, for one—call this Smað home and Men its friends, but others have no share in the suchness of this world, bearing valid grudge against the Heron's humble staddle, and can make war upon it without having to live with the aftermath.

"And should one of them place Man beyond the Heron's circles, King—and I ask this without knowing the answer, nor wanting some such one—were it better for a kingdom of Men to ally itself with these outlanders than to seek peace with its own neighbours? Were an alliance with dragons better than leaving some room for the bears, or holding back the hunt of a thing nearly killed off? For though the wyrms and the trolls, the thurses and other monsters found their making at the hands of other Powers, their natures are as fixed as those of any smathly souls, and they will sting if embraced, however earnestly they may they sue for peace. For unlike the hungry wolf who snatches up an unwatched child, and hears in its cries no sound different from those of any other prey, there are abominations at work who know the difference, and who lust for evilest chances, and who are patient, and crafty, in their search for its troves."

And at that speech, Knaks loosed a noise that from a lesser man might have been a snort, but from him threw up a wall without doors. "You have scattered many leaves in my path, priest—and with pretty breezes, from the outlandish taste of your words. Let me crush them all, and I shall at last hear my Wyehead's tidings.

"You say the Heron's Age is a fellowship—a samening, you might call it, were your tongue better tuned to the sweep of Man's meanings—where gods work together, for the greater good than any one of them might bring about on his own. You thought your words careful, but it rang clear that you deem this a better thing than kingship, which I forgive you, priest, but only because it neither touches me nor takes me unawares. There is a saying in the court of Brac about this, which makes a game of the old words and the new, and it says that something sameworked is samwrought—that is, something done by many is only half-done. Too many cooks spoil the broth, as they say of the kitchen, and of something slightly less worthy of a pecking-order than a *government*, as you call it.

"And as for whether thoftship with fiends is choicer than brotherhood with wolves, you say you ask without willing some right answer, and yet again your ox's tongue breaks faith with you.

To ask "were it" is to ask my will of it, priest, not the sooth of it, and to sunder me from truth. Again, though, I forgive you." He half-raised the Evertux, now full again. "You ought to thank the brerdsmed warming my heart—a brew of Men, mind you, not of bees.

"But I drift. Hark to this, priest. A war may be fought on many fronts, and against foes who themselves are foes. The land might be harmed by both fire and water, but none can make thoftship with one against the other. No, priest. Man is alone in the louring bleak, and onely in every way, and as he keeps what is his in the threat to come, he will fight with the unbounded strength of his own wit and learning. Every craft he has ever known or found, every blade, mail, and weapon ever built or glimpsed—these are the shelves of his warhoard, and the ways he might use them are the ways of every chart he has drawn or read. And should these not be enough, we shall dig up every inch of dark lore we once knew and banished, and buried close to Hell, and we shall set its shoulders toward our foe, and unleash it. For these are the bolt-holes of cornered Man, not to burrow or cower, not to spit or howl or chew off the limb snared, but to mend his broken bow with his own heartstrings, and ere his spark is snuffed out to fit to it and hurl forth everything at his back, be it his home and the very world he leaves. *That*, priest, is the way of Man, and that is why we shall not bend to your Heron's trough. In the end, we shall die on our two feet, upright as Men, or he will bow before us."

There could be no stiffer curtain to this play, and the priest, whatever his mind, resumed his silence, and shrank back among the seated without seeming to move at all. Again, as it had done seven times ere now, the room stilled. Before this the lulls had been hot ones, quietly stewing in the smacks of everything left unspoken. But this stillness was cold, and left those within it shrunken. Not even the hearthfire seemed willing to touch it, and glowed without warmth or light, like a reminder of sunshine, or a burning torch upon the wall of a tomb.

The brooding are not barren, however. They hide what they hatch. Among the theows and hofmen who tended to the King and knew his ways were thoughts aplenty, and all of one breed. They were of the man who had banished the kingly hounds from his throneroom, and so broke with his longfathers, who had seen them at the foot of their beds, and even with them to the needhouse[49], where kings are most unsafe. They were of the man who now seldom rode any of his horses, least the six-legged Thridslip, offspring of Woden's own steed, who could gallop upon screes, and climb cliffsides, but who also knew a hundred words of Braccish, and prattled like a two-year-old. They were of the man who, what is more, kept his hengests[50] hitched far from earshot of any meaningful talks, and who leaned more and more upon seeing stones and dreecraft for his correspondence than upon *Knaks-hawk*—the doughty network of swifthawks and bringdrakes his House had bred and fought to build, which, no less than might of weapons, made strong the Onelatching of the Bracsriche. And, more than all the others, they were of the man who had weighed the striking of the boars and badgers from his house's sigalders—the carving out of his heraldish tokens and namesakes from all the kingly shields and helms and breastplates from the islets of the western Kúloys to the easternmost marches of Ignam. It was after drinking he had done so, and at a mell much like this one, but he had said it nonetheless, and such a mighty bell cannot be unrung. Instead of the beastheads, he deemed, he would have etched words of might—staves of Man's own making—akin to the wreathrunes of Shebril, and the stark, slashdrawn badges of the Houses of Trebell. Into the rims of shields he would inscribe the most stirring words from the lays of the Knaksmen, and the sagas of the Nethrishmen, of the eddas that breathed into their hearts, and of all the scopship around heroes and men who have won everlasting names.

Their thoughts were of the man who forbore the byname of Boar for now, but few saw it lasting, and looked for the day when he called slurs even the thegnly handles of *lion* and *eagle*, all one with *ass, swine,* and *louse.* No fourlegged wight, no matter how trustworthy, had found a haven from his hatred. The soarcats of Tymnig, though truer to the throne than many a Knaksman and eastern underking, had not been called to the Isentron in years, and the King had not called upon them at home in Pandressey, not ever, and many feared their friendship had soured. The cunningest beasts he now saw as halfbirths—blunders born between worlds—and had banished them from his lorddom, and even from his heart, be they

---

[49] *(AK):* privy. An indoor outhouse.
[50] *(AB):* stallions; horses.

the crows whose speech he knew as a birthgift, or the heleth-hounds who, wandering against the wolves, had overnighted at times at the Isentron, asking only for a bed by the gleeds, and a friendly word with the King or Kween.

These, the brooding thoughts of the court, were not shaped by godtroth or ill will. Of the Heronstroth and His Age, they knew less than the King or the Heron's priest, and could not say whether either side was rightful or wrongful. No, it was not the truth of it all that they brooded upon, but rather the sadness—the sorrow of a friend who knows someone beloved to be cheapening himself. Worst of all was that Knaks himself seemed to struggle with it. Were those about him said to brood, the sullenness of the King himself was like the nursing of an unseen pack, the thrashing and feeding of which made his teeth to grist, and his eyes to glaze as it drained him.

Stiffening, he sat up in his chair, and now spoke as a carven mouthpiece of the Isentron itself. "Tell me now, Wyehead, the tidings you bring."

All winsomeness at an end, Ivrik returned to himself. As Wyehead he sat more easefully than he had as a man. "Bayerd is lost, King. Not only are we pushed back, but we cannot see inside. Our birds, our men, our dreecraft—none of them break through. It is as though the very earth is working against us, and Man is the only thing it will not hire."

Knaks nodded once, and his face stayed cold. "As I knew it," he said. "My soothsayers—they warned me ere you tried it, and made it known to me ere you came. But I needed to hear it, you see, for wisecraft might be warped, and the word of a staunch witness is as close to the thing itself as one might be brought."

Bayerd—backward Bayerd, with its dizzy ways and olden livelihoods—with its amber-dredging and peatburning and its unKnaksish kinglets who asked too little to be unthroned; its blue fogs and tired gods; its tung, which like a bonfire crackled and spat, but whose warmth was a hallowed hearth to whoever had slogged across the moors that ringed its lakelands.

Bayerd—Shebril's better brother the Knaksmen called it, mindful of the fight each had offered in the Onelatching, and thankful Bayerd had not, unlike Shebril, fielded women and beardless, as though facing the very hordes of Ferine, and not the neighbours and landlords they'd known for hundreds of winters beforehand. A few and skirmishing folk, they weirdly warred playfully, like to youths with wooden swords, waylaying and cackling and running away, and laughing at their wounds as though caught and earned in some dizzy but wifewinning stunt. They'd trapped and they'd raided and sneaked into tents, stealing horses and boots and painting the boarhelms pink. The *Coggaskelta* some called it, a warfare of old tales, where every man was a story, and a thread among webs, and not a mailshirt full of moving meat to be slaughtered by the thousands. And because neither they nor the Knaksmen had been hateful in their task, but fought busily, like whistling workers at deadly but needful work, they saw one another no more scornfully than the miner sees the slouching caveroof, or the bridgebuilder the swallowing gap, and they fought only enough to prove themselves, and be done, and not take each other out of this world.

With fellow Man, they knew the limits. Their warpath had a hedge. For Bayerd was marchland to nightmares, edging the Unfondlands that hid Ferine like a sea, and whose fogs threatened great, clawing waves which all at once might rise, and rip the southeastern shires from the landcharts. Overnight these holdings might swether, without sound or flash of struggle, like ships thieved from their havens, and not until travellers sought them out would they find all the roads in lying broken and frayed among wilderness, like moorlines chopped, and end-burnt to stump off. Such a thing had befallen many a marchland of Ráma, though not yet Knaks, nor the Bracsriche. But the tales had gnawed and fretted many kingdoms before the eastering of the Nethrishmen, among them those of the Bayrdish themselves, whose lands had once stretched further toward Ferine than where they now stood.

"And so it seems," Knaks muttered, though looking in on himself, "that all my lioning of yoredays has brought them slavering to the walls of today. Were it that this was a foe we had once faced, and thrown down, and not one from books too brittle to read. Of yore I think of Briyim, whose wreck left no witnesses. I had kinsmen there."

"We await your will, King," the Wyehead said. "The eastern wereds have made herewicks along the edges of Ignam and Pyndamir, and hope to keep in what we might not drive out."

"They will hold those lines," Knaks said, telling secrets to his beard. "I have readied us for this, as I know you've heard tell."

"Yes, King. The sellswords—the teerseekers, rather—who now gather in the elderburgs." The Wyehead was swift, but not eager, to right his word for them, choosing the same one Knaks himself had written in the lathing now posted everywhere between Kilko and the Kúloys.

Knaks caught his discord and threw something back in a glance, and the Wyehead found he could not read it. All he could tell was that it was a barbless look, sharp but unentangling, and that within moments the King had drawn it back within himself, left to a sulk—whether of gloom or malcare or of that mighty breastwhelm of uneasiness the Braccish called *yeth*—no one save Knaks could know.

The great door to the chamber burst open, and the hearthfires bellowed as a body of the King's housewered stormed past its threshold. Five men they were—four wyemen and a wizard—and Ivrik's three marshals were with them. Both Knaks and his Wyehead leapt to standing, the King's chair toppling backward and thundering down, which would need two men or more to upright again. Though the breach spoke of trouble, the housewered halted just inside the room and awaited acknowledgement. Their eyes swept the walls as those seated and at rest began to build sounds of worry.

"What is it?" Knaks bid of them, his voice ringing off their mail.

"King, Kween," their headward spoke from beneath his helm. "Some uncouth thing has been found within the Leafapanz. It took eight spears and lies dead, but we do not know whether it came alone, nor how it gained the Rim unseen."

The Blue Boar bristled, and his mantle, though it might swallow several men, seemed all at once to strain. "Bring me my sword!" he bebode. Again the Rings became an iron-knuckled fist. "Bring me Unriven. And bring me the Whelpwroughtskin, that I might show this landleaper the comelitheness[51] of the Isentron."

Ivrik shuddered to hear those mighty names uttered, but also thrilled a little to think that he might—unless the King be talked down from his halfdrunkenness—see the best of the Ringgear wielded. Alack and thanks, the housewered would have no such wanthrift as to see the King rush weaponed but unmailed into the bowers of his own grounds, to pick a fight with a dead thing, or worse, a baitgoat.

---

[51] *(AB)*: hospitality

At no time during the riche of this Knaks—nor likely, the riche of his father—had the Leafapanz been gained by any bogey, for the great garden was girt by the Rimberg of the Starbowl, that mighty hoop of hills thrown up by the blast of that fallen star of iron from which the Isentron's own walls were shaped. The Boarsman spied the coming of all from its bulwarks, whose crests were finned with battlements, and horned with towers, from whose heights they trusted no newcomer, neither man nor bird, for what he seemed. And the land about the Rimberg was blasted and barren for many hundreds of furlongs in all bearings, its scrub and creeks hiding nothing, even unto the burgship of Kraterpol, which was a city of dreemen. As for those Outsiders and dreeish things whose skill was to go unseen or to take otherworldly paths, watch over their eldritch domain was given to the Boar's wizards—the Black Tusks—whose sentinels were themselves seldom seen, and whose wered was a single field of black at one edge of the Kingly Houseshield.[52] Their beady eyes were everywhere, from the elderburgs through backwaters to those nameless forlorn cloisters where they were said to practice black trollship and witchcraft—things forbidden from any dreemen in Knaks but them. Even in these wastes, however, the more wholesome Boarsmen might be found, in bodies of rangers like the *Magernatt*, roving among the kingdom's furthest flung folk, whose feelings towards Knaks, however luke or cold, would never go so far as to let a monster make its way untold toward the Isentron.

That all these eyes might have overlooked something was more than unforgivable. It was unthinkable. Ivrik's teeth gnashed behind his beard. His arm felt a stump without a blade at its end. He wanted to fight, and alongside his King, but the Isentron was its own world, and he had no sway here. It had its own Boarsmen, who were brought up here, and though these kingsmen thegned at the marches to gather the wounds and bloody wisdom the peace of the Rimberg kept at bay, they were never swapped out, and knew the homely quirks and crannies of the Starbowl and its fastness as only sons who once toddled there might do. So it was that the wereds of the Isentron held sway over all other Boarsmen inside the Rimberg, their ranks overshadowing elselanders, their learning of that uncanny stead went so far. But, Ivrik reckoned, a sword went through a

---

[52] The royal coat of-arms—distinct from the Boar's own Kinshield—representing, among other things, the various divisions of the Knaksish military.

fiend's flesh the same here as out East, and he should be thrice thurse-fucked if he stood by like some bondsman while others clashed for his King. His toes fidgeted, working the thews of his lower legs, and he felt still the daggers that lay sheathed along their lengths. He had two of them, and they were no butter knives.

No matter the mayhap, the headward at the door was cool. "My King, as he knows, by the laws of his own blood, is given leave to come down once we have made fast the Rimberg, and the wizards put their ferrets through all dreeish warrens." He looked to the Black Tusk, who nodded and went across the room to do something at the window.

Knaks seemed to grow, stacking and blackening like the ashcloud of a fireberg. He thrust the Evertux into Oyvarr's hands. "Housecarl, bring me Unriven. Bring it me lest I make new halls to the weaponhoard where I keep it."

The laws were allbinding, but the King was allwielding. It baited the old saw about something that could not be stayed meeting something that would not budge. The headward stickled, the two kept to their squabble, and amidst the gathering uproar of it, Ivrik made his way to the window where the wizard was murmuring his tradecraft. Though the trollman—as Harandrishmen were wont to call them—did not look away from his uncanny deed, nor show any other token of welcome, he spoke to Ivrik, his words grumbling out from the pulleys of whatever weird task strained him.

"Do not worry yourself, Wyehead. The problem is not the what of it but the how. The thing that came upon us in the Laufapanz, it was more startled than we were to find it there."

Ivrik eased up a little. "You are saying it was lost?"

"Yes. An anomaly, not part of a design. At least, not yet. I cannot school you in the science of it, not in a fortnight. But have our word."

Ivrik wondered how he might take the word of a man half of whose words he did not understand. He tried to peer out the window, but it was more a loophole than an eyethurl, and he saw only that silty twilight where night and the hearthshine mingled. Meanwhile, in the chamber behind him, a monstrous chair smashed against a wall. The King, it seemed, had set his will above the lawly writs of his forebears, and would atgo this threat, whatever it might be, and however foreslain. Ivrik, for the life of him, could not but ween the mighty Man hacking apart a heap of meat, spittle in his roar, Unriven cleaving into dirt, till he stood there puffing before the steaming mince of it. Knaks and his wered billowed from the room, leaving Oyvarr and the rest of the court within, Ivrik's men among them. Housewards stood at the threshold to keep things as they were, and to eke out and uphold what was left of the law.

Ivrik nodded at his marshals, who nodded back and knew the score. They would sit tight until he, and not the housewards, bid them do otherwise. As for the other hoflings and hirdmen in the room, they cinched themselves into knots long tied, and tried as they might to find something in the tidings that had not been said. Among those who did not speak, and who stood with no one, was the Heron's priest. Though on his feet, he kept his place at the ironwood board, leaning upon its edge, kirtle furrowing where it bunched. His eyes, both youthful and old, staring wanly into the silver grains, as though he would scry there, or dowse, either to see what was happening outside or to find within it the wells of loathing the King had sipped to spit upon him. He looked up, as though feeling the Wyehead's thoughts—not like a Man, Ivrik thought, but like a deer startled drinking—and the two kept their eyes locked longer than was hovely, with Ivrik, for sake of hoveliness, the one to break it.

At the chamber's farthest end, he saw the Kween. It was hard to miss her, head and shoulders above her thuftens, whose ring of headscarves seemed like the stones that rim a smoldering campfire. He thought better of drawing next to Oyvarr, whom he did not know well. She was a shieldmaid in a pinch, as was every Kúlish woman, and she was moreover the drotning of her island folk, and athelborn, which meant she was stronger in a fight than at least the worst Boarsman. Still, she was an elselander here, now and till death, and followed the inland laws as painstakingly as on broken glass. Ivrik met her eyes, and again, but their inner wrath was a flame, and needed to flicker. As by a draft, they seemed drawn to the door of the bridebower, wherein she would indeed keep weapons ready, likely the Grindknife[53] itself, which was her own, and not, like Unriven, something kept in a fastened heedern.[54] Should a fiend tear through the bricks and wood to come at her, Ivrik would make a wall of himself before the Kween, as was his oath, but he could not help but to think he might be getting in the wrong one's way, and

---

[53] *Kúlish*: Grindaknívur, which is also the generic term for a blade the Kúlish folk use to slaughter whales (*grindar*).

[54] *(AB)*: guarded storehouse; secret armoury.

damming back a flood the better to let loose. And so he tarried, getting no more than a stingy glance when the trollman left too, and was made for the first time to feel the shame of the herd, to which the herd itself was dull, but for a sheepdog was worse than a whipping. The great head of the Ever watched them all from its shadowy roost, its dead black eyes reaching across the room to fall somewhere near the wooden carving of Morgenmece, the kinslayer. Ivrik beheld the fiendish boar and felt the stirrings of a deep shudder.

Wrack and bane were not afoot at the Isentron, at least not yet. He felt such things as one feels a dampness in the weather. But something unhappy lay beyond the highbergs, beyond that toothsome skyrim whose walls had always soothed him till now. Its thrashings had begun in Bayerd, but now it was burrowing. How far its warren reached, and where its head might break through, he had only his whats to needle him. For the Boarsman and the heleth in him, restless and loveyearning, it all pledged a chance of dear worth—to stare down an outland foe, one not seen in centuries—and either overcome it, or better, wrixle deathblows[55]. But the Man in him, and the orchardlord, they balked at the cost. He who so begrudged his homeland its bite now found its teeth rather soft, for at least the weather and blights were hardships he knew, and not weird things whose reach was a six-fingered arm. Though there were some who saw monsters as a rightful share of the wilderness, and others, like the King, who wrote them over wholly to the eldritch, Ivrik saw the two as one, and likened such fiends to the wildfires of Harandril, which had a foot in both worlds, and would, though shaped of something Man knew and needed, eat his land down to its bones.

Beneath the teeth of such a foe, Ivrik foresaw the suffering of all the Fergh, of all life red and green, and knew not the right thing to hope for. Whether to flood the marchlands with the whole strength of Knaks, and so lay low this monster in its cradle, or to let it feed, and swell, to go up against it on the Wyeride[56], fullgrown and dreadful and maybe unstoppable, for all the stakes, for all time, to Hell with everything else.

The Wyehead sighed, and gristbit, willing his blood to carry away the brerdsmed, whose giggling froth he now found too much like piss upon the dark calm of cool thoughts. No matter. Nothing

---

[55] *(AB)*: exchange deathblows; each be the death of the other.
[56] *(AK):* The final battlefield of the Ozmen (Hálish *Vígrið*).

that would happen here would be his call. So he settled into himself and waited, his thighs, aching so much from the ride only a while ago, now aching only for the ride back to Bayerd.

The King would come back in a fivespell—the Timekeeper told it to the trice—and would say nothing of what he had seen, save to the Kween. It was plain, however, that what he had seen had touched his cares deeply, and would shape his thoughts for a long time to come.

VI
Unæwful
Lawless

For two days they had been in Eksar, and Toron had seen nothing.

That is, he saw only glimmers—flashes that rose in the darkness and vanished, like white-bellied trout snatching flies from the face of a pool. Colours burst and bled, and not simply with his thoughts. Turning his face towards heat brought a gloaming to his eye-night, just as the opening of the doors to the inn's hall, in the morning when they faced the dawn, lit a torch behind his mind's black curtain.

There had been a final flicker of things before the thoftship gained the burg's western gates—of painted arches straddling the square, their ribs overlapping like too many bracelets on one arm; of timber-braced stone; of still, blue banners, and of many, many folk. They'd hurried along beneath a bower of slender trees with trunks wrapped in scarves and leaves the hue of flame, their branches trailing white streamers. Trimmed for a holy day most likely, but he still wasn't sure the trees weren't dressed and breathing—some weird, woody thede from the forlornlands of which he had never heard tell. In truth, he had hardly given a thought to it at the time, and only in the restful hush of the days since then recalled these last sights. Set before the guttering of his senses, the dread that he was dying of his wounds, and the mutilated but fragrant bundle of woman slumped across his lap, it had all been overlooked. Now that he had time, and the reassurance of life and swift healing, he wanted nothing more than to step out-of-doors open-armed, and to fill his dry feelings to the brim from the wells of the elderburg's menning.

He heard the city's gab and rattle. He whiffed its heady stew, which changed with the wind. Sometimes it was of baking and smelt-reek, other times of woodsmoke and manure, but always sundry, and always mingling with the hearty smells from the inn's own kitchen. He felt the warmth of the heatblower, a wondrous thing of both magic and smithcraft. The evenness of its heat was like a spring day, and so unlike the breath of a hearth or campfire, where one is hot in front and cold behind, and one must move and turn one's self before its flames like one cooks a piece of meat. He felt the sanded-smooth faces of tables, and of handles within his hands, and of wool between his toes. Clean bedding held him, a bliss of softness and of the mayweed with which everything was washed. Uncaring of any ambush he lay within them naked, and the pleasure of their embrace was heavens beyond that of any portqueen[1] a hungrier man might have hired. He had not yet shaved, and would not try it till the dressing was off his face. He had bathed long though, and twice, the waters baked by the same underground wonderworks that gave breath to the steamhouse across the way.

That sauna the Chaldallions only seemed to leave long enough to look in on him, and to have the innkeep or one of his daughters brew another pot of their acrid-smelling tea to drink and sweat out again. It cleansed the body they claimed, and helped with their own healing. Their wounds, though not as crippling as his own, had been fierce, or so they told him, and they promised not to strike out into Eksar until everyone was whole once again. Toron had nonetheless roused each morning to find them gone from their room.

He had hardly minded, waking not to the dawnshriek of birds, nor the groaning of trees in cold wind, but inside the muffler of walls and roof, with no dew in his hair, and no grudge in his bones. It was not wet moss or mud that received his first steps, but rather wood milled by men. He had felt his way downstairs, fingertips relishing the ribs of the wainscoting, seeking the post of the landing that led between floors. The rail of the staircase he had jiggled on its brackets—unrepaired since their last visit—and he had stumbled over the nosings of the treaders, which were new, but stuck out much too far. It made him wonder again about how he'd do as a woodsmith here should he hang up his swords and put down roots. Downstairs in the hall he had tasted the city as well—its meats free of scorch and smoke; its breads soft enough to be torn, and not broken like clods of dirt; and its water, dippered from barrel to cup, tasting nothing like the old leather of his waterskin's innards.

---

[1] *(AB): courtesan.*

He had seen no one, but the tokens of folk were everywhere. Voices and footsteps, and the scents of bodies both unwashed and perfumed. The strangely slow, lilting flow of the Eksarish Allmal, which made every statement questionlike, but seemed blithe whether it was answered or not. Such speech, he'd heard tell, along with much else of the Teakenmalish ways, was owed to the Timebriar, for all those born in the Whorl grew up alongside ghosts. Whenever Teakenmalers chanced upon a newcomer, they approached him as a likely shade from the past, rootless among centuries, who might not understand all it was told. So it was that the wordhoards of Teakenmalers were steadier than those of outland elderburgs, where the rich and the learned treated their tongues as any other share of their bodies to be decorated—flaunting stylish ways of speaking which buried all their innermost meanings. No, the folk of Eksar did not—as with those of Entogor and Tayamot, and the five western townships—prune their quide[2] as a gardener does the shrubbery. Instead they spoke plainly, though that plainness was strewn with old rubble.

In Eksar, speech went undressed, but its nakedness was invulnerable, like that of an old ox glimpsed tenyear-after-tenyear in the same hillside meadow, gathering wool and wisdom, never taking shelter from the rain—steadfast, immortal. Its meanings were old but not olden; they could not be overturned. It went a little against this steadiness that Teakenmalish words, when written down, had no firm order of letters. Its writings showed more variety than even in Brac and Landon, where the juggling of old, new and middling wordforms was bravura—like painting with as many colours as one might find. Teakenmalish writings were among the hardest to read in the kingdom, rafting among the Whorl's eddies of time, and having fostered bookish tungs and dizzying thews of expression that nary an elselander might know for his own. Happily for the outlander, there was no chance of hearing such bookspeech put to breath among the streets and markets of Eksar. Only in the hofs and selds[3] of that burg might one find speech to dizzy the ears, and even there was as play, or as a strange sort of scopship one lord in twenty suffered to hear.

---

[2] *(AB):* phrase; verbal expression; way of speaking
[3] *(AK):* courts and halls.

But here the thoftship was as far from that kind of stead as one might get and still be indoors—a humble inn in Eksar's southwestern sheet, not far from the western gates through which they'd come. The Stitchmeal Sark it was named, after an old story of thildiness, where a thrallgirl assembles a lordly garment of bits she had gathered over the years from the floor of the castle her prison, and, fooling the doorwards during a feast, escapes to freedom. At the Sark, there was no gleemanry, no smoking of pipes, and no stronger drink than saraf—which the Chaldallions snickering called *runk*— and which was served only at daybreak. The want of song and spirits was owed to the four taverns down the road, with which the innkeep pleaded no gain in competing. Moreover, he said that too many an Eksarish inn hazarded the comfort of its overnight guests for the coin of local drunkards and merrymakers. In those words lay the sedefulness[4] that marked the innkeep and his daughter as Heronites of some stern branch. While they did not lack for mirth, they kept their own enjoyment of spirituous things to fixed corners of the year. And it was indeed sedefulness rather than righteousness; lodgers at the Sark who wanted a bit of song and ale were urged wholeheartedly to seek it, but to return for a quiet night's sleep once the fun was over, and to find a tray of saraf at their door the next morning.

It had been lack of gold that had brought the thoftship to the Sark the first time around, and where the innkeep—as a Heronite, and with Toron's word that the cat knew when to step outside—had let Gorrh sleep indoors. Though their wallets were now heavy with the weird offwhere gold of Sherk-narsk-wirth which Níscel and the folds of their own clothing had gathered under Eksar, they picked the Sark freely, and welcomed its humble airs even as they yearned to heal and to explore the burgish wonders beyond. So it was that Toron leaned upon his elbows at a table in the front hall, a stein of green tea between them. Its fumes moistened the bandages about his face as he listened to the heatblower breathe, to Kurtisian sigh, and to the passage of revellers beyond the walls he could not see. Gorrh covered a good swath of the floor nearby, peering out from that place between wakefulness and sleep which everyone mistook for sleep itself. Stoneware clunked beneath water as someone washed the evening's crockery.

---

[4] *(AB)*: abstemiousness; self-restraint.

Gorrh's nod of mind. Boards creaked beneath the approach of footfalls. One of the daughters.

"Would you like anything else before we let the kitchen fires out?"

Aldessa, the eldest.

Kurtisian made a farting sound with his mouth. There would have been a wave of his hand too. His tired *no*.

"Thorn?" he mumbled, all but asleep.

"No, thank you. This is good."

The swipe of a wet cloth on wood; the woodflowery scent of her hair as she leaned past him. She had used too much of it, whatever it was. His eyes, were they unbound, might have watered. The blooms of its stock were wild, but they were the fruit to a cooling pie; he could smell every step of their cultivation—the cleaning and crushing and brewing, the decanting into bottles boiled and ribboned, the hawking of them beneath colourful awnings, their swapping for man's mintage, the beauty bethought with its every uncorking.

His nose reeled, long given to the whispers and mere traces of things amidst the cold, quiet tangle of aftersummer smells. He shuffled against the urge to horse-snuff it all in.

"If you need anything through the night," she said. "You know our door."

And she left. Kurtisian chuckled, half-heartedly lewd, and the two men went back to not speaking for some time.

Toron drank his tea slowly, the flavours and the heat a riot of feeling in his mouth. Even now he fought to calm himself, to batten in the doors that kept him closed, to keep from weeping like a castaway who has at last made it to friendly shores. Much had changed with him since last he was here, and to be alone with hearing was to be alone with the chatter of one's minning. He'd been warned that the kind of healing he'd received might play tricks on his mind, and he had no doubt that the Briar made it worse. It was hard to tell how much worse, however, for so gently did it churn together the past and the now that the eddy could not be felt, and revealed itself only through the thickening of what it stirred. Níscel, Shard, Rhianys, Dhandhar: they were but the surface of it, and every hour he saw their faces and heard their voices with more life than he had done even in the most joyful dreams, and cruelest nightmares, since their deaths.

When he sat still he sank deeper. Memories brushed against him in the darkness that were so old he knew not when he'd first met them. Harandrish things, many of them: old neighbours he'd met as a toddler, now surely long dead; things he'd seen and done as a boy in the woods, things gathered before he'd had words to name them. He saw his dogs run living before him, and the day he'd seen them laid dead on their balefires. Shaggy cattle snorted beneath the bearded branches of his homestead. Cats blinked at him from under the house. And when he slept, he fell out the bottom of it, and not only saw his father and mother but also spoke to them again, and woke up with his bandages wet, for he did not know if it was a forgotten memory he saw or something he'd done new in a place beyond sorrow.

From the first morning here he'd wanted to tear the dressing from his eyes, if only to vent his soul but also to water down with the addition of new sights the stuff he found tarring up his mind. Three days he must wear them, he'd been told, and he'd asked why it was the Chaldallions had hired such slow healing when they'd had the coin for swifter. They'd thought he was dying, Justinian had pleaded, and that the *pullula*[5]—or so the Chaldallions kept calling the girl they'd found mangled among the bushes—was already dead. Moreover, they did not know their choices. The burgwards at the gates had gone for the closest help they could find, and returned with three acolytes from the nearby sickhouse. They were Heronites of a kind, ministering to the farmers and their livestock who lived among the foothills outside the city. And so they had been able to tend to Gorrh as well to the Men, setting Kurtisian's wrist and balming Justinian's cuts, and stitching up the many biteholes that oozed upon the tuskcat's coat. As for the wargening sickness that such bites were said to carry, nothing was said or found.

The matter of Toron's blindness had been more weighty, Justinian had told him. The wound had been in his brain, and not simply in his eyes. As for their foundling, her body showed no tokens of life—no breathing, no heartbeat—and while the healers insisted she wasn't far off, it was beyond their own powers to lead her back. They'd sent a bird to summon their highest priestess from the Medthkirk of the Heron at the city's eastern end, a stern but softspoken woman whose voice Toron recalled in shards. She'd

---

[5] *(L)*: little hen; chick; girl.

prayed to Sownatch-Lebley as she worked[6], and sharp smells had come about.

"This maiden is not of Mankind," she had said, though Toron had somehow already known that. "She is of the fayfolk, a dreeish wight from the Otherwhere, and the Heron's lechning will not restore her. So be it. I can work this too."

And with that she had called upon raw, regenerative magics, which were to her chosen ways brutish, but in which she was needfully learned, just as every craftsman from carpenter to cook knew the means of patching and salvaging the stuff with which they worked, should they lack the setting and the stores to right it properly. As she shaped her spells, the acolytes had explained that there were healers in Eksar who worked only with such dreecraft, but these were no more healers than the florist was a creator of blooms. Such magics spliced and grafted, and dressed with alien salves, and did all within their might to draw the thing on which they worked out of the world in which it had been raised and into one that merely ruled it. While much hastier, the women claimed, such healing brought many perils, for just as the waxing of a life is so much more than the growth of its flesh, and meant weathering and toughening and altering to withstand life's blows, so did the hastening of health risk lapse, and dependency upon whatever splints and ropes had advanced it. The Heron's true healing, they'd whispered, was persuasive and wholesome, encouraging the body to do what it knew how to do, and to lead itself back to the state it knew ere it had been led to ruin. And more so than any worldly wort or leechcraft, the Heron's soundness was healing without scars, a refreshing of the meat and bone that banished hurt, as well as the shadow of weakness and pain often left behind.

It was on the heels of this lecture, Justinian had told Toron, that Kurtisian had held out his good hand to the woman, his fingers and thumb pressed together. She looked at it, then at the other, which she herself had treated and dressed.

"Is this one hurt as well?" she had asked, taking him by the wrist.

---

[6] SAU-natch-leb-LEE, Healing Deity of the Vitalic Pantheon. Though She is one of Bluharyn's consorts, She is reputed to be a refugee from an uncertain Age. The etymology of her name is unknown. Among the Knaksish, She is represented as a robust woman clad in hemp and accompanied by a symbolic triad of creatures: the maggot (recovery), starfish (regeneration) and termite (immunity from disease).

Kurtisian had shaken his head. Hungry, tired and in pain from the bite-wound he wouldn't disclose, his face was colder and more miserable than that of a griff chained out in the sleet. "This is me giving you your famsapping brochure back," he said. "Now hurry the Hells up and finish what we hired you for."

And they had, in silence. They had taken their fee—their alms, though they called it—and they had gone. Fifty gildenbits, or just over half their wealth. Most of it had been to requicken the stranger, though the thoftship had never openly made the choice to do so. Both Chaldallions had grumbled about it until the second day, whereafter they began to see the boons of which the priestess had spoken. Justinian missed old scars that had healed with the new wounds, and the knuckles on Kurtisian's left hand were unflattening themselves, regaining the knobs they'd long ago lost to punching things. Toron, meanwhile, was forced to endure the flood of memories his mending brain sent into his thoughts, whose debris scratched at the edges of his mind like driftwood. All the while, the woman whose fading life had chanced them the Heron's best healing had yet to regain her senses, and lay in her own room upstairs, looked in on every hour by the innkeep's youngest daughter. Out of some propriety Toron had never before met in them, the Chaldallions let the stranger be, and did not once peer in on her, vowing to wait until she rose on her own, and sought out her rescuers of her own will.

Of course, they could not be sure she would not try to flee unseen, but for that there was no remedy. Though Gorrh kept watch over the common room day and night, and would sense it even if she tried to escape through her own small window, she was an Outsider, and for all they knew might have the means of blinking herself from the itness of this world without needing to lift the bedcover. Before that happened, though, Toron and the Chaldallions had some questions for her. They were not pressing ones, nor needful, but had to do with the path by which they'd come, and on which they'd found her, and which they'd learned after stepping onto the Swansbawn could not be tracked back on.

That path, rounding once and plunging suddenly downhill after their battle, had sent them through an overgrown bower that seemed to empty itself onto another road. It had been larger but just as desolate as their own, and other than the birds and the wind and the rushing of faraway water, nothing could be heard as they drew near to it. But as they pushed out from beneath the thicket and emerged thankfully onto the wide thoroughfare, a world of menning had roared up around them, blinking into shape out of nowhere. It was then that they knew, as they had forethought, that they had been led to Eksar on a fairyroad. To the wayfarers who met them it seemed as though they had stepped out of hiding among the bushes at the foot of a cliff-face, even though the bushes were much too meager to hide them. Those travelers started at the sight of the band, thinking them highwaymen springing their ambush.

Witless brigands they would have been, however, to have done so within sight of Eksar's western gates, for the thoftship was threatened within moments by three griffmen, who alighted before them grimly, and demanded to know their business and how they had come there without being glimpsed before then. It was, moreover, by the eastern gates—by way of the Swansbawn—that elselanders came to the burg. Only countryfolk came by the western side, to which there was no road from outside Teakenmaley. Ten more griffs gathered overhead as Justinian had settled things, laying out their goodwill, and digging from Gorrh's lopsided saddlebags the kingly leaflet they were answering. The bulletin seemed a tired matter of angst among the watchmen, who after conferring said the paper did nothing to shed light on their stealth. And there, Kurtisian had given leash to his own weariness, naming the two failing lives among them and the staggering, bloodied beast who carried both, holding up his own misshapen wrist, and nodding toward Justinian's deeply gouged chest.

"A guide brought us here," he said through the pain. "And I want him more than you, if you find him. We're staying at the Stitchmeal Sark. Follow us there if you want."

And he began to walk again. It might not have worked anywhere else, but it worked in the Whorl, where misgivings were sleepy, and trust was not grudging. Not only did they let the thoftship go, but one of the watchmen also flew ahead to the gate, bidding one of the wards to fetch healers to help these would-be heleths of Knaks, and to join them at the inn, if not meet them on the way. It helped too, Justinian shared later, and when Kurtisian was not there, that the guards seemed overburdened, and unwilling to tarry. Aside from the others who came in answer to the call, the Swansbawn was reportedly choked with caravans, while the skies, merely flecked with griffs on their last visit, was now peppered with flying things.

Eksar was a haven after all, and many of the highborn and wealthy merchants who wintered there seemed to have chosen this week to do their snowbirding.

The burgwards of Eksar were not true Boarsmen but their own wered, and answered to the Burgreeve. The Burgreeve himself answered to the Ealdorman of Arsask, who made his home in the burgship, and was in some way kin to Knaks himself. Unlike the kingly burgs of the east, however, Eksar could not petition the Isentron for more men when it felt itself overwhelmed. Even as its numbers trebled, the city had to make do, and for that the Burgward was a limber body, donning and shedding bulk with the seasons, like a bear, and leaving most of the city's working men with some knowledge of, and pride in, their hometown's wardship. This meant countless regiments and divisions—some acknowledged by the Burgreeve, and others run wholly underground—but it also meant the eyes of the law were everywhere, and that the frankfrith[7] of Eksar was owed to more than just the soothing daze of the Timebriar.

Of Urien, they would later learn, there had been no sight or token. He had simply vanished. As for the fairyroad on which the changeling had led them, it might no more be found again than one might leap from a bluff and hit the same bird twice. Brought about in an elsewordly time and place, the roadways of the fayfolk threaded like spidersilk among the coarser fabric of Man's itness, showing and unshowing themselves with the slightest wrinkling of the While. Some said countless realms lived in such a way among the folds of Being as Man understood it, and that these folds were greater than the face of the World as it seemed—as though Ráma itself were a crumpled cloth, and if seized by the corners and drawn taut might show itself twice, or ten, or endless, times larger. For many, such a thought went beyond ease, if not the loosest grasp.

So it was that most of the hazards such a condition threatened—that, for one, unwatchable roads reached past the stoutest walls and sharpest eyes of Man's domain—went ignored, so long as those walls and eyes seemed to work most of the time. On Urien's fairyroad, however, the thoftship had not been alone. The manshfretters and the wolfmen, whatever their aim, had been there as well, and would have stood within a bowshot of Eksar's walls had

---

[7] *(AB):* the common peace.

they travelled a hundred yards further from where the thoftship had dealt with them. Whether the two packs of fiends had been in cahoots or were at odds, and whether they were coming or going, only the foundling might tell, though she too might simply have been a traveller, and her own band suffered the same end that Toron and the Chaldallions nearly met.

Whichever it was, there was no going back. The Outsider would either awaken and talk, or she would vanish without a word, leaving the memories of that elseworldly crossing to haunt the three Men like a dream they'd all somehow shared.

The table jolted, and Kurtisian mumbled something in no language. Toron lifted his head, but of course could see nothing.

"You say something?"

Kurtisian mumbled again, then spoke drowsily. "Falln asleep. I'm goin up."

"Good night."

"If my brother's inebriated when he comes back, tell him to be quiet. And alone."

"Inebriated?" Toron had caught the outland word before, but tonight found his mind too open at the ends.

"*Drunk*, Thorn," Kurtisian said simply. He seemed too exhausted to be brusque about it.

"Will do. If I'm still up."

Kurtisian grunted, and the legs of the stool grunted against the floor. "We'll all be up again if he's not quiet. Or alone."

Toron scratched his eyebrow beneath the dressing. A burst of light slipped beneath them, white-bright but acheless. "I'm taking these off tomorrow," he said. "First thing. And we'll all go out."

"Yeah," the other man said. "I might take mine off upstairs, I think." A sniff. "Been sweating into it for two days."

He began to make his way toward the stairs, but Toron, borrowing Gorrh's ears again to make sure no one else was in the room, called after him. "And when do we begin having to worry about wrapping you up in silver rackans[8] if we hope to live through the night?"

It was a sharp way to put it to him, and Kurtisian halted in mid-step. The Southerner laughed to himself, and it was not wholesome.

---

[8] *(AB)*: chains; bonds (also *rakenteie* [rackan + tie]: bonds specifically).

"You worried?" The question was dark, but Kurtisian had painted it. Toron had known him long enough, and heard his brother heckle his plays often enough, to know when he was putting on black airs.

"Yes, but about you as well."

Kurtisian *aww*ed.

"What I mean is that I don't think the burgwards would be unready for you if you burst into the streets howling and half-shifted. You might get away with ripping out a few throats in Barrin before making it to the woods and freezing your balls off overnight in there, but not here. You said so yourself. The burgwards are panned up in good ply[9], and their weapons are dreeish. This is an elderburg, not a backwater. There's a school of wizardry. The ealdorman's wife heads the derking of Friga and half the wardwereds are likely given to Tiw. Wolves are for Locky, if your godlore's stale, and the Ozmen eat wolves for breakfast.[10] You wouldn't last one full moon in this valley. And, yes, after all that, I don't much like the thought of being next door to your room. Both as meat, and as someone who was seen coming in with you."

Kurtisian considered this, or at least took the time to appear that he did. His decision to try to keep whatever strain of lycanthropy the wolfman might have passed along in its bite had been made almost immediately after he'd been bitten, or so he'd claimed. There were, after all, many different kinds of wolfmanry afoot, some of whose evils yielded to strong will and wortcraft, and which carried with them a whole host of special crafts—things such as nightsight, beastspeech, and vastly strengthened senses of smell and hearing. Keeping in mind that their lupine adversaries on the fairyroad had shown full mastery of their wits, Kurtisian clearly hoped that a few months of practice might leave him able to assume a bestial form at will. As such, he could indeed become a fullblown, throat-ripping monster, or he could choose to wargen halfway, carrying on as hairy, fairytalish version of himself, with a vest and growly voice, and likely—for his sarcasm—remaining the most biting wolfman in Ráma without needing to sink his teeth into anyone.

---

[9] *(AK* expression), a play on *panoply*: encased in good armour.

[10] *derking of Friga (AK/AB):* cult of Frigg; *wardwereds (AK):* regiments of the city guard; *Tiw (AB):* warrior-god of the Ozmen, Týr to the Hálish; *Locky (AK):* trickster-god of the Ozmen; Loki to the Hálish.

Of course there was also the chance—and a more likely one, Toron felt—that whatever the man was letting into his blood would boil him slowly from within, in time to blister his outsides and twist him into a shape unforetold by what had carried it. The look of attery things such as snakes and spiders gave no foretokening of what their bites did to you. Were the wargening something helpful, it would not be a worry, but a boon. The awful tales would not have been told, and men would line up to be bitten.

Kurtisian sighed windily. "Prime. First thing tomorrow then, I'll find a sage who can at least identify what strain I might have picked up. If it's a bad one—I mean, a very, awful bad one—I'll have it removed. I'm sure they have people that can do that too. Fassy, spassy.[11]"

Toron scoffed through his nose, even as Kurtisian himself might have done. Being unable to see his thoftman's face had made him bolder with the moody southerner than he might otherwise have been. "'If it's a very, awful bad one'," he said, throwing back the dreeman's words. "Like the kind the Heron's own priests didn't see or heal? The kind you might pick up on fairyroad midwhere, and not a place anyone here knows of? That kind of strain? So who makes the call? Or need I ask?"

"No," Kurtisian called back easily, the stairs beginning to creak as he climbed them. "You don't."

The inn's building was a hollow, yawning place, dry and bare-walled, and Toron heard every move the man made until he reached his room and shut the door. Gorrh grumbled from his half of the hall. *What an ass*, the cat said, or would have. *He did not know the thing he was feeding.*

Toron agreed, but there was nothing for it. The Chaldallions were not bound to him, and there was nothing keeping them on but choice. It was the strongest misgiving Toron had about coming to burgs such as Eksar—that they all might see better ways to live and forsake the winning road they sought. They all knew tradecrafts, and had fallen back on them for short times when booty had been scarce. Even now, and with a little gold in their wallets, they meant to do some odd work around the burg if they could, if for the simple and unusual pleasure of it rather than for the silver. Last they were here, Toron had done some woodwork among the river docks, and

---

[11] (*AC* expression)*:* easily done; 'easy-peasy'; 'Bob's your uncle'.

Justinian had found ready openings as a bodyguard to the rich elselanders who called Eksar half a home. Kurtisian had learned that his cradle knowledge of the Linguish made him useful to the students of Eksar's wizarding school, many of whose dreeish writings were in that tangled, outland tongue. He was not, of course, given leave to see their grimoires, but rather helped with drills and glosses, and with the Linguish fables they had to read as beginners. Not many colonials strayed inland from the Sundarsund, and that Kurtisian might carry Linguish words into the Allmal and back again as swiftly as he read was a thing of wonder to them. Most of them— especially those among the library-taverns of Shiremansairy where he went to hawk his services—were children of powerful families, with deep, deep pockets.

For the three men, the chance to do these humble things was dear worth, but not in the wistful way that troubled minds see them—that is, as a break from much heavier work. They were instead dear worth in the same sad way that a draught of cheap ale was beloved by a thirsty tramper—as a taste of largesse, and of menning however coarse. Strange and damning was the thought that happy toil might be choicer than their chosen livelihoods—that indeed they might yearn for those leeward lives who in turn dreamed themselves far beyond shelter, in search of teer, like those who scratch leafy and faraway things onto the walls of their prisons.

It was a thorny hedge to his selfworth, but a hedge nonetheless, that their teer was still in the making, and not so whimsical as a daydream. To the homespun mind, the life of the wandering swordsman was nothing but fun and fresh air, days given to a game—bloody but harmless too, somehow—against foes who burgled and bungled, and gave up sprays of gold with their ghosts. Bewitched by these weenings, none cared to ponder how much more glorious it might be to wear clean clothes, to eat round meals with one's kin, and to have a home with six sides, than to spend weeks slogging through bracken and weather for the chance to fight things that ate children. Towns and hamlets were safe, but every time they burged, there was a chance they would not leave, at least not all together. That Toron hazarded them anyway said a lot that he pretended not to hear.

Time passed in blindness, which was time whose length he could not see. Creaking, the inn settled onto its groundwork and seemed to fall asleep along with those in it. Eksar had no curfew, however, and merrymakers kept passing by, rattling their knuckles and noisemakers across the windows and doors, bidding happy whatever to those within, goodwill too drunk to be rude. Faraway music he heard in the lulls, and the lowing of horns, and the knelling tinsel of small bells. Whether holy or worldly all had meanings he did not know, and he sat within their wash, sipping his tea as it lukened, like a child beneath the skirt of a ballroom table.

A whisper came across the board; the scent of blooms, no, of potpourri, a florilegium of mayweed and amaranth, and something familiar he could not name.

A woman's voice bid him good evening.

Toron leapt, knocked over his tea. Gorrh geysered up, stood boiling.

"Who's there?" Toron asked, as calmly as he might. His blades, every one of them, were in his room.

Again a murmuring, a moment of silence, then the answer. She was the one from up the stairs.

A lie. Toron bristled. There was more than one voice. One—the whisper—seemed to be advising another before it spoke.

The voice whose words he heard was very pleasing—as smooth as down, and just as soothing. But in the same way that such stuff must be plucked and winnowed, there was something about it that seemed made up, and unwonely, and more like the sounding of harpstrings than speech. He fought to understand this, and held still for a moment, the mounting drone of Gorrh's growling like a madness creeping in.

Again came the whisper, and this time he heard it well enough to know it for what it was. It too was a woman's voice, one spoken so low beneath the breath as to hide its tones. It was not so low, however, that it might hide what made it odd—it warbled a little, and rasped, and though was truer to a breath of flesh than the first, it spoke in no tung he understood. But within its wake came words he did know, and in the voice that had first greeted him. She was the one in the bed, it said. Someone had brought her here, and she did not know who it was.

Only one, Gorrh told him. *One, but with two voices.*

How? Toron shot back, and as he and Gorrh met eyes in the Rine, they told themselves this was not unforeseen. The woman was from the Otherwhere—whatever that meant—and might do things beyond their ken and calm. Nonetheless, Gorrh was not a Man, and had no more often been startled than a topmost hunter was hunted. To let in a new world was to threaten old laws, and here was someone from a world that put no stock in a tuskcat's nose and ears.

"It was us," Toron heard himself say. He had no grounds for fear; he'd done nothing to her, and she with her stealth might as easily have killed him as spoken to him. "We found you on the fairyroad outside the burg and carried you here. You had been attacked. You were dying, or dead, or—" and he recalled the acolytes' qualms, "—somewhere in between. We fought some manshfretters and wolfmen on the road before we found you. Maybe they did it, I don't know. My eyes—" and he fingered the dressing about his face "—I lost my sight. They're healing now; I should see again tomorrow or the next day. But I wasn't the one who spotted you. We—Gorrh there, and I—bore you to this inn, where the Heron's priestess brought you back. You've been in that room for two days, under the care of one of the innkeep's daughters."

The long hush that followed was the sound of one tasting, and with great care, what one has been fed. Who she was; whence she came; what she made of her predicament; he had hints to none of these things, and though he'd been told she was unMannish, he knew far too little of the Otherwhere to make anything of that. In truth, such a dizzying thing only threatened to muddy what he might know, and he did his best to stand aside for now, and not seek to understand anything.

The murmuring again. A single word from the sound of it.

She asked him who he was.

He became aware of the tea dripping onto his lap, into the warmth of the earlier spill he had not felt at all. "Toron the Belkol, of Harandril. We were on the same road, and we found you."

The murmuring voice repeated the name to itself, and in a way that left no question about its coming from Beyond. Not one of the consonants seemed to fit in its mouth, and the sounds of the selflouds that strung them together were much too slight, like locks of hair binding the links of a heavy chain.[12]

Thorn the burning coal, the second voice then sounded, shaping the sounds better than he himself might have done. Of the next gray land.

---

[12] The usual *AK* terms for 'consonants' and 'vowels' are *midlouds* and *selflouds*, respectively—*midlouds* because consonants must be spoken amid vowels to be fully articulated, *selflouds* because vowels can stand alone (as in *I, a, uh*, etc.).

It was then that he understood. The second voice was carrying the first into his own tung, reshaping even names, which should have stayed as they were spoken. Whatever the mistake, he was pleased, having never known before the full meaning of his aughtname[13], nor that of Harandril, which even for Harandrishmen had always been a rune among words.

She then asked who are we.

None of the three words had any more weight than the others, and Toron thought at first she meant him and her, or perhaps something deeper, like the place of Man amidst all that was. "We? Oh—the ones who found you. I, the tuskcat at the door, and two others."

The murmuring, louder this time, more pressing. Who were the two others.

"One is upstairs. The other is at a tavern down the road."

Louder, not a murmur at all. Who are they.

"Brothers. Kurtisian and Justinian Chaldallion, from the Southern landholds. I'm sure you wouldn't know them."

He heard her huff, but whatever her thoughts the answer stilled her for a time, and Toron was left to feel the unsettling thing he was in. If she were to walk away now, he might pass her by in the weeks and years to come without ever knowing it.

She spoke again, repeating what he had said about finding her on the road. Which road was he talking about? Was it the road to the city?

The question made Toron wary all of a sudden, though he could not say why. It seemed less forward than those about their names, and they had not hidden from anyone how they had made their way here. Even the burgwards knew. Nonetheless, he felt something hard beneath the face of it—perhaps not barbs, but the bones of a sharp, pressing care. He handled it carefully.

"We headed into Teakenmaley—"

She broke in right away, asking what that was.

"Teakenmaley? The Crown. It's a whorlberg in the east of Arsask. We're in Eksar, an elderburg, in the middle of it."

She kept silent, and he reminded himself what she might be.

"Arsask is a Medth—a share—of the Kingdom of Knaks. The greatest share. We call Arsask the Crownsmedth, as the home of the

---

[13] *(AK)*: family name; last name.

King is in Arsask as well. The Isentron. To the northwest of here? Kraterpol? The Starbowl?"

She made a noise he could not name, and no words followed it.

"Knaks?" He said again. "Was once called the Bracsriche? On the northwest of Ráma? The landbody of Ráma?"

Nothing still. His wonder of her dizzied him. It sat with him, though uneasily, that she might not know of Arsask, nor of Knaks, nor of the Bracsriche, all being realms of Men, and whose borders and business might be to her own country much as the swap and skirmishing of shucks and bushmen were to his. But Ráma—Ráma was one of the greatest things for which he had a word, a thing vast beyond the boundaries of his own mindsight, uncharted by his thoughts, trembling upon the shelves of his word-hoard like a chest that, despite its outer size, was endless within, and might swallow any who lifted its lid. Even Shard and Dhandhar were of Ráma, or nearby to it. The Southern landholds of the Chaldallions were just below, and spoke a Norrámish tongue. Ráma. No one he had met, or could think to meet, went further than the fringes of the word.

Aside from *itness*—which meant all things, but was a word only, and not a name—there was only one nemning he knew that went beyond Ráma, and still named a thing that might be touched, seen, and measured. He had heard it first upon the knee of his mother— glinting amidst the hoary yarns of the Ossalore like a single strand of a comet's hair—and its weight upon his mind had staggered him, teaching him then and ever since that words and meanings stood not always one before the other, and might swap places, with all the fairness and legardemain of a magician's cards.

He pitched that word now.

"Smað?" he said.

And with that, she spoke again.

Smað, she said, she knew tell of, and he felt his mind lighten a little. It was not beyond likelihood that her people simply called his lands by other names, perhaps hailing from the broken isles west over the Sundarsund, which were said by godlore even older than the Ossalore to have once been joined to the world of Men. He had never been one to press, however, and did not know what to say or ask next. So he went on with what he reckoned she would want to know, or what he would want to know were he in her shoes.

"We came from the south about a fortnight ago, from a town called Barrin, where we met a pathfinder who showed us the way.

We would have come by the Swansbawn, but it was too far north, and we would have had to have spent gods-know-how-many days backtracking up to the northeast. We were in Shebril before that, and Ignam. We don't use the highways very often, and Justinian's godtroth keeps us from going by air."

He had not yet finished this before she asked to know who the pathfinder was. Though he knew not its words, her true voice was sharp, and clipped, and would brook no waffling.

"His name was Urien. He was a swapling of a kind. Fayfolk. I don't know much else about him."

She asked where Urien was now, and a whisper of a shiver went through him. She had spoken the name, and it had not been carried over into new words. He opened his mouth to answer her, but felt a trembling creep into his chair. It was Gorrh, growling louder, at him more than at her. He was warning him to make up some ground, and to stop baring himself.

Toron cleared his throat. "It's all right. I'll tell you all that. But why don't you tell me who you are first? I think you owe us that at least."

And with that, and the hesitation and unease that met it, he had the first feeling that someone was indeed sitting before him.

"*Kwall-le kwee-andeh,*" said the first, as he heard it.

But the second said that her name was 'Vail.'

"Vail," Toron said, not trusting his tongue with the first. "It is good to meet you." And though he had found it was not the way of men and women anywhere outside of Harandril, he reached out his hand, and shook the long fingers she placed, after a few heartbeats, within it. Her skin was warm, or his was cold—he did not know which—and although it was clear she did not know what a good northern handshake was, she hid none of her strength, whose measure startled him.

"Good," he said, releasing first, and bidding Gorrh sit down. The cat did so, but only to his haunches. "Why," he went on, "do you speak with two voices?"

When she answered, the murmuring went on for longer than before, and had not yet finished before the second voice began, and lapped over it. She said, as he had already gathered, that only the first was her own voice. The second belonged to the magic she used to carry her own words into his tung, which she did not speak well. It was not the best of its magic, and she had to choose to say small things.

Toron nodded. Shard had used this kind of dreecraft before, though it had allowed him to speak in his own voice. "Is this the way you understand my words as well?"

Yes, she replied, but that magic was easier, and lay within her own mind. His words were not changed, and she heard them just as he spoke them, but their meaning was made clear to her even as she heard any unknown words. It would help her with time to learn, she said, as well to understand what he said right away. She asked if he had any magic, *magic* being the word she used.

"We call it dree or dreecraft here," he said, shooing away the southern term, which most Knaksmen would not have understood, and which he had not heard himself until he had met the Chaldallions. He found it odd that the spell with which she spoke, despite being otherwise clear, had used *magic* instead. "We call it other things, too—wizardry, tivership, galdercraft. Halsing, I've heard. Whate. Witieng. Wiel. Some of them not so loving: trollship, sidden. But no, I don't have any. I only know some of its names because I've met some who do."

And heard what others have called them, he nearly added.

Vail spoke again, her second voice beginning shortly after. Then magic, she said, was a thing that was feared in this place. She reckoned she should not wield it lest she come to harm.

He had not said as much, but she had read him well. "You ought not to wield it openly," he said. "It's against the law here, and in most other burgs. Called Dreebreach. Though it really rests on who is around to see it. It's not—"and he lowered his voice a little—"it's not something Knaksmen look kindly on. Dreecraft, that is. You see it everywhere, even in the hands of the Boarsmen—the King's men—but it's not something you can talk about freely. Not like the weather. Not even the gods, for that matter."

It is forbidden, she put it.

"No, not all of it. Some of it is. Dreecraft that raises the dead, for one, or charms that move a man against his own will. Such things go against what is rightful—in this kingdom and everywhere else I've heard tell of. That does not mean that wizards don't use them. Outside of those things, I can't say what is lawful where. Every Medth and burg has its own laws. Some of the northern townships do not suffer dreemen within their walls. Others, as Eksar once was, simply do not allow the wielding of dreecraft. I've heard the

Ringburgs nearest the Isentron admit dreemen but not dreeish things. Weapons, rings, books, cloaks, and everything else that might be bewitched must be left in the Boarsmen's heederns. It keeps folk away more than anything, as I don't think many who own things of such dear worth are willing to take the chance. I wouldn't."

She asked of the æw. The question—the word—staggered him. Among the bones of Aftheksis he last had heard it, when Shard had spoken it in the naming of Avarnok.

He opened his mouth to answer, but then bore to mind that he had not said the word himself. Though he knew its meaning more or less, he did not know if he had ever spoken it out loud in his life. Clearly, and again, one or the other of her speech magics had reworked something he had uttered, either honing it or blunting it or otherwise shaping it to settle more smoothly amidst the ready quide from which the magic drew its terms. He found it unsettled him to hear magic making these choices, having always believed its glammer to have lain in cold perfection, more alike to the ministry of the seasons than to the ministry of Men. And yet here was a very token of its partiality, and proof beyond dent of twain that some thinking thing lay behind its workings. Whether that thing had been there only in the beginning, assembling the spell like the orthanksmith builds a cunning device, or whether it lurked there now like a hidden hireling, ear outstretched and lips fidgeting, he could not tell. Uneaseful enough it was to be speaking to one Outsider he could not see.

"The æw," he said, overmouthing the sound. "I reckon you might call it the way of things, but it's more like an unwritten law." He sighed and tried again, his hands wheeling before his blindfold as if seeking to spin the roughness of the likening into finer stuff. "It's...it's the difference between something everyone knows to be wrong and something that is wrong only because a law says so. The first would be wrong even if there weren't a law against it."

He was unsure whether that made sense, but Vail's true voice answered quickly, and confidently. The æw is a belief, then, whereas the law might simply be a rule.

"Yes...yes." Not wholly, he thought, but good enough.

And magic, she came again, is against the æw.

"Yes. Some more than others."

Because, she said, it is unnatural.

"Yes. Unnatural. We would say 'unwonely', but yes."

Vail laughed then, and unlike her voice it was not a pretty sound. If the æw was for nature, she said, she knew its face, and might already name a great many things it frowned upon. Sarthing, for one, and much ado about it. With who, what goes where, and so forth.

She went on a little more, and what Toron found most striking was not the sudden swing of their talk into matters of lovemaking— or simply hamelock[14], as she shaped it—but that it had swung there lustlessly. It was as though the farkind woman discussed something that had no bearing on either of them; neither the weather on the moons nor the worth of Tarmaterizish wool might she have yondthought more carelessly.

Toron was no tippamare, as Harandrishmen called those who were squeamish to bawdy things. Dirty thoughts were puddles even on the highest roads of life, and though he'd found Harandrish ribaldry to be humble next to that of other Medths—aiming higher, for wit, than for the splashes sent up from of its filthiest depths— he'd never felt or feigned distaste for lewd talk so long as he was not its spring, or the heart of it was light Had he done otherwise, the Chaldallions would have been unbearable to him, as they had often been to Rhianys, who like Toron was not merrow, but who, having been no barmaid either, had had a seemly woman's boundaries. Vail, however, seemed neither turned on nor put off, standing as far outside those feelings as she stood outside Mankind itself.

Still, it was not until now that Toron first began to wonder what she looked like, and indeed how she was shaped. What the Chaldallions had said of what they had seen was flattering, though they'd not said much, and that was unlike them. She was lithe, not much to her. Smelled good. Her face, they'd said, was a red ruin, and it was hard, even for most prurient mind, to look south of that. If indeed she had healed, they'd have no such qualms and would tell her top to bottom like auctioneers at a slavemarket. But they were not here. Indeed, she might walk out the door this very night, and they might never catch another glimpse of her. To help him he had only Gorrh, whom he knew would have told him if she had two heads and a whale's gut. To deeper matters of comeliness, however, the cat was stone-blind, about as fit to tell Mannish beauty as Toron was to know a lion worth bedding. As for the simple things from which comeliness was reckoned, the tuskcat could not speak to those

---

[14] *(AK)*: sexual intercourse.

either. Her Otherwhereness muddled his whats, dizzying his waymind[15] and blunting a wisdom whetted only in this earth.

Was she old?

For Mankind, most yes.

But did she look old?

She looked odd.

How tall is she?

A woman's height.

What did she wear?

Clothing.

Thump, thump, thump, went the cat's tail.

What of her hair?

Hair-coloured.

Gorrh could have answered that one. Toron understood from the Rine that the tuskcat's sight for hues was unlike his own, but the beast might nonetheless do what he had done before when asked, which was to liken what he saw to things Toron already knew. Green was of leaves and grass, blue an open sky, snow white, blood red, and so forth. It was not a flawless way of doing it—it erred at times, and it forgot the richer hues of things—but it worked in a pinch, and was better than nothing. But Gorrh would go no further, and Toron held off on pushing it. Though the beast was at all times on edge, it was rare he became grumpy. The hunter did not enjoy the crippling of his whats, and loathed the otherworldly thing that was teaching him such helplessness. Toron bethought himself of the Rinesight to catch a glimpse of the Outsider, but thought the better of it. He had not harnessed the knack since being wounded, and feared the ache. Moreover, Gorrh was grudging, and there seemed no way of doing it that was stealthy enough. Though it smarted him, the man gave himself up to the thought that he might never lay eyes on the farkind being before him. He tossed the regret Gorrh's way as he might have tossed a good boot the cat had chewed apart.

I don't believe she's going anywhere, Gorrh shot back.

What makes you say that?

Can you not feel it of her?

I can't even see her.

She's afraid. It's rolling out of her.

Afraid? The thought of that had never come to Toron.

---

[15] *(AK)*: orienteering; sense of direction.

Less now, but still barely holding herself together.
Her voice didn't show it.
The dreeish one. It's a cover.
But she'd not kept herself hidden in her room. She'd risked speaking with him.
I think she's doing it only because you can't see her.
You might be wrong.
Gorrh huffed. *Wherever she's from, I don't think she knows how to get back. Someone that afraid, she would have done it already. She's trapped. I can read that, at least.*

Vail interrupted them then, though she could not have known that she did so. She asked Toron's forgiveness, saying that the æw, by any name, was not odd among the Wheres. She had to be careful. When in Rome, and all that—he understood.

Yes. Well, no, he didn't understand the last bit, and she'd misspoken the name of the world—Ráma was *RAWM-uh*—but then the saying hiccoughed in his mind, and in its place he heard another, which he knew from childhood.

One must howl like the wolves one is among.

A lull followed, soundless. But for the smell of her, he'd have thought she'd blinked away. He struggled to find something else to say, but nothing seemed right. Where she stood with him, with his world. Everything he might ask her seemed unhovely—a hard rap at her door, a Boarsman's boot lodged in the jamb. What do you look like? No. Where do you come from? No. What are you? Gods, no. And though at the time he'd had no thought as to how long the choice might own him, he'd made up his mind that either Vail would tell him these things on her own, or he would never know them. It was the most careful kind of friendship he might put forward, one the Harandrish called *gyensidey*, where trust was built not upon shared openness, but by heeding the other's boundaries. Though the slowest to grow, it stood to be toughest in the end—thildy and unneedy, onely but unlonely.

She spoke again, and Toron listened for fear in it. He heard only weariness. She asked whether she might go back to her room. Her insides ached through to her outsides, and she needed more time to regain her strength. He turned up his hands, as if to show they held no chains—why seek my leave?—and was glad for once to hear the stool scrape on the wood. She asked, from further away, what they had paid to mend her, and he found he could not shrug it away as much as he wished. To them, fifty gildenbits had been as close to a wyrmbed[16] as they were likely to come. It had been an almsdeed to bring her here, but the deed had bled them out. The Chaldallions had grumbled enough already, but it was hard, even for him, not to see it for a feespilling.[17]

But what to do? She had not asked to be brought back to life.

Vail asked whether there was a word in his tung for the gold someone might owe for having ended a man's life. Toron thought about it, and said such a thing, or near to it, was called a wergeld.

It seems, she said, I owe you my own wergeld.

Then she was gone. The sound of her shutting the door to her room was the only token that she hadn't indeed swethered out of the itness. Toron was alone for only a moment, however, when the door to the inn grunted open.

"It is magnificent," the newcomer announced to everyone awake and asleep, "to be able to shit indoors."

And like churchbells chasing away trolls—but the other way around—any blissome thoughts of the farkind woman fled.

"Justin," Toron played, making his arms to grope about. "Justin, is that you?"

The southerner erupted with piratelike laughter, then tripped over one of Gorrh's oustretched legs. He didn't go down, but the sound of him staggering shook everything.

If what he was could be called inebriated, then the Harandrish indeed had a word for it too.

Swinedrunk.

"Your brother told you to be quiet," Toron said, turning on his stool "and alone."

"No, and no!" he bellowed up the stairs like a mad ox.

But Gorrh said there was no one with him.

"Was at The Mong and Poot downna road," he said. "Whadda place they ran out of fuckin…"

A bloodshocking crash. He had fallen to the floor and wasn't moving, only giggling in a way that said he wasn't likely to pick himself up again. Toron was left to ponder what it was for a place to run out of fuckin.

---

[16] The heap of gold on which dragons are said to sleep. (*AB* expression): fabulous wealth; a helluva lotta money.

[17] *(AB):* waste of money.

He slid carefully from his stool, and Gorrh's tail gave a thump
goodnight as he made his way toward the stairs. Tomorrow was a
Tiwsday, he reckoned. A cheapday, as they called it, when the
sellers without shopfronts, and the growers and craftsmen and others
from outside the burg were free to set up their stands wheresoever
among the Grensteads[18] they wished. As it came back to him, the
cheapdays were a hoot, full of sights and merrymaking, with steadly
food, and song, and many other things he wouldn't need his eyes to
find bliss in. They would see with the morrow whether he—and, less
likely, Justinian—was up for an outing.

Outside the frost-etched window, the dogs continued their
mournful hag-hymn, baying an answer to the wolves and
wilderhounds who watched the city from the cliffsides. Bristling and
black against the lighter hues of the highbergs, the chimneyscape of
Eksar slowed its breathing stack by flute, the last quills of smoke,
like the howling of the hounds, trailing lines into a sky shocked with
stars.

---

[18] *(AK)*: the burgyards—or city plazas—of Eksar Arsask, of which there are nine.

VII
Teer and Blead
Tear and Bleed

No nightmares straddled him while he slept. Not at first.

Instead, Toron drifted gently into the arms of a sweven, and saw before him neither fiends nor sorrows, but a slow sweep of blissome things. He beheld all his thoftship, as they had been, now were, and might be in the yet-to-come, standing as one beneath a banner of three hues, its token the curling rood he had first drawn on the banks of Timil Insee. Together they strove, in a quest for teer and min, together, upon a world that swallows the lonesome and folkless. Together they grew—like the great stands of aspen trees on the borders of Nagland, which link arms beneath the earth, and however battered cannot be uprooted, and though beheaded never slain.

Their pack swelled. Their strongholds bloomed across the badlands, like the outermost outposts and cabins of the Harandrish rangers of old, but never to be forsaken as those had been—not as Toron had found them in his boyhood, slumping empty-eyed and mossy in the wastes, too frightening in forlornness to go near. Not so the fastnesses of his heroes. Their beacons shone out; their pools overlapped, swimming with hope and trust; and among them no darkness, no depths of shadow where evil things might spawn and resurge. In the elderburgs rose their headstables, which oversaw their doings and made known to everyone—to the ealdormen and the burgreeves and the lawmakers and the athelings and the everyday burgdwellers—the full sweep and tale of their deeds. Scops fought over words for it. Songs poured from the alehouses. Together they won, from the swallowing earth of this fleeting life, a name that would outlast their bones.

He saw them brought together for a painting, gathered upon a bluff backed by stormclouds and all laughing to see how swiftly the artist might catch them before the heavens opened up. Long ere this they had mopped the tears from Bayerd, standing where the King's own Boarsmen had fallen. They had hunted their foe to the heart of the Unfondlands and come back without loss, their swords wet and glorious. To the Kingdom of Knaks itself they next had turned, to the north and to the marchlands where maneaters still throve, and every pathless unknown they had hiked and made safe. Into every black hole they had thrust their torches, unthorned every bramble, rinsed every ramshackle of the lurking undead.

Those years had been rugged but not unkind. Toron wore a full beard, the flaxen whiskers iron-thorned, his scar nearly hidden beneath their briar. Gorrh sat beside him, his jaw likewise white, his eyes a little deeper in his skull. But whereas the tuskcat had lankened slightly, Justinian had only grown thicker, standing proudjawed in a tasseled southern vest. The great valleys of his brawn had filled in a little with the sediments of age, the meat of his arms and legs less bulbous than beefy. Kurtisian was there, to the side and to the front of his brother, the larger to appear to the artist who sketched them, on his face irredeemable smugness, a six-foot *Carno* across his shoulders like a yoke. Between the brothers knelt Níscel, her golden fur gleaming, silkened as only the marvelous shampoos of her homeland might have made it—or so she had complained while she lived. Her face, though, was unreadable, even to one who had learned to read it. Her copper eyes, half-screened beneath her coiffed forelocks, reached out with an emptiness that was abyssal. Toron felt the first chill prod the dream, a shudder of the mind that garbed itself in a sudden gust of the wind.

He looked elsewhere among the gathering. He saw Rhianys, and she too wore a look he could not unriddle. Her hands were up before her chest, and a cantrip swirled between them. The glassy light of it played across her dress, a true enchantress's gown, one which she had never owned, nor had the wealth to buy, but which, he now saw, the world indeed had owed her. To her right stood a mighty incarnation of Shard, his face hidden beneath his scarf. His lithe limbs were clad in blade-finned mail, black and white, his hands upon the pommels of two flaming swords he had pitched into the dirt. The flutter of their yellow-black flames showed the breeze. Dhandhar was there, gloved in some dreadful gray adderhide, and Urien too, to whatever end. Others were there whom Toron did not know, at least not yet—odd others, a dozen or more, some prinked like playfighters, decked out in ways and with such weapons that seemed utterly unworkable in a fray. There were fayfolk—at least two—their wings inked with henna, and a great mazebull[1], a white one, with a halo and an axe. The Reaper was there, or so it seemed. This was a scythe-wielding man, tall as a thurse but thin as a sapling, wrapped in dusky blue, and hooded. The rest of the gathering stood pleated into rows, the better to crowd the bluff, some peaking out from behind others, their faces bodiless but with names no more knowable than those in full sight. Chests pouted; weapons bristled; siggertokens dangled from their belts.

After long years of selflessness, of warding the weak, and bringing law to the wilds, they had become hailed as Norráma's greatest champions. Endeared to the athelings, hallowed by the Ozmen, they drank the mead of dwarfs, and ate the apples of Idunn, and knew neither ignorance nor elderness, building for themselves a great citadel among the clouds, upon a thunderhead made fast and everlasting by epic magic. From its ledges they watched the turning world far below, their ears cocked to its hum, awaiting cries, forever on call, the dayshift, the nightshift, their winged steeds and airships at the ready.

Time shimmered past—in the tenyears, in hundreds. Borders wrinkled. Dynasties fell. But their thoftship did neither. Still their number grew, but not recklessly—not with the spurts to bring rickets, nor the bloats to turn flab, but pickily, with tastes never to be rushed by need. Some came to them. Others they sought out themselves. Either way, those harvests they put through an endless winnowing, then over and again screened the chafless, so as best to weed out the brashest and thickest, and to shed the tincake swordsman Toron had always loathed. And though this made slow

---

[1] *(AK):* minotaur.

the outgrowth of their thoftship, its waxing was like that of a tree-bole, which gnarls and toughens where it does not swell, and becomes steadfaster and more woundproof though its look changes little. By the end of it their band was no mere body of fighting men and women, and no simple culling of the swordhandy, but a thrilling crowd, awesome even at rest. Their smiles might open clouds, but their threat, like the bristling of a wolfhound, was a shibboleth, whose very sight flushed the bad from the good.

And so stood these paladins, indelible and legion, enlisted forever into open war, laying low bane wherever it rose, freck[2] against freak, the black blood of whose foes turned to gold upon being opened to air. And as their good name became etched ever deeper into the face of the world, so grew the warrens it reached—nethermost hells, sunless since the Source, whose chasmic worms and crawlthings shook off primordial slumber, and snaked forth into leetlairs to conspire against them. So the stakes grew, and pierced all scruples, and to their bowstrings their enemies nocked everything imaginable—beasts of myth, blackest magics, and cabals whose roots reached the crownburgs. The Unsung welcomed it, and kept to their codes, for in following laws to withstand the lawless, one proves the mettle of menning, and the bestness of all that Man makes.

But they had to work harder to win, mining every wit and shaping what-ifs, until every scrap of leisure became a frill, every waking standstill a chance to better themselves lost. Their souls hummed with purpose, upon their chords every battle a hard-strumming hand. The masters of all Man's arts flocked to them now, vying for a share in the upkeep of mankind. Time became teaching; to live was to learn. And what they learned emptied out every flask of lore, then wrung it, then unstitched it from within and added new more material, bringing new ways and unbeforetold crafts, such as hand-to-hand with dragons, in which no mistake might be yielded.

In the depths of an arena rimmed by stands full of onlookers, Toron saw himself grappling with the mammoth Justinian, a dreeish girdle of strength buckled about his own waist. They all had such belts now; they went on and off at their bedsides like stockings. Other trappings, such as their magical rings of warding, and the skin-sigla that branded and tracked them, stayed on at all times.

---

[2] *(AB):* warrior; hero.

The swordsman went low, wrapping his arms about the Sumo's thigh, its girth so thursish it was all he could do to lock his hands behind it. Chortling, Justinian took a few steps, a father giving his son a ride, then threw himself forward and pinned the moppet to the dirt with his knee. Toron's grunts became laughter, then turned to gritty yelps as his thoftman bore down. The swordsman twisted and pushed. The belt of strength grew hotter, its magic burned so fiercely, but still it did not help him.

The Allmetal dangled in a mockdance above his eyes, and Toron muttered something in Linguish. Baited, Justinian stooped to hear it, and when he did, Toron shot out. He seized the holy medallion by its chain and pulled—had he been walking the Fenriswolf on a leash, he would not have brought the devil to heel with any less strength. The links stretched. They shouldn't have, but they did. Justinian's eyes followed shape. The Sumo lost his head and scrambled for it, and when he gave up his balance Toron found room to lodge his legs. Still pinned on his back, he kicked into the big man like a grasshopper, and with his enchanted strength threw him skyward like a lobstone. The priest's arms wheeled, his look sparkling with mirthful frustration as it retreated from view.

A wincing hush grew as the boulder came back to ground. Its impact jerked the drapecloths on the arena's walls; pebbles leapt amidst the dust. Justinian lay there, legs apart, groaning theatrically. He raised his head then let it fall again. Toron baited him from afar with the Allmetal, jangling it on its broken chain, then held the siggertoken aloft for all to see. The onlookers boiled up into cheers. He stared into their highest rows and was blinded by the sun.

Then the arena was gone. He found himself in a meadow, vast and rimless, up to his waist in silver grass. The wind was alive with seedtufts and the greensweet smell of fennel. The sky was a haze of gray wool through which the sunlight came as an even glow. He blinked, and looked at his hands. They were young again. Nothing else of his own self did he see or remember there.

Two women stood upon a high swell in the grassy sea not far away—a mound he could not have told from the feathery flatness until someone had strode atop it. He saw the two more clearly than he ought, as if through the Rinesight rather than with his own eyes. He knew both of them.

Rhianys was as she had been earlier—not as she ever was in life, but in a likeness gilded by the memory and loss of her. Her face was a pale puzzle, her hair the wild flutter of a blackbrown flame. Rising above the grass, her pose was stiff in its bawse-hued gown, cinchstrings switchbacking on both sides up the front, lightning bolts leashing breast to womb. She blinked coldly. Her hair was the only thing else that stirred.

Next to her was Vail.

Toron knew he had not yet laid eyes on the farkind woman, and he could not, for the wimple whipping about her face, see her fully now. Somehow, though, he knew her on sight. She stood coiled up in what looked to be a single sheet of white taffeta, a cloth Toron had only seen once before. Much of what she seemed belonged to a woman of Mankind. Her yellow hair was long and brindled; her skin, where bared, was the even, peach-golden hue of one often outdoors and underdressed. Her body narrowed between the chest and hips; she had ten fingers, a nose, and two each of eyes, arms, and legs.

The look of her was not unpleasing, least of all to the eyes of a man, which she seemed shaped to hook. And yet there was something off about her, something faint that Toron felt, though it took time to search out and name what it was. That Rhianys stood nearby helped him see it. Although dealt like a manness, Vail's dole was awry, stretched in some places, too slight in others, like a woman of Mankind glimpsed through cunningly bent glass. She was much taller than Rhianys—who after all was not tall—but she was also lesser, as though made that much taller from the same share of flesh. Her legs were overlong, half again the wonely length, their full reaches wrapped and washed by the wind. Where they met, her trunk was sparse—more like a hub for the limbs than the lifehouse of a mayly[3] mother. Her ribs had only a little more girth than her head, and her breasts were small, making her shoulders seem somewhat broad, though they were likely no wider than the everyday. Her arms looked soft but nimble, and were not overlong like her legs. No veins crossed the bones of her hands, which were otherwise a woman's hands in every other way. Her neck, though, was swanlike, at the very brink between lovely and eerie, while her eyes, her eyes leapt—her eyes, howsoever oceangreen at the rings and sealpuppish where black, albethey moist and dazzling, her eyes were phantasmal, something twice her size peering through them

---

[3] *(AK)*: potential; possible.

from within, pressing its own, unseen face to the inside wall of hers, which it now did, and blinked strikingly—her eyes were great, wide-open windows, whose look was, and which looked in on, the otherworldly. Their gaze was inescapable.

She was a wonder to witness, each part of her a token of an ugliless elsewhere, their assemblage proof of another creation, breathing, breathtaking, and unreinventable. Even here in a dreamscape she seemed smuggled in, contained within a phial just her shape, the breaking of which might wither her, like an orchid bared to winter. Whether such a thing could happen, her bearing showed no worries. Her faith in her beauty was fearless, her chin up and chest out, one hand loose, the other akimbo, the lines of her hips and shoulders tilted to thwart one another. She shifted smoothly with the heartbeats, swapping her weight from one foot to another, tilting her head to match, varying her stance as though hearing goddesses tell her to do so. Rhianys seemed to watch her, maybe to shrink a little, and to say the Ignish woman could not hold a candle to the Outsider was to withhold a reckoning of each woman the stage seemed built to compel. Even so, and on grounds beyond his own leanings, Toron could see that the game was crooked, and that shortsighted indeed was he who fell for it. Whatever stock of womankind Vail belonged to, it was the echo and not the voice. She was the oil to Rhianys's whole flower—unearthed, pressed, and steamed, its essence poured into a body-shaped bottle, there a ghost to haunt the senses, flawless in what it lacked, and not in what it bettered; made not begotten, mannekin not maid. Rhianys was the winterbloom whose world Vail could never survive.

Toron had known from childhood that all swevens taught something. So it was that he felt a stroke of smugness here, the overmood one is given by unlocking something without needing the keys. All at once, however, he found himself standing before Vail, or her before him. Rhianys was gone, and the knowledge ripped through him that she was the dead one of the two. And to see the farkind woman up close was too much. To see her see him so close was too much. Her radiance was not sunshine, but elfshine—a wild, jealous kind of brilliance that suffered no peers, but brought forth in its baskers every shoot of love and self-loathing, every weed and bloom both, till every thought was a tangle, and every light but hers strangled out. Her eyes, those great, green-shored pools, drowned him headfirst.

He reached for her. The wind gusted. The veil about her mouth flashed open and shut. What he saw turned his blood to ice.

He backed away.

She reached for him. Her eyes sorrowed, then hardened, as if to trap him in their freeze.

Their hold was too mighty.

Their moons ruled his tides.

He fought them, and he failed.

The air rotted around them.

He awoke and felt himself again in the bed into which he had laid himself the night before. Sunlight pushed softly against the wrappings about his eyes, gleaming through in strips where the dressings had worked themselves loose with his tossing. He was in Eksar Arsask, at the Stitchmeal Sark. Someone was cooking breakfast, and the sounds of rousing burglife murmured at the walls. A din of voices, footsteps, clopping hooves and rattling wainwheels sounded from the streets below and afar. The hammer and clatter of building rang through the streets, a griff screeched overhead, and the tolling of churchbells wrestled above the roof-thatch. Ravens honked, horses nickered and dogs barked at them both. Vail; the meadow; the feelings of dread and helplessness; all were gone in a blink—all, save for the foul smell that had come in at the end. That stayed, and it seemed to be billowing onto him.

What was that?! Fergh and Hern! Was someone emptying his dinner into a chamber pot two feet off his headboard? Had he in his blindness been given a room that was also the inn's needhouse? Toron had never trusted such buildings, which he had never heard of until leaving home, and which he called indoor outhouses. Such a dig was best kept outside, along with the unhousebroken beasts whose business it shared.

The smell kept coming, wave after wave of it.

That was it.

He had to see.

With two fingers he split the slack of the wrappings and risked a look. The thrill of finding his sight given back to him, healthy and hueful, was swallowed quickly by the first thing he saw. It was a great, panting maw, hanging open above his head—all white-yellow fangs and shearteeth, rooted in pink, running backwards into darkness, a lolling rug of a tongue at its floor. A hot, gutsy stench was what it spoke, yelling fumes of the uncooked meat that had stood overnight in its depths. It was not until Toron knew what he was smelling that he retched at having sniffed it so nosily.

He rolled to shelter and battered the tuskcat with his pilliver[4]. Never one to take a prat, Gorrh axed the bag of feathers with his head and speared it with a tusk. Both fighters snarled and pulled, and the sack burst. A winter of duckdown settled upon the room, and the fight was at end. The two eyed each other grudgingly through the feathers.

Gorrh spoke through the Rine. *You were upset.*

Toron stood from his trench on the bed's other side. So wake me with a blow to the head, not by throwing up on me.

I was fishing in your dreams. The closer I came, the more I saw of it. I believe, had we touched, I might have stepped into it.

As I said, a blow to the head.

Toron stood and stretched, breaking the last of the sweven's cobwebs. It bothered him that he had been so hasty to unriddle it, and been taken unawares by its hidden sting. This was the Timebriar after all, which threw heaps of its muddling bracken upon every signal fire, clogging the paths between message and meaning which otherwise and elsewhere were clean. If indeed through the twisling and snag of the Briar it still sought to teach him something, he had misunderstood it. He had looked inwards, whither everyday swevens tended. What the dream had betokened went beyond himself. This he understood. This, and that he staved off its hounding at his own peril.

Toron had his eyes back nonetheless, and he let his sight frisk in the sunshine, whose light the half-open window of honeyglass split into two shades of gold. He took the time to look himself over, rubbing and prodding at the many blackblue leals that had bloomed upon his hide since last he saw it. Not too bad, all things reckoned. A man had been much worse after going toe-to-toe with four manshfretters. He felt a heave of pride, a heavy new tale upon his bookshelves, and marked with the settling of that thought that his head no longer ached, but seemed to float, as with giddiness of one fully healed, whose life is filled back to overflow him. He took his breeches off the floor and put them on while standing, buckling his belt before pulling his tunic over his head. It was his clean one, and

---

[4] *(AB):* pillow.

it was, from the smell of its underarms, still clean. He had changed shirts yesterday, having had to grope through his saddlebags. It had been hard to find blind, and to wrestle with the heavy saddle that lay, needing mending, in one corner of the room. Had the Chaldallions sneaked a woman's kirtle into one of the bags, he'd likely have put it on all the same. Tuger and Mortha leaned upright in their sheaths nearby, baldrics trailing out like tails, the modest mathom of his hoard. His swordstaff, too tall to stand, lay at the foot of the wall. He had not thought to see it again, and he was glad to see them all. He checked that they'd been cleaned and was stunned to find they had been. Pity had made the Chaldallions generous.

The boards beneath his feet quivered with the deep pitch of a man's laughter as he made his away across the room to the washing bin. He dipped in to dampen his face, making sure beforehand there were no telltale globs of spittle in it. On the wall before it hung a looking glass, mean of kind and dim with years, into which he peered. He was neither shocked nor saddened to learn that the Heron's healing had not wiped away his old scar. He saw also the untended shrubbery of his hair, and a dirtjawed beard, and meant to find a bathhouse and a barber sometime before that evening. He sat on his bed to put on his boots, then taking up his swords he slipped the belts over one shoulder and bundled up his breastplate in his cloak to bring with him.

It took this whole time for Gorrh to pull the speared pilliver off his tusk. When at last he got it done, the tuskcat sat there, blinking in the sundust, that twitching halfbreed of boredom and readiness making the rounds through his hide.

Is everyone up? Toron asked.

Yes, but not long. The younger Chaldallion is ailing a little.

Toron laughed aloud, which was something he tried not to do out of Rinespeech. It made him sound woody as a squirrel tree to anyone nearby. Furthermore, Gorrh never understood why he laughed, and often believed Toron was making fun of him. One of the first things the man had learned with the latching of the Rine was that the tuskcat's feel for kidding was rooted wholly in scorn, with no twig of it given to blitheheartedness. It stood to follow that a hunter of prey that was itself prey to nothing would not have been endowed with any share of self-belittling silliness. No behoof did it offer, like boldness for voles. All that mattered was pride, and the loathing of shame that was its flipside. Such a thing was too flat to give way, and Gorrh would not suffer to be squeezed.

Toron all but hurried from the room, and ran into Vail. All limbs and locks, she bounced staggering from him, and caught herself on the railing that edged the middle floor. Below them was the stir of the morning rush it overlooked, the breakfast after a holy night, the dishes rattling and daughters nattering as they sought to keep abreast of it. As it had been years ago, they were the Sark's only help, doing the work of barmaid, housemaid, and everything odd and between. The innkeep called them his wee squirrels, a word he must have picked up off a Landishman. His daughters hadn't liked it when they were wenchels, and they liked it less now that they were young women.

Toron stammered his sorry, and Vail smiled carefully at him— with her mouth, which he could see plainly was not fiendish. What he saw of her before him the sweven had not lied about, but it had overstressed her nonetheless, singling her out of the world's mingle, whose shared whereabouts were no one's island. Here, walled in roughhewn softwood and amidst the whiff of cooking eggs and woodsmoke, her otherly winsomeness was what it was—stunning but not staggering, as many a woman's was, with a face like that of highborn child's doll. Her eyes were extraordinary, yes, both in size and hue, but the green of them did not sparkle with an inner light, nor were they any greater than those of Urien, whose huge stare had struck Toron as babyish. Her hair was tied up in a crooked horsetail, and a little stringy. Her nose was small, her lips a little thin, with a chin that hardly began before it ended, and gave everything of her face to her gaze. She was dressed not in taffeta, but in a blue shift made of wadmal, which she found too short all over. The sight of her selfawareness as she pulled its hem back past her knees was not at all like the dryad he had dreamt. Of all things, it was her height that caught the eye most. She was only a hair shorter than he, who found himself looking down onto most men, and seemed even taller for her thinness, which two days without food had stressed. He rummaged through his head for a trinket of small talk, which Harandrishmen were the worst at. Gorrh step out into the hallway behind him.

"Have you slept well?"

Toron kept it in mind that she did not speak the Allmal, and wondered whether her tung-switching magic needed to be kindled before she might understand him.

"Yes, I thank you," she said, and with her own voice. It was a young woman's voice, though heavily stooped by the moulds of some farkind mothertongue.

Her newfound knack for the Allmal did not take him unawares. She was of the fayfolk, after all. It did, however, remind him that she was something of a guest beneath his sky, and though he had things to ask and business of his own, there was nothing that could not wait until they had all sat down together, and picked their morning meal. If, that is, she ate.

"Have you met the rest of us?" he asked, waving toward the stair at her back. Whatever Justinian's health, he could hear the big man laughing somewhere.

She looked warily into the hall below, and he recalled Gorrh's warning. *She's afraid. It's rolling out of her.* Now that he beheld her, however, she did not strike Toron as being afraid, at least not thoroughly. The tuskcat's mistake did not take him unawares either. As with his blindness to the many hues of funny, Gorrh was nosedeaf to the full sweep of fear, his huntermind stirring at the first whiff of it, his heartlessness swelling with the love of its weakness, swatting it to and fro in his thoughts like a mouse. Whether awe or dread or pang of worry, it was all one to him—the mindblood of one wounded, to be found and straddled, for play or feast. It was a nearsightedness the both of them had worked to reshape, but it seemed they had far to go, for what Toron saw in Vail was less fear than caginess, and of the same kind that Gorrh himself often showed when made to walk in Man's world. Though her eyes felt about for hints, they peered out from an impenetrable stronghold of self-mastery, one whose weapons were all drawn and readied, but which gave nothing away of their strength.

Vulnerable was the last thing Vail seemed. At least the dream had gotten that right.

"No," she said at last, drawing the word out. "I woke, and I waited. This room I stayed inside it until now."

Her eyes searched him for understanding, but her mouth said no more. Toron bethought himself of their talk last night, and it came to him that he still might be the only one she had spoken with since coming out of her long swoon.

"Well, unless you have somewhere to be, come down and sit with us a while. We shall not keep you any longer than that."

She nodded, and let him lead her, and after he shut the door to his room and turned the key, they went down the steps into the hall. It was full of talk and clatter, and the bustle of its hues was lovelier than fall leaves. He had forgotten that the walls were sheeted with luterwood, which was the rich yellow-red hue of laxflesh[5]. Cloth webs, woven in bright threads, gave scarves to the beams of the ceiling, and dust swam in the airy streams of the heatblower, glittering in the sunlight, whose glow flashed at the honeyglass windows whenever flying things went past beyond.

All the chairs were full. The heavy longboards had been dragged away from the walls, as they were every morning and night, and twenty guests or so—half of them men and half women—were gathered around them to eat. Toron and his thoftship had hired all the Sark's rooms, so these folk were neighbours, or lodgers from another inn. Some, for their dress, looked to be from outside the burg, and had likely overnighted in their wains, which they'd left at the gates or in the Grensteads. Some looked tough, and fidgeted as Toron, and then Gorrh, came off the groaning timbers of the stairs,

---

[5] *(AK)*: the meat of the salmon.

but none had the mellow smolder that marked fighting men to be feared. None, save the Chaldallions, who were sharing a runt of a table near the hearth. They stooped about it open-legged, like ogres playing a boardgame, and defended their steins of saraf with both hands. It was dear worth here, that drink, and potent, though they called it the dirty whoreson of coffee and soma. The skimpy devilishness the brothers' talk had put into their faces disappeared when they saw Vail, and both of them stood up, which Toron had not thought was in them.

He had not been blindfolded for long, but he found the sight of the men otherwise than what he had seen in his mind whenever they had dealt with him over the last two days. Brighter-eyed they seemed, and more at home, with near to no token of the wounds they had taken three days ago. While they had seldom been ones to whine about bushwhacking, not even as southern winlanders[6] amidst the rough of the middle North, there was no hiding their thrill to be back in a burg. Kurtisian was in his black armour, which he often slept in. His cloak was off though, and its lack left *Marat* bared, peeping out from its booksheath between his shoulderblades where most men kept their swords. Keeping it there meant Kurtisian could not sit back into his chair without discomfort, but it was annoyance he bore, having that alien ally at his back. As for the *Carno*, it was nowhere to be seen, but that meant nothing of a weapon that came and went at a word. Justinian wore his own clean shirt today—a vast hemp garment, laces open at the chest, which in a pinch might double for a tent or a sail. The Allmetal lay tangled up in its strings, a titan blinking up through the mesh. Its captivity fooled no one.

Both brothers stared fixedly at Vail, and if they saw Toron had his eyes back, they made no word of it. He told them her name, and they each told her his. Vail nodded slightly at both, then looked at Toron, then back to the Chaldallions. She lifted her hand to them, and they shook it without a trace of amusement. Toron saw they were captivated, at least for the time being. Maybe it was the saraf, he thought, glancing down into their cups.

Wood dragged on wood as Aldessa brought two more seats out from the back of the inn, from that walled-off share of the bottom floor, with its kitchen and larder, that lay beneath the upstairs rooms. The dark, sharp-chinned maiden was the first of the innkeep's

---

[6] *(AK):* grapegrowers and winemakers. Also called *vinlanders*.

household Toron saw again up close, and indeed she had gathered a few more winters than the single year he himself had known since last being here. From the looks of it, and something like the squirrel she was nicknamed, she had stored them all in her chest, which strained at her rain-gray dress in a way that might have seemed sultrier if Toron did not believe it to be the one of the only garments she owned. Heronites were a picky flock when it came to what weaves they wore, the banlaws of which Toron did not know, save that they took a lot of silver to meet. As the oldest daughter, Aldessa was in the worst weeds of it, so to speak, hopeless for hand-me-downs, with a widower father. As such, her budding frame was more likely to burst the stitches of her own clothing before it loosened the pursestrings of a man who did not want to see his firstborn's womanhood, and moreover who lacked a friendly woman who might have shaken his eyes open to it.

The closer Aldessa drew to the thoftship the slower she went, always keeping someone between herself and Gorrh, whose fur she never stroked. Knowing her unease and having been scolded for toying with it, the tuskcat plodded over to the nearest corner, turned around three times and flopped onto his side. Crockery rattled, and Aldessa kept to her path, keeping her eye on the great, flicktailing heap of him. She put the chairs where they were needed. Toron thanked her, laying his cloak and breastplate within reach and unshouldering his swords that he might sit more easefully.

Staring open-mouthed at the farkind woman she had helped to care for, Aldessa seemed no less bewitched than the Chaldallions by the sight of her up and about. Fayfolk were not seldseen among the roads and settleships of Knaks; they kept shadowtowns here and there, and indeed there were kinds of butterflies and songbirds and other thisworldly creatures one was much less likely to lay eyes on. Even among Outsiders, however, Vail was something else—fished up from the deeps of the Otherwhere, from far enough away that whatever her lot called itself, the tungs of Men would have no name for it. *Flocklore* was the word for that handling of knowledge that told one kind of thing from another, dealing everything from fish to rocks, from trees to clouds into bins of what made them unsame. It told oaks from elms, and silver oaks from mossy oaks, and those into even narrower pockets of being, fitting bulkheads throughout the great Lifeboat of Frumth and Fromship, telling onely from sundry from All. Men, and fiends too fell within the ken of flocklore, but Vail stood beyond its books, a hue unknown to the rainbow. She was of the fayfolk, yes, but that word was a catchall, scooping and not sifting. Of the wise of this world, only a Wherewalker—a wizard whose dreecraft carried him to other itnesses—might sketch the family tree to which she was a branch.

They were seated, and Vail lowered herself awkwardly, her legs keeping tightly crossed and turned to one side, towards Toron rather than Kurtisian, whose twain she sat between. She did not turn down Aldessa's offer of saraf. Nor, Toron groused to himself, did the girl ask how she might pay for it. Why not sell her a horse while you're at it? The fee for the woman's healing had been in the neighborhood of fifty gildenbits, which was likely more wealth than the Sark saw in a year. He had no way of wringing that gold back out of his foundling, nor, despite her talk last night of wergelds, did he mean to find one. It was not being too stingy to pull shut the pursestrings he had already stretched for her.

"Good and sunny out there today," Justinian said blithely. For someone who had likely drunk an ocean of mead the night before, he did not look so bad. "A little cold though."

Kurtisian snorted. "How would you know? Did you wake up in a ditch this morning?"

Justinian's eyes, having been aimed somewhere over all their heads, settled slowly onto his brother like ash. "I left the window open, and it felt a little cold."

Loath he was to admit that he had awakened where he had collapsed, only a few yards from where he now sat, having been surrounded with cordons by the innkeep's daughters, who were getting ready for the morning rush and had not expected him to arise beforehand. Toron nonetheless felt that the priest's face seemed darker than irritation owed it, and saw with a deeper look that a slight shadow of the blow he taken from the manshfretter indeed still lay there. If there were other welts, his shirt hid them, and it came to Toron that his thoftman was not wearing the unwonted thing simply to be humble.

Kurtisian half-turned to Vail, who was at his right elbow. "How about you, Vail? Does it get cold where you're from?"

She regarded him without turning her head. "In places. And you?"

Kurtisian opened his mouth to answer but then halted, like a man who leaves his next footstep hanging in midair. His lips closed again, and he yielded the grudge-grin of one outplayed. Thankful that his thoftman's brashness had been rapped so early in their talk, Toron smiled to himself and watched Aldessa add a few small logs to the nearby fire.

"Kurtisian and Justinian are from far to the south of here," he said, shaking his head when the innkeep's daughter looked up and pointed to herself. "They're mostly northern blood, but a long time ago when there was a lot more fighting than there is now, some folks living near the sea loaded up their ships and headed down the Sundarsund to get away. Hundreds of them, maybe thousands. A handful of kinglings went with them. They forsook their kingdoms, which were likely to be pushed into the sea anyway, and I reckon bought new lands among folks they had traded with for hundreds of years. They fought for more lands, and over time, those lands became new homelands."

He was careful to pick small words, that Vail might better understand him. It came to him nonetheless that he could not have been able to put it any other way, nor answer with anything further were she to ask. Though it seemed but the nutshell, it was also the meat of what Toron knew. Níscel had spoken more of the South than the Chaldallions, who in turn seemed less tight-lipped than simply unwitting of its yorelore. Shard had spoked of them as well, though the Highbred seemed only to have come up through those many, many lands the Knaksish in their unknowingness called the South, and not begun his life there. Toron was in over his head even to broach the thing. Those landholds were so far away, and indeed so unlike the only world he had walked, that they might as well be the otherworldly Elfhome of the Ozmen tales—whence Vail had come, for all he knew.

Kurtisian, however, saw new room for swagger. He leaned back with hands behind his head, as far as *Marat* would allow him. "Homelands of a kind, Thorn. We still don't know what real ties are kept between Salpes and the North, or what flags are flown just to keep the emirs and the shahs and the rajahs and the pharaohs and all the rest of them guessing at our strength. It's like a blowfish. All bristles and hot air. We're supposed to be friends now down there, but the South is full of jackals. Smiling enemies. Fawning politeness is a code to a lot of them, not a gesture of friendship or subservience. To this day, it throws us off. And that's when you get a talwar across the trachea." He laughed, brought the front legs of his chair back to the floor, and reached for his cup. "Or a khanjar through the cranium."

"Or a jambiya in the junk," Justinian added.

Kurtisian finished his sip and looked at him with bitter disappointment. "A jambiya *is* a khanjar."

"No. It's smaller."

"Trust me."

"How about a shamshir in the shkull?"

Kurtisian groaned and finished his saraf. He sat back and stretched, eyes shining.

Toron ducked in and around to look at Vail. "Are you following any of this?" Because he wasn't.

She sighed, murmured something to herself, and moved her hands as though stirring smoke. The air startled a bit, and she murmured again. "I am following it now," the second voice said.

The men all looked at each other, the Chaldallions' smirks full of scofflawry. Toron was much less at ease.

None of them truly knew how the laws governing Dreebreach worked in Eksar, how they were broken, or how the wielding of magic was even nosed out. There was a school of magic and however many priesthoods, all of which would have some freedom or leeway. Rhianys had done some last they were here—though quietly—as had Kurtisian to summon the *Carno*, and Justinian every time he gripped the Allmetal. Bethinking himself of those deeds, Toron recalled seeing magic done on the streets as well, though of the harmless sideshow kind which the burgwards overlooked. Altogether it told Toron that Dreebreach was reckoned by the breadth of it, and not simply by its happening. Some folks—Vail among them, according to the Heron's priestess—were dreeish in their very blood, and might no better snuff out those flames than still their own hearts. Furthermore, Eksar had to be full of dreemen by now, the King's lathing about Bayerd giving no ban against them, who were many among the roving teerseekers of the land. Were none of that so, and were the warlock-wereds of the burgwards indeed sniffing about for any hint of magic—peering into seeing stones with clawed fingers fidgeting—the thoftship would find out soon enough.

The men sat not speaking for a time, with the wolfsheepish looks of a gang of knaves whose dirty banter has been scolded by a bystander. Vail stared down and about like they did, but her eyes were drawn over and again to the windows, whose golden glass was throughshinely and not seethrough[7], behind which flashed the shapes of things she seemed less than eager to meet. Her look darted back in from time to time, by chance meeting theirs, though Toron knew not whether she did this to fluster them or simply that her glance was too striking to be stealthy. They did not speak again until Aldessa had come back with Toron and Vail's cups of saraf, and asked what they would have for breakfast. Vail smiled wanly, and let the girl—who seemed to believe that she hardly understood a word of the Allmal—pick for her. She chose berries and oatmeal, the simplest thing they had, which came sprinkled nonetheless with pimmusk, the red-brown cride whose tang was hard to put in words. Aldessa swore she would love it.

"So we'll head out today," Toron said to his thoftmen once she had gone. He took a slow pull of his drink and wiped his mouth with the back of his hand. "Go to the Burgreeve's, see what we need to do there."

The swallow seemed to wash straight from his throat to his blood, like a single wave that splits among many waterways. Saraf was not simply an upper but what the wortmongers called a *sheenleef*, flooding the cellars of the mind with its shining waters on which only the lightest of one's thoughts floated. Both sharpening and dulling, it was a fitting drink of Teakenmaley, and Toron still found it funny that the innkeep had something against dealing in booze but not this.

The Chaldallions nodded serenely and added nothing. Justinian brushed a piece of something from his shirt.

Vail asked what it was they needed to do at the Burgreeve's.

"I don't know," Toron answered, his face open. "But if you're asking why we have to go, it's why we're here." He patted himself down a little for the half of the leaflet they had taken from Booril then recalled he had left it in one of his saddlebags.

Justinian spoke up. "There's some kind of trouble in a border province to the south of here. Monsters, brigands. It isn't clear. The King's men have been pushed back, and he's put out a call for men. It said to come here and to make ourselves known to the Burgreeve, and he'd take care of us until we're sent."

---

[7] *(AK)*: translucent, not transparent.

Vail nodded and answered with a few words in her own tung. And this is what you do? All of you? She looped them together with two swings of her hand. Those brisk movements brought the strong smell of mayweed, with which the clothing she wore had not so much been washed as seeded.

The Men all nodded. Toron nearly said something—a few words to whittle down what she might have meant—but chose against it.

You are sellswords, she said.

Toron had seen its shadow rising, but the name slapped him nonetheless. He flushed.

"No. There has already been a call for them, and that is not the one we are answering here."

Justinian's face was innocent when he mentioned they had not even known of the call for sellswords until after they had seen the bulletin they were answering.

Vail looked from him back to Toron. Then what do you call what you do?

Toron said, "We are teerseekers."

Vail looked bewildered.

Kurtisian snickered. "You heard it right."

"Tear and bleed," his brother added.

Toron shook his head, and stared back into the hearth. This was an old bit of wordplay they were prodding him with, and its nub grew duller every time.

"Glory and renown," Kurtisian yielded. "More or less. Gods forbid we use words no one can mistake."

Teer and *blead*.

The words were of old Braccish stock, with *tir* shared by the Northway tungs, among whose outland folk it was also the name of the fighter-god *Týr*, whom the Braccish called Tiw the One-handed. Found but in books and heard only in scopship, *teer* and *blead* were for higher things—words kept clean and sharp, above the wear and tear of everyday speech, like to one's best clothes and heirloom blades. Their meanings were not marks to be hit, but rather stars to be chased, to keep high one's head in this game of life Man could not but lose in the end. And for this there was a grimmer edge to the Chaldallions' ribbing than they knew, one that Toron had never made them aware of, and which he was less likely to do as time went on.

Teer and blead. He had not taken the twain from a saga-book, nor from a storied web in a throneroom, nor from any lofty wordwind he'd overheard among athelings. He had seen the words gouged into a shield, in runes rather than staves, lying tarnished in the high wastes between Harandril and nowhere, its owner known only to the wolves he had fed. The finding of it had not stung Toron, but it got into him nonetheless, and for weeks it lay in him like a dead meal, like rocks sewn into his belly. Only months before he had come across the body of a hanged outlaw where no men were known to live, but not even that melting nightmare had bothered him as much as this did. So it was that his southern thoftmen took his withdrawal from their kidding for sulk when indeed it was for something dreadful—something so grisly that he had stuffed its true memory like the body of a proud kill, swapping its offal with sweeter smelling insides, as one might do the corpse of an angel, devastating to behold but too dearworth to abandon.

Such thistles were the only crop Harandrish soil had yielded without fail, the bounty of a land whose staggering beauty swallowed more than it gave man to eat. Its cold embrace was mother to every belief he now held.

First among them was a saying.

No min, never been.

The Chaldallions had rolled that one around in their mouths too, but seemingly in earnest, for what they offered in translation was not venomous, nor anything phlegmatic, but rather a pearl, one whose polish took the edges off its homespun northern quide.

If you are not remembered, you never existed.

And for the sake of that pearl, he forgave them their cheek over it now and again. So long as they sculled the Lethe[8] together.

Vail nodded. So you are helpers of Men.

Toron liked that better. "Yes. We want to help wherever it's hardest."

For glory. For teer.

"Yes."

Vail's eyes lost some of their softness. Though those soul-windows might not give away her story, it was clear they could hide nothing of her feelings.

Is this glory your only fee?

"Well, no. A man's got to eat."

"And sleep in featherbeds," Justinian said, luxuriating showmanly in his chair.

"And pay for the healing of strangers," Kurtisian added.

Something twitched on Vail's lips. She turned herself toward the fuhrbido a little, but still did not face him when she spoke.

But are you godsmen? A king's rangers? Are you lordless thegns? Whose teachings do you follow? To what or whom do you pledge troth? Do you seek to do good, or do you seek simply to do well for yourselves?

Justinian looked bored. "Why can't you do both?"

As outcome, you can. But I ask of the input. To seek to do good is selfless. To seek to do well is selfish. What most drives you, the deed or the glory?

"Both," Kurtisian said, recrossing his arms.

Vail sighed and nosed at her drink. So far she had not drunk any of it, but seemed content to warm her hands on its cup's clay walls, cradling it to her breast like some beloved trinket she feared they would take away. Toron kept his knees toward the hearth and watched her stir over his shoulder, bewitched at how even the slightest shifting of her hands and feet was unlike theirs—not so

---

[8] One of the Rivers of the Underworld in southern godlore, the waters of which bring oblivion, and which the dead drink in passage to forget their earthly lives.

much budging as drifting, as though loosened to a current that flowed past her always. He chewed the insides of his cheeks. This early prying chafed at him, though he did not get the feeling she was being willfully meddlesome. She was far from home, groping to get the lay of the land, and to learn something of the outsiders who had, seemingly on no grounds beyond the good will they could not spell out, carried her back from the gates of death. Holding those thoughts made him thildier than he would have been, and he suffered it to choose his answer carefully.

"Some good things are harder to do than others. Take the things men call *good deeds*." He smeared the two words as he said them. "Good deeds are feeble things. Almsdeeds. They're no harder than the choice to do them. Help an old man to his feet. Fetch a child's doll from the stream where she dropped it. Hold the post straight while your neighbour hammers it in. You're not a good person to do these things. You're an arsehole if you don't do them. You know it. The wretch you snub knows it. So whatever thanks you get for doing them is not clean, but brought forth from the ready grudge of the owed, like a blossom grown on a dunghill.

"And *selfless*? A good deed is only selfless in that the deed blesses itself. The doer? He's a shoe to its foot. He is to be grateful for the chance to do something anyone else should have done. You ask me, this isn't what good is. It's a mean burden a man steps under whenever he is around other men, and which the strong end up shouldering the most of. It's a weakling's cheaping founded on warped shrift.

"What we seek to do is a better kind of good. It's the only kind of good that the strongest ought to have a share in. Most folks, they work selfishly to bring themselves somewhere that doing good gets easy. It's an afterthought, a copper tossed in a beggar's lap. It does not pain them. It does not drain them. It's a thrill of pride, a spring off the head of someone on his knees. That's not what we want. We want the work and the deed to be one, to do the kind of good that puts an end to evil, whatever shape it takes. That's what we want to do. The greater the better. We want to hunt the wyrm to its hole. Stare down the thurse. Make the troll eat fire. We want to drag the wolves back dead through the folds they fed from. That's a kind of good few seek to do, and fewer can bring about, for the simple truth that a mistake means you're dead. But those who die trying are still

held up as better men than those who run the mill. And the ones who
pull it off? They're something even better."

He felt a flutter of blitheness, whose wings spread for a soaring
mood. Before they could get away on him, though, he recalled again
the trenchant grounds for this speech he made, and all his lift
foundered. Instead, a scornful laugh burst out of him, unforetokened,
like the sudden boil of mud whose thickness hid its simmer.

"That you end up being loved for doing something does not
mean that doing it is selfish. Neither is it selfish to make a living off
something folks would give anything for. This kind of good, the
kind not anyone can do—it is the help no man sees coming, so he
doesn't feel it is owed to him. There is no ready grudge for his
fellow man, only hatred toward the fiends or ill hap that put him in
his need. Maybe he has hope, but it is not the same as a right. The
only thing that grows cleaner love for help is hopelessness. To lie
bitten a thousandfold, awaiting only death. Begging for it, maybe.
To see the healer coming when all trust in chance is lost—there is
nothing more wholesome to the heart of Man. And to rekindle a life
in the darkness, its fire is the most worshipful teer under heaven. It
is what gods did in the beginning. It is a deed akin to Fromship[9]
itself.

"So I ask you, what is an almsdeed to this? And what
grassfeeder's eyes sees them both as one? They are as unlike each
other as a puddle and a cloud. Only from below, to the
puddledrinker, does the cloud seem the same. And that the deed
might be shorn of its teer? Only a sheep could up with such a cud. It
will become true the day a sheep takes down the wolf for itself."

He brought his cup to his lips, and with it hid his gloating smile.
He was glad he had had the mindlifting drink to hand, the float of
which had uncramped his thoughts, and let him paddle the clutter
into a winning shape. It was not like him to spell himself out, not as
it was with others he had known, whose upbringings and livelihoods
had taught them the readiest frameworks of mathelcraft[10]. As he had
said more than once, he'd rather build buildings than build speeches.
So it was that he felt he had done well here, and got from Justinian a
rosy nod and high cup. Kurtisian he did not twist to glimpse, but the
lack of a quip bespoke the fuhrbido's unanimity. As for Vail, she

---

[9] *(AK)*: Creation; Genesis.
[10] *(AB)*: rhetoric; oratory; the art of speaking well.

said nothing for a while, but her head wawed a little, either the better to roll around what she had heard, or more likely in some riddling gesture shared only by her kind. Having now uncorked his mind, Toron found his pride curdling rather than curing, knowing that, as a faywoman, she might have many times his years behind her, in which likelihood it was the words and not the depth of the thoughts that gave her pause. He recalled a saying his young father had let him in on—*age is nothing to boast of; you get it for free*. As a piece of wisdom belittling elderhood, it was a rare bird, but Toron took it as given that it didn't touch fayfolk.

Their morning meals came, and they ate without word, their dishes on their laps, the sounds of the other guests giving cheer to the lull. Kurtisian ate loudly, as was his wont. Justinian, it seemed, had asked for but a single helping, and the morsel was a sorry sight before him. The only clear sign his guts were unwell, it was like watching an ogre chew off only a man's fingertips and chase away the rest of him. Vail sniffed at hers first, then dug in without qualm. The wooden spoon was too broad for her mouth, forcing her for seemliness to take small bites off the top of each scoopful. Toron poked at his eggs, which he had had softseethed[11], and soaked up the yolks with dark bread. He ate them at every chance he found, for it was hopeless to bring them on the road. Though they had been nothing to him as a boy who had learned to toddle chasing chickens, he now found that the lack of them was making him into a bit of a dotard, as he found himself eyeing the speckled gray shells on Kurtisian's plate, and wishing he had got his unbroken too.

The berries were less wondrous, as the roadsides and thickets of Knaks were often bursting with some kind or other, and he had on more than one day eaten too many for his own good. He had had them when a child as well, but had been made to pick them for his mother too many times, being scratched by thorns, stung by bees, and dived at by drunken birds. Twice he had had to flee from bears whose cubs he found picking alongside him, getting away thanks only to his dog, and coming home to a mother he had thought worse than the bear for more or less laughing at him and calling it all the unsung hazard of gathering the North's most fought-over fruit. Where Eksar differed was in the kinds of the berries, few of whose names he knew and not all of which looked akin to those of

---

[11] *(AK)*: soft-poached.

Harandril. The sharp smack of them was homey enough, though, and they were garnished with a white ream called sheermilk, which, though sweetened, was much like *skyr*—a cheese thinner than butter which his neighbours had made, and for which his father had swapped handiwork. This he washed down with a drink from the ewer Aldessa had set on the floor, whose waters were from the Gungnissa, and which were as cold, and sharp, as the spear said to have carved that watery road. Gorrh watched them chew with tail switching, which was the cat's way of drumming his fingers. Although he himself had been fed, and well, since coming to the burg, he knew today was the day they would set out upon its sea of Mannish business.

As their meal neared its end, Vail mumbled between nibbles. This matter to the south, what is your plan?

Toron laid his dish on the floor and sat back with his saraf once more. Before he might answer, however, Kurtisian did so, the dreeman's mouth still half-full.

"We told you already. We go by the Burgreeve's and proceed from there."

But how is it that you proceeded in other work like this?

Justinian's smile was jocular but his look no less impatient than his brother's. "What do you mean?"

Work like this. Teerseeking, as you called it. And fiendslaying, which is more the gist of it. So you find work, as you have here. There is some devil, or a pack of them, preying on a town, or stalking a countryside. How do you ready yourselves? How do you choose your weapons? How do you go about fighting something?

Kurtisian belched a little before replying. "We make sure our weapons are with us, and we go hit the monster with them until it dies."

Vail laughed, the spring of it showering the men's own chuckles. Unlike last night, it was a delightful sound, auditory ambrosia, like no laughter learned beneath Ráma's suns. To hear its fetching chime was to grin like a dullard, and Toron felt a gale in it, one that might move him to leap overboard anywhere, to swim what deadly stretch, to dash himself at the rocks nearest its blissful song, giving all but his ears as the toll. As soon as Vail clipped it, he began to yearn for it, yet it was more titter than peal, and he wondered what strength lay in its fullest breath, and what breed of elfkind she was to own such a gift. From the look of her, she did not wish them to know—

not at all—and she bit down hard upon that glee, like one who hides too late the crooked teeth that shame her, hating the happiness that caught her unawares.

I speak, she went on, of the learning behind your craft, and the doing of it. It is a trade of a kind, yes? As with hunting and cobbling and woodcutting?

The three men looked to one another, and with bobbing heads thwore to agree.

Then how do you carry it out? What is the way of a fiendslayer in this kingdom? Walk me through a day of your work.

Kurtisian readied himself to answer again, the rogue in his look unchanged from his last remark. Toron spoke over him.

"It all hangs on where we are, and how we get word. We've answered calls, like the lathing for Bayerd that brought us here. Other times folks have come straight up to us when they saw us coming through, telling us that a household a few days out has not been heard from in weeks, or that some goonish troll has set itself up under a bridge they need. Or else townsmen have been going into the woods and not coming back out. Sometimes, it's been happening for months, or even years, folks being picked off. It's more like that with the outlying steads, that they offer to hire you when they see you. Not enough swords come through for anyone to bother putting out a call."

"That," Justinian put in, reclining again, "and they don't have the money in the first place."

Toron's smile was empty. "Some towns are simply too far out to know what is wrong with them. Folks are born and die there, never seeing a better way. They'll believe anything they grow up with and never know their unhappiness for suffering. It's why fiends prey at the edges of menning, and seldom at its heart. Watch any herd being hunted, it's the stragglers get picked off. There are fiends, longlived ones, who've made marchland hamlets what are well-nigh their own sheepfolds, the folks inside their livestock. It happens more often than the heartlanders think, and it's gruesome to see what it does in the long run. The stakewall grows thicker. They lock the gates at night, giving no heed to the screams outside. You only come upon such a town by mistake or by taking an old road for days, and when you come through the gates they look at you like you're in on it, as though you'd have to be to have gotten there. And if not, it's as though somehow you'll make things worse for them by staying. You know something is dead wrong, but most of the folks won't tell you what it is. As I said, most don't know it for wrong. But there's always one or two folks, outcasts of a kind, who'll talk to you when no one else is watching them."

Vail wobbled her head, and he knew it for a kind of nod. Then you are wanderers. You wander widely, and at the marches, to find this work.

"We do. We must." Toron cleared his throat, and looked over his shoulder at the other breakfast guests. "We are not alone in what we do. There are others, some much better off than we are. The Boarsmen are the greatest of them, and though they're fiendslayers, they're not what we call teerseekers with the same meaning. Frithkeepers is more like it. They're kingsmen, and they fight to uphold the calm. All teer in this falls to the King."

Then I take it, Vail followed, that there is little love between teerseekers and Boarsmen.

Toron scoffed through his nose. "That's putting it lightly. What work we find for ourselves, they see it as a kind of deerjacking from the king's rightful grounds. That, and you're showing the Boarsmen up in some way, finding the blind spots in their wardship. We're a walking likelihood of shame for them. That's another thing that tells sellswords from teerseekers. Sellswords the Boarsmen hire. To do dirty work; as baitgoats; to help bring wainrows down godforsaken roads. To kill yourself, to boot. I've heard of them putting up gold to go stick your head in a hole, wherever they've lost men at the mouth of some den somewhere, and they don't know yet what they're up against."

"Makes sense," Kurtisian cut in, and yet again not unwryly. "You've seen the armour they wear. Those helmets, and those shields with boar's heads on the bosses. It's probably not easy patching bite marks in those. Then you have to hand that gear on to the next poor recruit and hope he doesn't notice the bloodstains."

Yet, Vail countered, the King sent for you this time. Sellswords and now teerseekers. The both of you.

Toron nodded, and the offness of it had not struck him until now. "The Boarsmen are overwhelmed in Bayerd, the lathing says. Them, and the sellswords they hired earlier. The wording is aboveboard, and there's nothing swikeful about the stakes. They don't have the men to deal with havenseekers, watch the borders, and drive out the threat all at once."

And you say, Vail continued, glancing at Justinian and recalling his words, that you do not know what kind of threat this is. Fiends, outlaws. That it's not very clear.

"As clear," Justinian said, winking, "as a muddy day."

It sounds to me, Vail's second voice translated, that you are being asked to go stick your heads in a hole.

Toron finished his saraf and handed the empty stein to Aldessa, who had come to gather up their dishes. "If the lathing was all there was to it," he said, "that would be so. I have a feeling that a leaflet and a pocket full of hope were all the sellswords had to work with. But we're not to be sent to Bayerd on that alone. We were to come here to be given further tidings and some sort of backing—whatever that means, I can't reckon. A weapontake maybe. What is clear is that the King needs a third kind of man to deal with whatever is ailing Bayerd, as the first two weren't good enough."

Or filling enough, Vail said. Something that bites a whole kingdom, it might be hungrier than two helpings, no?

Chortling, Kurtisian slapped his knee, the display of it a show, but the sentiment genuine. "I like her. I like this one."

Toron licked a tooth with lips shut. "As I said, we mean to hear more once we see the Burgreeve."

Vail huffed out one side of her mouth, another gesture whose meaning he lost. She began to speak more swiftly. I do not ask these things to be unhovely. But it seems you go about your work with very little in the way of readiness. Of teer and death, I cannot tell which you are truly seeking, or which will find you first. And you are all so young. You are what, in years? Hardly half again out of youthhood? The game is so barely begun, you cannot know the odds of your play. How often have you won with these ways of yours, and how often have you been set back?

Toron and the Chaldallions withdrew their eyes from one another, for what she had put among them had many edges and was nowhere safe to touch. The hearthfire popped in the hush, and Gorrh's tail gave a great thwack. It was saying something that even the tuskcat was feeling lousy by her questions, for whom the best and only readiness was being stronger and doughtier than one's foe.

"Six of one, half a dozen of the other," Kurtisian at last caroled through a sigh. "Though everyone's a lanista[12] among the

---

[12] *(L)*: a trainer and manager of gladiators.

spectators." He picked at his cuticles and looked half her way. "We've answered a lot of questions about ourselves, Vail."

Her sincerity seemed unfeigned. And I am grateful for your courtesy.

"Hey, courtesy is my name."

I ask only in that I seem bound to you for a time, in repayment of my wergeld, as it were. She looked to Toron and smiled, and it was a sight much like the sound of her laughter. You must have some skill in your work, or fortune must favour you, for you to have delivered me from the Dwimmersithe.

Justinian's brow twisted. "You mean the fairyroad?"

She spoke the same word she had before—which was something like *theehaseersha*—but her dreeish voice gave another. This time it was not Dwimmersithe, but Waywindle. Again she tried, resulting in Whereleet, and again, giving Warptrod. Twice more she said it, becoming angrier—*theeharseersha, theehaseersha*—giving Wridegrot and Earthedder, and finally *theeharseesha-tic zykeshalot!*—which gave 'the goddamned Fayroad'. I'm sorry, she said, eyes burning beneath a blear. This magic is not the best of its kind.

If it had been a mule and not a spell, she'd have kicked it. The men chuckled merrily, and she saw the warmth in it, though she had to look nine ways first.

I come from Outside, she said, if that be not naked to everyone. From far Outside, the hiccoughing of this magic tells me. I listen to it go through its wordhoard, and it finds few settled meanings. That tells me something of your minds, for words and wordings are not the same. A world may have many of one, but few of the latter. It is what tells scopship from hard knowledge. Never mind. I shall tell you of myself, but to lay it all before you will take time, and you will have to grasp it loosely. All that can wait, however, as you have business here, and I have nowhere else to be.

She giggled at that, and it sounded a tad unhinged. Justinian threw Toron a hairy eyeball.

Let me help you, she said. I know some things, of the fields if not the grasses. Things are not the same here as I am wonted to, but you would be startled to learn what is shared among Wheres. Let me help you.

She fixed Toron with her stare, and Kurtisian, behind her, shook his head at him with all the gusto of an actor aiming for the back rows.

Toron did his best to look like he was mulling it over. "Well. Can you fight?"

Everyone can fight, she said, though not all of us might throw a sound punch or wield a two-handed sword. I have my magic, the knack of which I shall regain here. It is a lot like learning to walk again, but on a small boat in high seas. And I have other tricks. But if you speak of weapons, I am a marksmaid. If I can shoot it, I can score with it.

"Anything?" Justinian said. "Like bows and crossbows, and— other kinds of bows?"

And many kinds of throwing weapons, yes, though I would see what you have at hand before staking myself. Come. There must be somewhere in this city where I might prove my worth to you.

Toron was not about to lie, either to himself or aloud, that he did not like the thought of the Vail's thoftship. But he knew next to nothing of her, and what trust he lacked on his own behalf went deep into unhealed wounds. It was not simply that she was a lady, though she did seem frailer than most. The Harandrishmen had not the qualms of elselanders about the fitness of their wives and sisters to work and fight alongside them, though it had nothing to do with fairness, nor with the tales of shieldmaidens and walkyries they grew up on. There was nothing aforethought about it— there simply hadn't been enough folk to go around in Harnadril for the men and women to name the work for one side or the other. Not even the Ignish were so heedless, whose women were born touched by wild dree, and Rhianys had needed time to see that Toron truly did not care about her kinness[13], so long as she didn't make its weaknesses theirs.

But Rhianys was dead, as was Níscel. Though Shard and Dhandhar were no quicker, the losses of the women had been worse, and Toron found he could not shake it—what he'd heard called the shepherd's shame. It had sent him deep into the root cellar of his beliefs, to go through every store, and to distrust them all for stunted. Harandril was a hard land, but humble. One broke faith with simplicity at a risk to one's life. Too narrow was its bed, too shallow its earth, for the roots he had grown there to hold true everywhere else. His own groundwork he could not reshape or do over, but he still had a choice over who he let through his door.

---

[13] *(AK):* gender.

The hush drew out, and faces sharpened in wait. "Gods, Vail," he said. "Why should you even want to come with us? We don't ask it. We're only three men, and the fellreeps[14] bloody all our dreams. We've left nothing behind us but bodies, our gold is dwindling, and our hearts are hardening against those we only ever wanted to help. We came to Eksar on a walking swoon. Had we not come across the lathing we answer, the gods only know where we'd be."

Such a plea crawled out naked on the heels of his speech about teerseeking and do-gooding, and though Toron had forethought otherwise, Vail was as dumbfounded as the Chaldallions to hear it. Her allseeing eyes searched his face, and their ancientness shone through. The disparity was too lovely, and out of nowhere he felt his heart ache for the undeathless, whose wisdom means withering, the body and the mind swapping strength. The faywoman broke her gaze and took a final pull of saraf, biting her mug with a *clink*. She held it there for a while, between her teeth, then put the vessel down, where it was caught nigh on the bounce by the youngest of the innkeep's daughters. The girl had come to see the Outsider, ogling her shamelessly as she stacked their dishes.

Aldessa, grudgingly, made her sister known to Vail—Sealith was her name—and Toron took the break in their talk to acknowledge the misgivings his thoftmen were hurling at him. It was Hell, he showed them with a shrug, that he would have to catch from them later. There was no turning the woman down here, save to forsake her at the inn, and , were that to happen he did not believe that Vail would be there when they got back. No, she was not their ward. Unless she was. They had smuggled her into their world, both sides in the dark. She knew no more about where she was than they did about where she had come from. Whether she knew how to get back; whether she wanted to get back; there was no shooing her toward something she had not broached herself. If they were to be rid of her—if, after today, they indeed wished to be—it would have to wait till the morrow.

"Excuse me, friends," Justinian announced of a sudden, rising. The air tightened at once, as though the lifting of his voice and person had sent it all in a crush to the walls. He glowered over the heads of his seated thoftmen, at the room full of guests he alone had

---

[14] (*H* expression): The fellreep, or ptarmigan, is a symbol of misfortune among the Nethrishmen, akin to the albatross of southern lands. To dream of fellreeps fighting is to foresee a violent end to one's life.

been facing. The three men he addressed had been heading for the door, and they did not halt so much as freeze. They stood there in what was less a hush than the sound of noise yielding, the only other voice the hoarse whisper of the heatblower.

"I've noticed," Justinian said to them, his tone false-friendly, "that you've taken quite the shine to my ladyfriend." He traced the line between them and Vail.

Though the threesome looked leathery enough to take a couple of blows, they were not fighters, and went unarmed. They balked at once before this man-mountain and his weird swettling of their tung, at a loss for one word to give back to him.

Toron and Kurtisian arose then too. The legs of their seats scraped the floor, which in many an alehouse was the first sound of any good brawl. Kurtisian was clearly up for it, and Justinian looked ready to spew ash and molten rock. But this was no alehouse, and the fight would be neither rightful nor fair. Toron saw the fear, not simply in the three men they threatened, but in all the guests watching. Some indeed were cowering, their cups in their hands, and he felt the shame of a thug, becoming angry with the brothers for not backing off as well as for showing the recklessness to shit where they were eating. Sealith and Aldessa, who only a heartbeat earlier had been chattering merrily before Vail, now cringed upon what they felt was to become a slaughterpath, clutching each other as the heavens came down around them.

"Put it in some milk, you two," Toron gristed at his thoftmen, careful not to call them openly by their names. "What have they done?"

"Gawping at her since you came down," Justinian muttered, the floorboards whimpering as he shifted his weight. "And staring holes into the back of her head the whole time we ate. Just got sick of it now."

Somehow it had slipped Toron's heed that Vail herself had stayed seated. She had not even looked around, but kept her back to all this, not wholly frozen, but hardly stirring—a little like a fawn who believes itself unseen. The easiest thing to see was that she wanted no share of this business.

"It's all right," Toron said to the men awaiting their doom. "Go."

They left, throwing out the door and wedging themselves through its frame. Were the inn a burning ship and the doorway its lifeboat they could not have fled or squeezed harder. The sounds of

the burg beyond were near to a racket, which unheard till then
showed the wonder of the inn's luterwood walls. The nearest guest,
an older man, arose to close the door again. He walked slowly,
sideways, eyes down and hands up, all of it carefully chosen to show
Toron and the Chaldallions that he wanted no quarrel. The sight of it
brought Toron's shame to self-loathing, to see a working man who
had come in for a humble morning meal now believe himself the
yisel[15] of outland tyrants.

"Your meals are all on us," he said to the room, though there
was little strength in his voice. Few cups went up in thanks.

"Except for the saraf," Justinian joked, at least halfway. Toron
only shook his head and gathered up his swords by their belts.

The innkeep came out of the kitchen, seeing the affrighted hue
of his daughters and looking wary of whatever he'd missed. Drying
his hands with a dishcloth, he cast his frown toward the
Chaldallions, whose hackles had yet to slacken, and then at Gorrh,
whose tail thumped two wounded beats at the slight. In truth, the
tuskcat was the best behaved among them, wherever an outburst
would catch his hide the spears of ten burgwards.

Toron tried to soothe the innkeep with a balmy smile and a
wave, but the house owner walked over and spoke to his other
guests first. What they said to him Toron did not hear, at least not
word for word, but whatever they told, it was so much starch to the
hardness of their host's eyes. Toron felt himself wilting, amazed at
how much being in the wrong might shrink a man.

"They're telling on us," Kurtisian leaned over and whispered
churlishly. "It's because you softened on them, you know."

Toron said nothing as he fished the goldbag from his cloak and
squeezed its dwindling heft with all the unease and tenderness owed
an ailing ballsack. He hardly had the time to untie its knot when the
innkeep loomed in from the left, a storm in his stride.

Before he and Toron might have words, however, a white wall
rose between them. It was Vail, and she lay before their host, in the
voice that was her own, a plea meant to teach the thoftship her
worth. Though halting, the traipse of her words was not at all
rickety, instead wobbling, deliciously vulnerable, as though made to
totter on high heels. And the voice itself—it walked like a river at
low water, its sparkling breath made to grind through the narrows of

---

[15] *(AK):* hostage.

the throat and tongue that kneaded it. This was not the way she had spoken with them all earlier, nor with Toron outside his room. This was a hunter's knack, whose weakness was bait, like to the babyish wailing of bergcats, which draws its prey far beyond the help of its turf and herd.

All she said was that they were sorry, that they didn't want what had happened to happen. That, or something close to it—the choice of words itself carried no weight. The dree was in her speech, a magic which, shapeless as a fume, might have hid in any shell, needing no waving of the hands, nor a pinch of this or that to let out. Whether its workings were weakened by dearth of the Allmal, only she knew that, but what was bare to all was the crippling dint of it— like to an embrace which, though begun as a token of love, might be overdone, and made to crush and kill. Toron did not see her face as she spoke. But he saw the man she spoke to, and the uncanny thing she was doing to him. Toron watched his colour carried away by her words, the hues of flush and umbrage both, mote-by-mote, like pollen to an unseen swarm, till the man hardly seemed to know where he stood. By turns, his look slackened, then warmed, then slackened again, then gave a start of dread, which flashed and was gone, as though beneath the flow of her words something swam, which he saw too late before it spilled into the depths of him and sank in. He wobbled there slightly when her words had ended, not wheelingly like a drunk, but as the breeze moves a dry stalk of barley. With one hand she brushed his bare arm, and what was left of his strength fell away, harvested, like an ear of corn to the touch of a slingblade.

He stammered something, forgiving them through and through. He was to blame, he swore it. He all but begged them not to worry themselves. He met Toron's eyes, but the man's mind seemed rootless. Of anything, he looked like someone overwhelmed by new tidings, who struggles to keep abreast of a smaller thing ere at hand. Toron asked his reckoning of the breakfasts he had bought, and the innkeep waved it away with his dishcloth. Toron was firm and bestood his pledge, becoming more and more uneasy. He fished out some of the lighter coins and offered what had to be ten times what the food was worth. Again the older man stickled, and again, until Toron dropped his own hand onto him, barreling his gaze into that fidgeting face, and making his will known as a foreman does with a dimwit.

The innkeep blinked his sad eyes and held the Harandrishman's stare for what became an unseemly stretch of time for two men who meant neither to kiss nor kill each other. He looked to Vail then back to Toron, who stepped fully between them. Again, something flashed across the man's windows, which was darker than before, but then he saw his daughters, all three of whom now were there, and a weight seemed to lift from his cares. He won himself back long enough to say he would put it in their ledger, then drifted back toward the kitchen on a cloud of befuddlement. The guests went back to their meals, only a few of them still muttering, and the daughters made a huddle over how silly their father was being.

Aldessa opened the ring of them and passed some of their twitter out to Vail. I think he likes you, she said. Sealith tisk-gasped, knuckling her sister's shoulder. Vail smiled blithely at the girls. Her eyes switched to Toron, and their gaze was like a nudge now, something he knew he'd feel even with his back to her. She had yet to quench their dree fully, however it worked. Cannily he met those eyes, grateful that everyone had mistaken the innkeep's thralldom for mere fluster. What Toron had seen, however, had not fooled him—what was no less than a reaping of manly strength. The swing of her scythe had gone for one neck only, and would not have touched anyone else. As though nosing his rebuke, Vail turned fully toward the Harandrishman, and he found himself staring into the embers of whatever it was that had melted the man. It was a weapon, of that there was no doubt—a ravishing onslaught of loveliness whose brunt was aglow as it cooled. Like a wind-quenched wick it faded, that which was not light, but rather a fairness to make lemmings of men. Her face, though still fetching, was only its shadow and tinder. Were she a woman of Mankind, he weened, she'd have arched an eyebrow. As it was, she deepened a dimple instead.

It was elfshine. His dream had not been wrong. This was a perilous creature that stood before him. The only frayn unanswered was whose side she was on.

Toron still had his wits about him, and he was willing to trust her for now. She might have unsheathed that weapon at any time ere this—to rob or to beguile them—but instead she had wielded it only to help, and to right a woe she herself had had a hand in. Besides this, he saw no worth to her in their serfdom. This was their world, but they were little less outsiders in Eksar than she was. They held no sway here, nor anywhere else, worth the steering of it.

That her glammer seemed wild was his foremost care. It was not harnessed, and it leapt without forewarning, to her or to others. He had felt it lap at him, as had the Chaldallions, as had the three men who had not kept their eyes off of her. Its bite, were it let slip, might rip a man's heart out.

He gathered up his breastplate, and sought the collar amongst its edges. He pulled it about his breast. "How would you feel," he asked her, slipping on his baldrics, and buckling them tight, "about donning wriels before we go?"

Her look, he swore, was playful. "Ree-ells?"

The Chaldallions, ready at the door, nodded their approval.

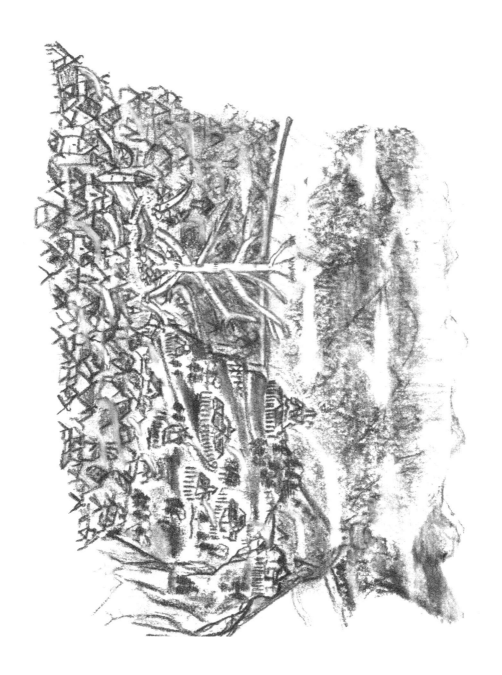

VIII
Equinox
The Day and the Knight

The onlookers sent up a hearty cheer as the play[1] drew to a close, and the players fell out of their roles to receive the acclaim with toothy grins. Their wain creaked and wobbled as they all came back to its stagedeck—the Norns, gods and guildsmen alike—and bowed all in a line. Some blossoms were thrown, and a few of the players lifted their children up with them, but in five heartbeats they were scurrying again, hastening to batten everything down and move on to the next Grenstead. The wain carrying the next guild's play came grumbling around the bend of the ringroad behind a team of black-antlered oxen, and soon the canvas weavers and awning makers were off as well, their own float chased southeast. The guildsmen clung to its edges onehanded and waving, like blithehearted vikings clambering up gunwales to board. With hands and words alike, they steered the crowd's eyes to a booth at the edge of the Grenstead, one half-hidden behind heaps of firewood, though it was clear from its brandmark and tall, hueful awning which one they meant. Waiting inside the little stall was another man, about his shoulders a telltale cloak, who in the time he had before the next play began, was egging the onlookers to come buy the guild's amazing new ware.

The thoftship watched the crowd split and split again, some of it drifting to the booth, some following the old wain, others thringing toward the new, some standing by to watch the next play, and still others going back to their business.

Justinian sniggered, looking toward the booth and shielding his eyes against the sunfall. "Funny how well those plays work."

Toron bent a grin. "You want one too now? So do I."

He chose not to tell the Chaldallions how foggy he had found the speech of the play. As southerners they had nimbler tongues than

[1] For the stageplay "The Gift of Canvasgard," see Appendix B.

his, and could handle the more Linguishlike Allmal with the same ease as they did the Knaksish. Toron had followed the drift of the play's tale, but much of its depth had been lost on him. Its quide was not Teakenmalish either, for though the Teakenmalers had a way of speaking that was at times too thick for Toron to see through, the words of the play were more elselandish than anything, and had likely been written for the ears of rich and well-taught chapmen, many of whom flew in from the seaboard burgs of the Sundarsund to winter in Eksar. Few of those traders bothered to peddle goods in Teakenmaley themselves—the deeply landlocked whorlberg lacked the mobs and wealth to make convoys worthwhile—but many bought things there to bring back west in the spring, making winter the sowing time for Eksarish wares. It was still too early in the year for the awningmakers' song to have found the right ears, or the right pockets, but as the guildplays happened only once again before spring, this was likely a harrow run to make smoother the pitch that would be coming in the months ahead.

Toron's eyes walked the wide clearing that was Eksar's westernmost Grenstead. Though not yet crowded, it was still early, and what with a holy day followed by a cheapday, a great crush was already in the making. The burgyard was a waymeet for three different thoroughfares, but that groggy lake of folks seemed unbothered by the wheeled and fourlegged things wading among them, and simply opened and closed again to let it all through. The knock-and-clatter of hooves was jarring, for though the floor of the Grenstead was a wheel-friendly patchwork of shaved bedrock, greenswards, and grouted slatestones, it rang out thunderously when beaten. At those times when many hoofs landed at once, the sound that leapt back from the inclosing faces of the cliffs was like the earth cracking open, and it became no wonder that luterwood, with its knack for dampening dins, was so soughtafter by the burgdwellers as lumber and hedges. Small stands of the gray-skinned softwoods could be found throughout Eksar, but outside the burgstead they only grew in one grove, at the very heart of Teakenmaley, within a sink of a valley Knaksmen called the Reamswell. It was a ghostly wold, and those who went in came out odd, but the timber was worth its weight in silver, and there was no lack of woodcutters willing to stake their health on it.

The Grenstead of the Gates where it was sold was nonetheless the lowliest of the burgyards, fronting as it did the western outskirts of the valley, where no lords lived, whence no rich wayfarers came and whither none went. It did hefty business, but it was workmanly trade. Most of the crops, the meat, the wood, the raw thrums from which cloth was woven: these and other goods were brought in and sold at the Gates, or right outside them if the wind was not too grim. There was another Grenstead with gates on the eastern side of Eksar, but it was called the Grenstead of the Swan, receiving as it did the Swansbawn, by whose highway came the choicest crides, trinkets and outland weaves. And so while the Swan made for the preened and winsome face of Eksar Arsask, the Gates at the rear were more needful for the burg's good health. To that end, there was some longstanding wit among laymen that a fetching face was no good without a working arse, and that the farmers were fainer to live behind the walls of a walled city than far out in front of them.

As it was, the Gates were a warehouse and a hive both in one. A little of its stock went to single buyers, but most of it went in bulk—thrown in great sacks and bundles off one wain and onto another, often that of a broker, who then sold to middlemen in other Grensteads, the whole it of it slowly shedding from one edge of Eksar to the others. It was all gruff reckoning and finger-dulled gold, that business, and only on the holiest of holy days did farmers and woodcutters and other outdwelling laymen suffer it to be decked out with burgish trimmings and silliness. Such a time was now, where the Grenstead was set about with bright scarves and flowers and singing, and other things better meant for those with more time.

Of the godtroths at play, Toron knew little. As with how men reckoned time, their ways shifted from Medth to Medth, and even steading to steading, and he had long ago given up trying to keep track. There was the Heronstroth, yes indeed, which was everywhere now, and likewise the Oztroth, which cleaved to an older, bloodier understanding of the world than was handy for most Knaksmen, but would never step aside. There were other troths as well, and steadfaster gods, some of whom seemed to mingle with the new—as did Sownatch-Lebley—and some who did not—as with Osyus the Orchardlord, whose old wooden ofgods stood at roadsides only between Kawsvad and the old border of Harandril. All had their worshippers, and all brought their own blessings, but working men bent their knees and backs for weightier things than prayers, and Toron had always given it to the salt of the earth to take holy things with a grain of it. The awnings sold on this cheapday had nothing to do with the hues still flying from yesterday's holy day, but together they gave cheer to the otherwise dour Gates—like the chuckle of an old sire who is piled upon by children too merry to be scolded.

Kurtisian took a loud breath, which seemed to brace him. "We ought to buy one," he said, nodding toward the awningmakers with mouth mockthoughtfully pursed. "Pick some colours, set up our own booth. *Heroes for hire.* I'm sure we'll find work. Upend a washtub in front . Make Vail dance on it."

Toron's laugh came out dryer than a griffon's lips. "We'll end up with a little too much work that way."

Vail eyed them over the crest of her wriels, which they had made from a wimple, scarf and cloakpin. It had taken a few goes to get it right, along with Sealith's small fingers, but it looked good enough, and, better yet, it did what they needed it to. Following her ears and fastened to the hair she'd bound in a horsetail, the garment covered her lower face and much of her neck. By chance it was near to the same dusky hue as her cloak, which they'd had to borrow from Aldessa as well. They hadn't wanted to take any more of the young woman's clothes, but they were in need, and she had pressed, saying she had no chores outside the inn today that her sisters might not do in her stead. Toron got the feeling she would lend Vail her teeth if the faywoman asked for them, but he thwore to the offer, wanting to leave without further ado. The garment lacked a hood, which the Eksarish goodfolk shunned as thievish, and which was bound to draw the very heedfulness it was meant to hinder. So it was that the garb did nothing to hide Vail's eyes, and even hawked them a little, laying them atop their wall of dark cloth to beam like two suns cresting a mountain together.

Her height was no help either, her head rising far enough past the shoulders of Toron and Kurtisian that there was no cluster the three men might shape that might hide her from all sides. Only Justinian made for such a screen, in whose shadow all of them might huddle when the suns were right. But he was only one hedge of their yard, and for his own looks drew as many stares as Vail might have. All in all, she seemed made to catch the eye, and it was not long before Toron disliked the fretting it did them, and how watching for oglers took his mind off the otherwise easeful and long-missed sights of the burg itself. At least she had doused her tung-switching magic after they had left the inn, and until they had got a better feeling of the burgwards' mindset towards Dreebreach. The law might have been tightened or loosened with the coming of the teerseekers, or it might lie as frayed as it was the last time they were here. He hated to have taken its help away from her—her only candle in this dark world—and without which she seemed hunted. Whatever the way, Kurtisian did not carry the *Carno* either, though that was not the same as leaving it behind.

Toron spoke to her, picking his words one by one. "Are you good?"

She blinked once and nodded slightly.

"Tired? Thirsty?"

Her eyebrows bent like bows, and she shot him a look. Toron hid his smile, glad to find her ear for the Allmal—her own, and not the dreeish swapman's—to be hearing things between the words. Sweetening his wit to bait her laughter would take more time, though, if indeed it was honey that lured her, and not salt. She was like no one he had ever sought to draw out, and might sooner answer to rowan, or rosemary, than to roses. He reminded himself of her winters, however many tens or hundreds she had behind her, knowing it a number with which her youthful looks broke every last bit of faith, at least as Man's shortlived eyes might see them. He recalled a snatch of scopship he'd seen etched on the wall of a kirk in northern Landon, and which he had never forgotten. It called laughter

> *the splash of us playing in mortality's tears,*
> *a cistern which deepens with wounds and with years*
> *overflowing, and flooding, and dragging us down*
> *till one day we enter to play and we drown.*

If that were so, what in the Wheres might an undying maid find funny? All told, he had not an inkling, and weened his wit might seem to her blunter than a child's, whose mind has yet to tell rote from meaning.

She looked away from him easily, her eyes skipping across the sharp peaks of the Whorlberg. Toron, on the other hand, looked down onto the sturdy roofs they ringed, heaving out a grateful sigh that he didn't have to worry about the coming weather for a while. Nestled between the bushy toes of mountains which themselves soared and dwarfed, Eksar Arsask was not a mighty steading, at least not in the way that Sundarwick and Thunors War and Bighthalf and

Bracshof were mighty steadings, with all their looming, leering stoneworks, their endless weaves of bridges, streets, and stairways, their towers straddling the few open places among them like trolls caught in midriot by the suns. On the whole, the halls and homes of Eksar were stavebuilt, and their roofs stayed within a stone's throw of the ground. Their doors were wide, and dazzlingly carved, and their gables were whimsical, with heads like the prows of longships. There was glass in most of the windows, which could not be said of many Knaksish burgsteads, but the buildings were not the lofty wonderworks of elsewhere—not leaping at the eye from afar but sitting quietly to be come upon, like sleepy stags wallowing in the mist.

The roads did not squeeze and skulk between the buildings, but had wide lolling berths, which along with the Grensteads showed the boon of a burg built nigh from scratch—one which had followed a layout, and had not grown through the slow upcleam[2] of a creeping sprawl. Furthermore, Eksar was a winged city, like Kraterpol nearest the Isentron, and others in the Medth that griffs and feathered horses called home. Flying steeds were everywhere, able to take their business upwards, dealing its crush across an endless choosing of upper routes, and to thin the wayflow on the ground so as to make walking and waingoing easy. So it was that the cleverest things about Eksar's layout might only be acknowledged from above— either from the saddle of an airborn griff or from the cliffsides overlooking—where the landings and rooftop courtyards of another half of the city opened their hands towards those not bound to land. That crafty upper shelf was mostly for the burgwards and wealthy folk, though Eksar had not the numbers nor the towers to make a whole world of its heights—not like Thunors War, whose lofty reaches split overlings from underlings, the one kind having wings to reach its airy islands, the other kept to the sunstarved depths of an aboveground netherworld. A man on foot did not have to be as wary of falling filth in Eksar as he had to be in Thunors War, but he was not wholly carefree of it. There was no shame in walking, but it was safer to fly. As a Landish saying had it, nothing shits on the eagle.

The thoftship had never beheld Eksar from the sky, nor any other burg, though they had all of them seen mightier steadings, and more wondrous. After Aftheksis, they were not easily overwhelmed. Only

---

[2] *(AB):* accretion; accumulation.

two buildings in Eksar showed true orthankship. One was the Burgreeve's seat, called Awklindhome, which they would see today. The other was the Medthkirk of the Heron, called the Sapling by its priests and many less flattering things by nonworshippers. Both buildings resembled great trees, but neither one could be glimpsed from the Grenstead of the Gates, whose sweep was in the lap of a great, richly housed hill called Shiremansairy, or simply the Airy. That rocky hump, all crags and grassy ledges, reared up out of the valley floor like the head of an earth-god rising, the falltime suns dealing and splitting its shadow across the breadth of the Grenstead. They flickered often, those suns, as things flew through their beams, and made the daylight seem a guttering candle. Few at their business in the burgyard seemed bothered by that winking, save those who were not wonted to it, who kept startling, and showing themselves foreigners.

Among those most skittish were the thoftship, who began to grow abashed of their flinching. Gorrh, at one time, leapt straight up, which, unlike the flickering sunlight, the burgdwellers were not so easeful about seeing. Folks fled from it a little, and four burgwards on griffback swooped down at the stir. Again Toron and the Chaldallions found themselves in a coop of spears, and hastily had to lay it out who they were. Kurtisian barely kept his mood, and Vail, at the thoftship's behest, shrank in behind them.

The burgwards asked nothing further once Toron had shown them the king's lathing. They did, however, send the teerseekers on their way toward Awklindhome, where they said a booth had been set up to log their names. There the Bookmen would also give them further tidings. The thoftship were also bid, though not in so many words, not to wander the city like any other boarder or wayfarer. Sellswords to the king—and *sellswords* was the word their headman spoke—were somewhere between guestworkers and interlopers in their eyes, and would not be suffered to misbehave. Toron had a hot answer ready for the ward, who left his griff too much rein, and let it lunge and snap, but the Harandrishman swallowed it. There was something like a grudge in the watchman's eyes, whose loathing Toron was not wonted to finding in Teakenmalers. It did not yet come to him, as it would in a few days, that the halfblown hatred of hired guards for teerseekers might have its seed in shame—that the armour bought for guards by toll-gathered gold should seem to them in needfullest times both shelter and burden, keeping its wearers from harm by keeping them from the worst of the fray, while selfmade men were free to fight for their own.

After the griffs had taken flight again, and came about and again to make sure the outsiders were on their way, the thoftship grudgingly bent their steps towards the southern inlet of Eksar's middlemost ringroad and began their long walk toward Awklindhome. There were three ringroads all told, one nested within the next, which looped about the whole burg like the ripples of a stone dropped in water. The ringroads did not touch every share of the burg evenly, for Eksar was not itself round, but shaped rather like a twoheaded axe. Its great wings swept out to the east and west from an inner belt, the better to slot it between the two scree-spills that slouched out towards each other from both sides of the valley. As it was, there were some nooks in the outermost boroughs of Eksar that might catch and bewilder a newcomer, but it was hard to get lost on a ringroad, which always ended right where it began. The burg had straight roads as well, which were as spokes to the ringroads' wheels. Best among them was the Boarsrun, which cut straight across the settling east to west, and halved every ringroad, or should have done were it not for Shiremansairy in its path. Had that haughty halfberg been flattened or lifted away, the thoftship might have taken the Run straight to Awklindhome, which stood within its own Grenstead at the very heart of Eksar. Instead, they had to go around, though the sunshine and crisp fall were not unwelcome things to linger in.

They went without speaking a word for a time, though each had his own wherefore to do so. For Toron, it was the twin whelm of thoughts and happenings that buried his tongue between them—as though the stout walls of Eksar themselves had given way, and the screes that pinched its shape thundered in upon him. Headiest among the crush were the simplest sights and sounds, which staggered his brain. The blue of the sky singed his mind. Every clop of a hoof was a pickaxe, its strike chipping at his soundness. Ravens squawked, cocks crowed from afar, and the carrier hawks made their dry screeches. Birdsong might have soothed him had there been any, but few songbirds came anywhere near Eksar, whose skies were thick were griffs and other feathered meat-eaters. Their only haven was the Medthkirk, whose belfries were a mighty aviary, about whose honeycomb of inlets feathered things made a shapeshifting cloud and a great white mess on its eaves.

The thrill of finding himself healed veered toward fright, and the worry that he'd been given not healing but an all-yielding newness that would wince and bleed with everything that touched it. As the flood of saraf crested, however, he found it difficult to bethink himself of anything dreary. He strove to walk off his cares, and to ready himself as they made their way to Awklindhome, the sight of whose orthankship he feared would leave his softskinned mind squalling. As it happened the touch of the breeze about his head was not so unsettling to his wits as the things flooding his eyes and ears, and he put the new strength of his mind into willing the wind a rinse, and carrying away the things that weakened him—even as a backyard blacksmith might do, who quenches a newbuilt ware in a running stream.

As for the Chaldallions, their silence was of a much more peaceful sort. Accustomed to cities, and those larger than Eksar, the brothers were much more at ease among buildings than Toron, reverting to odd habits and tastes which only the mightiest and most open northern burgs might indulge. Food and fun were half of it—after months on the road of simple meals and card games, they now refused to tolerate either. The rest of it was mood. Like housecats met outdoors, the two seemed aloof on cobbled streets, back-shelving everything and everyone they already knew to make space on the table for the fresh and unbeforeseen. Toron had marked the shift in them often enough that he knew it for wariness as much as for sightseeing and gameseeking. He had asked the brothers about it once, when their minds were at ease and they were most likely to give a full answer.

To be *urbsavvy*[3], as Justinian had called the mood, was to know that the city was a world built by men, where their values, though invisible, had greater might and sway than the seasons and storms in the world built by gods. Things happened in cities that had happened nowhere else, and people lived there who had the mastery of it all. There were wonders and pleasures, of course, some honed to sharpness unbeforeknown to the rustic and smalltownsman whose own tastes were dulled by pursuit of need. But there were dangers as well. The worst a brigand might do in the woods was to lie in wait among trees or to build a trap out of things gathered from the land

---

[3] *(AC)*: citysmart, streetwise. A Knaksish calque, heard in the coastal shires of the Sundarsund, is *burgwise*.

and sharpened. But in the city, every mind could be sharpened, and every encounter become a pitfall. Every population was a potential army, whose hearts became less knowable the further one drifted from one's own country. Just as woodland creatures, however swift, are crushed upon the highways trying to cross the paths of things beyond their ken, so too were simple men shattered by the city's unforeshadowed machines, unable to shape themselves to its grind. Laws and customs; faiths and taboos; the games of statecraft whose rules no one taught; all might serve to entangle a careless man, and find him jailed or worse, where a careful man might simply have avoided this district, or that gesture, or that language, or in some cases the city altogether.

Toron had found the speech slightly goading, and more than a little overwrought. He wondered at the sorts of burgs the Chaldallions had in mind, since no city they'd seen in Knaks had been so baneful by a third. He himself was a roving elselander, and more travelled than most of his countrymen, but he was not a wanderer among lands, and had never left Rámish shores—not even for Tymnig, Bayerd, or the Kúloys, which were the only Medths he had yet to see. What peopled pits of snakes one might find in the colonial south he did not know, but he felt he knew enough of burgs not be foolish in any, which was near enough to being urbsavvy for his understanding. Perhaps the whole likening was little more than a clever flipside of that storytelling citydwellers owned, which was to haunt every forest and countryside with horrors for the thrill, forgetting that city streets at night were much quieter than woods, and misdeeds less likely among woodsmen. Had Justinian's aim been to unsettle him, it had missed Toron's heart. Though he did not trust the cities, he did yearn for them, and Eksar, he'd decided since returning, he loved. Its hurry was mellow, and did not cloy his relish for it.

The ayflood of the Gungnissa could be heard even through the busiest bustle, its waters gurgling through the stonewalled trench man had troughed it in. The river came into the valley far to the east, whence it stepped down from the highbergs, from the great tarn of Whitchwelkinsmere, as a staircase of waterfalls. From there it switched and scrithed from one side of the valley to the other, making islets in its middle and hollowing out ledges on its sides, galloping through Eksar from northeast to southwest and plunging into caves no man had fully sounded. Said to have been gouged out

by Woden's spear as he wrestled overhead with the thurse-hags of
the Wild Hunt, its groove was much deeper than its width, and had
been easier for settlers to span than to ford. Bridges of rock and
timber made high humps across it, over whose railings oldtimers
fished all year, smoking the deep-bowled pipes known elsewhere in
Arsask as Gungbowls. It was for the goldlax and rainbow shoat that
they baited their hooks, but there was sturgeon in the water too.
Some were old enough to have their own names, gliding in and out
of minning into the depths of the river and its caves, and becoming
ghosts among the deepest roots of the Timebriar.

The ayflood slowed enough in places for swimming and sculling,
and there were docks here and there by which men shipped goods.
Its windling path had also shed a handful of lakelets over the
hundelds, whose banks men strengthened with pilings. Those pools
froze hard in the winter, and men set out onto them then, boring
holes through which to fish. Other than that, only the oddest of folks
set foot in the Gungnissa east of Eksar, whose mistiest arms had
caught more fishermen than fed them. The hauntingness of
Teakenmaley was not ghastly—not like a drowned wreck or a
graveyard—but its loneliness ached, and whomever it took to its
breast it kept him there a long, long time. A missing soul might wash
up or wander out of the mists again many tenyears later, sometimes
having aged, sometimes not. For that, the heartache of mourning was
lighter in Teakenmaley, its weight aflutter with the mothwings of a
weird, mad hope that the lost might one day be found again. It was to
this hope, or this hedge against hopelessness, that some said Eksar
owed its name, but others gainsaid that, swearing that the walls of
Eksar were full proof against the kidnapping nettles of the
Timebriar, and that the burg was a haven, beyond which only fools
and scops might dwell.

However proof they were, it was inside and in sight of those
evermanned walls that the thoftship kept their way, walking the rim
of the slowly bowing street, well beyond the dash of wheels and
hooves. Only three furlongs or so did the ringroad warp to the
southeast before it came upon the Gungnissa, its nighness shown by
a wide break in the buildings and the mist rising softly in the gap.
The houses edging the ringroad were wealthy ones—the shops of
thriving craftsmen, and guildhalls, with open doors and hueful
signboards, with hitching posts and wide, upheld eaves. All gave
wide way to the path of the river, whose shorelines were ribbons cut

from a village green, with trees and shapely flowerbeds, and lawns where folks might gather. In summer and spring these belts thringed with outdoorsmen, but the riverwind was sharp today, honing the fall crispness sharp. Only a handful of women and children loitered beneath the yellowing boughs. Shining through the breaks among the trees was the white-brick mill on the east bank, its wet black waterwheel chewing into the flow, the groan of its timbers a murmur amidst the threshing of the river's neck. The bridge itself came into sight, its gate a bower of maples, their long-fingered branches reaching high over the road like the arms of a toll-gatherer. Oakwerns leapt feverishly among them, their fun loosening leaves which featherfell onto the cobblestones and traced the bridge's threshold in drifts of deepred and gold.

Toron spoke over his shoulder to Vail, whom for her hush and ghostly way of walking kept startling him by still being there. "You can cross running water, yes?"

She nodded, blinking once. If she got it or if she smiled he didn't see either.

"How about you, Kurtis? Showing any weaknesses to weird things yet? Silver? Garlic?"

The southerner flexed his hand. "You think if I were a vampire that I'd have been able to drink that runk this morning? Blood couldn't be much harder to swallow than drow urine."

"So you're not feeling like a howlish man yet."[4]

Kurtisian looked mockwearily towards him, who it was plain had been holding onto that one for a while.

Justinian nodded toward the bridge. "There's some kind of roadcheck going on up there. The wagons are backed up on the other side."

Through the trees, at the very peak of the bridge, a knot of burgwards came into view. They seemed to be halting everyone, wains and those on foot alike, and taking their time going through their belongings. Toron sighed and looked overhead, and though the burgwards on griffback who had badgered them only a short time earlier were no longer making loops a hundred feet above, he could tell their flock by the shape they flew in, and saw them dipping and wheeling not much further away.

---

[4] Toron is punning on *Hálishman*, which is pronounced almost the same way.

"It wasn't like this the last time we were here," he muttered. "I reckon a lot of folks in Knaks don't feel the same about teerseekers as the King does."

Kurtisian adjusted *Marat*'s shoulderbelt. "You make it sound like the King needs to like us in order to want our help. The way I read that post, he's in a corner, and it can't be easy for an atheling to cry damsel."

Toron sighed even deeper. Among the southerner's many maddening habits was to utter something wayward and unaforesaid as though he had felt it all along, and kept to it himself until it was most unhelpful. As such, his lurking wit did not waylay Toron, but the thought that the King might feel the same about teerseekers as the Boarsmen he headed did not sit well with him, and he wondered why it was that he had always reckoned the Rings to be tenderhearted towards freeswords such as himself.

If there was anything to blame, he deemed it was tales. The Kings of Knaks were kin to the Ozmen, or so most Knaksmen believed, and the Ozmen were kingless loners who struck out into unknown lands, and at untried foes, with no more than one or two thoftmen at their sides. They pitched no banners, and they founded no burgships. They were seekers, and sounders, with hands stained by the blood of fiends not by the ink of laws drafted to herd and fleece lesser men. Though the Æsir-gods of the far north were not outwardly the same as the Ozmen, their marrow was one, and there was as little seemliness in an Ozmannish royalty as there was in a brick-and-mortar church of the Heron, whose breath was in all living things. The upsidedownness and bad faith of Man's world was not something Toron felt would ever catch him so unawares as to throw him, but he was shaken by this thought that his King might be so proud as to begrudge the help of men he had asked for.

As it happened, the check on the bridge was not so ill-mannered as the run-in at the Gates, nor did the burgwards seem very mindful of them. Their true prey, the thoftship was told, were unlawful things hidden in the stagewains of the guildplayers, as well as bands of smugglers who sought to pass themselves off as guildplayers themselves, and whose wains were hollow shams. The wards' headman seemed bored to death by the whole thing and stood off to one side, barking at his underlings from time to time and picking loose mortar from the bridgerail's capstones to drop into the river-fork below. While the thoftship waited to be let through the anvil-jawed man took enough of a shine to them to explain that smuggling in Eksar was most often done by road, not only because wains hid and carried things better than flying steeds, but also because the griffs of the watchmen had an uncanny knack for smell.

That led Kurtisian to ask what kinds of things were being smuggled in, which the headman did not like. He nonetheless hinted at a haggard struggle between athelings, wizards, and priests at the lawhouses over which of Teakenmaley's many mindfloating worts and dreeish bloomlife ought to be banned, which steered through tolls, and which freely peddled. Saraf, when asked, he called a *neithertwain*, which he said was a lawly word for something that fell between the rules. Though by the word and soul of the law it was likely a drink that ought to be forbidden, too many folks loved it—lordlings and burgwards among them—and the Wardhelm of Eksar was not a man to mistake all lawbreak for wrongdoing. You have the look of the drink, the headman added, his stare like a striking snake. And seemingly pleased thus to rattle them, he told his underlings to let them through, and they made their way past the row of wains to land on the Gungnissa's eastern shore.

From the peak of the bridge they had glimpsed a limb of Awklindhome as it reached out from behind the great crag of the Airy. The gnarled shakes on its walls had caught the sunlight as a beaconlike flare, but for a short time the building went unseen again. As the ringroad southered it grew slowly back into sight, its long, boughlike wings seeming to shoot up and wave like the weird Teakenmalish tree its craftsmanship had meant to reproduce. The *awklind* was a wetland hardwood, akin to the willow rather than the linden. Its trunks forked like the necks of a hydra, some of which bowed and dove back into the earth, reemerging at odd angles with leaves of a darker hue than those of the central trunk. As such, the tree had the look of the eight-armed devilfish that lived only in the faraway seas, but most Teakenmalers had never laid eyes on such a nicker[5]. They had named the tree after the awklinnorm—a seldseen lakesnake, many humped, that once swam the Whorlberg's tarns.

As a likeness of that amazing tree, Awklindhome was not flawless. It lacked the telltale leaves and tendrils, and its rind, though wrinkled right, was white instead of gray. By the reckoning of many, the building looked more like a sunbleached antler half-buried, and

---

[5] *(AB)*: water monster.

because it rose within the lee of Shiremansairy it was easy to see the nearby knoll as a gravemound, and to call Awklindhome the horn of some thursish elk barrowed beneath Eksar. Some said Woden had brought it down from the Wild Hunt with the same blow he had gouged out the Gungnissa. Most folks called this silly, but there was no gainsaying the dreeishness of the building with its many outleaning steeples, none of which needed cantilevers to uphold them.

No layman or dreeless workfroding might have drafted or overseen the raising of such a wonderwork, but there was no wonder about how Awklindhome came to be. Eksar Arsask had a school of magic, though only its students knew where it was. The Burgreeve's lineage had long been entwined with the wizards who ran it, so much so that all of his kinsfolk were said to have a touch of the craft. Such a thing was queer among Knaksish athelings, who were Oztrothers in both faith and blood, and wont to see magic as witchcraft and sidden, however handy they were at times. That the Burgreeve's kin were also the grimmest backers of Dreebreach did little in Eksar to soothe any household misgivings about the fickle fairness of lawmakers, but those with any insight saw the strain beneath that double standard, and praised the Burgreeve for standing up to the dreemen so openly, who might otherwise have made Eksar a romping ground for their eldritch learning.

Awklindyarth in which Awklindhome stood was less a Grenstead than a garden, with many bowers and nosegladdening bloombeds, and carvings of elders atop wet banks of springstones. The thoftship had wandered through its nooks and bowers a handful of times when last they were in Eksar, but they had not been back since. Like Awklindhome itself the Grenstead seemed more for show than for business. Its many sights made for slowgoing, even without booths and peddlers. The Gungnissa cut across the burgyard slantwise, whose path Awklindhome straddled with two footings. There was a wharf beneath its archway, though none had ever seen the Burgreeve come in by the ground floor. Like all the wealthiest burgfolk, he went by wing, and Awklindhome lent its boughs to a steady coming and going of griffs and carrier hawks. The tips of its many limbs widened and hollowed into spoon-shaped landing decks, its uttermost heights weaving together into a windle of a courtyard that lay flat and open like a tableland. The whole of it stood a little higher than Shiremansairy and swayed slightly in strong wind.

Those in the burgship who could not already see Awklindhome from their doorsteps had only to walk a short way to find it. As the saying went, every street was awkly in Eksar, which was to say that Awklindhome, as the hub of its spoke-and-wheel roadnet, might readily be reached from anywhere in the burgstead. The Burgreeve himself was no more at hand than any other steward or atheling, and met with no one unbidden, but all were welcome to Awklindyarth, so long as they did not dawdle overlong, or hawk goods. The Burgreeve's housewered was a baldrish lot, and said to be much more blithehearted than the rest of Eksar's burgwards. Their smiles showed no fewer teeth than other watchmen, however, and no one mistook their friendliness for lack of might.

After the bridge, the road wound only a little further east before a great choking crush of oncomers began to build. The din of it muttered and shuffled, and though its gathering spread the full breadth of the ringroad, it did not seem to be getting anywhere. When the thoftship made the bend they saw that the throng was indeed moving, but very slowly, and was pressing itself down a much narrower spokeroad that led north off the ringroad's inner rim. Straight as an arrow shot the street toward Awklindyarth, and at its end an unbroken glimpse of Awklindhome's full awe and orthank— as though the radiance of its craftsmanship had burned a path straight through the lesser buildings around it, and that path troughed its wonder right into them. The spokeroad seemed an alleyway next to the wide sweep of the ringroad, and hemmed in by sheer walls. Despite this lessening, its wayfarers were no fewer, and the thoftship had to time it right to cross the oncoming stream and to slot themselves into the crush creeping toward the Grenstead.

It was late enough in the morning that the falltime suns had lined up above the road and like ruthless hunter-gods loosed their lightning upon those corralled within. The sunshine drenched the manmade gully, its beams bursting open against the whitewashed eaves and the steel fittings of the unlighted lamps. Everyone shrank into squinting as they inched forward, and the great bright tree at the end of their tunnel was a hereafterlike sight, the flying things about its boughs like the errandghosts who fulfill gods' ministrations. But like all things heavenly, that loveliness was brittle, and fled at the first touch of an unclean thing. There were rough men among the wayfarers, and ill-mannered beasts, the likes of which had had no forerunners on the ringroad and at the Gates.

Justinian snarled as a man in black mail led his horse straight up through them, and the thoftship had to split in two to keep from being trampled.

"Hoy there, son," barked the Sumo. "Keep that thing's hooves off of mine."

Gorrh gathered down, as a geyser before it blows, and Toron knotted his fingers into the tuskcat's withers. To be bumped aside by a slab of meatlife, indeed one that showed no fear of him, was about the worse scorn the great hunter could be shown. The horse must have been spellbound, Toron told him through the Rine, or wearing some dreeish tack, to have been led past a flesheater without a care in the world.

"Why the hells is it so crowded here?" Kurtisian bellyached above the din. "Aren't there around ten other streets that lead to the same place?"

Someone answered from nearby. "They're all clogged up too, my friend. We headed round this far to find another way in. This one's moving quite well, all told."

They looked around, and a red-bearded awnsman smiled alongside them. His words had a throaty Braccish trill, and he wore the sark of some burgward wered from outside Eksar. It was dark brown, and had an olden hint about it. Then he was gone, folded into the depths of the evertwisting rope of folks, steeds, and farecrafts[6] which wove slowly but tightly northwards. The thoftship pressed back into their own knot, but keeping it tied was not easy. There were wains among the traffic, of whose wheels and hooves they had to be wary, but the greater bother came from others on foot—men in ones and two and gangs near to ten, most of them cloaked and hooded like thieves, and elselanders clearly, who like the horseman earlier seemed utterly fearless of the toes they might be stepping on.

The presence of Justinian seemed no deterrent, not simply because his mass was less impressive among horses and wains but also because there were men who saw him and did not care. At first Toron was simply rankled by their manners, even a little scoffblithe, but when he was pushed aside from behind like a hedgeshrub, and a thurse of a man went past him without so much as a wink at Justinian whom he outsized, Toron smelled the unwashed death in the stranger's wake and began to see the throng for what it was. He

---

[6] *(AK):* vehicles, including chariots, wains, and coaches.

was shoved aside again, and again, as the thugthane's companions
followed their leader. There were siggertokens on all their mail—the
teeth and claws and manes of slain nightmares—and across their
backs was some godforsaken thwarsebreed of sword and axe, with
blades like the cleavers of butchers, and over a foot wide. These men
were not of Mankind, at least not fully. Other blood was in them, and
had watered the uncanny growth of their bones and thews. Few
doorframes in Eksar might have taken their shoulders, and though
their legs were short, their arms were overlong, and their fingers
nearly dragged as they walked. The reach and strength of their
swing, Toron weened, and with those weapons, would be fell indeed.
Not even the Allmetal, he believed, would be enough to turn them
aside.

The last of the devils looked back as though smelling his
thoughts, and Toron felt the swipe of its cold eyes. Little else could
he see through the gaps in its headgear but the press and crowd of
bony outgrowths within, like a barrel of crabs with one stave
missing, whose insides scrape and reach for release. Toron's blood
ran to ice, his heart lurching with the clog, break, and rush of it.
These men were so near to fiends he knew not how they had found
leave to walk the streets of Eksar freely. He looked up, eyes straining
into the gleam, and saw the tens of griffmen overhead, some in
flight, others perched upon the wide, wallless walks that made a
maze across the roofs of the burg.

For the first time in a while, Vail spoke. "You're not at all alone
I see."

It all became clear to him then—the bitter greetings of the
burgwards; the wariness of the innguests towards his thoftship; their
being shooed toward the eastern half of Eksar. This was the swarm
of teerseekers the king's beacon had brought in, and whether full of
smiles or cloven-hoofed, all comers had been let in to answer it.
Toron peered, and strained, and saw that fewer than half the hooded
heads belonged to Mankind. They were most of them men, but many
of their kinds he had no names for. He marked breeds of fayfolk, and
mannishkin both great and small—dwerrows and risslings, halflings
and halfthurses, and beings that nearly passed for Men, but whose
looks were off by a little—some with horn-nubs like fawns, others
with noses too broad or too thin, some with brows too flat, others
with hair too bright—and he wondered at the bodies hidden beneath

their cloaks, which might have wings, and which might have four arms, or tails.

Then there were those who looked Mannish, but who clearly had been brought up in other folklands, and who showed the quirks and trappings of their adopted herds. Such fosterlings stood out more for seeking to hide their differences less, maybe believing their blood a password that would see them embraced by any Men who shared it. Were that the hope, it misreckoned with Knaksish kindness, which grudged not the outlanders for themselves, but rather those who brandished their outlandishness like an open banner. Cloaks covered all, which was why there were so many, and why outlanders who did not wear them got the worst of it.

Not far from Toron was a young woman whose bone-ashen hair told her out from the hoods like a torch. Her longsword and armour were odd, and her swagger it seemed was unwelcome. When she turned, she showed great green eyes.

"*Patrz, gdzie idzieszl!*" she snarled at the crush.

Her tung—Tarmaterizish? Toron did not know it. He marked others who stood out less than she, but whose whiff of offwhereness was even greater—a roundheaded lad, hair limed starfishlike, carrying a blade that looked like a great, black key; a tall, dour man in a wide-brimmed hat and a cloak-like leather coat, the sandalwood handles of his weapons peaking out from stubby sheaths at his belt; a man whose hacksword had a grip like a handcrossbow, trigger and all, which he held over his shoulder like a fishing pole—*Taikutsu-sugiru* he sang, over and again, till someone told him in the Allmal to shut it; a sturdy redyellow-haired man with bare feet and shirt open, a cloth-wrapped bundle hanging from the end of a stick he carried; a green-skinned youth with blue-black hair, his body draped in a hide the hue of raspberries. The small, spotted horse he led was the only wonely thing about him.

Who these folks were, what struggles and godtroths had shaped them, what networks of itness their brushing of shoulders here bespoke—Toron recalled that the Braccish had a word for the kinds of riddles, soul-dizzying, that stirred heaven and meanings. *Ghost-rounish*. It had been a bodiless word when first he had heard it. Not at all had he understood, nor weened, what it touched on. Now, and since Aftheksis, he knew all too well, and it sickened him that such a swime as this had been so aforefelt by other men as to have earned a name he was learning only now.

He knew that many thedes other than Men had homelands among the Medths of Knaks, as well as in Tarmateriza to the northeast and the forlornlands south of Trebell. None had their own kingdoms, at least none that the kingdoms of Men acknowledged, but some had a share of self-wield, which is to say that they were left alone. Among these were the soarcats of Tymnig, the hulsetrolls among the foothills of the Wottrámish Alps, and the goblin kingdoms with which they skirmished[7], but all their lands were hinterlands, and far beyond Man's craving and easy reach. As for the other thedes, many had been chased into the shadows with the coming of the Nethrishmen, or had been dwindling since long before. Many were seen as holdovers from earlier Ages, to be thrust aside by Man's needs and creeds. Not even the Heron was said to have much love for them, many of whom had dreeish blood, and a foot in other Wheres than this one.

Toron felt nonetheless more bewildered in their midst than threatened, having met enough unMannish outlanders to know that the world was far wider than the landcharts, even by the reckoning of this single Where. Somewhere on this Smað, likely not far from Ráma's own shores, there were lands where Men were as seldseen as Elves, or wholly unknown, while among the yondermost stars were steadings utterly beyond Man's fathoming, where firehuddlers and ironbeaters such as Knaksmen might crumple slackjawed before the shining cities of the deathless. What addled Toron was not so much their being here, these farkind folk and outsiders, but rather that so many of them should know or care enough of Man's world to come to the help of a king of Men. Were they all simply wanderers by choice, as Shard and Níscel had been, or something more akin to castaways, as Vail was? Either way, their grounds for seeking thanks were not the same as those of Men, much less Knaksmen such as himself. They were more likely tangled with bitter roots, and hid other crooked things, which with the first watering of grateful tears would creep forth, like worms and toadstools after a stiff rain.

Not for the first time, he wished Shard were here. Toron's will was bullheaded, full of snort from the gates, and yet it was slowed by the cling of whatever bracken it had gathered strength to storm through. The Highbred had always known what best to believe to

---

[7] Among the goblin kings of the north are Yukki-tuk, Hyba-jobo, Doobla-badda, Baga-wo-wo, and Baga-voo-doo, whose antics have been immortalized in songs for Knaksish children.

keep going, and how to knead the will to a suppleness neither too hard nor too tender. That one's thinking might so readily reshape truth was an uncanny wonder to the Harandrishman, and he begrudged men the gift of it, to swap the way of things for the way one looks at things, to let out truth like a mooring line, and not be dragged down by its anchor. What unyielding truths Shard had ever held to, these were lost with the man. It seemed that his outlook was as limber as his body, leaving Toron, who prided himself on keep his back to the bedrock, with cold pride indeed.

The thoftship inched in, and the sunwashed shimmer showed the full reach of the gathering. Its creep enclosed the foundations of Awklindhome, and squirmed about the trees of its garden like a frogspawn-choked tide. There were thousands, with hundreds on this spokeroad alone—thousands of lordless selfseekers, unknown and unhovely, with dreeish crafts, gear and weaponry, all jostling and overpiling one another like so many piglets fighting for a single teat. Were they to brawl, or even a third of them to uncloak as invaders, the burgwards would soon be overwhelmed, and though Toron believed the weaponhoards of Eksar held deadlier things than spears, he did not ween those things could be wielded without wide-wasting loss. The King had called for this gathering, but no need seemed great enough to warrant such recklessness. So stricken with worry was Toron for the burgship he loved that he forgot that he was here on the same grounds as the rest of them.

The Chaldallions showed qualms as well, their tsking and cursing rising slowly above their breaths. So affected was Kurtisian that he consulted Toron's leadership.

"What do we do, Thorn?"

Toron looked back the way they had come, but even as he did so, he had to keep moving forward. "Well, we can't swing around again."

"Why should we want to?" Justinian asked. "We have to sign up somewhere in there, yeah?"

Jostled from behind yet again, Toron made a fist in Gorrh's fur. "Yes, but why are there so many here? We couldn't have all chosen to come on only this day. The king's lathing was out for how long before we saw it? Did we all happen to reach Eksar at the same time?"

Kurtisian shrugged, now feigning the nonchalance to foil him. "Bulletin shouldn't have been up for that long before we found it. And it's likely that whoever saw it made a beeline straight for the city. And the way we came in? With the time we took to recover? I wager we're all here within a few days of each other."

They got their answer when at last their share of the flow crept out from between the buildings of the spokeroad and onto the Grenstead. There they bobbed and jostled like so much shipwrecked flotsam, staring out across a sea of heads and spears and the hilts of swords sheathed on backs—a sea broken only by the misting gap of the Gungnissa running through Awklindyarth, and the trees and hillocks and buildings rooted to its grounds. The Grenstead was fed from eight sides by spokeroads, and nearly every one of them poured people. The odd one out was the lane to Shiremansairy on the westernmost flank, which was gated, and guarded, and led nowhere through. Its reaches could be seen against the side of hill itself, far above the lowland rooftops whose midst the rock thrust from, switching back and forth upon ledges delved out and built up, over cleft-spanning bridge, and linking the many homes whose owners likely had little want of it. Housewards watched the mighty flood from the walls of every one of those buildings, as did the burgwards at the gatehouse below, whose body had been strengthened this day, unless twenty of them was the wonely number. It didn't seem to have made them any healthier. The burgwards of the Airy looked sick to be standing there, they whose daily task had ever been to mind a single door. Lapping at their threshold was a tide of hungry killers, and wading through that surf were giants whom all of them together might not bring down or even wound—great devils of mail and brawn, sunk to the waists and chests amidst their lessers, upon whose boil riders looked less horsed than beached, clinging to odd-shaped rocks just above the toss of other men.

"Fergh and Hern," Toron blasted. "And this is only one burg." He recalled the king's lathing, and the wide gap between the blocks of writing where the name of Eksar Arsask had been written in another hand. It was not hard to see that the same leaflet had been made out maybe hundreds of times, and dealt out from one side of the kingdom to the other, nailed up on walls between Tymnig and Shebril with the name of the nearest elderburg scratched in at the last. They had understood this from the beginning, but they had not reckoned on the scores it should mean. Never before might they have foreseen that the well-swept wilds of Knaks should hide much less feed so many scavengers. The call, it seemed, had been more of whistle than a voice, the kind only one creature hears. It had brought forth from the shadows a slavering pack of them, like a dinner bell beaten above the heads of the starving.

Sundrily they might have struck awe, these petitioners, but any legends they carried were hidden beneath the shuffling beggary of their crowd. Whatever tales and talents and heirlooms they bore seemed as things clutched to their breasts in flight, from wildfire or war, now fingered numbly in this soup line, to be put up for pawn at the chance of room and board. That they should behave themselves so well in this herd bespoke not courtesy but brokenness. They were unplighted thanes after all, and rightfully unhinged by that independence. No path was too lonely for such onely men, whose whats were so bent as to whip them away from the flock, the faster to put their backs to it, and to shun any brand for the burn it was, the better to find the monsters that sent herdminded folks huddling. To see solitaires clustered wrought a weird kind of shame—to find their uniqueness dispelled by the common need that had brought them together. It was not lost on Toron that he was one of them, nor that among the goldilocked outlanders and black-mailed wyelords there should be men like himself—Knaksmen whose lust for teer he felt was more trustworthy, and unentangled with hidden troths. But rather than rightful, he felt belittled. Instead of pride, he felt the boiling mad mingle of this cauldron thinning his own worth, as though beneath the surface and silence of its brew every morsel bled to flavour it, and he had not the gist to withstand it. Howsoever unheralded, there were great heleths here, some of them with many times his own years, and as many more wins under their belts.

He was a dreamer, but not by day; he held no misbeliefs about his standing. No one in his thoftship was green, but nor were any of them fully out of their buds. His swords were dreeish, a little, and he knew how to wield them, in a way. Kurtisian and Justinian were better off than he, but the great powers they'd found roadside would never gallop without the right carrots. For the first time in months Toron was thankful for his scar, and for the rugged right it gave his look. From his earliest days, he had spurned tales of unscathed heroes for the yarns of softhanded scops and coalbiters, knowing that a man who steps from the swordstorms ever handsome was as likely as a man who comes off the fields with fingernails ever clean. The more he browsed the faces about him, the truer he knew that insight to have been, glimpsing cloven lips and shredded cheeks, crooked noses, and more than a few missing eyes. He saw scars so plentiful, they seemed less carved than woven, the grisly warps and wefts of nornish websters, whose looms were the skulls beneath. What flailing nails that flesh had withstood—what nightmarish sights those eyes had seen—Toron could only shudder to fathom. And whether it was mana or the soulshine of their teer, the betterhood of these slayers blazed over him, and burned off his own worth like a shallow lake beneath the heat of every sun.

He rued their coming here, their step into this stir. From the day he'd learned to walk, he had been taught that only dead fish follow the flow, but by the reckoning of that saying the stream only went two ways. Never before had he seen it, even after a childhood spent up to his knees in creeks and spawning pools, that those who swim upstream must in the end find themselves in schools of the strongest, and fight harder fights than any before. There was no way out of it. The stream foredoomed one's choices. Its banks could not be leapt.

He would have to find carefuller words to live by.

The thoftship kept heading forward and was thankful to find that the crowd was not so thick as to stay them. There were small windows in its shoals, and many of the folks within its flow seemed wayward, not knowing whither to go or whether to go there, milling about with its swash from one side of the burgyard to the other.

There were some wains as well, slowly drifting through, though word seemed to have gotten out that those on wheels should keep clear of Awklindyarth, and there were not many. The drowsy draftneats yoked to them were not wonted to the smells of bloodthirsty men, nor of their steeds, some of which had never suckled milk, and rather were scaly like snakes, or feathered, or dreeish thwarsebreeds like griffons. Every now and then, a carthorse or an ox would spook, and a throb touched the dark crowd. At these times, griffmen would hook out across the spate from their perches at its edge, their shadows shooting across its shoals like the dart of fastswimming things. For the most part though, those burgwards stuck to the sides, as though watching a run of molten fire whose fumes should be shunned as much as its touch.

The path of the Gungnissa which split the Grenstead split the crowd as well, but there was no higher ground from which to overlook it all. Not even the bridges made for a perch, which were flat in Awklindyarth, not humped as they were on the ringroads. Save for the spray of the river, it was hard even to see where those crossings lay. Though men thronged their timbers as they did every other stretch of ground in the Grenstead, only the tighter shamble of their swarm, and the closer pack of their heads, showed the wedging on both banks. The murmur of their speech was steady but undinsome—the cool thildy hum of business, with little feeling or small talk yielded.

Kurtisian looked to his brother. "Do you see the booth the guards were talking about anywhere? Over by the doors of the treehouse, maybe?"

Diminished by Awklindhome and up to his shoulders in armoured men, Justinian did not seem a great deal bigger than the one who consulted his height. "There are some banners through the trees over there." He pointed. "The ones with the red leaves, around what I think is the main entrance, but I can't tell from here if they're decorations from yesterday or if they're meant to show us where to go. We'll have to cross the river to get a better look. Thorn?"

Toron shook his head. Gorrh was too low in the crowd for the Rine to be any help. As of yet, the two knew only how to use it to see through each others' eyes, not to swap eyesight. Had they the knack of that, Toron might have climbed onto the cat's back and peered far enough ahead to see where they needed to go.

"It seems to be where the crowd is drifting," he said hopefully, though he found trying to find the right lines to slip themselves into was like trying to boat swift water at night.

After a while they neared one of the bridges. Its railings were low, its timbers groaning beneath the feet of a hundred men. The waters of the Gungnissa narrowed far below, choking on a handful of sharp, stony eyots. There it became less a river than a frothing rent in the Grenstead's flagstones whose mouth would chew up and swallow anyone who fell into it. The spray was enough to dampen those who passed over it, and the bridge was forever wet, though its wood must have been swapped out often, for it showed no rot. Upstream it was calm as it flowed out from beneath the splayed feet of Awklindhome, and widened into something of a lakelet. This was also an outlet for the locks—seldom manned or hired—by which barges and skiffs made their way down around the white water.

By the time the thoftship had crossed the one bridge, and landed on the sword-shaped islet between the river and the locks, the suns were nearly one overhead, and forbearance was thinning. They said next to nothing to each other, behaving as though they were among betrayers who would wield against them any word or gesture. Awklindhome became athlier as they neared it, its wonders clenching as it reared, showing off its countless lookouts and tinted windows, which from afar had seemed as knags and eyes upon its bark. They stepped beneath the shadow of its longest bough, which indeed was wagging slightly in the winds above the rooftops, but the unsettling wonder of that sight seemed the only thing their time yielded as the end of the row they followed stayed hidden behind its many, many coils. The hueful trees of Awklindyarth, thickest about the manor's gates, hid some kind of inner business, but the crowd seemed to eddy about the Grenstead rather than shoot towards its heart. Its swirl was too tight, and indeed too threatening in spots, to be cut straight through. The likelihood of being stuck in its whirlpool all day was clear to everyone, whose sighing and murmuring became an unbroken hum, spiked at whiles by coughing and the outcries of beasts. The racket of hammers drifted down from the docks upstream. Mad laughter leapt from a window. The Burgward's griffs, perched or wheeling high above, seemed like buzzards waiting for them all to drop, their feathers ruffling coldly, their tails switching, their weird shapes black against the daylight.

Kurtisian leaned past Vail, muttering into the midst of their thoftship. "This is ridiculous. Do we have to do this today? Why don't we come back in a few days, or get up earlier tomorrow? It's not as though the caravan is going to leave without us."

Toron kept weaving from one foot to the other, and waited to be pushed from behind. It was how he had been walking since they stepped onto the bridge—like a doll, wobbled to and fro by a child's hand. "I'd at least like to know a little more about why we're here," he said. "They'll have to tell us something up there. Someone must know."

Kurtisian drifted back to both feet as they all shambled forward a step. He spoke louder. "That's what I don't understand. Why doesn't someone at the front just climb a tree, or better yet, come out onto one of those balconies up there and give us the details? We'd still have to sign up one-by-one, but there's a lot they can tell us all right now."

"Maybe they don't want the whole burgship knowing those things."

"You hokering me? You think it wouldn't get out anyway, or that some of these people aren't just townfolks or newsmen sneaking in for an earful? There's no way in the Hells the Rings could keep it a secret. On top of that, there was nothing secret about the bulletin we're answering. Anyone could read it. Everyone knows the kingdom's in some kind of trouble. Everyone who sees us knows why we're here. I think it's possible the inkfingers manning the rolls up there don't know anything more than we do now."

Some nearby hoods shifted to listen in, but not too stealthily that Toron missed it. To keep his answer from their earshot, he tried leaning across Gorrh's shoulders, which stood like a hill between him and the rest of his thoftship. For the height of them he gave up, and leaned across the tuskcat's low-lying head instead. Justinian bowed forward a little, forcing Vail, who walked before him, to do the same. The shuffling huddle of their conspiracy, which included the great, tawny face of Gorrh, was no subtler to those around them than if they had discussed things at the top of their voices.

"We haven't spoken with anyone about this yet," Toron whispered loudly. "And we won't know anything until we reach the booth at the front of this row."

Kurtisian threw a hand towards Awklindhome, nearly striking a bystander. "What booth? Where? We can't see anything through this. For all we know, this snake's eating its own tail."

Toron shook his head. "There must be some who have gotten

there and come out again. Have some tholemodeness—some…some patience! You have somewhere better to be?"

Kurtisian's eyes went wroth, but he looked away and walked it off, half the while licking the insides of his teeth. More time passed. They crossed the bridge over the locks, and began to inch their way around the northwestern rim of the Grenstead. They passed the inlet of another spokeroad, and though its throat was not as choked as their own had been, the tightening wind of the crowd wrung from them any hope the flood might be drying. The suns swapped sides of the sky, and Starmath's brighter burn began throwing down the shadow of Shiremansairy. Their bellies grumbled, and the hopes giddied by saraf went down hard into the gloom. Still no one spoke. Only the burg offered noises, tossing them in from afar like rubbish. The line reeled round, threatening to send them behind Awklindhome.

At length Kurtisian turned turned back in. "Is it so hard to believe this thing's just poorly run, and no one's talked enough to find out?" He leaned in closer, stumbled, and caught himself with Gorrh's right tusk. The cat growled but forbore it. "Look at these poor bastards. Look at them! Look at him, over there. He's so tense, he'd make a better stableboy. He could use his asshole to pry off horseshoes."

"Hern, Kurtis." Toron dared not look, lest he find the meant man to be eight feet tall and all ears.

"Look. Thorn. Better yet, listen. You ever heard so much silence? No one's talking to anyone else. They've got all their cards so close to their chest, they're all so bitter to be here for the handout, I doubt they can even think straight. People like us, we don't come begging. We wait for the world to turn beggar and come to us on its knees. Or that was the dream, anyway. Till we started starving. No one's happy to be here; everyone here's got a mouthful of crow. And when shame irrumates pride, you think you deserve everything that gets thrown in your path. I guarantee, no one's asking. They're just taking what they're given."

Justinian leaned heavily on Gorrh as he walked, the better to avoid staggering and collapsing onto Vail. The tuskcat didn't like that either, but Toron kept it to himself. "Thorn, you know Kurt and I went out exploring a few times while you were on the mend. We didn't come out this far, or we'd have seen this mess. But even where we went, just north and south of the Gates, all we got were the same snits and scowls. No one seems to respect why we've come. Even at that village near Sherk-narsk-wirth, they treated us better."

Toron looked to each of them, then to Vail, who offered nothing beyond her penetrating stare. They were right. There was something foolish about all this, about the pride which kept them sheepish and herded. He looked next to him, and behind him, and no one met his eyes. It was as though they were all invisible to one another, or mirrors they could not bear to peer into.

"Forgive me," Toron spoke to the hood alongside him. "Do you know where this leads, or what we learn at the end of it?"

The hood turned. Yellow eyes candled within. "*Nee*," said the mouth, a ditch in their glow. "And we have been back three days."

The Outsider's own thoftmen turned their gazes upon him, three of them, their own eyes kindling, the hues green, and blue, and a hue he could only call sunset. He felt himself quiver, but he pushed back.

"Three days?" Toron said. "As in, you have been here, got nowhere, and come back twice more?"

"Yes," the Outsider answered. "That." It was clear he would say no more, at least not without a fight.

Kurtisian turned to his right, to a man next to him. "How about you, handsome? Any idea why we're going in circles?"

The swordsman was of Mankind, and he chuckled heartily. "Your words are odd to me, outlander. But I see what you ask. And no, like the fellow yonder, we have been back twice, and come no closer to the end." He leaned in closer, and the mighty depth of his voice belied his small, shaven chin. "Some of these men around us, they overnight here, never leaving, sleeping under the stars, if indeed they sleep or need it. Not all of them are Men, as you see."

He caught sight of Vail as he uttered the last few words, and it was clear he didn't like what he saw. He pulled back into his own thoftship, and his friendliness blew away like smoke. Toron found his choosiness odd—to warm to an outlander, but not an outsider—but the man had told them enough, and they needed him no further.

Kurtisian looked from the man to Vail, whose eyes, trained ahead, showed the unseeing fixity of someone tucked behind a drape. The fuhrbido's thick eyebrows quivered, and a heavy scraping breath left his nose.

"You see," he pressed, turning back to Toron. "They might as well be bleating. Or making a lemming noise. Hey, *fra*! What noises do lemmings make?"

Justinian removed his arm from Gorrh's back and returned to his full height. He saw the game, and a hard sparkle went across his eyes. "I think it's a pipping sound. Like, *peep! peep! peep!*" He swung his gaze between the two teerseekers they had spoken to, both of whom heard him, but neither of whom yet seemed eager to react. Instead, they passed words to their own companions, whose sharp edges skewered the breaths they were hidden under. Toron's blood leapt, and Gorrh, who felt the brittle calm cracking, shot a warning through the Rine. *There are fell men among us,* he threatened. *And not all of them, nor their steeds, are what they look to be.*

"When have you two ever seen a lemming?" Toron answered, trying to pick from his thoftmen's talk the coolest coal there was. "I've only ever seen a handful, and that was near north of Hellgrindel.[8]"

Kurtisian nodded thoughtfully now, head high, and without the slightest jitter of showmanship. To see him so given over to his game meant big trouble, for he was a fiendish agitator, or as Justinian had once called him, a master baiter. His teasing, Shard had once warned, could provoke a stone to throw itself.

"Yeah," he began at last, "but the tung has its own memories. And nothing I ever saw in the south beats a mouse that's said to piss itself on the heartbeat, and walk off a cliff just because the one in front of it does."

All around them now, Toron saw heads leaning in, and the fidgeting twitches of anger taking shape. *Not here*, he prayed. Half-men hulked at every edge. Even when he squeezed his sight to blur, all the weapons became quills in the air, the spears and helves rising as from a landscape overrun with pokepigs[9]. And somewhere in the gullet of his brain, where his tongue, nose and soul brushed roots, he could taste all the dree fuming at the rim of Eksar's mana, like so many weird herbs and crides dealt and readied for the cauldron.

This would be no alehouse brawl.

These were not men who weighed and doled their strength with a miller's stinginess. They did not spar with their foemen, but gutted them, beheaded them, and burnt them to ashes. These were fiendslayers and daredevils, wonted to the kinds of fights they'd have lost without giving their all, and a little of their morrow selves

---

[8] An exaggeration on Toron's part; *Hellgrindel* is one of the names of the wall surrounding the icy Hell of the Oztroth faith.

[9] *(AK)*: porcupines

to boot—won only with the kinds of blows that loosened the marrow in their bones, and had no care at all for the bystanding world. Toron's thoftship would be hard put to it even to overlive such a clash, and that would only be the beginning. Worse would come when the Burgwards moved in to put down the uproar, by whatever ruthless means they brought to bear. At the very best of all ends, the thoftship would be thrown into the hell of every dungeon and forgettery[10], put in stocks smithed to hold the worst wizards and devils, the shit dripping down their broken legs, till the day their dooms were chosen by a ring of chalk-skinned warlocks whose sink into dreecraft had eaten through every tie with the Mankind they judged.

Toron looked for some means of forestalling that lot, and marked only the three griffons roosting on a low rooftop a hundred yards or so away. Neither they nor the burgwards standing at their sides had yet sniffed the bloodshed he felt coming, and by the time those men had even taken their saddles and become airborne, it would have been well underway. He thought quickly, and saw another spokeroad only a little up ahead. At his egging, Gorrh slowed, drifted back, and came up around the thoftship's right flank. He and the tuskcat now had Vail and the Chaldallions between them.

"And something else—" Kurtisian began, and with that Gorrh leaned hard, and banked them hard north towards the spokeroad.

The move had its own hazards, as Toron foresaw even before he felt himself being driven like a ploughshare through a battlefield. His body dug its furrow through the tightly packed earth of brawn and mail, and was scratched by the touch of more than a few spikes and open blades. Eyes of wrath came up like bulbs; there were some swearwords, and more than a few shoves. Someone, with a kick, tried hard to trip him, and worse, the hawk and mist of spittle, which nearly did him in. But he made it the win not to strike back, and whetting his share with *forgive me*'s and *make way*'s and *need a needhouse*'s he cut a path through the crowd and led them off the Grenstead to the near shelter of the spokeroad. It was far narrower than their own had been—indeed, more of a backway between those buildings that looked onto wider spokeroads east and west. On its path lay a single thread of men, all waiting to be woven into the

---

[10] *(AK)*: oubliette; the depths of a dungeon in which one is forgotten, and left to die.

coiled rope from which the thoftship had only now untangled themselves. The road was walled in, as the other had been, but one of the walls soon showed them a gate whose hollow opened into a yard full of busy washer women. The women themselves seemed less happy about it, but they had no weaponry, and suds instead of scars. They might as well have been lambs napping on a sward for all the frowns and muttering they made. Nonetheless, one of them dropped her washing in the tub three of them were sharing, and headed briskly for a nearby door.

Toron took the chance to settle his guts with whatever time they had before she came back with some warden or other.

"Smooth, Kurtisian." His mouth tripped and lathered on the full outlandish name he seldom spoke. "Get us all killed at the hitching post. You blasted fliteyearn."

Kurtisian grimaced lazily. "I don't know what that means."

Toron took one more breath and straightened up. His fist rose, trembled, and slowly, like the growth of a shoot, uncurled one finger. Toron hammered it, and again, into the dreeman's chest. Kurtisian didn't like that, but some inner part of him seemed to know he had earned it, and he took it quietly, even as his eyes hardened with each knock.

"Everyone back there," Toron began, keeping his words low and out of others' reach, "they all kept it together until you got there. For days, some of them. You heard."

"All I heard was *baa*. A lot of flatus and b'latus.[11]"

"Yes, you said that already. Or something like it. I hardly heard you by the end, over the sound of the teeth grinding around us. No one is glad to be there, least of all men like us. But they're hovely enough not to shit where they eat. Hern, even sheep don't do that."

"But the lion," Kurtisian grinned, his eyeteeth fanging out, "he shits where he wants. And if that's where sheep eat, so be it."

Toron felt the others watching him. There was much he would say.

You're not a lion, Kurtisian. You're a sheepdog, and you're gnashing at the flock too often. You're flirting with the wolves you've taken an oath to hate. I don't want to see you put down. I don't want to have to help do it.

---

[11] (*L* expression): a great deal of bellyaching and/or blather; a whole lot of pissing and moaning.

But he gave breath to none of that, which was nothing he had not thought before. Gorrh heard it, and agreed, he who was closer to a lion than anyone, but who could muzzle his less hiresome self at need, and with a greater will than many men wielded.

"There are healthier ways to stand out than by setting yourself on fire," he said instead. He had never heard its like before; it came to him like a whisper from another Where.

But Kurtisian only smiled, flexing his fingers as if practicing an upcoming snatch, and rubbing his once-wounded arm through the black mail. A voice, loud but aquaver, called out from the nearby postern, and told them they had no leave to be there. They stood in the garden of so-and-so, who was such-and-such to the Burgreeve himself, and they would be put in bonds if they did not go at once. Kurtisian jeered.

"Whither now, Thorn?" Justinian asked, his smile pursed and neutral.

Toron looked over at Vail, who kept up her ghostly half-thereness and gave no token of understanding anything that had been happening. Though it was a hush more welcome than her stir at the inn, Toron could not help but feel she was watching them, taking it all in with the hard heart of loregatherer, as though her wriels were a blind, the seer herself unseen behind them. He hardly blamed her. Save that she walked among them, she yet had no stake in their gamble, and little did he ween she might wish for one now, being better off unfastened, the likelier to dodge the fallout of their foolishness. She seemed with her cool bearing and hidden strength to befit the king's teerseekers more than they did—were it that Kurtisian was wrong, and the crowd of freeswords behind them indeed best embodied that calling.

And on that, Toron recalled the one other thing they might do that day barring another go at Awklindyarth or seeking a sage for Kurtisian's lycanthropy. Back at the inn, Vail had called herself a marksmaid, and bid them find somewhere she might prove herself. At the time, he had meant only to bring them out of Eksar into the western foothills, to scratch rings and bull's eyes into tree trunks with knives, and mete out how far away they were with footsteps. As for shooting weapons, he had the small crossbow he would have lent her, but that shoddy thing made up the whole of their dart-throwing weaponhoard. It was not worthy of a sharpshooter, and the thought of handing it over, were Vail as good as her word, had wrought Toron's shame to ready its tinder.

But as luck it would have it there was an avenfeld[12] not too far from where they now tarried—a wide field where the burgwards honed their fighting skills, and which the thoftship had happened to pass by when last they were in Eksar. The yard was not inside the burg's walls, but hard up against its northern middards, in a pocket delved out from the scree. Arrows seldom strayed from its pit, and griffonriders might drop weapons into its rubble without killing any burgfolk under them. It was also a playstow of wooden sword dummies and shooting marks, with wrestling rings, weights, and runs full of hurdles and climbs and crawls. In the air above it hovered lists and other things where the griffmen bettered their griffmanship, steering their winged steeds through hoops which never stayed put, and between walls and thick logs that swung and leapt to hinder them. All of it was meant to simulate a chase among buildings and trees, into whose thickets running thieves often fled. Such courses were called *flightgoes*, and while other business in the avenfeld stuck to the clearing itself, the griffon drills went out across the scree, whose rocks did not catch thrown riders softly. The slope was steep enough, however, that those who fell seldom died, which made the rocks kinder than the grass of the more easterly avenfelds, where the flightgoes floated high above flat earth.

The spokeroad on which the thoftship found themselves led straight north, towards the great, crumbling mountain face at whose chin the avenfeld lay. The pale berg seemed brittle in the midday, like a dried fin of bone, no more so than where it shed its scree, whose outfanning run of rubble looked to have buried a great stretch of the city's midst. But this was not so—that wreck was a dwimmer[13] only—for the shape of Eksar was built to seem pinched, its northern and southern walls bowing in to catch the landslips. The bergs had been molting long ere the founding of the burgship, always peeling a little at a time, and never giving way in murderful heaps. The flinty clatter of its sloughing was an everyday sound to those living and working nearest the runs. The worst of it were the hair-raising thuds of those few runaway clods that, having the right

---

[12] *(AK)*: training-ground, exercise-yard. A comparable term is *playstow*, which is more specifically for competitive athletics. An *oretstow* or *oretfeld* is a place for fighting contests only, including what would elsewhere be known as an arena.
[13] *(AB)*: illusion.

weight and shape, made it all the way up to Eksar's outer wall. As for the burgwards sweating in the timber-crutched clearing beyond that wall—those who toughened their fingers with bowstrings, bruised each other with wooden swords, and tore white-knuckled handfuls of feathers from their griffons' napes—they were clearly less safe from the screes than those within them. But Eksar's other avenfelds, shooting fields, and swordstables were far away, scattered across the burgstead and broken up amongst oft-quarreling weaponlords. Some of them only welcomed one or two wereds, and shunned the others. For many of the wards in the humbler boroughs, the narrowmindedness and petty foemanship was not worth the time. They gladly chanced a rock in the head to forgo the infighting, and moreover to do everything in one field.

Though Toron winced to foresee any further hassle it might bring them, he brought it up to go there. They all agreed, being halfway there and having few other choices before them. Leaving the washer women, whom the Chaldallions thanked for their trouble with florid bows, the thoftship followed the spokeroad further away from Awklindyarth, seeing the line of teerseekers dwindle and at last give way to everyday burgfolk. A wide berth and as little heed did those people give them, who here seemed more wearied by the sight of their ilk than frightened or enthralled. Groups of old men went silent as they drew near, and chewed their pipes. Mothers gathered their children close; servants about their business stepped off the road and trod the sedge nearest walls. Toron knew that much of their wariness was for Gorrh, as well as for Justinian, but so few of those they passed bothered to meet his own eyes that he wondered what they saw when they looked at him—whether a fellow Knaksman who fought for the welfare of the kingdom they shared, or some untrustworthy outlander, like the hundreds of hoods making a moat around Awklindhome. Or maybe it didn't matter to them where he had come from, only that he had swords on his back, and a wound-twisted smile, and that he walked beneath a black cloud of thrack the likes of which Arsask had not known since the Onelatching of the Bracsriche. Maybe he was more wraith than a righter of wrongs, and all the worse for walking in daylight. That he fought what they feared made him no less its harbinger.

Nearly all the buildings the spokeroad passed had their backs to it, and what the thoftship looked upon as they walked were the waindocks and trade doors of some of Eksar's richest homes outside the Airy. The halls showed stonework here, and were not simply stavebuilt. Some went three floors up, with wide upper windows, and slates on their roofs. In the yards below, hirelings split wood and stacked it under eaves; scullery maids threw scraps to chickens; dogs barked from behind stone half-walls. There were horses and donkeys and oxen by the tens, and sheds bursting with hay, some yards well swept, others in clutter and mess. The smells were of smoke, and leafmold, and dung, though none of it a reek, but rather sweetened by a hint of some bloombalm or other, for which dreeish pomanders, hanging from silver stands, were clearly owed. A few of the homes boasted gardens, with stumblestone pathways among the fronds, and ornate hooded wells that looked better for wishing than for water. A young woman read a book on a bench before one of them, black hair piled high, her eyes faraway. She hardly looked up as the thoftship went by.

They crossed another ringroad, and the buildings cheapened. The woodwork became grizzled, and some of the walls between the yards went tumbledown. The barking of dogs was sharper here, whetted by hunger. Men snarled at the hounds from the shadows. Beneath sagging eaves, water stood black in old tubs. Workfires glowed, and hammers fell against metal. Saws snored hard against wood. Lowly smiths wiped their brows and looked up, haggard eyes white against the grime. What they saw did not touch them, and they went back to their swenk without word. One after another, these homely worksteads went past, some of whose craftsmen—like the wheelwrights and nailsmiths—were shown by the rows and crates of what they built. Others made things too onely or odd to be known in passing, such as axlepins for wains, and gear for holding the flasks of wizards and druggists over open flames. Two women worked spinning wheels, bags of gray wool at their sides, humming and seemingly unbothered by the iron reek and din on all around. Other yards were empty, though there were lights in the onlooking windows. Still others seemed wholly forsaken, with dark stretches of building, dusty and bleak, like gaps in the menning.

After this, the road opened onto another Grenstead, Eksar's northernmost, which they had never before seen, and whose name they did not know. The face of the mountainside loomed so near as to scowl upon it, its upper ridge like a brow, its frown hidden beneath the great beard of scree. The Grenstead itself was not flat, but pitted at its heart, in whose shallow depths lay a fuming

shantytown of booths and stalls, where chapmen and buyers rubbed
shoulders with the draftneats. The smell and bustle were raw, and
unlike elsewhere. No silver pomanders fought the reeks, which
stewed freely. The barter had a cackling edge to it, and the
burgwards looked rougher. The only griffs were high above and to
the north, these the first tokens of the avenfeld, who made their way
through the flightgoes above it. The buildings at the outer rim of
Eksar were humbler than those in its midst, and stood no higher than
the burg's walls themselves. So it was that the thoftship could see
the hues of the griffons clear against the rocks, their heavy bodies
bobbing and banking to get around the hurdles that hovered about
them like hummingbirds.

They stayed to the edge of the Grenstead's marketplace, which
seemed glad to stay to the edge of them as well. They did have a bite
to eat there, buying a small heap of flatbread-wrapped meat the
monger called wraywhelks, which the Chaldallions thought sounded
revolting. Kurtisian said they had a similar food in the south, but
much better, and that these northerners had bastardized them on
import, and washed off all the spices, like everything. Justinian had
agreed, but wordlessly, unable to speak between the throat-galloping
gulps that would have disgusted a python. The thoftship ate while
sitting on the cheapstow's halfwall, and Toron had sat looking the
other way. All mischief at Awklindyarth aside, he was beginning to
find their burgsprung choosiness a bother—to have slept on dirt for
weeks on end now to grumble about the pebble under the featherbed.
All he wished was to stroll easefully for a while, and gratefully, but
they'd put the pebble in his own shoe.

Once they had finished and crossed the yard, they had only to
follow the spokeroad onto another ringroad, and by turning east
come within sight of the avenfeld's door by high noon. Like the
Grenstead, the ringroad was the outermost of its kind, and would
carry them about the whole rim of Eksar, at great length bringing
them back to the Gates where they'd begun. As it was, they were
only on it for two toes of the day before stepping off it again, and
making their way up the small street between barracks to the
humble, near hidden, doorway of the avenfeld they sought. Sturdy
but everyday it looked, like a mousehatch in the wall, the scree
coming down so hard beyond it, that it seemed as thought the stones
would come flooding through if they opened it. No one stood watch,

and the three burgwards leaning on their spears and chatting in the yard nearby said nothing as they approached.

"They weren't too glad about us being here last time," Toron recalled. "But they let us in for three silvers. All I have are golds and coppers. They likely won't take copper, and I'm not giving them gold. Do either of you two have any?"

Justinian nodded, and went for his wallet. Before he reached it, though, the door grunted open on its heavy hinges, and a party of teerseekers came through. They were swordsmen all of them, with cloaks draped over their arms, and faces flushed from drilling. The laugh they were sharing dried up at the sight their own kind, but they nodded manfully and left the door open for them. An awesome din came rolling out, which the high wall and foot-thick door had muffled almost fully. The thoftship entered, and found themselves flocked by peers yet again.

Had it been empty—and it was not—the avenfeld would have been a sight stirring enough. A hollow sink amidst cascades of stone it was, the spill of its walls held back with great beams, save in a few spots, where the rubble had leaked through into drifts. Stretching half the width of a Grenstead, its rolling grounds were a patchwork of grass and dirt, with plots staked off from their neighbours. Small outbuildings stood here and there, their smokestacks piping, the brands of Burgward wereds upon their walls. But what best struck the eye were the whimsical strings of buildworks running to and fro—high, runged roosts linked by railless bridges, and lofty gallows whose beams trailed many ropes, and other crafty oddities, upon whose shuddering networks the shapes of men scurried like squirrels, and skirmished wherever they met. Elsewhere stood ringed marks and straw men for the shooting. Dummies hung from crossbeams in rows, their bodies swordbitten and spilling. Haystacks stood by to restuff them, and all kinds of fightgear lay about like the grown men's playthings they were. Rooted in a pitch at the field's western edge stood a pair of orthankful wooden mockfiends for tilting at, whose limbs spun to unhorse careless riders. Eksar was not a burg known for its horses, however, and the pitch lay lonely, its dirt and dummies undented.

The best of the avenfeld was for the griffons, whose riders entered the flightgoes from a great, towering loft—a wonderwhim of craftsmanship whose landing spidered up the walls of scree by dint of the timbers that framed it, and reached a deck across the

stonescape like a falconer's arm. Beyond it floated the amazing
gauntlets of the flightgoes themselves, whose parts were steered as if
by unseen hands. Great sheets of wall axed up and down; others
winked open and closed like shutters; rings spun slowly on edge;
rows of logs waved like trees caught between tiltering winds. These
and other things hindered the paths of the fliers, their trends shifting
to thwart the ease and foresight of both rider and steed. How these
wonders stayed aloft only the wizards who had set them there might
say, but their kinship with Awklindhome was plain, and spelled out a
fellowship between layman and dreemen that was like few other
steadings in Knaks.

Had it been empty, the avenfeld would have been stirring. As it
was, it was busy, and the sight of it churned the mind toward awe,
for those who chewed up its turf were no wet-eared kids, but men of
steel, with shows of skill and of strength far beyond the reach of any
dabbler. Which of them were burgwards Toron could not tell, for
few wore their sarks here, instead doffing their hues at the sheds or
leaving them behind, the better to mingle in brotherhood. What
Toron knew, and no two ways about it, was that many of those here
were teerseekers like himself, who seemed to have found the
avenfeld on their own. As in Awklindyarth, the easiest to pick out
were the ones too great or small in body to be fullblooded Men. But
there were others whose bearings and deeds, even watched from
afar, were well beyond those of a burgward—or a Teakenmaler or
Knaksman for that matter. Some were much too swift; one
swordsman seemed as he sparred to twitch from one stance to
another, like a chipmunk, rather than to flow. Two others raced each
other up ropes more briskly than a man might walk the lengths of
them. Another man pummeled a punching bag, and the sound of his
blows said the bag would not hold out for long. Crowds gathered
wherever these odd ones played, the whoops and heartening cheers
of the onlookers utterly unlike the hush and uptightness of what the
thoftship had met elsewhere.

Whether these teerseekers had already got the goods on Bayerd
and were readying themselves for the sending, or whether they had
chosen to come here and keep limber rather than grow stiff upon the
floor of Awklindyarth, neither seemed so weighty as the gold they'd
struck upon, which was the goodwill of fellow fighters.

A man half-watching one of the skirmishes at a nearby ring
broke away and came up to them. His fifty or so winters had fallen

on sturdy ground. His hair was gray, but only, it seemed, because all their copper hue had seeped into his eyes. Though unmailed, he showed no fear of them, and his friendliness was as rough as a dry lick. Toron remembered him at once as the groundskeeper of the avenfeld. He wondered if the man remembered him.

"Help you folks?"

"We have a marksmaid," Toron answered, "wants to do some shooting. We have silver."

The groundskeeper waved away his offer like he might shoo a fly. "No need. The king's heleths are welcome here. Freely." His eyes pried among them. "You bring a bow?"

Toron felt the pang of the beggar. "No. We thought we might borrow one."

"A marksmaid indeed if she can hit the marks with any bow she picks up."

The words seemed goading but his smile was warm, and Toron knew well that fighting men were often poor judges of how sharply their wisecracks fell. He opened his mouth, but it was Vail who spoke.

"I am, lord," she said, her wriels rippling over her mouth. "Give me any."

The groundskeeper nodded, pursing his lips against delight. He looked over his shoulder and back again. "Any other time afore two weeks ago I might have said you're drawing the longbow already, lovely lady." And he chuckled at that one, which he'd clearly had in his quiver for years. "But in the past fortnight I've seen outlanders work enough wonders on these fields it's all I can do but wait to see it. The shotpaths are at the rear, behind the row of hayricks yonder. Shoot east only. As for borrowing a bow," and he looked at Vail like a thirsty man swallows water, "you give a knock on the shed with the blue hand on its side. That's the brandmark of the Drac Ottumnar, best sharpshooters in the mongs. Any of their beards in there, I'll give my fingernails they don't all shove their best gear at you all at the same time."

She gave a kind of bowing nod, and Toron and the Chaldallions thanked him. They began to head past, and to pick out a way among the many crowds and pitches. They'd only left the groundskeeper a few steps behind when he called out to them again.

"Last you men were here, round four years ago, you had another lady with you, no? Had the look of a galdernorn?"

He remembered them indeed. Rhianys too. Toron would have been gladdened to hear it, were he not bewildered by the word the man put to her, and trying to tell whether the name of galdernorn held any scorn in Arsask. It did in Harandril, but only a little, and only for the loathing dreecraft suffered there. There were so many words among the Medths for those who did magic—some dirty in their meanings, others dirtied by ill will—that it was hard to say what was meant without knowing the speaker.

Slowing but not halting, Toron nodded. Justinian made a little noise to show he was impressed.

"What made you remember us?"

The groundskeeper thrust his chin toward Gorrh as he headed back to the ring he had been watching before they came in. "You see something looks like a bergcat fucked an ox instead of ate it, that's not a thing you forget."

Kurtisian gave one of his slow, mock-thoughtful nods. "Well put," he said.

"And no dree!" the groundskeeper barked above the uproar, his finger raised. In a nearby ring, a fighter in a full-length hauberk was thrown like a sack of corn.

They all of them, the whole of the thoftship, cast their eyes upwards at the flightgoes, whose shadows fell and twisted across the pitches all around them.

"But we're outside the city!" Kurtisian protested. "What about those things up there?"

"No dree! None! I don't care if a mage stuffed your ass full of lightning somewhere, you keep your knees crossed!"

"Gods damn it." The fuhrbido's fingers curled and twitched. The *Carno* would have to stay where it was.

"Odd that he remembered Rhianys and not Níscel," Justinian remarked. "She was here too, yeah?"

Toron did not know why, but he needed to think about it, and not only a little. Yes, the kattid had been with them in Eksar. She had hardly left his side. He found himself troubled by the insider burglary of that forgetfulness—a kind of which one finds in dreams, when beloved things are stolen from the mind for the sake of carefreedom and makebelieve, and the dreamer recalls them with dread well in, aghast at the harm his carelessness might have wrought. In dreams, however, there was no harm done, and it was an impish playwright who tampered with one's memories. But in the waking world such forgetfulness was unwonely. Was it the Timebriar, or Eksar's own haven, that kept back thoughts of Niscel, or had the Heron's healing gone too far? No, if anything his hindsight had been more sorrowful these three days, their windows freed of overgrowth. Maybe it was the saraf, whose sheenleaf no longer floated like beaten gold, but now crunched beneath the feet of his plodding thoughts.

They made their way toward the rear of the field, choosing wide leeway wherever they found it. Men clashed, wrestled, and drilled all around them, some in the pitches, others in rings of their own. Dirt flew. Weapons whipped out of thongs like sprung traps, and not all of their blades were wooden. The musk of sweat lay thicker than the woodsmoke in spots, and the smell of some men was staggering. Most only stank, but with others the strength of it was staglike, boasting, making itself known in a way older than speech, even as the nose and tongue themselves share a single root. Unhovely were some, their fog so befuddling, and like thurses and manshfretters more akin to the wild things teerseekers fight than to the clothed homeowners whose love and gold they sought. For one's blood to catch a whiff of such wights was to be dragged back into a world of fire and hides, where the seeds of Mankind glinted within the brains of things not wholly Men, and menning was a puzzle yet to be rinsed and put together. It was some wry kind of doom that washed man found himself a weakling against such beastly throwbacks, and to win needed every shred of orthank he might come up with.

And dreecraft, as any dreeman might tell, was the best of that cunning. Hatred of it was selfslaughter. It did not follow that in finding a better tool than all the others, Man should cut off the thumbs that let him wield it.

The shotpaths, as the groundskeeper had called them, were drawn across a single sward at the furthest reach of the avenfeld, up against the screewall itself, whose mighty timbers seemed a weir before its flood. Only in one spot had the stones found a way through, and slouched out in a great heap whose edge the groundskeepers had dragged out a little to mark the shotline. On the western end was a shed, its little smokestack blowing heat, the blue brandmark of a close-fingered hand on its wall. Its door stood open a little. To the east there were ten marks, at widening stretches from the shotline. Half of them were strawmen, and half of them shotspoons—the latter the ringed wooden bull's eyes Toron knew best. The closest of the marks to the line was ten yards, and had as a backboard one of the same timberwalls that floated above in the flightgoes. It was for beginners, and for weapons other than bows. The other marks, which had no backboards, were from twenty to two hundred yards away, staggered so as to lessen the likelihood of a man being caught in the neighbouring shotpath when he went to get his arrows back. Twenty men or so had gathered there at the paths, though only half of them seemed to be shooting. Arrows whistled; their heads stabbed wood. Feathers stood from the middlemost marks.

The thoftship made their way up the mild slope and came to a halt in the wide clearing between the shed and the shotline. The grass beneath their feet was flattened but not churned, and the gear around them—the racks, the boards, the handcart for bringing marks onto and off of the field—seemed more weathered than worn. As with riding, marksmanship in Eksar went to the griffmen, and fewer burgwards cared to shoot from their feet than those who esteemed marksmanship on the wing. Only a handful of hawkeyed and iron-thighed burgwards were good enough to call themselves flying bowmen, however, and so lordly was their skill that near to no one else sought out their livelihoods, believing it time wasted, and better given to weapons they might come to shine with. Learning to shoot from a griffon's back was nonetheless done outside the burg, where stray arrows did much less harm.

"You know, it is quite the place," Kurtisian said, putting his back to the mountainside and taking in the whole breadth of the valley. From the rise they could see both of Eksar's gates, as well as all its lordliest buildings. Awklindhome shone, aglow next to the dusky hump of Shiremansairy, but they could also see the Heron's Medthkirk to the southeast, a black needle of a tower, more like to a spear than the Sapling its byname. To the west, they saw like a fallen star the last shimmer of the Gungnissa as it went underground, flowing beneath the feet of the southern mountainside whose face was the twin of the one at their backs.

"I dreamt of it often," Toron said, "when the road seemed longest." He unshouldered his swords one by one, and with his free hand kneaded the spots their belts had numbed.

Kurtisian gave him one of his dry, strained looks. "I don't mean the city. Except for a couple of things, the place is another Knaksish backwater. I meant the training grounds. Even in Salpes, I didn't see anything like this. Those griffon courses up there? I'd love to give them a go one day. How about you, fra?"

Justinian took his brother's ribbing and snorted in acknowledgment, but the Sumo's mind was elsewhere. He was watching the bowmen at the shotline, and was transfixed with one in particular. "Thorn," he said, his fingers fishing blindly for a piece of his thoftman to grab. "The one at the end. Look at him. Look at his *bow*."

Toron's eyes were not as sharp as Justinian's. Even so, he spied the archer his thoftman meant—a shooter on one knee, wrapped head-to-toe in shieldcladding[14] yet, who was sending his arrows down the shotpath nearest the screewall. Such an outfit as he wore was seldom seen in Knaks, but they were not wholly unheard of. Their end, as Toron understood it, was only to shell men up like oysters, and with great swords send them against one another, to see who shucked whom first. He had never known of anyone to shoot in them, or to walk around much for that matter, but the mark the bowman arched for was a light smear against the faraway grass. It was the yondermost there but one, and well over a hundred yards out from the shotline.

"The one in full plate?" Kurtisian asked.

"Not just full plate," Justinian said. "He's wearing his famsapping *helmet*. With his famsapping visor *down*."

"And gauntlets," Kurtisian noticed.

"And he has not missed." Vail put in. "Not one shot."

She's right, Gorrh confirmed, and Toron said aloud.

Kurtisian squinted. "Not one? How? I hardly see the damned target."

Vail stepped out in front of them all. "Not all of them are in the middle," she said, and louder than before. "But they are all in the rings."

The man let off one more shot, and the flight of it sounded weird, like a child's first try at a whistle. He turned to look at those who were speaking about him before it struck home. He had more than enough time.

"Ah, my judges," an avenging voice spoke. "When shall I ever satisfy you all?"

---

[14] *(AK)*: plate armour, as opposed to chain or leather shieldwear.

They understood its words, but its speech was amiss. Though perhaps made by lungs of flesh, it had not been borne by them. It was too loud for its depth, and its depth seemed bottomless. Rather than shoot from mouth to ear, the voice seemed to plunge from helm to earth, and to barrel through the underground, rolling up into the bodies of its audience with an eruption of stonebruised sound. It startled them to hear it, who were at first unsure whether it had come from the armoured man at all. But the helmet moved with the words the way any speaker's head would have, and he propped himself to his feet with his bowlike contraption, and stood inviting an answer. He looked down the shotline, and when he looked back to them again, there was a face within the helmet, one not at all like the coldblooded doomsman his voice had presaged.

"Well?" he said, now with another voice. It was that of a man now, and friendly, though no less firm. The other they would come in time to call the *helmsrerd*. "What of that last one?"

Vail craned her neck a little to look, though Toron had a feeling that was for show. She had likely watched the arrow land, if not seen the very woodgrain split open.

"It is in," she acknowledged. "A good shot."

The man inclined his head, and twirled his wrist with a flourish as amiable as it was mockcocky. Turning back to himself, he then began to tinker with his bow in some way, every and now and then glancing toward the avenfeld's fighting rings as some excitement began to build there. After Vail, Toron had had enough of hearing two voices in one soul, and would have gone back to their own business, but the farkind woman herself seemed entranced by the stranger, and kept her way toward him.

The thoftship had followed, and so it was that they made the acquaintance of Melgard, who by almost every indication was not of their world. No less ghost-rounish than the other strangers Toron had seen at Awklindhome, he introduced himself first, and gave them all his hand to shake. Toron hid his wonder at that manner of greeting, which till now had belonged to Harandrishmen alone.

He was clearly Mannish of thede, at least the share of him they could see above his shieldwear—an older man, perhaps twice their own years or more, with crowsfeet at the temples and his forelocks dwindled to a single, iron shock. Even his smile showed him to be a man of war, with the creases of one ever gnashing at the fray, and though these lines were deep indeed, they seemed to slacken themselves like hackles, and yielded to the good breeding of a gentleman. The only thing that refused to be housebroken was a certain glint in his eyes, which however much he lifted his brow to open himself seemed to withdraw further into their kennels—to crouch there with unrepentant hardness, patiently waiting out the decorum to which they had been brought.

It was at the edges of Melgard's face that all familiarity ended, however, for that was where his shieldwear began. Up close it was little like the cumbersome metal shell to which Toron had first likened it. It was piecemeal, yes, but its joints and segments were much more numerous, as though to ease the have-at-it of the wearer rather than to hinder him. Nowhere did it swell or jut or spindle as pieces built asunder might do when at last put together, but showed a wondrous evenness and flow, like something cast in a mold, which only one man in a thousand might wear. It had no straps or buckles, which would have looked mangy upon its sleekness, but was held together with a limber weave that was neither chain nor cloth, but some himely thwarsing of both. A mighty webbing of stays wrapped the body, rising into flanges about neck, the better to turn away blades and to uphold the lifehouse against the crush of ungodly jaws. Those who had not foreseen the latter of the two purposes might have been forgiven—save for the halfrings of bitemarks that gouged the breastplate collar to waist. Whatever had done that damage, it had been no queenling's lapdog.

The helm seemed one block, though deftly shaped, and bared Melgard's face between the sideburns. The visor from earlier was nowhere to be seen, even with nowhere to hide, and at the crest of the headgear was a single socket which clearly had once held some plume or other token. The gauntlets, like the cladding of the body, were marvels of suppleness, the hard plates floating atop a softer weave, with battered cloutstuds at the knuckles. Their wrists faulds did not overlap the sleeves of the forearms but wedded with them, even as the footwear met the lower legs. There was no hint of how the wearer might take any of it off. Of all, it was the steely silver hue that seemed woneliest to Knaksish shieldwear, but at closer look even this was strange. It was bright but somehow dull too, like the burnt glass of an old lamp, which might be kindled from within and made to glow, though the flame seem a smudge. The sunlight warbled on it as the man stirred, and though the armour had to be heavy, and clunked where it hit itself, Melgard's movements were nothing like those of someone overburdened.

He claimed in earnest to be an imperial knight, of a realm so far away that if one bored a hole straight down through the core of Smað and dived out the other side, one would still be thousands of furlongs from its shores. It was, he said, a vast country, with sundry climes and kingdoms from everwhite to evergreen, and provinces such as his own, where winters did not lay the land to sleep but rather two kinds of bloomlife swapped reigns.

For all the wonders the shieldclad man spoke and showed that bore witness to the truth of his claim, Toron knew not how any of it might be true. West of the Sundarsund were the broken isles of the Yonderstrands, but they were stormracked, and lonely. East of Tarmateriza and Nagland were other kingdoms of Ráma, whose names Toron did not know, but which the kingly chartwriters did. Neither the folks of these lands nor their ways were so hidden from lore as to make Melgard one of their sons. South were lands aplenty, but one could tell those folks from their tungs and looks, and wonts, none of which was like those of Knaksmen, save maybe in the loosest ways. There were the Southern landholds of now-lost northern kingdoms, of which Kurtisian and Justinian were sons, but even the Chaldallions looked less Knaksish than Melgard, whose eyes were gray like a Hálishman's, and whose skin was so pale it seemed likelier to catch flame beneath the suns than to brown. No, Melgard had not hailed from the south, but nor was he from further north—from Hála, or from one of the handful of island jarldoms and free commonwealths everyone threw in with that kingdom. Though the cunning smithcraft of Knaks's brotherfolk there had been fostered by the unpitying cold, and might have yielded such a wonder as Melgard's bow, the Hálish still had nothing like the knight's shieldwear, which could not have been more dreeish if it had been quenched in Meem's well[15]. No, the Hálish distrusted dree, more so even than they did the weather, and could not have suffered to smith such a thing even had they'd had the knack of it.

North of Hála was the sea. And north of that was death.

What Toron weened of the unknown wastes at the world's edge he threw in with what he had heard of Ráma's own heartland, whose

---

[15] *(AK)*: A wiseman of the Oztroth godlore, to whom a well of wisdom is attributed. Known as *Mímir* to the Hálish.

share in Bayerd's loss he had done his best not to think about. Things maybe seen by Men but never lived through—fiendhaunted karsts, and firebreathing bergs in whose bowels lived devils so great that thurses were to them what Men were to thurses. Seas thrashed by the flukes of meat-eating whales, above whose wet hell went a corpsejam of thunderheads whose black bodies split and dripped lightning. As for diving out the other side of the earth, such was a depth of wayfaring Toron could neither follow nor fathom. Indeed Melgard had said the word *Smað*, but Smað as Toron knew it was less a landchart than a weave upon the itness, undone at edges, with no beginning and no end, its warps trailing off into seas and stars and dread. Beyond the soundness of its fabric, the yolks of brooding nightmares mingled, and half-shapes arose—fanged faces straining at the skins between worlds, and claws scratching their names on the shells that kept men from madness.

It seemed to him more likely Melgard came from another Where alongside this one than that he came from somewhere else within it. Though it dizzied one's waymind, it was the only answer to unriddle his thoroughly Knaksish looks, and that his mothertung was the Allmal, like their own. Whatever the sooth of it, he showed them, painted on the riser of his bow, an image of his homeland—of purple alps, and gorges watched by eagles, and a wine-red river in emerald footlands which flowed beneath the walls of a palace white as foam. In beholding it, Toron did not know what to wonder at first—how such a lovely etching might be made at all, and whether the whimsical thing it graced was indeed a weapon. It looked like something out of a mad gnome's workshop, only it was sleek and wieldy, and it clearly worked.

Stretching forty inches from end to end, its body was not whole, but in three pieces—the riser in the middle, and a supple limb fastened to each side. Despite the shiny woodstuff of which they were made, the limbs seemed simple enough, recurving like swan necks away from the riser, until their tips forked. Between each pair of tines was a trise, or a pulley, axle-pinned in the same way a wheel is housed at the front of a handcart. These wheels were not round, however, but oblong, and about their slotted edge ran a long, onely kind of drawstring which did not follow a single path. Instead it went back and forth several times, looping into two other trises and crisscrossing in the middle. Such a thing might have tangled were it not so taut, and its cords kept apart by dint of small arm reaching out from the bottom of the riser. It left an unacquainted onlooker unsure as to which of the three lengths was the one meant for nocking. Once one got above the whelm of it, however, it became clear that there were two strings, not one, and that the hindmost—with the bright red patch of paint at its middle, was where one nocked, seized, and drew.

No less a marvel was the riser itself, whose grip was molded for the grip of a hand, even as a cloth might be made to do if wetted. It had the strength of steel, however, and like the limbs kept a clever shape—leaning away from where the shooter looked through it, forming a sill on which the arrow rested, and an open window through which he aimed. Above that window, out of the way of the arrow but right in the path of the archer's eye, was a most cunning part of it, and what a Braccish smith might have called an orthankickle[16]—a framework of threaded pins by which the bowman fulfilled his aim. Fastened to the other side of the riser was a quiver as odd as the bow, whose row of clasps gripped the arrows like fingers, and held them heads-up. The blades of the arrowheads nestled beneath a single helmlike cover, their nocks only inches from the string that would throw them. And these were only the parts of the weapon that might be known from looking at them, for there were smaller, uncanny parts as well—among them brackets, and clips, and knobs for the twisting. In its own way, the thing seemed as eldritch as the *Carno*, and to hold more ingenuity than the whole world whose suns it had somehow come now to share.

When Vail asked Melgard if she might borrow the bow for their own shooting, Toron nearly laughed out loud. Whether or not the man might lend it to her, it seemed a beast that might as soon wound its handler if stroked the wrong way. And yet the knight yated, handing it over without hesitation, and bidding them all walk with him as he went to retrieve his arrows.

"I'd call them back another way," he said. "But our host wouldn't care for it."

"You mean with dreecraft," Toron said, and Melgard winked at him.

Kurtisian picked up his pace and drew even with Toron and the outlander as they headed down the long stretch of grass toward the shooting mark. Vail and Justinian trailed behind, both of them

---

[16] *(AB)*: an ingenious little thing, said of something done in miniature, or a tiny device such as a wristclock.

scrutinizing the treasure she had been lent. Gorrh, meanwhile, pitched his rump behind the shotline and waited, his ears and tail twitching. Something about the nearby scree bothered him, though he could not put his nose to it.

"I take it," Kurtisian said to Melgard, "you're here for the same reason we are."

"Answering the call of the King," Melgard replied. "Yes, I think a third of the city is here for that. And been here for a time, too, some of them. A fortnight, perhaps, maybe a little more. You've only just arrived, have you?"

"Three days ago," said Toron, "but today is our first day out of doors. How did you know?"

"I've not seen you at these grounds before today. They're not easy to find, and most of those you see here have been coming daily. Until further tidings arrive about our errand to the south, practicing here is the best thing we can do to keep ourselves out of trouble."

Toron felt his hopes kindle. "Further tidings? When did you hear there were further tidings?"

"Or any tidings?" Kurtisian added.

There came another uproar from the fighting rings, and Melgard slowed a little, craning his neck to see over hayricks separating the shotpaths from the rest of the avenfeld.

"One of my companions made it to the front of the queue in the central commons," he said, resuming his pace, "and learnt what he could, which was only a little more than what was written in the bulletin. The southern province has been overrun, and the King's men have pulled back. Everyone is waiting on the word of the King himself, including the scribes we met it seems, because there was nothing more they could do for us than to take down our names and offer us vouchers for inns and food."

Toron winced as the last burning beams of understanding dawned on him. He had only likened the crush at Awklindyarth to a breadline, but that was straightup what it was—droves upon droves of gleeless men, dreamwretched and starved besides, who peddled their fight not for love or riches, but for food and a bed to bleed on. It thoroughly unriddled the hush and bitterness of those gathered there, as well as the sheer scores of them. Times were bleak indeed for his trade, and pickings thin where swords made better almsbowls.

"And how long have you been here?" Toron asked.

Melgard reckoned for a moment. "A week yesterday."

"A week," Kurtisian repeated bleakly. "I'll be climbing the walls in a week."

"Or howling at them," Toron put in.

Kurtisian ignored him. "The bulletin was so urgent, who would have thought we'd hurry here only to wait?"

"A fair frayn," Melgard said. "Though I find things move a little more slowly here."

By *here*, Toron knew not whether he meant Eksar, Knaks, or the whole world of Ráma altogether. He chose to go back to the knight's own story. "How many are with you?"

"Five," the man said, "including myself. And you?"

"Four."

Vail spoke up from the rear. "So I am one of you now." Her true voice, as was its wont, lacked the hues that told its mood.

"I meant the cat," Toron lied.

"You did not," she replied, but it was hard to read that too.

Melgard chuckled. "A new recruit, I see. Well, I doubt you're the first party to find some new blood at this chance convention of ours. Myself, I only threw in with my band a short time ago. Not here, but not much before it. All young countrymen of yours, and promising swordsmen. They're down at the rings right now. Tugging a few beards, I'll hazard."

The crowd below boiled again, as though it heard him, and this time it was Toron who slowed to peer. The hayricks were high, however, and the gathering was too thick about the rings to see through—a hundred or more souls, burgwards and teerseekers both. So far into the pitches they stood, Toron wondered at the room the fighters in their midst had to work with. Every now and again the walls of onlookers warped and churned as someone was thrown against it.

"Your men have anything to do with din down there?"

Melgard chuckled again, but it was less blithehearted than before. "I'll hazard," he repeated. "Ah, here we are. You're right, milady. A couple of them are a little off. I'd have missed the crow, but not the orc. And I don't shoot crows."

They were still a good stretch from the shooting mark, but the bright red fletching of the arrows stood out against the weathered wood. Even Toron could see them, none more than a few inches from the black bull's eye at its heart.

"Good grouping," Melgard added, and his steel shoulders shrugged at the consolation. "Nothing wild. Believe it or not, I don't call myself much of a bowman."

The thoftship might have shared a wry look behind his back, were it not for the earnest shrift of the remark. From the mouth of anyone else it had been a boast, but the shieldclad man seemed proof against the overmood of selflove, though there was nothing meek about the humbleness that shunned it. It was strange whey indeed that kept all the starch but none of the lumps of what had curdled it, and Toron found the man's manner as otherworldly as his armour, shaped beneath wholly other suns.

"Then I'd hate to meet much of one," Toron said, "though I don't think I'd get my eye on him before he put an arrow through it."

Not too far behind them, they heard the hiss and rustle of an arrow skipping across the grass. The shooter in the neighbouring path had overshot his mark, but he and his fellows had shouted their sorries before the thoftship could even turn to leer at him. Melgard hardly blinked before waving back, and Toron weened it easier to be carefree when your clothing likely turned aside everything short of Woden's spear. They went the rest of the way to the mark, where Melgard carefully began wiggling the arrowheads free of the wood. The darts themselves were only a little less striking than the bow, and thoroughly its mates, with shafts made of metal light as wood, overlapping blades, and fletching that shimmered like the down at a hummingbird's throat.

"I can't say that I much care for throwing my good blades into solid wood. Cork, or even packed straw would be preferable."

"Can you sharpen them?"

"Oh, yes. I'll do that tonight. Here, milady."

He reached out and received the bow again, and they watched as he snapped the arrows one-by-one into the bracket of their strange quiver. When he was done, the ten of them stood alongside each other like the strings of a harp. Toron half-hoped Melgard would begin strumming them, and that the weapon would sound like one too. Instead, the knight handed it back.

"All yours," he said, and they made their way back toward the shotline, this time with Melgard, Toron, and Kurtisian in the rear. Vail and Justinian walked ahead, now marveling at the arrows and the way it all came together. Next to the Sumo, the woman in her cloak was like one of the holy day ribbons they had seen, undulating softly alongside the trunk of a thick tree.

"I hate to talk shop," Melgard said, his voice shedding some cheer, "though I'm quite sure it's simply talking business here. I have not spoken to many of the other adventurers since arriving. I was wondering if I might ask you what you know about the attacks to the south?"

"Not much," Toron said. "We came in from the east, and first saw the lathing in Booril."

Melgard waited a moment, then went on. "This province of Bayerd, where it's happening. What can you tell me about it, as a Knaksman?"

"Well, for one, that Bayrdish folk don't call themselves Knaksmen. They're not of the Nethrish thedes—the founding bloods of the Bracsriche, whose roots reach north."

Melgard nodded, considerate but also grave. "My companions have told me this. The Five Yoredrights of the Bracsriche, of which the Rings of the King are emblems."

What he said rang a bell in Toron's mind, and its knell loosened some fog. He'd known the Boar for the Rings all along, but never that the Rings stood for something other than the Boar. As it had happened time and again with Shard, an outlander stood to enlighten him about his own kingdom, whose lore had not come in with the air he breathed, as so many homeland sons seem to believe. Rather it came from wisdom and learning, which anyone frimdy[17] enough might gather. He knew then as well that the King likely did not reckon the Harandrish among those five founding bloods, for Harandril was the last of the Medths to have been founded when the Bracsmen swept east, and that the thedelore of the Bracsriche was one of the things that drove them to it.

Toron felt himself wayward, like one who has last been given a landmark and sees he been adrift for some time. The chill of it did not last long, however, before the bloodyminded selfdom of a Harandrishman wrapped its cloak back about him. He went on, eager to show what he did know.

"The Bayrdish are far kin to the Ignish, and to patches of folk in Shebril, and Pyndamir, all along the northeastern marches of Knaks. In Trebell as well. They have their own names for everything, and

---

[17] *(AB):* curious; inquisitive

they go by their own landcharts. We're all under the same king, but no one believes the King looks in too often, so the folks there still live a lot like they did during the Bracsriche, when they were their own kingdoms. Every Knaksman has heard tell that if you go in deep enough, you will find shires and valleys where they don't speak the Allmal, and if you go all the way to the outermost edges, you will find hamlets that have never laid eyes on one of us. I've never been to Bayerd, but I've seen enough in Ignam and Shebril to believe it."

Though Toron got the feeling that Melgard knew this too, the outlander seemed to be listening with his whole mind, with a thoughtfulness and welcome that wiped the world clean between them. The soft pull of his hearkening was like an ebbtide.

"Do you believe," the knight asked, "that these differences have anything to do with what is happening there?"

"No. If anything, it's the Unfondlands." Toron chose to spin the board then, and to ask Melgard what he knew, or had been told, of that nomansland the king's own lathing had blamed.

Melgard took a breath as his mind went through its rolls. "I have heard it called Ferine as well. It is the frontier at the heart of this landmass, this Ráma. Never won, and unexplored. Your kingdoms cling to the coasts, or are kept there, because of it. It is a land of monsters, where the dikes of this reality crumble and leak, and dark forces stack up like waves. It is also said to be the refuge of every foul thing that civilization has displaced since setting foot on this land." He then lightened up a little, and turned his head to Toron fully. "Have I chosen my words well, brother?"

"Well enough," Toron answered, though it struck him how like to Shard's the man's quide was. Were it not for the smorgasbord-Allmal to which he had become wonted through his thoftmen, Toron reckoned he would have a hard time understanding every third word the man spoke.

Melgard seemed relieved. "Good. I find choosing my words in this land a little like a tombraider's test, where I must pick the oldest chalice off the altar before the ceiling falls."

But with that, Melgard had lost him. Toron turned back to the dark matter at hand. "These things you have heard about the Unfondlands—that no one has ever won them, that no outfarer has rossed[18] past the merestones of our own kingdoms, or that fear of

---

[18] *(AK):* explored.

them has halted our menning—" Toron bit one cheek.

"They are wrong?"

"Not all. Some are. I am no yoreman[19], and my homeland is as far north of the Unfondlands as Knaks reaches. What I know has passed through many hands, but I can set you straight on a few things, at least. For one, the Unfondlands are not a single stretch of wilderness, nor do they make up the whole of the Rámish heartlands. From the seashore inward, there are many layers, each with its own name and tales. They become bloodier the deeper you go. From what I've heard tell, you are right to say that the kingdoms of Ráma cleave to the shores. I've heard of none that does not keep at least one foot to the strands on which its folk first landed, and to which it might flee at need. There are no inland kingdoms we know of, at least not anymore. Some may lie hidden. They'd need thick walls.

"Beyond this girdle of menning lie the marchlands, where the edges of each kingdom smear and thin. There are townships here, but they are small, and keep low to the grass, like motherless fawns. The folks who live in them know little of the outer world, and never stray far from their cradles. Such folks live throughout this land. Mine is one of them. But however lonely we are, we never worry whether we might be bitten off the rim of our Medth like a seal and swallowed one day. The neighbours of the marchlands are the Unfondlands, and this is where the shadows you speak of begin. Bold men fare across them. One such man was our friend.

"The Unfondlands aren't a single belt either, but a handful of wastes whose turf has been won and lost many times over. Some stretches of it have their own names—the Narfelds under Ignam, the Fretshaws off Landon, the Shamblemoors. However frightening these names might be, many of these wastes are said to be lovely. The Heronstroth would have us hold them more in awe than in dread. Their woods are mostly uncut; their waterways are unbridged. Mighty breeds of things live there, like great evers and tuskcats. Gorrh, there, was caught near the Unfondlands, and we've not seen another of his kind. There are fewer men there than in the marchlands, but some seek its wealth. Trappers try their luck, I've heard, but so do wortgatherers. No bigger harvests than those, but that doesn't mean a lot of reapers aren't slavering to get in. There's tell of endless plenty, with rich soil, and boundless groves, with trees

---

[19] *(AK)*: historian.

unknown to druids and woodsmiths alike. Some say every hill hides a motherlode, with hoards of athelstones so thick they stick out from the dirt.

"The wrecks of old kingdoms are there. Knaks has never been driven back from any land it has won, but I know the Bracsriche had landholds they lost there. A shire called Warnland comes to mind, and Thalasp. Koostoma as well. The earldoms of Gecce and Helsendir. I know little more than the names. Some may belong to other lore. But this is where the layers become bloodiest. A lot is said about the lives lost to the Unfondlands, but not so much about the killers. The way the tales tell it, it is as though the ground up and swallowed them one day. One tale every Knaksman knows is of a land once called Briyim. Even in Harandril, we learned it as children.

"Briyim was said to be a small inland riche of nine kingdoms, which lay up against the southeastern flank of Knaks. Over the hundelds it grew, gathering land slowly and driving back the fiends that called them home, even as the Nethrishmen did when they swept around the Wottrámish Alps from the north. One night, it is said, the overking boasted that the mustered trumes of all Briyim could, if he so bid, overtake the whole of the Unfondlands. Not only that, but that he ought to do it. Yes, on the morrow he would begin. And he raised his cup in pledge. It is not said how this hearsay came to be known, for only one soul overlived what came to pass.

First to see what happened were the errandbirds of the outer kingdoms, Knaks among them, who came back to their keepers with their scrolls still tied to them. When the wizards reached no one through their dree and seeing stones, men were sent on foot and by wing, who saw from afar the glow of Briyim's downfall, and felt settling on their shoulders the ash-snow of its ruin. Those who kept going found the skyline empty of the overking's stronghold, the gap in the bergs like a mouth ripped of its teeth. Those who dared go closer met the shattered hollow of the elderburg, and saw the rubble strewn from one edge to the other, as though the steading had been gutted up by the talons, and rolled across the valley like dice. Furlongs of woodland lay crushed and burning beneath it. Rivers choked, and the suns were smudges beneath the reek. The only witnesses sped homewards, and spread tidings everywhere they went.

"Men went back, but nothing was found. Briyim was no more. Every steading in every kingdom had been delved out and mangled, with no souls left behind. Only a handful of lonesome hamlets and homesteads were found untouched among the wolds, but these had been forsaken, many with food still upon the boards. Not one body was ever found. Briyim, for all its might and wealth, was banished to the deadbook, and time, as always, went on. Some say three hundred years have passed. Some say five. What everyone agrees on is the lesson. You don't go too deep into the Unfondlands. And you don't lay stakes to them. Or they'll come for you first."

"A cautionary tale," Melgard murmured. "But is it true?"

Toron turned up his hands. "I'm the wrong one to ask. As I said, I'm no yoreman, and I've never strayed south of Ignam. If it is true, the wreck of Briyim should still be there for all to see."

"Then you believe its teaching holds something for Bayerd."

"No. Maybe. I don't know. Of all the things you said about the Unfondlands, there is one thing I know forsooth. The worst fiends of Ráma fled there with the coming of Men, and have lashed out every now and again for hundelds. But Bayerd is neighbour to the marchlands, not the Unfondlands. Its reavers have been seen, and fought. The king's lathing said the Boarsmen are overdrawn, not overcome, and that many Bayrdsmen will not leave their homes. It is all too outstretched to carry the earmark of whatever thing unmade Briyim. But there is another name you spoke. *Ferine.*" The word seemed to tip backwards as Toron spoke it, and sent a trickle of icewater down his backbone. It was not a banword, not like an oath, or the Heronstroth's nine Hights of Unlife, but no one seemed to speak it very often, and its touch upon his tongue was unhappy.

"The kingdoms of Ráma, the marchlands, the Unfondlands— they are the meat to a heartland no Man has seen. It is this innermost place that we call Ferine, of which is said the frightening things you've heard tell, and worse. Even if it had something to do with what is happening in Bayerd, the King would likely not name it, lest few answer his call. It is a wrekin of horrors, whose fumes are the soul of every bloody tale we tell here. And Briyim stood nearer to it than any other share of menning in this world."

The crow's feet deepened about Melgard's eyes. "Then you believe that what is happening in Bayerd is indeed uncanny."

Toron's sigh was a peeved one, as at the buzzing of a fly one has swatted many times. "I don't know. What is said of Ferine, such things are said about a thousand dark valleys inside Knaks's own borders, and of Harandril my homeland besides. I call a lot of it stuntspeech—folks around their hearths spinning yarns, quickening shadows, saying the cloak of this Where is fraying, and that the devils are crawling in. I've seen enough to know that its seams can be unstitched, but I've seen more bad things in the here and now, for which there is no meaning any tale can give it. You ask me, there are some bad things waiting for us in Bayerd, but I don't think they're anything Nethrish steel hasn't cut down before. What I don't understand is why they rise now, why in our time. The Kingdom of Knaks was won and settled long ago, as anyone here can tell you. What fiends are left among the Medths, they are skulkers in the barrens, and the last lingerers of their kind. Some teerseekers might call Bayerd a gift until they give another thought to it, and look to whence their tide rises."

"And whither it flows," Melgard followed. They came to a halt then for they had reached the shotline, and Vail seemed more than eager to wield the bow. Her eyes bid them step from her path, and if she had been listening to the two men, she gave no token of it. Justinian, however, had the taut look one gets from finding something unpleasant in his food and does not wish to give himself away. As an outlander, he knew less of the Unfondlands than Toron did and had never discussed them to any depth.

Melgard put his hand on Toron's shoulder and looked him hard in the eye. "Brother, you have told me more than anyone I have spoken with about what we might be facing. My foremost hope is that we shall all be given more, and enough, before we are told to risk our necks."

Half-smiling, Toron nodded his welcome and felt the dizzying strength of Melgard's leadership. As for the man's touch, he was less welcoming. Word was that Knaksmen were given to leave to clasp each other only twice in their lives—when their fathers caught them at birth, and when they caught their own sons.

"There now," Melgard said, stepping over the rubble of the shotline and coming to Vail's elbow. She was taller than he was, or likely would be once his helmet and footgear had been removed. Toron and the Chaldallions backed up and gave them both waggishly wide play, as though whatever they did might cause them to burst into flames.

Melgard gestured as he spoke, mumming the movements he bid of her. He did not seem to presume her incompetence, however, nor fear any injury either to his weapon or to himself. "It looks like you've got it down. Sit the arrow on the ledge—that's it. And nock it to the paint—very good. Now br—"

The drawstring thrummed, barely before Vail had raised the bow at arm's length. She could not have drawn it more than a few inches. Even as it happened, however, it was clear she had done what she meant to do, for the arrow did not stray, but floated down the shotpath toward the mark, her gaze chasing it like a scolding. It struck the wood, and half a heartbeat later they heard its knock.

Toron passed on what Gorrh told him. "It's in. Right the middle."

Kurtisian squinted, the twist of his lips incredulous. "Really? But she didn't even look down the arrow."

"Now it's fallen out of the wood," Toron told them. "It didn't stab deep enough."

Melgard's smile, though admiring, was wary. "Try another one, milady."

Vail unclipped another arrow and nocked it. This time, she raised and drew the bow fully, but as she released, Melgard bumped its lower limb with his elbow. The arrow went off high into the neighbouring shotpath. Vail glared at the knight ferociously, but only for an eyeblink. She then put her gaze forward again, and everyone watched as the stray shot righted itself, banking leftward like a living thing and finding the mark in the same spot as its forerunner. Even from afar, they could see the whole arrow, which had not met the wood straight on, but stood askew upon its face like a halfopen door.

"Dree," Toron said.

The other shooters had seen it too. As was the way with everything Vail did, they seemed more charmed than put off by the sight, and chortled wryly, as though having found someone cheating when nothing of their own was at stake.

Vail turned to her own company, the edges of her eyes slicing past the bow's owner. "No, it is not. It is a doing of the mind only. If I wanted dree, I would not need this thing." She shook the bow like a naughty kitten.

Justinian crossed his arms. "Looked like dree to me."

"It is not. It is like with thoughts, like my mind makes my body do—" she opened and closed the fingers of her free hand, "but it goes out there, to other things."

"Psychokinesis," Melgard translated, though into a language they knew even less.

"Well, I think you're going to have to teach that word to our hosts," Kurtisian said. "Because there's a bit of a uproar building down there."

They all looked south, where the crowd about one of the rings was breaking open like an anthill. Something was churning out of its heart, and those who could not get out of the way hastily enough were knocked to the ground and overrun.

"That's not for any of us," Justinian said.

But Melgard said, "it might be."

The shell of men burst at its northern end, and the bickering of steel rang out of it. Two fighters staggered forth, told from the rest by their hustle and hotfootedness, and their path spun through the flow of onlookers like an eddy through the froth of a stream. They were still fifty yards from the shotpaths and heaped in with bystanders, but even so the thoftship could see that one of the two was much bigger than the other, indeed bigger than a man born to a woman had any right to be. His head was topheavy, and though his limbs were overlong, he was nearer to lank, and not oxbuilt like the grim thurses they'd seen in Awklindyarth. Toron knew him for a troll, whose folk are called by that name whether they carry all its blood, or but a sprinkling. He seemed not to have a weapon of his own, but went after his foe with open hands. The lesser of the two men, though doughty, was on his heels. He gave ground step-by-step, steel flashing, and was soon overtaken. Their open violence shrank at once into a slowly wrestling knot, which trembled as it tightened. Lusty oaths squeezed out of it, every word of them heard as the crowd hushed for the outcome. Limbs flailed, a sword went flying. The tangle of them spun—once, twice, thrice—and a third of its mass broke loose. The smaller man was thrown northwards, not as a man is thrown in a wrestling match, nor even as a bushel of corn is thrown onto the deck of a wain, but as a stone—egg-big or less—is thrown by a youngster over a high wall. The man did not flail as he hurtled, and his flight had been graceful but for his lack of wings. As such, the warp of his path from upward to downward brought winces to the faces of onlookers, some of whom loosed groans as he struck the ground. As luck would have it, he met a hayrick, or at least the edge of one, and so dodged the worst of it. He was slow to unbury himself, however, even as it became clear his foeman was not done with him. The angry troll made his way up the slope toward the shotpaths, his lumbering steps like something out of a child's make-believe, but somehow not funny.

The hayrick into which his prey had dropped was less than twenty yards from where Melgard and the thoftship stood. Two other things had come to them in the meanwhile. The first was that no man narrower than an ox, no matter what was in his blood, had the raw might to hurl another so far without the help of dree. The other thing, no less troubling, was that the dree-wielding strongman had not meant for his prey to find such a soft landing. As such, he had meant to shatter a lot of bones, and from the sounds and slowness of the man finding his feet amidst the hay, one could tell he had not wholly missed his mark.

The leatherclad troll built up as he neared, showing a short black beard and a wreath of braids about the bald patch on his head. His brow was a hedge of black thorns, beneath which his eyes were mere glints; his nose was swollen into the likeness of a turnip, as with those of old men who have been drunk their whole lives. Its shape was clearly inborn, however, and along with his bulk gave away his unMannish stock. All in all, he was ugly as a bulldog with a mouthful of shit, and might have been twenty years old or fifty for all that ugliness told of him. Toron's soul shuddered to look upon him, and to bethink itself of the man, or worse the woman, who'd been made to yield such a child.

The brawler's steps gathered storm as he closed the gap between himself and his game. Everyone who saw it watched. What was happening was not lawful, but not even the groundskeeper, seemed willing to step in. Only a few men stirred at all, among them a handful who pushed toward the front, and tangled with each other. They were the thoftsmen of the two fighters, it seemed, but none would make it in time. The troll hauled his quarry from the hay, and gripped him by a scruff made of jerkin.

"Yaw skreethit arsebirth," he brogued. "Yaw slit me nyooken shron!"

He wiped his nose with the back of his free hand, and it came away bloody. The snuffer of his was so mottled, one might not have marked the wound otherwise.

The lesser man might have whimpered, but he put enough throat behind it to make it a growl. "Call us even," he was heard to say.

"In tha darkest crotch o'Hel," the troll heaved back, and he was so angry he seemed not to know what awful thing to settle on next. He fnasted through his nostrils, befouling his foeman's face. He looked around for what was in reach.

Toron was only a little aware of Kurtisian saying his name—that they might want to do something—but the madness of the giant's hatred had scared away time, and whatever gruesome doom he meant to deal seemed a forgone deed. To leap into its path, even had they been swift enough, were to uproot themselves from godsgiven refuge, and to struggle toward a harm they'd been spared. Such is the vegetation of the bystander, whose idleness is like ivy, and though alive cleaves to the dead walls that give it uprightness.

The troll gave up looking for something worse than his knuckles and slapped down his foe, tabling the broken body between his feet like a log for the skinning. His fist rose like an axe, but there were no flies on Melgard. In a blink, the knight was there, and with a haste more dreeish than the troll's own strength. He might have put that speed into a blow, but he did not. Instead, he took a blow across his arms, which he raised even before he had put himself between the doomsman and foredoomed. There was a flash, a bone-shaking thud, and another sound, like that of a bullwhip breaking glass. The troll staggered a few steps back, as though bumped by the haunches of a turning workhorse, and fell to its own arse in the grass. Melgard kept going past the man he had saved, though only a little. The stroke he took had driven most of his forward thrust downwards, bending him like a nail hit by too heavy a hammer, and buckling his body for all its mighty shielding. He never lost his feet, nor did he quite drop to one knee. Instead, he walked off the shock of it in the few steps it took to come about, every footfall becoming firmer, until he stood sentry before the wounded man.

The troll was slower, but only for wariness. He rolled to his knees and rose to his full spindling height, facing the fight rings as though for cheers. With another wet blast of his nose, he turned, and with braids bouncing it stalked up to stare down its meddler, his legs making the same, laughworthy stomps as before.

Melgard stood his ground, not as a statue but as a man, which is to say that he gave the troll a few wary inches and kept for himself some room to act. He did something else as the goon barreled up,

which few saw, though all beheld its outcome. He flicked his head in
something like a nod, as someone with full hands might do to lower
his hat, or loosen her forelocks. It seemed nothing, and no words
went with it, but it brought the visor back to his face, wherever it
came from—whether it shot downward like a dropgate housed
unseen within the helm, or blinked into the window fully formed. An
unbroken shroud of silver it was, as uncanny as the cladding it
complemented, with no slits or holes, letting nothing in, though no
one doubted its owner saw everything.

As for the troll, he was no cavedwelling sot of his kind, but a
wanderer and teerseeker himself, and had plainly seen enough of the
world to know a powerful foe when he saw one. It was not one
against one, this match, but him against the whole world of cunning
and orthank from which the steelshelled champion hailed. Whether it
was for the ebbing of his anger, or that he'd had time to think things
over on his arse, the troll stood posturing before this foe he dwarfed
by three feet, and did not lash out right away.

"Your match with this man is over," the helmsrerd proclaimed,
and that voice was more dreadful than the troll's. "Deliver one more
blow, and a different contest will begin."

Melgard was weaponless, but no part of him seemed unarmed.
Those few on the avenfeld who saw the face of the troll saw its will
balking, the dripping of its nose drumming atop the tension. Things
might have soothed themselves, but for the hounding of the troll's
henchmates, who with their unseen numbers had busied the
companions of the wounded man, and sent three of their own
bursting from the thicket of onlookers to howl and bait their own
fighter back to bloodlust. They were not trolls themselves, these
men, but wargish knaves all of them. If they saw the touchwood
smoking between Melgard and their own fighter, they showed
nothing but a wish to blow on it. They called their man spitted meat,
that he liked it from both ends. Their swords they waved about them,
limbering up their own arms even as they goaded their swordless
friend to slaughter.

"Hie ya from my path," the troll said to the knight.

"No. This was not a fair contest."

"Yawr seekin fair fights, yawr in the wrong trade."

"This is not a battlefield. Not yet."

"I'll crack ya. Old man. Them nicey weeds. Yaw're all the mince
under that."

The troll's voice tortured speech. Its words were like finery bubbling to the surface of a pot into which civilized men had been thrown fully clothed. But the helmsrerd only chuckled.

"You can try. You'll find it's not worth the aches."

The troll bit his tongue, but his fellows kept egging him. It seemed empty madness, that the law of Eksar did not somehow take shape and drop on them like a gavel, but indeed the whole thing happened in but a few twinklings of the suns, and burgwards above and on ground were already stirring to fasten back the peace.

Many things came about at once. All Hell crashed at the gates.

The wounded man in the hay, in his shame, threw a rock he had found. It struck the troll, and shattered its brittle restraint. The goon trembled once, bellowed, gathered, and leapt. Melgard tensed, the helmsrerd roared, and a white light burst from the sleeve of his vambrace. His hand was engulfed in a blizzard of dree, and something appeared in its grasp. The troll's cronies surged; Toron reached for Tuger and Mortha. The *Carno* came at last, licking with steam the ready hand of its master, and Justinian called for the strength of Seisuma, his bare feet sinking an inch into the sward. Vail, the swiftest of them all, loosed an arrow.

But one thing happened that overwhelmed all of this, and brought breaking Hell to a standstill. Atop the heap of scree from which the shotline was drawn, something mighty roused, and stepped from behind its screen with a scream like nothing upon Ráma. Everyone stopped, and their faces were dragged north to it, for the apparition of this awesome creature began like a premonition of the eyes, a sense that the weave of the world was balking. What they all saw was the air itself rolling, like something prodding, no, molting, the very membrane of reality. The sunlight runnelled, and streamed from its protrusions like rainwater with no place to pool. A film melted away, and before them all stood a living engine, winged and silver. It looked a dragon made of metal, horned like an ox, with a single wide burning eye, and fitted to its every joint and limb was an implement of death, whether the hookblades at its fetlocks, or the blunderbusses yawning atop its wingspurs. Its fourlegged core was about that of drafthorse, but its long neck and tail, and wide, menacing wings, made it seem three or four times greater.

Gorrh gathered down, and the Chaldallions swore dirty love to the gods. Toron froze with his arms craned backwards, and was nearly clubbed by Vail as she brought the bow around. Scree shifted and clattered as the wyrm slipped down from the ungolden heap on which it had lain stealthing, and though the thoftship had been startled by its appearance so near to them, it was clear from the beginning the wyrm meant to move past them. The many plates of its hide, which overlapped with its movements and did not fold, looked to be of the same stuff as Melgard's shieldwear, and blushed the same paradoxical brilliance, like a dark cloud with a storm playing within. It told two things right away, this shared cladding— that the dragon was Melgard's steed, and that Melgard's shieldwear likely had the same knack for going unseen. As for whether this walking weapon had been welded together in a workshop or hatched from a steelshelled egg, no one who beheld it here could tell or fathom. All that mattered was the arsenal with which it rigged itself from one corner of its body to the other—weapons which kept unsheathing and unholstering even as it walked—until the animal itself became more their hub than their wielder, and tottered beneath the overkill like a peacock waddling beneath the weight of its own magnificence.

The troll had seen it too—indeed, he had been one of the first—and had stiffened in midstrike, but it was hard to say whether it was the sight of the armed horror that had arrested him or the blade Melgard had shoved up under his chin. With one hand, without looking, the knight threw back his free palm, and the wyrm halted its advance. It stood there, one foot still raised even under the tonnage of its weaponry, and waited. Its body whirred softly as it balanced.

Burgwards mustered behind the troll's henchmates, some in their sarks and others in unmarked clothes. Many teerseekers lent a hand, and griffons began to swoop down out of the flightgoes. A stakewall of swords and spears half-ringed the unhovely knaves and began to close on them, the law of Eksar cinching shut. They were told to lay down their weapons, which they did, but not before some hardheaded dawdling. One of them swore ears full of dirt, not for having been thwarted but for the arrow sticking out of his thigh. Its fletching was redder than a culver's eyes. Vail, though distracted at the last moment, had not missed.

As for the troll at the head of them all, he stood frozen at the end of Melgard's blade, quivering only with his breaths, and what was left of his anger. His hands, having been raised to strike, were now open-fingered.

"Yaw said one more blow," the troll squeezed out carefully, as though his chin were a peeled egg upon a knifetip. "One's not fallen, care taw reckon."

The helmsrerd did not reply, and griffmen alighted roughly on both sides of them. The griffons smelled the fight cooling, and mourned the lost slaughter with croaks and down-bobbing heads. To the stenchless wyrm up the hill they gave little heed, as though blind by the nose, or to things standing still. Their riders slid from their saddles with dree-dampening shackles at the ready. The thinness of those irons was laughworthy—they seemed more bangles than bonds—but the metal of them was glassy and black, like the stone spat by firebergs once polished. The sight of them swallowed mirth as well as their touch did dree, and the look of them told the difference between shackles that had been enchanted once built, and those shaped straight from dreeish ores themselves. That the watchmen near the avenfeld had kept such dearbought gear at hand said they had been waiting for this kind of thing to happen, or that it already had.

For a wink, it seemed the young wards would slap a set on Melgard too, but with an upward nod the knight banished his visor, and showed them a face so dour and righteous that no further wrongdoing could be done. The burgwards nonetheless looked toward the weaponfraught dragon, which stirred only as the breeze caught its wings, and seemed if anything even more unsettling now that life looked to have fled it. Others watched the beast from their griffs high above, keeping a good stretch away, though it was clear to anyone who cared to send their eyes among the beast's bristling arsenal that there were things there that could shoot them all down like gamebirds.

Their watchfulness was not fear, however, for Melgard had been in Eksar a week, and those of the burgwards who had not yet laid eyes on the creature had heard about it, and all knew it for a steed loyal to a thegnly man. What none of them had foreseen were these hundred hidden claws now bared, and they drew back out of wariness, as from a nettled cat whose spells of fiendishness come in with the wind.

"Vigil," Melgard called out, and the wyrm's head gave a twitch. The glede of its eye flared back to life, as though its name were the pump of a bellows. "Vigil, stand down."

The beast took a step back, and the soft whirring of its innards rose to a whine. With the sound of twenty swords being whetted at once, a storm touched the steel forest upon its back. Blades and muzzles swung up and withdrew, some into slits unseen, others into housings beneath its hide and whose plates slid across their openings as hatches. Some went away easily, as tools to beltloops, while others such as the great barrels upon its wings seemed first to undergo lessenings of their own—their parts sundering and nesting, and sidling together like window sashes before fitting into the narrow holds meant for them. All the short while it took, the dragon tilted this way and that, widening nooks in its body at need and shaking down all the freight like a man making room at an eating match. When the last weapon was stowed, however, it was hard to say whether the process or the outcome made a sight more marvelous, for though small compartments stood here and there upon the dragon's body, everything had folded smoothly into its holds, with no sharp edges other than the feet and horns. What stood before everyone, and settled to its haunches on the grass, was something majestic and no longer meatmincing. Had the pokepig a knack of storing away its quills, and thereby shrinking to a third of its former bulk, it could not have done it so strikingly.

The burgwards watched slackjawed, as did the troll, who could not risk slackening his own jaw. The awespell was broken when the three companions of the troll's foe at last reached their friend's side, having taken wide paths about the griffons which stood still and bewitched after seeing Vigil demilitarize. They were young men all of them, younger even than Toron and the Chaldallions. Melgard shifted his footing a little to keep half an eye on them as well, lest they come at the troll themselves. They looked to have had their own scuffle, however, with marks about their eyes, and bloody lips. They called to their friend and fussed over him, who croaked back swearwords and showed no will to get to his feet. As for the two onlooking burgwards, they weren't much older then those four, and kept their eyes gummed to Vigil, the black shackles lowering as their arms limpened. Melgard called the helms back to themselves with an order honeyed by helpfulness.

"It's his girdle," said the outlander, "under his jerkin."

One of them passed the other his shackles and dutifully stepped beneath the embowering shadows of the troll's open arms. Gingerly he undid the bottom fastenings of the goon's sweatstained leather sark, drawing back the flaps to expose a drab, but no doubt dreeish, girdle. Dusky of hue it was, the thick tongues of its buckle shaped like fangs. A snaking of filigree that might have been writing wound about its three rows of holes, and the whole thing was cinched up so tightly that it cut into the troll's flesh. Beerflab lapped over and under it, thick and wirehaired, like bread dough kneaded on the floor of a dirty kennel.

"I'm taking this off now," the burgward said, and set his fingers to the buckle.

The troll growled like a dog whose meat is reached for, and Melgard put the sword a half-inch deeper into its neck.

"One more blow," he reminded, and the goon simmered down again. His thick wrists were locked in irons, behind his back in the Knaksish way, and the dreeish girdle of strength was peeled from his waist with the help of two other griffmen who had alighted nearby. The troll said nothing as he was spun and led away with his fellows, of whom there were six, but those men made enough of a racket on his behalf. They were heleths, they cried out, and the king's own guests. They had the paperwork to show it. The Burgreeve himself was beholden to them! Someone told them to shut up, and the crowd of burgwards built up around them, like more snow to a snowball, as they neared the doorway back into Eksar. The troll's scalp nearly scraped the lintel, and by the time they all went through, the avenfeld had given up half its folks. The griffmen stayed behind, however, and spoke amongst themselves. Only once the door had slammed shut did Melgard fully lower his sword and turn to the friends behind him.

Laying down his weapon, the knight knelt.

"Where does it hurt?" he asked the wounded man. His voice was grave.

"Pride ain't too good."

"I should hope not," muttered one of the man's friends, a knobby-nosed fellow with black locks and a beard red as rust. "We told you not to fight him again. You could see it in their eyes they had something up their sleeves."

"Or under their jerkins," said another, who at once looked sorry for his lame wit. He shook his head and looked off down the valley, his eyes gathering shine. "Blast it, Rinse. I'd a bad feeling about today. We ought to've stayed at the inn. I ought to've said some-thing."

Another man, the smallest of them, and beardless, swatted him in the ear. "Shut your upper hole, Ath. You're already putting him in the ground. He's beaten up, is all."

"Yeah, beaten up," the wounded man snarled. "Like a sack of whelps beaten up against a wall. Having a hard time getting my legs to answer me." He roared then, and nearly sat up with the strength of it. "Where were you three sheepsarthers!? Where were you!? How about you, Melgard!? Up here playing with your bow." He fell back again and fought back sobs.

The one called Ath leapt up and began to walk in fretful rings. In the meantime, Melgard had somehow removed his gauntlets, and was working his way up the man's legs, feeling the bones and looking towards the waist as a threshold he did not wish to have to cross.

Toron watched them and listened, and though he felt somehow drawn to their plight, he knew not what he might do to make anything better. His thoftship seemed likeminded, and stood emptily milling, all but for Gorrh, whose mind was nailed to Vigil. Things built like beasts and given souls by dreecraft were not unknown to the tuskcat, but never before had he been so close to such a thing, and so nakedly startled. With Vail, that made for two slaps to his nose in two days, and showed the stakes between Heronlife and the Outsiders whose dreeish ways blunted every what the Heron had honed in them.

So bewildered was the thoftship by what had happened, or might have, that they hardly heeded the four griffmen who came up to them, leading their steeds by the bridles. If they did, they mistook the meaning of their approach for something friendly, and missed the shackles the burgwards had fished out for the meeting.

"You will all come with us," their headman told them. He was no small fry and looked Toron head-on. Nor, however, was he any Justinian, and even a child could tell that the lawman begrudged the Sumo that manliness. Such ill will, said his simmer, was not to be trifled with. He'd already helped to shackle one thurse today.

"For what?" Toron demanded, but he already knew the answer.

"Dreebreach. All of you."

Kurtisian snorted. "Even the cat?"

Gorrh growled, having at last found something to pull him away from Vigil. He stalked the griffons without taking a step, and the black hearts of his eyes grew full. The griffons were unruffled. There were four of them, and the tuskcat, however great his might, could not take all of them.

The headman ignored Kurtisian's remark and sent his eyes to the *Carno*.

"You want it?" Kurtisian said. "Here."

"Get that sidnish thing away from me. Lay it on the ground and put your hands behind you."

"Well if I do that," the fuhrbido returned cheekily, "you won't be able to see what I'm doing with them."

One of the other helms spoke up, asking who it was that was making the ground shake. He looked hard at Justinian.

"Lucky guess," said the priest. "It'll take a moment to stop it."

"You'll stop it now."

Justinian's nostrils grew bullish. "Son, believe me, I haven't done a thing yet. Every rock these walls have dammed up, it's begging to be let out. I can hear them, all lowing like a herd in a burning barn. Rocks came from the heart of the earth, see, and they all want to go back home. At the very least, they want to hug the ground, press their ears to the door. I could have brought down this whole slope with two taps of my little toe, but I haven't."

"You too," the headman told him. "Hands behind you. And that neckring—take it off."

Justinian played the dimwit. "Well, lord, I can't do that with my hands behind my back."

Said the first burgward, "take it off before you put your hands behind your back."

"See, that's kind of difficult to do too," Justinian replied, "because my arms are so big. I can't reach behind my own neck. Look."

"Then spin the ring around until the clasp is in front."

"Like this?" He dragged the shimmering Allmetal from one side of his collarbone to the other.

"No."

He was making gulls of two of the burgwards, but the other two were having none of it. They dropped their shackles and went for their swords, and Toron, burnt out and fed up, went for his. His thoftship had done nothing wrong, and if they were going to be taken in so roughly, he would give that deed some fitness. The sight of him drawing inflamed the headman to hatred, and both gnashed for the chop, but two voices stayed their fray, one cry from each side.

One belonged to Vail, who having thrown down the bow, ripped aside her wriels. Her elfshine burst forth, and the strength of it was reckless with desperation. It was from fear that she did it, she later told them. Fear of their chains—and of their laws and judges whose ways were unknown to her—which were to be fled with every wile if they were at all like those of her homeWhere. Onto the embers of her elfshine she had upended the whole flagon of her dreeish essence. It did not so much flare up as explode, and such radiance, like the sunlight, no eyes of flesh had been made to endure.

All those who looked were forcefed the lotus of its glammer, filled to strangling with it, of a creature seeded and fullblown with eldritch and perilous beauty. They felt the fight leave them, flashsteamed by the heat. Had they looked a blink longer, their blood woud have boiled in it, and their minds had cooked, their souls forever slack to the leash of thralldom.

But the other voice vied with it, whose manfulness was its counterpart. That other was the helmsrerd, and it seized them like the hands of an Allfather knelt to set them straight.

"No," it told the burgwards. "You will not take these people away. Not for my sake, and not for justice, whose blindness is not so blind as this."

They watched, stunned and shamed, as Melgard strode towards them. His gauntlets had been restored, his visor again had been lowered, and his face was nothing but a mirror. Like a wingless errandghost he seemed, saintly and impervious. The burgwards, foreweakened by Vail, were sapped by his words, and they stood like castaways after a deadening swim to shore. Their drawn swords fell like hewn weeds, their tips sticking into the dirt. Vail, her own sway in slack, stooped to retrieve the bow, and regathered her wriels against her face as a barechested woman might do her bodice.

"They're—" the headman began, then broke off. Half his winters looked to have been lost in the undoing of his anger, and he seemed a meaty manchild in borrowed gear. He pointed weakly at the *Carno.* "It's Dreebreach."

"That had already been done," quoth the helmsrerd, "and the culprit has been led away. There is no breaking the same breech, least of all for those who have leapt in to mend it. Mine was the

greater part in it, and yet you did not approach me." It might only
have been a stray lick of the sunlight, but the sheen of his shieldwear
swam. "Why not, I wonder."

As he reached the outer ring of them, his visor retracted, and
Melgard removed his helmet. To see the aging man beneath that
stainless shell bled out his lordliness somewhat, but his look was no
less steely, and by then he had gained an upper rung. He cradled his
helmet in one arm, and put his hand to Vigil's muzzle as the
creature, shuffling along on its belly like a dog, craned its long neck
toward him. The sight and strange sounds of its movements upset the
griffons, whose open-winged rearing dragged two of the burgwards
to their knees. The thoftship stepped back, but Melgard did not
flinch, and instead watched the disarray like an inspecting captain,
reproachfully stroking his own, placid mount. The helms scrambled
to soothe their steeds, and in so doing lost all face, or what had been
left of it. One of them dropped his sword.

The headman brought his griff to heel first, hauling the hawklion
back down to all fours with a jerk so reckless, he was nearly caught
beneath its talons. Had it been a horse and not a meateater, he might
have followed up with a blow to its jowl. Toron and Melgard
wrixled glances as the burgwards slowly stowed their swords and
picked up their shackles. The knight's stealthy nod told him to keep
cool, for by now it was more than clear that these hotheaded wards
had taken it upon themselves to do this whole thing, and had not
been bidden to do it by a higher-up.

"Have it your way," said the headman, though he did not meet
any of their eyes. "But you'll leave us with the names of your inns.
And you'll give your free pledge not to leave the burg till the Ward
has given leave."

"The Stitchmeal Sark," Toron shot back. "In the southwestern
sheet, near the Gates." He had not yet put his own swords away, but
kept them pitched, draping his fingers across the upturned pommels
as a hunter might do his hounds' heads.

"All of you?" the burgward hazarded a sweep of his eyes. "And
her—?"

"Yes," Vail said. She still clutched the loose end of her wriels,
but the way she stood, and with one hand behind her head, she
looked less dishevelled than sculpted. If anything, vulnerability
made her even more perilous, and it was uneasy to behold how a
thing trapped might chew off its paw and step free even nimbler than

before. The burgwards shunned the sight, and kept their eyes down, even as wolves do when their queen goes past.

"I do not overnight within the walls," Melgard informed them. "But three of my companions will be at the Naughtaloss. The other, I fear, will be at the Heron's Church next door. I shall take him there myself. As soon, that is, as I have seen these friends of mine gone freely."

The headman opened his mouth to say something further, but seemingly thought the better of it. He nodded to his men, and they all made a strutting cockshow of getting back onto their griffons, from whose saddles they were only a little taller than they had been on foot. They said nothing to the beasts, but must have done something—the griffons' wings seemed to span the whole valley as they spread. With a few catlike lopes the steeds leapt into the brawny, loftchurning climb they called flying, and were soon among the flightgoes they swung into for one last bit of swagger.

With their retreat Melgard wilted a little, as might a man do given devastating news. His face crinkled into a wince, and he leaned against the mount he had been stroking. Their kindred armor rasped together, and the wyrm's neck wobbled as it took his weight. For a moment, he looked a rickety grandfather catching his breath at a stile, but it was a weakness soon swallowed as the knight forced it back down inside him like a draught of something scalding.

"You all right?" Justinian said.

It was something Toron had thought too meddlesome to ask.

"Yes, thank you," the knight answered, but as he straightened he bit down on his lip, and kept it between his teeth until his helmet was back in place. "My friend with the temper," he added, after spitting it out again, "he gave me a little more of a lovetap than I was ready for, that's all. But that's the worry with magical strength. When you're dealing with size and muscle, you can make a good guess as to how powerful something might be. With a magical item, you never know. That girdle, it was no librarian's backbrace. I would never have taken such a blow if I'd had another choice."

Vail brought him his bow, which he seemed to have all but forgotten. He did something to collapse it, then somehow clipped it to Vigil's flank, the dragon's wide, visorlike eye studying the newly come woman all the while.

"Do you need help?" she asked. "With your friends?" She looked back at the thoftship, who nodded their willingness.

"No, no," he said. "I'll be fine. Excuse me." But as he began to lead Vigil toward his fallen fellow, his gait was not right.

Everyone left in the avenfeld watched him, neither speaking nor stirring as he helped the wounded man's companions lift their suffering friend across Vigil's withers. That young man, who had never ceased his complaints, quieted down after Melgard leaned in to whisper to him.

The wind gusted a little, and golden leaves lifted from the grass. The fiery wells of the sky poured down from their cornflower heath. It all seemed so much dinge, however, with that silver pair in its midst, whose hide caught every bustle and shimmer, and threw it back brighter and more cleanly than the hands of the world that first shaped it.

"Hoy, Melgard," Kurtisian called out.

The knight turned, one foot planted to mount.

"Yes, Kurtisian."

The fuhrbido sent his hands toward the panorama, and by that gesture somehow framed its every wart and sorrow—that which was, had been, and was yet to come.

"Why are you here?" he asked.

Toron peered over at his thoftman. It was a strange thing to ask, and what had shaped him to ask it, he did not know. Maybe he had thought they would never see the knight again after this.

For his part, Melgard chuckled, and there was more to its sound than politeness. Something in the question he had understood, something dark, but for all its pertinence to the gallows, he kept a dreadnought spirit, however drained its maintenance left him. He finished climbing onto Vigil's back, and fitted himself in. There was no saddle but instead a recess like one, with wide open channels for the thighs and legs seemingly hollowed out of the creature's ribcage. There were no stirrups, but pegs, which stuck out like horns. In all, they received their rider so ergonomically, there could be no further mistaking whether Vigil had been built or born. Melgard checked his points, drew his passenger closer to his thighs, and leaned across that cargo like a batten. He secured one gauntlet into its grip, whose slots were found on either side of the dragon's collar. There were no reins.

Melgard looked back toward the thoftship, and his face was again a silver shroud. Vigil's wings began to gyrate, and the bystanders backed away.

"Is that not clear?" quoth the helmsrerd. "I am dead. And this? This is the Afterlife."

The silver sails began to blur, and their drubbing met the whine of whatever power drove them. Melgard and his passenger seemed as ghosts behind their flickering walls, whose gusting bedeviled the Knaksman's long hair and clothing. Dirt, but mostly hay, rose into a prickly cloud, and everyone within twenty yards sent up at least one arm. None wished to turn away.

With the slightest of hops, Vigil was airborne, his legs and tail dangling, his hummingbirdlike flight lifting him by the nape, with the wind playing no part at all. For the all the racket and flurry, it was the smoothest of ascents—no tearful god might have taken a soul to its bosom more gently—and when it rose high enough to cross the wall and rooftops, its lift shifted forwards, and the droning steed made a beeline for the Medthkirk. Hardly a glance did Melgard's fellows spare Toron's thoftship before following on foot, gathering up dropped gear on the way.

When at last they had gone, Toron put away his swords, and the weight of what they'd nearly done staggered him. His hand sought Gorrh, and he all but fell into the nook of his haunch. There he stayed for a time, his head against his arm, breathing the outdoorsy smells the tuskcat's fur caught like burs.

The walk back to the Sark was long and speechless. Though nothing ruinous had come of what happened, the thoftship seemed to find shame in it, and at those other plights by which they'd been caught unawares the same day. Eksar, at one time mellow enough to seem sleepy, now seemed fretted and folkstrained, its walls become too small for the hungry swarms that lodged behind them.

They'd sought the burg out as a stepping stone, whence the headlong leap of Bayerd, but little had they foreseen the dangers of the stone itself, and what they fallen into already.

They called it *The Itsslag*, the Men who first came upon it.

Even through the dust, they saw it essentially for what it was. They likened it to a blob of smelt from the Forge of Creation. And not knowing what more to do with it, they left it where it lay. The autochthonous thedes—the firstfolks—of Wottráma used it for rituals. Their writings, still undeciphered, can be found on nearby stones. What they did with it, and if it did anything for them in response, we shall likely never know. Nature has since changed hands, perhaps many times over. What phenomena worked for them—whether science or magic—will no longer work for us.

Nethrish dreemen discovered it on their own, and only afterwards learned that the locals already knew of it. Those wizards were drawn to its beacon, whose signature is neither magical nor natural, but quintessential—the muted radiance of some fifth kingdom which is grandfather to them all. There was no rush to claim it, for it was one of many such places in Ráma, some more promising—and better guarded—than others. And when at last they came, it seems they were disappointed by what they found. If not then, then after their experiments had ended.

At first, they sought merely to activate it, treating it as some sort of artifact, or a dormant cell. When that didn't work, they chipped shards from it, and installed them in constructs—in the pommels of swords, in the chests of golems, in the eyesockets of the blind. They powdered it in mortars and fed solutions of it to the sick and dying. They subjected it to lightning, to dragon's breath, and to that auroric combustion of mana laymen call spellfire.

Its energies hummed like a beehive, both the whole and its fragments, all of them in rhythm, and no matter how far we sundered the pieces of it. Its power, its potential for something, was unmistakable. But everything we did with it, every use to which we put it—nothing had any effect.

Time passed. For years we lost interest.

The annals do not tell us the name of whoever foresaw or dared to slice it in two. Nor do they say how it came into his mind to fill one half of its open geode with shimmering ichor, and to drown the black crystals inside. At first his colleagues believed it was quicksilver he had used, but when they learned the truth, the warlock's name was scraped from the records. It was no mercury that fluid, but errandghosts' blood. That he was able to get his hands on so much of that heavenly helver gives a clue as to his conspirators. He has since disappeared. One can hazard a guess where, and of the price of the secrets shown to him. They did him no good.

There was debate over whether to keep intact what he had done. But done it was, and as is sometimes so, great evil effected the breakthrough that scruples could not. Across its face, and in thousands of spots, the silver liquid dimpled and ringed.

Imagine the night sky spread before you on a table, but silver instead of black, and every star drummed by one raindrop. Every few seconds, some of them—say half—are struck by a new droplet and send rings washing out across the field. Some of these wavelets meet and stack, as they do in a puddle or washtub. Others pass right through each other, like wandering ghosts. They widen, these rings, but few walk the whole field, for some of the stars are as breakwaters, and warp or obstruct the wavelets that touch them. Still other stars annul the rings completely, bursting them like bubbles. A heartbeat later, different stars throb, and send out their own rings. Some do it quite often, others seldom. Many never do, or send them out so rarely that my eyes have never seen it. Some stars, when touched by the rings, answer with their own. There are pairs, or groups, that talk only to each other. At all times, however, the field simmers.

Their business is the bustle of the Multiverse.

It took time to recognize that what we beheld was a Wherescape—a kind of map of the Planes, or some shred of a corner of it, where the energies and forces of the Quanta could be seen to diffuse, and to touch other realities. Look upon it, and observe the hidden commerce of all Being. There are springs of purest force—here, and here—which radiate only, and others, like our own itness—which may be here, or perhaps here—which are irradiated by them. Whether a physical stuff such as a fire, or a spiritual value such as the Heronstroth, they all have their wellspring somewhere. Their essence flows into the emptiness, into the godless hinternaught beneath all things, and there it cooks together, and acculturates. Their confluence is the kitchen of worlds. And those worlds become the crucibles of their own essence.

We called it the Mirror of Wheres, our little tableau, this microcosm of the Macrocosm whose business is so hypnotic that its students must look away as often as they peer. It is not a portal, nor can we scry in it. It is but an observatory, much to the disappointment of those dreemen who gave their lives to its study, who stared into it until they went mad, till they swore they could see inhuman shapes hunched behind it, which stirred that empyrean cauldron, and licked its batter from fingertips a billion miles long.

When it became clear we could not soon wield what we learned from the Mirror, most turned away from it—for the second time—and put their work into more gainful fields than Wherelore and planar cosmography. We are not ignorant men, we the northern magi. But we are Men, and we are heir to shorter lives, and narrower ken, than almost every other thede our journeys through magic have come across. The devils, fayfolk, and Intelligences whom we dare at times call upon, or compel, to assist us, we know many of them reside offwhere, which laymen in their benightedness call one place—the Outside or the Otherwhere. But the wise know Creation to be manifold, perhaps to outnumber the stars. The dizziness of it sickens our mortality. It is too much for us to fathom.

Were all the grains of dirt and sand on Smað made into a single anthill, our world would be but one of its chambers, and most of us blind within it. Even with torches, with enlightenment, we might come to know only a few neighbouring cells, and what we might learn is more likely to humiliate than to uplift us. What is worse, we might lose ourselves, or be in turn engulfed by the chambers we invaded. The walls are there for a reason, and once perforated might never be patched. For that, dreemen would sooner put their gifts to the here and now, manipulating others, and piling up power, than to gamble it all against the infinity of the void. They have not turned their backs on the Mirror, but as before, ere the *Itsslag* was cloven and charged with angel's blood, they await word of something useful to their own ambitions, from those more patient men who keep watch, and homefires burning.

I of course do not feel as they do. But I've had a lot of time to think about it.

For these two years, I have watched the Mirror, and carried out my scholarship diligently. It is lonely, and it was not my first choice of projects, but it came to enthrall me, even as the stars did when first I looked on them as a child. I have done my best to add to the lore, whether through new observations, or by honing old—and I believe mistaken—conclusions. It is a little like doing mathematics without knowing all the numbers, but believe I've identified numerous material planes, and am well towards developing a method by which to tell planes of matter from those of energy, time, and space. I've spoken of my work only once before, at a moot in Kraterpol, to which I was summoned to speak on that method. I was flattered beyond words to be invited. I was never a promising student, having abstruse interests, and no stomach for politics. Once I began to speak, however, and was met with sighs of disappointment, it became clear that the Highwise had mistakenly believed I was heading towards a new kind of breakthrough, by which they might gain some control over the whole domain to which the Mirror was merely a kind of seismograph.

The most unhovely of those dreemen was a Wherewalker who saw no soundness in charting what he called the lawless and immeasurable. You seek to map the oceans on their own tideflats, he said, and in the wettest sand at ebbslack. The planes were too many, and too volatile. They observed no constants. Wells of their influence dried up. Their beacons went out like candles all the time. And whenever that happened, those less than gods were left in the lurch, trying to recall a color the rainbow suddenly lacks. As such, he said, the Wheres must be exploited, not explored.

The *Itsslag* he dismissed as a primitive oddity, likening it to a rod of glass pulled from stormblitzed sand. And the Mirror, he said, was useless, lacking the dimensions by which to tell even the configuration of the Wheres it portrayed. To the complexity it alluded, it was as a cavepainting—cultivating wonder, but teaching nothing.

The man was a pig, a trufflesniffer however pale and sinister, who stuck his nose into other earths only for the treasures he might find there. Like many, I suspect, the Multiverse threatened his selfhood, and cheapened his singularity.

Only a fool sees expendability in the myriad. Multiplicity makes something more precious not less. Variety is insurance against annihilation.

I went back to my work, dejected but not dispirited, the words of the naysayer whispering in the silence. Despite the Wherewalker's claim, I had never observed a Where simply to blink out of being, though their rings often hiccoughed, or were stayed for a time. From what I had observed, the dimples upon the field were more or less stable, though endlessly, and unpredictably, at play.

Tonight, though, the Mirror did something unprecedented.

It brought me to contact the Highwise for the first time.

Three hours into my observations I looked away from the rippling pool to reset my vision. That I peered into a stony halfshell of celestial blood all day no longer troubled my heart, but the monotony had never ceased to trouble my eyes. The walls of the observatory are decked for this, however, with colorful webs, and shelves full things to knead the feelings back into weary, silverblinded sight. I am still young, and have not yet turned to the goggles, but I find the gimbalthwart very helpful, by which I can observe the Mirror comfortably from above, and adjust my position with the wind of a wheel.

I prodded the life back into my eyes with the sight of the stuffed devilfish I'd named Fondler, looking him over from one arm to the last, and by flexing my eyelids for another brainful of tedium. I had been focusing on four smaller dimples in the Ans-Three sector—the rim of the Itsslag had been incarved with one axis of runes and one of staves on opposite sides, by whose coordinates we singled out specific shares of the Mirror. With the use of the Timekeeper, I was meting their exchanges, and found them to be passing their rings in circle east to west, as a circle of children play catch with a ball. Nothing went to one until his fellow before him had caught it. Such a thing was not unique upon the Mirror, but it was seldseen enough to warrant further study.

I sharpened my leadstick and waited for the Timekeeper to tap the top toe. But when I looked back to the Mirror, something ominous had already begun.

It began as a string of ripples drifting in from the edges. From all sides they came, and crawled across the dimples—as though someone had gripped the *Itsslag* and shaken it, only the ripples were not bent like its rim. Straight they crept, as banewaves to a long beach. Perhaps they were indeed rings, but of a scale off the map, and simply too great to show their curve. No dimple warped or stayed them, and when they met, they overlapped, but did not change their paths. They crossed the Mirror, and all, for a moment, was as it was before. Then, in the Thurse-Nine sector, the Mirror boiled. Just once it did so, producing a raft of froth like frogspawn. Then those bubbles burst. I felt the splatter on my cheek. It burned like ice. Their rupture sent ripples back across the Mirror. Again, no dimple altered them. And once they reached its periphery, the Mirror began to behave as though none of it had happened.

The only thing I knew was that I needed to let someone know of it, someone much higher than myself. Not those bastards in Kraterpol. Not the pedants in Eksar. Dared I go outland? To the trollmen of Hála or the sorceresses of Tarmateriza?

I could not think.

The Highwise of the Starbowl. The Black Tusks. They were not the most powerful body of wizards in Norráma, but they were more trustworthy than most others. They answered to the King, and I was, after all, a Knaksmen. At least I had been one, before dreecraft made me an outsider to most of Man's domain.

I scrambled up the steps to the seeing stone. I opened the callbook, but I bungled the incantation. I wiped the stone and tried again. This time it went through. The black silica swirled then crawled into shape. It was a man I had never met before.

"Yes," he said simply.

I introduced myself, and told him I headed the Itsslag observatory near the Oathshoals. He asked me how he might help me. There was menace, and impatience, all about him, but he kept his courtesy and did not spurn me out of hand. I told him what I had seen, and I did not mince my words. The Mirror might only be an instrument, I said, and powerless to manipulate the happenings it told, but to begrudge the tale its deafness were mad—tantamount to rejecting a soothsayer, or one's own eyes.

These were my preoccupations, however, and the wizard listened to them impassively. He repeated back to me the report I had given, nigh to the word, as though rehearsing lines for a play he soon would stage. Yes, I told him. That was it. Then he asked me something for which I was not ready.

What I had seen. He asked me what I believed it meant.

I stammered. My answer trailed off into nonsense. In my years as a theurgist, I had only ever been tested, and never consulted, by a superior. But the sudden flattery of it was like the bubbles on the Mirror themselves—bobbing up from the arcane depths like some useful salvage, glinting like pearls upon the slick, only to burst, and to show themselves devoid of all certainties but queasiness and fear.

The Tusk restated himself. "You are the nearest one to an

authority on the object, brother. What do you believe this phenomenon portends? A cataclysm? A conjunction? You must have some hypothesis."

It was neither of those things. That much I knew. The first pertained to one world only, the second to two, and for what I had seen, set against the godwearying immensity of the Wherescape, they were two words whimpered to a storm. I felt the air clap about me, even as it shocks beneath a thundersome blitz. Perhaps it was only fear at the ignorance I was about to profess rather than lie. Perhaps it was something else.

"I do not know what it portends, High One. But I am afraid."

IX

And so trapped between Sheol and Abaddon, he undid his flask, and poured out into his eyes the Well of Worlds, that he might see a way out. But all he beheld was a Catch-22 at the cusp of infinity, whose stewards were two, though their names be legion—Scylla on one side and Charybdis on the other, the Devil and the Dead Sea, Fire and Wormwood, Solar Nova and Cosmic Entropy. But beneath their raiment he saw there was only Etymon and Eskhaton, the Truth and the End, through whose gates every path must lead, and who will not be cheated.

- from the *Umbrantomia* of Mimsley
The Library of the Unwritten

A garden of weeds.
Breath without air.
The wealth of dead worlds.
Worlds without Men.
They were meanings dispossessed, countries without borders, pictures without edges or frames. What they signified, no fingers might point to them. Only minds could do that.
And the world had lost its minds.

He had turned the coin from Aftheksis over and over in his hand, and pondered it in the torchlight. He did not know whether it was gold, and he would not bite it to find out. It was something. Yellow as honey, faceted, and smoother than a first freeze. There was a waterfowl on one side, and a woman's head on the other. The writing was embossed rather than engraved. As with all the coins, he could not read it. He left it on the table and put his stein over it so that only the barmaid would find it.

Easy come, easy go. Well. Easy go, anyway. As a drinkpenny[1], it was as lavish as they come. The girl, were she thrifty, might not have to work for a year. More likely, it would get her into all kinds of trouble. That was up to her.

The stuff haunted him, that offwhere reaf they'd shaken from their boots and clothing on the slope of Sherk-narsk-wirth. It had

---

[1] *(AK)*: a tip; gratuity left at a tavern.

been their one reward, and they'd not meant to come away with it at all. At the time, in the waking swoon in which they'd been left, he recalled much less of how they'd ended up with it. Over the months that followed, as he had handled those unwelcome keepsakes, the other raven returned to him, as it were, and hidden doors creaked open in the depths of his mind, doors from whose sills no light had crept. Dark things crouched behind them, which the gold brought crawling—like the wights of plundered barrows, who wanted it back, and knew it to the last coin.

It bedeviled him, that orphaned wealth. Its craftsmanship mocked his menning; its writing wormed at his brain. Its faces were the worst. Whether of Men or of beasts, they stared out at him like things stuffed alive and lined up behind glass. How he might get by without it; where he might find more; hunger; cold; even beggary—these things worried him less than those faces. Though he would not throw it away outright, he wanted to be rid of it as soon as he could. He left the beerhall as the gleemen were beginning their song.

Leaving the beerhall.
It was his last memory of the living world.
Before it emptied itself of everything but him.
Since then he'd known only stale solitude, holed up as in shipwrecks upon the seabed of the Whenwhere, in whose sunken cabins are a little air, though more hell than haven. Why and how he had come there, he had no answer. It was all he could do to deem he'd drunk too much beer and fallen headlong into the Gungnissa, to be swept away underground and become tangled among the roots of the Timebriar forever.

The first place he found himself, he still had no name for. There had been no one there to tell him nor had he ever met anyone. It was a world of one, and such a world had no need of names. He had talked to himself for a while, tending to the garden of language in case a visitor showed up. But ere long the weeds crept in, and he could no longer tell them from the flowers. It grew unkempt, then feral. A howl and hello were the same.

It was a wasteland, this place, but it was no wilderness. The trappings of other people were everywhere. There were homes with plastic siding, and cars in the driveways—infinite, repeating rows of them, overlapping like the bellyplates of an endless serpent, whose length dripped into cul-de-sacs, and looped into crescents, and sprawled against faraway hillsides on which nothing grew. A single sun drifted past, and at night a single moon. The stars had been different. But these were novelties devoid of wonder. They seemed old already, and long owned, however absent the landlords.

He had met its like before, this civilization without tenants. But unlike Afthecksis, this one did not show the dwindle of ruin. The lawns neither withered nor grew. The milk in the fridges did not curdle. Instead of unpeopled, it seemed out of sync—its time forever troughed, like a body caught in the hydraulics of a river rapid. There was no change, neither progression nor decay. That he had become an old man in its midst seemed unfair.

It made even less sense that he'd never managed to escape this suburban hellhole in an entire lifetime, but he could not tell how long that lifetime had lasted. Whether he had sought its edges for years, or whether he had amassed all his decades in a few hours, monotony had blurred the difference. His life here was more a memory than it had been an experience—as brief, and as tedious, as his reflections cared to leave it.

He knew the place should have terrified him.

Quiet woods were one thing. There was a lot that might hush them, all natural things. Winter, for one, and incoming weather. A hunting cat might pass, its scent chasing away everything for hours. You might feel watched when the woods are quiet, but nothing watches you when the woods are empty. In the cities, it is different. The alleys, the streets—at night, they seem darker than any grotto, than any bower of deadfall. The banks of windows peer, haunted hives, like the exoskulls of dead spiders, crawling with the shadows of old, alien thoughts. When the woods are empty, there is nothing unseemly about it. When civilization is empty, it is the void that watches you.

And yet as he wandered there, and aged, the strangeness of the place never disturbed him. Fear, like a flavour, was a vessel upon a tide. Without change, there was no store of feeling to upset. What he saw, what he heard, what he touched—he perceived it all and felt nothing, as though his mind lay on a table, anaesthetized in a cell, to whose windows his senses pressed typewritten reports. When at last he died there, he could not tell it from torpor. The robes and scythe whose touch he'd craved fell simply as a gloaming, as a gathering of darkness imperceptibly slow, of which he was not aware until he'd sat up from it.

Where he found himself then was back in Ráma, and himself, neither elsewhere nor elsewho, but both in the lee of life's breath. There was change here, but no course—only the slow, dry scuttle of decay. In time he called it the Waning, and it was the last name he gave anything.

There he had grown old again, or simply waned with the years. At least the world had done it alongside him this time, and for that he felt a kinship with it that gave him some company. But unlike the world, which had neither a heart to stay nor a breath to smother, he knew they could not take that companionship to the grave. One would at last have to rid itself of the other, and he wanted no part in that contest.

As he'd felt the ache of his bones last longer into the day and saw the hair on his hands begin to whiten, he decided two strawdeaths was too many for any northman, even the only one left. He resolved to end himself, and in the only way like battle the last living thegn might devise. He would hurl himself from on high, and in the fall find his teerful last fight. It was the one foe left to him— the downpull of the earth—whose deathstroke was long enough, and thrilling, and not a slow smother like sickness or drowning. To descend fully armoured, a bearded star, headfirst and gleaming, and with the impact delve out his own grave, swords driven hellward, the final fuckyou.

He would do it from Awklindhome, within sight of where it had begun. It was a long time getting there. But at last he had come.

The light was hot, and settled like soot upon the burg. The dry trough of the Gungnissa gaped like a narwound, and the springs had long ago run dry. The bleached stavebuilt halls lined the streets like so many barrows, the tallest staring dumbly across the gutted thatch, over the unmanned walls and out into barrens. Among the trees' bony limbs, their hollow eyes found nothing green. No oakwerns leapt, no deer nosed the underbrush. Beyond the borders of that tangle, the ground lay bare and untrodden. Upland, lowland and midland alike—they were all one in waste, all a ruin of unstirred dust broken only by plant bones and pierced by the gaunt, crooked whorlberg of the Crown. The great, coiled range melted into a sky the hue of stone. What was once Eksar Arsash, elderburg of the last kingdom of Men, lay withering beneath its dome. No griffons flocked its heights anymore, and the sky was hollow without them.

A single set of footfalls knelled, ringing out not because they were heavily laid, but because they vied against nothing. They belonged to the Old Man, to the gangrel soul who had woken here long ago to find the world thedeless—its redlife reaped, its greenlife throttled, and himself the throwaway of that harvest. Born along by bones whose knees buckled with every step, weighed down by a rucksack hung with two rusting swords, he headed past the inn, past its rotted awning and warped-open door. Within lay the hall, and the hearth, and the stairway to the room where it had all begun, wherein he had roused from one emptiness to another, leaping up with all the lightness of a sleeper dismounted by his nightmares, and having his joys waylaid by a waking world much crueller.

Hobbling around he took some time to look the building through again. He did not know why. Maybe, beneath the ashes of his hopes, there was some cinder of longing—to find some token, some hint of a wanderer: a heel of bread half-eaten, a bedroll indented, a glob of spider's blow among the beams. He found no such thing, and he went along his way.

He had taken the ringroad nearly all the way around, much further than he needed, nigh to the westernmost Grenstead. Now he went back, turning north onto the innermost spokeroad and following it east back nearly to where he had begun. He passed through another burgyard and went until the ringroad was crossed by a street wider than any other in Eksar. At their waymeet stood a marker, and upon its weathered post was a crossbeam bearing staves.

Rinyarunyas, it read. Arsaskish. *The Boar's Run.* The writing stayed him in his tracks.

He felt his lips weave, his tongue shape his breath. Sounds came from his mouth. The letters burned his brain as he stared at them, sinking into his mind like a branding iron.

Of all the rubble of the World of Life, the sight of buildings he could suffer. To brush his fingers across the cheeks of a carving he could bear, and he had hardened himself to walking roads that once had swarmed with wayfarers. To look upon the soundshapes of writing, however, was something he could no longer withstand. With a wail he struck at the post. Its dry rot shattered. The marker fell to the ground amidst the bleached flotsam left from when the river had flooded. He watched it there, lying upside down between his feet, until his madness flattened out. He shambled away.

He saw the smear of himself pass in dirty windows, and he

kicked a stray pebble under a slouching wain. More buildings drifted past. Many were like open ribcages, their thatch gone or sinking like flesh, their smokestacks sticking up out of the bones of their trusses like spears that had rained down and killed them. He came upon a hall which in the Days of Life had been a merry stead. It had been the last place he had lingered before the Fergh forsook him, and he could not help but wonder, yet again, if he had done something there to earn what had befallen him. It was so long ago, however—two lifetimes now—that he could hardly call it back to him.

He kept on to the west and followed the road into the deadburg's silent heart. His eyes he drove skyward and dragged them through the bramble of lightfall. He felt the heat rake his brow, the spots grow across his sight. It was an old wont of his, done at one time in hopes of spotting birds or flyersby. He did it now only to remind himself, through the unease the deed wrought, that he still lived. To stare into the suns brought no other feeling. There was no bracing warmth, no pledge of new spring. Whichever daystars they were, they were long dead, their bodies crackling on the spit of the rolling skies. Maybe they had been unsouled on the same night everyone else had been taken. Or perhaps, having never been freed from their workspells, they had died of exhuastion, and simply drifted now, steersmen slumped open-eyed against the helms of their ship.

Not everything had withered right away. Even as a great star that, dying, spends its last bit of life in a selfsplitting burst, so did some things make a breathtaking show of their deaths. For many years after he awoke, streams had gushed like mad, fed by the melts of the deepening heat. Many of the Whorl's valleys had flooded when icecaps old as the bergs themselves thawed and came washing down the slopes of Teakenmaley. They filled the high tarn of Whitchwelkinsmere beyond its stony bowl and brought the Gungnissa itself to spill its banks and floodflats. For a time, Eksar Arsask had become a city of waterways rather than of roads, but the floods soon dried up. Firebergs had belched into the faraway skylines, hurling aloft their foul reeks and blitzing tongues of flame. Ash had snowed, and weeks went by without day. After long the black sky bleached itself again, and daybreak came back, but the heat had only worsened. Though the Old Man was sure that it had at last steadied itself, the world's fever was greater now than any the Days of Life had ever known. It was the same all year, with no winter between them—a Fimblesummer, but godless and neverending, and no Racking of Ranes to give it meaning.

As for the Heronstroth, its teachings had foretold the world would end with an even greater fight than the Wyeride of the Ozmen—when all the Fergh, good and evil alike, would come together as a single, mighty gestalt, and withstand the Dwolma of forgottenhood, the devourers from Outside, though the Here-now be broken beneath its hoofs. But there could be no such struggle without life to furnish it. Wherever it was the Old Man now languished, wherever it was he died and again, it lay beyond the ken of prophecy and faith.

Prayed as he had for it, there came no snow and no wind. Nor with the heat was there any cloud, mist or dew. On the upended wain which was the World, day and night were the only wheel that still turned steadily. But that steadiness worked no ease in him, for when the suns sank down behind the bergs, they dragged across the land a cloak of night blacker than the gums of Hell. Unlike the day and its searing suns, the night sky went unbroken by light. No moons could be seen, nor the wicks of any stars. For the first few years, he had dreaded the dark, which fire did little to banish. He'd shuddered as its gloom crept across him, its darkness seeping into his eyes and his ears like the embalming ooze of a bog. Before the suns fell, he'd fastened his back to a wall, or settled into a trench, or put himself anywhere else he felt at all shielded. There he'd awaited the kind of blackness that bedevils one's hearing, where every thought gropes for sounds, and every fear breeds one.

In such a state he had hearkened for any hint of stragglers. There had never been any, though it had been hard at times to tell the stillness from his own breathing. After a while he began to look forward to the night on the same grounds he once had feared it. The starving madness of his whimsy, of longing whipped to a lather—they pestered his mindsight selfmurderous, till he imagined that somewhere out there, something with a face prowled for him alone. But when the suns lifted again, he found himself as alone and unharvested as he had been the day before. His skin remained unchewed, and there were no tracks in the dirt to hearten him.

There was no fleeing the nothingness. He found the Timebriar dead, its ghosts gone with it. Everywhere he roved, whether among the bergknots far inland or the southernmost shores of the Rámish landbody, he found only a scab without edges. Not once in those long farings had rain rinsed him, nor had a bellow of wind blown dust into his eyes. Though uncanny, there was a kind of soundness in it. Such things seemed too lusty to happen here. Weirdest of all was that he had never felt one pang of hunger nor a dry stitch of thirst. Though he ate and drank things here and there, he found them dead on his tongue, which led him to believe he might be a ghost. Then one day he cut himself badly and bled harder than a ghost had any right to. Another day, he broke his leg. Both wounds healed in time, though he knew not how his body found the means. Sleep he still knew, and in it dreams, but those things only made the fickleness of this neitherwhere seem hateful, given to him with an ancient snicker. So it was that even to lay himself down in a painted room was a torment, howsoever the hues leapt at his eyes—with trees like green clouds, and uproarious blue brooks, and fiery blossoms, and rainbows of birds on the wing—he could not forget the godlessness beyond, hearing its croak within his few lingering needs, its slither through the marrow of his bonehouse.

For years that had wrung and at last dried him out, he had nursed the hope that somewhere, maybe deep within a grotto or on the shores of a faraway land, there stood a kingdom where folks like himself had been drawn. There they took heart in their fellowship and raised the last stronghold of menning. They found means to wall out the emptiness, to make it a haven of meaning. All that was good crowded into it, as things flock when the world has a single corner left. There, the body revived—food found its smack, and water its quench. Women. Women. The siren songs of the flesh would be welcome.

But the Old Man's lonely path went ever on, he slowly gave up his faith, and lived only because his heart kept beating. His feet had blistered in the search, and his soul had curdled for want of clean hope. Its last croak had come outside a hamlet, when he had taken a shovel and dug up a graveyard. There hadn't been many bonechests. Most of the dead must have been buried without them, bare to the dirt like seeds. It was not the way of Harandrishmen to lay their dead under the earth to be wormfeasts, but rather to ash them on balefires. So it was that the digging both sickened and wearied him, but he found not one body. The earth was just earth, and the chests were empty.

Up to his waist in a pit, he folded over and retched. What came out of him was hope, and he left it in the open grave. He knew what it was to believe that the only worthwhile thing left to do in the world was to find its loveliest place, and to die there.

The lonesomeness by itself he might have born without much fretting, but the lack of cold and hard work here had gelded him, and left him without those tasks and struggles that best hushed a busy mind. The fights to stay fed and keep warm had won northmen the proudest siggertokens of their menning, and shaped Harandrishmen from birth to balefire. Now that these throes had been taken from him, he felt adrift, lost upon a tale whose meanings, whose worth, turned every touchstone of life to salt. Whether he was a doll in some Thing's playhouse, or a mouse put to the untangling of a maze, the unfaithfulness of both the setting and his own body made it clear he was trapped in some sour bubble of the Whenwhere, and not in any world open to the winds.

He had walked to the heart of Ferine—or so he believed, since there had been no one there to bless or witness the feat—and come back from that dreaded land without having glimpsed so much as a crow. He had sculled the full breadth of the Sundarsund, thwarting neither kraken or maelstorm, and found on the Yonderstrands no fight to greet him. No friendly arrows whistled; no threats from other tongues. Within the soundless glades and skeletal thickets of that land, he came upon many grand burgships, but their only dwellers were forlornness and the wrack. He had reached Hála, the brotherland of Knaks, on whose shores the first keels of the Nethrishmen were said to have landed, and whence the Harandrishmen had come. At one time Hálish landholds had reached into the mighty glaciers themselves, those lockswallowing iceflows which peered between the starscraping peaks of the Wottrámish Alps into Knaks itself, and Harandril. But the Old Man had found only a flood, its menning all molten. How so much ice had thawed so hastily, he could not say. Many weeks he had spent ferreting through the halls that were left—halls that once had met warrens in the ice, and led down into underburgs, which were wonders, and bustling havens during Overwinter. Laid-open mouths riddled the mountains now—hundreds of them—like the nest-holes of mud swallows greater than the dragons.

Many were the lands whose names he never knew. Though he saw many markers, their tungs were shaped by other writing than the Knaksish staves, and no teacher could be hired to unriddle them. He had sat in the throne rooms of twenty or more athelings, and swum in mountains of their gold. He had slept in the beds of queens, beheaded the carvings of emperors, and smashed against kristal walls the heirlooms of Ráma's oldest bloodlines. He could boast of being the world's utmost man—its wittiest, its strongest, its handsomest, its wealthiest. Once, in a fit of madness in the royal library of Trebell, he had written out every one of them he could name. It was shortly after this that his eyes would no longer suffer the sight of writing, and he had thrown away the roll somewhere between Toronsness and the Firth of Toron.

One land he could never bring himself to see was his cradleland. Though it was not unwonely for Harandril to lack folks and burning homefires, the withering of its evergreens and the throttling of its creeks threatened, amidst all the uncaring that he bore, to show him something truly dreadful. No lowlands gray with pussywillows, no new grass wobbling beneath the meltwaters of spring—to see its sky without eagles would take the last of him apart, and there was enough of him left to know to keep away.

He had weighed faring south beyond Ráma, to see the lands of some of his lost thoftmen, but by then he was feeling his years and had at last chosen against it. He'd coasted north again, following the seaboard back to the dead strandburg whence his boating had begun, and eastered back inland on foot. Now, however many the years since he had left, he was here again, and the only thing that had grown since he had left was the reach of the waste.

The Old Man looked over the many shops as he headed further down the way, minding the shelves behind their windows and peering past the shutters. Though coated with dust, everything was still there. Silks and athelstones. Candles and yellowing lorebooks. He called to mind taking this way long ago, his steed-brother on one side, an Ignish woman on his arm.

The white hope of youth, so like a pearl. Small but hard. Shiny, with no edges. Built up and polished within the smiling oyster of childhood. Laid bare to the scrabble of the world.

He remembered the streetwaifs—or maybe they all had homes, and were but impish knaves—and how they would single out the elselanders, and try to pick their pockets. One of the more darling ones would sidle up with board full of trinkets for sale, all limed down for a hasty flight. Another would slip beneath the blind of it, slitting open pouches or snipping away satchels. Unless the tinkling of coins on the pavestones gave them away, the littles thieves were all gone before the prey knew he'd been plucked. He'd watched it done to others; none had ever tried it on him. He'd been a big man, with a wont to scowl and an ugly fightwound on his cheek. His swords were always in full sight, and his meateating steed did not look sluggish. He recalled passersby, their looks both fearful and overawed, this in a burg full of griffons and wizards and other things that tended to stiffen necks from turning. He was shy to stand out at the time, but in hindsight he should have been proud to cut a swath.

Another bygone sorrow, another insight past hope. Himself rushing down the street, stumbling, screaming, driven mad by hatred and bewilderment, putting his fists through the honeyglass, crying names into the shadows.

Being forsaken by the world had addled him, but being stripped of the Rine had torn a share of him away. He'd not felt its loss in the Other Place. But here, where he'd left it, it was as though he'd awoken with mind in midslaughter, his brain freshly carved. Gorrh had been cut away, as truly as a limb, and however he had done it to stagger off the butcher's block and live on, the chop had taken too much to overcome. His head had been gutted, his skull half-hollowed out, the innards of his wits too many to close off. He'd stitched them all in and let their drear mingle, puddling into a slough through which his every thought now waded.

The shadow of Awklindhome lay upon the roadstones, its edge like a crooked doorsill. The draining of magic from the world had left the dreeish house without its most needful thews, and at some time after he had gone, one of its thickest arms had broken away and shattered much of the Grenstead beneath it. The hole it had left in the building yawned, showing girders and other wooden bones. The remaining branches of the treeshaped tower hung unsteadily, and groaned. Their walls folded and buckled, the lath peering through wherever the shakes were gone. Behind the building lay the blocky halfberg of the Airy, still warty with the houses of once-rich men. Its gates, seldom open in life, were still shut.

He made his way across the burgyard, skirting the heaps of rubble and taking the two bridges across the dry gash of the Gungnissa. Both crossings had been spared by the fallen limb of Awklindhome and were still whole. He was glad to see it, for he would otherwise have had to climb down into the riverbed and somehow make his way out again near the locks. As it was, he had only to follow the wear in the slatestones, which marked the path to the thursish house's front gates. It led first through what was left of the garden, its trees open-armed like flayed fiendish skeletons. The carvings of thegns and elders still stood atop their springstone heaps, but the stones had not flowed in half a hundeld, not since the Gungnissa had dried up. The bloombeds stood beneath them like chests of dirt dragged in for the bodies. Where the garden had ended, the slatestones became choicer, and paved the path between hedgecrested halfwalls and the outer gates of Awklindhome itself. There were two such gateways, both open. He had left them that way.

The loopholes in the burgwards' booths watched him go through and cross the brown tongue of lawn up to the doorstep. His knees smarted as he went up the sprawling stair, whose path was cloven, and arched over the dry lakelet the building once had straddled. Little boats lay on its bed, oars still on their benches, the strakes fallen from their ribs. Climbing, he wove his way past the stone anlikenesses that stood on each landing. Like teerseekers they looked, doomed by the stony stare of some snakefiend within.

Turn back, their open mouths might have said.

Or come in.

We don't care.

His fingers brushed one of their footstones as he drew near to the front doors, and it broke away like snow where he had touched it. It had been dreeish stuff, that stone. Most likely these carved men and women had been watchers, through whose eyes burgwards peered from elsewhere. He recalled that the ground floor had seldom been needed, which was why the path through the garden was so narrow, and the steps to its threshold so cluttered with ornaments.

He looked at the dust on his fingertips, whose chesils magic once had held together. How came things to wear away without weather, and why had the wooden walls overlooking the burgyard fared better than this stone? There had to be some wherefore to it, some song he might sound out. Dragged out from its den, care twitched once, grudgingly, and crawled back into the depths to die.

He dusted off his hands and stepped past the doorsill of Awklindhome. Even with the sun drifting down through the hole left by the fallen steeple, it was dark inside the great hall. He put his shoulder to the heavy doors, and pushed them open a few feet more. His eyes settled to the gloom. Through the halflight, over a wasteland of floorcloths and housewares, he saw the lowermost steps of the mightiest stair he had ever beheld. In all his wanderings, he had seen longer and wider, but none more striking. Even amidst shadows and ruin, it scorned to seem less than he remembered. Like a whirlwind made wooden it twisted down from on high, rising the full height of Awklindhome and followed all the way by a ring of hangcloths many-hued. Each had to weigh tens upon tens of stone, but in the vastness of the well they seemed like so many ribbons let down for wishing.

In a spotlight girt by shadows the staircase slowly found its shape, and watching it the Old Man was confronted with the memory of something else, from two lives ago, as it was dragged from the darkness into being. The strength of the recollection shook him, and his hand sought support. He'd not felt its like in forever, and he knew he was on the right path.

But the rucksack dragged at him as he climbed, and his bonelocks nettled at the task. Every step up seemed a stroke swum down, which the pull of the earth, and the float of the body, seeks to undo. He had to fight for every treader, as though through the risers between them fleshless hands sought his ankles, and however weak their grasp needed to be shaken off. Around and around he went, paying no heed to the walkways branching off into wings. Light stabbed through their windows, and riddled their long halls with spearshafts of light. They seemed the throats of slain serpents as seen from within, their hides perforated by the spears of errandghosts.

Up and ever up he climbed, the light below shrinking to a fog, till he came into the burning, blinding flood of where one of its wings had fallen away. Through the yawn of it he looked eastward over the rooftops, over the landings and ledges and catwalks and perches whose muddled maze was broken only by the steeples and millvanes in their midst. A winged city he'd heard such burgships called, with two floors—one grounded the other aloft, the two seldom mingling, save when then upper sent its buckets into the wells of the lower. He'd heard the griping, but Eksar hadn't been so bad. There were no thralls, and there'd been no curfew. The frankfrith was in earnest. No witches were burned here, and doomed outlaws were not put to death before crowds. Since waking he'd felt sorry only for himself, but he knew now that Eksar had not earned what happened to it either.

Throttled and woebegone, its deadeyed menning lay faceup between the bergwalls of its bonechest. Maybe he ought to burn it, to put an end to its wretchedness.

He didn't care anymore.

Far away he saw the old Medthkirk of the Heron sticking up above everything else. How like a tree it too once had looked, and so holy to boot, with flocks of white birds going round and round, shimmering, like a ring of light. Dark and a husk now, its blessedness was gone, and it looked more like something it might as well always have been—a dagger, driven into the heart of the very world its Lord had sworn to protect. Whether the Eld had been better off under other gods was a thought that fretted him less now than before, which had been very little. He was but a Man, and could not undo the fall of a single leaf. Far mightier than he, and weaker, had been swept away all the same.

He had borne this in mind as the ache of his body became as ungodly as the land that would not let him ease it. Where no soothing worts grew, and nothing he had found on healers' shelves had been of any help, the years had ground his bones more ruthlessly than any ogre might have done, and left him nigh halt for days on end. Booze had worked for a while, until one day it hadn't. After that, he had drunk everything, hunting its poltergeists through mead and ale and every firewater he could find, but all of it was soulless, and turned to biting, dingy water.

Only a little further. A little further to the darkness at the top of the well.

The winding stair ended at a landing in the midst of a lightless room. He inched forward into its murk, and it took him a while to find the last flight of steps that would take him to the roof. Here too he made his way among carvings and other standing riches, at whose edges he groped, and against whose faces he leaned for help. More than a few things he knocked from their showboards and heard them break against the floor. He wondered what they were, set here in the highest reachest of an atheling's keep. The heirlooms of the heirless, the birthrights of those never to be born. The shards of them crumbled beneath his feet, and those he could not crush he kicked from his path lest they throw him.

He met a wall at the top of some steps, and heaved. The wall shifted, and light drew sills on three edges. The door budged with all the willingness of an old root. He felt something burst inside his shoulder. The door took that wound as an offering, however, and let him through. He stepped, one arm limp at his side, onto the uppermost roof of Eksar.

The bergs enclosing the valley were indeed far loftier than Awklindhome, but only from the ground one might tell it. From the roof of the tower itself, their heights seemed even. Higher than the peak of Shiremansairy lay the open landing on which the Old Man found himself, and he looked down onto the dry scalp of that halfberg, even as the highborn there had once looked down upon everything else. Of the buildings below, none seemed bigger than a fist, and he saw in their sweeping rows and spoke-fed ringroads all the orthank and foresight put into their layout. Beyond each set of gates lay the parched trough of the valley, which, as he turned from west to east, he could see nearly to its ends. The Swansbawn by which he'd come lay like a worm in the dust, while the western road whose name he'd never learned seemed little more than a thread—an iron stitch that had outlasted flesh it once had mended. Beyond its reach lay outskirts of the valley he would never see, with their farms, and dingles and lifeless hidden hamlets.

He bethought himself again of Aftheksis, and how the Dwindling, for leaving behind livestock, seemed kinder than the Waning. The Dwindling had been unlike the Waning in many ways, but in neither of his forlornnesses had he shaken the inkling that what happened in Sherk-narsk-wirth had had some bearing on this doom. He swore an oath with care's corpse to look into it should he leap to his death and wake up again. Then he put it from his mind, and from the windless heights of his dead menning's wonderwork he drew an emboldening breath.

The stairhouse from which he'd stepped was set into a hedge—a tall tangle of manmade bough-thatch that edged the open loftyard like the halfwall of a nest-rim. Though he could see through the hedge clearly, he would have to push himself through it, and he chose to ready himself now lest he snag at the brink. The rucksack he unshouldered and let fall. His old swords, lashed to the sack by their baldrics, clattered against marmstone tiles. His one arm still worked a little, though it would not go up too high. As it was, he found the strength to take his mailshirt out of the sack and to pull it over his head. It settled heavily on his collarbone and fitted very poorly, having been bought for a much younger, and brawnier, self.

He fingered its flawed steel. Trails of its sheen came off under his nails. He held out his thin arms and beheld the uneven lengths of its sleeves. Better stuff by far he had found in his wanderings. The same was true of his swords, whose dreeishness had brought them to awful ruin.

Good old Tuger and Mortha.

Chewer and Biter.

Both now toothless, their bitterness gone brittle.

The Old Man picked them up one-by-one and unsheathed them. Tuger, mangy with rust, left half himself inside the scabbard.

Beyond the girdling hedge of the loftyard his foeman lay waiting. He pushed through it, and its stalks gave way like rotted wicker. He made a path to the brink. There he looked down, and to his sunken eyes the buildings now seemed a mustered army. Its graying rooftops were as helms, its reekless smokestacks like a forest of spears. As for Awklindyard below, its weapon was its emptiness, and more deadly than any other. The marmstone crunched beneath his boots as he shuffled closer. Clods of them broke off and went down before him.

Fitted out for his closing fight, he toed the threshold. Very nearly he walked straight off. But at the last his will misgave him, and he drew back shuddering. A raven of min had come back to him just then, from two lifetimes ago, of when he had found himself stranded on a height even greater. His thoftmen had stood alongside him, and together they overcame something they could not have. That ghastly ordeal had made a laughing-stock of every fight and precipice that followed it, and this was nothing to unseat it. Though the world lay before him with arms splayed open, he could not, try as he might, believe it a beckoning. There was no fight here, and no good death. There was only selfmurder, whose shamefulness was one of the only things both Ozmen and Heronites agreed on.

To the Hells with them both, he wanted to cry, then to leap. There could be no sin in a world of dead gods. His Ozmanry was the lukewarm kind of Harandrishmen, not the blood worship of the Yoredrights, and that the Heronstroth had reckoned suicide among its Nine Hights of Unlife should bind him no faster here than a rope of sand. Yet it would not be banished, this upheaval of the æw within him, which angered him all the more for bursting forth from a lawhouse hollow till now

But then a lighter Min came to his other shoulder, and its whispering taught him the way around. His swords he cast aside, and his mailshirt he took off again. All three he threw off the edge.

Then putting his back to the brink and bending over, he pressed his knuckles to the floor for steadiness and shuffled backward, till his heels overhung the emptiness, and his toes were all that kept him from the fall. His thews stretched and his knees cracked as he slowly stood up again. He lifted his arms as high as he could. A smile ghosted beneath his beard.

He had played this game as a child, on the wharf over the lake down the valley from his homestead. A grizzled, rickety thing of unknown years, the wharf had always won—even in the late fall, and when he had fought it fully-clothed. That was so long ago. The thing had to have rotted away even before the Waning began. Though this landing was its stand-in, he begrudged it none of its former wins, knowing not how he could have won a game that only ended when he lost. Today they would win together, and his fall would become his uplift, come Hell or high water, though Walhall be shuttered and forsaken.

Having weakened for so long beneath the weight of his doom, he soon felt himself dodder, and the fall tip him toward it. He never yielded, but fought it the whole way. Even through the blitzing dim of all things coming to an end, he could now recall many a time making his way back home from the lake, soaked and shivering beneath wind-tossed pines, to dry himself before the fire, and his mother's sighs. These mins were dearworth, and spoke louder than any had in years. When all things were said and done, and for all his restlessness and teerseeking, his thoughts went back to his beginnings, seeking the soft hand of the boy, and not the nod of the hardened thegn. How those small fingers tugged at his lifelust even now, begging like an almsman for something to keep it going even for one more day. He hearkened to its plea, and for a heartbeat he wavered.

What he heard was richest music.

The kind that sings fiats to the void.

Its minstrelsy had met his ears once before, and like much of that time lain forgotten until now.

He arched his back like one racked as at last the downpull won him. His fingers curled into hooks, but no weft of the Weave did they find. Stretched but unbroken, he threw back his head to leer at his painmaker. Like a Northman, laughing at the spear that has impaled him. And with a last breath of this world, he tipped backwards. Everything leapt away.

His long ghostly hair reached after it, locks and beard alike.
What he saw was enclosed by that mad fluttering ring, whose ashen
flames were the balefire that burned away all that was dead in him.

Faces flashed, of everyone he'd known. They rose upon the swell
of a darkening sea, like lanterns of flotsam, their fire behind glass.

But it was too high, the heave of them, and they flickered upon
its surge.

And behind them something terrible, like the approach of a
wave onto sleeping lightless harbours, whose blackness rushes to
engulf them.

The pain and years loosened. A strangling rope gave slack.
Youth found its breath again, and filled its lungs.

He was somewhere else, somewhere dark. A whorl of murk lay
ahead, throbbing light like a ghostly heart. Its beating showed the
lines of a hallway. There was a breeze, and it was cold. He clapped
his arms about his body, which was naked but for his underwear.
Someone screamed from nearby. A girl. There were words in it, but
a storm crashing overhead broke it up, and he heard only the fright in
its trilling.

The hallway was not empty. Shapes inched into it—first one,
then another—stepping in over thresholds he mistook at first for
hellish gateways but saw with the settling of his mind were only
rooms. The first incomer swung its gaze towards him and through
the dim showed him two burning eyes. Their fire was not bloodhued,
however, but blue, and he knew them at once.

"Kurtisian?" he thought aloud, and his tongue was so much meat
in his mouth. "Kurtisian Chaldallion?"

"Thorn?"

The man he'd thought long lost to him was naked from the waist
up, which was not like him. On the road, Kurtisian had slept in his
black mail, which clad him from ankles to throat, and taken it off
only to wash himself. Here now he wore only breeches, and his pale
body shimmered in the blink of the fog. His thick locks, undone,
hung about his wide shoulders like a mane. They were heavy on
Toron's neck as the men staggered into one another, and less
embraced than beached themselves. The sturdiness of one, the
suchness of the other, was for each castaway an island onto which he
crawled shivering.

"What the Hells?" Kurtisian kept uttering.

Toron said something too, but he'd forgotten what it meant. His ribs heaved to keep his heart in, whose riot flooded his bloodroads, and his skin felt to stretch, as though his newfound youth had overfilled an old sack. Tears out of nowhere fell burning down his face, and behind Kurtisian's neck he looked at his hands, which were smooth again. He clenched them into fists, and thick ropes of his best years' brawn made their knots inside his forearms. All his strength had come back, and would see him again wield twohanded swords two at once. From somewhere in the deepest shelves of himself, laughter found some tinder. Its ignition felt weird in his mouth. His tongue wandered through his cheeks, wonderstruck through the giggling, and nearly tripped on his own teeth, all of which were back where they belonged.

Another foundling stepped from a doorway, and his body seemed to fill the whole hall. The way he splintered the light at its end brought a word to Toron's mind—*moonmurkening*—what Harandrishman had called it when clouds dimmed moon and stars. He'd forgotten it where the world had snuffed all those candles out. Justinian saw him too, and such a starving smile cracked the southerner's face that Toron knew they'd all been bled through the same oblivion. The priest leapt toward them, the Allmetal phosphorescent, one arm oaring out and scooping to hug her a bug-eyed woman along the way, who was so thin next to him she had lain hidden among the tracery of the shadows. Their compassion they heaped together, in a standing tangle of limbs and shuddering.

"It was a dream," Kurtisian said, staring down the lengths of his arms. Tensing the muscles and tracing the veins with a finger, he whispered it again. Neither Justinian nor Vail said a word.

Toron looked around him, at the walls, at the unmarred wainscoting and open beams.

The inn. The Stitchmeal Sark.

Indeed, they were here, but what he had lived through, it had been no dream or nightmare. He had suffered every breath and heartbeat of that dead halfwhere. The burning heat still lingered on his scalp. The snap and flutter of his clothing as he'd hurtled down from Awklindhome.

He beheld his thoftmen, and did not trust them to be themselves, for he had awoken here once before and found the world not as it should have been. He saw himself bound to a wheel which was going around again, maybe never to stop, till his soul itself wore away.

Hardly had that dreadful thought begun to sink in when an unearthly wail tore through the building. From somewhere outside it came, but like shrillest thunder its sound seemed everywhere—haggish, bansheelike—the guttering howl of a witch, hissing out from the oven in which she burned. No lungs of flesh might have made it, whose keening crawled into their ears, and to gruesome thralldom put their mindsight.

Death, slaughterful and ruthless.

Burgsteads put to tooth and claw.

Houses broke open like eggs, their living innards dragged out and half-eaten. The bodies of children bleeding into the dirt where they'd played.

The fiendish din of it brought them all to their knees. They clamped hands to their ears, and ground their teeth to mill it off. Hardly heard from open rooms came the tinkling burst of honeyglass windows, whose shards fell through dust drifting down from the beams.

But then the wail stopped, as though slapped from the fanged mouth that winded it. In its wake came a deep, throbbing whistle, which Toron could only liken to the dive of a horsegowk, or snipe. He heard it clearly through the shocked hush, and again, as though hunting after the evil thing it had dumbfounded. Hues flashed through the fog. Then came the yelling of many men, and the long, thickening cry of someone falling from a great height. Horns rang out, and bells, bells, everywhere. Everything in Eksar seemed to cry out for help.

At last aware that something was happening outside, Toron leapt up. At once he felt the quickening of the Rine. Its homecoming filled him, like five waterfalls leaping into a single pool. The floorboards groaned as Gorrh, his brother and steed, padded down the hall, more bewildered than any of them yet with hackles up, and bristling against the uncanny thing all about them.

Another scream, from very nearby. A girl. The same thing he had heard on awakening. There was a word, and this time he caught it.

Vaddi. Arsaskish. *Father.*

It was one of the innkeep's daughters.

As one the thoftship charged toward the light at the end of the hallway. They had meant to find the clutch of rooms where their hosts kept their own bedsteads, but when they pierced the murk, they found those rooms were no more, and nearly fell to their deaths when the floor led off into emptiness. Past the misty curtain, the southern half of the inn had been shorn clean away.

A girl stood at its edge. It was Sealith, the youngest. Where once her father and sisters had slept, there lay a great pock of a pit, into whose depths the thoftship peered from the open ledge of the inn's upper floor. Half a furlong wide that hole stretched, and down fifty feet, but with the cleanest of edges, as though carved out by a fishknife and unplugged. All that had once lain within its reach—the houses and buildings, the mill, the sauna, the trees, a great stretch of the ringroad—everything down to the bedrock was missing, without so much as a shred of rubble left behind. Its emptiness gaped up at the stars, like the open mouth of a corpse. The leaking of groundwater, and of severed rushes, babbled in its sink.

No one spoke as they stared across the gap, and saw many buildings like their own whose walls had been hewn wide open. Like the hollow backsides of dollhouses they looked, their insides split into rooms, whose inner reaches yawned black against pale walls. Hearthfires flickered in some of them, and stunned folks staggered about. Next door but one, a few tens of yards to the south, a splash and run of bright red stared out from white sheets. Someone's bedstead, it seemed, along with the someone himself, had been half-inside the ring the moment it had been carved away. He had not been the only one. From somewhere to the north came the cries and clattering of a horse pulling half a wain, a sound soon overwhelmed by the rumble of collapsing stonework. To the south and east, great tongues of smoke lolled up over the rooftops, flaming at the roots, and the night stank of their burning breath.

But for all the amazing wounds gutting the land, it was overhead where every onlooker's eyes were hardest drawn, where a clash played out whose bearing on the wreck of Eksar they would not know for some time. Something was up there, fell things, things swift and so dark that the night itself was not black enough to hide them. Ink against tar, they kept to the ditches between the stars, and were it not for the burgwards who fought them, and died, and for the winged, silver champion whose dreeish blunderbusses made the night wink dawn with every firing, none might have glimpsed them at all. As it was, the nameless things tore apart griffman and griffon alike, and made their bodies rain blood upon the burg they sought to defend.

But there were no flies on Melgard.

The harder he was put to it, the harder Vigil shone, as though friction were fuel to his brilliance, like a shooting star once it plunges past the lid of the sky. The fell things spun their web about him, and the wyrm's wings axed through its devilry. Their magics locked horns, two worlds touched wires, and each leapt arcing from the other. Still the fell things closed, and the shots of his weapons came faster, and faster, until their staccato resolved into a single roar, and the whitehot burn of their many barrels made a constellation whose name was Invictus.

"Fergh and Hern," Toron whispered. "We have to help him."

But as the orphaned girl they'd nearly forgotten alongside them sent up another brokenminded scream, it was all they could do to take her into their fold, and swear to keep her safe, all watching on idle at the warring of angels far far beyond their reach.

Nid yn unig y diwedd ond hefyd y dechrau
An Epilogue that is also a Prologue

He lay there awhile and listened tfo the downpour of the rain. It played its fiddlesticks upon the roof, the puddles in the grass, the thousand thousand fronds upon the marsh. There seemed no face of the world it could not find and turn to fun and minstrelsy. No thunder interrupted; no flashes tore its gray wool. There were no storms in Ignam. There was only the dampness, ever thickening and thinning, swapped up and down endlessly between the clouds and the wetlands.

When after a time the rain had not died down, he climbed to his feet and pondered the next leg of his wanderings.

Homeward, he chose. Harandril was still so far off, and he was unlikely to last the way alone. But he could not stay here.

He put his things back into his rucksack, tying his bedroll under the flap. His sword he uncovered from beneath some firewood. Two baldrics lay there, and two scabbards. Tuger filled one of them. He hadn't the heart to throw away the empty one.

He donned his cloak, then the swordbelts, followed by the rucksack. No matter how carefully he did it, the straps always tangled now. It was the lack of the other sword.

A sigh hobbled out of him, and he stepped through the doorway of the woodshed. Past the eaves he drew his hood, and the mist, churned to cream by the drubbing of the rain, was warm against his face. The greenlife all about him was explosive. The homestead and its yard seemed but a hollow in its sea, with raindrops rollicking on every leaf, and woodbine glistening on the walls its creepers engulfed.

He lowered his head, worried his footgear would not keep the puddles out for long. When he looked up again, there she was, staring at him from under a hood of her own.

She was not startled, not even a little. In her hands she had a dish of something covered against the rain. Steam crept from beneath its lid. Its smell was heavenly.

"You are away," Tesog said, peeved. "Wherefore? Why? The tale you owe is not told out."

He gaped down at her. "You know me still," he said, and nearly choked on it. "You still know who I am."

Tesog narrowed her eyes at him, as though what he'd said smuggled a slight. "Forgetting is not me," she said, and stepped past him toward the woodshed.

He watched her eyes leave him. A few feet from the doorway, she turned back again.

"Are you with me?" she asked. Her wet forelocks clung to her brow like woodbine. She was barely a woman, but had the bearing of a woman who always gets her way.

Toron's eyes welled, and something opened its wings inside him.

"I am," he said, and followed her back into the shelter.

"I am."

Appendix A

Glossary

What follows is a comprehensive, but not exhaustive, list of the novel's new or special words—including names, places, terms, idioms, and others—which the reader will have encountered in the text. Many but not all were given footnotes on their first occurrence, in hopes of promoting eventual fluency with the novel's language. In hindsight, however, the footnotes alone seemed insufficient, and a more convenient means of looking up a recurring word was needed than flipping back for the original gloss.

This is not intended to be an encyclopedic glossary. Many of the translations and definitions found below are far from perfect. Some words—such as *blead* and *bloot*—are much more complex than their entries suggest. Some reproduce the original footnotes themselves. Still others have been expanded to include information—as well as other terms—not found in the novel's text. This imbalance must suffice for now. Such an index as this threatened to become its own creative project, and to attach a vast new stage of work onto what was the novel's essentially finished product.

Not everything is glossed that might have been, and some entries may seem superfluous. Terms such as *burglife* were deemed self-explanatory or transparent enough through association with existing glosses, and do not have their own entries. Other words—including *aphelion* and *palimpsest*—can be found in normal dictionaries, but are defined here for the sake of convenience. The reader should also keep in mind that while the entries are itemized uniformly, the languages and their speakers have different characters. Speakers of the Braccish Allmal, for example, traditionally create compound words at need, many of which don't necessarily need glossing, but which lack the currency and semantic depth of longstanding terms.

For further clarification, readers are encouraged to consult the 'Languages of the Story', which can be found among the prefatory materials of this book.

Abbreviations

AB – Braccish Allmal
AC – Colonial Allmal
AH – Harandrish Allmal
AI – Ignish Allmal
AK – Knaksish Allmal

B – Braccish
L – Linguish
H – Harandrish
I – Ignish
K – Knaksish

Entries

Abaddon – (**Saffish Allmal**) According to Safish belief, Abaddon is a place of destruction; a bottomless pit from which there is no escape.

Abois of the Fosswolds – *Landish* poet of the first century of the *Kingdom of Knaks* after the *Onelatching*. Court poet of *Seagrim*. Also known as the *Baying Bard*. Known for composing the *Blavor*.

adderhide – (**AB**) snakeskin; reptile hide.

addersnake – (**AB**) venomous snake.

Adlergriff – draftgriff; the largest of *Knaksish* griffons, bred for their strength, and their hardiness in heavy winds and other foul weather. Called *Stormskyer* in *Harandril*.

æmettig – (**B** *unoccupied; unemployed*)

æw, the – (**AB**) natural law; an unspoken way of things.

Aftheksis – Both an extinct mountain civilization and its capital city, known for its marvels of engineering and metallurgy.

Aftheksish Reekgish – extinct mother tongue of the people of *Aftheksis*, traditionally written in the *Rekghnakghlokh* script).

Aglæcan þær grislic aglæca guðode – (**B** *There, horribly, one hero slew another*) a line from the *Orgeldream*, engraved beneath the oak carving of the duel between *Morgenmece* and *Blæc-hafoc* outside the *King of Knaks*'s bedchamber.

Airy, the – see *Shiremansairy*.

Aldessa – An *Arsaskish* maiden; eldest daughter of the innkeeper of the *Stitchmeal Sark*.

Allmal (the) – the common language of the *Kingdom of Knaks*, also sometimes known as *New Braccish*. Allmal is more inclusive with its vocabulary than Braccish, however, and lacks the same etymological boundaries.

Alleverwood, the – the *World Tree* of the *Heronstroth*, upon whose branches all the families of animate things are ordered and arranged.

For an expression involving the Alleverwood, see *scared off one's branch*.

Allmaller – a magical item that translates spoken language into the *Allmal*.

Allmetal, the – A holy medallion, marking the wearer as a follower of *Seisuma*, and granting him the powers of that *godtroth*.

almsdeed – (**AB**) charitable act.

Almuhit – both a language and a script; the alphabet in which a number of southern languages are written (only one of which is actually called *Almuhit*); *Biten al-Yasan* is another.

anlikeness – (**AB**) statue; sculpture; artistic representation.

Ansend – the larger of *Norráma*'s two autumn suns. The other is *Starmath*.

aphelion – point of orbit furthest from the sun.

aredman – (**AB**) rescuer; saviour.

Arsask – The largest province (*Medth*) of the *Kingdom of Knaks*. Because the *Isentron* is situated here, Arsask is also known as the *Crownsmedth* and *Kingsmedth*.

Arsaskish – of *Arsask*; the *Mannish* peoples (*thedes*) of Arsask; their languages.

arung – (**B**) esteem; honour.

arveth – (**AB**) difficulty; hardship; adversity.

Arwill – a *Booknap*; a *Bookman* at the *Isentron*; assistant to *Blacwell*.

arwydd – (**I** *sign; manifestation*) the gift of magic.

Ásatrú – (**Hálish** religion of the *Æsir*) the Hálish *Oztroth*; the body of story, practices and beliefs surrounding Oðinn, Þórr, and the other Gods of their pantheon.

Ath – a young *Knaksman* and *teerseeker*, a *thoftmen* of *Melgard* in *Eksar Arsask*.

athelborn – (**AK**) of divine blood; marked by greater size than normal specimens of its kind.

atheling – (**AB**) nobleman; highborn. Some distinction is often made between an *atheling* and an *athelborn* – the former a matter of rank and the latter a matter of blood – but not always.

athelstone – (**AK**) gemstone.

athlier – (**AB**) nobler. Comparative of *athly*.

athwart – (**AB**) across.

athly – (**AB**) noble; of or like an atheling.

atstandand – (**AB**) attendant; member of a retinue.

attery – (**AB**) poisonous; venomous.

aughtname – (**AK**) last name; a family name that is passed down unchanged from generation to generation. Few Knaksmen have aughtnames.

Avarnok –a cosmic executioner, as told in the mythology (*godlore*) of the *nyhhrdoiv*; a creature sent to annihilate those peoples who refuse to mingle with the world.

avenfeld – (**AK**) training-ground, exercise-yard. A comparable term is *playstow* or stadium, which is more specifically for competitive athletics. An *oretstow* or *oretfeld* is a place for fighting contests only, including what would elsewhere be known as an arena.

Avonlays – (**Shebrish Allmal** *river fields*) most fertile region of the eastern *Smilkameers*, known for its many orchards and winyards.

awklind – a tree native to *Teakenmaley*; a wetland hardwood with many trunks, some of which bow, re-enter the ground, and emerge nearby with leaves of a different colour than the other trunks.

Awklindhome – A wondrous tower in *Eksar Arsask*, built to resemble an *awklind*-tree; seat of the city's *Burgreeve*.

Awklindyarth – The centremost market plaza (*Grenstead*) of *Eksar Arsask*, location of *Awklindhome* and the gates to *Shiremansairy*. The *Gungnissa* cuts through it from northeast to southwest.

awklinnorm – a legendary lakesnake (freshwater sea serpent) of *Teakenmaley*.

awnsman – (**AB**) A Braccish term for those men who, by some blessing or gift of blood, are able to grow thick, mighty beards, and like to dwarfs and heroes of legend, might tuck them into their belts or weave them into braids as thick as wrists.

ayflood – (**AK**) – river.

azflesh – (**AK**) carrion; dead meat.

Baga-voo-doo – a *Norrámish* goblin king of legend; told of in children's songs.

Baga-wo-wo – a legendary *Norrámish* goblin king, known as the overthrower of *Yukki-tuk*.

baitgoat – (**AK**) a lure, meant to draw out a predator.

baldrish – (**AK**) jovial; good-natured; easy to like.

balefire – (**AK**) a funeral pyre, on which a body is cremated. The folk of *Harandril* use balefires almost exclusively, seeing the burying of their dead to be wormfood as inhumane.

banewave – (**AK**) a great, killing wave, whether tsunami or tidal wave.

Barrin – foothill-village of eastern *Teakenmaley*, south of the *Swansbawn*.

Bastet/Bast – southern goddess whose dominion is *kattids* and other felines.

bawse – (**AB**) a reddish-purple color.

bawsy – see *bawse*.

Bayerd – southern province (*Medth*) of Knaks. Marchland to the Unfondlands.

Baying Bard, the – see *Abois of the Fosswolds*.

Bayrdish – of *Bayerd*.

bearsark(er) – hide-wearing mad warrior, comparable to Hálish *berserkr*.

bebide, to – (**AB**) to command; to order.

bebode – see *bebide*.

benny – (**AC**) okay; fine; good enough.

berg – (**AB**) mountain. See also *highberg*.

bergcat – (**AK**) mountain lion; cougar.

berg-gap – (**AK**) mountain pass.

Beskak-lin – (**Aftheksish Reekgish**) ignorance; unknowingness.

'better the baddy the bleader the boot', the – (**AB** expression) the bigger your foe, the more you take home (even if you lose).

Bighthalf –an *elderburg* of the *Kingdom of Knaks*; a port-city of *Brac*.

bitelamb – (**AK**) something harassed because it is particularly vulnerable; an easy target.

Biten al-Yasan – both a southern *Mannish* people and their tongue. Biten al-Yasan is traditionally written in the *Almuhit* script.

Black Tusks, the – the wizard-*wereds* of the *Boarsmen*.

Blacwell – Head Bookman of the *Isentron*.

Blæc-hafoc – (**B** *black-hawk*) A Braccish atheling and betrayer, who conspired with *thurses* to overthrow the kingship of his uncle, *Morgenmece*. Morgenmece slew him in single combat.

Blavor – (**Middle Braccish** *The Blue Boar*) a lay of the first century of the *Kingdom of Knaks*, which tells of the rise of the *House of Knaks* and its wars to unite the *Braccish Empire* under a single crown. Composed by *Abois of the Fosswolds*, a Landishman.

blead – (**AB**) inspiration; enthusiasm; success.

blink, to – (**AK**) to teleport.

bloombed – (**AK**) flowerbed.

bloomlife – (**AK**) flowering plants.

bloot – (**AB**) sacrifice.

Bluharyn – The Lord of the *Eld*; *God of Life in All Its Shapes*.

Boarsmen, the King's – the king's soldiers; the royal military. Its divisions are known as *wereds*.

Boarsrun, the – A major street in *Eksar Arsask*, linking the *Grenstead of the Swan* to *Awklindyarth*. Called *Rinyarunyas* in the Old Arsaskish tongue.

bonechest – (**AK**) coffin; casket; ossuary.

bonelocks – (**AB**) joints.

bookland – (**AK**) land granted by writ rather than inherited, conquered, or bought; a kind of benefice.

Bookman – (**AB**) a scholar; an archivist. Also an official title; the Bookmen are the lorekeepers of the *Kingdom of Knaks*, and are represented by a bound scroll on the Kingly Houseshield.

Bookman King, the – see *Brac the Sleepless*.

Booknap – a *bookman* of middling or lower rank.

Booril – a town in eastern Arsask, near the border of Shebril; an *edgeburg*.

Brac – western province (*Medth*) of the *Kingdom of Knaks*; seat of the *Bracsriche*. Pronounced BRAWK.

Brac the Sleepless – An Braccish *atheling*, ancestor of the *King of Knaks*; also called the *Bookman King*.

Braccish – of *Brac*; the *Mannish* people (*thede*) of Brac; their language.

Braccish Empire – see *Bracsriche*.

Bracsey – island off the northwestern coast of *Brac*; also called the Brock's Eye.

Bracshof – elderburg of *Brac*; foremost seat of the *Oztroth* in the *Kingdom of Knaks*.

Bracsriche, the – Also known as the *Braccish Empire*; the dominion that would, with the *Onelatching*, become the *Kingdom of Knaks*.

Brakwyrm's Coils, the – see *Teakenmaley*.

Brasmat, the – see *Seisuma*.

brerdsmed – an alcoholic beverage, brawny kin of burned wine.

bringdrake – the courier dragons of *Canocshafoc*.

Briyim – a former *Rámish* empire (*riche*), legendarily lost to the *Unfondlands*.

Brock's Eye, the – see *Bracsey*.

brockwolf – (**AK**) wolverine.

burg – (**AK**) city. Not to be confused with a *berg* (mountain).

burg, to – (**AB**) to stay in a city or town.

burgreeve –(**AB**) mayor; ruler of a city or town.

burgward – (**AB**) guardsman of a city or town.

burgwise – (**AK**) knowledgeable in cities; street-smart (**AC** *urbsavvy*).

burgyard – (**AK**) plaza; city commons. *Grensteads* and *sigyards* are examples of burgyards.

burnaddle – (**AK**) fever.

byname – nickname, another name.

Byornsgrav – (**H** *Bear's grave*) A lordly manor in the *Smilkameers*; the seat of the former *yarls* of *Kyaribo*, from whom *Ivrik* is descended.

Byornsvey – (**H** *bear's road*) foremost hall of the yarls of the Kyaribo, built upon the shore of Timil Insee.

byrnie – chainmail shirt; hauberk.

canicula – (**L** *little she-dog*) bitch.

Canocshafoc – The *Kingdom of Knaks*'s country-wide network of messenger birds and draftgriffs; essentially the country's mail service. More commonly called *Knaks-hawk*.

cantrev – an administrative borough of *Ignam*, comparable to a *shire* in *Brac* and a *filk* in *Harandril*.

cantrip – the simplest of magical spells, whose effects are comparable to parlour tricks.

Carno, **the** – a *fuhrbido* sword; Kurtisian's weapon; a moon-shaped eldritch blade which he summons by name.

Cascade de sylve – (**Trebellish** *Fosswold*).

Chaldallion, Justinian – male human of Southern landholds; a *Sumo*; member of the *Unsung thoftship*; younger brother of *Kurtisian Chaldallion*.

Chaldallion, Kurtisian – male human of Southern landholds; a *fuhrbido*; member of the *Unsung thoftship*; older brother of *Justinian Chaldallion*.

chapman – (**AB**) merchant; seller.

chartwriter – (**AK**) mapmaker.

cheapday – (**AB** *merchant day*) a day in *Eksar Arsask* when the sellers without shopfronts, and the growers and craftsmen and others from outside the burg, are free to set up their stands wheresoever among the *Grensteads* they wish.

cheaping – (**AB**) trade; market.

cheapstow – (**AB**) marketplace.

chirm – (**AB**) cry; shriek.

chthonian – underworldly.

clethman – (**AI**) swordsman; mercenary.

coalbiter – (**AK**) a layabout; someone who sits by the hearth all day instead of working.

cockhanded – (**AH**) left-handed.

Coggaskelta – (**Bayrdish Allmal**) the mischievous, swashbuckling approach to battle exemplified in Bayrdish folk tales, more bent on humiliating one's foes than killing them.

Colonies, the – see *Southern landholds*.

comelitheness – (**AB**) hospitality.

cornstone – (**AK**) granite.

crampadder – (**AB**) varicose vein.

cride – (**AK**) spice.

culibone – (**L** *good bum*) male prostitute; rent boy.

culver – (**AK**) pigeon; dove.

Cur verbum 'lupa' et pornam et lupum feminum adsignificat? – (**L** *why does the word 'lupa' mean both prostitute and female wolf?*)

deadhead – (**AK**) waterlogged tree or log, of which all but a small portion stands above the waterline.

dearworth or dear worth – (**AB**) priceless; invaluable.

deathlock – (**AK**) rigor mortis.

deerjacking – (**AK**) poaching of deer.

derking – (**AK**) sect; cult.

deus – (**AC**) a god.

devilclepper – (**AK**) devil-summoner; diabolist; practitioner of goetia.

devilfish – (**AK**) cephalopod; octopus; squid.

devilgrip – (**AK**) demonic possession.

Dhandhar – a *psyon*; a former member of the *Unsung thoftship*, who was killed within a week of joining.

'Nid yn unig y diwedd ond hefyd y dechrau' – (**I**) 'Not only the end but also the beginning.'

Djinni Kick – an *Ultrix*; a long-distance flying side kick.

Doobla-badda – a *Norrámish* goblin king, known in children's songs and tales as a trickster.

doomer – (**AB**) judge.

Drac Ottumnar – a regiment (*wardwered* or *mong*) of the Knaksish Burgwards, known for their archery skills.

'drawing the longbow' – (**AK** expression) joking; pulling one's leg.

dree – (**AB**) magic. Also, rarely, used for a magic-user.

Dreebreach – The crime of using magic where forbidden, as in *Eksar Arsask*.

dreecraft – (**AB**) magic use; the art and practice of sorcery.

dreeman – (**AB**) any magic-user; a word used by *magentiles*.

Dright – (**AB**) the nation; the people of Knaks. See also *Yoredrights*.

drinkpenny – (**AK**) a gratuity left at a tavern.

drosen – sediment; deposits.

drotning – (**Kúlish Allmal**) queen; lady of the people.

Drotten – (**AH**) Lord (an archaic title).

dwaledom – (**AB**) willful foolishness; something made up to avoid pain; a delusion.

dwerrow – (**AB**) dwarf.

dwimmer – (**AB**) illusion.

Dwimmersithe – see *fairyroad*.

Dwindling, the – erasure-like phenomenon observed in Aftheksis, where things seemed to fade away rather than decay naturally.

Dwolma – (**B** *confusion*) a word that signifies the chaos of the unknown; often used as a synonym for the End of Days.

ealdorman – (**AB**) head of an *ealdormanry*; usually an *atheling*.

ealdormanry – (**AB**) an administrative unit of land overseen by an *ealdorman*; ealdormanries often have the same boundaries as boroughs (*shires, filks, cantrevs*, etc), but it depends on the history and circumstances of the province (*Medth*) in question.

Earthedder – see *fairyroad*.

earthfarer – (**AK**) astronauts, travellers among the stars and planets.

earthyard – (**AH**) farmland; cropland.

edder – (**AK**) vein; artery.

Edem merdam antequam perdam – (**L** *I'll eat shit before I lose*). The fraternal motto of Justinian's wrestling squad, uttered together in a private circle which is closed to the *exercitores*.

Edgebane – (**AB** *Sword death*) Ancestor of the *King of Knaks* and former king.

edgeburg – (**AK**) a bordertown; a Knaksish town close to the border of another province (*Medth*) or country.

effiat – see Avarnok.

Eksar – see *Eksar Arsask*.

Eksar Arsask – an *elderburg*, and *headburg* of *Arsask*, situated in the heart of *Teakenmaley*. Also called Eksar.

Eld – (**AB**) Age, Era.

Eld/Age of Life – The current Age, of which *Bluharyn* is president.

elderburg – an ancient city, one whose original settlement has usually been lost to memory. Most of the *Kingdom of Knaks*'s *headburgs* are elderburgs; *Eksar Arsask* and *Kraterpol* are examples of elderburgs.

elderthegn – (**AB**) senior officer; high-ranking or long-serving warrior.

eldfather – (**AK**) male ancestor.

eldmother – (**AB**) female ancestor.

eldritch – otherworldly, from another plane (*Where*).

elefil – elephant.

elfshine – (**AB**) the perilous *glammer* of a faywoman.

ell – (**AB**) a Braccish unit of measure; 1 ell is about 18 inches, or the distance from a Man's elbow to the end of his middle finger.

elseland – (**AK**) hailing from a different Knaksish province (*Medth*) than the one someone is currently in. See also *elselander*.

elselander – (**AK**) someone from a different Knaksish province (*Medth*) than the speaker, but still a countryman. Someone from *Arsask* would call someone from *Brac* an *elselander*. Compare with *outlander*.

Entogor – a large township in *Arsask*, located in the east of *Teakenmaley*.

errandghost – (**AK**) angel; celestial winged messenger.

ettin – (**AB**) a kind of giant (*thurse*).

Ever – (**AB**) great boar.

Evertux – the drinking horns of the *King of Knaks*, fashioned from the tusks of *Evers*.

exercitor – (**L**) wrestling instructor.

eyethurl – (**AB**) window.

færgryre – (**B** *terrible horror*)

fairyroad, a – an interplanar route; a *midwhere* road.

famsapping – (**AC**) an execrative adjective. Its original meanings have been debated; all of them are terribly offensive.

farecraft – (**AK**) vehicle.

farkind – (**AB**) exotic; foreign.

'fassy, spassy' – (**AC** expression) 'easy-peasy'; 'Bob's your uncle'.

feyness – (**AK**) imminence of death.

feck – (**AC**) faeces; shit.

feespilling – (**AB**) waste of money.

felefedborn, the – (**AK**) children born as multiples, such as twins, triplets and quadruplets.

fell – (**AH**) mountain.

fellreep – (**AH** *ptarmigan*) The fellreep, or ptarmigan, is a symbol of misfortune, much like the albatross. To dream of fellreeps fighting is to foresee a violent end to one's life.

Fenriswolf, the – The fell wolf of *Ozmannish* godlore; destined to devour *Woden* at the *Racking of Ranes*.

fenroot – a *Norrámish* swamp plant with an acrid, ginger-like flavour.

Fergh – (**AB**) Life; the animating force.

Fergh and Hern – (**AK** expression) 'O my God'.

Ferghsmith, The – See *Bluharyn*.

Ferine – The interior and frontier of *Ráma*; a hinterland stalked by nightmares. Buffered by the *Unfondlands*.

ferly – (**AB**) sudden; unexpected.

ferrow – (**AB**) a form of *fergh*; life; the animating force.

fayfolk – (**AK**) general name for a vast host of magical peoples whose domains seem to exist halfway between here and elsewhere.

Fiddick Morwa of Lakeland – *Bayrdish* warrior, undefeated in battle; known for never turning down a fight, but also for hiding his identity in order to avoid them in later years.

fiend – (**AB**) any monster.

fightwound – (**AK**) scar, typically on the face.

filk – (**AH**) an administrative borough of *Harandril*.

Fimblewinter – (**AK**) the monstrous winter of *Ozmannish godlore* which will presage the coming of the *Racking of Ranes* (**Hálish** *fimbulvetr; Ragnarökr*).

Five Western Townships, the – five settlements in *Arsask*, situated in the western half of *Teakenmaley*. The Western Townships are distinguished from other settlements in *Teakenmaley* for being particularly remote; two are accessible only by water, and one only by air.

flatus and b'latus – (**L** *blowing and bleating*) complaint and/or blather; 'pissing and moaning'.

flightgo – (**AK**) floating obstacle course in *Eksar Arsask*, in which griffmen practice their flying.

fliteyearn – (**AH**) needless provocateur; shit-disturber.

flocklore – (**AK**) taxonomy; classification.

floorcloth – (**AK**) rug; carpet.

fnast, to – (**AB**) to blow; to blast.

folkfullest – (**AK**) most populated. Superlative of *folkful*.

Fondler – a stuffed octopus (*devilfish*) at the *Itsslag* observatory in the *Oathshoals*.

footgear – (**AK**) boots, footwear.

forgettery – (**AK**) oubliette; the depths of a dungeon in which one is forgotten and left to die.

forlornlands – the haunted ruins along the western coast of *Ráma* below *Trebell*, said to be the *midwhere* kingdoms of faeries and other outsiders.

Fosswolds – a region of southern *Landon*, known for its natural splendor.

fra – (**AC**) brother; bro.

frankfrith – (**AB**) the common peace.

fraudatrix – (**L** *cheatress*)

frayn – (**AB**) question.

frayn, to – (**AB**) to learn by inquiry.

freck – (**AB**) warrior; hero.

freethorp – (**AB**) independent village; unsworn to any House or *yarl*.

Fretshaws, the – (**AB** *devouring woods*) a stretch of the *Unfondlands* bordering *Landon*.

frike, to – (**AB**) to dance. Appears in some regions as *freek*, much to the amusement of elselanders.

frimdy – (**AB**) curious; inquisitive.

frithkeeper – (**AK** *peace keeper*) Boarsman who maintains peace rather than fights in a war to bring it about; some question such a distinction.

fromkinnish – (**AB**) primitive.

Fromship – (**AK**) Creation; Genesis.

frover – (**AB**) consolation; benefit.

frumth – (**AB**) creation; created things.

'frumth and ferrow', the whole of – (**AB** expression) all of living creation.

fuhrbido – an eldritch class of warrior-wizard. *Kurtisian Chaldallion* is a fuhrbido, wielding the *Carno* his blade and *Marat* his grimoire.

fulfilled – (**AB**) completed; perfected.

fullfremed – (**AB**) perfected; fully made.

furlong – Knaksish unit of measure, about an eight of a mile or a fifth of a kilometre.

Gaia – an earth goddess of outland *godlore*.

galdercraft – (**AB**) a kind of magic.

galdernorn – (**AK**) sorceress.

Gatherdsburg – town in southeastern Arsask.

Gecce – a former earldom of the *Bracsriche*, lost to the *Unfondlands*.

geomancy – elemental magic involving earth.

Gifts of the Eld – the qualities of life unique to the *Eld of Life*.

gildenbit – gold piece; the highest denomination of Knaksish currency.

ghost-rounish – (**AB**) spiritually mysterious.

gimbalthwart, a – (**AK**) a nonmagical observation apparatus, suspended by ropes above the object under study, and whose position can be adjusted with the use of winches.

Gladhome – the dwelling place of the *Ozmen*, in which stands *Walhall*.

glammer – an illusory kind of magic; like a *dwimmer*, but more spectacular.

gleed – (**AB**) ember; glowing coal within a hearth.

gleeman – (**AB**) minstrel.

gleemanry – (**AB**) minstrelsy.

goddy – (**AK**) marked by reverence for gods, but not priestly.

godling – anything less than a god, but close to it; halfgods; titans.

godlore – (**AK**) mythology, but also theology.

godtroth – (**AK**) divine pledge; commitment to a god or gods; religion.

goldlax – (**AK**) a salmon native to the waters of *Teakenmaley*.

Gorrh – greater tuskcat, Toron's steed, to whom he is bound by the *Rine*.

graxroot – a mountain plant, prized by some for its gritty, peppery *cride*.

grede, to – (**AB**) to sound; to make a noise.

greenlife – (**AK**) plants; flora.

Grenstead – the market plazas of *Eksar Arsask*, of which there are nine.

Grenstead of the Gates – westernmost market plaza (*Grenstead*) of *Eksar Arsask*, onto which the city's western gates open.

Grenstead of the Swan – easternmost market plaza (*Grenstead*) of *Eksar Arsask*, which receives the *Swansbawn*, and onto which the city's eastern gates open.

griff – griffon.

griffman – (**AK**) griffon-mounted soldier.

Grindknife, the – (**Kúlish** *Grindaknívur*) an heirloom weapon of the *Kúlish athelings*; *Kween Oyvarr*'s own sword.

gristbite, to – (**AB**) to gnash one's teeth.

gud – (**H** *god*)

Gungbowls – (**AK**) deep-bowled pipes smoked in *Teakenmaley*.

Gungnissa, the – (*Gungnir's river*) middling-sized river flowing through *Eksar Arsask* from northeast to southwest.

Gwyr o bant – (**I** *people from away*). Used by the *Ignish* to refer to both outlanders and elselanders, but usually the latter.

gyensidey – (**AH**) referring to the kind of trust built not upon shared openness, but by heeding the other's boundaries.

Hairn – contraction of *Heron*.

Hála – northernmost kingdom of *Ráma*; usually includes the several independent *jarldoms* and commonwealths of the northwestern coastlands, most of which speak the Hálish tongue.

halfbirth – (**AB**) freak; a creature outside the natural order; a term of abuse in the *Eld of Life*.

halfMan, the – see *Shard*.

halsing – (**AB**) a kind of magic.

hamelock – (**AB**) sexual intercourse.

handshoe – (**AB**) glove; mitten; any hand-covering.

hangcloth – (**AK**) tapestry; curtain. **AB** *web*.

Harandril – former northernmost province (*Medth*) of the *Kingdom of Knaks*. Now a *neitherland*.

Harandrish – of *Harandril*; the *Mannish* people (*thede*) of *Harandril*; their language.

Hattic – a *Mannish* language of eastern Zaota.

havenseeker – (**AK**) refugee.

havenwick – (**AK**) refugee camp.

Havsikt – a Knaksish name for *Avarnok*.

haw – (**AB**) hedge; enclosure; partition.

headburg – a major city, usually the capital of a *Medth* or *shire*.

Headmedth –The province (*Medth*) of *Brac*, ancestral seat of the *House of Knaks*.

healend – (**AB**) hero; saviour.

heatblower – a wondrous appliance combining magic and engineering; used for heating in *Eksar Arsask*.

hearsome – (**AK**) audible; pertaining to the sense of sound.

heedern – (**AB**) guarded storehouse; secret armoury.

hekatonchires – the hundred-handed ones of southern *godlore*.

heleth – (**AB**) hero

Hellgrindel – (**AK**) one of the names of the wall surrounding the icy Hell of the Oztroth

helmsrerd – (**AK** *helm's voice*) The voice of *Melgard* with his helmet on and visor down.

Helsendir – a former earldom of the *Bracsriche*, lost to the *Unfondlands*.

helt – (**H** *hero*) champion; great man.

helver – (**AK**) blood; vital fluid.

hengest – (**AB**) stallion.

herewick – (**AB**) army camps; bivouacs.

Hern – contraction of *Bluharyn*.

Heronite – any priest of *Bluharyn*.

Heronlife – natural form of life, as distinguished from unnatural forms such as that of *outsiders*; characterized by the *Heronstroth*.

Heronstroth, the – the religion surrounding *Bluharyn*; fealty to the Lord of the Age.

High One – see the *Highwise*.

highberg – (**AB**) lofty peak; colossal mountains.

Highbred – A byname for *Shard*, hybrid.

highroad – a major road, usually leading about and between provinces.

hight – (**AB**) "who call yourselves/themselves…"

Highwise, the – the highest order of wizards; not an official organization, but a term by which others, including lower ranking wizards, refer to them. Individual Highwise are often called by the honorific *High One*.

himeliness – (**AK**) secrecy.

himely – (**AK**) secret. Compare to *dighel*.

hinternaught – (**AK** *back-nothingness*) the void that is the background and canvas of Creation.

hirdman – (**AB**) retainer.

hof – (**AK**) court; temple.

hofling – (**AB**) courtier.

hokered – (**AB**) fooled; duped.

homefast – (**AB**) domestic; homebody; stay-at-home.

honeyglass – (**AK**) an amber-hued glass, more translucent than transparent, whose light is softer than colourless glass.

Hopehold – a village in *Teakenmaley*.

horim shakulim – (Safish) bereft parents; parents 'widowed' by the loss of children (sg. *horeh shakul*).

horsegowk – (**AK**) a marsh gamebird; a snipe.

Housecarl – (**AB**) a title; a *thegn* of the *housewered*.

houseshield – coat of arms.

houseward – (**AK**) private guards.

housewered – the king's own Boarsmen; the guards of *Isentron*.

hundeld – (**AK**) century. Also *yearhundred*.

Hyba-jobo – a *Norrámish* goblin king, best known in song as an exile.

Hyge / Hidge – (**B** *Thought*) The first of *Woden*'s two ravens. The other is *Myne/Mune*.

icerain – freezing rain.

ickle – (**AB**) glacier.

ictus anteprimus – (Linguish *the blow before the first*). See *Lightning Punch*.

Idun – a lady of Hálish *godlore*, stewardess of the apples which the gods eat to maintain their youth.

'If mine comes back' – (**AB**) '*If I recall correctly…*'

Ignam – easternmost province (*Medth*) of the *Kingdom of Knaks*.

Ignish – of *Ignam*; the *Mannish* people (*thede*) of Ignam; their language.

inerd, to – (**AB**) to occupy; to take possession of.

inghast, to – (**AK**) to instill, especially in an unsettling way.

insee, to – (**AB**) imagine. Compare to *ween*. Not to be confused with **AH** *insee*, which is a lake.

irrumator – (**AC**) look it up; it's pretty bad.

Isabitra – (**Hálish Allmal** *Ice bitress*) Princess of Hála, who became

Isolas, the – see *isole scusawappi*

isole scusawappi, le – The *Shoeswap Islands*; the rocky archipelago, known for its soaring bluffs and manors, to the east of the Colonial mainland. Commonly referred to simply as *le isole*, and *The Isolas* or *The Islands* in the Colonial Allmal.

itrem – (**AC**) again; one more time.

Itsslag, the – (**AK** *Slag of It*) a mighty geode, believed to be smelting refuse from the Forge of Creation. Cut in half, its crystalline bowl filled with angel's blood, it began to behave as a *Wherescape*. Also called the *Mirror of Wheres*.

Ivrik the Byornlab – Knaksish *Wyehead of the East*; highborn of *Harandrish* blood whose family exiled themselves from that province and resettled in the *Avonlays* of *Shebril*.

jambiya – an exotic *elseland* dagger.

jarl – (**Hálish** *earl*) a kind of chieftain, whether of an independent *jarldom* or in service to a kingdom; in *Harandril* they were known as *yarls*.

jarldom – (**Hálish Allmal**) domain ruled by a *jarl*.

Jezi Baba – a witch of *Tarmaterizish* lore, known to fly in a mortar. Also *Baba Yaga*.

Justinian Chaldallion – see *Chaldallion, Justinian*.

kadu plant – the bamboo-like equatorial plant from which Shard's scabbard is fashioned.

katkin – see *kattid*.

kattid – sapient race of cat-people to the south, known for making excellent merchants and thieves.

Kawsvad – a town in *Shebril*, within sight of the *Three Ayfloods*.

khanjar – an exotic elseland dagger.

Khibak na –(**Ogrish** of the fairyroad) 'look again'.

Kilko – Town in northeastern Ignam, known for its library.

kingsburg – (**AK**) a royal city; not necessarily a capital, but a former seat of a king of the old *Bracsriche*.

kingsman – (**AB**) noble servant of the king; thegn; Boarsman.

Kingsmedth – see *Arsask*.

kinness – (**AK**) gender.

kirk – (**AK** *church*) temple; place of worship.

kith – (**AB**) acquaintainces; friends.

Knaks – either the *King of Knaks* or the *Kingdom of Knaks*. Pronounced both as KeNAWKS and NAWKS.

Knaks, the House of – (traditionally *Canocs*) Braccish family of *athelborn*; the founding House of the *Kingdom of Knaks*.

Knaks, the Kingdom of – *Mannish* kingdom of northwestern Ráma, formerly the *Bracsriche*. Ruled by the *King of Knaks*.

King of Knaks, the (title) – ruler of the *Kingdom of Knaks*, whose seat is the *Isentron*, and who wields the *Ringgear*. Also called the *Rings*.

Knaks-hawk – see *Canocshafoc*.

knobleeks – (**AK**) a tough, gnarled strain of wild leek (onion-like herb), known for its extremely strong flavour.

knocking stable – brothel; whorehouse.

Koostoma – a former inland kingdom of *Ráma*, lost to the *Unfondlands*.

Kraterpol – an *elderburg* in northern *Arsask*; the city closest to the *Isentron*.

Kris's Cusp, the – a region; the tip of a very long, undulating peninsula on the eastern coast of *Zaota*.

Kúloys, the – archipelago in the *Sundarsund*, a province (*Medth*) of the *Kingdom of Knaks*; ancestral home of the Kúlish manfolk, of whom *Kween Oyvarr* is *athelborn*.

Kurtisian Chaldallion – see *Chaldallion, Kurtisian*.

Kwall-le kwee-andeh – (**Vail's speech**) the name *Vail* gives to herself. *Vail* is the translation of this name.

Kween – (**AK**) queen; title of the wife of the King of Knaks.

Kyaribo – former region (*filk*) of Harandril, among the footbergs of the *Wottrámish Alps*. Only one filk lies further north.

lamh-alef – in wrestling, an illegal combination anklehold leglock, developed for use against opponents much larger than one's self; named after the *Almuhit* character the wrestlers resemble once it is locked in(Ⴥ). It is bynamed the *not-of-knots*.

landchart – (**AK**) map.

landhold – (**AK**) colony.

Landish – of *Landon*.

landmeter – (**AK**) a surveyor.

Landon – southernmost province (*Medth*) of the *Kingdom of Knaks*; a *marchland* of *Trebell*.

Langblod – (**H** *long blood*) *Harandrish* pony, bred for its hardiness to cold weather.

lanista – (**L** *manager/trainer of gladiators*)

lathing – (**AB**) summons; invitation.

lawdeemer – (**AK**) judge.

lawly – (**AK**) legal.

laxflesh – (**AB**) salmon meat.

Leafapanz, the – (**AK**) the great, disorienting woods surrounding the *Isentron*.

leal – (**AK**) bruise; welt; wound.

leaming – (**AB**) beaming; gleaming; radiating

learninghouse – (**AK**) any school.

lease-shower – (**AB**) an infiltrator.
lechning – (**AB**) healing.
leechcraft – (**AB**) medicine; a discipline dedicated to healing.
leethcraft – (**AB**) poetry. Also *scopship*.
leetlair – (**AK**) communal lair; a den conjoining others.
lestword – (**AK**) a contingent warning; an 'or-else'.
Library of the Unwritten, the – an endless library of the *Otherwhere*, said to contain every book ever dreamt or imagined in the multiverse.
Lightning Punch – an *Ultrix*; an extremely swift punch, too fast for most eyes to see coming.
limed – glued.
Linguish – a *Mannish* language, native to the southernmost lands of *Ráma* and its colonies.
Locky – a trickster-deity of the *Oztroth*, and occasionally of the *Ozmen*; as aspect of the Hálish *Loki*.
loneharriers – elite soldiers of the *Oztroth*; warriors slain in battle and chosen to dwell in *Walhall* until the *Racking of Ranes*.
longmeech – (**AK**) a Braccish longsword.
looknow – (**AK**) bulletin; posting.
lorddom – (**AB**) government; rule.
luterwood – a leaf-bearing tree of *Teakenmaley*, gray-skinned, known for the bright, yellow-orange colour of its wood and its knack for dampening noise.
lying fee – (**AB**) money up front; ready money.
magentile – (**Colonial Allmal**) a non-magic-user.
Magernatt – (**H** *meager night*) Rangers of *Harandril*, who wandered the wastes and maintained outposts in the darkest corners of that land.
Man/Men – human(s).
mana – the life-breath of magic; that fuel that is drawn in and consumed by the casting of spells.
mandrel – pickaxe.
manfolk – race of humans; the *Mannish* peoples.
manness, a – (**AK**) female human.
Mannish – pertaining to humans.
manshfretter – (**AK** *man-devourer*) ogre.
Marat – the grimoire of the *fuhrbido*, from which he learns his spell-like attacks (*Ultrices*).
marmstone – (**AB**) marble.

mathelcraft – (**AB**) rhetoric; oratory; the art of speaking well.

mathom – (**AB**) precious object; treasure.

mayly – (**AK**) potential; capable.

mayweed – (**AB**) chamomile.

meary (pl. **mearies**) – (**AK**) a kind of sausage.

Medth – province of the *Kingdom of Knaks*, of which there are nine (ten including *Harandril*): *Arsask, Bayerd, Brac, Ignam*, the *Kúloys, Landon, Pyndamir, Shebril*, and *Tymnig*). Medths themselves are divided into smaller units, whether regional or jurisdictional. There are many, many such units, among them earldoms, yarldoms, boroughs, *shires, filks, cantrevs*, and others.

Medthkirk of the Heron – a temple in *Eksar Arsask*; seat of the *Heronite* order in *Arsask*, and one of the foremost seats of the *Heronstroth* in the *Kingdom of Knaks*. Also called the *Sapling*.

meinwen y coed – (Ignish *maiden of the wood*) nymph; dryad; rusalka.

Melgard – *outlander*-knight; the master of *Vigil*.

melltith – (**I**) a curse.

meng, to – (**AB**) to mix; mingle.

menning – (**AK**) civilization; culture.

merestone – (**AK**) border-markers

mereswine – (**AB**) dolphin; porpoise.

merrow – (**AB**) tender; delicate.

Merry Yearsday – (**AK**) Happy Anniversary.

mete – (**AB**) proper; apt.

mickle – (**AB**) great in size; mighty.

middards – (**AB**) middle contents. Compare *innards*.

middenerd – (**AB**) middle-realm; middle-earth; the land of mortal men.

midloud – (**AK**) a consonant; a nonvowel.

midwhere – (**AK**) liminal; between planes *(Wheres)*; often used of *shadowtowns* and interplanar routes such as *fairyroads*.

Meem – (**Hálish** *Mím / Mímir*) a mysterious sage among the *Ozmen*, to whom a well of wisdom is attributed.

min – (**AB**) a memory recalled.

mindfires – (**AK**) inspirational ideas; learning that brings about epiphanies.

mindfloating – (**AK**) pharmaceutical.

minning – (**AB**) the process of remembering.

Mirror of Wheres, the – see the *Itsslag*.

mockfiend – (**AK**) dummy-monster, used for target practice and other exercises.

mong – (**AB**) a division of a *wered*. A company or regiment.

Mong and Poot, the – a tavern in the southwestern corner of *Eksar Arsask*, near the *Grenstead of the Gates*.

monkstow – (AB) monastery; monk's hermitage.

moonmurkening –(**AH**) the dimming of the moonlight by overcast clouds.

Morgenmece – (Braccish *morning sword*) Name give to two athelings; one a Braccish ancestor of *The King of Knaks*, who was forced to slay *Blæc-hafoc*, his sisterson (sororial nephew), in combat. The other Morgenmece is the eldest son of the King.

Mortha – *Biter*. One of Toron's two-handed swords, shorter and stockier than *Tuger*.

mujahid – (**Biten al-Yasan** *one who fights in holy war*).

Myne/Mune – (**B** *Memory*) *Woden's* second raven, the partner of *Hyge / Hidge*.

namelore – (**AK**) onomastics, including genealogical etymology.

Narfelds, the – (**AK** *corpse fields*) a stretch of the *Unfondlands* bordering the south of *Ignam*.

narwound – (**AH** *corpse wound*); a lethal wound – a wound that dooms someone to become a corpse.

Naughtaloss, the – a luxurious inn in the eastern share of *Eksar Arask*, next door to the *Medthkirk of the Heron*.

Nawpont – (Ignish *Nine Bridges*) The major bridges of *Ignam*, which unite the province (*Medth*) by roads.

needhouse – (**AK**) privy; toilet.

neeser – (**AB**) spy.

neitherland – (**AK**) disputed territory; a land forsaken or being fought over.

neithertwain – (**AK**) something that falls between categories; a gray area.

neten – (**AB**) beasts (frequently used of cattle and other livestock).

Nethrishmen – the *Rámish* northerners below the *Wottrámish Alps*. Descendants of the *Rámish Northmen*.

nicker – (**AB**) water monster; any monster.

Nine Hights of Unlife – The names of nine concepts (including both thoughts and deeds) which are anathema to the *Heronstroth*. Suicide (selfmurder) is one.

Níscel – a female *katkin*; member of the *Unsung thoftship*.

Niskers – *Níscel*'s cat, which she brought with her from *Zaota*.

'no good merchant has the stores that will match his spirit to sell them' – (*kattid* saying)

'no min, never been' – (**AB** expression) 'if you're not remembered, you never existed.'

nodus textoris – (**L** *weaver's knot*). A wrestling hold involving the opponent's knees, which when applied forcefully might dislocate both joints.

nonjuloft – (**Rivrish** *karst of memories*). A conception of the *Timebriar* which holds that the phenomenon reaches into the mind as well, and does not simply involve the external landscape.

Norráma – (**AK**) the north of *Ráma*; a geographical term (not linguistic, national, etc). *Knaks, Hála* and *Tarmateriza* are all Norrámish countries.

Norrámish – of *Norráma*.

Northmen, Rámish – a *Mannish* people (*thede*), the predecessors of the *Nethrishmen* who did not fare south. Very little is known of them, save that the *Hálish* and *Harandrish* are their closest descendants.

Northway speech, the – the old tongue of the *Rámish Northmen*.

Nothingmaker, the – see *Avarnok*.

not-of-knots, the – see *lamh-alef*.

nyhhrdoiv – a southern people *Shard* names as his womb-mother's, and whose myths name *Avarnok*.

nyosinger – (**AH**) spy.

oakwern – (**AB**) squirrel.

Oathshoals, the – the mainland portion of *Tymnig*, or, more specifically, its only habitable area—the low-lying finger of coastland reaching out toward *Pandressey*.

offsend – messenger, emissary. Also called a *send*.

offwhere – (**AK**) from another plane (*Where*); not from Here.

ofgod – (**AK**) an idol.

óhøviskur – (Kúlish *unhovely*)

Olallishmen – the first Harandrishmen to cross the Wottrámish Alps; legendary founders of *Timil Insee*.

on idle – (**AB** expression) in vain.

'One must howl like the wolves one is among' – AH expression.

Onelatching, the – the unification of the *Bracsriche* under a single crown, whereby the empire became the *Kingdom of Knaks*.

onely – (**AB**) unique.

onhere, to – (**AB**) to imitate; to mimic.

onput, to – (**AB**) to add; to augment.

Ontoclast, the – see *Avarnok*.

orfkin – (**AK**) cattlekind; bovine.

Orgeldream – an epic poem, the work of many poets, which tells of the bloodshed and joys of the earliest *Nethrishmen*.

ormete – (**AB**) vast; nearly immeasurable.

orthank – (**AB**) skilfulness, cunning and ingenuity, especially in matters of engineering. *Orthanksmith* is the Braccish word for both a master architect and an engineer.

orthankickel – (**AK**) an ingenious little thing, said of something done in miniature, or a tiny device such as a wristclock.

orthankship – (**AB**) the practice and/or product of *orthank*; can refer to both alchemy and engineering, including chemistry and physical products of ingenuity.

Ossamen – the Harandrish *Ozmen*; euhemerized (humanized) aspects of the *Oztroth* pantheon.

Ossalore – Harandrish story-cycle; the body of old sagas surrounding the *Ossamen*.

Ossa-Tor – a hero of the *Ossalore*; euhemerized (humanized) aspect of the Braccish Thunor and Hálish Þórr.

Ostasgard – a large township in northeastern Shebril, the seat of Knaksish administration in that province (*Medth*).

Osyus the Orchardlord – agricultural deity of the *Heronstroth* pantheon, whose idols are seen at roadsides throughout the *Smilkameers*.

Other Place, the – a mysterious suburban pocket of the *Otherwhere*, uninhabited, in which *Toron* lives out a lifetime.

otherland, an – (**AK**) a country of the *Otherwhere*.

Otherwhere – (**AK**) the Outside; general term for any external plane of existence.

outdale – (**AH**) outlying valleys; remote lowlands.

outlander – someone from outside the *Kingdom of Knaks*. Compare with *elselander* and *outsider*.

outsider – someone from another plane (*where*) or reality (*itness*).

overking – (**AK**) emperor.

overlive, to – (**AK**) to survive.

overmood – (**AB**) pride; arrogance.

Overwinter – the deepest part of winter.

Oyvarr – Kween of the *Kingdom of Knaks*; an *athelborn* of the *Kúloys*. Wielder of the *Grindknife*.

Ozmen – The foremost tribe within the pantheon of the *Oztroth*, including *Woden* and his family.

palestra – (**L**) wrestling school. Called a *wraxl* in Braccish.

palimpsest – recycled parchment; manuscript material whose inks and dyes have been scraped off in preparation for new writing.

Pandressey – The island portion of *Tymnig*, ancestral home of the *soarcats*. For its weird geography, climate, and inhabitants, Pandressey is believed to be a transplanted *otherland*.

'panned up in good ply', to be – (**AK** expression) encased in good armour; fully protected.

pantex – (**L**) gut; paunch.

pathice – (**L**) recipient of sodomy; the bottom.

Pedica me – (**L**) sodomize me (an execration).

pilliver – (**AB**) pillow.

pimmusk – (**AK**) a red-brown spice.

pokepig – (**AK**) porcupine.

prat – (**AB**) trick; wile; joke.

'Prime' – (**AC**) great; perfect (often facetious).

privy-ningler – (**AK**) outhouse queen; gloryholer.

psyon – a psionicist; a mind-mage; a wielder of powers such as telepathy whose basis is in the psyche, and not in magic.

pullula – (**L** *little hen*; *chick*) girl.

Pyndamir – a central province (*Medth*) of the *Kingdom of Knaks*.

Quicklife – see *Fergh*.

quide – (**AB**) phrase; verbal expression; way of speaking.

rackans – (**AB**) chains; bonds (also *rakenteie* [rackan + tie]: bonds specifically).

Racking of Ranes, the – (**AB** *torment of the Powers*) the *Ozman* eschatology; the End of Days of the *Oztroth*.

Ráma – northern continent (*landbody*) of *Smað*, of which *Knaks* is a kingdom.

Rámish – of *Ráma*.

Rámish Northmen – see *Northmen, Rámish*.

reaf – (**AB**) booty; plunder.

Reamswell, the – a ghostly, forested valley at the heart of *Teakenmaley*, where *luterwood* is harvested.

Red Collector, the – a Knaksish name for *Avarnok*.

redball – an *Ultrix*, allowing the *fuhrbido* to hurl spheres of concussive energy.

rede – (**AB**) counsel; advice; plan.

redlife – (**AK**) animals; fauna.

reese – (**AK**) a kind of giant.

Rekghnakghlokh – a script, or *staffrow*, in which the *Aftheksish Reekgish* language was traditionally written. An alphabet of straight lines, its only remnants lie among the tablets of the Aftheksish capital's lorehouse.

'Nid yn unig y dechrau ond hefyd y diwedd' – (**I**) 'Not only a beginning, but also an ending'.

Rhianys – female human of Ignam; magic-touched; late member of the *Unsung thoftship*.

riche – (**AB** *empire*)

Rimburg, the – the outer wall of the *Starbowl*; a ring of hills and low mountains, the outermost ramparts of the *Isentron*.

Rine, the – the bond joining *Toron* and *Gorrh*, of which there are four particular knacks.

Rinesight, the – a knack of the *Rine*, by which *Toron* and *Gorrh* are able to see through each other's eyes.

Ringgear, the – the five heirlooms composing the legendary arsenal of the *King of Knaks*.

ringroads, the – the four concentric circular roads of *Eksar Arsask*.

Rings, the – Usually refers to the *King of Knaks* himself, but specifically the five rings he wears on his right hand; the emblems of the *Yoredrights of the Bracsriche*.

Ringsmedth – The province (*Medth*) of Arsask; home to the *Isentron*.

Ringwall, the – the ring of cliffs and ramparts surrounding the *Isentron*, which is the outer rim of the *Starbowl*.

Rinse - a young *Knaksman* and *teerseeker*, a *thoftman* of *Melgard* in *Eksar Arsask*.

Rinyarunyas – see the *Boarsrun*.

Rioter, the – see *Upstormer*.

rissling – (**AK**) a lesser giant; a half-giant.

rizzing – (**AC**) kidding; joking.

ross, to – (**AK**) to explore.

rother – (**AB**) an ox; a bovine animal. See also *orfkin*.

roun – (**AB**) mystery; secret. Cognate with *rune*.

runk – the Chaldallions' unflattering term for *saraf*.

rush – (**AK**) conduit pipe.

Sallupus – A settlement of the *Southern landholds*; inland hometown of *Kurtisian* and *Justinian Chaldallion*, known for its vinyards and winemaking. Also called *Salpes*.

Salpes – Knaksish form of *Sallupus*.

samening – (**AB**) congregation; assembly; union.

Sapling, the – See the *Medthkirk of the Heron*.

saraf – a spirituous drink, akin to coffee.

sark – (**AK**) shirt; tunic; shirt of armour.

sarthe, to – (**AB**) to fuck.

sarthing – (**AB**) fucking.

saxknife – A simple Knaksish shortsword.

'scared off one's branch', to be – An idiom of the *Age*, or *Eld*, of Life; the *Bluharenites* postulate the existence of an enormous, *eldritch* tree (the *Alleverwood*) upon whose tier-like branches is arranged the hierarchy of all living things. From Its trunk extend branched for every order of creature, and upon each branch is housed the Progenitor and Archetype of each, from whom all living descendents draw their character. For a creature to be "scared off its branch" is thus for it to behave in a manner either atypical, or akin to some lesser type of creature.

scavenger's daughter – an implement of torture, which essentially folds one in half.

scoffblithe – (**AK**) showing good humour in difficult times; bouyant.

scop – (**AK**) a poet. Known as a *skald* in *Hála* and *Harandril*.

Sealith – An *Arsaskish* maiden; youngest daughter of the inkeeper of the *Stitchmeal Sark*.

sedefulness – (**AB**) abestemiousness; self-restraint.

seethed – (**AK**) boiled.

Seisuma – an elemental God of the earth; a minor *Power*, not of the *Heronstroth* pantheon. His followers, known as *Sumoi*, wear the *Allmetal*, and are able to manipulate the earth.

Seisumite – (see *Sumo*)

selcouth – (**AB**) rare; seldom met.

seld – (**AB**) hall; residence.

seldseen – (**AB**) seldom seen; rare.

selfloud – (**AK**) a vowel-sound.

Selfmurder – (**AK**) suicide; one of the *Nine Hights of Unlife*.

selfwill – the freedom to determine one's own path, as opposed to it being dictated by some faith or Power. Said to be one of the *Gifts of the Eld*.

'serve with blead rather than to rule with blethefulness', to – (**AB** expression) to serve enthusiastically rather than to rule timidly.

Sesh'mak-howrool – (Eastern Kattid *foundlings of the yellow sands*). Name the kattids of the *Kris's Cusp* call themselves.

settling – (**AK**) any settlement, whether thorp or city.

shabshuck – (**AH**) the savage *underthurse* known as a troll to most Knaksman; to the *Harandrish* and other northerners, however, *troll* refers to hulking, clever folk not too unlike themselves.

shadowtown – otherworldly, *midwhere* settlement; shadowtowns are known both for fading into and out of reality, as well as reappearing in different places.

Shamblemoors, the – a stretch of the *Unfondlands* bordering *Bayerd*.

shamshir – an exotic outland sword.

Shard – see *Thyrsabyn-Sairtys*.

Shebril – northeastern province (*Medth*) of the *Kingdom of Knaks*. Also a *marchland* bordering *Tarmateriza*.

sheenleaf – (**AK**) a pharmaceutical plant.

sheermilk – (**AK**) a sweetened variety of *skyr*.

sheerteeth – (**AK**) incisors.

sheet – (**AB**) corner; district.

shempy – (**AC**) silly; tacky.

Sheol – (**Safish Allmal**) A realm of the dead; the Hell of *Saffish* beliefs.

Sheolish – see *Sheol*.

***Sherk* (the)** – a poem describing the wreck of *Aftheksis*, from which the *Unsung thoftship* learn of *Avarnok* and his whereabouts.

Sherk-narsk-wirth – (**Aftheksish Reekgish** *rock of white mist*)

shieldcladding – (**AK**) plate armour.

shieldwear – (**AB**) any armour, including *shieldcladding* (plate armour).

Shiremansairy – the wealthiest district of *Eksar Arsask*; a gated hill, or hog's back, overlooking *Awklindyarth* from the west, upon which stand many mansions and great halls. Also called the *Airy*.

Shoeswap Islands – see *isole scusawappi*.

shotpath – (**AK**) division of an archery range, a single target at its end.

shotspoon – (**AK**) shooting targets.

shower – (**AB**) a spy. See also *lease-shower*.

shuck – (**AB**) unknown monsters; bogeymen.

Shûme-ho – original (abandoned) form of *Sumo*.

Sibakhe khua! – (**Ogrish** of the fairyroad) 'I have the child!'

sic et non – (**L** *yes and no*)

sidden – (**AB**) a derogatory term for magic; evil magic.

sidnish/siddenish – (**AK**) thing of evil magic (*sidden*)

sigalder – (**AB**) devices adorning coats-of-arms and other heraldic and house symbols; charms intended to bring about victory.

siggersorrow – (**AB**) anguished victory.

siggertoken – (**AK**) trophy; memento of victory.

Sigyards – Great gathering places at the hearts of the Hálish *headburgs*.

sile – (**AK**) pillar.

silvern, to – (**AK**) to line with silver; to put silver in.

Singrim – second Knaksish underking of *Landon*, contemporary with *Abois of the Fosswolds*.

skald – (**AH** and **Hálish Allmal**) poet.

skeevy – (**AC**) left-handed.

skin-sigil (pl. **-sigla**) – (**AK**) tattoo.

skoal, to – (**H** the *skoal* being a bowl from which one eats without a spoon) to drink to one another; toast.

skyr – (**H**) a cheese thinner than butter, comparable to yogourt. See also *sheermilk*.

sleen – human fleshmeat.

slingblade – (**AK**) sickle-like blade for harvesting.

smack – (**AB**) taste.

Smað / Smodth – the whole world, of which Ráma is but a single landmass.

smial – (**AK**) burrow, as of a small animal.

Smilkameers – valley region reaching from northwestern *Shebril* into southeastern *Harandril*; farmland of rivers and lakes. The Similkameer is also a river in that region.

smithcraft – (**AB**) handiwork; manual craftsmanship.

smittle, to – (**AB**) to infect; pollute, befoul.

snowbirding – (**AK**) traveling to a warmer climate for winter.

Soarcats, Tymniggish – the intelligent winged bergcats of *Pandressey*; longtime allies of the *Isentron* for aid in past wars. Now feared estranged.

Sofe – *Níscel*'s white horse.

softseethed – (**AK**) soft-poached.

soma – a *mindfloating* beverage; holy drink of the *Heronstroth*.

'something sameworked is samwrought' – (**AB** expression *something done by many is half-done*).

soothfastness – (**AB**) truth; fact.

sotship – (**AB**) folly; idiocy.

Southern landholds – the colonial lands south of *Ráma*; former kinglets of Allmal-speaking lords. Also called the *Colonies*.

Sownatch-Lebley – SAU-natch-leb-LEE, Healing Deity of the *Heronstroth* pantheon. Though She is one of *Bluharyn*'s consorts, She is reputed to be a refugee from an uncertain Age. The etymology of her name is unknown. She is represented as a robust woman clad in hemp and accompanied by a symbolic triad of creatures: the maggot (recovery), starfish (regeneration) and termite (immunity from disease).

Spark of Life – an *Ultrix*; by which the *fuhrbido* is able to generate light and radiate heat with his hands. Used by *Kurtisian* in the underdark of *Aftheksis*.

spellfire – (**AK**) a magical phenomenon; the spontaneous combustion of mana, which causes radiance similar to an aurora.

spokeroad – (**AK**) the streets in *Eksar Arsask* radiating out from *Grensteads*, and connecting the ringroads like the spokes of a wheel.

spore up, to – (**AH** expression) to track down.

springwell – (**AK**) fountain.

staddle – (**AB**) estate; foundation; establishment.

staffcrafts – (**AB**) learning; esp. literary arts.

staffrow – (**AB**) alphabet.

stakewall – (**AB**) palisade.

Starbowl – the impact crater in whose heart is the *Isentron*.

Starmath – the smaller but brighter of the two autumn suns. The other is *Ansend*.

stemband – (**AK**) vocal cord.

stent – (**L** *let them stand*) that which holds something up; a reinforcement.

Stitchmeal Sark, the – A small inn in *Eksar Arsask*, located in the southwestern quarter, not far from the *Grenstead of the Gates*.

stone – a Braccish unit of measure, equal to fourteen pounds.

Stormsky (pl. **Stormskyer**) – (**H** *storm cloud*) see *Adlergriff*.

stoundmeal – (**AB**) from time to time; in spells.

strandburg – (**AK**) coastal settlement; beachtown.

strawdeath – (**AK**) dying in one's bed; considered by some strains of Northmen and their beliefs to be an ignominious way to die. Others disagree.

strind – (**AB**) generation.

stringdoll – (**AK**) marionette.

stuntspeech – (**AB**) foolish talk.

suchness – (**AK**) characteristic; quality.

sum – (**L** *I am*). The very state and recognition of being.

Sumo (pl. **Sumoi**) – priestly follower of *Seisuma*.

Sundarsund, the – the broad, perilous strait separating western *Ráma* from the *Yonderstrands*. Believed to have been created when the landmass of *Wottráma* was torn in half by a cataclysm.

Sundarwick – an *elderburg* of *Arsask*; a coast city on the *Sundarsund*.

Surtskrone – see *Teakenmaley*.

Swansbawn, the – the highroad into *Teakenmaley* from the east.

swapling – (**AK**) changeling; a childlike kind of *fayfolk*. See *Urien*.

swapman – (**AK**) trader; translator.

'sweet smacks sweeter after salt', the – (**AB** expression)

swenk – (**AB**) toil; labour.

swether, to (**AB**) – to disappear; to vanish.

swettle, to (**AB**) – to make clear; to pronounce.

swettling (**AB**) – pronunciation; manifestation.

sweven – (**AB**) a vision while asleep; often the neutral term between a *dream*—which is joyful—and a *nightmare*—which is distressing.

swey – (**AB**) noise; din.

swikedom – (**AB**) deception, fraudulence; treachery; treason.

swikeful – (**AB**) deceptive; treacherous.

swime – (**AB**) vertigo; disorientation.

swink, to – (**AB**) to toil; to work.

swordstaff – (**AK**) a lance.

talwar – an exotic elseland sabre.

Tarmateriza – a kingdom of *Norráma*, which shares its western border with the *Kingdom of Knaks*. A brooding land of deep valleys and dark stone, Tarmateriza has few dealings with its neighbours. Its rulers are rumoured to be witches and warlocks, who have little interest in worldly affairs.

Tayamot – a river town in *Arsask*, situated in the southwest of *Teakenmaley*.

Teakenmaley – a *whorlberg* in *Arsask*, known for containing the headburg of *Eksar Arsask*. Also called the *Whorl*.

teer – (**AB**) glory; renown. See also *teerseeker*.

teerseeker – (**AB** *glory seeker*) adventurer. The term is often disputed; teerseekers usually distinguish themselves from sellswords, who fight for money, and not for heroic ambitions. Sellswords have been heard to question why the two incentives should be considered mutually exclusive, while Boarsmen tend to consider them all sellswords.

Tesog – (**I** *hot weather; sunny*) *Ignish* peasant girl, younger sister of *Rhianys*.

Tes – see Tesog.

Thalasp – a former inland country of *Ráma*, lost to the *Unfondlands*.

thaning/thegning – (**AB**) a noble service; the act of a thegn.

thede – (**AB**) a race, a people. Comparable to a folk.

Thede-Eater, the – (**AK** *eater of peoples*) a name for *Avarnok*.

thedelore – (**AK**) anthropology; study of peoples.

theeharseesha-tic zykeshalot – (**Vail's speech** 'the Goddamned fairyroad').

thegn / thane – (**AB**) a warrior, typically of noble station.

thellich thildy thegn – (**AB** *such a patient thegn*) phrase from a Braccish lay, celebrating the hardiness in mind and body of the ideal *kingsman*.

theow – (**AB**) a free servant; distinct from a thrall.

thinkress – (**AK**) female philosopher.

thoftman – (**AB**) an ally, a comrade-in-arms as well as a partner in toil.

thoftship – (**AB**) band; fellowship; especially in difficult matters; partners in misery; a *thoft* is a bench on a rowing vessel, upon which men sit and grip the oars. A *Thofty* or *thoftman* is a companion.

thofty – see *thoftman*.

tholemodeness – (**AB**) patience; forbearance; putting up with something.

Thorn – see *Toron*.

thrack – (**AK**) violence; force.

thrackful – (**AB**) violent.

Three Ayfloods, the – three chief rivers of the *Avonlays*, including the Caramayas, the Olannish, and the Tweelameer.

threst – (**AB**) to twist; writhe.

thridfather – (**AB**) father's father's father; great grandfather.

Thridslip – The six-legged steed of Knaks, offspring of Woden's eight-legged horse.

throneburg – the city-seat of the king.

throughshinely – (**AK**) translucent.

thrum – (**AB**) fiber; cord.

thuften – (**AB**) maidservant; handmaid.

Thunderfist – an *Ultrix*; a mighty punch which collides with a thunderclap.

Thunor – an *Ozman*, an aspect of the Hálish *Thor*.

Thunors War – an *elderburg* of Brac; chief city of the Brock's Eye (*Bracsey*).

thurse – (**AK**) a giant.

thursish – giant-like.

Thusandells, the – see *Teakenmaley*.

thware, to – (**AB**) to agree.

thwarsebreed – (**AK**) crossbreed.

Thyrsabyn-Sairtys – male outlander; also called the *Highbred*; member of the *Unsung thoftship*.

tidesong - A song of a certain length, sung in order to measure the precise passage of time. Many of the Knaksish folk still use them; in the burgs, however, they have largely been replaced by *Timekeepers*.

Tidewonder – see *Timebriar*.

'tie me a hangknot' – a Knaksish idiom admitting culpability; 'you got me', 'so sue me'.

tightfear – (**AK**) claustrophobia.

Timebriar, the – name for the temporal phenomenon of *Teakenmaley*, which causes time to fragment, flicker, and resurge.

Timekeeper – a wondrous device, by which time is told to the moment.

Timil Insee – (**H** *Tenmile Lake*) Lakeland *filk* of *Kyaribo*, ancestral homeland of the *yarls* of *Kyaribo*; Timil Insee is also the name of its foremost lake.

timmer – (**AI**) season of the year.

tippamare – (**AH**) a squeamish person; a prude.

tithe, to – (**AB**) to agree to.

tivership – (**AB**) wizardry.

Tiw – A warrior-god, one of the *Ozmen*; an aspect of the Hálish *Týr*.

Tiwsday – second day of the week in the *Oztroth* calendar used by most of Knaks; named for *Tiw*.

to boot – (**AB** expression) as well; on top of that.

toe (of a daytime) – about ten minutes.

toll-gathered gold – money collected through taxes.

Toron the Belkol – male human of *Harandril*; leader of the *Unsung thoftship*.

Trebell – a *Mannish* kingdom of northwestern *Ráma*, located on the coast of the *Sundarsund* immediately below the *Kingdom of Knaks*.

trise – (**AK**) pulley.

trochlea – (**L**) arm-and-pulley device used for loading heavy weights; essentially a crane.

trollman – (**AH**) any wizard (usually derogatory).

trollship – (**AH**) black magic, the dreecraft of a *trollman*.

troth – (**AB**) fealty.

trume – (**AK**) army.

Tuger – *Chewer*. One of Toron's two-handed swords; longer than *Mortha*, and much more difficult to keep sharp.

tung – (**AK**) language; code; system of meaning (distinct in broader ways from a *tongue*).

Tusker's Airy, the – a mountaintop stronghold in *Teakenmaley*. Built by giants, it is now a garrison of the *Boarsman*.

twaining dole, a – (**AB**) a dichotomy; division into two.

twiborn – (**AH**) twins. *Twiborn two-edged* are fraternal (nonidentical) twins.

twisling – (**AB**) a division; a forking.

Tymnig – northwesternmost province (*Medth*) of the *Kingdom of Knaks*, comprised both of *Pandressey* and the *Oathshoals*.

***Ubrantomia* of Mimsley, the** – a travel narrative contained in the *Library of the Unwritten*, describing the odyssey of a mythical *Wherewalker*.

uhter – (**AH**) any monster; comparable to *fiend* and *shuck*.

Ullris – (**H** *wooly giant*) Harandrish drafthorse.

Ultrix *(pl.* **Ultrices***)* – (**L** *avengress, she who punishes) name for the spell-like attacks contained in* Marat. *Also called* Wreakresses *in **AB** (*Ladies of Pain*).

unæwful – (**AK**) unnatural; against the natural order.

unBraccish – non-Nethrish; usually used by Knaksmen to refer to the peoples (*thedes*) of the *Kingdom of Knaks* who are not descended from the *Five Yoredrights*. These include the *Ignish*, *Shebrish*, and *Bayrdrish* peoples, as well as many others in enclaves among the provinces (*Medths*).

uncuð – (**B** *unknown*).

underking – (**AK**) king whose country is part of an empire.

underthede – (**AK**) people who are subject; subordinate folk.

underthurse – (**AK**) ogre; any large humanoid monster larger than a man but smaller than a true giant.

Unfondlands, the – the belt of unclaimed land surrounding *Ferine*; the wastelands of countries ousted from that region.

unhiresome – (**AB**) monstrous; savage; uncivilized.

unhovely – (**AB**) discourteous; unfit for civilization.

unMannish – nonhuman.

unplighted – unpledged; unsworn; un(be)trothed.

Unriven – the ancestral sword of the *King of Knaks*, forged for and wielded in the wars of the *Onelatching*. The foremost of the five pieces of the *Ringgear*.

Unsaid, an – (**AK**) a blasphemy.

Unsung thoftship, the – party of *teerseekers* led by *Toron the Belkol*. Members past and present include *Dhandhar*, *Justinian Chadallion*, *Kurtisian Chaldallion*, *Níscel*, *Shard, Rhianys* and *Vail*.

unthildy – (**AK**) impatient.

Unwinn the Unyielding – *Braccish* hero of yore, known for never having lost in battle, and dying a strawdeath despite his best efforts.

unwonely – (**AK**) unnatural.

upcleam – (**AK**) accretion; amassing.

Upstormer – the mighty *Ever* whose head is mounted on the wall of the *Isentrone*'s throneroom. Also called the *Rioter*.

urbsavvy – (**Colonial Allmal**) streetwise; city smart.

Urien – male *swapling*; pathfinder who led the *Unsung thoftship* into *Teakenmaley* on a *fairyroad*.

ust – (**AB**) storm.

Vaddi – (**Old Arsaskish** *Father; Daddy*)

verso pollice – (**L** *with thumb turned*).

Vigil – a wondrous mechanical dragon; the outland steed of *Melgard*.

viloma – (**Vakhish**) unnatural thing; perversion.

Vitalic Age – the *Eld of Life*.

Vormsbal – a lake township in *Pyndamir*.

waingoing – (**AK**) wagon travel.

wainrow – (**AK**) wagon-train.

waleberries – purple berries that grow in *Norráma*; akin to blackberries.

Walhall – the Valhalla of the *Ozmen* in the *godlore* of the *Oztroth*.

walkyrie – (**H** *slain-chooser*)

wanderyear – (**AK**) a year of young adulthood spent wandering, the purpose of which is to find one's rightful place.

Waning, the – the slow, inconsistent decay of the *Other Place*.

Wardhelm of Eksar – head of the *burgwards* of *Eksar Arsask*; captain of the city guard.

wardwered – (**AB**) regiment of the city guard (*burgward*).

wargening, the – (**AB**) lycanthropy; the disease by which one contracts wolfmanry.

Warnland – a former shire of the *Bracsriche*, lost to the *Unfondlands*.

Warptrod – see *fairyroad*.

wastumly – (**AB**) fertile; fruitful.

waterspitter – fountain gargoyle.

waymeet – (**AK**) intersection.

waymind – (**AK**) orienteering; sense of direction.

Waywindle – see *fairyroad*.

Weave, the – the fabric of reality.

ween, to – (**AB**) to imagine.

weening – (**AB**) imagining; vision; fantasy.

wenchel – (**AB**) child; little girl.

wered – division of a military unit; a company or detachment.

wergeld – (**AB**) compensation for a man's life.

wetherwardness – (**AK**) variability; inconstancy.

whate – (**AB**) divination magic.

whats (pl.) – (**AB**) instincts.

Whelpwroughtskin – the legendary wineskin of the *King of Knaks*, made from the hide of one of the runt-whelps of Frecky and Yerna, *Woden*'s wolves in *Walhall*. Filled with the milk of the she-wolf, it sends its drinker into a terrifying battle-trance. No one who has drunk from the Whelpwroughtskin before battle has ever been defeated. One of the five pieces of the *Ringgear*.

Whenwhere, the – (**AK**) existence; space-time.

Where – a plane; dimension.

Whereleet – see *fairyroad*.

Wherescape – a layout of the Planes (*Wheres*); see the *Itsslag*.

wherewalker – a dimensional traveller.

whilom – (**AB**) at times; occasionally.

Whitchwelkinsmere – the great tarn of *Teakenmaley*; the source of the *Gungnissa*.

Whorl, the – see *Teakenmaley.*

whorlberg – a mountain crown; a coiled mountain range.

wiel – (**AB**) a kind of magic.

wifkin – (**AK**) female kind.

wight – living being; any person or creature. Distinct from the undead monster.

Wild Hunt, the – a supernatural phenomenon; a mysterious and destructive congregation of Gods and other outsiders who appear rioting across the sky. The passage of the Wild Hunt has shaped landscapes, and worse.

winsomeness – (**AB**) pleasantness; merriment.

witherspeech – (**AK**) opposition; dissuasive talk.

witherwin – (**AB**) opponent.

witherword – (**AB**) opposite term.

without dent of twain – (Knaksish expression) without a doubt.

withsake – (**AK**) reaction; contradiction.

witieng – (**AB**) divination magic.

wlitifast – (**B** *enduringly beautiful*)

Woden – Patriarch of the *Ozmen*, also called the Allfather. An aspect of the Hálish Óðinn.

wonely – (**AB**) normal; habitual. At times, *wonely* can also mean 'natural.'

woodroad – (**AB**) elevated roadways supported by log frameworks.

woodsmith – (**AK**) carpenter; woodworker.

woody as a squirrel tree – (**AK** idiom) crazy.

wordhoard – (**AB**) vocabulary.

workfroding – (**AB**) engineer.

World Trees – cosmic trees, including *Yggdrasil* of the *Ásatrú*, and the Alleverwood of the *Heronstroth.*

wort – (**AB**) herb.

wortcraft – (**AB**) herbalism. Also known as *worting.*

wortmonger – (**AB**) herbalist; seller of herbs.

Wottrámish Alps, the – the range of insurmountable highbergs separating *Hála* from *Knaks.*

wrake – (**AB**) revenge.

wratts – (**AB**) ornaments; trinkets.

wraywhelk – (**AB**) an Eksarish foodstuff; a flatbread-wrapped meat; a wrap.

Wreathrunes of Shebril – a cryptic writing system of *Shebril*, seen engraved on many stones.

Wridegrot – see *fairyroad*.

wriels – (**AB**) face-covering; wimple.

wrixle, to – (**AB**) to exchange; to swap.

wursts – (**AK**) sausages

wyehead – (**AK**) Knaksish military rank, comparable to a general.

Wyehead of the East – field commander of the *Boarsmen* throughout the eastern *marchlands* of the *Kingdom of Knaks*, including *Shebril*, *Ignam* and *Bayerd*.

wyelord – (**AK**) warlord.

wyeman – (**AB**) soldier; military man.

Wyeride, the – (**AB**) the final battlefield of the *Ozmen* (Hálish *Vígríð*).

Wyrd / Weird – Fate; one of the Three Sisters of the *Oztroth*; a norn.

wyrm – (**AB**) dragon.

Wythdeg – Large town in central Ignam.

yarl – (**H** *earl*) highborn of Harandril; chieftains of the *filks*. Comparable to the *jarls* of *Hála*.

yate, to – (**AB**) to agree to, say yes to.

yepship – (**AB**) cleverness; cunning; artifice.

yeth – (**AB**) surge of anxiety.

yetted – (**AB**) poured.

Yggdrasil – the *World Tree* of the *Ásatru*; known also as *Wodengest* in the *Oztroth*, but more often simply called *Iggdrasil*.

yiselry – (**AB**) hostagery.

Yngmwn – (**I**) Ignam.

Yonderstrands, the – the coast of the *Sundarsund* opposite that of western *Ráma*.

yondthink, to – (**AB**) to contemplate; to reflect on.

yondthought – see *yondthink*.

yorechewn – worn away with great age.

Yoredrights of the Bracsriche, the Five – the five olden peoples whose blood is mingled in the *House of Knaks*.

yoreland – a lost country of olden times.

yorelore – (**AK**) history; old knowledge.

yoreman – (**AK**) historian.

ythe – (**AB**) wave.

Yukki-tuk – a *Norrámish* goblin king.

Zaota – equatorial continent (*landbody*) of *Smað*, known for its deserts, jungles, and various *unMannish* peoples, including *kattids*.

Appendix B

"The Gift of Canvasgard"

A bustling Grenstead in Eksar during a cheapday.
Enter Barast and Holplis, two brothers who are chapmen. Their
booths are neighbours to one another.

Barast: By Hern, a lovely day it is!
Arvakr and Alsvin trot above
With leisure, Hati unpursuant.
The haelons warm the buyers' blood
And heat their festive coins red-hot.

Holplis: It does indeed, my merry friend.
So thick doth waft the lilac-smell
That every breath is candy-sweet
And even geldings sigh for love.
See petals drift from th'Heron's vault.

Barast: I mark them, Holplis, brother dear;
The Gungin giggling catches them
And wears them as a train pastel.
The strings of viols titter along
With birds who serenade all eared.

Holplis: Behold the thrillèd flush of cheeks!
Titania smiles in every lass
And Aonghus crowns the lads fourfold
With thoughts of naught but kisses sought.
The vernal fruits lay ripe to sow.

Barast: A day more opportune ne'er came
Before a pair of baldrish men
Whose necks ere wear the wreath of Frigg
And now whose blood is agèd cooled,
No more can quick the yeast of love.

Holplis: 'Tis true, my merchant sibling fair;
Such wares as ours be tinder dry
Afore these hungry, hearty flames
Which burn the cheeks and loins withal.
No dealers stand to profit so.

Barast: My tables overflow with balms
To heal the lovesick but preserve
The love: papyrus, th'elvish kind,
And Ar'bol's[1] softest vellum scrolls,
This paper from Tymnigian birch,
By soarcat reaped from valleys hid
To man. Anointed all with scents
T'enthrall the senses, surmount sense,
And that's without the precious inks
I have here too. Such florid tints
As blush and sky, so churned and thick
Like buttermilk that only quills
Of peacock, merl or Blodeuedd owl
Suffice t'apply it. Them I have.
Pastoral, urban, sonnet, ode,
It differs not if epigram;
Inscribe one word in any tongue,
Enrapt the hind will swoon hamstrung.

Holplis: These braces mine are likewise lush
With lures and hooks for angling harts.
Calligraphious goods attract
The lettered ranks and Muse-besought
But olden charm has this stock here:
These pretty feathers for the locks
And coloured ribbons frayed at ends
Which catch the air like heather-grass
And wave to all who see. Look these!
They're beads of glass nigh dewdrop size,
By faery-glaziers blown and stained.
Each core is eyed and will receive
The threads of hair if rightly coaxed.

---

[1] Aribol, homeland of the Aribolgrínn.

Coiffeurs but two possess the craft
Within these walls, to whom I have
Indentured me and stand t'enrich.
So light these dainty baubles be
That breezy hands will pick them up
Fantastically and 'twill redound
As tinted bubbles dancing 'round.

Barast: Most favourably our wares do stand
And we shall peddle hand-in-hand.
The crier now I haste to pay
By tongue to crack the stags our way.

(Exit Barast)

Holplis: A fruitful day it stands to be!
And so it must, for not a cupe[2]
Remains betwixt our purses both
Committed not to lay this out,
These treasures of the choicest kind.
Aha! The cry, it comes! I set.

*(A muffled announcement begins from somewhere offstage which
is quickly overwhelmed by the keening of wind)*

Holplis: What's this? What's this? A roguish gust
Come stealing down into our glen
From out the alp-diverted blasts
To like a lusty demagogue
Induce to arms the gentler blow
And make a mob of masses kind?

(Enter an Aeolian[3] and His fan-weilding attendants)

Aeolian: Too placid be this urban seat,
Alike a craven hunkered down
Behind an esker 'pon the field

---

[2] A copper piece
[3] A wind god

Of blood whilst others prove their right
To live by facing full the brunt.
My breath, blow forth and bluster loud!
My airy hordes, dishevel and sack!
Though it hath not the wintry hooks
Of Idunn-sere Thiassi's force,
It yet will yank these boarflags taut!

(His attendants begin waving their fans)

Holplis: Oh, merciful Bluharyn! Such
A gust ne'er drove the argosies
Which plowed the breakers of the Strait
To bring these goods to port! Now see
Those trinkets scatt'ring all
Before my helpless eyes! To sky
The feathers disembodied fly
And fingered ribbons wave goodbye!
Oh callous Norns, see how my beads
Escape these trays like fluff-winged seeds,
Rejecting order, selfish brood,
And tethered not to rightful strands
But drawing off my thread of Fate.
Bewail me Joy, for I am lost!

(Exit Aeolian and attendants)
(Enter Barast, preoccupied)

Barast: Received your ears that zephrous snort
Alight came hurtling down the Run?
Such beastly breaths belong not here
But at the hooves of Ode's Great Hunt.

(He notices Holplis's empty stands)

Reverèd Fortune, brother mine!
So handsome didst thy produce prove
That ere I come from yonder fount
You have dispensed it all and now
Are on your knees in bliss?

Holplis: Oh, woe!
'Tis true I genuflect before
The Fortune-Gods but not to thank
Or praise! Th'old wolf I am, I roll
To show my underside that They
Above might kill or leave me loan.

Barast: How mean you by this, Holplis man?

Holplis: Oh, Barast brother, I am done!
That dreadful horn you lately heard
Was as a blast dispatched by Whom
Not but the eagle-feathered Him
Who swallows corpses! And whiles
The merchandise of yours lay cached
Behind this coign, all my effects
Were by this blow most cruelly blought
Or sent to suit the Sky unbought.

Barast: For rue!
(he turns to audience)
What vicious work was this
That spent my brother's fortune so?
Was it indeed the fault of winds
Whose Sires we know yet cannot stay,
Or was't the songbirds Odish[4] which
Forsook poor Holplis, counseled not
When's chose this full-unhindered spot?
Them both my shoulders bore when 'round
This corner I took mine; Esconced
'Thin dikes of brick full-windy-proof
 But welcoming a windfall.
(To Holplis)
Hear
Me, wretch I love so dear. Your tear,
Now wipe it 'way. In moments, Fate
Will be rewove, for now one half

---

[4] Odin's ravens.

Of mine is yours and still we vend
Together.

Holplis: Noble is your grace,
O blood! Behold! Omitted seems
The gust, withal did not subdue
Amour but sent the shivering dames
With rosy cheeks and pert-nosed breasts
Into the eager arms of beaux.
The bellow did as bellows do
And thus we stand the stronger!

(Thunder cracks)

Barast: Gods,
It cannot be! Yon cloud, it drifts
Athwart the sunny firmament
As swift as foam upon the Gung!
Portentous-dark with flashing paunch,
 It seeks t'unturd itself upon
Us like some doomy gull! Away,
Despoiler!

*(Thunder cracks again. Enter a Rain Goddess and Her
attendants with pails)*

Rain Goddess: Pleasant is this glen
And inset place of Man! How strong
The efflorescence burgeons, blows,
And steeps its perfume in the air!
The vernal sugar puckers lips
Of all with blood to nose it. But
There is none like a playful rain,
To set the hearts athrob aflame.

*(The Goddess's attendants prepare to empty their pails.
Cringing, Barast and Holplis cry out, but the water does not yet
come)*

Rain Goddess: I'll gloss the skin of every pair

And set upon the flags a show
Of dancing pearls through which they'll foot
Enchanted. Hands entwined, they'll laugh
At how their weeds are sod nigh sheer
And step beneath cascading eaves,
Amid the smell of blossoms damp,
The tang of soakèd stone, and catch
With one another's mouths their gasps
At life's ebullience.

(Again, the attendants ready their buckets and again, Barast and Holplis
*   exclaim with anguish. Yet again, however, the water does not come)*

Rain Goddess: Fruits more doth
I grow by this than-

Holplis: *(Yelling at the sky and shaking his fist)*
On with it,
Thou fat, unbidden, farting punk!

(The attendants empty their buckets, leaving the brothers and their displays soaked)
(Exit Rain Goddess and attendants)

Barast: That thunder was the knell of death
For our prosperity.

Holplis: Not just,
But our posterity as well;
So deeply buried in arrears
That when our seed returns to light
The scions will be hatred-stunt
And pruned of enterprising buds.
And as for now, we should be pleased
T'escape our bankers with two limbs
Attached intact. Come on. We'd best
Prostrate ourselves without duress
Afore 'em.

Barast: Fie! 'Tis true, all true!
I kick at Thee, thou woofing Fates!
Thou mangy, thicket-hiding thieves
Who skulk aforth to steal my fleece!

Holplis: For naught, Barast. I ere have whipped
Them so. 'Tis all to do to hang
Our heads and by our salt transmute
To dye this spilt and rain-cut ink,
Whereby imprint the only mark
Upon this square we'll make.

(They weep)
*(Enter the three Norns, Hoary Urd with Her back turned, hooded
Skuld facing the audience and youthful Verdandi standing sideways
to gaze upon the brothers)*

Skuld: Be these
Here sobbing, snotting capons those
Who so severely pecked Our names
It echoed down stout Yggdrasil
And ringed the waters of Our spring?

Urd: Methinks their tears as brine didst cure
Their tongues to hide wherewith they whipped
Us in the ether but find now
Themselves garroted by'm. What say
You, Sister Presently?

Verdandi: Oh Past,
This twain I pity nonetheless;
So thoroughly ensnared within
Their silk that they appear as prey
And not the spindles.

Urd: A brocade
Most poignant, I'll dispute it not.

Skuld: What smoke and mirrors, weeping hearts!

I'll none of it. To choke their throats
We came anon and though their state
Extenuates their blasphemy,
So far I'll not oppose Myself
To rue them now instead!

Urd: In want
Of heart are You, Our third, as was
The one of clay who wades the mist
Upon his kiln-delivered birth.
In Valkyr's armour too oft dight
Of late You've been, wherein You change
Your silver looks for youthful gold
But sky-careering makes You cold.

Verdandi: Indeed. Blind Hodur sees that though
These men upon Valhalla wilst
Not look, a baldrish pair they are
Despite, not hawks but hawkers be,
Dispensing toys of love to which
The hardest goats are softest kids.

Skuld: Reply Me then with 'bah!' If Hod
Spies Baldur in these two, I say
To give Him stem of mistletoe,
Direct Him forth and have Him throw.

Verdandi: How dim and bleak the Future is!
 For shame! Herein be lovelorn life:
Perpetual, crepuscle gray,
Horizons smoke the brands of war
Alone which highest thrills the beast.
A sphere one-poled is not equipped
To spin amain and soon would crash
And skid and dash itself against
The others like a top among
Too many twirled.

Skuld: What can We do?
Their webs We can unravel just

Enough to set them fresh within
This square but 'tis inside the weaves
Themselves, by crossing warps and wefts,
That memories are formed. With them
Undone, the pattern coarse will only be
Restored.

Urd: And weather We no more
Control than they. Our skills confine
Our aid alone to constructs of
The loom.

Verdandi: By Me, I have conceived
the means by which We might pin down
Success! Lachesis told me last
We spoke of marvels mercantile
For which Her dedicated realm
Is famed. Above the sparklies, scraps
And rubbish of an hundred lands
Which, altogether dumped, excite
The moneyed crows, there stands aloft
A fabrication most superb:
A simple frame o'erlaid with weave
The same as wings the ships of wind.

Urd: Design most paradoxical!
The textile which impresses aught
Can also it dismiss!

Verdandi: Indeed,
It is a most amazing stuff.
So stout, 'twill last a polecat's age;
Not Thor himself could tear it twain.

Urd: Phenomenal! 'Tis true a cloth
And not th'impenetrable hide
Of some unsaga'd brute?

Verdandi: 'Tis cloth, dear Past. By troth, 'tis cloth,
And wove right here within Eksar.

But its distinction does not end
With that. Moreover, it is dipped
In special wax whereby it doth
Repel the unrelenting rain.

Skuld: Oh, Balderdash! If such a weave
Existed even, no one but
The king whose pockets stretch more deep
Than Jezi Baba's jaw could stand
To buy enough to roof a hen.

Verdandi: The same I'd say if it were not
Erroneous extreme; Perhaps
Astounding most of all, this stuff
Affords Affordability.
'Tis cheap as flax from which it's knit
And but a little more for toil.

Skuld: It sounds too good to be for truth;
Auspicious great, suspicion grows.
If 'tis not weak and 'tis not dear,
I say 'tis then unsightly gross.

Urd: Again You look for storm to chase
The sunny day!

Skuld: Did Men not do
As much, they'd never thatch their homes
Or store their crops, believing all
Their summers amaranths and not
The sharp-tailed thistles.

Verdandi: Both of which
When rooted firm are common weeds,
Dependent on the whims of clime
As any fragile grass or bloom.
That is, until the shears enclose
Upon their necks and by behead
Immortalized. Such is the gift
Of plants that taken from the ground

They can become most helpful things
And flout Your pessimistic law.
To vanquish now Your final doubt:
This cloth repulses only's much
As merchants wish to make it do,
For dyes of all the Bifrost's shades
Can by its skeins be drunk.

Skuld: Resigns
Me to this fabric's eminence,
Which even Loki would admit!
Its name, Verdandi?

Verdandi: *Canvas*, 'tis,
Because its temper can subdue
The elements to vassalage.

Urd: The day is thinning, Sisters two;
If We're to act, let it be soon.

Skuld: Agreed, dear Fate, Our spinning calls
And Ratatosk unwatchèd crawls.

Verdandi: Above these men We'll raise a roof
And like a runner hang it down
On either side and thereby proof
Their wares to clime, their souls to frown.
But first t'undo this dismal woof
And stay the loom until We've flown.

(The Norns rotate their formation counter-clockwise until Urd faces the brothers)
(Enter the Guildsmen whose tunics are emblazoned with the emblems of the Awning Makers' Guild. An awning-tent is swiftly and silently erected thereby.)

Urd: How splendid swift their tasking goes!

Verdandi: What cheery grins and cheeks of rose!

Skuld: What outdoor place could not use those?

(Exit the Guildsmen)

Urd: A Palace Fibrous stands afore,
Impregnable to blow and pour.

Verdandi: And now these two essay once more
Though unbeknownst of what before.

Skuld: To Urdar's edge We now restore
And none shall claim the Norns ignore.

(Exit the Norns)

Barast: Most favourably our wares do stand
And we shall peddle hand-in-hand.
The crier now I haste to pay
By tongue to crack the stags our way.

(Exit Barast)

Holplis: A fruitful – Ho! What's this about
Mine head? A sort of tailored cloak
It seems at first, though't doesn't hide
Our goods but rather like a trim
Of pretty lace about a page,
Enhances their appeal. Wherefrom
It came I have no clue aside
From wisdom of the faery realm
Whose dusty denizens oft slip
The boundary through to here effect
What looks to our magentile eyes
As miracles and chance.

(The wind keens)

Holplis: By chance,
There lows a bullish wind within
The breeze so softly grazing here!

Oh sailcloth, batten down these wares
Somehow and save me from the plank!

(Enter the Aeolian and His attendants)

Aeolian: Accursèd Norns, You caulk in vain!
This curragh I shall wreck again!

(The attendants begin waving their fans)
(Enter the Guildsmen with escutcheons made of canvas)

1st Guildsman: We charge Thee back, Thou braying ass!
Athwart our craft You shall not pass!

2nd Guildsman: Against its mail you dash your brains
For scarce a bod can find its grains.
Now back to sky, now back to Hell
And tell the Others of your quell.

(They rush the Aeolians and His attendants, driving Them away)
(Exit the Guildsmen)

Holplis: The wail is spent and yet I float!
My livelihood remains intact
Behind these shield-efficient drapes
Whose stitch-testudo barely shook
Beneath the airy ram's assault!

(Enter Barast)

Barast: It all is set – By Odin's eye,
What is this stylish hood the likes
Of which ne'er mitered nuptial priest,
Encircling us like halo halved
and tilted plumb?

Holplis: I recently
Myself beheld its stately arch,
And while I wondered at its charm,
Perforce did come a brutish wind

To demonstrate its twofold good;
The billow-breath, afoam with dust,
Didst hurl itself against this vault
And was deflected without harm
To neither goods nor combèd bob!

(Thunder cracks)

Barast: A rain? Amidst this sunny blue?
Oh, antlered kine, I envy you,
For when some wagging beast doth stand
Amid the grass upon that land
Of yours, you can at least before
It strikes make break for safer shore!

Holplis: Do not disheart before the pain;
Despair has force enough to torque
The rack without you slackening
Or shackling yourself. Look here!
So densely woven is this screen,
It seems a solid thing. Mayhaps
The shower's like the gust and will
Be turned aside.

Barast: Although I doubt,
I have no choice; eccentric cloth,
Protect these dear, unbouyant wares
Against the coming flood!

(Enter the Rain Goddess and Her attendants)

Rain Goddess: Oh, Fates
Of North, You twin My work! The spring
Has thawed the tundra of Your hearts
Indeed when caissons You dispense
To foundered, thick-hulled argosies.
Well, I'm a privateer of sorts
When't comes to keeping Dana moist;
Submerse I must the fleets who care
For none but blithe and cloudless days.

Amour needs rain as all seeds do;
Corollas, ambergris and wreaths,
Whyfor would float besides?
Thus I repeat My erstwhile act
And soak this place in Heaven's glaze.

(The attendants ready their buckets)
(Enter the Guildsmen, their escutcheons raised)

1ˢᵗ Guildsman: Abhor we not the stuff of love
 But things are harmful from above;
 Your rain like hail and sleet and snow
 Is oft no better than a bow
 Discharging darts at downward train.
 Why else would anyone complain?

2ⁿᵈ Guildsman: Bombard us then if drip Ye must,
  Just speed it up and spare the fust!
  You'll find, however, that our craft
  Will stand like Gimli while it's strafed.

*(The attendants discharge their buckets onto shields, which
withstand the water)*
    *(The Guildsmen drive the Rain Goddess and her attendants
away)*

Barast: Conferred from High this substance was,
Alike the flame which Rexans claim
Was granted by an elder God
Who for the deed was caught and chained
By Those who kept us cold at nights
And chewing uncooked flesh.

Holplis: I deem,
Therefore, we share this gift in kind
With others needing its avail:
All those who think of fawning to
The Gods of wind and rain.

Barast: Its name

Unwittingly you've caught! It shall
Be called an awning, then, for those
Who thought of fawning ere it came.
And now, my brother, comes the tide
To which this shield is not so proof.

Holplis: Amen, tis Men! With that I pay
Oblation to Whoever dawned this day!

(He tosses a handful of feathers into the air just as the two merchants are swamped by customers)

The End

Acknowledgements

There was never any doubt about whom *the Unsung* would be dedicated to, but the number of people who helped along the way, both directly and indirectly, has grown over the years. I'd like to thank those who never gave up on it, especially as life and learning stepped so heavily into my original vision.

I took a huge detour through academia and met some great people—some no longer with us—who gave my love of language the tools my imagination needed: Alix Carrel, Ian Cameron, Ian Pringle, Roland Jeffreys, Ian McDougall, Máirín Nic Dhiarmada. There are others: Bob Argall, who first showed me *Beowulf* and *Paradise Lost*; Hefina Phillips, who was so gracious as to correct my Welsh, and to offer suggestions that greatly improved the book's Ignish. Now that I've named all these teachers, most of whom were never aware of this project of mine, I must stress the standard liability—all errors and infelicities remain my own.

I'd also like to give a shout-out to David Cowley and all the anonymous Anglish/Ednew English people online. You guys are my thofties.

I'll leave it to others to detect all the influences and tributes *the Unsung* is full of. Some of them might be missed, but few can be mistaken. Stay tuned for the next installment, where Gorrh can be heard to declare, *I'm no cringer*.

Kurtis never got to see the finished novel. He nonetheless enjoyed reading many early pieces of it over the years, and his enthusiasm kept me building them.

About the Author

Harley J. Sims has always been a wanderer between worlds. Raised in rural western Canada, he studied languages and literature at Carleton University and the University of Toronto, earning his PhD in English in 2009. Now a recovering medievalist, he found his academic experience points weren't much good for leveling up in the real world.

Working in his parents' heavy-duty repair shop when he began his studies, and as a bouncer while he finished, Harley has also enjoyed gigs as a commercial fisherman, translator and book reviewer, as well as teaching Tolkien and Fantasy at every opportunity. His articles and reviews have been published in newspapers, online, and in scholarly journals both in Canada and abroad, and he has appeared on national radio and television programs to discuss issues of language and other topics.

The Unsung is his first novel.

He currently lives on a mountainside in British Columbia with his wife and two children. He can be reached online at www.harleyjsims.webs.com.

Made in the USA
Columbia, SC
18 September 2018